I0822278

A CURSE OF WINGS & GEMS

a BRIDES OF THE DRAGON KINGS novel

A CURSE OF WINGS & GEMS

a BRIDES OF THE DRAGON KINGS novel

S.D. HUSTON

LITERARY DAWN PRESS

Contact Info: www.sdhuston.com
Cover Design by Jacqueline Sweet & S.D. Huston
Edited by Malcolm Bradley
Edited by Nissa Leder

CONTENTS

Evermist
The drakelock
Therossium Mountain Range
Aelunis
Mariskust
Nordrun
Mellan Ocean
Nivoch
Lucror
East Agondray
Virdis
Central Agondray
Drakkon
Sun temple
Cyaneus
Zaheel Mountain Range
Siren's cove
Meridonali
Bellafuria sea
Agondray
The fire isles

Elemental Magic

PRONUNCIATIONS

People

Adria / Adriavata (AH-dree-uh / AH-dree-ah-VAH-tah) – derived from Illyrian "adur" (water) + Sanskrit "vata" (wind, air) meaning "wind of the sea"
Airian / Airi (AIR-ee-uhn / AHY-ree) – derived from Welsh "Eirian" (bright) + "arian" (silver) meaning "bright silver"
Alariel (AH-lah-ree-EL) – derived from Arabic "Ala" (exalted, sublime) + Hebrew "-riel" (of god) meaning "exalted energy of god"
Anjali (AHN-hah-lee, AHN like "on") – Sanskrit meaning "divine offering"
Aqirun (AH-key-roon) – derived from the Latin "aqua" (water) + "runa" (secret or mystery) meaning "mysterious water"
Avi (AH-vee) – shortened version of True Name; meaning "night dew"
Aysima dal Aybek (AYE-see-mah dahl EYE-bek) – Aysima, Turkish meaning "she who possesses the beauty of the moon" + dal, Korean meaning "moon" + Aybek, from Ay- Turkish meaning "moon" and Aibek, Kyrgyz meaning "moon masters"
Belian (Lian) (BEH-LEE-ahn) – derived from the Turkish "balian" meaning "king or lord"
Bian (BEE-ahn) – Chinese meaning "ever-changing fate"
Brac (BRAHK, Rhymes with "rock") – shortened version of True Name; meaning "strong arms"
Bryn (BRIN, Rhymes with "win") – derived from the Welsh "Bryn" (hill or high place) + Old Norse "bryne" (fire); adopted by Sun Fae to mean "celestial fire"
Carina (kuh-REE-nah) – derived from the Italian/Latin "carus" meaning "dear or beloved"
Cassia (KAY-shuh) – from Greek "kassia," a type of cinnamon tree, symbolizing

spice, warmth, and exotic strength; used as a name to symbolize "alluring presence"
Cephus (SEE-fus) – derived from the Greek "Kēphos," meaning "rock or strong foundation"
Charisse (shah-REES, REES like "peace") – derived from the Greek "charis" meaning "grace or kindness"
Cielan (SEA-eh-lan) – derived from the French "ciel" meaning "sky or heaven"
Cyrillus (sih-RILL-us, RILL like "thrill") – Greek meaning "lordly, masterful"
Edmar (EHD-mar, EHD like "bed") – Old Norse meaning "wealthy sea"
Emira (Emmy) (eh-MEE-rah, MEE as in "meet") – Arabic meaning "princess"
Eurynome (YOU-rih-noh-mee) – Greek Goddess of Water-Meadows, meaning "mistress of the floodplains"
Galerius (guh-LAIR-ee-us) – derived from the English "gale" (strong wind) + the Latin suffix -erius (indicating stature or quality) meaning "mysterious wind"
Galton (GALL-tun) – English meaning "owner of rented estates"
Glacius (GLAY-shus, GLAY like "glacier") – derived from the Latin "glacies" meaning "ice or frozen"
Grigor (GRIH-gor, GRIH like "grit") – Armenian meaning "watchful, vigilant."
Isamore / Isa (EE-sah-more, EE like "see" / EE-sah) – derived from Old Norse "isa" (ice) + Old Irish "mór" (great) meaning "great, mythical ice"
Jayasurya (JAY-ah-SOAR-yah) – Sanskrit meaning "victorious sun"
Jesi (JEH-see, Soft "J" like in "Jewel") – shortened version of True Name; meaning "one formed from water"
Kalden (KAHL-den, KAHL as in "call") – derived from the Old Norse "kalda" meaning "cold or chill"
Kyran (KY-ran) – from Kiran, Sanskrit meaning "ray of light"
Lida (LEE-dah, LEE like "lead") – derived from the Greek "leda" meaning "beloved"
Malala (mah-LAH-lah) – derived from Pashto "malal" (grief) + Spanish "mal" (bad, wrong) and "ala" (wing) meaning "one with broken wings," symbolically representing powerlessness, sorrow, or lost potential
Lutine (LOO-teen) – from French Folklore meaning "the tormentress"
Mithya (MYTH-yah) – Sankskrit meaning "illusion or unreal"
Morcant (MORE-kant) – Welsh meaning "sea circle"
Morvella (more-VEL-lah) – derived from Latin "maurus" (dark) + "velum" (sail) meaning "dark tide"

Najla (NAHJ-lah, NAHJ like "lodge" but with an "N") – Arabic meaning "one with beautiful large eyes"
Nereus (NEH-ree-us, NEH like "net") – Greek sea god, meaning "wise one of the sea"
Nira (NEE-rah) – shortened version of full name that means "burning wrath" and "fiery rage"
Nuria (NEW-ree-ah) – derived from the Arabic "nur" meaning "radiant, light"
Owen (OH-wen) – Welsh meaning "young warrior"
Rafiq (rah-FEEK, FEEK like "peek") – Arabic meaning "gentle friend"
Rin (RIN, Rhymes with "win") – Japanese meaning "cold, dignified, severe"
Rivus (RIH-vus, RIH as in "river") – Latin meaning "stream" or "river"
Rythnor (RITH-nor, RITH like "myth") – derived from Greek "rhythmos" (flow) + Old Norse/Saxon "nordr" (north) meaning "the flow of ice"
Sargon (SAR-gon, SAR like "car") – Akkadian meaning "true king"
Solvrev (SOLV like "solve" and REHV like "rev") – meaning "silver fox"
Sygilla (sih-JIL-lah) – partly derived from Scylla in Greek mythology, adopted for a meaning of "wounded beauty"
Tarinor (TAR-ih-nor) – derived from Sanskrit "tarana" (crossing water) + Old Norse "nor" (narrow sea) meaning "guide of the narrow sea"
Thrandmir (THRAND-meer, THRAND like "grand") – derived from Old Norse "Thrand" (strength, boldness) + Arabic "Mir" (prince, leader) meaning "The Bold Prince or The Powerful Commander"
Vamphyr (VAM-fear, VAM like "vam-pire") – derived from Slavic "vampir" (vampire) + archaic English "vampyr" meaning "vampire"
Vayushin (VY-oo-shin) – derived from Sanskrit "Vāyu" (wind, air) + Slavic "-shin" (from "sin," meaning "son") meaning "Son of the Wind"
Yolande (YO-lahnd, LAHND like "wand") – French variant of "Yolanda," derived from Greek "Iolanthe" meaning "violet"
Zane (ZAYN, Rhymes with "rain") – derived from Hebrew meaning "God is gracious" + Arabic meaning "beauty" or "grace" meaning "gracious beauty"; in the mythology of the Winter Goddess, Zane symbolizes the graciousness of winter and the icy beauty of snow

Places

Aelunis (AY-loo-nis, AY like "fate," LOO-nis) – derived from Aelius, from the Greek "helios" (sun, to symbolize celestial bodies) + luna, from Latin (moon)

meaning "the moon in the heavens"
Agondray (A-gone-dray, A like “bay” and DRAY like “tray”) – derived from Gondr, Old Norse meaning "way" + -dray, from "dregr" (Old Norse) meaning "pull" meaning "way of the kings"
Cyaneus (SIGH-ah-nee-us) – Greek meaning "blue of the sea"
Drakkon (DRAH-kon, DRAH like "draw," KON like "conquer") – derived from the Greek "drakon" meaning "dragon"
Khalanthrax (KAH-lan-thraks) – derived from the combination of Arabic "khalid" (eternal, immortal) + "hadid" (iron) + Greek "teichos" (wall) + Latin "arx" (citadel) meaning "the Iron Fortress"
Malustra (mah-LUS-trah) – derived from Mal-, Latin meaning "bad" + -lustra, Latin meaning "forestland" meaning "cursed forest" or "bad forest"
Mariskust (MAH-ris-kust) – derived from Mari-, Latin from "mare" (sea) + -kust, Dutch/Swedish meaning "coast" meaning "sea coast" or "maritime coast"
Mellan (MEL-ahn) – Irish Gaelic for “lightning”
Meridonali (MEH-ree-doh-NAH-lee, MEH like “met”) – Latin meaning “southern”
Nilamora (NEE-lah-MOHR-ah) – derived from Sanskrit "nila" (sapphire) + Hinidi "nilam" (blue sapphire) + Latin "ora" (shore, border) meaning "the Sapphire City"
Nordrun (NORD-run, NORD like “north”) – Nordr-, from Old Norse/Saxon meaning “north”
Novacor (NOH-vah-kor) – derived from Latin "nova" (new) + "cor" (heart) meaning "new heart"
Paxsylva (PACK-sihl-vah, SIHL like “silver”) – derived from Latin "pax" (peace) + "sylva" (forest) meaning "peaceful forest"
Sarineton (SAW-ree-neh-ton) – derived from Sanskrit "sarin" (noble) + Old English "-ton" (town) meaning "noble town"
Virdis (VEER-dis, dis like “this”) – derived from the Latin "viridis" meaning "green, lush"
Zaheel (ZAH-heal, ZAH like “saw”) – Arabic meaning "sure of heart"

PROLOGUE

EDMAR

The midsummer sky gleamed like molten gold as Edmar soared, his dragon wings slicing through the warm breeze. Below him, the sea lay deceptively still, but it could turn in an instant. Just like his curse.

Another bride by chance. Another death. The curse would force his hand soon, as it had for a thousand years. At times, its oppressiveness threatened to crush him.

For now, he reveled in the freedom of the sky. Each wingbeat sent ripples through the air as he glided toward Siren's Cove, a hidden paradise nestled among turbulent waves where the mermaids sang at dawn and dusk.

He pushed forward. Sunset loomed, dragging his dreaded transformation with it. The curse stole his wings with the fading light, binding him in human flesh. Yet this evening, like so many others, he would risk it. For the mermaids' song.

He'd made this flight countless times.

As the cove came into view, his heart quickened, and he angled downward, cutting through the humid air. The chaotic surf gave way to calm waters around the rocky island. Mermaids, their jewel-toned tails glistening under the fading sunlight, gathered in song, their voices weaving together in haunting harmony.

Thoughts, feelings, none of them his own, threaded into his mind. Subtle at first, like a soft breeze, then stronger, flooding him with desire and longing, tempered with pain. Their song filled him with more than music, whispering of the mermaids themselves.

The melodies wove through him, threads of light in the darkness until one mermaid shattered the spell.

She sat on a coral throne, sapphire-blue hair cascading down her back. She was unlike the others. Her curves more pronounced, her stillness more unsettling. While the others swayed and sang, she remained motionless, her emerald eyes fixed on him alone.

The music faltered, the other voices fading into the background as if they'd never existed. The gaze of the mermaid held him captive. She didn't move, didn't blink, but her presence seemed to grow. Filling the space between them, pulling at something deep inside him.

For a moment, he forgot to breathe. Longing stirred in his chest, but not just for her beauty. It was her stillness, the way she observed him, with a warmth he'd been missing until he found her.

She belonged to him, and he to her.

Then a visceral twinge alerted him to his impending change. Sunset was near. He had to return to the safety of his kingdom before the curse forced his transformation.

I have to leave her. He growled at the idea, but he didn't have a choice. Reluctantly, he tore his eyes away and beat his wings hard, flying back toward the coast, promising himself he'd find her again.

Then the sky darkened. The wind turned.

The storm struck.

Purple lightning slashed across the sky, and the air crackled with static. He swore, banked left, and tried to outfly the storm. But the clouds rolled in faster than any natural storm, churning above him as if summoned from the depths of the ocean.

He dodged the first bolt, then the second, but the third struck him in the chest. Pain seared through him as magic coursed over his scales. His wings locked, and before he could recover, the world spun, and he plummeted toward the churning sea.

Darkness claimed him before he hit the water.

He woke on the beach, the sand cool beneath his bare skin. His body was human now—naked, vulnerable, weak. For a long moment, he stared at faint stars against descending twilight, disoriented, until he heard the soft splash of water nearby.

A shadow loomed over him.

The curse stirred, scratching through him once more. Compelled change, shifting between his human and dragon form, was merely a symptom of his unending torment. An invisible band constricted around his chest, familiar claws sinking into his flesh like old wounds reopening.

No. Not again.

His next wife had been chosen.

A bride by chance, not by choice. A prisoner of his fate, picked by the cruel magic that dictated his every move. If he didn't marry her before the lunar cycle ended, the curse would claim his life. But marrying her meant her death, just like all the others.

Then the nightmare cycle would repeat. Unbroken, eternal, merciless.

She knelt beside him, and his breath hitched. It was *her*, the mermaid his heart called to. Her emerald eyes caught the dim light, searing into his soul, far more intense up close.

His heart stuttered as his gaze swept over her. She was naked, too, long legs in place of her tail, sapphire hair spilling over her shoulders, silver swirls glowing faintly on her skin.

This mermaid—this woman—was the most beautiful creature he had ever seen. An immediate, powerful attraction that went beyond physical desire. The curse's binding force tightened around his chest, warring with his own emotions.

"No," he whispered, the word breaking as it left his lips. *Not her.*

She flinched, her eyes flashing with something that looked like sorrow and pain.

The thousand-year-old spell had chosen her, demanded their union. A fate that meant her death. Yet something else stirred within him, a strange sense of rightness, an unfamiliar pull toward her. A spark of hope ignited.

Can she be the one to finally break it, to free me?

Hope, such a fragile thing, flickered in his heart. Maybe, just maybe, she was different.

"What's your name?" His raw voice cracked, and his hand trembled as it brushed the wet sand. "Please. I need to know."

She didn't answer.

Instead, she touched the glowing red gem embedded in a gold band around her throat, the source of her power. It pulsed in time with his heartbeat, its dark crimson light thrumming with ancient magic. She winced, clutching it as though in pain.

His chest tightened further, a silent reminder of his fate. That he must marry this woman or die. He forced himself to sit up, ignoring the protests in his body.

"You're hurt?" He struggled to focus through the confusion. The storm, the lightning, the curse. It all swirled together in a blur.

Her lips pressed into a thin line. She said nothing, but her eyes flickered with something—anger? Fear? He couldn't tell. But he needed to understand.

The gem's light intensified, and she recoiled as if she couldn't bear the pain anymore. With a final look, a look that seemed to hold a thousand apologies and a lifetime of sorrow, she rose and turned toward the sea, her bare feet leaving soft impressions in the sand.

"Wait!" he called.

But she continued, the gem's glow expanding, enveloping her as she dove into the churning waves.

He collapsed back onto the sand, gasping from the snap in his chest. The curse's tight band felt gone, severed.

How?

Silence fell over the beach, broken only by his ragged breaths and the distant crash of the ocean.

His chest ached, not from the spell, but from the sudden, hollow absence, as if something vital had been torn from him. He had lost brides before, all claimed by the curse, but never like this. Never had it relinquished one.

Never had a bride left so abruptly.

Never had one been so silent.

Never had the curse let one go without a death.

What does it mean?

CHAPTER 1

EDMAR

Twenty-five years later...

Edmar missed flying with the stars.

The vast expanse, constellations stretching beyond sight, the wind beneath his wings. Freedom. He hadn't known it in a thousand years. The curse had stolen his dragon form at night, along with the hope that he might ever find a love truly his own.

Every year, that dream faded, worn thin by his fruitless search for the mermaid. And yet, part of him resisted. His fate couldn't be to marry, then mourn, again and again. He wanted more than duty. More than a fate-bound marriage. He wanted a choice. A partner. Someone who saw him, not just the king, but the man.

He soared through the snow-choked morning, his wings slicing the frozen air. The cold didn't bother him. He was an Ice Dragon, a creature of Winter. But this was more than cold.

Below, Kalden's once-vibrant land lay entombed in white and gray, its villages skeletal remains of their former selves. Winter had stolen its breath. Its people dwindled. Its crops lay buried beneath ever-deepening ice. The curse took its toll, not just on Kalden, but on the innocent humans he had sworn to protect.

His heart ached. For Kalden, for the humans, and for himself.

He didn't want another wife chosen by fate. Another love twisted into obligation. He wanted more. To love freely, without invisible chains tightening around his ribs, forcing his heart to accept what the curse dictated.

But the curse didn't care.

And time cared even less.

His own kingdom had not yet starved, but the creeping freeze at his northern border with Kalden strangled vital trade routes, and fewer ships arrived each passing season.

He angled his wings, descending toward the jagged white peaks of the Therossium Mountain Range, the Beast's Bones. Sharp and unforgiving stone jutted toward the sky like the ribs of a long-dead titan.

Kalden's cave sat atop the shortest peak in the range. The Dragon's Perch. A perch, meant for watching over one's domain.

Kalden had used it to disappear. A twenty-year prison of his own making.

As Edmar neared the cave's entrance, the air thickened, heavy with frost. Ice crystals coiled in midair, stirring an unnatural gust of snowfall. He grimaced. The curse always reacted when he and his brothers were near each other. A worse storm would come soon.

With a sharp exhale, his breath turning to mist, he prepared for what would come next. He'd allowed his brother to wallow too long in his grief.

Tucking his wings, he dove into the cave, landing with a heavy thud. Snow kicked up in his wake, swirling and bringing an unmistakable crispness into the cave. Pebbles and loose rock cracked beneath his claws as he strode deeper inside. Tendrils of ice slithered from the entrance, gripping the walls like skeletal fingers.

Morning's weak light barely reached the cavern's maw, leaving shadows to coil in the corners. His dragon's sight, glowing teal in the dimness, quickly found his brother. He approached the black dragon, a hunched shadow on a bed of stale straw.

Kalden! His voice thundered through their shared link, firm, unyielding.

A low growl rumbled from the shadowed mass. Cobalt eyes flickered, cold light cutting through the dark. The slow scrape of claws against stone echoed in the cave. *Leave me be.*

The weariness in Kalden's voice twisted something in Edmar's chest. He despised watching his brother sink further into misery. He knew this pain, had felt the sting of loss himself many times. But unlike Kalden, he refused to let it break him. He buried it instead, locking his sorrow deep in the ice of his mental Frostlands.

One day he would find a way not just to endure the curse, but to break it. He had to. He wouldn't let the curse snuff out every chance at love, his brother's or his own. *You know that won't happen.* He lowered himself into a squat beside Kalden, his tail sweeping across the floor. He noted the smell of damp, old straw, a pungent aroma adding to the scent of cold stone. *Besides, these storms are combining with Rin's, creating havoc in my lands. Don't you have any care for the humans? For everyone living in Agondray?*

Rin was their oldest brother, and the only one who had never given in to the curse's demands.

The people will forget I even exist.

He knew his brother too well. Kalden did not say this because he did not care. He said it because he cared too much. Because grief had hollowed his brother out from the inside.

This is what happens when you stop hoping, Edmar thought to himself.

Too many wives lost. Too many funeral pyres. Kalden had surrendered twenty years ago, retreating into his beast. Was this Edmar's future, too? Would he one day retreat to a cave, decades slipping by, too heartbroken to try again?

That hollow desperation in Kalden's eyes was a mirror Edmar refused to face. And yet, here he stood, forced to watch his brother slip into despair after a thousand years of suffering.

He glanced toward the cave's entrance, where the snowstorm raged. Kalden's words echoed in his mind, the fear that his people would forget him. *If there are any left after all this, I'm sure they will.* His exhaled breath added to the cave's already biting chill. *Dragons were created to protect the humans, and we are the Dragon Kings. It is our duty to take care of them.*

Kalden turned his back to Edmar, a gesture of utter defeat, retreating from a world he no longer wished to face.

Edmar's wings twitched. His brother's melancholy sent a lance of pain through his chest, but he refused to give up. He hardened his tone. *From the moment Rin allowed his beast to take over, you became the eldest brother. You should lead by example.*

I'm following Rin's example.

Rin had lost himself to fury and heartbreak long ago, triggering the first great wave of ice that had locked down the entire eastern side of the continent. He had loved the woman responsible for their curse—the Snow Princess. Now, no humans lived in his kingdom. No one lived there at all.

Edmar's tail lashed once, striking the ground. *And where will that leave Agondray? We are supposed to be the protectors of humanity!*

Kalden remained silent, but his claws twitched. A small, involuntary movement. A crack in his otherwise frozen demeanor.

This was never who his brother was. Kalden had always been the sensitive one, the one who had felt each loss too deeply. The part of him the curse had sunk its claws into, slowly tearing him apart, bride by bride, year by year.

The curse was a cruel tormentor, and it had broken something in Kalden. But not everything. Not yet.

The brother Edmar once knew—the one who had cared too much—was still in there somewhere, buried beneath the grief.

Edmar softened his voice. *Your people are starving. Homes and farms have become ghosts of activity. Fields empty after so much snow and ice.*

He watched for a reaction, but Kalden only remained still. His brother's heart still beat, even if it was weary, even if he wished otherwise.

He continued. *It's been twenty years, brother. Time to end this.*

At last, Kalden responded. His voice raw through their link. *I can't do it again.*

A pang of sorrow tugged at Edmar. He knew what that meant.

Kalden had loved each and every wife, deeply, desperately. And the curse had stolen them all.

Edmar had endured his own heartbreaks, but at least he had found moments of happiness with each bride. At least he had his Frostlands, the mental stronghold where he buried the worst of his emotions. Kalden had nothing. No way to escape the pain. No way to lessen it.

The wind whistled through the cave, and the snowstorm intensified. Time was running out. Edmar swept his spiked tail through the accumulating frost. *It's a full moon tonight.*

The words seemed to drain Kalden further. The Snow Princess's curse was bound to the lunar cycle, always waiting for its moment to strike. If they met a bride by chance, they had until the end of the cycle to marry her.

They had learned long ago that avoiding women entirely was the only way to delay it. But delaying wasn't the same as breaking it.

And finding a bride by chance on the first night ensured they would have thirty days and thirty nights to convince her to marry.

They couldn't force her. But if she refused...

They would die.

Kalden didn't move, his voice softer now with his repeated request. *Leave me be.*

Edmar had no intention of listening. Despite his compassion, he couldn't let this continue. He loved Kalden, and he would no longer allow him to hide in his cave. *Kalden, we need you. I need my brother back.*

For a long moment, there was no reply. A bitter wind howled, funneling snow into the dark corners of the cave. The silence stretched so long Edmar almost thought he would get no answer. But then... *I wish she would just let us die.*

His gut twisted. It wasn't the first time he'd heard this from his brother. But it never got easier. *Even if we weren't cursed, we're immortal.*

Kalden surged up without warning, claws latching onto Edmar's shoulders, his grip strong enough to crush mortal bone. *She stops my hand! I beg of you, kill me. Let this misery end.*

Edmar snarled and wrenched himself free. *Stop! You're no coward, and I won't have it.*

Kalden slumped onto the straw, the fight draining out of him as his wings folded tight around him. *What's the use?*

That look in Kalden's eyes... Edmar had never seen him so defeated. His great form seemed so much smaller in his despair.

Edmar forced down the sick feeling in his stomach. Duty demanded he save both Kalden and the mortals who depended on them. *Even if you can't find the will to marry anew, even if you can't do it for your people, do it for us. Your family. Think of Mother and Father, and what they would say to you.*

A tremor ran through him. The memory of their parents was a bittersweet ache, echoing across the centuries.

What if this time could be... His words trailed off. He'd always clung to the slight chance that one day, a bride might break the Snow Princess's hold on them. Perhaps it was naive. Yet hope was the only thing left. He wished he could impart some hope to his brother, even the possibility of finding something real within the confines of the curse.

Kalden's eyes gleamed in the dark, and for a moment, a crack seemed to spread through that wall of grief. *Who can survive the Dragon's Kiss?*

The Dragon's Kiss, a requirement to break the curse. No human could withstand a kiss from an Ice Dragon, cold breath stealing their warmth, so finding the right bride in Kalden's kingdom would prove difficult.

Then forget about what can't be done right now. Find your bride by chance so your land can thaw out. Guard your heart if you need to, but save the people. Don't forget what happens when we refuse the curse's demands.

In the beginning, it wasn't just Rin who had defied the Snow Princess's will. They all had. And in response, the Little Ice Age swallowed Agondray, burying the land in ice and snow. Humanity had barely survived.

Finally, Kalden exhaled a long, ragged breath. His wings drooped, shoulders sinking, resignation in every motion. *Fine, I'll put out the Dragon's Call.*

Relief filled Edmar. He covered his eyes, rubbing away the sudden moisture collecting there. He hadn't been sure he could pull his brother back from the edge, or make him want to live again. But Kalden wasn't safe yet. Not until he married the bride the curse would soon send.

He grimaced at Kalden's preferred method of choosing brides. *Barbaric, but it works.*

But what about me? The thought burned at the back of his mind. He told himself he still had time. That he wasn't as lost as Kalden. That he could afford to wait, to search for his mermaid. But how long could he chase a ghost?

Kalden's breath curled into the cold air. *You put out the same call with your Blind King's Bluff Ball.*

His throat tightened at the reminder. He had once hoped that the mermaid might be different. But she had fled before he could begin to know her.

Had she felt the same pull toward him that he had toward her?

It didn't matter. He had to let her go. His kingdom needed a queen, and the curse wouldn't wait forever. His people had already endured two years of worsening winters. He owed them more than his longing for a woman who had vanished beneath the waves.

He would host another ball. The women of his kingdom would come willingly. *Unlike yours,* he thought, glancing at Kalden.

The curse was cruel, demanding randomness or outside intervention to act. Kalden had resisted for decades, isolating himself to avoid triggering the magic that would bind him to a new bride. But time was running out. Already, his brother's kingdom turned to ice.

Edmar had seen the toll firsthand. His own land still bore the scars of the mermaid's escape. One year of endless winter. One year of loss before the curse forced his hand, choosing another bride to keep the frost at bay.

But the mermaid's choice to leave sat uncomfortably in the back of his mind, because Kalden's bride would have no such freedom. She would be compelled to answer his call, bound to him whether she wished it or not. Yes, she could refuse to marry him, but she would have no choice in being chosen. And that involuntary fate made Edmar want to roar in protest.

Yet he held his tongue. The curse bound them in ways no mortal could truly understand. Kalden turned his face to the stone wall, retreating into silence once more.

At least he had agreed.

Edmar rose, his footfalls heavy in the cavern's stillness. The storm outside thickened, fresh ice gathering in the air, the curse whispering its relentless demands. Kalden would summon his next bride. Edmar only prayed his brother would survive it.

But Edmar's duty here was done. His path lay elsewhere.

And he wasn't ready to give up on the mermaid.

She had fled once. He had let her go. But if there was even a chance of finding her again, he would chase the stars themselves to bring her back.

Yet, the next full moon loomed. If he wanted to save his people from a creeping winter, the ball had to happen soon.

Maybe he had a few days. A few days left before the curse bound him for another twenty years. A few days to decide between duty and the ghost of a woman who had once saved his life.

If he found her, stars above, he wouldn't let her slip away again.

CHAPTER 2
EMMY

Five days later...

Life was pain.

Only two things brought relief.

Hold absolutely still or use her magic.

But even the thought of using her magic, a gift of her merfolk heritage, filled Emmy with terror, her stomach twisting.

Her breath caught. The memory of her mother's death was still raw, her magic's fire acid, bursting free, searing her mother's skin.

Even as it burned through skin and scales, eating down to bone, her mother's voice had been calm, absolving. *"It's not your fault."*

But ten-year-old Emmy hadn't understood. Not until it was too late.

After that, she had learned to hold still for nearly two hundred years. Until today.

Now, fire acid simmered beneath her skin again, awakened by the journey from her royal prison to this land meeting with the Seat of the Dwarf, ruler of all dwarves in Central Agondray.

Under the cover of night, the Seat of the Dwarf's mountain loomed ahead, its wide, yawning mouth carved into the Zaheel Mountain Range. Behind her, the brackish river lay dark and still—the only path home.

Before her and the other merfolk, the Seat of the Dwarf sat on a throne of stone and gems, his gold crown glinting in the firelight. Warriors flanked him, their weapons ready, rough features cast in flickering torchlight.

Icy wind stirred through the clearing. She willed it to brush her bare skin, the only barrier between her and the cold a simple seaweed wrap around her wide hips. Anything to quiet the fire acid raging inside her. She longed to scream, to unleash the power that terrified her, the force that had taken her mother's life.

But her scream wouldn't be just for the pain. It would be for why she was here, standing on land covered in winter, surrounded by Land Bound, boxed in by mermen warriors on all sides.

Today, her father, the King of the Seas, intended to barter her away like a rare pearl, offering her to the Seat of the Dwarf. A creature as alien to her as the land itself.

"Your daughter is... remarkable," the Seat of the Dwarf said, his rumbling voice as cold as the surrounding peaks. "Such beauty, and a gem so rare. Painite, is it not?"

Her painite. Her power. Her curse. The deep red gem rested in a gold band around her neck.

Standing between her and the dwarves, her father inclined his head, his tone polished but distant. "It is. The rarest of our kind. But let me not continue to interrupt the little humans."

Another group had arrived first, standing just north of the river. They huddled together, but one stood out. A towering Earth Fae with a black gem glowing at his neck, just like hers.

Strange. Only merfolk magic was tied to their gems, always worn at the throat. Fae had no such need to access their innate magic.

A thin-voiced human man spoke. "Baron Cyrillus of House Galton thanks you for the recent trade and would like to continue."

"If Lord Galton continues the supply of money, I will see he receives uninterrupted shipments." That was the Seat of the Dwarf's rumbling voice.

The human bowed. "My father, Lord Galton, would ask if you'd allow our Earth Fae a chance to inspect the mountain where you find your supply for the valuable resource in our trade agreement?"

The dwarf's sudden bark of laughter startled her. She flinched, a barely perceptible movement, but pain tore through her body. She fought to keep her expression neutral, swallowing the moan rising in her throat.

Every movement, no matter how small, triggered the fire acid in her veins. It spread through her muscles, coiling like a living thing, waiting to consume her. Only stillness kept it at bay.

The Seat of the Dwarf leaned forward over the two-handed battle ax on his lap. "Your father is an idiot if he thought I'd allow any stranger into the domain of my people."

The human raised his hands. "I apologize for the assumption, Your Majesty. My father was just interested in—"

Her father tapped his trident against the ground twice, both ignored. Even after giving space for the human to speak, he bore little patience. His final trident slam interrupted the other male, who finally realized the danger he was in as a mere human testing the tolerance of the King of the Seas.

"King Cephus, Seat of the Dwarf, the humans have spoken long enough, and I have a counteroffer for the trade agreements. I offer my daughter in marriage in exchange. We will also offer one-tenth of the jewels from our sleeping merfolk."

Her breath quickened. At last, her father had spoken the words she had dreaded—offering her as a bride, her worth measured in jewels and minerals.

Why is my father doing this?

"This is new." The Seat of the Dwarf's voice barely hinted at surprise.

Unable to move and track conversations by sight when her magic forced her stillness, she had long learned to listen for the smallest shifts in tone.

"We hope we can come to some resolution agreeable for all parties?" The same Land Bound man spoke with an arrogance that hardly suited a fragile, magicless creature.

"Silence, human!" The prongs of her father's trident glowed against the snow, pulsing with magic.

Her father was the most powerful here, but this was a treaty to the Seat of the Dwarf. The King of the Seas wouldn't gain any favors by dominating the meeting.

The human's voice notched into a higher tone. "How dare you? I'm Lord Samael, son and heir of Lord Cyrillus Galton, the wealthiest and most influential man—"

"I said, '*Silence*'."

None of this made sense. Merfolk rarely dealt with the Land Bound, and they certainly never needed to trade. The seas provided everything.

Why would her father marry her off, knowing the risk? *Unless that is his plan.*

The Seat of the Dwarf had no idea what she was. He couldn't know. If he understood the curse in her magic, he wouldn't be so eager, dreaming of the wealth she could bring him.

He couldn't know she'd likely kill him.

Her throat tightened, the urge to scream again rising inside her. Why couldn't she demand answers? Why couldn't she refuse? But mermaids didn't question. They obeyed.

Mermaids and mermatrons were bound to their mermen. First their fathers, then their mates. An invisible tether ensured their obedience from birth.

That same tether linked mermen to their females' gems, allowing them to track their mermaids and mates at all times. Her painite, a deep red Fire crystal, pulsed within the wide metal band around her throat, its glow a warning of rising magic.

Her father shot her a wary glance but continued speaking as if nothing was wrong. The mermen warriors edged closer, their gazes sharp with unease.

No one wanted her magic to burst free.

She suppressed a shudder. The mermen hated they couldn't control her magic. To them, mermaids were possessions to be guarded, not individuals with a will of their own.

Mermen enjoyed a freedom she would never know. Their gems belonged to them, their fates their own to forge. But she would be passed from one master to another, her magic a weapon to be wielded by someone else, her desires irrelevant.

Her painite, the rarest gem among merfolk, gave her dominant magic but also unbearable pain. She wished she had been born with a useless garnet instead, a gem with no power in water. At least then, she wouldn't be a threat or a burden.

One of the merman's gemstones glowed blue, radiating protective magic. His power couldn't contain hers, but he would shield the king if she lost control.

Yet how could she stand there while her father handed her to a dwarf who had no idea he was accepting a death sentence wrapped in seaweed?

A ripple passed through the clearing, the air shifting as if sensing an unseen force. Murmurs stirred among the gathered crowd.

Heat pulsed from her gem as she instinctively turned toward the commotion. Pain lanced through her muscles, fire acid surging in warning. She forced herself still, dropping her gaze, struggling to breathe through the tension gripping her body.

The whispers grew louder. A storm's shadow passed over the moon, swallowing its pale glow. Her heart stuttered, and for a breath, her fire acid flared, her control slipping. She clenched her teeth, forcing the magic down, swallowing the pain.

Then, the wind carried three words through the icy air, clear as a prophecy.

"The Dragon Kings..."

All of them...?

The words crackled through her like lightning, but she remained frozen, a prisoner in her own body. Her heart pounded, a frantic drumbeat against the silence of the snow-covered clearing.

Memories surged, breaking free like waves against the shore—blue-green eyes, hauntingly beautiful, a voice as soothing as the ocean's lull, the day she saved a Dragon King from certain death.

She had relived that day endlessly, trapped in motionless decades, longing to see it again.

Now, *he* might be here.

One of the four Dragon Kings, rulers of Agondray alongside the dwarves.

Her pulse quickened. Through a break in the mermen surrounding her, she finally dared to look up.

It was him.

He stood tall in his human form, his sharp gaze sweeping the crowd before settling on her. Ocean-colored eyes locked with hers, and a sense of familiarity swelled within her, as if she had always been meant to find him.

Twenty-five years was long enough to forget childhood fantasies. But not him. Not the only Land Bound she had ever met.

Does my Dragon King recognize me, the one who had once saved his life?

Did he realize she was being sold, a pawn in her father's ruthless game?

Fire acid flared in her muscles, and her knees buckled. She caught herself before she fell, but the effort sent a tremor through her limbs. Her gem pulsed brighter, a red stain against the snow.

The mermen warriors stiffened, their fear tangible.

Panic clawed at her throat. She had to regain control. She bowed her head, closing her eyes, focusing on the meditation techniques her mother had taught her.

"Focus, Emmy, breathe... let the calm flow through you, like the still waters of the deep."

Slowly, she inhaled. *Hold. Exhale.* Each breath a battle, a brief reprieve from the agony coiling inside her. Her mother's voice faded.

The pain ebbed, but his presence filled the void, stronger than ever. *My Dragon King.*

He was here—with two of his three brothers. The fourth had not been seen in centuries.

A low, smoky voice cut through the rising clamor. One of the Dragon Kings spoke. "Long ago, a Seat of the Dwarf went to the true king and queen of Agondray and offered trade rights to a new mineral. Dwarven snow."

She sharpened her focus. Dwarven snow—the third ingredient in black powder. The conversation unfolded like a game of strategy, a careful exchange between the Dragon Kings and dwarves, a clash of power and secrets she barely understood. She listened as accusations flew, as the smoky voice of the one Dragon King hinted at a dangerous game being played.

A blast of icy wind swept through the clearing, snuffing out the torches. Darkness swallowed the space.

She tensed, bracing for pain. But then, blue light flared around her. The merman's protective magic shimmered, his gem casting a translucent barrier over the gathered merfolk.

As quickly as the chaos had erupted, it faded. The humans fled the snow-washed clearing, and the dwarves withdrew into their mountain, vanishing into the yawning stone entrance.

The Dragon Kings spoke in hushed tones, their words lost to the wind and the shimmering barrier. Her father turned to her and the merman warriors.

"Aqirun, stay with the princess. The others will come with me."

But Aqirun hesitated, torn between obedience and his duty as protector. "Your Majesty, it's too dangerous. We shouldn't enter their domain uninvited."

He meant her father shouldn't enter the dwarves' mountain.

Her father growled, frustration thick in his voice. "You know I have no choice."

"As your Protector, I veto your decision."

"Then we all go."

She hid her grimace, keeping her head bowed. She would rather stay here than get dragged into their argument.

"No." Aqirun stood firm. "It's too risky. Think of your daughter."

But he wasn't concerned for her safety. He feared her magic. They all did.

"May the depths consume you, Aqirun!"

Her father wanted to follow the dwarves, but his resolve wavered. She could hear it in his voice.

"I hate this wasted time," her father said.

Aqirun's voice softened. "If I may, Your Majesty, the Seat of the Dwarf has seen your daughter. He knows what you offer. Further communication can be done by courier."

"This is too important for a courier."

"Then I suggest leaving the princess behind next time."

Even with her eyes closed, she felt their stares, the breath they held. They hated the risk they had taken bringing her here—and they would not take it again.

The journey from the ocean depths had been a silent, agonizing procession. Carried in the arms of her father's mermen, she had endured the jarring swim by pouring all her focus into suppressing her magic.

But if they'd left her behind, she never would have seen her Dragon King again. Not that it mattered. The Dragon Kings would leave, too.

Despair twisted in her gut. *Is this it?* Would she never see him again?

"King Sargon, King of the Merfolk, King of the Seas," a familiar voice called out. *His* voice, a gentle cadence promising intimacy, a brush of his words on her lips. "I want to talk to you about your daughter."

Hope flared to life, fragile but burning.

But as her heart raced with anticipation, another emotion crashed into her like a tidal wave—fear. Fear that her magic would spiral out of control, that she would hurt him as she had hurt her mother and the others before she had learned to suppress it. That she would lose him before she ever truly got to know him, despite the life she had once saved.

The Ocean's Lament, her people's song of sorrow, rose unbidden, humming through her bones.

She could not risk being near her sweet Dragon King.

She could not bear to be the reason he died.

Her father's voice was cold and dismissive. "My daughter is not open for discussion."

Hope withered, replaced by relief. The memory of her mother's screams as her fire acid consumed her kept Emmy chained to her fate. She was a danger to everyone she loved.

But the Dragon King persisted. "Is there nothing I can say to change your mind?"

Her father laughed coldly. "No."

The King of the Seas was stronger than her Dragon King, stronger than anyone here.

Yet she could not stand still much longer, knowing everything she could never have. So she focused on the darkness behind her closed eyes, the cold beneath her feet, the wind whispering through the clearing.

The Dragon King's voice pulled her from the darkness. "Then perhaps I'll make my own terms."

CHAPTER 3

EMMY

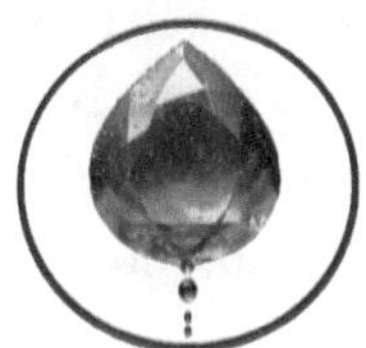

Emmy's eyes snapped open, her heart hammering as the Dragon King stepped closer. Against every instinct screaming at her to stay still, she lifted her head, pain igniting through her body.

Agony flared, fire surging through her veins, but she gritted her teeth and breathed through it. She'd endured worse. And for this moment, the pain was worth it.

Her pulse roared in her ears as their eyes met. His gaze held something that stole her breath. Fleeting, yet real. The same connection as before.

Recognition. Yearning.

The memory struck like lightning—the storm, his fall, the raw agony of holding back her magic to save him.

Now, standing before him, her gem pulsed with barely contained power. And she knew, with certainty, she couldn't go back. Not to the prison she had endured for nearly two hundred years.

"Enough of this," her father snapped, his voice slicing through the moment. He raised his hand, signaling to the guards. "Take her back."

She wanted to scream. To tear herself free. To stay. But she didn't dare move. Not when her magic clawed at the edge of her control, waiting to explode.

A useless dream.

Her heart ached, a reminder of her brokenness.

She didn't have the power to choose him. She wouldn't risk his life just to feel his embrace, to know what it was like to be so close to another without sensing their disdain or dread.

The mermen hauled her toward the brackish river. A low growl rumbled from her Dragon King.

"You would force her into this?" His voice cut through the night, rich with authority.

His gaze never wavered. Then, the water swallowed her whole. The current pulled her down, muffling the world above, but not the ache in her chest.

In the river's cold depths, her body transformed, legs melding into a tail. A merman tucked the cloth from her hips into a seaweed bag. Merfolk didn't wear clothes.

They swam, gripping her tightly, steering her toward the caves and sea channels leading back to the Mellan Ocean. Her mind screamed in defiance. It couldn't end like this.

She might never see her Dragon King again, but she would not marry the Seat of the Dwarf.

She couldn't.

For two centuries, she had searched for a way to control her magic, but this marriage changed everything.

If she didn't act now, she would never escape. She would never be free.

She refused to continue living like that.

She would escape. And find a way to sever her magic.

After that, she would find her Dragon King.

She would rewrite her fate, even if it was only a daydream.

With a sudden burst of strength, she tore free from the unsuspecting mermen and shot into the dark sea channels. Searing pain ignited with every stroke. Her gem flared, casting blood-red shadows along the tunnel walls. Fire acid swelled through her veins, but she forced it down through sheer willpower, knowing it wouldn't be enough soon.

Shouts rang out behind her, but she didn't—couldn't—stop. Every movement stoked her magic and pain, but even fleeting freedom was worth the agony. She steeled herself against it and pushed forward.

Keep going.

She dove deeper into the tunnels, the cold pressing against her skin. Her muscles, weak from years of confinement, protested, but she forced herself forward.

A tunnel branched off to her right, dark and uncharted. It beckoned her deeper into the unknown. She darted inside, heart hammering, power surging, coiling, demanding release. She was running out of time.

Years of stillness in the Little Palace had kept her magic contained, caged. But now, with every movement, pressure built inside her, rising to an unbearable peak. A white-hot glow pulsed beneath her sea foam-green skin, turning her flesh translucent.

She cried out.

She turned and released a torrent of fire acid. A blinding blast of energy rushed through the tunnel, rock shattering as the passage behind her collapsed.

Agony tore through her. She screamed, nausea crashing over her as the explosion's echo faded.

Darkness crept into her vision, cold and beckoning. Weightless, she let the current carry her deeper into the tunnel.

But she had little time. Her father would find her through the link in her gem. Just as all fathers could with their daughters until they were mated and the tether passed to another.

She blinked against the lure of a dark void, her determination sharpening with a sudden, unsettling awareness.

I'm not alone.

A magnetic force tugged at her, resonating with her magic, growing stronger with each stroke of her tail. Her gem throbbed at her throat, a beacon of heat in the abyss.

Then the ache of her magic returned.

The tunnels twisted and turned, the water growing saltier, the air thicker. Countless channels wove beneath Agondray, many mapped by her father. Not that she had ever seen them. Daughters knew little. The Sea King's daughters knew even less.

She only knew what Gilly, her best friend, had said to her in secret.

But something else guided her now, pulling her forward, calling to the power in her gem.

Pain pierced through her muscles, fire acid coiling beneath her skin, throbbing in time with the pulsing energy ahead. It crawled through her veins like lava across the seabed.

Tunnel walls narrowed until her broad hips grazed the rock. Panic settled in her chest.

She closed her eyes, flipped her tail, and delved into a meditative state, willing her fire acid to calm.

Give to me.

She startled at the voice in her head. The voice of what had called to her. It was alive.

Electromagnetic energy vibrated in the water, her tail's lateral line sensitive to it. She swam faster, pain nearly doubling her over, bile rising in her throat. Dark red light oozed from her gem.

At last, she emerged into a vast, circular cavern.

It was breathtaking. Walls shimmered with incandescent crystal veins, sapphire-blue water stretched below, and above, the ceiling glowed like a mosaic of living anemones.

And at the center, floating like a luminous moon in the abyss, pulsed a massive, egg-like structure, alive with energy.

Her heart pounded as she drew closer, senses overwhelmed. The egg, diaphanous yet filled with swirling, otherworldly energy, emanated warmth, a song of power calling to her. It needed *her* magic.

Fire acid fought for control, rearing through her limbs with sharp, burning stabs. Her skin lightened again, turning translucent. She thrashed against the encroaching burn, her vision blurring.

A figure plummeted into the water from the cavern above, stopping silently beside the egg. A woman.

Black feathered wings stretched wide, their edges wavering in the shifting currents. Black and silver hair billowed around a face both beautiful and terrifying. Black eyes, dark and shiny, like twin mirrors reflecting the dim, blue-tinged light.

An aural energy, also black, like flowing smoke, flickered over pale skin. A sword in her claw-tipped hand, a blood-red smile, and sharp fangs. Looking at her was like staring into the face of death itself. Yet, she emitted no electromagnetic pulse. No sign of life.

This specter didn't move, didn't breathe. Her presence, cold and menacing, radiated a silent warning for Emmy to stay back.

Fire acid erupted, a burning tide Emmy could no longer control. Agony cracked through her bones. With a guttural scream, she released the torrent of dark red power that both washed the egg and was absorbed by the egg. Its form shimmered as it drank deeply of her power.

Then the egg reached back through her stream of magic, traveling against the tide of her searing energy, reaching into her very being. An overwhelming, invasive void drawing her magic's essence, drinking and consuming her fire acid.

The pain ebbed, replaced by a strange emptiness, an eerie sense of peace. Her body grew heavier, sinking toward the cavern floor. Darkness pressed at the edges of her vision, but before it swallowed her, a thought surfaced.

How powerful must the winged woman be to guard a creature that could drain magic like this?

As the darkness took her, she felt two sets of strong hands yank her back into the tunnel.

And in those final moments before oblivion, a vision surfaced—the face of a girl. A powerful, ancient soul within the egg, still calling for her, still demanding more.

Chapter 4

EMMY

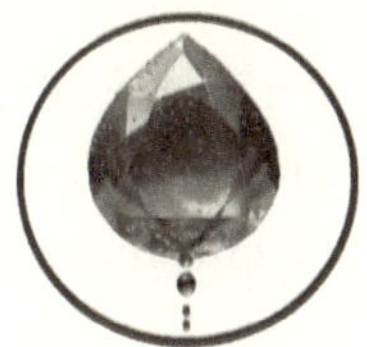

Emmy woke to the familiar glow of painted constellations on her chamber walls and coral ceiling.

Back in the Little Palace.

A shadowed memory of the cavern lingered behind her eyelids. Someone had brought her back, cold hands as impersonal as the chains now binding her to the bed.

The Little Palace, a gilded cage far from Opal City, was her prison, built to contain her power. A place she rarely left.

Of course, she hadn't escaped. Her father had found her. Chained her down again.

She calmed the ache in her chest by recalling the stories of the stars. Her younger sister, the only one who didn't fear her, had painted the constellations, each brushstroke a quiet offering. Anjali's gift eased the longing in Emmy's heart, but still, she yearned for a world beyond her reach.

She had glimpsed the twilight stars only once—twenty-five years ago, the night she saved her Dragon King. A beautiful man beneath a sky full of stars.

Now lying trapped beneath the waves again, she couldn't even float near enough to touch the stars painted on her walls.

Other mermaids adorned their tails with jewels, precious metals, and oyster shells, symbols of status. Her tail bore only chains and heavy stones, anchoring her to the kelp bed. They hooked into her scales, dull against the iridescent colors shifting between deep purple and sea-green, like fractured fluorite.

For nearly two hundred years, *this* had been her existence. But she hadn't forgotten her promise to herself. She couldn't live as this prisoner anymore.

Unless... Had the egg-child drained her completely? Maybe her fire acid was gone.

She twitched her tail, then froze. The pain was dull but still there.

My magic isn't gone.

As if sensing her wakefulness, the coral wall unfurled, its branches spreading like a sea bloom. Two mermaid servants glided through, followed by a warrior merman who took his post at the entrance. His wary gaze swept the room, carefully avoiding hers.

The servants also avoided her gaze as they set down two glass cages filled with bioluminescent lantern fish. Their soft, shifting glow dimmed the painted constellations. Fear tightened the servants' mouths as they lifted her from the bed and settled her into the seaweed-cushioned rock chair by the window.

Hastily, they shoveled a bland, soupy seafood mixture into her mouth. Nothing that required chewing. Can't risk her magic building. Their eyes darted to the gem at her throat, watching for the faintest shimmer, the smallest shift.

Decades had passed since her fire had scorched a servant's hands, but they hadn't forgotten. She couldn't remember a time when she hadn't been feared. *What would freedom be like?*

The coral wall unfurled again, and King Sargon entered.

His presence radiated cold authority, an undertow of power that rippled through the room. Aqirun, his ever-present shadow, stood at his side. Trident in hand, Sargon dismissed the servants with a glance before settling his sharp, unforgiving gaze on Emmy.

"You will explain yourself, Emira." Anger laced his command. "Why did you swim away?"

She stayed silent, finding solace in the painted stars. He didn't truly expect an answer. Not yet. But his question meant Gilly would arrive soon. She would speak for Emmy, as she always did.

"Do you think this is a game? You brought shame upon our family. You will never again be allowed such freedom. Not until you are safely bound to the Seat of the Dwarf."

She met his cold, unyielding gaze. There was only hatred there. Najla had been the love of his life; he had despised Emmy since the day her mother died.

Like all mermen, Sargon's coloring—from head to tail—was muted browns and blacks beneath the waves. But on land, she had learned, their hair and eyes shimmered with jewel tones, their skin softening to pastels. Mermaids, in contrast, were always vibrant, born to attract mates. Silver streaked through Sargon's tail. A mark of his ancient lineage and power, setting him apart from other males. That same silver traced faint, swirling patterns across his torso and arms, barely visible but undeniable. A mark shared by all his children. A symbol of their heritage. Their unquestioned right to rule.

With his trident in hand and the blue agate that inspired loyalty and compelled truth, none could rival his power. None except the Sea Witch, a grotesque being Emmy had only seen in rock drawings.

The coral parted again, and Gilly entered, her rare black tail shimmering. The only mermaid untouched by jewel tones. She bowed, reverent, yet still managed a conspiratorial wink toward Emmy.

"Your Majesty," she said, her voice melodic compared to Sargon's harsh tone. "I came as soon as I was summoned."

His gaze lingered on Gilly, a flicker of past desire in his eyes. Once, he had hoped to make her his wife. Until she had chosen another.

As Emmy's best friend, Gilly was one of two people in Emmy's life who didn't fear her. Emmy had thought she knew everything about her, except she had never met Gilly's mate. Her friend rarely spoke of him. But then, Gilly was fiercely independent, more than any mermaid Emmy had ever known.

Sargon pinched the bridge of his nose, exhaling sharply as Gilly straightened from her bow, expectant. His dark eyes roamed over her full curves, lingering at her small waist. Some of his irritation eased, replaced by something else. A sigh of old, unfulfilled desire.

Emmy had always envied Gilly's slender grace. She had curves too—full breasts, wide hips—but no merman would dare claim a mate who could kill him with a touch.

Sargon waved a dismissive hand but his gaze sharpened on Emmy. "Tell me, Gilly. Why did she think she could defy me?"

Gilly's quartz necklace pulsed as she slipped into Emmy's thoughts. A flicker of anger crossed her amethyst eyes before she spoke. Her gem granted her a rare gift—the ability to read minds.

Emmy told her everything: the meeting with the dwarves, her impending engagement if her father got his way, seeing her Dragon King, escaping the mermen, and then finding the strange egg and winged woman in the cavern.

Then a flicker of happiness lit Gilly's eyes, confusing Emmy. Was her friend happy to see her married off like a sack of seashells? But the happiness vanished, replaced with anger, and Emmy wondered if she'd imagined the mirth.

"The marriage is not to her liking, Your Majesty." Gilly's voice lowered. "She's afraid of hurting someone."

"What else am I to do with her?" Sargon's voice echoed against the walls of her prison. All her sisters, save herself and Anjali, had been married off already decades ago. "She is a danger to everyone. No one wants her. No one will risk their life for a creature like my daughter."

He's right. I am a monster. I'm so tired—of hurting others, of watching everyone fear me, of Gilly and Anjali dedicating their lives to helping me.

Her gaze drifted to Gilly, heart heavy. *I don't want to be a burden anymore.*

She, Anjali, and Gilly had spent years searching for a way to control her magic, to break free from the curse that imprisoned her. Every path led to the same place. Dead ends. Despair.

Except for one. The one Emmy had refused.

"And what would this marriage accomplish?" Gilly challenged, meeting his gaze. "Their execution? You would condemn your own daughter to that?"

Sargon's face hardened, his eyes cold and calculating. He rounded on Gilly, his fury sharp enough to make her flinch. "She will obey. She will marry the Seat of the Dwarf and finally serve this family—this kingdom—as she should."

No. Her fingers twitched, straining against the chains biting into her scales. She was not a pawn, not a weapon to be wielded and discarded. She would rather die.

There's only the one way out.

One she dared not think of. One Gilly had whispered of in secret.

A single chance to break free. To live without fear. Without pain. Without loneliness.

Her heart pounded as she looked at her friend.

Understanding gleamed in Gilly's amethyst eyes. Then a small, knowing smile.

A dangerous plan.

Her only hope.

Chapter 5
EDMAR

Despite the enormous stone fireplace dominating one wall, the Emerald Palace's Council Hall felt cool and cavernous. Green marble floors remained cold underfoot. Edmar didn't mind the chill—he preferred it to the summer heat—but the high-backed wooden chair was another matter. Hard. Unforgiving.

He had walked most of the night, leaving the Zaheel Mountain Range and the Seat of the Dwarf behind. A hot bath should have been waiting for him, a chance to soak away the tension knotting his muscles. Instead, he was here.

Through the tall, double-paned windows, he watched the night unravel as the first light of dawn approached, the Mellan Ocean a dark smudge on the horizon. Another hour at most. What he wouldn't give to watch the last stars fade.

Instead, he must attend this council meeting.

"Your Majesty, we must speak of the upcoming Summer Solstice celebration. As you know, this is a sacred time of year. When the power of the sun is at its strongest, we must honor the Sun God with our prayers and offerings."

One of humble origins, Father Jayasurya had risen through his unwavering faith and wisdom. Now, as the abbot of the Sun Temple, he looked at ease in his bright orange robe and golden mantle. Ornate oil lamps touched a shine on his brown bald head.

"How long before the solstice?" Edmar struggled to focus, distracted by his memories of the sapphire-haired mermaid.

After all these years, he'd finally found her, and she was still so far away from him. The curse hadn't picked her again, not like it had twenty-five years ago when she'd rescued him.

No telltale sign of tightness in his chest.

Father Jayasurya cleared his throat and spoke in a firm, but respectful tone for the whole council to hear. "Three days, Your Majesty. We must ensure that we have enough supplies and decorations for the celebration. I propose we allocate an additional budget for—"

Lord Mithya interrupted the abbot. His thin lips curled into a sneer on his reddish-orange face. "Do we really need to spend more money on this frivolous celebration? We already allocate a significant portion of the kingdom's resources toward religious ceremonies and festivals. Surely, we can make do with what we have."

Other council members sat around the large wooden table. Most were humans like Father Jayasurya, but his Treasurer, Mithya, was a full-blooded Sun Fae. His hair shimmered like woven strands of golden light, each thread pulsing with subtle energy. Only full fae had hair that moved.

Absently, Edmar rubbed his temple. As his Treasurer, Mithya would be responsible for the budget, but he couldn't ignore the celebration, either. Father Jayasurya looked entirely unhappy in his seat across from the Treasurer.

As he rested his hand on the polished table, teal scales peeked from beneath his sleeve, overlaying his powdery-blue skin. Nearly three years without a wife. If he waited much longer, he would continue to evolve. Until he looked like Kalden, more beast than man in most lights.

Father Jayasurya arched an eyebrow, his gaze sharp in his wrinkled face. "The Summer Solstice celebration is sacred. We must honor the Sun God and give thanks for His season."

Mithya waved a dismissive hand. "I understand its significance, Father, but we can't ignore the kingdom's finances. Reckless spending will empty our coffers."

The other council members shifted uncomfortably, all except Rivus, his only true confidant and friend, who frowned beside him. As Marshal of Cyaneus, Rivus secured the kingdom. Edmar had already briefed him on the meeting with the Seat of the Dwarf, his thoughts were likely on that, not a festival.

Still, Edmar couldn't ignore the solstice. The abbot had likely raised this before. With more Sun Fae migrating to Cyaneus to worship at the Sun Temple and see the Sun Stone, their traditions had to be upheld.

He looked Mithya in the eye as he spoke. "Father Jayasurya raises a valid point. The Summer Solstice is an important event for our people, and it is our duty to ensure it is celebrated properly, especially in these times."

When Mithya's gaze flicked to his teal scales, Edmar pulled his hand back, tucking it beneath the table. Few knew the truth of his lineage. A secret he and his brothers guarded against Summer Fae assassins, who had culled their kind long before the curse ravaged them.

Of those present, only Rivus knew his secrets—secrets his Marshal had already been aware of when they first met as comrades on the battlefield.

A thousand years ago, the Snow Princess cursed him and his brothers, forcing them into an endless cycle of fate-bound marriages. He had long since accepted that part of his life, but not the cold hand it laid on his heart.

No one else knew his history. To most, he was an enigma. A being of uncertain lineage, whispered about in speculation yet never questioned, never challenged. His kingdom had flourished for centuries… or at least it had, until the last twenty years.

Rivus studied him now, waiting for an announcement he had long been pressing Edmar to make.

It was time he married again.

Agondray's eastern lands remained frozen because Rin refused to marry. Kalden had resisted, too. Now, Agondray suffered, winters lengthening, trade routes closing. Mithya had reason to be concerned.

He had to fix this. First, his visit to Kalden a few days past seemed to rouse his brother, who had found his next bride by chance already. Except that the girl, Airian, refused to marry him. If Kalden didn't convince her, he'd be dead with the next full moon.

But now, it was his turn. He had found his mermaid again, but her father had refused him, shutting him out before he could even try. She was beyond his reach. He bit back a sigh. "Additionally, it's time for the next Blind King's Bluff Ball. I must take a wife again."

Rivus nodded, relief clear in his expression, pleased that Edmar was finally listening to him. At least someone cared about Edmar's fate. Not all his brothers were as fortunate. Only Kalden had a confidante in Bryn, his former nanny turned steward. In fact, it was Bryn who had urged Edmar to speak with his brother, unable to rouse Kalden herself.

But now, he had to put his duty first, as it always had. The ball would bring the kingdom's noblewomen before him, and the curse would choose his bride.

But the weight in his chest told him what he already knew. His heart had already chosen.

The curse had not.

Not the sapphire-haired mermaid. Not the princess of the sea.

Mithya scowled, his narrowed eyes shrinking further between the sharp angles of his pinched nose. "And how much do you intend to allocate to all of this, Your Majesty?"

Edmar gave him a patient look. Of his brothers, he was the level-headed one, the measured one. Emotions—especially useless ones—had no place in his decisions. A waste of time.

Emotions went to die in his mental Frostlands, a vast, frozen wasteland where nothing ruled but the cold.

Like the gloom expanding in his chest as he thought of the mermaid.

She had saved him twenty-five years ago and asked for nothing in return. No favors, no titles, no power. Just a fleeting act of selflessness. That was the kind of person he wanted in his life. Not like his council members, who schemed for influence. Not like the women who attended his balls, their eyes set on a crown rather than the man who wore it.

Very few people in his life were trustworthy. His brothers. Rivus. Father Jayasurya.

That was enough.

He sent this new gloom to his Frostlands, the icy vastness swallowing his emotions.

Edmar exhaled slowly, unwilling to waste energy on Mithya's skepticism. "We'll combine the Summer Solstice and the Blind King's Bluff Ball this year. It will save costs, but allocate enough for what Father Jayasurya needs."

He didn't want to prolong the distasteful topic and handed the discussion over to Rivus to discuss rumors of the Dwarven snow and all Edmar had learned from the Seat of the Dwarf. His thoughts drifted back to the mermaid while the council deliberated over Rivus's plans.

She was immortal, as he was.

Might there be a day when he could claim her as his, just as he felt it in the depths of his soul?

As the meeting drew to a close, Edmar rose and thanked his council members for their time. They filed out of the room, but he hesitated, going to one of the long windows, lost in thought.

Rivus cleared his throat. "You'll need to get to your cave soon."

The Emerald Palace perched high on the cliffs, overlooking the restless sea. As the tide receded, it revealed a small, secluded bay. A hidden world carved between rock and water. His cave lay there, at the end of a winding flight of marble steps that led from the palace to the sea.

"I'll walk the beach instead." Edmar hadn't been to Siren's Cove in weeks. Seeing his lost mermaid reminded him of how much he enjoyed flying over the ocean at dusk and dawn. He glanced at Rivus, who knew about his coming transformation. "I thought you had left already. Don't you have a new paramour waiting for you?"

"Ah, a certain woman on your mind."

"The curse didn't choose her again." He'd told Rivus everything, including seeing the mermaid again.

"Perhaps it's not time."

Maybe.

But that didn't stop his thoughts of her.

Chapter 6

EMMY

An hour later, Gilly returned with Anjali, whose turquoise eyes shone with worry. Of all Emmy's sisters, only Anjali dared to come near her. The only one who truly cared. They looked nearly identical, except for Anjali's slender frame and eye color.

As Anjali swam closer, the soft chime of delicate oyster shells strung along her tail accompanied her movements, a gentle melody that echoed her status as the youngest princess. Precious metals glinted in the shifting light, woven into the translucent fins of her tail.

Anjali wrapped her in a gentle hug.

"I'm so sorry." Her whisper resonated faintly in the water. "I fear the day Father makes me marry."

Emmy stilled, closing her eyes as she inhaled Anjali's scent—fresh water lily, sweet with a hint of lemon. The Ocean's Lament, the melody of their people's grief, swelled within her, but she swallowed it down. She wouldn't burden Anjali with its sorrow.

She loved Anjali for accepting her, cursed magic and all, expecting nothing in return.

If only she could do the same for her sister.

All their older sisters had lost their first husbands. Not to cursed magic like Emmy's, but to Sargon's ambition. As the highest ruler, he sought to dominate the smaller kingdoms, especially those guarding the Sea Veins, the vital trade routes connecting the underwater realms.

Sargon married his daughters to kings along the Sea Veins. Then, he sent his new sons-in-law to war, ensuring their deaths in battle. With their husbands gone, his daughters inherited the kingdoms, but control of their gems and their autonomy reverted to him, their father.

In this way, Sargon didn't just rule his own kingdom. He ruled the Sea Veins. That was how he became King of the Seas.

There was nothing Emmy could do for her sister's future marriage, unable to change their subservient fate to their mermen.

"Don't waste your pity," Gilly said, slicing through the tenderness. "Emmy won't be marrying anyone."

Anjali pulled back, confusion flickering through her worry. "What do you mean?"

"Tonight." Gilly's voice dropped to a whisper. "Emmy escapes."

"Escape? But where?" Panic flashed across Anjali's face.

Don't tell her! Emmy yelled the words to Gilly in her mind.

Anjali would never understand, never allow her to seek the Sea Witch—their greatest threat. Although the monstrous creature hadn't been seen in her lifetime, tales and legends spoke of her continual war with the King of the Seas, seeking control of all merfolk. No one believed the Sea Witch had given up, even if she was hiding.

Gilly shook her head. "It's a secret. For your own safety."

The way Gilly said that last part seemed to taste bitter in her mouth.

"I don't care about safety! I just need to know she'll be alright."

"You will," Gilly assured her. She fixed Emmy with a firm look.

Her heart ached. While she wouldn't miss this prison, she would miss them. She projected the image of herself singing the Ocean's Lament at dawn, a beacon in the ocean's vastness.

Gilly relayed the message, her brow furrowed. "She'll sing at dawn. Every dawn, until you find her."

Anjali's eyes widened, her hand tightening around Emmy's. "But her magic—"

"We'll find a way," Gilly promised, though doubt flickered in her gaze.

Love and worry shone in Anjali's turquoise eyes, and for a moment, Emmy wished she could freeze time, hold on to this feeling of being loved.

Anjali embraced her once more before departing. "Be careful, Emmy. Please."

Gilly squeezed Emmy's hand. "I'll come when the kingdom sleeps."

Her friend's words echoed in the silence of her chamber long after she'd departed. *Get rest.*

But rest eluded her. Every shadow, every creak of coral, became the swish of her father's tail, his inevitable knowledge of her plans. Coming to stop her. Coming with more chains.

The Little Palace was a tomb of perpetual twilight, a gilded cage where she marked time by the hushed routines of her fearful servants.

The hours crawled by. Emmy clung to the memory of Anjali's embrace, the warmth of her sister's love a fragile beacon in the cold depths. A love she didn't deserve. A love she endangered with every heartbeat.

But she had to try. For Anjali. For herself. For a life beyond the suffocating grip of her magic.

I'm so tired of being the monster everyone hates and fears. Her gaze fixed on the star constellations painted on the walls.

Only one path remained. She had to take it.

Hours later, as the servants retreated with their glass cages of bioluminescent lantern fish, a shadow flickered at the coral wall's entrance.

It was time.

Gilly moved swiftly under the painted constellations, her amethyst eyes gleaming with determination. Her touch was sure, her fingers deft as she unfastened the chains. She hooked an arm around Emmy's soft waist, and she swam them out of the room.

In the hall, Emmy's usual guards drifted motionless, a servant or two among them.

Are they dead? she asked through their mental link.

"Asleep."

They left the Little Palace behind, slipping through the open sea.

Emmy hadn't realized how close the Sea Witch's lair was. So close to Agondray, to her Dragon King. The thought unsettled her, swirling through her mind as Gilly pulled her through the currents.

The silence stretched between them, broken only by the rhythmic beat of Gilly's tail and Emmy's ragged breaths.

Fear gnawed at Emmy's resolve as the Sea Witch's lair loomed ahead.

What if she kills me without hearing me out?

"Be reverent."

Stories she'd heard from Gilly and Anjali flashed through her mind. The Sea Witch, the ruthless being who claimed to be the first mermaid, but looked like a monster.

"She's not a monster!" Gilly's vehemence startled Emmy.

Who is she to you?

Gilly shook her head, refusing to answer. People deserved their secrets. Emmy wouldn't push.

"Just remember your father meant for you to die," Gilly said, her voice low and urgent. "He planned for you to kill the Seat of the Dwarf, then let the dwarves execute you in revenge."

Her father's men would have done the same.

A cold knot coiled in her gut. Her own father had planned her death.

"He never even considered the Longing. He knew you'd be dead long before it took hold."

The Longing. A slow unraveling, a madness that crept in when merfolk were severed from the sea for too long. It ended the same way. Death by their own hands.

"He's never cared about you."

They swam south for another hour, until a dark cave loomed ahead. Her insides turned to salt water with her fear.

Gilly gripped her shoulders. "I can't go any farther. The Sea Witch doesn't tolerate strangers. This is your bargain to make."

Can I trust her? Will she help me... or destroy me?

Terror slicked cold scales down her spine. She drew a slow, steadying breath, then met Gilly's gaze. *In case I don't see you again...*

"Go," Gilly urged, her gaze intense. "She's waiting for you."

Gilly pushed her toward the cave. "Find your destiny."

Thank you.

Emmy plunged into the darkness. The cavern's entrance narrowed, the water cold and murky. Silence swallowed every sound but the slow beat of her heart.

She swam deeper. Her magic stirred, an ever-present threat coiling beneath her skin.

Her gem pulsed, a muted heartbeat of red light in the abyss.

Her tail's iridescent purple and green hues illuminated, her skin's faint swirls glowing softly, like bioluminescent whispers in the dark.

Then she saw them. Hundreds of them. Glowing, seaweed-like plants, swaying in the current. Their moans echoed through the cavern, a chorus of lost souls blinking mournful eyes up at her.

The Garden of Souls.

A graveyard of the lost. Trapped mermaids and mermen.

They had come to the Sea Witch seeking favors. When they failed to uphold their bargains, she claimed their souls.

Their stolen magic fed her, each loss making her stronger.

Her heart slammed against her ribs as she pushed forward, fire acid threading through her muscles like molten wire. A whimper escaped her, a pitiful sound.

The tunnel constricted around her, and pain erupted. Magic surged, white-hot, locking her muscles mid-motion. She clenched her jaw, shutting her eyes against the agony.

Breathe.

She forced herself into meditation, sinking deep into her center, inhaling slowly. Exhaling slower. Bit by bit, the fire acid dimmed, retreating like embers buried beneath ash.

Her nerves still screamed. Two days of unchecked magic had left her raw, scoured from within.

Finally, she pushed forward, emerging into a vast cavern, taller than it was wide, its jagged walls riddled with crevices and crannies overflowing with strange relics.

Shells and gems. Bones and skulls. A dragon's talon, its surface blackened and cracked. A human skull, its hollow sockets watching.

She drifted upward, the eerie collection glinting in the dim light.

"Welcome, Daughter of Ruin."

The rough voice startled her. A bolt of pain lanced through her, and she barely swallowed a gasp.

An enormous shadow undulated out of the darkness.

She prayed. *May the Sun God and his Seven Sleepers keep me safe.*

The creature chuckled, drifting into the oculus's pale light. Thick, inky octopus legs intertwined with four mechanical limbs, each ending in three razor-sharp claws. Their tips bit into the rock, supporting a bulbous body.

The Sea Witch came to rest in front of Emmy, her massive face nearly the size of Emmy's entire body. Her voice rumbled through the water, low and scornful. "The gods couldn't care less for their creations. Least of all the merfolk, Little Mermaid."

A thick metal belt circled her waist, flashing in erratic bursts, emitting low, woofing pulses. From the torso up, she looked very much like merfolk, save for the gleaming metal plates fused to her flesh, curving over one of her rounded breasts.

One amethyst eye—eerily like Gilly's—gleamed with something ancient and knowing. The other was a metal tube, extending and retracting with a faint mechanical hiss. A red light burned at its center, a cold and soulless gaze.

You can read my thoughts? Emmy continued floating upward.

The Sea Witch's voice slithered through her mind. *All those with direct god blood can see your thoughts.*

See? Interesting. So it was more than just hearing words. She would have loved that ability, to have lived life through another's visions while she'd been a prisoner, trapped in her immobile body.

The Sea Witch sighed, a deep sound that lifted her full breasts. If she had been a mermaid once, she would have been one of the most beautiful. Emmy could see it in the marred but delicate lines of her face, the softness of her full lips, her daintily pointed chin.

"Beauty is a curse." The Sea Witch's voice held no nostalgia. Only certainty.

Heat crept up Emmy's cheeks. Of course, she had heard that thought too.

"Tell me why you have come. Does the Daughter of Ruin seek to end her own misery?"

Daughter of Ruin. She had called her that before. Was it because she had killed her mother?

"That and so much more," the Sea Witch said. "But I'm bored with your questions. Say something before I change my mind about not adding you to my garden."

Internally, Emmy shuddered, but she rushed to mentally communicate her innermost desire. She flipped her tail to halt her upward float. Fire acid bubbled in her veins with the slight movement.

The amethyst eye gazed down at her painite's soft red glow. "I will take your magic if that is what you truly wish, but it will come at a price."

Anything.

"You will have to be dedicated."

I will be.

"Hear me out first."

Emmy didn't respond, not wanting to delay the time until she no longer felt pain, that she was no longer a threat to anyone.

"You must collect all the Gods' Stones and bring them to me. Will you do that?"

Most had been lost to time and legend. Only the Sun Stone remained. She had no idea where to find the others. But none of that mattered if she still had her power.

I will do this if you can help me control my magic. Otherwise, I cannot move without pain or killing those around me.

"I can help with that." The Sea Witch lifted a hand to pull Emmy back down from where her body naturally floated again. "A spell to temporarily sever your connection to your magic, but that will change your natural being. You'll be powerless like all humans, but existing as neither a mermaid nor a human."

Not a mermaid?

No swimming in the ocean without needing the air above water. No Ocean's Lament? She wouldn't be able to fulfill her promise to her sister to let her know where she had gone. But without her mermaid's voice, without the magic woven into every note, how would her sister ever find her?

The Ocean's Lament was more than a song. It was a language of longing, of emotions too deep for words. And now she wouldn't be able to sing it.

"In some ways, you will still be a mermaid. But you will not breathe water, and you will not sing. We cannot risk unleashing the true destruction of the Daughter of Ruin upon the Land Bound."

But no pain? No destructive magic?

"Partly." The Sea Witch lifted a blue hand, one metal-tipped finger catching the dim light. "This is only temporary. Like all temporary magic, it will wane and return with the moon's cycle. As the moon waxes, your power will creep back, little by little. And when the full moon sets, everything will return. Every ounce of pain, every flicker of destruction. That should keep you motivated."

How would she gather all eight stones in less than a full lunar cycle? *Do you know where the Gods' Stones are?*

"You will retrieve the stones one by one using the Sun Stone, and deliver them one by one so that I can refresh the suppression spell I'll use on your magic."

And then you'll make my spell permanent, the severing of my magical connection?

"When you've delivered the last stone, I'll use their power to free you forever."

Hope built the first wonderful flame in her chest. She could do this.

"Good." The Sea Witch smiled. "Then let's begin."

The water darkened as the Sea Witch raised her hands, swirling tendrils of magic coiling between her fingers. Glowing sigils bloomed in the currents, vanishing as quickly as they formed.

An iridescent lavender light engulfed her, pulsing in time with the inaudible rhythm of her spell. The pressure in the cavern shifted, heavy with power, thick as the depths of the ocean itself.

Something about the magic felt familiar, but her attention strayed with the Sea Witch's next words.

"I'm sure you're aware of the Sun Stone's location?"

Everyone knew it was in the Kingdom of Cyaneus, resting for over twelve hundred years in the Sun Temple.

The kingdom of my Dragon King. That familiar giddiness when she thought of him enhanced her anticipation.

But stealing from her Dragon King dampened her spirits.

The lavender cloud pulsed. "The Sun Stone will glow with your truths. Use that knowledge to locate the Metal Stone."

Sun Stone to Metal Stone. *Then return?*

"Yes, Little Mermaid." The cloud of magic crackled with energy and hung in front of Emmy. "Now prepare yourself. This transition will not be easy."

The lavender cloud surged forward, swallowing her whole before she could speak, before she could prepare.

Agony erupted. Not fire acid. Something worse, unlike anything she'd experienced. A hot knife shearing her skin from her body. A molten blade slicing through her body with blistering precision, cutting through her tail, carving through muscle, scraping off scales.

Then—nothing.

No air. No breath.

Her lungs seized. She was going to die.

A black force coalesced beneath her and shoved her up and out of the cavern.

Emmy flipped her tail, only to find flailing legs had replaced it. These she kicked, barely moving in the water as she had been able to with her tail.

Then Gilly was there, hauling her up and up.

Oxygen depleted from her new lungs. Her world shrunk.

The Sea Witch's voice echoed in her mind. *Another note, Daughter of Ruin. Your pain is from a curse linked to your gem* and *your body. Some pain may still plague you.*

What?

CHAPTER 7

EDMAR

Edmar strolled along the beach, the countdown to his forced transition at dawn ticking in his mind. Soon, he would take to the skies in his dragon form, soaring over Siren's Cove, eager to hear the mermaids sing. He loved their songs, ethereal voices weaving skyward, reaching for the stars before vanishing with the rising sun. They always lured him closer.

Maybe this time, he'd see her—the mermaid who had saved him, the one who haunted his dreams.

The one he longed to claim.

A sharp, piercing screech split the air. Instinct propelled him into a sprint.

Two figures grappled at the water's edge, one eerily still.

Waves crashed over them again and again, obscuring them in the distance. Edmar prayed he wasn't too late as he rushed toward them.

He reached the spot where they had been, but they were gone.

Drawing a sharp breath, he dove, kicking deeper with frantic urgency. Shadows lurched ahead.

A striking mermaid with dark purple hair and blue skin caught sight of him, clutching a limp human.

The mermaid yelled at him. "Help her!"

Gripping the unconscious woman, he surged through the shifting currents toward shore.

The mermaid disappeared, and he wondered why she hadn't just taken the woman to shore herself? Perhaps she couldn't handle the Longing.

Merfolk weren't meant for the land. Except that his mermaid, her father, and the other mermen had been out of the water for a while without being affected. It was possible his limited knowledge of the phenomenon couldn't answer his questions.

Finally, they broke the surface, and the woman was a dead weight in his arms. But he was strong enough to clear the water and collapse on the sandy beach.

He lifted his head, still breathing hard, and shock stilled him.

Skin the color of seafoam, hair like sapphire waves.

But she wasn't breathing, her chest still.

He sprang into action, tipping her head back and clasping his mouth to hers, breathing into her, knowing his cold breath wouldn't kill another creature of Winter, the mermaid. His mermaid.

This was not how he imagined their first kiss.

With one hand over the other, he placed his palms on her sternum and compressed hard and fast.

"Breathe, Princess!"

Panic stole into his heart, and he felt it cracking. He couldn't lose her now.

He blew breath into her mouth again, then back to compressing her chest. Her body arched in a jerky movement, and he turned her to the side. She heaved saltwater onto the sand, coughing violently, her shoulders convulsing.

Praise to the Sun God.

After several moments of vomiting water, she fell back to the sand, emerald eyes fixed on the lightening sky.

And now that the threat to her life had passed, he assessed her fully. Water-logged curls clung to her pastel skin, doing little to hide her nakedness. Her large breasts rose and fell as she gulped in air. Warm air rolled off the ocean and across her hardened nipples and chased goosebumps down her body. Down to her soft belly and broad hips, dipping into the valley between her legs. The only thing she wore was on her neck, a wide gold band with a dark red gem.

Embarrassed by her involuntary exposure, Edmar dragged his gaze away, whipping off his white shirt to cover her.

The movement caused those emerald eyes to roll toward him. Her lips parted with surprise. He jerked as if to rise, realizing just how close they were. He was on his knees, his body pressed against one of her hips, one hand braced in the sand as he leaned over her, the other frozen mid-motion, still gripping the shirt he'd started to tug over her.

But she reached up to his hovering hand and threaded her fingers with his. His shirt slipped off a shoulder, revealing nearly all of her breast, but she seemed unconcerned.

He groaned inwardly.

Having dreamed of lying beside her voluptuous naked form so many times over the years, seeing her like this—so close, so exposed—was exquisite torment. He was too much of a gentleman to take advantage of the situation.

Instead, he swallowed the lust raging in his blood, and he tightened his fingers with hers. His mermaid. Heat radiated in his chest, and a feeling of lightness filled him.

And the feelings fled just as quickly.

The curse still didn't choose her. No tightening in his chest, pinpointing his way to her.

He swallowed his disappointment.

No matter. She was here now.

He moved a strand of hair off her forehead. "Are you alright?"

Her eyes widened, but otherwise she didn't reply.

He frowned, thinking about their few interactions and when he'd first seen her with the other mermaids singing at Siren's Cove. She hadn't joined in the singing, hadn't even spoken to him when he woke on the beach after she'd rescued him.

The irony of rescuing her back wasn't lost on him.

"Are you able to speak?"

She opened her mouth, closed it, then tried again. When she spoke, it sounded silvery and ethereal, a light musical tone, how he imagined angels would sound. "I can. I just haven't spoken very much in my life."

A small line appeared between her eyes, but it was gone seconds later. He wondered at that and her revelation of speaking so seldom. What kind of life did she live as a mermaid, as a mermaid princess?

But was she even a mermaid? How else could she have lost her tail, her ability to breathe underwater?

He leaned closer to her. "I thank the gods for bringing you to me, but we have to stop meeting like this."

Her emerald eyes widened, then a slow, knowing smile curved her pink-hued lips. "Especially if you take twenty-five years to return the favor of me saving you."

He burst out laughing at her response, and her smile stretched further.

Then he remembered the last time he'd seen her, just the night before, when he'd visited the Seat of the Dwarf. "Do I need to worry about your father coming for you?"

Edmar would gather the largest army to protect her from her father, knowing he'd probably die, but he'd rather die having his mermaid in his life than live without her again.

That is, if she wanted him. *Does she feel this same intense connection, as if we belong together?*

His heart stopped for a painful beat when he thought she might not want to stay with him.

"No," she said, her voice breathy. "My father cannot find me."

Joy restarted his heart.

Now if only the curse would choose her and give him a chance to break it.

"Are you here to stay, then?" He wanted to ask if she was there to stay with him, but he was afraid of a different answer.

She nodded.

"Then you must attend the Blind King's Bluff Ball in three nights." Perhaps the curse would pick her among the ladies of the kingdom to be his bride by chance.

"Ball?"

Balls meant dancing, so it was likely she had no clue what a ball was. "A party, with lots of food, drink, and dancing. Please say yes, you'll come."

Her eyes glowed in the dawn's soft light as they met his. "I want to learn to dance."

It wasn't a yes, but he heard her eagerness. Every part of him ached to touch her then, to press his lips to hers again but in a proper kiss, but he chided himself. *She's a princess, for gods' sakes, treat her like one.*

"Come," he said, "let's get you back to the palace. I'll find you some proper attire, and later you can tell me how you lost your tail."

"Proper attire?"

"Clothes. I know merfolk feel no qualms about nudity, but it's important for those of us who are Land Bound."

She shrugged, seemingly unbothered. But he couldn't have a naked goddess roaming the palace. Well, unless she was in his chambers...

He shook his head in disgust. Since when had he started thinking like his youngest brother? Zane was the womanizer, not him.

He helped her stand up, and she promptly fell into him, his shirt slipping to the sand. Instinctively, his arms wrapped around her to keep her from falling.

His breath hitched as her bare breasts pressed against his chest, the contact igniting a firestorm of desire. Almost all thought left his mind as blood rushed to another part of him, that part growing hard against her belly.

His hand snaked into her thick hair, fingers grabbing a fistful to pull her head back. Lowering his gaze to her large, upturned eyes, his breath was caught by her otherworldly beauty, a heart-shaped face gently sculpted, every facet rounded. Her soft body against his, and it felt so right.

Her lips parted in the same anticipation he felt, but he withdrew his hand from her hair. She tried to stand, a shy smile gracing her lips, but her legs buckled, and she would have fallen if not for his arms.

With one hand steadying her, he bent to retrieve his shirt, and a sharp pain shot through his shoulder, making him hiss. A reminder of his curse. He'd gone too long without a bride by chance. Teal scales shimmered in several places over his sky-blue skin, but small hardened lumps also formed along his shoulders.

He forced the discomfort away. He couldn't afford to be distracted with his lips inches from tasting the mermaid's naked beauty.

Quickly, he held out his shirt for her.

She gave him a challenging look. "I don't want that on me."

Part of him hurt, as if her statement was about not wanting him, but he thrust the thoughts into his Frostlands. "I'm taking you back to the palace, so you must wear the shirt."

Resigned, she nodded.

Trying to be as discreet as possible and keep his eyes up, he held the shirt for her to slide her arms into the sleeves, then buttoned it. He scooped her into his arms.

"Sorry," she muttered once he had her settled. "I'm not used to moving."

Not used to moving? Did she mean walking? That made more sense.

"I will be your legs until you're used to yours."

She hid her face against his bare chest, and the feel of her lips on his skin made him suck in a breath. Desire flooded him again, blood pounding in his ears, drowning out something she said.

"What?" he asked.

"I'm too heavy to carry."

He frowned, acutely aware of the soft flesh beneath his fingers. If he could, if his actions wouldn't dishonor her, he'd rip his shirt away and feast on her body, worship every inch of her with his lips.

He didn't say any of that aloud. Instead, he said, "You're perfect."

She was quite shapely compared to mermaids he'd seen over the years, but he'd told her the truth.

She was perfect to him.

CHAPTER 8

EMMY

His name was Edmar. She'd learned it in her studies, but hearing him say it aloud made it feel real. More than just a lesson. Before dawn forced his transition, he settled her on a boulder, his arms lingering, his sea scent still clinging to him even after they'd left the water. He'd already told her it wasn't common knowledge he was a dragon. She'd keep his secret.

Then he leaned over her to speak into her ear. "I want to know more than your name, Emmy. I hope you'll tell me more tonight."

Goosebumps had prickled her skin, and she shivered.

As the sun breached the horizon, golden light engulfed him. His form shimmered, lifting. Bones realigned, skin hardening into gleaming scales. Magic reshaped him, mesmerizing—and just a little terrifying. She watched, breathless, as his wings unfurled, their vast expanse casting a shadow over her. He was magnificent. She almost forgave him for the scratchy material he made her wear. *Almost.*

Nearly twice the height of a man, the dragon inhaled deeply, his chest expanding. Then he reached for her, drawing her into his arms. Even though everything about him was hard-scaled with sharp angles and razor-tipped claws, he held her with the utmost care. His chest was surprisingly soft and warm.

With a running leap, he took to the air. She swallowed a startled yelp and embraced the reality. She was finally soaring through the skies she had only dreamed of. The sky that became home to the stars she yearned to see.

A thrill shot through her as they ascended. Wind tore through her hair, the sun kissed her face, and exhilaration flooded her—a boundless, intoxicating freedom. Below, the world spread out like a masterpiece on a coral canvas of soft pinks, purples, and oranges under the shimmering gold of the rising sun.

Her fingers explored the supple skin of his chest, and a low rumble vibrated beneath her touch, his growl. Muscles contracted and relaxed as his leathery wings swept through the sky. Her heart soared, beating in time with the powerful strokes. She never wanted this flight to end.

Yet a crushing weight settled on her chest. She was here to steal from this man, from his kingdom. For a moment, she entertained the idea of telling him everything. She tilted her chin up to take in the dragon's majestic head, searching his glowing blue-green eyes. Could she?

The dreams she had of him made him kind and understanding, but who was he really?

She only had twenty-five days until the next full moon. Hardly enough time to know if he could be trusted. She couldn't keep her Dragon King, and a painful ache settled in her chest.

If she could still sing the Ocean's Lament, it would rumble in her chest already. No song to express her sadness. She also couldn't create the tears the Land Bound made. Not entirely a merfolk anymore, but not really a human either. *What am I?*

Sadness locked inside her, catching her breath with no relief.

They crested a towering cliff, revealing the Emerald Palace below. It looked exactly like the stories she'd heard. Bright marble walls veined with long, curvy lines of crystallized green minerals, polished to a mirror sheen, reflected the sky's changing colors. Lush gardens of verdant foliage and vibrant blooms surrounded the palace, their fragrance mingling with the salty ocean air.

The dragon swept past the palace and soared over the city, a crescent of vibrant life nestled against the curve of the palace gates. She gazed down at bustling streets, towering structures, and colorful throngs of people. A world of motion and sound, like Opal City's waterways between coral and stone buildings but louder compared to the tranquil depths of her ocean home.

He swung lazily back to the palace. Towers and turrets rose into the sky, their spires glistening in the strengthening sunlight. Flags bearing the city's emblem, a stylized compass rose with a blue aura around it, fluttered proudly in the breeze.

As they neared the palace, they descended, then landed atop gravel squares surrounded by a courtyard of vibrant flowers and tall trees. Two humans waited for the dragon's landing. The first man was older, dour-faced, his gray hair pulled back. He wore practical black and white attire, the emblem of the compass rose stitched on his chest.

The second man was younger, with a friendly smile and a hint of mischief in his warm brown eyes. Silver streaked his shaggy brown hair, a touch of blue woven through the strands.

As Edmar uncurled her from his arms and lowered her to the ground, pain lanced through her feet. Each step like walking on needles and shards of glass. She winced and sucked in a breath.

While it smarted, the pain didn't compare to the agony she'd felt before. Her painite didn't glow. No fire acid in her muscles. This was the only pain she experienced—just in her feet—and if that was all, then she could live with it much easier than her previous life of torture.

The dragon's massive, clawed hand encircled her waist, covering most of her torso. She felt small in his grasp, but she knew he only meant to steady her. Muscles she rarely used ached with fatigue.

The sour, older man stepped forward, his shrewd gaze scrutinizing her. "Another soul saved?"

She raised her brows, wondering if rescuing strays was a habit for Edmar. Perhaps she wasn't that special to him. Not that it should matter, because she couldn't stay. But a part of her heart squeezed.

"I'll see that Yolande takes care of your new stray, dragon. See what jobs the girl is suited for." He shook his head. "Wonder what the king will make of this one."

When the older man offered a hand to her, the dragon threw a wing around her, lowered his head, and growled. Icy breath misted in the warm air, leaving glistening drops of water on the large, sharp teeth in his mouth.

None of it scared her. She knew her Dragon King wouldn't hurt her.

"Oh-ho, Grigor, I doubt this one's just another stray." The shaggy-haired man bumped the back of his hand on the older man's shoulder. His warm brown eyes also surveyed her, but she felt less judgment from the perusal.

Then he bowed and held it, only raising his head to meet the dragon's gaze. Edmar relaxed the wing but didn't fully raise his head or hide his fangs.

"May I see to your guest, dragon friend? I'm sure she'd welcome a nice bath and sensible clothes."

Now the dragon stepped back, but his taloned hand still curled over her waist. The nicer man raised from his bow and tilted his head. When he offered an extended arm, the dragon finally released her and let him take over by sliding his arm around her waist.

The loss left a void within her, but then she wobbled on her feet, pain sharp in her soles. She barely caught herself by grabbing the front of the shaggy-haired man's shirt.

The dragon growled again.

"Calm down, dragon. I have no designs for your woman. We'll take care of her, keep her safe, untouched."

With a smile on his face, he gave Emmy a wink. Unable to resist, she returned the smile. She liked this man, whoever he was. She liked he called her the Dragon King's woman.

The dragon leaped into the sky with a low rumble. Filled with awe, she craned her neck to watch him. He was just as beautiful as the first time she had seen him.

"I'm Lord Rivus, this kingdom's Marshall, and that there is Grigor, the Emerald Palace's steward." He spoke as he drifted them toward a beautiful arched entrance into the palace, the wooden doors ornately decorated with intricate metalwork and studded with precious gemstones. "May I have the honor of your name?"

"Emmy."

"And would I be correct in my assumption, Princess Emmy, that you are the daughter of the Sea King?"

She was surprised. She'd always been told the Land Bound knew little about them because the merfolk avoided interacting with those above the surface. Or perhaps he knew about her from Edmar. That made more sense. It also meant that Edmar had thought of her enough to talk about her to this man.

That made her spirit sing. "I am."

The older man coughed, a forced sound. "My apologies for my hasty assumptions, Your Highness."

When she glanced at him, a bright pink color rose under his brownish-yellow skin, a similar change in the way coral blushed beneath the caress of the sun's rays.

Frowning, she wondered what he'd done wrong. If it was offering to help her find a job, she understood. Everyone had to contribute to society in some way to keep it running smoothly. Having magical gems helped… unless one had hers. She had been nothing but a drain on her society.

No wonder her father had wanted to get rid of her.

Well, she was gone now. A burden lifted from his kingdom, a daughter of the powerful Sea King, who could offer nothing more than her death.

Chapter 9

EMMY

"We'll arrange a tour of the Emerald Palace, and if you're interested, our magnificent capital, Virdis..."

Rivus kept talking, but Emmy's mind drifted, captivated by each new sight. A sense of romance underlaid by power hummed in the intricately carved stone walls, their delicate motifs and sculptures whispering tales of valor and love.

They entered the Grand Hall, a vast and opulent space, supported by elegant marble columns. It dwarfed anything she'd ever seen. Sunlight streamed through stained glass windows, painting the polished marble floor in a kaleidoscope of colors. Tapestries and murals whispered of stories she'd yet to hear.

The first painting, a massive canvas spanning the length of five mermen, captured a battle of epic scale. Ice Dragons, griffins, polar bears, and wolves stood on one side, balancing on an ice shelf. They faced off against a fiery horde of Ember Dragons, Sun and Fire Fae, and a phoenix, all wreathed in flames.

She longed to linger, but Rivus guided them onward.

"Yolande," he called across the hall.

The cavernous hall bustled with people, cleaning, straightening, and working on projects. Rivus's voice caught everyone's attention, and one by one, the hall fell into silence as they looked at her.

A plump older woman wove through the workers, making her way forward. She patted her violet hair in place as if ensuring the high bun on her head was still there.

She'd heard humans were mostly muted in color, similar to Rivus and Grigor, although Rivus had some blue in his hair. But this human was anything but muted. Besides the hue of her hair reminiscent of the twilight sky meeting the ocean depths, her skin shone as a deep red-brown color like the prized ribbon kelp forests.

"My lord," the older woman said, as she bowed to Rivus.

"Please take charge of Princess Emmy's care. The king would like to see her tonight when he returns."

"Of course, my lord."

Rivus turned her to him. "The housekeeper here, Yolande, will take care of you. Whatever you need, please ask. Edmar would see that you lack for nothing."

She blinked, surprisingly at ease in the woman's care. Yolande reminded her of home, despite her being human, as evidenced by her aging and rounded ears. The immortal fae had pointed ears.

"You don't say much, do you?" Rivus asked.

She opened her mouth, waiting for pain to hit, then remembered the pain was gone. Temporarily, at least. "I haven't been able to speak for a long time."

He shrugged with a good-natured smile. "That's okay. Edmar likes to talk, so the two of you should get along just fine."

Once more, warmth filled her with the idea of being with Edmar and listening to him talk. She returned his smile.

Rivus handed her over to Yolande. Despite her shorter stature, the woman possessed surprising strength, easily bearing Emmy's weight.

Her chest tightened when she remembered none of this actually mattered.

She wasn't here for her Dragon King.

She was here to steal the Sun Stone.

Only after her magic was gone could she come back to her Dragon King, if he still wanted her after she stole the Sun Stone.

Happiness bled out of her as the older woman undressed her and put her into a large water container found within a set of interconnected chambers. Yolande and a younger maid, who introduced herself as Lida, used scented "soap" to "wash" her.

Merfolk never bathed. But as she stepped from the water, her skin scented with unfamiliar florals, she finally understood the ritual's significance of a "bath."

Afterward, they struggled to dress her in a long, flowing white garment.

"It's just a dressing gown, Your Highness. Until we find you suitable clothes." Lida had chased her around the room and now frustrated tears gathered in her eyes.

The sight caught Emmy, never having seen tears before. The distraction gave the woman enough time to slap the fabric over her head.

"Why do I need to wear anything?" she asked.

Yolande ushered her to a chair in front of a table and a mirror, while Lida tied the front of her gown all the way to the base of her throat. When Lida reached for a handled instrument with stiff hair on one side, she plucked at the top ties, undoing them.

Lida huffed while gesturing to the mirror. "Look, Your Highness. White looks great with your green skin and blue hair."

She stared, mesmerized. The mirror was so crisp, so flawless, unlike the hazy reflections of the Little Palace. It was as if she were seeing herself for the first time. Free from chains, her skin glowing in a way it never had. She looked... different. Almost beautiful.

While the women worked the handled instrument—a brush—through her long sapphire curls, she grabbed chunks to inhale. Her hair had never smelled this good. She recognized tingling hints of coconut beneath the flower scents. She knew what they smelled like from her one visit to Siren's Cove, but the others she didn't know.

Eventually, the women pulled all her hair out of her hands as they plaited it into one long braid, then rolled it up so that it didn't brush the floor. Somehow, she'd also missed one of them tying her dressing gown closed again.

"How did you grow your hair so long, Your Highness?" Lida asked.

While Lida didn't remind her of home like Yolande, her affable nature put Emmy at ease. Lida was brown-skinned like most humans, but there were differences from the mermen's brown coloring that Emmy wasn't used to seeing.

Back home, mermen's muted tones camouflaged them in the ocean depths, leaving little variation. Here, above the ocean, it was as if the vibrancy of this world under the bright sun promised nuances to make each human unique.

The women waited for her answer to the question. She was at a loss for how to respond as she had done nothing other than exist, and exist quite poorly, according to her culture. She shrugged—a new motion for her. Her attention was drawn to her reflection in the mirror, causing her to miss their reaction to her response, and she shrugged once more.

Her smile stretched wider.

She'd never been able to smile without pain.

Abruptly, she touched her face, feeling the smile, the texture of her skin on her fingertips, the silkiness of her lips.

There were so many things she could do now. She could wink an eye. She could wiggle her ears. She could clap her hands.

A yawn overtook her.

The women exchanged knowing glances.

Yolande leaned over her shoulder. "When was the last time you slept, honey?"

When had she slept last? "Three nights ago."

No wonder she was tired.

Both women exclaimed aloud, hands crossed on their chests, but didn't ask her questions about why. Perhaps that was rude, so Emmy offered an explanation that made sense without giving away the real reason she was here.

"Two nights ago, my father wanted to sell me in marriage to the Seat of the Dwarf. I didn't have a chance to sleep, and I swam away last night."

"Would you like to sleep now, Your Highness?" The younger woman gestured toward the large structure against the far wall. It looked like what they used here for a bed, but it was huge.

"I would like that," she said.

When she tried to stand, sharp pain lanced up from the soles of her feet, and she fell forward with a yelp. Heat coursed through her cheeks when she caught herself on her hands and knees. Seconds later, the women bent to help her, asking if she was alright.

She shut her eyes, having forgotten that her new existence wasn't exactly pain free. She'd have to work through this limitation if she was going to steal the Sun Stone.

Lida tucked an arm under hers to help her stand, and that's when she spied Edmar's discarded shirt on the floor.

Inhaling deeply and bracing herself, she took a step forward, balancing on her tiptoes to lessen the pain.

After several steps, she finally reached Edmar's shirt and swept it off the floor.

"I can take that, Your Highness." Yolande held out a hand.

Her words stung. Emmy thought through why that hurt, and she realized she'd never owned anything worth having.

Rocks and chains.

But Edmar had gifted her this shirt. She didn't want someone to take it away from her. But if they made her give it up...

Lida sensed something of her distress. "Keep it, Your Highness. There are plenty of shirts in the palace."

Yolande nodded at a look from Lida. Then they tucked her into bed, exclaiming over her lack of sleep and need for rest. They checked her for any injuries from falling, and she couldn't help but think about how nice everyone was to her. Yet she planned to take the God's Stone from their kingdom.

She was an awful person for what she would do.

But she had no choice.

At least, that's what she told herself as she shed her dressing gown, curling around Edmar's shirt. His ocean scent wrapped around her like the tide.

CHAPTER 10

EDMAR

"Her maid said she'll be here soon. Stop worrying." Rivus shot Edmar an exaggerated look, brow lowered, lips pursed, clearly fishing for a laugh.

"You look too much like the wolf like that," Edmar said under his breath, though he rewarded his friend's efforts with a chuckle.

They sat in his private dining room, capable of seating twelve, with low lighting on three walls, the fourth a collection of floor-to-ceiling windows. The table was set, but food waited for the arrival of the princess.

His steward reported that Emmy had slept soundly after her bath, not rising all day. He'd sent the request for her to be made ready and brought to dinner, wanting badly to go to her chambers himself. He didn't want to seem overly interested and scare her, though.

He agonized over the dinner arrangements. Did she prefer lavish feasts or quiet family meals? He chose a more intimate setting.

It would be just him and her, along with Rivus, in case he faltered in the conversation.

Sweat collected beneath the collar of his emerald silk tunic, the color chosen to match the same vibrant green of her eyes.

Wiping his hands on his dark brown trousers for an innumerable time, he bolted to his feet and strode over to the darkening windows, glancing at the stars.

For the third night in a row, he would miss his observatory. He thought of bringing up his love for the stars, but it was likely too soon. Maybe he could find some way to bring it up in the natural course of conversation with her.

When he looked over at Rivus, his friend shook his head, knowing his thoughts.

"Do. Not. Bring. Up. Stars."

Edmar raked a hand through his hair, silently cursing Rivus for knowing him too well. "It's hard enough finding things to talk about with women," he said, "and she's not just any woman. She's a mermaid for gods' sake. What do they talk about?"

Rivus chuckled. "I imagine they talk about the same things everyone else does. Food. Family. Fashion." He winked. "Perhaps a few juicy tales from the deep."

"But..." Edmar's brow furrowed. "What if I tell her a joke, and it falls flat? Would she think I'm an idiot?"

"For the love of the goddesses!" Rivus laughed again, the sound reassuring. "I don't think conversation is going to be a problem. Relax. Be yourself. And maybe try not to stare at the bountiful chest the gods favored her with."

Edmar frowned at Rivus but forgot why the moment Yolande's voice drifted from the hall.

"Didn't I tell you? I knew you'd like the dress. You look beautiful, honey."

Then he heard her sweet, melodious voice. "The sea doesn't care what we wear."

"Us Land Bound folks are a bit more complicated. Running around in just your skin will make all the men go crazy."

"Then they should learn to control themselves."

A breath later, she was in the doorway looking in.

"As they should, Princess," Rivus said.

Edmar barely heard him.

In that moment, breathing became inconsequential. Simply seeing her was enough to sustain him, as if she had become his very reason to exist. He could have forgotten how to breathe, forgotten he ever needed to, and it wouldn't have mattered. Even if he'd suffocated, he wouldn't have cared. Her presence in the same room filled a void he'd never known existed. She was an angel, his completion.

Sweat prickled his palm, reminding him he did, in fact, need to breathe.

He dragged in a ragged breath as he saw all of her—her sapphire hair, braided and twisted into intricate patterns, didn't touch the floor but still hung down her back and over the white dress. The empire-waisted dress perfectly complemented her sea foam-green skin, and the flowing material and low neckline barely covered her gracious curves.

Yolande offered a little support as Emmy came fully into the room, and he wondered if she felt the same magnetism between them. Her wide emerald gaze never left his as she glided forward, stopping just before him. Behind her, the housekeeper quietly withdrew.

"Princess," he said, nearly in a whisper.

"Just Emmy, Your Majesty." A slight smile curved her lips, and he loved the lights that danced in the depths of her large eyes.

How long they stood there looking at each other he couldn't say, but then he remembered his manners. He held up a bent arm.

"Are you ready to eat, Emmy?"

Her smile widened as she slid a hand into the crook of his elbow.

He helped her into her seat, noticing that she seemed to walk much better now, although it looked like she walked on her tiptoes beneath the long dress.

When the servants brought platters piled high with steaming food—roasted meats, colorful vegetables, and fragrant breads—Emmy's eyes widened, her stomach rumbling. She picked up a golden-brown roll, its buttery crust gleaming, and took a cautious bite.

Her eyes closed, a moan escaping her lips, and desire shot through him. He wanted to be the bit of butter she licked from her lips.

"This..." she said, her voice breathless, eyes locked on the bread. "This is divine! What magic makes this?"

Rivus laughed. "Just a simple roll, Your Highness."

"Simple?" She shook her head and lifted in her chair to pull her feet under her onto the seat. Bracing her hands on the table, she leaned over and reached for another. "This is beyond anything I've ever tasted! You Land Bound have mastered the art of food."

Servants froze as they laid out more dishes.

Even Rivus, who sat across from her, halted with his wine glass half raised to his mouth, one eyebrow cocked.

Edmar nearly laughed. What princess did anything but sit prim and proper at the supper table?

But then his eyes strayed to how far she leaned over. The top of her gown barely contained her rounded breasts, the fabric straining, and he wanted to jump up to cover her.

He constrained himself by roughly barking at her. "Princess Emmy."

Immediately, she stopped, wonderment draining from her whole body. She slipped back down to her seat, but kept her legs tucked under her as she lowered her eyes.

Silently, Edmar cursed himself. He had to have more patience. She wasn't from his world and wouldn't understand how much she could affect others, especially when it came to the body and nudity—something that didn't concern her at all.

Rivus set his glass down and swept a hand over the table. "Tell me what you want, Your Highness, and I'll get it for you."

Her dark lashes swept up with excitement back in her emerald eyes. "Can I have everything?"

"Whatever you wish."

Rivus took her plate and added a garlic biscuit and a couple of pieces of cut ham. Then he handed the plate to Edmar with a pointed look.

Edmar mouthed a thank you and added a little of everything on the table. He set the plate in front of her. "Perhaps after dinner we can go for a walk or take the rowboat out."

Those long eyelashes lifted to him. "I'd like that."

He breathed a sigh of relief as her shoulders loosened. But as they ate, he realized something troubled her. Her eyes darted around the table, looking at their hands where they held utensils, her fingers awkwardly holding her fork. She didn't know how to use it.

Clearing his throat to gain Rivus's attention, he put his own utensil down, picked up a biscuit to tear it in half, and stuffed a rolled-up piece of ham between the two pieces before chomping down on it. "A wonderful ham sandwich."

Rivus did the same.

Soon, Emmy followed suit with a relieved grin on her face. Until she took a bite. Her eyes rolled back, and she audibly moaned.

The sound shot through him, making him acutely aware of his body. It would be indecent of him to stand at the moment. He shifted in his chair.

Rivus laughed into his wineglass. "The food is that good, Princess?"

"You have no idea." This she said around another mouthful of bread and ham.

"Always nice to see a woman with a healthy appetite." Rivus took another swallow of wine, but laughed again when Edmar moved in his seat to find a better spot.

Emmy lowered her hand with the bread. "I hear a joke in your voice. Is there a lie to what you've just said?"

"Oooo!" Rivus hit Edmar on the arm. "You better watch yourself with this one. You won't be able to hide anything from her."

Edmar frowned at him but lightened the look toward Emmy. "What he means is that the ladies of court pretend they live on sunshine and gossip while food is only a waste of time."

She folded her hands in her lap, nodding as she swallowed hard. "I was never allowed to have any food I wanted, and most of what was fed to me was so bland, seaweed would have tasted better."

The tightness in her shoulders loosened when she stuck out her tongue. "Sunshine probably tastes better."

He smirked.

Again he wondered at the life she led beneath the waves, not allowed to speak often and unable to even choose her foods and eat for herself. He imagined she must have been like one of his cousin's pretty dolls. Isa would take them out occasionally, dress them all up and brush out their hair, only to set them on display until she was ready to play with them again.

"Fed to you?" Rivus asked. "What kind of world did you come from?"

Noticing her panic, Edmar slid a hand across the table toward her, hoping to distract her from Rivus.

He lowered his voice so that she knew his words were for her. "None of those women hold my attention."

Her chin dipped toward him, and she also lowered her voice. "Who holds your attention, then?"

"Only you."

CHAPTER 11

EMMY

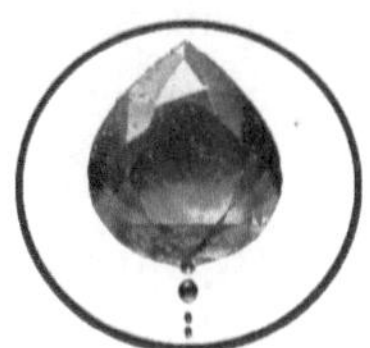

From the moment Emmy entered the dining room, she was drawn to Edmar with an overwhelming urge to be close to him. His tall, lean form by the window, the light-blue glow around his ocean-colored eyes, captivated her. The scattering of teal scales along his hairline and on the back of his hands reminded her of the magnificent dragon he became during the day.

She couldn't deny the pull she felt—a profound sense that she belonged here, with her Dragon King. Yet, despite the enchanting evening and enjoyable dinner, her thoughts remained fixed on uncovering a way to claim the Sun Stone. She knew now the magical artifact wasn't at the Sun Temple, but she didn't want to raise suspicions and question the maids gossiping about it.

Beyond the Sea Witch's quest, another call haunted her. The child from Agondray's depths. She'd invaded Emmy's dreams today, urging her to return, a plea conflicting with her task.

The child had absorbed her magic once before, but the effects hadn't lasted. She couldn't afford to lose focus. She dreaded her magic's return, its danger to everyone, and the agony it brought her. The thought alone made her nauseous, while the prospect of failing and becoming another lost soul in the Sea Witch's garden loomed ominously.

She forced herself to focus on her dinner, swallowing another bite.

"It's a sound request. The pack will probably have more information." Rivus ran a hand through his shaggy hair, a note of worry in his voice.

"I assumed as much. I wouldn't have asked if I didn't need the information." Edmar stared out the windows at the night sky.

"I understand. It will be done, Your Majesty." Rivus tilted his head down in deference. "Do you mind if I take my leave now?"

Edmar looked over the food and at her.

She smiled.

She loved it. Smiling without pain. Such a simple thing. Yet she'd spent a lifetime suppressing any movement. This could be her life. If she completed the Sea Witch's request, she'd be free to live like this forever. With her Dragon King.

But if she stole the Sun Stone from Edmar's kingdom, would he still want her the way she wanted him? The bargain with the Sea Witch might cost her everything. There was a reason she'd resisted going to the monstrous creature for so long—her bargains never led to anything good.

"I think we've finished." Edmar stood. "Thank you for joining me and the princess for this meal."

Rivus rose. The two men crossed arms. Although both were taller than her, Edmar still stood at least a good clamshell or two taller than Rivus.

But where Rivus was broader in the shoulders and in his hips, Edmar was all lean muscle. She'd been surprised by just how toned he'd been when he carried her, the muscles rippling without effort while he walked them toward the cliff with the Emerald Palace perched on top.

Rivus gave Emmy a mirthful smile. "Beware tonight. You may get either the Blue Angel or the Blue Devil."

With her confused frown, he bowed toward her. "The food and company were pleasurable. Have a wonderful night, Your Highness."

"You as well," she said.

Then Rivus strode out of the room.

Once more, Edmar offered her a crooked arm. She hadn't really known what it meant earlier when he made the same motion, but it seemed she'd chosen the correct response before, so she sighed—because she'd have to stand and feel the pinprick of a dozen knives in her feet—and took his arm to be led through the palace.

Her heart fluttered at his strength, at his irresistible ocean scent.

The sensations helped combat the torture in her feet, but like she'd learned before, she walked on her tiptoes to minimize the pain.

"Can you explain to me how you came to be here, Emmy?"

Her heart jumped. What could she say without raising suspicions? She measured her breath leaving her body, slowing it down like she did when she meditated. "I had to leave."

They crossed the Grand Hall, surrounded by its opulence. It was breathtakingly beautiful, yet torturous to realize that while she felt she belonged here, it would never be hers once Edmar discovered her true purpose in his kingdom.

"I understand your why. But how?" His gaze fell to her with open curiosity. No suspicion. "I saw you in the water without a tail. That's not really possible, is it? Because you're a mermaid."

As a servant opened one side of the double doors leading out of the palace, she wondered if he could read lies in words the way she did. Perhaps it would be better for her to say very little.

He paused at the palace doors, his gaze searching hers. "I won't force you to reveal your secrets. I don't want you to feel unsafe," he said, his voice low and reassuring. "But I hope one day you'll trust me enough to share them."

Trust was not forgiveness. Even if she trusted him, it didn't mean he'd forgive her for what she had to do—or that she could forgive herself. She just couldn't risk him interfering with her quest, a mission to protect him and everyone else. A mission to end her life of pain.

But she could reassure him in another way. "I feel safe with you."

He offered his hand, and she took it, noticing a few scales on the back of his hand as they stepped out into the warm night air. Her heart picked up the racing pattern again, but with excitement this time.

No matter that knives speared her feet, she felt happy right now. With a lightness in her step, she descended the stone staircase after him. They wended through moonlit gardens, adorned with ancient statues, fragrant with blooming flowers and the promise of adventure.

She squeezed his hand. "I used magic to make myself human. Well, somewhat human. I'm not entirely human, nor a mermaid, anymore."

Under moonlight, silver highlighted the top of Edmar's dark brown hair as he considered her words. His hand twitched in hers. "You never want to go back to being a mermaid?"

Being a mermaid meant suffering and pain. It meant a life of never being close to anyone because of her power. She would mourn the loss of her core identity, but if severing her link to her power meant she was no longer a mermaid, then she would take that life.

However, if she told him all of that, he might have more questions she wouldn't be able to answer. So she shared a different answer, one that was also truthful. "Mermaids may not choose their own mate. They must accept whoever their father or male relatives pick for them. I wanted something different."

"At dinner, you asked who held my attention." A soft blue glow entered his eyes. "I would turn a similar question on you. If you wanted something different from the life and mate your father had chosen for you, do you know what you'd want?"

She dropped her eyes, hoping he mistook her hesitation for shyness. His question was far too complicated. She knew what he wanted her answer to be.

Everything within her yearned for that to be her answer. But that wasn't her reality. Instead, she reached for an answer that would both be true and allow her to keep her real reasons for using the transforming magic hidden.

She met his earnest gaze, hoping that he believed her. "From the moment I saw you flying in the sky, I knew I wanted to be with you. It was like I was supposed to be yours."

It was true once. It just couldn't be true anymore.

However, it was the answer he needed. He smiled, and his eyes dropped to her mouth.

Warmth spread through her, and she tilted her chin up. He wanted to kiss her. She felt it in the strain of his body, and the thought thrilled her. She'd never been kissed before, and she would love for Edmar to be her first.

But then he audibly swallowed while his gaze focused past her, up at the sky.

She began to recognize this motion from him when he looked away, up at the stars, seeking something in their luminosity.

He was worried.

She looked away from him, her heart a frantic drum against her ribs. If only he knew how much he should worry about what she would do.

Chapter 12

EMMY

Edmar led her along a torch-lit cobblestone path to a weathered dock jutting out over the moonlit waters of a broad river.

"Lunarclaw River. Named for the werewolves' mother of the Water Clan." His voice was a low rumble against the quiet lapping of waves. Silver light shimmered and bounced on the water's surface.

She basked in the cool breeze whispering past her, rustling the fabric of her gown. She longed to shed the restrictive garment, but she knew better than to challenge human customs. Not yet.

"After you, Princess." He gestured toward the rowboat. His fingers interlocked with hers as he helped her aboard. The weathered wood creaked softly beneath her feet, the boat swaying gently with the rhythm of the river.

He settled into his seat at the oars, the palace, with its towering spires and marble floors, receding into the distance as he pushed them away from shore.

She inhaled the scent of pine and river water mingling with Edmar's unique aroma, a hint of briny sea air that quickened her pulse. For a moment, it felt like they were the only two beings in the world.

"Tell me about you, Emmy," he said, his voice a gentle murmur against the quiet cadence of the oars and the soft lapping of waves against the boat.

Crickets sang from the banks, a distant owl adding its haunting notes.

"I have five sisters."

"Favorite sister?"

"The youngest, Anjali." His smile seemed to tease her, so she felt the need to add more information. "We are much alike, in temperament and even in looks."

"I've never seen another mermaid as beautiful as you."

A thrill coursed through her, and she wondered why he hadn't kissed her earlier. She measured her breath, seeking calmness. In that moment, she heard Edmar's steady breath with the strokes of the oars. It was a comforting rhythm.

"Brothers or sisters?" she asked, although she knew he had three brothers, the other Dragon Kings, Ice Dragon shifters.

"Three brothers."

"Favorite brother?"

"I love them all equally. It's not right to pick favorites."

The look of superiority on his face seemed to hang suspended in time until he cracked with a laugh.

"Oh!" She tossed a handful of water at him.

Water sprayed the front of his emerald tunic. He released an oar to clutch his chest. "You wound me, Princess. I may not survive the night."

"Then you better be quick and tell me your secrets before you expire."

His mouth dropped open in shock, then he burst out laughing. She joined him. She exulted in the feeling of euphoria that filled her just from such a simple act.

Beneath the water's surface, close to the boat, Gilly swam on her back, looking up at her. Her laughter faded, and she gasped.

"What is it?"

She lifted her head so he wouldn't spy her friend. "I've just never been so free to laugh like that before."

"It seems to me that you've been bound by so many rules," he said, his brow furrowed. "Not always allowed to speak... to choose..." He trailed off, his gaze meeting hers, a question in his eyes.

Emmy's heart twisted. *He pities me.* She had a sorry life, but she'd deserved it. *Daughter of Ruin.* She didn't deserve someone as wonderful as Edmar. Especially since she had to steal from him.

Gilly reminded her she was not here to play.

She pushed past the emotions threatening to overwhelm her. "There is so much I've yet to experience. So much to see about this world. Like the Sun Stone. I thought to travel to the Sun Temple to see it, but then the maids said the God's Stone is no longer in the Sun Temple?"

"It's on its way here." He stroked the oars, correcting their drift toward the bank. "But it will arrive in time for the Blind King's Bluff Ball in two nights."

The ball he'd asked her to attend. "I'll get a chance to see it?"

"It'll be guarded in the chapel after arriving. Back when the Moon Fae offered it as part of their peace treaty with my parents, pirates stole the stone. We take a lot of precautions now. So it'll be on display during the ball until..."

His gaze drifted to the sky. Worried again. About what? *He can't know I'm here to steal the Sun Stone, right?*

"Please hold nothing back from me," she said. She needed to know what he knew.

He blew out an audible breath through his nose. "Until my new queen is chosen."

New queen?

But he'd asked her to the ball. Why would he do that but not ask her to be his queen?

Perhaps he has already chosen his queen. That would explain why he hadn't kissed her.

Pain lanced through her.

Idiot. And she couldn't help the idiot words that came out of her mouth next. "You're getting married to someone else?"

Of course there was someone else. That was what he'd been worried about telling her. This news should make her happy. Now she could steal the Sun Stone without getting too close to him.

Still... She frowned. At dinner, he confessed she was the only woman who'd caught his attention...Maybe he was also forced to marry, but who was forcing him?

"I will be." His simple confirmation stung.

No other explanation.

Heat flushed her cheeks and neck. She wasn't mistaken in his interest. Unless he was terribly good at faking it. Or he wanted something from her. Or he suspected her.

Whatever the reason, anger surged within her, and for the first time in her life, she could let it show. "Is this what you do?"

"Pardon?"

"Spout sweet words. Sway women to fall in love with you, then trap them in a boat so they can't escape your spell?"

He shook his head. "Everything I've said has been true—"

"Hardly, if you're marrying someone."

"Please, Emmy. This isn't my choice, and I know you understand that."

"Then... then... What do you call it...?" She made a motion with two fingers running along her hand. "Run away with me."

What in the eight hells am I thinking?

She couldn't run away with him. The Sea Witch's spell would wear off, and she'd risk his life. She also risked the Sea Witch taking her soul for her garden.

His lips flattened into a grim line. "I cannot run away as much as I might want to. I would place everybody here in danger if I didn't do my duty."

"And you always do what is right?" *Why am I pushing this?*

"Always."

"You must have such pride in yourself." It hurt. It hurt more than the piercing of dozens of knives in her feet.

He released the oars and scooted toward her, grasping her hands in his. She tried to pull away, but he wouldn't let her. "I don't know how to be different. I cannot run away from my kingdom. You possess a strength I lack. If I ran, the life of every human in my care would be at risk. Would you really want me to be a man who'd choose to run?"

Gods, no. She wouldn't want him to choose her over even one life, but the thought still fractured something deep inside. Her well of sadness filled with more tears she'd never be allowed to cry or sing away.

She couldn't look him in the eye. "Who is your new queen?"

He released her hands, but his body visibly tensed. "It's not decided."

Not decided, but definitely not her.

Torment squeezed her chest, and she bit her lip. She saw Gilly again, then. Her friend barely visible, with only the faintest lavender glow from her black tail.

Get over yourself—is what she would tell herself if she were Gilly. Swallowing the hurt, she lifted her gaze back to his. "Who are your choices?"

"All the eligible ladies in the kingdom."

"Am I not eligible?"

"That is tricky to answer without putting your life in danger. My next wife will be chosen at the ball, but I do not get to be the one to choose her." He looked up at the stars. "If I had the choice, I would select you without hesitation... that is, if you would have me."

It didn't make her feel better, but it strengthened her resolve. It didn't matter if she was chosen or not, as long as she got the God's Stone. "Can you show me the Sun Stone when it arrives? I'd love to hold it."

"I have no control over the God's Stone. It's a holy relic, vital to my kingdom. Father Jayasurya safekeeps it safe in the chapel until the queen is chosen. When she's chosen during the ball, the queen is the only other person allowed to hold the Sun Stone to ensure she is the true choice."

"Only the chosen queen can touch the Sun Stone?"

"Something like that."

He gave her an odd look, his gaze sharpening with curiosity. She needed to stop before she raised his suspicions. If he truly intended to marry someone else, she had to protect herself.

What woman in her right mind wouldn't leave immediately?

Except she was on a boat. In the middle of a river. And she didn't know how to swim without her tail.

"Why are you so interested in the Sun Stone?"

So much for avoiding suspicion. An answer formed quickly in her mind. She touched the jewel on her neck, letting her fingers linger. "I'm curious about the connection between my gem—a Sun Crystal—and the Sun Stone."

He seemed satisfied, and his shoulders loosened.

It was then that they both realized just how close they had come to each other. Their knees had shifted to either side, with one leg resting against the other's. He gazed down, watching as he clasped her hands again and slowly turned them over, exposing her palms. He lifted one hand while dipping his head.

His lips a breath away from the soft skin of her palm, he said, "Am I swaying you to fall in love with me, Emmy?"

Her breath halted, waiting for his mouth to touch her.

His lashes lifted, his eyes glowing as they peered up at her. "I will cherish you for as long as you allow me."

Then his warm lips pressed against her wrist.

A shock of desire skittered through her. Her pulse thrummed beneath the delicate skin where he brushed his mouth.

Over the years after her maturity, she'd experienced the same biological cycles as other mermaids in which her body yearned to mate and create offspring. But it had never been something she'd been allowed to do. She'd learned to ignore those drives, and so they diminished.

Now her whole body felt on fire from her Dragon King's kiss.

A good fire.

Yearning coiled low in her belly, a delicious heat.

He shifted to kiss her other wrist while looking up at her.

She let out a sound that was half sigh, half moan.

The sound shocked her as much as it ignited something within him. He pulled her forward, and one hand cupped her head.

He dipped his head, lips hovering over hers. "Tell me to stop."

"What?"

"Tell me to stop right now, Emmy. Tell me not to kiss you when I'll probably marry another woman by the end of the week."

She should stop him. A sharp pressure gripped her chest.

No matter who he married, no matter who he loved after this moment, he would always be her Dragon King.

"Don't stop," she whispered.

He released his breath and slammed his lips over hers.

The boat lurched, and they tipped over into the water.

Chapter 13

EDMAR

Edmar dove under the surface after Emmy the moment she disappeared. He found her quickly, struggling and sinking. She flailed her arms in the water. Her skirts tangled in her legs.

He grabbed her hand and kicked to the surface. But a moment after her head popped up next to his, she slipped below again.

He yanked her hand, then wrapped his arms around her from behind. "Quit fighting me, Emmy."

Immediately she became immobile, as still as when he'd seen her at Siren's Cove and at the meeting with the Seat of the Dwarf. She was very good at not moving—he wondered if she was even breathing.

He kicked them backward toward shore. When his feet touched bottom, and he judged she could stand in the water, he released her.

She trudged a couple of feet through the muddy bank, then fell on her knees and coughed up water.

How had she held that in until now? With one hand lightly stroking her back, he said, "I'm so sorry, Princess. I'm not sure what happened."

He shouldn't have kissed her, yet the urge to do so again was overwhelming.

She grimaced. "Mermaids don't make great swimmers as humans."

He chuckled, understanding her frustration. It would be a huge adjustment, he imagined, losing such a fundamental part of her nature.

As her cough subsided, Emmy glared at the soaked fabric clinging to her legs. With a frustrated growl, she ripped at the hem, tearing the ruined garment away.

He tried to stop her, arms flailing. "What are you doing?"

"This stupid dress almost killed me."

Gripping her shoulders, he halted her, her glare burning into him. "I would never let that happen. Do you understand me?"

Her glare subsided as she took in his words.

No matter who he had to marry next, he would do everything in his power to ensure nothing hurt her. "Perhaps we should head back?"

Resigned, she nodded and attempted to rise. He slipped his arm around her waist to help her. He didn't miss the wince of pain crossing her face. "Are you hurt?"

She shook her head, stepping away from him. He deserved that. He should have never taken advantage of her feelings for him just so he could kiss her.

She drew her hair forward and wrung water out of it. "It's just these new feet and all my sore muscles. I'll get used to it."

Her mention of her feet drew his attention downward, and his breath caught. Everything froze in this moment.

There he stood on the shore, moonlight filtering through the trees and illuminating the landscape and the woman before him. Silver light reflected off her wet, almost transparent white dress. The thin, wet fabric clung to her body, revealing every curve and contour. Edmar's heart raced as he drank in the sight of her.

This version of her tantalized his senses more than finding her naked in the ocean. Tracing the delicate droplets clinging to her skin, he wondered how he'd ever be attracted to anyone else ever again. He lingered at one water drop right at the center of her bottom lip.

A silent struggle battled between his innate respectfulness and the depths of his emotions for this woman. The woman he'd dreamed of for over twenty-five years. The king within him grappled with the man who yearned to hold her close.

He thought of himself as a gentleman, but he longed to take her in his arms right then. Yet he hesitated. The desire to shield her from the pain that would inevitably come when he was compelled to marry another, and the longing to surrender to those surging emotions, tore at his resolve.

His fingers curled involuntarily at the thought of touching her, and he finally loosed his breath, all too aware of how often he forgot to breathe around her. "We can't go to the palace like this."

"No?" Her musical voice was low, her chest rising and falling with deep breaths.

Is she feeling this same intense urge—to bridge this distance between us, to feel that spark again, like when we'd kissed?

"I wouldn't want any other man to see you like that."

"And how is that?" Unexpected vulnerability shimmered in her eyes, a vulnerability mirrored in the ripped, soaked fabric clinging to her.

He stepped closer, one hand gently reaching for hers. He hoped his touch offered subtle reassurance, a silent promise that conveyed both his respect and affection for her.

"A vision in moonlight. A temptress calling to me."

Their shared gaze never wavered, and when she tilted her head up to his, he found her unspoken permission. He pulled her fiercely against him, her wet dress a thin barrier between him and her heat. He sucked in a breath, desire hardening his body.

His whole body strained to do more as he pressed a tender kiss to her forehead.

"Gods give me the strength to resist," he whispered over her head with his eyes closed.

Soft fingertips brushed his cheek, drawing his eyes down to hers. The stars reflected in her gaze. It melted his defenses. He should push her away. Save them both the heartache that was sure to come.

But in that stolen moment under the waning full moon, Edmar surrendered to the love and desire within him, allowing the river's baptism to wash away the barriers that had kept his feelings at bay.

He cradled her head, lowering his lips to hers, finally tasting her, licking the tempting water drop from her bottom lip. Her mouth opened with a faint moan. The sound ignited him further. His fingers clenched in her hair, and he plunged his tongue into the warmth of her mouth.

But then her breath was cool, nearly matching the coldness rushing from him, both of them creatures of Winter. It was a perfect combination of cold and warmth circulating between them.

Her arms wrapped around his neck, and she molded her body against his. His hands found every delightful curve. A faint scent of coconut mixed with flowers rose from the heat of her skin.

Desire bled through her moans as he moved his kisses to the top of her shoulder. A heady sensation overtook him, her scent filling his senses. Blood pounded in his ears. He needed her. *Now.*

No part of the respectful king existed as every hidden wanting of her burst from him. With hooked fingers, he pulled down the top of her dress and palmed her full breasts. He sucked one dusky green nipple into his mouth and rolled it between his tongue and teeth, tugging, before moving to the other one.

She arched into him, and he lowered them to the ground. Under the ethereal light of the moon, he kissed every inch of her exposed skin, feeling like he'd never have enough of her.

"Edmar..."

The sound of his name in her melodious voice tortured him, making every part of him hurt with the pain of not having her. She repeated his name between her moans as he teased her nipples again, sucking the tight buds into his mouth before alternating with a cool breath.

Her sounds and writhing body meant she neared a release he longed for, and he imagined ripping the rest of her dress away and burying himself deep in her, taking her, consuming her.

But that animal vision of himself sobered him.

She deserved better than to be taken in the dirt.

She deserved better than a man who would have no choice but to marry another.

How would she remember this moment, rutting on the riverbank while he was practically engaged to an unknown woman the curse would force him to wed? A curse he couldn't even tell her about without endangering her life.

Abruptly, he pulled the top of her dress back up, covering her, even if the wet fabric barely concealed the shape and darkness of her nipples. He wrapped his arms around her and tucked her head beneath his chin.

With deep breaths, he willed his body to calm down, wrestling for control over the desire pumping through his blood. He pushed every errant emotion into his mental Frostlands, his defensive barrier for all the worst feelings to afflict him and keep him from being the king his people deserved. Now his Frostlands would protect her virtue.

"Edmar?" Her voice muffled against his chest.

He closed his eyes with another deep breath. "I'm so sorry, Emmy."

Her stillness and silence drew his attention back to her. The moonlight emphasized her surreal beauty, and he cursed the fate that brought her to him again but didn't allow him to have her. "Please tell me you forgive me."

"Why would you need my forgiveness?"

"I shouldn't have taken advantage of you."

"But you didn't. I enjoyed it."

He shivered. *Gods, she wants me as much as I want her.*

"I don't know how the merfolk come together for such activities, or if you've ever been with a Land Bound man, but I rarely do anything like this. You deserve—"

His words tumbled out, fueled by embarrassment, but Emmy silenced him with three soft fingers pressed against his lips. "I have never been with any man. Merfolk or otherwise. But I see nothing wrong with what we did."

His eyebrows shot up. *A maiden?*

Could it be true?

How the fates were so cruel!

If she loved him, and they had been allowed to marry and fall in love twenty-five years ago, then she might have been able to break his curse.

She could have been the one.

Could be even now, except the curse refused to choose her again.

He'd always hoped for that outcome, even after a thousand years of being forced to marry over and over again, always to a bride by chance, a bride he wasn't allowed to choose. His brothers had lost faith they'd ever be free of the curse. Kalden, broody but sensitive, seemed to die a little death with each wife who passed from this realm. Zane, the ultimate playboy, chose a new woman every night, yet even he hadn't escaped the curse, though he'd had fewer wives than Edmar or Kalden.

Then there was their oldest brother, Rin.

He'd never married anyone, making his kingdom inhospitable to any but the hardiest of creatures.

Rin had loved the Snow Princess, and with her curse, he'd retreated from everyone. Even from his brothers. And now he was no longer human.

But Edmar had to believe that everything would be better one day.

But not today.

Fate laughed at him.

He had the perfect woman to break his curse. He'd probably always love her, but he never wanted to hurt her. Continuing whatever this was would lead to heartbreak for both of them.

Lifting the back of Emmy's hand to his lips, he murmured. "If you were my wife, I'd want to take my time with you. Make love to you the way you deserve."

"And I would have to be your wife for you to make love to me?" She arched into him, pressing her body to his.

His hand dropped to her hip to halt her movement.

Her lower lip caught between her teeth before she settled back. "I've never been allowed to do anything, and there is so much I can do now, so many firsts for me to try. And I want to be with you. I want this first time to be with you, Edmar."

"Gods," he said in a low murmur, closing his eyes. His fingers tightened around her hip. "I don't want to hurt you."

"You are not the guardian of my heart." Her hand snaked into his hair and tugged his head down, his eyes opening in surprise.

He stopped the forward momentum so that his lips were just above hers. Her breath touched his skin, not as cold as he'd expect from another creature of Winter, but still chilly.

He groaned. "Emmy..."

Lifting her head, she kissed him, but he kept his eyes closed, his lips still. He couldn't give her what she sought from him. It took everything within him to resist her, and when she realized he wouldn't kiss her back, she released him with a frustrated sigh.

She must feel this same intense connection between them, but he could do nothing about it. He rose and put several feet between them. When he didn't hear her move, he turned his head just enough to send his words back to her.

"We need to go."

A nearly quiet shuffle as she also stood. "Give me a moment."

Now he looked over his shoulder to see what she was doing. She walked to the edge of the river bank and crouched near the water, her head bowed. Muffled words reached him.

Edmar put more distance between them. Enough that he'd give her privacy for whatever prayer she offered, whatever succor she sought from the gods, but not too far that he couldn't see her.

Then he said his own prayer, asking for the strength to abstain from touching her again.

CHAPTER 14

EMMY

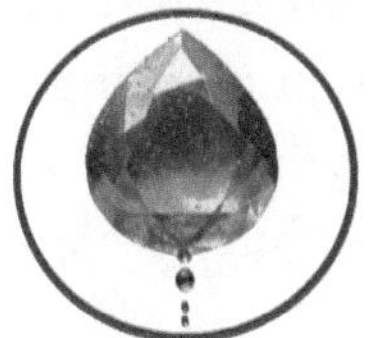

Emmy swept her hand through the river water and sang the beginning of the Ocean's Lament, her first time ever bringing the song to life.

"Beneath the waves where shadows linger
In our hearts, shades of fading gray,
Longing whispers in the ocean's song,
No tears, long unshed and kept at bay.

Sorrow wrapped in waves of our hearts,
A symphony echoing through the sea,
The Ocean's Lament renews our soul,
Release pain and let spirits roam free."

As the melody wove through her, she searched for the familiar soothing calmness, but it didn't come, leaving a hollow echo within her. No other merfolk would hear her Ocean's Lament, including her sister.

What else could wound her as deeply as the knives constantly digging into her feet?

Edmar felt the desire lying between them yet denied them the experience of coming together. And now she missed the opportunity to reach out to her sister.

"Emmy."

With a gentle ripple, Gilly's head emerged, water cascading from her sleek hair. Her eyes gleamed like polished amethysts just above the surface.

Emmy leaned forward. "I knew I saw you."

Gilly also saw her, everything in her thoughts from the moment she met with the Sea Witch and the bargain she'd made over her soul.

"Do you have the Sun Stone?"

That made her frown. She'd think her best friend would ask how she was doing first, but she knew her friend was just looking out for her. "It will be here soon. In time for a ball. I hope to take it then."

That pacified Gilly somewhat, but her dark brows lowered. Probably over Emmy's thoughts about the ball where a wife would be chosen for Edmar.

"This is no time to be kissing boys."

"I've never had the chance to kiss anyone."

"You shouldn't be kissing the king. I know how you feel about him and that way will only cause you trouble. Distract you from your real goals here."

"Before I can do anything with the Sun Stone, I have two days and nights. I want to enjoy these stolen moments before I no longer have the chance."

The mermaid blew bubbles on the water's surface. "Fine. Just don't forget why you're here."

"Believe me, I can't." As Gilly sank until only her eyes remained above water, she said, "Please tell Anjali where I am and that I'm fine."

Gilly nodded and submerged, leaving her to brush off her hands and join Edmar, sucking in a breath as she went to her tiptoes again. He offered his arm, the gesture familiar. She felt a pull toward his warmth but masked her longing with a studied gaze at the horizon, leaving his arm hanging in the humid night air.

Let him think she was mad... Well, she was mad that he hadn't continued kissing her, even though she'd been open about what she wanted. But she couldn't stand the idea of touching him if it didn't lead to more kisses, like the ones they'd shared already. She loved how his kisses left her breathless.

Back inside the palace, Edmar shielded her until a servant fetched her a blanket, then he led her through unfamiliar corridors. She still didn't entirely understand the obsession with clothes. They were a hassle, but the Land Bound set a lot of expectations and placed great importance on the different colored fabrics.

Admittedly, some dresses were very pretty, romantic even.

But right now, she yearned for the heat of his touch to melt away the layers of clothing between them. For him to continue kissing her as he had on the riverbank. Yet he stood before her, an unyielding cliff against her crashing waves.

"These are the doors to my chambers. You see down there," he pointed down the long, curving hallway of polished emerald marble filled with closed doors set at twenty-feet intervals, "is your door. If you need me, you only need to come knock."

Ah, so this is why he brought me this way.

She hadn't known her chambers were so close to his, even though she'd been told this was the royal wing. Could she use this to her advantage? Maybe sneak into his room later, when his defenses were down.

She really wanted to kiss him, to feel his lips on her again.

Excitement thrummed in her chest.

At the moment, he seemed to wait for her response. She mentally kicked herself. She was so used to no one ever expecting her to speak.

"Thank you, Your Majesty."

He frowned, then led her to her chamber door, where he turned and took her hand. Yearning welled within her. She wished he'd just get over his moral responsibilities to protect her and what he thought was the right thing to do.

His sense of duty and honor was admirable, but she could foresee it causing more problems for them.

He bowed to place a kiss on the back of her hand.

Heat touched her cheeks, more desire than anything else. "The riverbank seemed to wash away your reserves and sense of honor, didn't it?"

Those same lips had kissed her, teased her, only an hour ago. It had felt oh so nice. After a lifetime of being denied everything, she wanted to experience it all.

His tone resonated with his inner conflict. "Some tides are too strong to swim against, even for a moment."

Her body vibrated with the need to press against him, kiss him until he surrendered. There was nothing holding her back now. Her killing magic was gone, at least temporarily.

She kept her voice low, but allowed a mix of her vulnerability and a hint of challenge to bleed through. "Not all my tides are turbulent. Some... invite you to dive deeper."

The storm in Edmar's ocean eyes betrayed his steady reply. "And some depths hold treasures too precious to risk with careless dives."

He moved closer to her, the door at her back, and she thought perhaps he would kiss her, even after saying no. She raised her chin with a smile, but he only toyed with one of her blue curls, mostly dried now.

"I will send a maid to help you wash and prepare for bed. I hope you have a restful evening."

Hurt lanced through her. She didn't understand him at all. How could he deny this thing between them? "I won't see you again until tomorrow night?"

"Like this, yes. I'll be in dragon form during the day, with business to attend to."

She smiled, remembering his other form. "You're a very beautiful dragon."

His blue cheeks darkened with her praise, the color change intriguing her.

He cleared his throat. "Tomorrow night?"

When his gaze traveled to her lips, heat extended to her cheeks. But she only nodded, swallowing hard.

"Goodnight, Emmy."

His eyes never left hers as the door closed between them, then she was left with no audience as she peeled the rest of the dress off with a long sigh.

An hour later, after Lida helped her as promised, plaiting her hair into one long braid again, but giving up on making her wear a dressing gown, she flipped over in the huge bed for the hundredth time.

Should she go to his room now?

Then she second-guessed her plan. If she did this, would he stop resisting her, only to hate her in the morning for pushing him?

Curse his sense of duty and honor.

She truly appreciated that quality, but it hampered her desires. It also made it very clear she could never tell him about her quest. He would not allow her to give the Sun Stone to the Sea Witch.

She knew she wouldn't change his moral standards when it came to the God's Stone, but she might tempt him to kiss her again.

Giving up on sleep, she left her bed. Knives dug into her toes. Her muscles groaned in rebellion, but she wouldn't be deterred. It was manageable compared to the pain she'd felt all her life.

She paused, wondering if seducing him was wise. What if he threw her out?

If he did that, then she'd leave the palace.

There was no way she could stay here.

Except she needed the Sun Stone.

Her mind raced with uncertainty. But the more she considered it, the more she knew she had to act. This was the only chance to push past his walls, to make him see what they could be together.

Would tonight be the night?

She pulled on her lightest-weight dressing gown, leaving the top ties undone, and threw a brown cloak over it in case any servants roamed the halls. As she tied the cloak's sash, determination settled in her bones. After slipping on a pair of leather slippers, she took a deep breath and stepped into the dim hallway.

She turned toward his chambers and stopped.

There was someone already leaving his room.

CHAPTER 15

EMMY

The soft glow of oil lamps barely illuminated the blue-cloaked figure slipping out of Edmar's chambers. Emmy stilled, trying to breathe through the furious clench in her chest.

Did he reject me for someone else?

The intrusive thoughts clouded her reasoning until a flash of powdery-blue skin, between a dark sleeve and dark gloves, calmed her.

It was Edmar.

And now she noticed other details, a leather bag over his shoulder, his distinctive walk—long even strides that spoke of a subtle power embodying a presence others should respect but also one that took great care—as he turned in the opposite direction.

She followed, curiosity piqued. So intrigued, she barely felt the knives in her toes.

When he slipped behind a tapestry in a different hallway, she followed him into the darkness within, but she'd barely taken a step when an arm wrapped around her from behind and a sharp touch of metal grazed her neck.

She let out a surprised cry.

The dagger instantly dropped away. "Emmy?"

"Yes."

"What are you doing?"

Though she couldn't see him, the hard edge to his voice was unmistakable.

"I couldn't sleep, and then I saw you sneaking around. I was curious."

"Sneaking around?"

"What are you doing?"

A faint blue light brightened in his eyes, circling the irises. The glow highlighted the small space. Beneath his blue cloak, he wore a plain navy tunic with the same color trousers.

The circumstances, the light in his eyes, and his attire recalled Rivus's words from dinner. *Beware tonight. You may get either the Blue Angel or the Blue Devil.*

Earlier she had the Blue Angel. Could this be the Blue Devil?

He smiled. "Do you want to join me?"

"Yes." She didn't need to know what he was doing to know she wanted to do it.

He grabbed her hand. Anticipation surged between them as they hastened through dark corridors, ebbing and flowing like the ocean. His excitement rolled over her, and she couldn't help but laugh.

His deep chuckle followed, and his hand tightened on hers. She squeezed back. They slipped through a lower tunnel, leaving the palace. A finger to his lips warned of silence.

The exit expelled them into a damp, dark alley. He crept to the end of the alley and scanned the cobblestone street to either side. He turned back to her and pulled her hood up. With soft movements, he tucked her hair so that none of the sapphire strands were loose.

"We are now in Virdis, the capital city surrounding the Emerald Palace," he said in a low voice. His touch sent a shiver through her and goosebumps rose on her arms.

She returned his intense stare, appreciating the long nose and full lips. He had a very regal face, finer than the mermen back home, but strong in its own way. He swallowed, and his gloved fingers pinched the edges of her hood to adjust it. His eyes fell to her mouth.

She drew in a breath, her lips tingling.

Then he pivoted away from her and ducked into the street, heading to the right. Disappointment thudded hard against her chest, but Emmy followed him. He kept them close to the shadows of two-story houses lining the streets on both sides. Even though tall, evenly spaced poles with oil baskets remained dark, the waning full moon splashed a wave of light down the center of the cobblestones.

She studied the sleeping houses as they crossed several streets. The ingenuity of building upwards impressed her, maximizing space, yet these homes seemed like leaning giants, haphazardly constructed and patched, lacking uniformity. No part of Opal City appeared so desolate or different from house to house.

A musty scent of dampness from poorly constructed runoffs for rainwater provided welcome relief to the occasional whiff of waste. Combined with uneven cobblestones, it all conveyed a sense of desperate instability.

Her Dragon King halted, and she bumped into his back with a chuckle.

"Shhsss." A blue glow danced merrily in his eyes.

He crouched in front of one door and pulled his leather sack forward to rummage through it. She noted the city's emblem, a crude compass rose marking the door, which didn't appear on any other door in this section.

Emmy knelt beside him, her intrigue growing. The relief for her feet, aching from the knife-like stings, was immediate. He finally found what he was looking for. With the greatest of care, he set a brown paper package in front of the door.

He bowed his head. "May the Sun God and his Seven Sleepers watch over you."

After his prayer, he shifted to rise, but she laid a hand on his arm, then flirted her fingers over the package. "What is this?"

He laced his fingers with hers, pulling her to her feet before continuing down the street. His hushed voice added to their low footfalls.

"Humans rarely have magic, yet our world is full of it." He never looked to her as he turned down yet another street, then stopped in front of a new door scratched with the same compass rose marking. She bent down with him as he continued. "Dragons were created to protect the humans."

He found the brown-packaged gift he sought and carefully placed it on the door stoop. His hand hovered over it. "My brothers and I unwittingly killed so many humans during the Little Ice Age."

The Little Ice Age. A time before her. Crops withered, seas froze, and entire kingdoms buried under relentless snowstorms. All civilizations were affected, but Agondray the worst.

She frowned, disbelieving that he could be responsible for hurting anyone. The more she learned about him, the less she thought she'd ever know what Rivus meant about the Blue Devil. This man before her embodied honor with unwavering values and principles.

Lost in memories, he remained motionless for several seconds. He shook his head suddenly and pulled them to their feet once more after a quick prayer.

"We can do more for humans than just protect them from danger. We can aid them, help them have a better life."

Her breath caught as he hurried over a bridge and down another street. The sharp sting of knife points in her feet matched the rapid beat of her heart. "I think that's admirable. But why do all of this in secret?"

"Many reasons." He paused in his stride, his brow furrowed before he continued to lead them down another street. "Atonement, for those I inadvertently killed before realizing what I'd done. Because of that, I don't deserve to receive public accolades or praise. But also there's a certain joy and fulfillment that comes from anonymous giving."

The more she learned about Edmar, the more her heart felt torn, a maelstrom of admiration and an aching guilt swirling within her. Turmoil, her growing affection warring with her looming betrayal, settled uneasily in her stomach. But she didn't have a choice with the Sun Stone. If she didn't do this, no one would ever be safe around her again.

He turned, catching her shoulders in his hands. "Few know about my nighttime activities. If anyone knew the king ran the streets late at night, some who have ill intentions might try to intervene, try their hand at killing a king. I only brought you because you said you haven't been allowed to do anything before. I can't offer you everything you want from me. But I can do this for you."

She shrugged one shoulder. "Rest assured, I wouldn't jeopardize anything you do here. I know that what you're doing is bringing joy to others."

"And you're not afraid of being out here in the middle of the night?"

"Why would I be?" People always had to be afraid of her, so she'd never experienced the reverse, except with the Sea Witch. "I believe your specific words were 'try their hand at killing a king.' I believe them as you meant them. Others could try, but they wouldn't succeed. I have no reason to be afraid."

He chuckled, leading her to the next marked house. Here the homes were in slightly better repair than the others across the river, but some windows carried sagging flowerbeds with only weeds or a single flower for company.

This time he withdrew a slim envelope, which he could slip under the too-wide gap at the bottom of the door.

"No gift this time?"

He shook his head and led them into a narrow alley between the houses. Blocking her view of the street, he backed her into a wall and bent his head close to hers. The pounding of her heart thudded in her ears with his nearness.

His chilly breath whispered down her neck, and she closed her eyes, shivering as his words touched her skin. "This family lost a child. Nothing will ease their pain."

The resonance in his voice spoke of a deeper loss. She turned each syllable in her mind, hearing the tones, hearing how others spoke of loss, and then she knew what his was.

"You've lost a child?"

Closing his eyes, he leaned his head on the wall. A shudder rippled through him, and Emmy slipped her arms around him. He dropped an arm to her waist, holding her close. She wouldn't have ever guessed this pain haunted him. At times, he appeared open with his emotions, but several times tonight, he seemed to lock them away behind an icy look.

Her words were a whisper against his tunic. "I'm so sorry, Edmar."

Yet none of his pain had been visible there for anyone to see, not even her. She'd controlled herself all her life because she had to. But what caused him to hold those emotions away from himself. The loss of his child, his attraction to her? What else did he lock away?

He drew in a deep breath before launching away from her. "It's in the past, and we have to keep moving forward."

A false lightness entered his voice toward the end of his statement. Still hiding his emotions. Did he always push away negative feelings instead of dealing with them?

She'd never been allowed to process her feelings for her part in her mother's death. Maybe she could now. She could say something to connect to him through the pain of losing their family members, and maybe he'd feel safe enough to talk about losing his child one day.

Clasping hands to her chest, she gazed downward as she admitted what she'd done. She'd never said these words aloud. In her mind, she had screamed the confession, but she had never given voice to them. "I killed my mother."

Edmar stared at her, the blue glow in his eyes dimming. "I'm sure it wasn't your fault."

"Oh, it was." She laughed, hearing her own maniacal sound. It was the only sound her faulty body could make, unable to sing the Ocean's Lament or cry tears.

"Tell me about it." His voice was that gentle cadence again, promising intimacy, promising his full attention.

How much could she say without revealing her reason for being here? Even if she told him the truth about why she needed the Sun Stone, and she truly believed she needed it, his integrity and strict moral code wouldn't allow him to give her what she needed.

He knew a little about her magic, though.

"My magic is destructive," she said. "I knew how to control it, but that day, I was being willful. My mother paid the price for my inability to follow the rules that kept others safe."

Something seized her throat, and she felt like she couldn't breathe.

He cupped her face, his gaze searching hers. "Breathe, Emmy."

His voice always soothed her, and she followed his command to breathe. His glowing eyes brightened.

Did he look for tears?

She had none. She wanted them. She wanted her Ocean's Lament.

Both were denied to her.

"How old were you?" he asked softly.

She swallowed the thickness in her throat, a heavy weight choking her throat. "Ten."

"You were a child." The words were almost explosive in their defense of her.

Warmth flooded her while something tightened in her chest, tangling with the despair in her heart. She tried to banish the new feelings, but these foreign emotions choked her until she admitted what was happening.

She was falling for him.

"Kiss me," she said.

He started, surprised. His thumbs rubbed the top of her cheeks, his eyes on her mouth, and he licked his lips. "My restraint weakens when it comes to you."

"Kiss me," she said again. "I need to feel something other than this overwhelming sadness."

He didn't hesitate. His mouth was hot on hers, and they breathed each other's cold, sharing in their mutual desire for the other, sharing the pain of who they'd lost. His arms tightened around her, and she'd never felt more at home and accepted.

He slowly ended the kiss, his breath quick against her lips, but leaving her breathless once more. Her heartbeat eventually calmed with their stillness.

Then he spoke into their shared quietness. "Do you want to dance?"

Chapter 16

EDMAR

"Welcome to the Blue Angel Tavern!" Edmar swung the door open to a lively scene, pulling Emmy into a world of warmth and merriment. Candlelight flickered in the depths of her emerald eyes.

Oil lamps cast dancing shadows across the rough-hewn beams and a golden hue upon the jovial patrons. The air was thick with the aroma of ale and roasted meat. Strains of a lute and the beat of a drum filled the tavern, creating a lively melody.

He stopped in front of the polished wooden bar, his hand still holding Emmy's. A part of him feared she'd wander off, not realizing what a single female in a place like this meant. But part of him didn't want to let her go, either.

He couldn't recall the last time he'd acknowledged his son's death, six hundred years ago. He didn't like thinking about those days. He'd buried his grief beneath layers of duty and time, eventually yielding it to the tombs of his Frostlands' icy expanse, never to think about his son again.

Yet Emmy's presence, so vibrant and alive, created a subtle shift within his Frostlands, a deep, unsettling thaw threatening the frozen stillness, awakening what he had long thought buried forever.

Not tonight. He pushed the memories of his son deep into the icy recesses of his mind. Tonight was for Emmy, for laughter, for the fleeting joy of her presence.

Behind the bar, a stout, friendly-faced man with a neatly trimmed beard wiped down a mug, his round eyes on the musicians, his head bobbing to the song.

Edmar smiled and spoke loudly enough to be heard over the music and the raucous noise of the other patrons. "Owen."

The friendly man looked over, his eyes lighting with recognition. "Big K! Been a while."

Big King.

It was better than the bar's namesake, the other name Owen bestowed upon him. Rivus got a kick out of calling him the Blue Angel on his good nights, and the Blue Devil on the bad ones—the nights when his Frostlands failed to contain his darker side. He prayed Emmy never saw that side of him.

"Two for the back table."

The other man began to smile, then suddenly halted, and Edmar looked down to find Emmy pushing her hood back, large eyes gleaming at the crowd and the musicians.

Owen's hand gripped the mug harder, knuckles whitening, the amiable smile faltering. "I trust you know what you're doing, Big K, but mermaids are not usually welcomed here."

Emmy jerked, but he sidled protectively closer to her. Her hand linked with his, pressing her body into his arm.

He offered the man a wide smile. "Don't tell me you believe the old wives' tale."

While the mermaids' song at Siren's Cove often tugged at him when he flew over them, he'd never seen evidence of what Owen alluded to.

The stout man set down his rag and mug to lean forward. "No wives' tale here. Saw it myself. A siren's song can turn deadly."

Emmy spoke before Edmar replied. "What do you mean?"

The man pointed at her, his glance sliding sideways. "No singing here."

Heat spiked Edmar's tone at the way the man spoke to Emmy. "We'll not cause problems."

The harsh words caught Owen's attention, and whatever the man saw on his face made him bow. "My apologies, Your Majesty. I meant no disrespect. The Blue Angel wouldn't exist without you."

Nearly thirty years ago, he'd helped Owen's family with their poverty-stricken household. The tavern owner had been just a boy then. A mischievous boy who'd heard about a mysterious benefactor and tracked the Blue Angel one night to ask for aid. They'd been friends ever since.

"Quit that," Edmar said through clenched teeth. He didn't want anyone else to know he was the king. Not that his blue skin hid that fact at all, what with most of his population being brown-skinned humans, but no need to draw anyone's attention. If he pretended to be a commoner, most of his people were happy to oblige and indulge in his fantasy.

The man hastily straightened. "Again, apologies. I've seen it with my own eyes how a mermaid's song, the Siren's Call, made men turn on each other. So many died that night before a woman could kill the evil siren. We just don't want that type of magic here destroying the peace."

Emmy's grip tightened on his hand, but she lifted her chin. "You should learn to reserve your judgment. I am physically incapable of singing as a siren."

Sweat beaded on the man's upper lip. His round eyes grew larger as they darted from Emmy to him and back again. "You're right, my lady. Just watching out for the folk here."

Tightness coiled in his chest, a tangled knot of protectiveness, but he gave the tavern owner one curt nod. "Two mugs, Owen."

As he guided Emmy to the back of the tavern, he remained vigilant, alert to anyone giving her more than a passing glance. Silent fear surfaced, complicating his instinct to shield her. He might be the greatest threat to her. In the dim light, his shadow loomed large, a specter of the peril he posed to her heart. The attraction between them, as discernable as the tavern ale's heady aroma, was its own siren song, luring them to uncharted waters.

Waters where his looming nuptials threatened like jagged rocks, ready to shatter the fragile vessel of their burgeoning bond. How does one extinguish a flame that feels as vital as the very air he breathed?

Letting her go seemed impossible.

That would be a problem... but maybe for tomorrow night.

As they sat at an empty table in a secluded corner, away from the lively crowd, her large eyes turned to him. "What did he mean about mermaids singing?"

Does she really not know? She was a mermaid herself. His eyes narrowed, wondering how she hadn't at least heard the things he'd heard.

He leaned closer, his voice a low thrum mingling with the tavern's din. "Legends whisper of mermaids' songs, luring and commanding, weaving desire and action with mere melody and often causing death and destruction."

He watched her closely, relaxing when he saw no subterfuge in her emerald gaze.

Her attention drifted to the raucous conversation at a nearby table before sliding to the musicians. "And you believe this is true?"

He settled back, surveying the tavern. A few couples danced in front of the musicians. He couldn't wait to show her dancing.

"Stories always have a kernel of truth. Deciphering which part is true is harder, but if Owen says he's seen it, I believe him." He studied her as pure joy lit her jewel-toned eyes when more patrons began dancing. "You really know nothing about it?"

Sea-foam green fingers traced the dull gem at her throat, her lips pursed. "In the depths, our voices are bound, not by water, but by the wills of those who hold our gems."

Edmar considered the jewel she absently touched. Gems were the source of the merfolk's magic, but she'd said she used magic to make herself partly human, no longer a full mermaid. Did that mean she no longer had magic?

"The subservience transfers to the mate chosen for the mermaid," she continued, interrupting his thoughts. "We aren't allowed to choose anything for ourselves except for domestic things, like taking care of home and pups. The idea mermaids have unknown powers makes sense."

She drew a deep breath. He waited, patient. A barmaid dropped off two mugs of ale. Emmy immediately lifted the mug to taste the liquid. She drew back with a twist to her lips, and he laughed.

"That's different," she said.

He nodded with a smile and laughed again when she dove in to drink large gulps of the ale. When she wiped foam from her mouth, he prompted her. "Would you elaborate? Tell me how it makes sense that mermaids could be dangerous sirens in disguise."

She blinked slowly, long lashes sweeping up to reveal large eyes, lacking his mirth. "First, if mermaids were capable of such power, of course, we wouldn't be told, and it would be hidden from us. Our mermen wouldn't want us to control them like they control us."

"And second?" he asked when she didn't continue.

She shrugged. "Just thoughts."

"I like knowing your thoughts." He leaned closer to her, catching her floral and coconut scent.

"I've heard plenty of mermaids and mermatrons singing back home. None of their songs have ever convinced a merman to do anything he didn't want to do, so if this is true, what's the difference? Is it because she is above water or does the song affect only the Land Bound?"

"Interesting questions. Do you have a theory?"

She smiled, and his pulse quickened.

"I don't know if I'm anywhere near being right, but if this is true, what Owen is saying, then I would say it's all about power balance. Mermen didn't always control mermaids, but those were dark days, from all the stories. Have you ever seen the way dolphins mate?"

His brow lowered. "I can firmly say it's not something I've ever paid attention to."

She chuckled. "Well, when you live in the ocean, forbidden from doing anything, even mating dolphins become a source of entertainment."

"If you say so."

With a light hit to his forearm, she continued. "Several male dolphins will harass and separate a fertile female from her pod. After they have her isolated, they will forcibly take turns mating her, sometimes for weeks at a time. When she becomes pregnant, they abandon her and all sense of duty to the pup. It is said our race used to do the same until our Father God, Metallon, added the link between our gems and our mortal fathers, who became our protectors. This transfers to our mates, who stay with us to rear the young."

"How would that have given your females power on their own?"

"Perhaps it was never meant to be that way, but..." Her glance flicked to Owen. "Perhaps we have a power we forgot about. One that can sway any man."

The way she said it alarmed him, as if contemplating how she might use that power. However, she had assured Owen she couldn't.

"You really can't sing?"

Again, that shrug and a smile. She seemed to like to shrug, as if she delighted in the movement.

"That's not an answer, Emmy."

"The answer is not easy."

"Make it easy."

For the briefest flash, distress filled her eyes. Then it was gone. "We don't cry like humans. Instead, we sing this song that allows us to express our sorrow.

"No human can replicate it. There are notes and certain places in the melody that captures who we are as a people. Magic infuses the words, the sounds, the imagery. But as much as I've tried to call the tune forward, I can't sing the Ocean's Lament the way my people do. My magic is gone, and I can't even properly mourn my mother."

Her magic is gone. He had his answer.

The sadness that swamped her then took him completely by surprise. He'd never seen such a depression in her since he'd known her. For a moment, he was reminded of Kalden, who had hidden from the world for twenty years and had admitted to trying to take his own life.

He hadn't allowed his brother to wallow in despair, and he definitely wouldn't allow Emmy to either. He enveloped her hand in his. "Let's dance."

The first strains of a new song filled the tavern as he showed the dance's intricate movements. He exaggerated the steps for instruction while the song swirled around them.

"Alas, my love, you weave a tale,
Of fleeting hearts, both wild and free.
For I have known your charms,
In passion's transient revelry.

Scarlet whispers, sweet decoy,
Scarlet tales of tempting night,
Scarlet flames, desires untold,
Enchanting, Lady Scarlet's delight."

With patience and grace, he guided her hesitant steps until they flowed with the music. Her feet whispered across the wooden floor, and a spark of delight radiated from her smile to the tips of her fingers.

Pure enjoyment animated her as she effortlessly swayed and shifted into each beat. She gave herself to the music, unaware of how others gave her bemused looks when her cloak swirled around her to reveal her loosened nightdress beneath, exposing more than was decent. But he couldn't ruin her pleasure and spoil the night like he'd almost done at dinner the previous evening.

Immersed in the dance, she entranced him with her natural grace, the joy radiating from her. Her movements were like poetry in motion—the lines of her body, the unspoken words on her parted smile, the narrative in her eyes. The very essence of the dance had been woven into the fabric of her being, an inseparable part of who she was.

Effortlessly, she followed the music's cadence, as if she and the melody entwined in a harmonious embrace. It made him long to join the embrace. He wanted her more than he'd ever wanted any woman.

Once again, he'd forgotten he needed to breathe around her, until the dance drew them together again, her back pressed against his chest. Her hair brushed against his cheek. He finally took a breath, inhaling her scent of coconut and flowers mingled with the tavern's smoky air.

Their closeness brought a rush of heat, an intimate cocoon amid the tavern's cacophony, his words a soft murmur only she could hear. "When the gods invented dancing, they thought of you."

She lifted her delicate chin, her voice barely rising above the music, her breaths coming in exhilarating gasps as the dance liberated something wild within her. "I've never felt so free."

The pure and unbridled happiness radiating from her wrapped around him so that he only saw her, felt her, smelled her. He lowered his head with every intention of kissing her, but she gave him a sly smile and twirled away from him.

Her laugh echoed across the tavern and the space between them.

How would he ever be able to let her go?

Chapter 17

EMMY

Fire closed a tight circle around Emmy.

Wake up, wake up!

Heat licked her skin, bubbling with fire's intensity. Sea-foam green layers darkened and shriveled, revealing red muscle and white sinew beneath.

It was her mother dying in the fire.

Then it was her.

Fire acid burst within her, snapping and exhausting every sensory nerve in her body. She fell to the ground, writhing. A combustion roared in her ears. Acrid smoke filled her nose.

"Please," she cried into the darkness past the fire.

Soothing water cocooned her, and she sobbed, tearless.

Princess Emira. The woman's voice was lilting and delicate, a balm for her frayed body.

Slowly, she uncurled, tail straightening, and she opened her eyes. Sharp pain snapped beneath her skin. Then the dark red light of her gem radiated. Flowing lines of power snapped out of her, bowing her body.

She hung suspended in the familiar cavern, the huge clear egg throbbing before her, pulling at her lines of dark red magic. Power hummed inside the egg, beating in time to the heart of the being inside.

Come to me.

This was a mature voice. The voice that had said her name a moment before.

Yet her lilt echoed the childlike voice from the egg beneath Agondray's surface. But this time, she did not reach back through the magical link.

"Who are you?" Emmy asked aloud.

Your savior.

"What does that mean?"

I can protect you from your magic.

"What do you want?"

Come to me.

"Why?"

I'm ready.

"Ready for what?"

I'm ready for—

The cavern suddenly shook, and something threw Emmy across the water and into one of the cavern tunnels.

Darkness enveloped her. Her head knocked into the rocky wall, and she blacked out.

Cold woke her.

The blessed Mother Goddess had come to cradle her close.

Now her tearless sobs rejoiced.

She'd always heard Aqua, the Water Goddess, carried her children's souls to the afterlife herself, taking them from the Sea of Shadows.

Cold fingers smoothed her hair back on her forehead, and she opened her eyes.

A Water Fae cradled her head in her lap under the light of a bright noonday sun.

How she knew the Water Fae was not the Mother Goddess was a mystery to her, but perhaps it was the way the other woman watched her with hooded eyes.

Wary of triggering her magic, she sat up slowly and scooted back.

She sighed.

No pain.

And she didn't have her tail. Instead, she wore a simple, light blue gown she'd never seen before. She plucked at the fabric as she studied her environment and the woman.

This wasn't the ocean, but a garden filled with flowering plants and trees. She didn't know this place or any of the plant names, but everything smelled good. A warm sun sent hazy streams across white marble columns, which supported a roof over an open walkway circling the garden.

The surrounding building was pure white, a contrast to the vibrant garden and the woman beside her on the grass.

The woman was undeniably fae, her pointed ears and the way her hair moved confirming it. Strands of dark blue, shot through with greens and purples, tipped in white, flowed around her shoulders like living water, their movement both graceful and unsettling. Her lavender skin, pale and almost translucent, hinted at a heritage more complex than that of a simple Water Fae.

As much as she studied the woman, the fae studied her.

Emmy had no idea why she was here, but she was certain this fae held the answers. She'd wait her out.

A half smile touched the fae's lips, but her eyes remained cold. They were strange-colored. A dark blue, not at all like any of the jewel tones Emmy had grown up with. Instead, they looked almost gray in the shifting light so that the coloring was more of a slate blue.

"I don't know you," the fae said.

"Same." She rose, backing away from the strange fae, then raised her brow, surprised by the lack of pain. Absolutely no pain—no fire acid, no piercing knives in her feet.

This couldn't be a real place. *A dream?* But it felt closer to reality than her dream of the egg child.

The fae also stood, but didn't approach. She wore a white dress with silver accents and braids stitched at the collar and over her breasts. A much more luxurious dress compared to the one Emmy wore. Around the fae's neck, a long slender silver chain cradled a small white stone.

"Why does the Summer Child want you?"

Emmy shrugged, loving the fact it didn't hurt to move at all. "Who is the Summer Child?"

The fae crossed her arms. "Are you serious?"

Such petulance. Who did this fae think she was—a goddess? She snorted. "Why would I know who the Summer Child is?"

She had an inkling who the fae meant. If the fae knew where she just came from, then it stood to reason that the Summer Child was none other than the child in the clear egg who could absorb her Fire magic. However, she didn't know if she could trust this fae, and if the fae thought her daft, the woman might reveal something she might otherwise keep guarded.

"She's powerful," the fae said, "and you were in her chamber during your dream."

"Ah, so because I dreamed myself into that place, or somehow ended up there, then it must stand to reason that I know what's going on?"

"That's logical." The fae's purple lips thinned with impatience.

"Then I should know you according to that same logic."

The fae clenched her fists. "Stay away from the Summer Child."

"If I knew how to control my dreams, then I wouldn't be here with you."

The Water Fae waved her hands at Emmy, and the world began to fade. "Be gone with you."

CHAPTER 18

EMMY

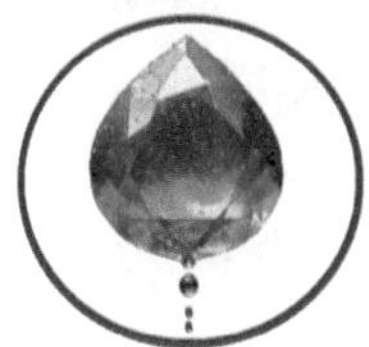

In her palace chambers, Emmy tapped her fingers on the table before the mirror, humming a few notes from the tavern music echoing in her mind. Lida pulled a brush through her long hair, separating parts into thick chunks.

Little of her dreams remained with her after she'd slept most of the day away, but she remembered dancing with Edmar until the last hours of the night. In her mind, she saw herself sweeping through each movement, and the words of the first song slipped from her lips.

"...I have known your charms,
In passion's transient revelry..."

"Princess Emmy!" Yolande paused at the doorway.

Lida laughed out loud.

The older woman strode toward her, a piece of lavender fabric draped over her arms. Emmy's eyes widened, remembering the fae from her dream, then narrowed at Yolande's frown.

"It's not decent for you to sing that," the housekeeper said.

Lida laid the brush aside, then gathered one separated chunk of hair to braid. "I think her voice is beautiful."

"Then she should sing something different." Yolande laid the fabric on the bed. "Where did you hear that song anyway, Your Highness?"

She giggled, unable to help herself. Lida's conspiratorial wink and the lightness she felt inside refused to bend to Yolande's reprimand. Plus, she wouldn't sell Edmar out. Let Yolande think whatever she wanted.

She didn't care as long as she spent more time with Edmar. She truly longed to see him again. To hear his voice, to see his smile. She'd enjoyed dancing with him last night, even though each time her foot touched the floor, it seemed as if she trod on sharp knives. She yearned for more moments like these before reality intruded with the Sun Stone's arrival tomorrow, in time for the ball.

Yolande turned to help Lida with her hair. "And why are you wearing *that* again?"

She fingered the buttons of Edmar's shirt, the one he'd given her to wear. "It's comfortable."

Before, she wouldn't have thought that true, but compared to the layers they dressed her in and the long dresses, this was better. The dingy white material hung off one shoulder and barely reached to her mid-thigh, giving her body plenty of room to breathe.

Yolande narrowed her eyes. "You shouldn't wear it when you have better options."

The woman clearly thought little of her selection.

"You'll have to take it off anyway for—"

Yolande became a frozen statue when Emmy took the opportunity to divest herself of the shirt. She stuffed the fabric beneath her bottom, knowing the housekeeper would likely jump at the first chance to remove the offending item and not return it.

"Well, then..." She patted her violet hair, as if reassuring herself the tidy bun was still there. The older woman looked lost for a moment, then she pivoted and left without a word.

Lida doubled over, laughing. "Oh sweet, goddesses!" She straightened and wiped away tears in her eyes. "I've never seen the housekeeper so flustered."

Emmy couldn't help smiling with Lida's obvious joy, even if it all left her bemused. "Clothes are truly an evil invention of the Land Bound."

Lida shrugged. "It's our way to be civilized, I suppose, and show off wealth."

As Lida finished with her hair, other servants entered with trays laden with dinner. All female servants, and they quickly looked away with wide eyes, her nudity shocking them as she rose from the chair, the sting of needles in her feet.

Nudity. A foreign word and concept to merfolk.

"Will I not dine with the king tonight?"

Lida pushed in her chair at the dressing table and straightened all the cosmetics. "King Edmar has a council meeting this evening, and you need to be fitted for your dress."

"My dress?"

Lida gave her a half smile. "For the ball."

Oh, that's right. The ball. She almost stuck out her tongue—a gesture pups loved, but one she'd never been able to practice. *How awful will this dress be?*

A small, unassuming woman entered next, her movements fluid and precise. Her dark eyes, large and owl-like, seemed to see right through Emmy, making her feel strangely exposed.

"Mistress Cassia, this is Princess Emmy." Lida paused for the small woman's bow, her dark hair threatening to escape its haphazard arrangement atop her head. "Your Highness, this is the seamstress the king requested for you. She creates the most beautiful dresses."

"I will touch you now, Princess Emmy." Cassia's words, a soft-spun whisper, emerged with unhurried assurance.

Uncertainly, Emmy looked to Lida, who nodded, so she said, "Proceed, mistress."

Cassia's deft and knowing fingers reached for Emmy's waist, her touch light yet decisive as she unfurled a slender strip of marked cloth, guiding it across her skin with practiced ease.

The seamstress barely spoke to Emmy while moving her limbs and telling her, "Hold right there."

Being measured and fitted felt like an odd dance, a constriction alien to her. Yet, there was a certain fascination in watching the seamstress work, her hands weaving through the air with a precision that was almost magical, turning the mundane task of measurement into an art form all its own.

But with the quiet woman working around her, Emmy fidgeted, earning a few frowns from the seamstress.

"How long will this take?"

"Not long, Your Highness," Cassia said.

Then perhaps she could eat. But would she see Edmar? Lida stood to the side, observing everything, waiting for any instruction from the seamstress.

"Will I see Edmar this night?" She couldn't help feeling he might be ignoring her, especially after their wonderful evening.

Lida spoke to a servant in the hallway, who hurried away. The same servant returned and whispered to the maid. With an enormous smile, she said, "He still wants to see you, Your Highness. He's asked to have you taken to the south garden where he'll meet you after his meeting."

"Oh." She supposed ruling took a lot of time. Her father had been busy when she was a young pup, but when she'd been moved into the Little Palace after... when she was ten, she really didn't know what that life looked like anymore.

"Don't worry. He's smitten."

Was she that transparent? Again, she fidgeted until Cassia smacked her hip.

Lida's lips thinned, but she said nothing. Emmy didn't blame the seamstress. It was a hard job to work directly with someone's person.

But while she was stuck here, she might as well make the most of her time.

"How is the next queen selected?" Edmar only said that it wasn't his choice. "Who chooses her?"

"Not a person. It's some type of magic." Lida stepped forward to hold her braids up from her shoulders, assisting Cassia as the small woman measured her shoulders. "The Golden Scepter with the Sun Stone."

"Magic decides?"

"It reveals the truth, Your Highness." Lida gently rearranged her hair, drawing some pins out of her pocket to capture escaped curls. "It's not exactly our place to question the king and how he chooses his queen."

If no one knew exactly how the choice was made, then there was no way to manipulate it.

Frustration welled in her.

Little Mermaid. The Sea Witch had been right to call her that, besides Daughter of Ruin.

What in the eight hells was she doing here, kissing her Dragon King and allowing herself to be dressed for a ball, when she did not know how to steal the Sun Stone?

She was acting like a lovesick adolescent, consumed by her first crush. Everything within her yearned to be with Edmar and for him to want her just as much, but she was here for one purpose—and that was not to mate her Dragon King.

Yet she was utterly lost around him. Her wits continually ran out of her head, her body lost all sense of decency, and her heart struggled to maintain a regular beat.

Lida clasped her hands, a wide smile on her face. "Mistress Cassia is making you a dress that will outshine all the other ladies. You'll see. The king is going to get the magic to pick you to be his queen somehow."

Why had her heart leaped at those words?

It shouldn't have.

Unless...

If I'm Edmar's queen, then when I finish doing as the Sea Witch asks, he'll have no choice but to take me back.

She needed to figure out how to make the magic choose her as its next queen. Then she could steal the Sun Stone.

But Edmar might hate her forever.

Chapter 19
EDMAR

Lord Rafiq, Edmar's Chancellor, slid a parchment across the table, the rustle loud in the chamber. "Here are all the eligible daughters from the noble families."

He fingered the document, his gaze not really seeing it. A sapphire-haired enchantress kept interrupting his thoughts. The image of Emmy dancing last night, her brilliant smile, and the kisses he'd stolen between songs remained with him.

How much longer can I deny myself?

His Treasurer, Mithya, cleared his throat, stealing him away from those consuming thoughts. The other man's golden eyes studied him with a frown. "I hope you haven't forgotten my daughter, Nuria, will be at the ball this year."

He'd forgotten.

He vaguely remembered Nuria, a young woman whose vibrant beauty hinted at her Sun Fae heritage. Her burnt orange skin and sunny yellow hair would surely endear her to the people who held the Sun God in high regard. Of all the places on the continent, many flocked to the Sun Temple to worship him.

However, he did not want to be tied politically to his Treasurer. The man would attempt to use the relationship to his every advantage. To many, he was just a crown to wed, pursuing him more for his position than for who he was.

To avoid yet another seeking to use him, he needed to choose Nuria first, before the curse decided she was his bride by chance.

By choosing a woman, starting an approach and truly opening his heart to the possibility of loving her, he somehow removed her from the curse's influence. This forced the Snow Princess's decree to find another, a bride by chance. That loophole was how Zane escaped marrying as often as the rest of them. After losing a wife, his younger brother spent every moment chasing women.

Edmar choosing Nuria would eliminate her from the curse choosing her, in the same way the curse had already eliminated Emmy as his next bride.

"Please have Lady Nuria wait for me in the south garden. After the meeting, I'll join her for a promenade."

The older man smiled and inclined his head, oblivious to his daughter's and his own thwarted ambitions. No one on his council knew of his curse besides Rivus.

He'd keep his promise to dance with her at the ball, knowing he wouldn't have to marry her after tonight. Plus, he always kept his promises, just as he would dance with the list of women on the parchment because it was expected. And he'd marry whomever the curse chose because it was expected.

Yet Emmy intruded on his thoughts again. The image of her sapphire hair working free of her braid while she twirled around the tavern filled his every thought. Her floral and coconut scent wafted over him, the memory so strong it was as if she was in the room. He stopped breathing.

He was to meet her tonight as well. She'd stolen nearly all of his reserve to put distance between them. He'd wanted her for so long. But in the end, the curse would separate them because it knew he wanted her. He realized he'd been foolish to think he could ever keep her.

Perhaps when she saw Lady Nuria later, the princess would finally understand that they could not be together, no matter how much they were drawn to each other, or how much they desired the other.

He slowly drew in a breath and rubbed his eyes, trying to banish her from his mind.

"Your Majesty?"

Realizing he had paused with his hand over his eyes, he shook the hand away and quickly scanned the list again, trying to see the names this time.

He failed.

Normally, he'd have contemplated these women, wondering who would be his next queen. Now a sick feeling settled in his gut. The Snow Princess's curse—a relentless cycle of unwanted marriages—was an awful existence. But he'd refused to let it break him.

Kalden could brood and wish for death, Zane could lose himself in a multitude of women, and Rin could hide himself from the world, but Edmar would not be defeated.

But this time, it threatened his sanity.

He wanted Emmy with an unnatural obsession, but how would it be fair to claim her while he wed another?

Unless I embrace the Blue Devil and take what I want.

No, he tried to avoid that part of himself. How would it be fair to promise his love when he would spend the next twenty years with his chosen bride?

He realized, with a start, that everyone stared at him, waiting.

They'd already discussed most of the important topics, with the list of eligible women being the last item on the agenda.

He sighed. "Thank you for the roster. I'll study this carefully and ensure each woman receives a dance. This council is adjourned."

The men pushed back from the table, happy to be done. He missed Rivus, but he'd sent his Marshal on a mission. Edmar wouldn't pull him back just because he needed a friend with an objective view.

But he needed guidance.

"Father Jayasurya, if you would please?" The abbot halted in following the other men from the room. "Would you mind praying with me before you leave?"

"Of course, Your Majesty." Father Jayasurya crossed his arms and bowed his bald head, his hands disappearing into the wide sleeves of his orange robe.

After nodding to the guards to close the door, Edmar's shoulders slumped slightly. He'd keep up appearances with his council, never showing weakness, but the abbot was the closest thing to a father he'd had since his own had died, though Edmar was over eleven hundred years older than the abbot.

"Father, I need guidance."

Edmar wasn't a religious fanatic like some in his kingdom, but he recognized the one god who still watched over the world. His creators, the Water Goddess and the Air God, had been in slumber alongside the other five deities for millennia. If the legends were true. And the absence of any god but the Sun God in recorded history lent credence to those tales.

The abbot nodded. "On what matter do you seek our Father's guidance?"

Edmar held back a wince. Sometimes it felt wrong to worship Solis, the Sun God. His true Father would always be Aeris.

"I must marry a woman who will bring honor to the throne." He couldn't say anything about the curse, but so far, the curse had chosen women who had brought joy, honor, and love to his kingdom. "But my heart is lost to another. I need the Sun God's guidance and strength because I must let her go in order to accept my chosen wife."

The abbot had listened with a grave expression, the one he wore the most often. "Kneel, my son."

Edmar bent to his knees in front of the man, who withdrew a reliquary, a tiny dark vial, from around his neck and slipped it off. His hands, calloused from years of manual labor and prayer, cradled the vial. He blew warm breath on it. A single golden spark bloomed inside. A drop of the Sun God's blood.

The air hummed with Solis's divine energy.

Edmar accepted the reliquary. The abbot then cupped his hands over Edmar's, and they both bowed their heads.

The abbot began the prayer, his voice resonating in the empty chamber. "Oh, radiant Sun God, whose golden rays grace our land with warmth and light, we beseech you, the eternal watcher. Look upon your servant, King Edmar, who seeks your wisdom in matters of the heart, entwined with the threads of duty and destiny.

"Blessed Sun God, illuminate his path and grant him the strength to release the ties that bind his heart to a forbidden love. May your divine light guide him through the shadows of doubt, and may he find solace in the choices that lie ahead."

Edmar swore he felt the Sun God's warmth travel from his hands to the rest of his body. The heat edged toward uncomfortableness, especially for one like himself who was a Winter creature, but calmness filled him.

His mind quieted. Her image receded. Her scent dissipated.

She was still here at the palace, and he'd see to her needs. She was a visiting princess, after all, and he'd do his duty. He'd ensure that she was taken care of, that she wanted for nothing.

He wished he could give her the life she'd always wanted to live, now that she was free of her father, whatever that looked like, but it wasn't his place to give her that future. The Snow Princess saw to that with her curse.

After hundreds of years, a burning anger rose in him. He'd kill the Snow Princess if she were in front of him right now.

As if sensing his agitation, the abbot continued.

"You gave us your blood for your light. Let its power infuse King Edmar with clarity and resolve. Grant him the fortitude to honor the path laid before him, to embrace the queen chosen by destiny, and to govern with a heart that beats in harmony with your celestial will."

He banished his anger to the Frostlands, embracing Solis's peace once more.

"May the Sun God's wisdom guide our beloved king, and may his reign be a testament to the divine order. In your sacred name, we pray."

Edmar echoed the concluding words of the prayer, "In the Radiant Name, we endure."

CHAPTER 20

EMMY

Emmy wandered the palace garden, the waning moon and stars casting a gentle glow over the cobblestone path.

Strategically placed lanterns emitted warm, flickering light, illuminating pockets along walkways. Everything seemed as fresh as it had been for the last two nights. The fragrance of blooming plants wafted through the air, creating a serene atmosphere. She trailed a hand over the flowers, the delicate petals whispering against her skin like a lover's soft caresses.

"Who are you?"

Underwater, Emmy would have tuned out the high and shrill voice, but it would be rude not to respond. She turned to face the speaker.

Before her, a tiny, fragile-looking woman stood like a stiff piece of plank wood. Her arms crossed in front of her, white-gloved hands tucked into her elbows. "Are you mute?"

Perhaps she should let the woman believe she was mute.

A second glance over the tiny woman confirmed it. The girl was barely more than a pup. The girl's burnt-orange skin and flaxen hair marked her Sun Fae heritage. A fancy blue gown and diamonds at her ears and throat spoke of wealth.

"Well, whoever you are, you must leave. I'm to meet the king here, and I don't want anyone else here to interrupt our time together." The girl flipped one hand at her like Anjali did when shooing away annoying shrimp hovering outside her window at the Little Palace.

Tiny fingers pushed back a strand of yellow hair, revealing the faintest glimpse of pointed ears beneath her veil. Very recent Sun Fae blood.

Her hair didn't move, which meant she was not a pure fae, probably either a mixed fae or a hybrid. Mixed fae resulted from the union of two fae of the same season, implying she might be a blend of Sun and Fire Fae. Alternatively, as a hybrid, she could be the offspring of a Sun Fae and a human, which could account for her distinct physical traits.

Emmy never had a reason to be jealous. No one had ever wanted her. But this young girl embodied everything she wasn't—a petite, young, pretty woman. Emmy was quite curvy and past her initial breeding days.

Then there was the fact the girl was here to meet with Edmar.

Had her Dragon King changed his mind about meeting her tonight?

Unease coiled in her stomach. Surely he would have said something. He was too thoughtful to have forgotten about her or not send a message.

"Lady Nuria?"

The young woman pivoted toward Edmar's gentle voice, a smile already widening on her face, and she bowed. "Your Majesty."

Emmy's heart beat a tattoo against her ribs as her Dragon King approached with his long, easy strides. Her gaze flitted between Edmar and the fae-blooded woman. The fae's elegance was understated, but a terrible reminder of everything she wasn't.

For a fleeting moment, she imagined a life without the curse, standing beside Edmar as an equal, their love a haven. But the fantasy shattered against the reality of her magic, a storm she couldn't escape.

Nuria rose from her bow. "My father told me to meet you here at your request."

Edmar's handsome face revealed little more than ice would, and something felt off. He didn't even look at Emmy.

So cold.

Her heart thudded with his clear message. He didn't want her.

Spending time with him last night had kindled false hope.

With a heavy heart, she stepped back, facing the bitter truth: her powers, like chains, barred her from Edmar's love. Love was a luxury she couldn't afford.

Edmar deserves more. He deserved the beautiful fae creature before him.

It was a silent concession to the cruel fate her powers had consigned her to.

He turned toward her, and a wave of heat surged through her body, a cruel mimicry of the fire acid always threatening to consume her from within. She couldn't help but wonder if yearning for Edmar was akin to playing with fire, where a single misstep could lead to destruction.

As she prepared to retreat, a vow formed in her heart. A vow she'd once made for her family and her people. If she couldn't have love, she'd ensure her presence wouldn't be a curse to those she cared about. It was little comfort, but it was the only solace she had. "I will leave you to your evening, Your Majesty."

"You can speak! Whatever is wrong with you?"

Ignoring Nuria, she met Edmar's gaze. A fleeting regret seemed to flicker in his eyes, but it vanished as his hand darted out to catch her arm as she passed. His touch sent a brief spike of fear through her—the fear of the danger she posed to him. Even though her magic was suppressed for now, closeness presented a risk.

She would have pulled away if not for his request. "Join us please, Princess Emira."

"Princess?" The younger woman fiddled with her gloves.

Does Edmar fancy this partial fae?

It seemed something was going on with him. She couldn't figure it out. She swallowed back all her feelings, keeping her face smooth. It couldn't matter to her. In the end, they could not be together. She'd wanted the opportunity to experience things with him, but it was obvious he was moving on.

Just as well. He'd hate her soon enough.

She nodded her acquiescence to Edmar's request, and he released her arm.

The other woman threw out her hands. "This was supposed to be our time, Your Majesty."

"My apologies, Lady Nuria. I'd forgotten my prior commitments. But please, stay and brighten our evening with your sunny personality."

The tones in her sensitive ears revealed them for a lie. What was the truth?

Had he changed his mind about spending time with her, or was it he didn't want to be alone with her?

Nuria straightened, shoulders back. She swept toward Edmar, ignoring Emmy. "I'm worthy of more than being a second choice."

Her chin lifted, and she glided away.

Emmy couldn't blame her. If she wasn't here for the Sun Stone, the hurt that had punched her in the middle would have been enough motivation to retreat as well.

What is he thinking?

She raised her eyes to meet his steady gaze, careful to show nothing. She was the statue she'd been her whole life, and she wouldn't show just how much he'd wounded her. Because hurt it did, and she cursed herself again for being an idiot.

He'd made it clear they had no future, but she'd at least hoped for his attention until she could steal the Sun Stone at the ball. She should have since put those feelings away. Her focus had to be on why she was here, certainly not to be kissing her Dragon King, despite her strong desire for him to make her breathless again.

She forced a smile. "Would you like to walk, Your Majesty? I would appreciate learning about the names of your plants here."

He inclined his head, and they started down the cobblestone path. At first, his wooden steps kept distance between them. She'd have to work on that, get him to let his guard down so she could find out more about the Sun Stone.

Immediately, she spied a cluster of unique flowers not more than a few steps ahead. Delicate blue petals shimmered in the moonlight. Her fingers floated over them, which radiated out from a thick, deep red center. "These flowers remind me of the red medusa jellyfish that emit an eerie blue bioluminescence when disturbed."

Surreptitiously, she peeked up at him, wondering if she piqued his interest. His half-closed eyes ran over her form. Was he remembering the way they danced last night?

She had never felt more alive in her life, and sharing that experience with Edmar meant something to her. She smiled at him now.

His face became unreadable again, a frozen mask.

Undeterred, she moved next to thigh-high plants. Feathery purple ferns cascaded together. "Look at these. They're not the same, but they remind me of the lilac Purple Coral. A very rare coral for its color, but they are immensely beneficial in providing a habitat for fish and other sea life."

"Those are called *Felicia Purpurophyta*, or more commonly, Royal Velvet Fern."

She tilted her head up at him, hearing the excitement creep into his voice where he'd been toneless before. He liked to share what he knew about the world. Although she needed him to loosen up, surprisingly, she found she enjoyed learning about the world from him.

Hiding a small smile, she skipped ahead, then paused beside a cluster of climbing vines dotted with closed buds. Further along the trellis, where moonlight touched the vines, flowers unfurled, their silver petals shimmering like captured starlight. "And these?"

A flicker of warmth softened his expression. He deeply inhaled the flower's fragrance, a faint smile playing on his lips. "Silver lilies. My mother's favorite." He brushed a petal gently, reverence in his touch, his voice a low murmur filled with longing. "Their fragrance, a blend of jasmine and vanilla, always reminds me of her."

He loved his mother. A bittersweet ache resonated in her chest. His unguarded tenderness, so opposite to the coldness he'd shown her this evening, reminded her of her own loss, of her mother. Sharp and unwelcome remorse twisted in her gut.

She forced a smile, tearing her gaze away from the ethereal glow of the silver lilies. "So beautiful."

Hoping distance might ease the tightness in her chest, she struggled to silence the whispers of her guilt as she drifted ahead to a set of clustered flowers. Their star-shaped blooms, their vibrant and alluring blue hues, released a sweet fragrance mingling with the night air. "The intense blue color of these reminds me of the blue sea dragons."

"Not really dragons," he said with a growl.

She chuckled but clarified for his benefit. "Sea slugs. Pretty ones."

He nodded to the clustered flowers. "Those are called Sapphire Stars."

"So beautiful. We don't have flowers in the ocean."

A new plant caught her attention, and she rushed to marvel at it. Edmar named it again for her, and she'd move to the next and the next. While his shoulders relaxed, his conversation remained limited to plant names.

How else could she get him to open up?

She paused in her flower perusal and looked up at him. "While I appreciate you indulging me, this doesn't seem to be what you really want to do."

The frozen mask fell in place. "I'm here for you, Princess Emira."

His unusual coldness puzzled her. *What changed since last night?*

She wouldn't let his indifference deter her. "What do you like to do?"

Under the soft glow of the moonlight, the hard planes of his face gave just a fraction. A slight thaw. When he lifted his chin to stare at the sky overhead, his whole body relaxed. "I love studying the stars."

Slowly, his lips curved into a smile, and her heart leaped.

"I always thought stars looked like the creatures in the deep oceans where their bioluminescence flashes, piercing the darkness." Her gaze traced the patterns in the night sky. She understood his fascination. The merfolk's origin stories captivated her. Now she wanted to know what led to Edmar's curiosity. "Tell me about them."

He gave her a hesitant look. "Stars are massive self-luminous celestial bodies of gas."

She raised her brow with his matter-of-fact answer.

"What?" he asked.

"That's interesting and informative, but I didn't expect you to talk about gas."

His face darkened as he looked away. "You're right. Gas is not an appropriate topic when talking to a princess."

She couldn't help it; she burst out laughing. A second later, he joined her.

It felt good to laugh. She had done so little of it in her life. And she was glad he had relented enough to laugh, too. But as their laughter mingled, a rapid thud of her heart reminded her of the precarious edge on which they balanced, the joy intermingled with a silent dread for the dire necessity of her quest.

With a shaky breath, she latched onto his arm for balance, her other hand pressed against her restricting dress. His biceps flexed, reminding her of the muscle packed into his lean body. She flushed, her laughter dying away.

An emotional tug of war played in Edmar's eyes, and before he could shut her out again, she pointed to a set of stars she recognized from her people's stories. "What do you call that constellation?"

He studied the sky. "The Harvest Basket. A woman named Alariel walked the lands of the world, teaching ancient men how to create nets to fish and women how to harvest mussels, clams, and sea snails. She gave many sea-faring peoples their god, Nereus, who was the one to teach her these things. Inspired by her devotion, Nereus crafted the Harvest Basket and placed it in the sky to remind the people of what she taught them."

He looked at her to see her reaction to the story, and she smiled with a nod. "We have a slightly different version of the story."

While gazing at the stars, she silently wished for a world as boundless and accepting as the night sky, where she could shine without fear.

"Tell me." Curiosity laced his voice.

A tingle spread along her skin as his cold breath brushed her cheek.

"We call that one the Silver Seashell. One day, a mermaid named Alariel became entangled in a man's crude fishing net near the sea's surface. She was on the brink of despair and sang the Ocean's Lament, our song of sadness. When it reached the ears of Nereus, the sea god, her sorrow moved him. When he freed her, he gave her the secrets to making better fishing nets.

"She was so grateful for his help but also fearful of what happened to her happening to other merfolk. For many days and nights, Alariel swam to every land, sharing her knowledge of these better fishing nets and how to find other prey in the ocean. Through song, she spread her love for Nereus. Her gift of freedom and knowledge resonated with the people and inspired them to protect the oceans while harvesting their bounty.

"Awed by her devotion, Nereus crafted the Silver Seashell and placed it in the sky to remind the Land Bound of her time with them."

When she finished her tale, he watched her in rapt devotion. "I didn't know the stories would be different, yet very similar. It makes sense, but too bad we don't remember that Alariel was a mermaid."

He scanned the sky. He found what he was looking for and pointed to a different constellation with twisting lines that looked like the number eight on its side. Two bright stars glimmered in the middle of each loop. "What do you call that one?"

She sidled closer, stepping just in front of him, and peered up at where he pointed. "Infinity. It's the sea serpent who looked into the future and saw a magical blight. He dug out his eyes to stop his visions and began to eat himself. He died before relaying what he saw, but Eurynome, the Goddess of Water-Meadows, took pity on him and placed him in the sky with his eyes set as those two stars as a reminder the future is never sure."

Edmar's eyebrows climbed higher on his forehead with the full story, and he looked at her in disbelief.

"Your story is different?"

"Not as dire, but just as sad." He lifted an arm over her shoulder to draw the symbol she knew as Infinity. With his nearness, the scent of the ocean washed over her.

"We call it the Serpent's Embrace. A tale of forbidden love." His arm lowered, brushing her shoulder. "A courageous Metal Fae warrior renowned for his loyalty to his kingdom was on a quest when he encountered a mysterious and enchanting maiden, a Wood Fae, who possessed a rare and captivating beauty, more stunning than all the other fae he had ever seen. The two fell in love, but it was forbidden for them to consummate their love for fear of the Chaos Lore."

The hitch in his voice vibrated behind her. He loved this story. The passion he imbued into the words struck deep within her, and she had to fight to keep from leaning back into him.

"The laws were unyielding in this respect, but their love grew. Their kingdoms had no choice but to intervene. A celestial serpent was summoned to separate them. He pulled them into the sky, his coils intertwining around them but separating them. This is the lesson about the price paid for a forbidden love."

She turned her head to look up at him with those last words.

Forbidden love. Is that what they had?

She could love him. It was so easy being with him. It wasn't forbidden in the same sense as the two fae from the story, but she couldn't allow herself to fall into those emotions. Theirs was a love that couldn't be.

He looked at her. He was so close, his warmth at her back.

She shivered. "Would you have thwarted the laws to keep your love?"

For one hopeful moment, his gaze softened and dropped to her lips. Then that frozen facade fell into place, and he took a step back. "It's just a story, Princess."

"Yes, just a story." She allowed her own years of practiced stillness to hide anything she was feeling. Once again, an idiot for asking. She knew his devotion and loyalty to his kingdom. He wouldn't sacrifice that for love.

This only confirmed why she couldn't trust him with her quest to rid herself of her magic. Swallowing the knot in her throat, she tilted her chin toward the sky. "Tell me about another one."

When he tipped his head back, a smile lifted the corners of his mouth again. He truly loved the stars.

"There!" He pointed to two stars, nearly touching. "The Phoenix's Dance. The stars waltz across the night sky, representing rebirth and transformation."

She chuckled. "Nearly the same for us! The Phoenix's Drift."

"Representing rebirth and transformation, too?" Excitement grew in his voice. She nodded with a smile, and he patted his pockets. "I should really write all this down for our records and for future generations."

Emmy peered back up at the stars. "The cluster of stars that looks like an eye—"

"The Dragon's Eye—"

"The eye of the first Ice Dragon—"

"Glacius."

"Yes!" Now she felt his excitement, too. When he pointed to a new star set off by itself, she blurted the answer. "The Moon's Tear."

"Luna's own tear—"

"When Glacius died."

She pointed to another set of stars. They compared stories, excited when they found similarities and charmed by any differences. She became so swept up in the conversation that the Sun Stone slipped her mind. Each new story fascinated her.

At some point, they spoke over each other at the same time, saying nearly the same thing, which sent them into a fit of laughter.

That's how Rivus found them. Laughing, hands on each other's arms, Edmar wiping away a tear. Though envious of that tear, she was delighted by how much she'd laughed with him.

"I never worried the two of you would find something to talk about." With his shaggy hair windblown and dirty traveling clothes, Rivus appeared to have just returned from wherever Edmar had sent him. He bowed with their attention. "Your Majesty. Princess."

Edmar's fingers lingered only a moment longer on her shoulder before he left her and engulfed his friend in a hug. "I'm happy to see you are unhurt."

She absently ran fingers over her skin where Edmar had touched her and sighed with the absence.

Not my life. But what would it be like to feel him touch her everywhere, even if it was just for one night? Regardless of who became his wife, she still wanted her first mating to be with her Dragon King.

Rivus returned his king's embrace, but his lips thinned. "The clan was not happy with my mission, but I've learned some interesting information."

His normally warm brown eyes flickered toward her. Interesting information he wasn't saying with her here.

Her time was up.

She had barely coaxed Edmar into relaxing, but her thoughts were consumed by what lay ahead. Tomorrow night he would choose a wife, and the Sun Stone remained out of reach.

More than his kiss needed to be stolen, and she still had to figure out how.

CHAPTER 21

EDMAR

Edmar tracked Emmy's retreat until she disappeared into the palace, his hand finding the nearest cold marble balustrade, his grip whitening his knuckles. It was as if he hoped the stone's chill might leech out the tumult within him, the fierce battle between a king's duty and a man's yearning heart.

"Still captivated by the mermaid?" Rivus asked, mirth lacing his voice.

He sighed, a sound more felt than heard. "If only the heart were free to choose, unfettered by ancient spells and the whims of a spoiled fae."

With a frown, he turned back to his friend and the Marshal of his kingdom. "Tell me."

The teasing smile dropped. "The dwarves are selling Dwarven snow to anyone who'll buy it, but I've heard something more troubling."

Centuries ago, the dwarves had held a monopoly on Dwarven snow, the crucial third ingredient for producing black powder. However, nearly eight hundred years ago, at the end of the Little Ice Age, they ceased its sale and distribution. Fear of the Snow Princess's wrath—after she decimated most of their supply—had driven their decision.

Why were the dwarves making Dwarven snow again? "Are they planning to attack us?"

New reports had come in just this day, warning of increased sightings of dwarven bands near Cyaneus's borders. Dwarven raids had declined in the last few hundred years.

"Not what I heard." Rivus shook his head. "They are using the black powder to create more tunnels deep within the earth."

"To be expected. That's how they find their gold."

"The rumor is that they are trying to locate a lost treasure or protect a treasure. Whichever one it is, it could give them the power to rule all immortals, save the gods, may their slumber be restful."

"Impossible."

"The Summer Child."

Edmar crossed his arms. "A fairytale nearly as old as the First Generation."

The First Generation. The first beings created by the elemental gods, like the first fae and Ice Dragons.

The Summer Child was supposedly a child of the two Summer gods and a woman of the First Generation. But it wasn't a creature of genesis or alchemy, something created by combining magics.

No, the stories claimed it was born through procreation, though how that was possible with two fathers remained a mystery. And the stories about it were wildly different, everything from it being alive in their world right now to being unborn to being dead within moments of its first breath. If it had ever existed.

He'd investigated a secret order built around the myth centuries ago, but his search yielded nothing.

"Maybe not a fairytale." Rivus narrowed his eyes. "If it's true, then we need to find it before the dwarves."

He threw up his hands, pacing a few feet away. He paused, his eyes drifting upward to the vast twilight sky, its expanse mocking the breadth of his kingdom below.

A king ruling boundless lands, yet a prisoner in an invisible cage.

It was a sobering reminder that, for all his might, the curse rendered him as powerless as any common man in his realm. "I will marry a bride soon."

Rivus nodded. "That's important."

Dread chilled him to the bone. Normally he welcomed the cold, being a Winter creature, but this was something so uncontrollable that if he gave it free rein, he'd be in a state of paralysis.

The weight of a thousand years settled on him as he once again turned his gaze to the sky. "I envy the stars. They are free to roam the heavens, unbound by the chains of fate and curses. To love as they shine, without decree or doom, to dictate their course."

Tomorrow night, he'd know who he was to marry next, and he would have to let Emmy go.

He should have already let her go.

"Still no sign of the curse choosing her?" Rivus asked, his voice knowing.

"No matter what I do, even deciding not to choose her anymore, the curse refuses to acknowledge that once it had picked her." A forbidden love like the one in the constellation. "I tried to trick it. I thought choosing another woman over her tonight would have been enough. Or maybe I simply didn't wait long enough."

Rivus sauntered closer, his face etched with sympathy. "I'm sorry, my friend. Truly I am."

He believed him. Their friendship spanned centuries, and Rivus had never let him down. Always there for him.

"I want her." He raked a hand through his hair, his fingers brushing against rough scales at his temple. Pushing the thought away, he clenched his jaw. He had to find a way to break free from this cursed cycle, to choose his own destiny.

"She feels like mine, but if the curse doesn't choose her tomorrow, I can't keep her." He pressed a hand to his chest, new scales appearing beneath his tunic, reminding him of his powerlessness. "It wouldn't be fair to whichever woman the curse selects. No woman should suffer the humiliation of her husband taking a lover. And it wouldn't be fair to place Emmy as the second woman in my life."

He balled his hands, ribbons of faint blue light arching along his skin. A brisk wind swirled over him. "She's finally here, and I can't imagine sending her away when the curse forces my hand again. But I must."

Rivus let him vent, an unusual indulgence for Edmar. Negative thoughts produced nothing and were abandoned in his Frostlands. But in this, he was losing. "I wish I could be like my brothers, but I can't."

He couldn't hide like Kalden or drown himself in women like Zane. He had to find his own way.

Rivus trusted he would fulfill his duty to his kingdom, and he would do what was right. He always did what was right. Yet he couldn't shake the feeling of longing that filled him. As surely as the heart beating steadily in his chest, he knew that same heart would forever be lost to the mermaid.

Rivus cleared his throat. "Perhaps you should enjoy the time you have left with her."

"And give her false hope."

"I know she can't be told about the curse, but prepare her for what will happen."

He glanced up at the stars he loved. "I have, but it's like it hasn't deterred her from tempting me."

"Perhaps she loves you as you've loved her all these years."

Could he be right? His heart lifted with the thought, but dropped just as quickly. "None of that changes that she cannot be in my life once a wife is chosen for me."

"She's immortal," Rivus continued. "The curse might choose her in the future."

"Do you think she'd want to see me again after I send her away?"

"That's a tough one to answer, but if she feels the same, maybe she will."

Or she'd be too hurt to ever forgive him. "How would I know?"

Rivus shrugged. "If I was in your position, I'd take advantage of this last night with her. One night of blissful passion could sustain you through decades of absence."

His magic flared. He had to do the right thing for his kingdom. That meant finding his next bride by chance and doing his best to banish the sapphire-haired mermaid from his dreams. "No. I can't do that."

"Fine. You concentrate on marrying your next bride, let the princess down as gently as possible, and I'll look into these rumors about the Summer Child."

He reined in his power, but it pulsed beneath his skin, a caged beast. He banished his emotions to his Frostlands. "As king, I would concur. As my friend, I'd ask if you would stay until my next bride is chosen. I could use your support."

A shadow crossed the Marshal's dark eyes, quickly replaced with a silver sheen. "Of course." Rivus laid a hand on his shoulder. "I'll stay for the ball, but what are your plans for tonight?"

"I need time alone to think through everything."

"And the princess?"

"I'll see her at the ball."

Rivus said goodnight, and Edmar strode back into the palace with every intention of not stopping until he reached his chambers. A cluster of chattering servants, their words punctuated with concern, drew his attention as he entered the Grand Hall.

Stone wings, tipped with talons, arched overhead—a sight he was not used to seeing in his Grand Hall. When a servant noticed him, he gestured to the others, and they parted, backing away and giving him a clear view of the dragon statue and a Water Fae man scowling up at it.

"Isamore..." Edmar breathed the name of his female cousin—the dragon. A woman he hadn't seen in over a thousand years.

Her statue looked like those ringing the Forbidden Barrier, an invisible, magical barrier around the Malustra Woods, which kept in dangerous creatures and protected the humans. But this particular statue of his cousin had never been part of the barrier.

He knew because he'd examined each statue, searching for familiar faces, for those he'd lost. Some of them were there. Family members and friends had been carved into the likenesses of the statues.

People long dead, transformed into stone. He and his brothers were the last Ice Dragons left... or so he'd thought. He'd hoped Isa and others, absent from Agondray when the Snow Princess's curse struck, had escaped its reach.

And he had not found his cousin Isa among the statues, giving him hope.

But it looked like the curse had caught up to her as her dragon statue bent a knee to him in the middle of the Grand Hall.

Sorrow twisted in his chest. For a moment, he wondered if the curse was not just a chain binding him to a cycle of loss that would never end.

Austere as usual, Grigor dipped a quick bow next to him. "The pirate just arrived in port and delivered Princess Isamore just like this."

His steward's disapproving tone made it clear he thought the Water Fae man, the pirate, was responsible for Isa's condition. Edmar knew otherwise. Or perhaps Grigor just detested the roguish visitor in the palace.

When Grigor looked to continue, Edmar held up a hand and approached his cousin's petrified coffin.

In her magnificent dragon form, Isa embodied the allure of their species. Even as a young woman, she'd been one of the rare beauties with plenty of suitors. She hadn't taken one before the Snow Princess's curse. Instead, she'd been traveling the world, searching for her parents who'd been lost at sea for decades.

But now she knelt before him, wings back, scaled arms outstretched, her cupped hands, one over the other, concealing something between her palms.

The midnight-purple Water Fae pirate, dressed in a forest green ruffled shirt with an open collar, belted over snug black pants, was familiar. He looked at Edmar. "She's got a message for you, Your Majesty."

He'd known this pirate long ago. "Brac?"

A Water Fae male with a B-name, just as most females had A-names, a clear indication of a man's subordination to women in the Water Fae culture. Edmar had always wondered why Brac kept his name after becoming a pirate. Either way, Brac had met Isa through his cousin's best friend, who was also a pirate. Adria had often visited before the Snow Princess's curse. He had served as her first mate until she married, at which point her husband replaced him.

The pirate man smiled, but sorrow dulled his clear blue eyes. Dark hair threaded with bioluminescent green strands waved slowly along his shoulders, like a calm abyss under night's embrace. "Aye, glad you remember me, or this could've been mighty awkward."

He glanced back up at the dragon statue with a hand on his sword's scabbard, slung low on his hips. "Swear on me life, I had no idea this was comin', and I'm furious she kept it from me. She asked for passage home, and I couldn't deny her that simple favor—at least 'til we reached port. But then..." He passed a hand over his eyes. "Couldn't stop it, could I? She knew all along... that damn Ice Queen, calm as you please, gave me your message afore she knelt like you see her now."

While anger roughened his voice, despair tugged down the corners of the pirate's mouth and eyes. He loved her. Brac loved his cousin. "I believe you. What was her message?"

"'Release the souls from the stones so the dragons can protect me from the Summer Child.'"

Another reference to the Summer Child. Perhaps he should take the threat seriously. He'd ask Rivus to find out more. "That's all?"

"Aye."

Edmar did not know what it meant.

Grigor cleared his throat. "Shall I have her set up somewhere else?"

Brac tensed, every part of him motionless except for the grip on his sword's hilt tightening.

"She's fine here. That way, our visitors can see her and pay their respects for my fallen cousin."

"I'm stayin' with her," the pirate said.

"With Your Majesty's approval, I'm sure I can find you accommodations in Virdis." His steward nodded while raising his chin to look down his nose at the Water Fae.

Murderous rage fell over Brac's face, his sword's blade whispering as it halfway left its scabbard.

"Stop being so pompous, Grigor. Find him a room here, close to Isa. Brac is my guest for as long as he needs to stay."

The pirate slipped the sword back into its scabbard and bowed, surprising Edmar. "Thank you for understandin'." Then a mischievous grin lessened the pain evident on his face. "Always figured you were the sharpest of the four dragon princes."

Dragon princes. A time lost to history, seeded in memories. Edmar should have never been a king. That had been Rin's job title. But then the Snow Princess had cursed them all.

Which brought him to his current situation. He empathized with Brac. His chest tightened with a heavy ache, while a bitter heat crawled up his throat. He pictured his Frostlands. He'd almost managed to subdue his emotions, but then he thought of Emmy. She stirred something in him, making it impossible to banish these feelings. Perhaps another visit with Father Jayasurya was needed.

"Grigor," he said, meeting the steward's steady gaze, "please see to our guest. That will be all for tonight."

"Of course, Your Majesty." His steward inclined his head in a bow, then strode away to start evening preparations for bed.

He took the long way to his chambers, passing Emmy's door. Pausing outside of it, he wondered what she was doing right now on the other side.

He could knock.

He could talk to her.

He liked talking to her.

But that may lead to kissing her.

He liked kissing her.

One night of blissful passion could sustain you through decades of absence. He'd spent two and a half decades without her, and he yearned for her all throughout those years. Maybe he could have this one night with her, and the next couple of decades would be easier.

Selfish desire. He could not use her for the night, then abandon her for twenty years.

He shook his head at the memory of what her lips tasted like. His duty didn't allow him to like kissing her, and he didn't want to hurt her, even if she protested his protection of her heart.

Centuries pressed down on him, a reminder of the gulf between duty and desire. The familiar chain of duty and destiny was as comforting as it was confining.

Remembering he wanted to be alone with his thoughts, he moved on.

Chapter 22

EDMAR

Edmar possessed an innate sense of the sun's movement, a visceral twinge alerting him to the transitions of dawn and dusk and his impending change. So when an unknown disturbance roused him, darkness enveloping the room, he knew without a doubt that it was the deep, silent stretch of night preceding the first light of daybreak.

His dragon sight pierced the darkness, and he saw her.

Emmy glided in, her dark sapphire hair trailing behind her, a faint iridescent glow swirling on her naked body like moonlight on water.

Heat surged through him, his heart pounding like a tempest-driven wave, echoing the chaotic rhythm of a sea in fury with every step she took.

I've yearned for this woman, for this connection, for choices I've never had.

With a start, he realized she saw him, too.

She met his gaze steadily, her merfolk heritage probably also granting her superior night vision. Then she climbed into his bed.

Alarm replaced the heat, and he started to rise. She pushed him back down, her palms warm on his bare chest. He let her.

"Emmy," he said, her name a whisper of breath. His chest tightened as she straddled him, settling over his hips, only a blanket between him and her willing body. He wore nothing underneath, and his body reacted to her nearness, her heat.

Instinctively, his hands gripped her hips. "What are you doing, Princess?"

The panic that flashed over her face almost made him smile. Brave, curious, bold. That encompassed everything he knew about her. But also innocent.

Her innocence highlighted the inner war between desire and obligation. Too much at stake. Not just his heart, but the fate of his people tethered to the curse. It was a burden he bore alone, and he mourned the duty he could not escape.

Yet, his thumbs brushed the crease of her hips, his fingers digging into her supple flesh. Duty and honor fled when he imagined pulling her over his hardened length. He bit back his desire with a long groan, barely constraining himself.

Her gasp, her quickly rising chest, drew his eyes to her perfect breasts. His hands whispered over her skin, cupping their weight. She shuddered. Her hair tickled his sides. Then she pushed his hands to her hips again so she could lightly skim fingers over his chest, skating over his scattering of scales, one fingertip scraping his nipple.

He jerked at the pleasurable sensation, and she smiled. He sucked in a breath, not realizing that he'd forgotten the simple act of breathing again. Something about this woman unraveled the very instincts that kept him alive.

"I wondered if you were as sensitive there," she said, her musical voice sounding like a dream. "I never knew such pleasure until you touched me the same way."

"Some find release through such stimulation."

"Show me," she whispered.

He longed to lavish his attention on her breasts, to suck and bite her nipples, teasing them, seeing if she could come, but he warred with himself. *This is wrong.* His heart wanted her, but there were too many reasons he should give her up.

A hot whisper brushed his mind, a reminder of his prayers to the Sun God. *The curse hasn't chosen her in the nights I've spent with her, so she isn't mine.* "Tomorrow, I announce my queen."

She chewed on her bottom lip. "I know."

"It won't be you."

Quick anger, then it was gone. She tilted her hips, grinding against his hard cock.

A silent crack appeared in his Frostlands.

Desire pounded in his blood.

He was losing control.

Without warning, he yanked her to him and rolled them over, trapping her beneath the blanket. When her coconut and flower scent filled his senses, he buried his head in the space between her neck and shoulder.

She squirmed under him. "Please, Edmar..."

Anger and desire fueled the fire within him in equal measure as he raised his head to look down at her. "You don't understand what you're asking for."

"I want you."

"No."

She hesitated at the heat in his voice, her large eyes dark as they stared up at him with uncertainty. "I know you want me. I can *feel* you."

"Gods, you're such a child. Of course I want you, but this... it means more..." *Why in eight hells is she angry?* "You can't be mine, and I will not take advantage of your naiveté for a single night of pleasure."

She shook her head, her lips tight.

He groaned aloud. "Why can't you understand I don't want you like this?"

He wanted all of her.

Her resilience and determination. Her courage to change her fate. The fire burning within her spirit. It inspired him, rekindled a belief in his own strength. The same fire, he realized with deep regret, that would see her through this, this pain he was inflicting.

"Like what?" The steel in her voice cut through his thoughts. "Pathetic and naked, begging for your touch?"

"That's not what I meant—"

"Do you realize I can count the number of hugs I've had in my life on my two hands? Before I got rid of my magic, everyone was afraid of me. I've never been kissed. I've never been desired by anyone. I just want to be wanted for once in my life."

Her words, though unsurprising given what she'd told him, pierced him. He didn't want to be another person rejecting her when he didn't feel that way. He'd live with this regret, but it would protect her from what she didn't understand. She may think this one night of passion would be enough until she realized they didn't have a future. One day, when she found a love she deserved, she would thank him for upholding his honor toward her.

"So yes, I guess I was childish to hope for your desire after kissing me on the riverbank, in the alley, at the tavern."

He'd made so many mistakes. "I shouldn't have said—"

She slapped a hand over his mouth. "I don't want to be insulted any further by your damn duty and honor."

Every time he'd dared to feel, to truly connect with any of his wives, to glory in the birth of his son, he'd been reminded that it had been fleeting all along. That eventually, his duty tore it away. The curse took his wives before their natural time, and nature had decreed his son an abomination, half human, half Ice Dragon, stealing the baby's breath before he'd lived more than a few minutes. He couldn't bear that loss with her.

She was perfect.

But she wasn't his to claim, even if he felt he should claim her in the depths of his soul, so he gathered every wild and consuming emotion threatening to destroy him, and he buried them in his Frostlands. Fully collected, he rose, grasping her wrists, and pulled her from the bed.

"We cannot have this," he said as he dragged her to the door.

Emmy yanked back, forcing him to release her.

She crossed her arms beneath her breasts, her chin lifting defiantly. "You cannot allow yourself one moment of true happiness?"

How could he explain a curse he was forbidden to speak to those ignorant of it? "Stop this, Emira."

"Why are you fighting our attraction?"

Looking at her—a naked, curvy goddess with wild hair and shimmering skin—his Frostlands groaned. When she saw his body's reaction, she smiled.

He clenched his jaw, and his brow lowered. She would never give up. He sought refuge in the icy embrace of his Frostlands. Small ribbons of his navy magic curled around him, and the air in the room chilled.

"I'm done." His tone sounded almost dead to his own ears.

Her smile faded.

"I don't want to see you again," he continued. "I will ensure Yolande understands you're to leave the palace before the ball tomorrow night."

The devastation on her face made him want to melt into the shadows, to get far away from her.

When she didn't move, he raised his voice. "Get out."

She fled.

Chapter 23

EMMY

Emmy sought the Summer Child in her dreams.

She floated in the water, tail swishing, but this time, there was no pain as she hugged herself.

The clear egg bobbed before her, the being inside more of a purple mass of tissue than human, with vague outlines of a head, legs, and a tail. In the center, a heart fluttered, with its beat echoing through the water and bouncing off the cavern walls.

Then the pale, black-winged woman dove into the water. Her black aura hummed, her fully black eyes watching Emmy. She held a sword, but the tip angled down just enough to offer a threat.

Emmy looked between the woman—was she fae with those pointed ears?—and the egg. She flipped her tail to move closer.

The winged woman held up a hand and a ball of red and black power formed in her facing palm. Nothing else. No other emotion expressed in her face or in her body.

It reminded her of the way Edmar shut off his emotions, retreating to an icy facade.

In the hush of her dream, Edmar's rejection stung anew, mingling with her longing. If only he could see beyond their circumstances, understand that even one moment together would give her one moment of belonging somewhere. She wished he could see beyond the necessity of duty to see the Emmy who sought a moment of true intimacy by his side.

But she belonged nowhere. No one wanted her. That's why she sought the Summer Child. *This child wants me, right?*

Perhaps she could be accepted in whatever world the child promised.

She faced the woman. "I have come because she asked."

The woman remained impassive while the female child in the egg spoke to Emmy. *Come to me in person.*

"Can you rid me of my magic?"

I can consume your power and keep you safe.

Not a long-term solution. Not like the Sea Witch offered.

She cannot help you either.

"She said she could."

Only your Father can help you.

My father? She couldn't mean her biological father. She probably meant the merfolk's Father God. "Do you mean Metallon?"

For many millennia, seven of the eight gods had vanished from the world, slumbering in unknown locations. Only the Sun God remained awake, so how would she find the Metal God?

Come to me, my child.

It sounded strange for this unborn baby, already more powerful than anyone she knew besides the gods, to claim her as a daughter.

"What would you ask in return?"

I'm needed, and I'm ready.

"Ready for what?"

Ready to breathe true life.

What did that mean?

I can give you what you seek...

The water shimmered, the Summer Child's heart pulsing, casting ripples through the dream. An image flickered to life within the ripples—a vision of Emmy, her skin aglow with the warm, controlled light of her magic, surrounded by faces both familiar and new. They did not flinch or flee. Instead, they reached out to her, smiles of genuine acceptance on their faces, warm embraces. It was a world where her powers were a source of wonder, not fear. A divergence of her grim reality.

Her breath caught at the beauty of the vision.

Then it faded. Other dreams followed, but she remembered none, until waking in the same garden with the same Water Fae from the night before. This time, they were both standing. For several long moments, they eyed each other without speaking.

Emmy could win this game. She'd passed two centuries without uttering a word.

The fae hesitated, then finally spoke. "Tell me about you."

"Why?"

"I see you don't trust me."

"I have no reason to trust or not to trust you. I don't know you or how I came to be here, although I'm sure you have something to do with that."

The fae looked down at her hands where her fingers clasped together over a semi-circular white stone strung on a silver chain. She took a deep breath before meeting her gaze. "I'm trapped in this world. Occasionally, I can tap into the realm where you were sleeping, and I can talk to people. Last night, I saw you in a nightmare and pulled you out. I had hoped to save you the anguish of that nightmare."

The vision of fire consuming her. That was the nightmare, but the egg had absorbed her magic. The child within had been asking for Emmy to come to her as she had done again tonight. Perhaps the fae didn't know she'd seen the child again.

Or maybe she was hiding what she knew.

She eyed the fae cautiously, sensing the undercurrents of a deeper story. "Why are you trapped?"

The fae's lavender skin paled to a dull gray. "Without meaning to, I've hurt the people I love."

Her words resonated with a painful familiarity. Emmy's life echoed with the same lament. A life marred by unintended destruction, the love she craved forever out of reach.

The woman continued, barely audible, her voice cracking with her confession. "It's my punishment. My actions... they led to tragedy."

Destruction. Fear. Loss. Guilt.

She knew those emotions intimately. Her heart twitched, an unexpected surge of empathy breaching her walls of distrust. For the first time since leaving the ocean, she felt a connection, not of desire, but of hope, a fragile hope that maybe, in this strange world, her past wouldn't define her future. Hesitantly, she extended a hand. "I understand your pain."

Her throat thickened so that no other words would pass but those. The death of her mother would haunt her forever.

The fae grasped her hand, an anchor. For both of them.

Emmy couldn't offer more right now. Her soul bruised. But this shared, quiet solitude of acceptance seemed to be enough.

Hours drifted by, with summer clouds crossing the blue sky while they lay side by side.

"I'm Malala," the Water Fae said, her voice low. Something also sounded untrue in her words. "Are you from the sea kingdoms?"

"Emmy," she said, while nodding. "Do you have another name?"

"Many." She sighed with a smile. "No fooling you. I didn't appreciate the names others gave to me in fear, so I chose this one myself. It means one who is grief-stricken and powerless."

Emmy understood. *Daughter of Ruin.*

"A wonderful name," the fae said, raising her hands to encompass the garden, "for one who has no power."

Sarcasm dripped from her words, but Emmy thought she detected another lie. "It would seem to me you still have some power. You've pulled me here to your realm twice now. Does that make you a Moon Walker?"

Perhaps that explained her light skin. She might have Moon Fae ancestry.

"I wasn't aware merfolk knew much about the Land Bound."

"Your people lived with us once, before they disappeared. Merfolk learned about all the magical races and creatures from them."

"Then it's true. The Water Fae are gone?"

"I believe that at last count, there were fewer than a hundred left on land." She wasn't sure why she chose her words so carefully, not revealing the full truth. Malala seemed to speak in half-truths herself.

If the fae could read lies like she could, she'd understand the nuances, anyway. However, she wouldn't be the one to give away secrets when the Water Fae hid for their safety.

"In the last eight hundred years," she said, "the Summer Fae and their allies have destroyed almost every Winter creature. Those who have survived are too powerful to kill or have gone into hiding."

The very reason she understood why Edmar did not share he was an Ice Dragon, only one of four left on the continent.

Malala's face clouded. Absently, she rubbed the stone on the chain around her neck. When she spoke, her words were low. "I have missed so much."

"Can I help in some way?"

Her slate-blue eyes trained on her. "Don't help the Summer Child. If she's allowed out, any Winter beings left will be hunted and killed."

"I'm not sure she can help me. Besides, I cannot escape my current quest without repercussions." *The Garden of Souls.*

"What quest are you on? Does it have something to do with you being in Cyaneus?"

She wasn't sure how Moon Walking worked, only having learned briefly about it. She heard nothing different other than genuine curiosity in the question.

But how did the fae woman know where she was?

Yet, she didn't think the fae could do anything to hurt her or stop her mission, and Emmy really wanted to talk to someone, to tell someone the truth. With fading reluctance, she unburdened herself. "I'm going to steal the Sun Stone."

The fae's dark brows rose. "Only one person has ever stolen the Sun Stone before. My great grandmother had to practically kidnap my great grandfather so she could get her hands on it."

Emmy recalled the story Edmar told about the Sun Stone when it had first come to Agondray. "Your great grandmother was a pirate?"

She laughed into her hand. "Yeah, she was a badass." She sobered. "How do you plan to steal the God's Stone?"

Emmy screwed her lips as she sat up, considering what to reveal. The fae woman also sat up, crossing her legs under her white dress, watching her.

"I need to be chosen as his next queen," she said slowly. Edmar had banished her, but she didn't plan to leave without at least trying to get the Sun Stone first. "Then I'll have access to the stone."

The Water Fae completely stilled in a wonderful imitation of how Emmy used to live her life. Then pink tinged her lavender cheeks. "You mean to tell me you plan to somehow get the king to choose you as his queen so that you can steal the stone and break his heart at the same time?"

She jerked as if she'd been slapped. She plucked a piece of grass. "I would never go out of my way to hurt anyone."

Malala laid a hand on her knee. "Of course not. I can see that about you."

Despite her caution, she enjoyed these moments, their bond, though rocky and fraught with complexities and hidden truths, offering a strange comfort. She understood the fae's guilt about her magic's destructive power. And it was nice to be understood in return, to belong somewhere, even if temporarily.

"But you need to steal the Sun Stone, right?"

"Yes."

"Then I'll pray for your success."

Wonderful.

She rolled her eyes—secretly delighting in this new movement—and smirked.

CHAPTER 24
EDMAR

The Grand Ballroom glimmered under the light of a thousand candles, celebrating both the Blind King's Bluff Ball and the Summer Solstice. Crystal chandeliers cast sun-and-moon reflections, while velvet drapes, woven with golden solstice symbols, adorned the walls in the royal colors of blue and silver.

"So many beauties," Rivus said, standing beside him on the raised dais.

Polished marble floors reflected the ladies' sumptuous gowns as they glided by, the rustle of silk and jingle of jewelry adding a melodic rhythm to the room. Bright sunflowers and golden heather, symbols of the solstice, crowned many of their heads, as soft music from lutes and harps filled the air.

Edmar usually loved this ball—the excitement, the beautiful women, the mystery of his future queen. But this year, combined with the Solstice's theme of renewal, the irony stung. While others celebrated light and new beginnings, his curse shackled him again.

Still, he searched for a silver lining. The women arrived knowing one would become queen, their anticipation a heady spice in the air. Their perfumes mingled with flowers and beeswax, and the murmurs of courtiers wove a hushed symphony.

Dressed in a midnight-blue velvet doublet, adorned with intricate silver filigree, he exuded regal authority. Yet the turmoil of his emotions expanded in his chest.

"I don't see her," he murmured.

Rivus raised an eyebrow at him. "I thought you told her to leave and not come to the ball."

His friend knew Edmar spoke of Emmy. "She hasn't left, though. I thought maybe..."

He'd stayed away all day as the dragon, unable to bear the thought of her leaving, only to discover she hadn't.

"She's really messing with your head."

Rivus also wore the dark blue colors of the kingdom, but his lack of adornments seemed to suggest he also lacked wealth, which was far from the truth. His friend didn't want to advertise himself as available.

He didn't fool the ladies, though. The moment the curse had chosen Edmar's bride, the very single Rivus would become a beacon of interest.

Pitching his voice low, Edmar said, "The curse is the real issue."

Rivus shrugged. "Maybe it's doing you a favor. What would happen if you married the Sea King's daughter without his permission?"

"Right," he said beneath his breath. He banished Emmy from his thoughts, shoving every memory into his Frostlands. *Time to find my bride by chance.*

Soft music filled the Grand Ballroom, fading slowly as he motioned to the musicians. Then he stepped down from the dais. Dresses of vibrant colors, from the deepest sapphire to the palest rose, swirled in a kaleidoscope of beauty as the women crowded closer to the front.

"Welcome," he said, smiling, arms opening wide, "to the Blind King's Bluff Ball. Tonight, one of you will become my queen, and I cannot wait to meet you."

Rivus followed him amid excited tittering and stopped at his side, a silk blindfold in hand, the symbol of his cursed quest for a queen.

He'd rehearsed this speech countless times over the centuries, careful of his words. The Snow Princess had killed those who shouldn't have known about the curse, even sending one of Kalden's brides to throw herself out of a tower window.

"I like to start with a game." He kept the smile to infuse the room with his usual sense of excitement. "I will dance with whichever women I blindly choose, but no worries for those not chosen. I promise I will try to dance with as many of you as I can tonight."

A rippling chorus of delighted gasps echoed in the ballroom.

He nodded to Rivus.

His friend tied the silk fabric around his eyes and backed away.

He adjusted the blindfold, relying on his heightened senses, which added to the anticipation—the ringing of his jeweled belt, the shuffle of fabrics, the soft sighs and giggles of the ladies surrounding him.

He busied his hands, adjusting the fur trim of his tunic as he moved forward. Then he stopped.

More fabric rustled, hushed whispers filling the silence. Rivus would ensure the women surrounded him—with the first ring consisting of the ladies from his roster. If the curse didn't choose someone right away, he was sure to pick one of them to dance with, satisfying the nobles of his kingdom.

"Ready," Rivus said.

He forced a smile. Music swelled, lilting lutes, resonant harps, and lively flutes. The perfect enchanting backdrop for the unfolding drama as he turned in a slow circle.

He waited for the tightening band in his chest to tell him he'd found her, his bride by chance.

Nothing.

This wasn't unusual, though. With so many random choices, the curse took time to pick one for him. But the ladies would be impatient, so he'd choose one himself if it carried on too long.

Raising his arms, hands out in front, he reached blindly for a partner. His actions felt mechanical, driven by duty, not desire. The music tempo shifted, echoing the heartbeat of the court as his search for a new queen unfolded in front of everyone. He navigated the sea of elegant ladies, his outstretched hands a silent invitation, guided by the soft sounds of slippered feet and rustling skirts.

His hands fell upon smooth, bare shoulders. She smelled of rosewater. Not the scent that haunted him, but he shoved those thoughts into his Frostlands as he untied the blindfold.

She curtsied, her head bowing. "Lady Charisse, Your Majesty."

One lady from his roster. Her father was the Master of the Royal Shipyard, a crucial architect behind the kingdom's formidable naval fleet. "Rise, Lady Charisse."

He slid a hand around her waist, took her hand in his other, and led them into the first step of the first dance. "You look lovely tonight."

"Thank you, Your Majesty."

The steps felt hollow, failing to forge even a fleeting connection. Lady Charisse moved with practiced grace, her every step and turn a true bearing of her upbringing in the court's refined circles.

A silent lament stirred within him. *For all the beauty and grace she possesses, she only wants me for the crown I wear.* All a charade, the same dance every twenty years, the same women wanting what he could offer them as the king.

The young woman was pretty. Her deep pink satin gown with golden embroidery along the hems and sleeves in flowing botanical patterns contrasted elegantly with her dark brown complexion.

But prettiness was a facade, a superficial layer concealing the true essence of a person. He couldn't help but wonder about the stories etched in the lines of her smile, the dreams possibly dancing in her hopeful brown eyes, the aspirations entwined with the strings of pearls in her raven hair.

In another life, free from this curse, might we have met differently? Could a spark have ignited, one not dictated by the whims of a curse?

Such thoughts were dangerous—frivolous, even, given his circumstances. Yet they fluttered through his mind like wayward butterflies, elusive and bittersweet.

He'd chosen her, not the curse, so she wouldn't be his bride. But he danced with her until the end of the song, after which he led her to the raised dais. There, Father Jayasurya waited with the Golden Scepter in hand. After guiding Lady Charisse to face the crowd, some hopeful for a new queen, others hopeful they still had a chance to become the next queen, he backed away.

"On this night, under the solstice sun's blessing, we seek the one destined to unite with the king." The abbot moved in front of the young woman. "Raise your hands, child, so that I may lay the Golden Scepter in them. Do not move otherwise. The Sun Stone, blessed by the Gods on this longest day, easily takes mortal lives if handled incorrectly."

Lady Charisse trembled, but nodded.

Then Father Jayasurya carefully placed the long, golden staff into her upturned palms and closed her fingers over the scepter. The top end of the staff cradled the black Sun Stone, which rose slightly above her.

The abbot stepped back, and he fell into his role. "Now repeat these words, Lady Charisse: I am the chosen queen of Cyaneus."

She swallowed with her nod. "I am the chosen queen of Cyaneus."

Nothing happened.

The black Sun Stone did not change, meaning she had spoken false words.

The abbot whisked the scepter away. Edmar gave her a bow before returning her to the crowd and setting himself in the middle of the ballroom again. This time, he tied the blindfold himself and started the process again.

Swishing skirts and delicate perfumes surrounded him. He touched gowns of velvet and damask, and encountered wispy lace and beads that clicked to the music. The ladies' lilting laughter pealed as he blindly felt for partner after partner, dancing with each new blind choice. One wore a trace of jasmine; another's pearl necklace clacked crisply.

The emptiness of countless dances, countless forced unions, echoed in the space between their hands. Each touch, a reminder of the curse's grip, the freedom he'd lost, the love he would never truly find.

And each exchange tonight brought him no closer to his destined bride. And none of them smelled of the combination of coconut and flowers he secretly yearned for. None of them danced as if the Gods themselves had blessed them.

None of them were chosen by the curse or were accepted by the Sun Stone.

Doubts, fueled by the sweet wine he drank liberally, began seeping into his mind.

When would the curse finally choose and end his misery?

If he had a bride by chance, then he could firmly put Emmy out of his mind and his life.

Adjusting his fur-trimmed tunic, he plunged once more into the shrouded sea of suitors, trusting his bride by chance waited somewhere in the darkness beyond his blindfold.

Chapter 25

EMMY

Intrigued by the blind king's quest to find his queen, Emmy had been watching the dancing from the start, hidden in the shadow of a hallway. She tapped her foot to the rhythm, yearning to join the dance instead of just observing. Her feet felt like sharp knives cut them with each tap, but she didn't care.

She imagined dancing among them, her laughter mingling with theirs, free from shadows, free from her magic's threat. A sharp pang of longing reminded her of the gulf separating her desires from her reality.

Edmar had told her to leave. She knew she didn't belong. Had her visit to Cyaneus been solely for him, she would have departed long ago. The arrival of her dress solidified her plans. She'd allowed herself to be prepared, despite Mistress Cassia's frustration.

Apparently, her waist had slimmed by *half an inch* since the fitting two days ago. Constantly moving now impacted her life. She would never be as slim as her sisters, but Edmar appreciated her curves.

In truth, she liked the way she looked.

With the dress taken in and fitted to her full-figured form, her hair and face expertly styled, she'd barely recognized her reflection.

The dress left her upper chest bare, save for two gauzy lilac straps that accentuated her breasts. Dark purple braided designs adorned the sweetheart neckline, continuing down between her breasts and around her ribcage. The silk beneath was dyed in shades of green, darker than her skin at the edges, but lighter in the center, creating a slimming effect.

Gathered at the waist, layered silk draped over her like a waterfall to the floor, cascading from emerald green to lilac. The layers united in front with a sapphire-blue braided panel, a river cutting through the center.

The dress was a masterpiece, silk rippling like water with every movement.

Lida had also worked on her hair for hours. A cascading waterfall of her sapphire curls interwoven with delicate braids, adorned with tiny, sparkling amethysts. Subtle twists and loops artfully pinned throughout created a sense of movement.

Lida finished with her face, applying a dark purple line along her lashes, a smudged lighter shade at the corners of her eyes. She ended with a pale peach color rubbed along the top of her cheeks and dabbed onto her lips.

"I look like a goddess," she'd said.

Yet, no goddess lurked in the shadows, scheming, gleeful at the king's failure to find his next queen.

In her transformed state, she dared to catch Edmar's attention, but reality soon dimmed that spark. If only Edmar knew the destruction she was capable of... he'd greet her with fear or disdain. The final shattering of her hope came with the harsh truth of her quest.

A presence materialized beside her as the Sun Stone remained indifferent to Edmar's ninth dance partner. Servants and latecomers had passed, but none had stopped, so she was surprised to find Rivus looking down at her with a friendly smile.

"Princess Emmy, you shouldn't be hiding when you look this lovely."

She blushed, her tongue tripping over her words. It was hard to lie about why she was hiding when the man was so clearly being nice. She really didn't make a good thief.

Not a good swimmer. Not a good thief.

One day, she'd have to find what she was actually good at.

"I didn't mean to startle you, Your Highness."

"You didn't, Lord Rivus."

"Please call me Rivus." He bowed.

"As long as you call me Emmy."

The music started into a new song, and she sighed internally. Possible bride number ten.

Rivus held up an arm. "Want to dance?"

She eyed him skeptically. *I am good at dancing.*

Hesitating, she looked at the smiling faces, yearning to join them, to laugh and dance without the shadow of her mission. But as quickly as the yearning came, it was squashed by the weight of her purpose here. She was not one of them.

He laughed, oblivious to her dark thoughts. "Oh, I know you want to. I watched you dance in place throughout the last set."

"You watched me?" she asked, her arms crossing.

"Hey," he said, holding up his hands, "I didn't know who you were at first. I just saw this beautiful woman all alone, without an escort."

"And how many other women here have blue hair?"

He crossed his hands over his heart. "I promise I don't have any nefarious thoughts. I know the king cares for you, and I wondered why you were here all alone." He swung his elbow up again. "Dance?"

She heard the truth in his words, but wondered if his sincerity extended to everything he said. Did Edmar really care for her? He was more worried about his kingdom than her.

And she was more worried about stealing the Sun Stone.

Except she was doing this to save her power from killing him or anyone else.

They just weren't meant for each other.

Despite her skepticism, the lure of dancing—and the opportunity it presented to learn more about the Sun Stone—persuaded her.

She slipped her hand into the crook of his arm with a smile. "Why not?"

Chapter 26

EDMAR

Edmar danced with another woman, the curse still silent. Never, in centuries of this ritual, had it taken this long. Usually, he recognized his chosen wife by the third or fourth dance. Once, it had taken five dances before the curse had tightened the band in his chest.

A weary sigh escaped him as he prepared to dance with the tenth lady, the sound lost beneath the ballroom's lively tunes. Each step, each turn with a new partner, was like walking through the pages of a book he had read a thousand times, knowing the ending yet hoping for a twist that never came.

Perhaps this time... Centuries of this charade had left him weary, yet his royal facade never faltered, the practiced smile masking his yearning for something genuine.

The woman currently in his arms was not the chosen one either.

Maybe he was drunk.

But that couldn't be it.

His youngest brother, Zane, was always deep into his cups by the time the curse finally thrust a new bride on him.

He moved through the dance, half-listening to his partner, wondering how many more times he'd have to play this game before finding his queen. Carefully, he turned his partner on the next step.

For a fleeting moment, amidst the sea of twirling dresses, a glimpse of blue, a spark in the darkness, stirred something within him.

Emmy.

Her name, a silent whisper in his heart, brought both solace and torment.

He stopped breathing and almost stumbled, shaking his head to clear the confusion and his reaction to her.

His heart pounded against his ribs.

He nearly lost his composure at the thought of her defiance. He had expressly commanded her to leave before the ball, yet the possibility of her presence intrigued him.

She hadn't left the palace. Her dress would have been delivered. She could have come. Only Rivus and Yolande knew of his command. It was unorthodox for a king to restrict an eligible princess, or any lady, from attending unless she'd ruined her reputation and wouldn't be a fit queen.

As he stepped with the music, he craned his neck, searching for her sapphire hair. When the music ceased, he finally saw her, engaged in lively conversation with Rivus. His eyes widened at finding his friend dancing with her.

The sight of her ignited longing and regret, but Rivus held her captive. She didn't even look at him.

An unfamiliar emotion—jealousy—wormed into his chest, his heart hammering, his breath constricting.

Just then Rivus caught his eye and offered a small, knowing smile, one that spoke volumes of the shared history and unspoken understandings between old friends. *"She captivates you, doesn't she, Edmar?"*

This silent exchange plucked at the contrast between his restrained exterior and the tumultuous emotions harbored within his heart.

"Your Majesty, does the dance weary you, or perhaps it is the weight of the crown tonight?" The gentle voice of the lady in his arms was tinged with curiosity and perhaps a hint of concern.

He looked down at her, his gaze unfocused. Her gray eyes held her question, innocent yet probing, which mirrored the internal battle he faced between his kingly duties and his personal desires.

With a jolt, he realized he was just standing there. He should escort her to the abbot. He offered his arm, leading her to the dais. Moving away from Emmy only intensified his distress, his breath short.

As the abbot carried out the ritual, he knew the curse had not chosen his dance partner, so the Sun Stone would show the truth of that, leaving him free to peruse the people watching them. His gaze met Emmy's over the heads of all the ladies and their escorts, and for a fleeting moment, he forgot the curse, the ritual, the weight of the crown. In her eyes lay the promise of a different story, one untold, free from the bindings of ancient spells. A surge of longing, so potent it stole his breath, filled him.

She was more beautiful than every other woman here. There was no other for him, and he'd missed her all day, as if he'd lost a part of himself.

He wished he could go to her, take her away—run away with her like she'd asked that first night on the rowboat. He moved closer to her, but a glint of candle flames on his teal scales held him back. The scales peeking out from his long sleeves were a reminder of his duty to the curse.

His jaw tightened, and he forced himself to look away, his heart aching. As quickly as hope flickered, it was doused by the cold reality of his fate.

Emmy was not his future. He had to stop torturing himself.

When the Golden Scepter was taken away and he led his dance partner back out into the crowd, he resumed the ritual of donning the blindfold. He took several deep breaths, trying to ease the pressure in his chest.

It didn't seem to go away, so he plowed forward by raising his hands, searching, but his inner eye still saw the beautiful vision of the mermaid. He walked forward. His breath became more difficult, so he instinctively turned right. Some of the pressure loosened. With each step, breathing became easier.

Satin, damask, velvet, and silk dresses rustled around him. The scent of the long-burning candles wafted between the women's perfumes. By now, the cloying smells had filled his nostrils so continuously it was hard to tell the differences.

The pressure eased as his hands landed on bare shoulders.

He smiled and began to untie the silk blindfold. "Congrats, my lady..."

The words died with his smile as realization dawned. The pressure he'd felt—it was the curse's sign, the constricting band that would remain in place until he married his bride by chance.

"Emmy," he whispered.

She frowned up at him, slowly blinking her large emerald eyes. "I never moved, Edmar, but you came straight to me. Are you sure you're really blind beneath that fabric?"

She wouldn't have. Unlike the others who had politely jostled for his attention, hoping to be chosen, he was certain she hadn't moved.

He hadn't been able to breathe—not solely because of Emmy, though she certainly had that effect on him. He hadn't been able to breathe because he'd located the one the curse had chosen, but he was so confused.

Why now?

"I'm not allowed to pick my partner. Only the magic chooses," he said.

"Does that mean...?"

"Yes, Emmy." Confusion be damned. It didn't matter how or why now, not when the curse had finally chosen the woman before him.

He smiled as it all finally settled in his chest. Accepting the twist of fate, Edmar embraced the reality. "You are my bride by chance, the one I'm to marry and to make Queen of Cyaneus."

Chapter 27

EMMY

"Raise your hands, Princess Emira, so that I may lay the Golden Scepter in them."

The abbot didn't warn her about handling the scepter. As an immortal, she could touch the Gods' Stones without harm, and use the hidden magic within each stone. But accessing the hidden magic took knowledge lost to time. Otherwise, each stone granted one power freely, and the Sun Stone revealed truths.

Trembling, she grasped the scepter. Unlike the other ladies, her nerves stemmed from a different fear. She could imagine a life where this moment led not to a crown of duty and deceit, but to lazy mornings in Edmar's embrace, laughter echoing amid the beautiful gardens, a belonging so profound it anchored her very soul.

Edmar could marry her—he would marry her if she didn't steal the Sun Stone before the wedding. Perhaps they could have had a simple existence. Her days measured by Edmar's smiles and her nights by the warmth of his arms.

His reassuring presence momentarily eased her fears as he stepped forward. She'd allowed herself the fleeting fantasy, but the dread of betrayal remained.

She'd wanted this. To marry him so she could steal the stone, but now, facing the reality of marriage to him, she quailed. She felt sick to her stomach.

"Don't be scared, Princess. You were already chosen."

But that's not why I'm scared.

The scepter, a symbol of control, mocked her powerlessness, a prisoner to her secrets and fears. The allure of what Edmar promised her reminded her she couldn't risk his safety. Her mother's death weighed heavily on her, forbidding any chance of happiness.

No Ocean's Lament vibrated in her chest. No tears came to her eyes. Instead, sadness swamped her.

She'd tried so hard to leave it behind in the ocean.

She'd enjoyed these last few days, but now?

He gave her an encouraging smile and stepped back, presenting her to the ballroom. She swallowed the tightness in her throat, forcing a smile.

"Repeat the words, Princess. I am the chosen queen of Cyaneus."

She opened her mouth to speak, but no words came out.

Edmar frowned.

She licked her lips and tried again. "I am the chosen queen of Cyaneus."

The black Sun Stone exploded with bright golden light streaming from its multifaceted surface.

Shielding their eyes, the crowd cried out as they fell back.

The Sun Stone's surging glow spotlighted her deepest flaw, not her affirmation as the new queen. Others might see the Sun Stone's acceptance, yet they were blind to the corrosive power lying dormant within her, ready to betray her claim to this throne and to Edmar's heart.

As the light dimmed, applause erupted.

When the God's Stone returned to complete darkness, everyone beamed at her, clapping and rejoicing at the proclamation of their new queen. It all felt so surreal—an echo of what should have been a joyous occasion.

The abbot reached for the scepter, but she held on.

I need the Sun Stone! Just let me take it before I break your king's heart.

The old man's forehead rose into mountains of wrinkles.

Everyone watched her. Waiting.

Edmar watched her.

She released the Golden Scepter.

Edmar stepped forward, his smile brighter than she'd ever seen it. Happiness danced in his ocean-colored eyes.

His smile tempered as he studied her. Concern etched in his furrowed brow, the gentle pressure of his hands enveloping hers, spoke of a tenderness that reached beyond the pageantry of their surroundings. "Are you alright?"

No. I must pretend I want this when I don't, but I really do. Does that make sense?

She blinked to shutter her thoughts. "I hadn't thought it was possible I could be chosen. You said..."

He raised her hands to his lips and brushed a kiss over her skin. So much promise. The rings of blue light circled in his ocean-colored eyes, like a beacon in a frothy sea. She stood to lose not just a king, but a man whose every look and touch whispered of a home she longed for.

"Neither did I," he said, his voice husky, "but the magic chose you."

He lowered their hands, but continued to rub his thumbs over her knuckles. "We will marry in three nights, if you'll have me."

If she thought they could actually be happy one day, she'd say yes a thousand times.

She wanted him without her power. But she couldn't have both.

The abbot departed, Golden Scepter in hand. But all eyes were on her. She couldn't follow. For now, she needed to maintain the facade of a devoted fiancée, despite her unresolved turmoil.

"Emmy, will you have me?" Surely he read her hesitations.

For a suspended heartbeat, the world muted, the clamor of the crowd, the orchestral melodies, even the palace itself fading to a distant murmur.

Her response intertwined her deepest wishes with her silent burdens. "My desire is to marry you and to keep us safe."

He smiled, turning to the crowd, his hand still clasped in hers. "My people, may I present your new queen, the daughter of King Sargon, the King of the Seas. The Princess Emira."

CHAPTER 28

EMMY

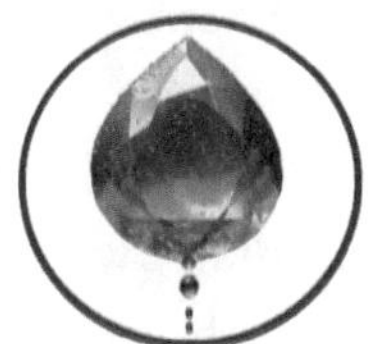

Emmy woke late the next day with the same dread from the ball. Underlying melancholy had dragged her back into her dreams many times. She couldn't marry Edmar. She wanted to. Every fiber of her being yearned to join her life to his.

But her eventual theft of the Sun Stone would create a rift as deep and wide as the ocean's largest trench. To marry Edmar would be to dishonor him, casting her as even more of a villain.

Her stomach quivered, and her hands shook.

She had to steal the Sun Stone and leave before she married him.

Lida's cheerfulness and a soothing bath couldn't alleviate her unease. Her skin prickled with discomfort beneath the maid's touch. Between dodging Lida's attempts to dress her and enduring the brush ripping through her hair, she finally snapped.

"May the depths curse you!"

"What's wrong, Your Highness?" Lida asked with more patience than she deserved.

Contrition filled her, but the same nausea shuddered inside. She pressed her lips together, swallowing the acidic bile climbing her throat. Retreating to irritation held her body's spasms at bay.

Moments later, Mistress Cassia arrived. The seamstress's gaze was intense and unsettling as usual.

"Time to make your wedding dress, Your Highness," she said, her voice a soft whisper.

Emmy glared, daring the seamstress to comment on her nakedness, but Cassia, as always, seemed to see right through her.

Cassia draped fabric over her frame, fingers deft and sure as she measured and pinned, the whisper of silk and rustle of lace filling the room.

The meticulous process left Emmy hot and restless, the dress constricting her, squeezing air from her lungs. She struggled to draw a full breath. "Why do humans insist on such restrictive things?"

"The king won't be able to keep his hands off you once he sees you in this," Lida said, offering a reassurance she didn't want.

Where once she yearned for his touch, she now trembled with nerves.

"The king will fall even more in love with you." Cassia nodded, her owl-like eyes fixed on her with an intensity that made her shift uneasily.

She turned toward the window. The endless blue expanse of the ocean, the sky darkening. She spoke aloud the words she thought of last night in the gardens. "Love is a luxury."

If he truly loved her, it would make her betrayal more devastating.

Sensing her distress, Lida explained the tradition of the wedding veil—a symbol of purity, lifted only by the king on their wedding night.

"Make him wait until your honeymoon," Cassia murmured, deftly arranging fabric over her hips.

"Honeymoon?" Her heart pounded.

"You and the king will embark on a voyage," Lida explained. "A tradition. He'll sail down the coast, introducing you to the people."

Cassia nodded. "The king does like to follow tradition."

Tradition, duty, honor. Those things were Edmar.

The room closed in on Emmy, the weight of the gown, the stifling air, the hint of a life and traditions that could never be hers.

A longing for the sea struck her, and she couldn't breathe.

She clutched her chest, doubling over, gasping for air.

"Your Highness!"

Someone brushed fingers on her shoulder, and she threw up a hand. "Don't touch me."

She closed her eyes and delved deep within herself. *Guide me, mother. I need you.*

It's not your fault.

But it was. She couldn't seem to exist without hurting someone.

Her betrayal loomed on the horizon, but it wasn't a betrayal of just Edmar but also of these people and their traditions.

Breathe, sweet one. Slow, steady. Hold.

Her throat tightened at the whisper of her mother's words.

I'm so sorry, mother. I'm so sorry that I couldn't have been a better daughter.

She slid to her knees and covered her face.

"It's alright, Princess," Lida said. "We know he loves you. That's why we didn't follow his orders to make you leave yesterday."

She shook her head. None of that mattered.

"The Sun Stone," she whispered, her voice hoarse. "Where is it?"

"It's in the chapel, Your Highness," Lida said, her voice hesitant.

Standing, Emmy caught her reflection. She'd wasted too much time already. It was time to do what she'd come to do. "Take this off, please, and tell me how to get to the chapel."

The women exchanged glances. Cassia swiftly removed the dress as Lida gave directions.

It really would be a beautiful wedding dress, perfectly complementing her green skin and sapphire-blue hair. The woman in the mirror was a stranger, a fraud, a queen of deception.

"Leave me," she said, her voice tight.

They complied, and as soon as they were gone, she rushed to pull on a plain dark gray dress, stuffing a similar one into a leather bag with any food she found in the room. Welcoming the knife points slicing into her feet.

Last, she grabbed Edmar's worn, dingy white shirt, the one he had given her on her first day on land. She held it to her nose, drawing in his scent, fortifying her for what she must do, then stuffed it into the bag, too.

As the last rays of daylight faded from the sky, she hugged the bag and headed toward the chapel, her steps firm, her heart pounding.

Edmar would be returning soon to his human form. She had to hurry.

The Sun Stone awaited.

And with it, the power to change her life.

Chapter 29

EMMY

Emmy's fingers grazed the ancient stone archway as she entered the chapel, nodding to the guard. She stepped lightly on tiptoe, but knives still stabbed at her feet. Each painful step echoed the deeper ache of her choices—the Sea Witch's spell, promised freedom.

Towering pillars and a vaulted ceiling reached upward, their shadows mingling with the incense-scented air. A realm far removed from her underwater home, which lacked centers for worship. She absorbed the chapel's reverence for the Sun God. She felt an ache of longing. For a place in this world, for a sense of belonging she'd never known.

Red candles with beaded wax cast a dim glow over gold and amber tapestries, the Sun God's mythical tales woven into their threads. In the chapel's hallowed silence, her resolve crystallized. Steal the stone and leave quickly.

I spent too long in bed, wallowing in my sorrow. Gilly would surely take her to task after warning her about kissing the king.

She strode toward the altar at the other end of the chapel. Perfumed oil burned in costly golden lamps around it. Silent shadows stretched across the space, only burned away by flickering flames. An effigy of the Sun God carried faint traces of exotic oils, which glistened on its polished surface. At the feet of the god lay the Golden Scepter.

She moved closer, absorbing the setup. She dropped her bag to the floor and extended a hand, fingers brushing the idol's smooth surface. Warmth emanated from the sun-kissed stone. Would the Sun God be this warm in real life?

Whispers curled from the Sun Stone's black surface, beckoning her. Overwhelmed the previous night, she'd missed the clear call. A rhythmic pulse, like a heartbeat, echoed between the Fire gem at her throat and the Sun Stone, a silent conversation of magic, both Fire and Sun magic belonging to Summer.

Drawn by the voices, she whispered to herself. "It speaks to me."

The voices intensified, eluding clarity yet spellbinding her. A lulling rhythm tugging her very essence into the stone's depths.

Power, it promised.

On the cusp of understanding, the whispers vanished, leaving her grasping for the fleeting connection.

Startled, she blinked out of her daze to find the scepter gone. *What happened?* But, no, it wasn't gone. Edmar held the scepter out of her reach.

She whimpered with the missed opportunity.

His voice, soft yet firm, carried a warning. "It called to you. But beware, Emmy. The Gods' Stones seduce those of us with magic."

Was her sense of loss because the power was beyond her reach, or because she had failed to take the Sun Stone before he caught her?

Maybe both.

Edmar leaned away from her to replace the scepter at the Sun God's feet. His ocean scent swirled over her senses as he straightened again.

Purposefully, her heels hit the stone floor, a hundred knife tips piercing her soles. She kept a cry behind closed lips, but her fingernails dug into her palms.

Unaware of her despair and frustration, Edmar bowed his head with closed eyes. His lips moved silently.

When he faced her again, she said, "Your devotion… It's a surprise."

His eyes traced her face with such intensity it stole her breath. Something seemed so intimate about this moment, alone in the chapel's stillness.

Goosebumps raised on her arms.

"I find comfort in my prayers."

"But the Sun God is not your Father."

He shook his head, part of his dark brown hair falling over his face and shadowing his eyes. "Maybe not, but he is the only one left to care for our world."

She admired his open heart and his acceptance of a foreign god, of the Sun Fae, even after the Summer Fae Wars, when the Fire Fae had repeatedly invaded Agondray as recently as two years ago.

Her heart ached to be encompassed by his same devotion.

She reached up, sweeping her fingers through his hair to move it away from his eyes, revealing a few teal scales. When her gaze met his, she recognized the hunger there. She froze. Then he crushed her to him and kissed her.

After his last rejection, she didn't think they'd find themselves here again so soon. She should reject him, for so many reasons, but she melted into the kiss, wrapping her arms around him, letting him steal her breath.

Could she have one blissful moment with him before she had to leave him?

"Please," she whispered against his lips, "don't say no."

Every beat of her heart was a word unsaid, a plea for closeness. She ached for his answer.

He tore his mouth from hers, his breath harsh, his eyes focusing on her. His embrace loosened.

In that pause, a lifetime of doubts whispered to her, curling around her heart like a vise. *No one has ever desired me, and even here, I'm too much, too dangerous. My very nature repels the good and draws in ruin.*

"For twenty-five years." Strain entered his voice. "I've thought of nothing but holding you, tasting you, making you mine."

"Then why haven't you?"

He released her, only to clasp her hands, his grip almost painful. "I love you."

She shook her head. His words had to be a lie, a beautiful, cruel lie.

The ocean in his eyes laid bare what he felt. This revelation should have thrilled her, yet it was a dagger twisting in her heart. He couldn't love her, not when he wasn't even aware of her treachery.

"Listen to me, Emmy." A sea of turbulent emotions layered in the tone of his words. "There are things I can't reveal, secrets I can't share,"—his fingers tightened around hers, a silent plea—"but what I can tell you is that I love you. From the ideal I held for twenty-five years to the reality I've come to know. It hasn't changed; it's only grown stronger."

Thunder rumbled within her, the sound a crescendo rising to block his words from her ears, to deny what he'd said. The need to steal the Sun Stone, to fulfill her bargain and escape this suffocating feeling, overwhelmed her. Her magic stirred within her.

It's too soon! Twenty days remained.

Dread seeped into her bones from the familiar threat of her magic returning if she deviated from the plan. She couldn't go back to that, to being a prisoner in her own body, a burden to everyone around her.

She closed her eyes, praying for control. It receded, almost too easily, as if she'd only imagined her rising fire acid. When she peered back up through her lashes, she saw the naked vulnerability on his face, and it almost broke her.

He'd confessed his love, and she'd remained silent, a statue, a hollow shell.

For one fragile moment, she let herself imagine telling Edmar everything. The warmth of his arms around her, his whispered promises to protect her, to help her carry the burden of her magic. But then the image shattered, replaced by the cold reality. He'd take the stone. He'd keep her safe in ways that would leave her powerless. And she couldn't let that happen.

She couldn't give him the answer he wanted to his declaration of love, not when it would shatter both their worlds. Instead, she lifted onto her tiptoes, her body trembling with the effort to hold back the truth, and pressed her lips to his, a fleeting, desperate touch.

He closed his eyes with a groan.

She moved her kisses along his jaw.

Then his hands landed heavily on her shoulders, pushing her back. "I need to know, Emmy. Do you love me?"

No, don't ask me that! A torrent of emotions threatened to overwhelm her as their gazes locked. It didn't matter if she loved him when she couldn't stay. And he'd hate her soon enough.

She took several steps back, his hands dropping. With a breaking heart, she adopted her composed stillness. Her throat constricted as she spoke. "I don't."

His pained recoil, the hurt in his eyes...

Her lies tasted bitter, poisoning her words. She almost couldn't handle it, and the urge to take them back clawed at her. Longing filled her, a desperate desire to tell him the truth, to fall into his arms and confess everything. But her purpose loomed heavy, pressing against her chest and stealing her breath. She had no right to love him, not when she was poised to destroy his kingdom.

"Do you even want to marry me, or was that a lie?"

She couldn't think of what to say, what words to ease his pain, what words wouldn't be lying.

His face became a frozen mask, his expression unreadable. His arms slackened at his sides. He gave her a sharp nod. "I see. Perhaps you've only been interested in my crown."

"No." At least she could be truthful about that. "I don't care about your crown."

Only a slight narrowing of his eyes. "Then what, Emmy? What do you want?"

Every truth came to her lips, but she couldn't let the words pass. All she'd wanted was one single memory of what his love could feel like before she had to forsake him. But if his sense of duty and honor to his kingdom, to his crown, wouldn't even let him take pleasure with her, there was no possibility that he'd just let her have the Sun Stone.

She squared her shoulders. "I can't marry you."

His mouth parted with shock, and he fell back further from her.

The space between them became a chasm, an abyss that swallowed any of their shared dreams.

His frozen facade locked in place with narrowed eyes. "We *will* marry in two nights."

"You would force me to marry you?"

In two quick strides, he yanked her into his arms again, one hand in her hair, pulling her head back. His lips hovered, his breath cold against her skin, her heart pounding, desire surging. She ached for him.

Something dark filled his eyes, more than desire. She shivered.

"Why are you lying to me?" His voice cracked, raw with unspoken hurt. "I can feel your heart breaking as much as mine."

"I'm not lying," she whispered, her voice splintering. "You can't love me."

"Why? What's holding you back?" His fingers tightened in her hair. "But you won't tell me, will you? You'd rather rip out my heart than risk giving me yours."

She locked all her words behind her closed mouth.

"Help me, Emira. Help me understand. You want me for what? For what pleasure I can give you when I kiss you? The pleasure I give you when I kiss you in other places?"

The images he put into her mind made her moan inside. Her hands fisted in his shirt. How did he make her feel so hot? *Gods, why does he have to be so...*

"There's more between us than that," he said.

"There isn't." There couldn't be. *If I tell him, he'll stop me. His sense of duty is too strong.* "We don't need to speak of feelings to enjoy each other." *And I can't go back to that life. I won't.*

"And that's all you want from me?"

"Yes." *Please, believe me.*

"I want more."

"Not a possibility." *Not if I want to live.*

"Why?"

"I can't." *I can't tell you.*

"Can't? What does that mean?"

"You have your secrets, and I have mine." *And mine will destroy us both.*

His eyes narrowed. "Will your secrets destroy my kingdom or just break my heart?"

Both. Nausea churned in her stomach. Why did he have to make this so difficult? He was forcing her to lie, to tell him something that he'd find believable, to push him away so completely that he'd never forgive her. *But if I don't, the Sea Witch will win.*

It left her no choice, so she hardened her voice, each word a shard of glass in her throat. "I don't want to be shackled by yet another man in my life. I've spent two hundred years ruled by my father, allowed to do nothing more than exist. There is nothing that could convince me marrying you will not be the same prison." Her hands loosened, releasing his shirt to push against his chest, but his arms locked her to him.

"You think I'd imprison you?" he growled, his voice rising. "That I'd limit you like your father did? Damn it, Emmy, I love you! Isn't that enough for you to trust me?"

Her composure shattered for only a moment, sending a fresh wave of longing through her. *Gods, this is torture.* She swallowed the thickness in her throat. "I don't want to marry you, Edmar."

Abruptly, he let her go. She stumbled against him, wincing from the stabbing pain in her feet. Though he steadied her with heavy hands on her shoulders, he didn't release her. He lowered his head, bringing his face close to hers. "Then leave, go back to your ocean."

Freaking seashells and clams! Could she win this battle without risking him sending her back? Fear turned her insides to salt water when she thought about the Sea Witch and her Garden of Souls. "I can't go back."

His expression hardened into a mask of ice. "Marry me or return to the oceans. Either way, I won't beg for your love."

Her heart fractured as the last thread connecting them snapped. She nodded, biting back a whimper. "Fine. We'll marry. But don't expect me to ever love you."

His gaze turned cold, lifeless. "Don't worry. I won't."

CHAPTER 30

EDMAR

Usually an oasis of icy calm, Edmar's Frostlands groaned a deep, guttural sound under the assault of a strange, unfamiliar heat. Emmy's rejection was a wildfire, scorching his frozen wastelands, leaving a trail of smoldering confusion.

Where have I gone wrong?

The curse chose her, the one he was destined to marry, yet a knife twisted in his heart. She didn't want to marry him. But he had no choice.

The observatory's wooden steps creaked. Peering through the telescope, he sighed. Only one person would come here to interrupt him.

He'd sought solace in his favorite pastime, in the celestial dance above. The smooth cold metal, the smell of ink and parchment, the ticking of precise mechanical gears from the astronomical instruments scattered throughout the room in the tallest tower of his palace should all have soothed him.

A glimpse of the Sea Serpent constellation, its eternal figure eight binding doomed lovers, reminded him of his own perilous dance with Emmy. She could be the key to breaking his curse, and her own salvation.

Only a maiden who loves you with a true heart can save you if she can survive the Dragon's Kiss.

As a maiden who could survive his Dragon's Kiss, his cold breath, she only needed to love him. Then he would no longer be forced to marry a bride by chance and be allowed to have command over his shifting. She wouldn't die a premature death either, as all brides by chance did. But one misstep could doom them. Her love, if it existed, had to be spoken before any physical consummation. She had to remain a maiden.

"I thought you'd be whisking your bride away tonight," Rivus said, stepping into the observatory.

He stared into the telescope, his gaze lingering on the void beyond. He'd meant to take Emmy on a midnight picnic, but that had changed with their conversation in the chapel. "Did you come here for a reason?"

"I thought to let you know I was leaving."

Jerking away from the telescope, he rubbed the scruff on his jaw. "I'm messed up."

"I could have told you that." Rivus laughed and leaned against the doorframe, the stairs behind him.

Edmar lit candles on the worktable, the beeswax scent reminding him of the previous evening when the smell had permeated his senses so thoroughly that he hadn't even smelled Emmy in the throng of women.

"What happened?" Rivus asked. Concern furrowed his brow.

"The curse."

Now that the curse had marked Emmy as its chosen bride, an invisible tether pulsed between them. He had a general sense of her location. Currently in the gardens, it seemed. The tether, though, was a constant reminder of his numbered days.

To avoid his death, one of two things had to happen: marry his bride by chance by the next full moon or send her away from Agondray. The last time the curse chose Emmy, she'd left Agondray. That allowed a reset, although his kingdom suffered a year of winter until the curse finally chose another bride for him.

"What do you mean? I thought everything was fine now."

Fine was a distant shore.

The moment he'd seen her in the chapel, all he could think about was kissing her. She consumed his thoughts—her smile, her wit, her love for knowledge, her fascination with the stars. Those things lay side by side with the sensual woman he'd come to know, her full-bodied passion he found hard to resist.

He flushed, embarrassed. He rarely discussed such things with his friend, finding it disrespectful. "It's not fine," he said, his voice tight. "She wants... things. And when I pressed her about her feelings, she said she didn't want to marry me."

"What are you going to do?"

"I've set a plan into motion, but I hope she chooses to marry me." He looked at his telescope, wanting to get lost in the stars again. His hands fisted at his sides. "But how can I hold back from fully loving her?"

"I don't see the problem." Rivus frowned. "If she marries you and wants you, enjoy your life together."

"You mean her shortened life?" He shook his head. "There's more between us..."

Rivus's careful study of him under a lowered brow made him pause. *What is my friend thinking?*

He dismissed the reaction as part of his own distraught state. "She won't admit it. If I give in to our desires before she loves me, she will die in twenty years."

"Edmar, as your friend, I must say that as much as I understand your dilemma, this is not the first time you've been here. How many other brides have you believed would be 'the one'? How can you be sure this princess is any different?"

That was the real question. "I don't know. She refused to tell me she loved me. Perhaps I've been wrong about her all this time. I mean, can a mermaid even love anyone? What do we know about the merfolk?"

"Not much," Rivus said, looking less worried. "They don't mate for love, but that doesn't mean they're incapable of it."

Maybe she just wanted to mate, nothing more, especially since she hadn't been allowed before. Considering her father's marriage arrangement between her and the Seat of the Dwarf, Edmar was the better option. And maybe that was all he was to her. A way to escape her father as the best option.

Yet she didn't want to marry him. "I don't know what to do."

Despair threatened an escape from his Frostlands.

Rivus stepped closer, placing a hand on his shoulder. "You have her, Edmar. Love her as you can and don't let the curse dictate your happiness."

He frowned. "You're saying I should just..."

Rivus's well-meaning advice clashed with the curse's harsh reality. He hesitated, afraid to risk everything on the chance of her love. He couldn't give in to his desire for her.

His friend nodded. "If she wants you and you want her..."

No question if she wanted him. *But does she love me?* He thought he knew the answer until she baldly told him she didn't. That hurt worse than a dozen punches to the gut. As if to confirm his fears, the curse tightened its grip on his chest.

He retreated a step, then another, as if physically distancing himself could somehow spare him the weight of his decision. He shook his head, a desperate denial of the no-win scenario before him. "I need to keep faith."

He murmured the words more to himself than to Rivus, clinging to hope still.

"So you'll marry her," Rivus said, his voice flat, "but refuse to touch her, for the short time you have, on the chance she might love you one day?"

...the short time you'll have with her...

The words hung heavy, but the gravity of his future with Emmy anchored him. Then, with a sudden burst of motion, he turned away, unable to face the truth in his friend's words. He swept a hand across the worktable in frustration, sending a scatter of parchments fluttering to the floor.

His lungs spasmed, stealing his breath. He bent over, catching a hand on his table, the other on his chest.

"Edmar!" Rivus leaped to his side, a hand on his back.

Without her love, he was condemning her to mortality. The band crushed harder around his chest with those thoughts. "I should send her back to the ocean."

If she returned to the sea, the link would break, and she'd escape the curse of a premature death, though the land would endure another year of winter. Then the curse would force him to marry another. But could he let her go again? He hadn't a choice the first time. He hadn't even known who she was.

Straightening, he shook off Rivus's hand, breath still ragged. "May the Sun God and his Seven Sleepers forgive me but I cannot let her go. Not again."

Didn't that make him as evil as the Snow Princess?

He'd keep Emmy, knowing she could die if she never loved him, and he'd never be able to tell her the truth. Revealing the curse to her put her life in danger. He pounded on his chest, trying to catch his breath.

"What will you do?" Rivus asked.

"I will marry her and hope one day..." A sharp pain of realization struck him mid-sentence, silencing him. He clutched at his chest, thinking his turmoil had stolen his breath.

But that wasn't it. The band constricting his chest came as a warning.

His hand shot out, gripping Rivus's arm with a strength born of panic, his knuckles whitening. "She's left the city."

CHAPTER 31

EMMY

Emmy's footsteps echoed on the worn trail, towering trees casting eerie shadows in the moonlit night. Knives dug into her toes, but her racing heart masked the pain.

A whirlwind of emotions drove her deeper, seeking solace in the forest's depths. The grandeur of Edmar's palace faded into the distance, a symbol of a future she had to forsake despite her desires.

He was not her future.

As much as she wanted him, she had to let him go. Leaving Edmar shattered something new inside her, but her very essence posed a danger to him. This painful acknowledgment propelled her forward, her resolve hardening with each step away from him.

She'd left behind Edmar and the Sun Stone, the opportunity to steal it unnoticed, lost. But the Summer Child offered an alternative with her promise to help. Emmy only had to locate the weird egg again.

Without her tail, she relied on the Summer Child's call. She closed her eyes to sense its beacon, which was like a pulse of life similar to the electrical energy her tail's lateral line perceived.

She followed it.

An hour into her journey, the forest lulled her into introspection, masking dangers lurking in the shadows. A sudden growl snapped her back to reality, revealing her vulnerability.

Ocean predators had been known to leave her alone, sensing her magic, but now she was defenseless.

Eyes, like moonlit shards, glimmered from the shadows. Clouds scuttled through the sky, casting the half-moon's pale light onto six dire wolves as they stepped onto the path, formidable silhouettes circling her, their predatory gazes gleaming.

She froze, her heart the only thing left working. It beat in her ears, her blood rushing through her body. Her magic, though chaotic and hated, had meant safety, so this feeling was new.

The wolves were tall enough to almost look her in the eye. Coats of white, silver, and indistinct darker hues. The one with the darkest coat, a silver saddle striped over its shoulders, advanced toward her. It snapped its jaws, a low growl in its throat.

Her gem glowed in response. An electrical pain shot through her blood. Only a single moment of agony, a reminder of why she'd left Edmar.

She whimpered.

The wolves closed in, their intent clear in their unwavering stares. The darker wolf's chilling breath wafted over her.

Her terror spiked, her gem pulsing, then a flare of burning torture ripped through her. She dropped to her knees, a cry escaping her.

The wolf lunged.

It slammed her back, jaws closing on her throat.

Her magic burst—a flash of red light striking the wolf's muzzle before its teeth broke her skin.

The creature yelped and jumped away.

She curled against the dirt, sobbing, tearless. From pain. So quick but debilitating.

But now it fled, once more suppressed by the Sea Witch's spell.

The wolves regrouped, circling closer. A distant rumble, then thundering steps, growing louder. Growls faltering, they turned toward the approaching sound.

A formidable white dire wolf leaped from the darkness, landing protectively over her. A defiant growl, challenging the other six wolves.

When the dark leader of the pack returned a growl, her protector wolf snapped its jaws in warning. The two seemed to communicate, their eyes glowing.

It wasn't enough.

The other wolves regained their confidence and circled even closer amid growls and sharp teeth snapping.

The ground rumbled anew.

A frigid gust swept through the wolves, swirling around her and her guardian. The strike thundered with formidable force. She ducked her head and closed her eyes in the whirlwind of dirt and debris.

The gale subsided, revealing a figure bathed in celestial blue light.

Edmar, astride a horse, rose from the saddle, his voice booming, "This one is under my protection."

The words echoed with enhanced magic, encircling him in a vortex of power. She momentarily forgot everything else as her Dragon King ushered the wolves back, so handsome in his fury. The wolves melted back into the forest.

Edmar leaped to the ground, rushing to her, and her wolf protector stepped away. He lifted her gently, his arms tightening protectively around her. Now that she was no longer in danger, her terror released, she trembled.

"Are you hurt?" he asked, his hands checking her clinically. His ocean scent sent her senses spiraling. His breath lay heavy on her cheek.

Even as her traitorous heart beat with glee and warmth flooded her, a sour taste filled her mouth. She struggled to win the war between her yearning for him and her need to flee, to protect him.

She shook her head while swallowing bile. "Thank you."

He didn't let her go, holding her shoulders. The half-moon slanted over the anger on his face, his features hard in a way she'd never seen.

"What were you thinking?" he demanded.

Her chin lifted with his tone, pulling away from his touch. She liked it too much. "Isn't it obvious?"

"But you agreed..." His jaw clenched. "I see."

She turned back to the path, determined to reach the Summer Child. The white wolf leaped in front of her, blocking her way forward with a growl.

"Emira."

Slowly, she turned to her Dragon King, wishing he'd just allow her to leave him so she could keep him safe, so she wouldn't betray him.

"You reject marriage," he said, his voice laced with disbelief, "but you want me to deflower you?"

Her confusion must have been clear.

"You want me to take your innocence?"

She couldn't answer him. He'd rejected her too many times for her to voice that she only wanted a single night of memories to sustain her until she became someone who wouldn't hurt him, both emotionally and physically.

"Is that all I am to you?" he said softly, pain in his words.

That was a sharp dagger to her heart. He meant so much to her, maybe too much. The words to tell him the truth of everything rushed against her lips, and she imagined the conversation they would have.

I need to leave you to protect you. My magic is dangerous and will kill you, just as it killed my mother.

Let me help you, he'd say.

Give me the Sun Stone so I can use it to find all the other Gods' Stones, which I will then give to one of the most powerful creatures in the ocean.

That wouldn't end well.

Or she could forgo the Sun Stone and reply with her alternate option.

I'm going to the Summer Child. The most powerful being I've ever encountered, who hides in the waters below Agondray. Oh, and a Water Fae from my dreams tells me helping the Summer Child will spell the end of all Winter creatures, which, as you know, includes merfolk and the Ice Dragons.

That second option made her gasp as she fully laid it out in her head. What was she thinking? She couldn't help the Summer Child even if it meant the end of her pain and destruction. She could continue with her previous quest or resign herself to the Sea Witch's Garden of Souls.

He wouldn't understand. He wouldn't help. Not Edmar, a man so rigid about honor and duty. She doubted he would even have any hesitation in stopping her—whether from taking the Sun Stone or reaching the Summer Child.

He'd take away her options, and she couldn't bear the bleak future that awaited her if she couldn't remove her magic. She couldn't tell him the truth, and he recognized her resistance to answering his questions.

His jaw popped, and a light blue ring circled his irises. "Would having me satisfy you?"

Yes!

He pulled her fiercely against him. His lips crashed down on hers, consuming, possessing. The shock of his action stunned her as his kiss laid a claim over her. It hinted at a desperate merging of souls seeking solace and surrender. Instant heat filled her, and she couldn't breathe as she twined her arms around his neck.

It was too much. She wanted his kisses, his touches, his possession. She wanted him, but she couldn't stay with him.

Despite her attempt to pull away, he kept her firmly in his grasp.

Instead, he bit the skin of her neck with a growl. "If you want me to make love to you here, right now, I will."

A soft whine filled the space between the trees, the white wolf waiting only a few feet away. Edmar sighed and lifted his head to look at her. Vulnerability shone in his eyes.

"My life was empty for a millennium," he said, his voice rough with emotion, "until the day I met you. For the first time, I understood the allure of a bright sun, because that was you. You are my light, and I don't want to live in darkness anymore. I love you, Emmy. Just tell me what to do so I won't lose you."

She opened her mouth, but did not know what to say. His words filled an emptiness inside her, too. More than anything she'd ever wanted in her life, beyond having her mother back, she wanted him, but whatever she promised him, or herself, would be a lie. She would not risk his life by staying with him. That had never been part of the plan.

She finally found the right words. "Let me go."

Her plea was more than a bid for freedom. She intended to confront her destiny head-on, and no longer be a prisoner of her magic, but a warrior against it.

Something shuttered in his face. It became the frozen mask she'd seen him wear so often now with her.

Abruptly, he released her to swing up into his saddle. He guided his horse close and leaned down to her.

"I can't do that."

Before his words sank into her brain, he scooped her up and held her to his chest as he turned the horse and sent them into a gallop back toward the palace.

CHAPTER 32

EDMAR

Edmar paced by the tall mirror in his sitting chamber, glimpsing his brothers' reflections. He spoke to his older brother, Kalden. "Sending supplies should ease your people's hunger. They should arrive in two days' time."

Golden rays stretched along the floor from a sun fallen beneath the horizon.

Rivus chuckled from his chair, swirling his drink. "Mirror talks, always less chilling than your ice storms, eh?"

No one laughed, all too aware of the curse's havoc when the brothers were physically together—fierce ice storms they couldn't stop until they separated. They relied on two-way mirrors for near nightly check-ins.

Kalden's husky voice, a voice deeper than any other Edmar had heard in his life, rumbled from the mirror. "Thank you."

Edmar halted his pace, and he faced Kalden and Zane staring at him where they suspended side by side on the surface. His tone softened. "It's the least I can do. I'm glad we have you back."

He would have done anything to coax Kalden from his twenty-year seclusion. He didn't want to see his brother end up like Rin.

Kalden's voice was tinged with regret. "Winters here grow harsher. The people suffer."

Edmar nodded as he resumed pacing. In recent years, those winters had begun to affect his lands. But once Kalden married his bride by chance, warmth would soon return to his realm.

"What in the eight hells is wrong, brother?" Zane leaned close to the mirror on his side as if he could see Edmar better.

Turning from the mirror, he clenched his teeth, exhaling a long breath. *Emmy's back, safe and guarded within these walls.*

The thought offered more reassurance than factual certainty.

Memories of her in his arms last night lingered. He would have done anything. Kissed her for hours, worshiped her body, brought her untold pleasure. If only she'd agreed to stay with him.

She hadn't made that choice, but he still would have done those things if she'd simply spoken or offered any explanation for refusing him.

He scrubbed at the stubble on his cheeks. *But silence?*

The silence gnawed at him, a contrast to the night when they'd shared stories under the stars, her laughter a melody in the dark.

He feared what her silence might mean. Her refusal to speak cut deeper than expected, silently challenging the belief that she was the destined bride who could break his curse. If she wouldn't talk to him, would she marry him?

As he paced, last night's desperate plan surfaced. A plan born not of certainty, but desperation. One she would learn of soon, but the choice remained hers.

Halting, he faced his brothers.

He opened his mouth to speak, but Rivus interjected. "Just girl trouble."

The jest, light yet edged with tension, drew a reluctant grin. He nodded, letting the levity ease the weight of the moment.

Rivus raised a hand, wiggling his fingers. "They've had trouble keeping their hands to themselves, but the wedding is tomorrow night."

Edmar stifled a snort, relieved the simplification deflected his brothers' probing. He didn't want to admit how badly he'd botched this. And he still didn't understand his mistake beyond refusing Emmy when she'd asked for intimacy.

What lady asks for her innocence to be taken without being married? But she was a mermaid. Perhaps their customs differed. He'd clearly erred grievously enough that she no longer desired marriage. *Perhaps she never had...*

He shot Rivus a meaningful look, murmuring more to himself. "It's not that simple."

Zane's sudden laughter broke through, mischief glinting in his eyes. "At least one of us has success with the ladies."

That was a jab at Kalden's stubborn bride by chance, who refused to marry him.

"You have a lady?" Kalden asked Zane.

As Kalden's deep query rumbled through the room, Zane responded with a sly wink, "Always."

"Yet you struggle with this one. Unusual for you," Kalden said.

Something dampened Zane's usual smile. "She requires more coaxing to appreciate my perspective."

Edmar was happy to have the focus off him and Emmy. "What perspective is that? Why she should join you under the covers?"

"Must be," Kalden said. "She troubles Zane by resisting his charms."

"You guys have it all wrong," Zane said.

Edmar smiled at his brother's slightly riled tone. "Then enlighten us."

"Maybe she saw what he has to offer and found it lacking." Kalden chuckled.

Hearing gruff and serious Kalden laugh was a miracle.

That made him smile harder. Even Zane laughed.

A knock drew Rivus to the door; Edmar held his breath. When his friend returned with a nod, Edmar squared on his brothers.

"I have guests to attend to. Please excuse me."

"Of course," Kalden said in his husky voice. He vanished from the mirror.

"Congrats on your impending nuptials, brother!" Zane broke the connection, the mirror darkening before reverting to its normal reflective surface.

Rivus shifted by the door. "Before you use your guests to threaten your bride, perhaps I could speak with her."

Edmar frowned. "What would you say?"

A deeper question persisted: Was he trying to win her for love, or to fulfill the curse? The ambiguity troubled him. *Couldn't both motives hold equal weight?*

But he refused to love a woman who didn't love him.

"That's between her and me," Rivus said.

"I'm not threatening her."

Rivus cocked his head, an eyebrow arching in challenge. "Aren't you?"

Edmar crossed his arms. "You know her refusal means she must leave Agondray. If she stays, I die."

"I do not want to see you die, but she's different."

"Right, she's a mermaid."

Rivus dragged a hand through his shaggy hair. "Something else is happening with her."

Edmar raised his brow, conceding that Rivus might have noticed something he'd missed. "Care to elaborate?"

Rivus wiped his mouth, choosing his words carefully. What would his friend hide?

Perhaps Rivus wasn't withholding information by choice. "Has your pack forbidden you to share?"

"When we caught her on the road, and her gem activated..." He shook his head. "They felt the same thing I did, but it's confusing."

This was unprecedented—Rivus and his pack agreeing, and also being confused. They possessed far greater knowledge of the world's creatures than the Ice Dragons.

"There's something about her magic—"

"Her magic?" he said, cutting Rivus off. "She has no magic."

"I'd agree. I haven't sensed or witnessed it before now."

He recalled Emmy's words. "She surrendered her magic to become human. She's not even a mermaid."

"Evidence contradicts her claims. She used magic last night. We all felt it."

Edmar hoped Rivus was mistaken. Otherwise, Emmy hadn't been truthful. But then she'd said she wanted to marry him at the ball, only to recant later.

What else had she lied about?

Rivus leaned forward, his voice a whisper. "She has magic, reminiscent of the Ember Wraith."

"The Ember Wraith?" Disbelief and curiosity mingled in his voice. "But that's just a myth, isn't it?"

Rivus paused, swallowing the rest of his drink in a long gulp, the gravity of his next words apparent. "Born from the union of the Fire and Moon gods," he said slowly, letting each word sink in. "A being of immense power and equal destruction. The wolf clans were created to capture him, and we chased him to every end of the earth until Chaos took pity, creating a realm just for him, the Celestial Firmament."

Edmar paced, attempting to reconcile these revelations with his understanding. "A creature of Fire and Moon?"

Fire was Summer magic; Moon was Winter magic. Gender imbalances among the Summer and Winter gods made those magics stronger than those of Spring and Fall. Summer had two gods, Winter two goddesses. Spring and Fall had one of each.

Opposing magics, opposing seasonal powers, both from the strongest seasons. It seemed improbable.

Such notions birthed tales like the Summer Child, another being of conflicting powers and a third parent, all highly unlikely.

"I've never heard of any creature surviving such disparate powers." Skepticism warred with awe. "But you see a resemblance in Emmy?"

Aside from a few enhancements from their gods, like faster healing and cold tolerance, Merfolk didn't inherit innate magic from their creators, the Water Goddess and Metal God. All their power resided in their gems.

Rivus's gaze held his, earnest and intense. "When she unleashed her power, we smelled a storm of Fire and Moon magic. Intertwined, yet volatile."

Rivus and others like him possessed a rare gift. The ability to identify the exact magic being used. Most magic users could sense magic, but unless it aligned with their own element, they couldn't determine its nature.

"How?" Edmar leaned against the wall, mind racing. "Wait, Fire magic? From what? Her gem's a Sun Crystal."

Rivus's eyebrows shot up. "That's not a Sun Crystal, my friend, but a Fire Crystal."

Emmy lied about her gem, too?

He closed his eyes, drawing a deep breath. Spider cracks webbed the ice of his Frostlands.

He hadn't suspected her lies, not once. *What else has she lied about?*

His head spun. Had his emotions clouded his judgment? She could be manipulating him.

He'd believed she cared, yet she'd tried to leave. Only his intervention had stopped her.

Unless...

"Is she working with the Snow Princess?" he asked, knowing Rivus couldn't possibly know.

It was the first explanation that made sense. Emmy possessed a Fire Crystal, and Rivus smelled Moon magic on her. Besides her Moon Fae ancestry, the Snow Princess had a source of powerful Moon magic to enact her curse.

Fear flickered in Rivus's dark eyes, quickly masked by consternation. "We don't know the source of her Moon magic. She might be unaware of it, or unable to use it, like your curse. You smell of Moon magic, but the source grants you no power.

"The clan is watching. A creature possessing both Fire and Moon magic, when it shouldn't be possible, means she's very powerful. Those conflicting powers could destroy everything, even the world. It's a wonder she's alive. The clan would kill her now, if they had their way."

Edmar straightened, growling. "They will not harm her."

Even if she was the Snow Princess's spy.

Rage filled him at the thought of anyone hurting her; he berated himself for his foolishness. She could have been sent to harm him, but he couldn't help loving her.

The curse linked them, but he'd never needed it to be drawn to her.

Rivus held up his hands. "As you've said. They'll wait and see, but if she becomes a threat, they'll act."

"If she becomes a threat, I'll deal with her personally." Edmar suppressed his anger. He couldn't be upset when meeting his guests.

"Let me speak with Emmy. I believe I know what to say without endangering her, so that when she sees your guests, she'll make the right decision."

Edmar nodded, willing to try anything to persuade Emmy. "I trust you."

Chapter 33

EMMY

Emmy entered the chapel for the second night in a row, immediately enveloped by the musty scent of old stone and heavy incense. Her guards stopped at the entrance, extinguishing any hope of stealing the Sun Stone. Even if she succeeded, Edmar would track her down again. He'd found her so easily the first time.

What can I do?

The Summer Child's incessant call, the threat of returning magic, and the prospect of a lingering half-life in the Sea Witch's Garden of Souls stole her breath.

Every choice offered only bleak outcomes.

She passed beneath the archway, tiptoeing across the stone floor. Flickering candlelight cast ghostly shadows, leading her to the lone figure kneeling before the altar, adorned with the Golden Scepter and the Sun God's effigy.

The unfamiliar cadence of human worship captivated her. Hushed prayers echoed, their words indecipherable, yet the reverence was palpable. Intrigued, she cautiously approached Father Jayasurya, his head bowed, eyes closed.

What would it be like to possess such certainty, to know your place in the world? To know where you belonged.

"Hello, Princess Emira."

The abbot's warm greeting pierced her heart with a bittersweet ache.

He is oblivious to my dangerous nature

"I apologize. I didn't mean to intrude."

"You haven't, child. All are welcome in the Sun God's Chapel, at any time."

Her gaze drifted to the Golden Scepter, cradling the Sun Stone.

"Shall I guide you in prayer tonight?"

She hesitated. The offer of prayer, a potential lifeline. *Can I find solace here, or will my presence defile this sanctuary?*

She'd never prayed to the Sun God, doubting he'd heed her. Yet desperation made her wonder if he might understand her need for his stone.

The weight of isolation, the yearning for belonging, pressed down on her. She opened her mouth to accept, but boots echoed from the far end of the chapel. Shaggy-haired Rivus approached.

"May I speak privately with the princess?"

Father Jayasurya bowed, hands clasped. "Of course, my lord." His gaze met hers. "If you desire that prayer later, you know where to find me."

Then he exited through a side door.

A chilling solitude descended, the stone floor seeming to grow colder as Rivus approached. She liked him, but something felt different today.

He stopped before her, eyes flinty, running a hand through his hair. Faint blue strands shimmered like silver in the dim light.

"Why did you run, Your Highness?" Rivus's voice was a mix of accusation and concern.

She remained silent, her composure strained.

"Tell me, do you even care about Edmar?" His question now carried a personal edge, as if the answer mattered more to him than he let on.

"I'm fond of Edmar."

His brows lowered, his voice deepening. "Tell me your true purpose."

Her breath hitched, sensing an unnatural tension in his stance. The chill of his breath against her cheek heightened the ominous aura surrounding him.

Is he even human? Why hadn't she questioned this before? Perhaps because it hadn't mattered—not until he appeared to be upset with her now.

Creeping wariness slithered down her spine. "I didn't come to hurt Edmar."

His hand shot out, seizing her throat in a crushing grip. She yelped, grabbing his wrist.

Her pulse thundered. Rivus's face contorted; his jaw elongated into a snout, bones cracking as they reshaped. A deep growl rumbled from his throat. She flinched as his nails sharpened into claws, digging into her skin.

She bit her lip against the sudden pain.

"Show me your magic, mermaid."

Her eyes widened, but she shook her head. *Will my magic hurt him?* Perhaps she shouldn't care what with his hand at her throat, but she did.

He yanked her closer, his face inches from hers, a horrifying close-up of his transformation. His features twisted grotesquely, skin rippling as if battling the beast erupting within.

His voice, a guttural snarl, struggled against his snout, distorting his words into an eerie echo. "Are you working with the Snow Princess?"

Who?

Panic surged as the line between nightmare and reality blurred, her magic sparking within. It was weak compared to its former strength, but she fought to control it. Rivus was Edmar's friend, and he'd always been kind. Her mind struggled to reconcile this brutal, unrecognizable creature with the man she had known so far.

Her magic sensed her distress, as it had in the forest. A tremble of fiery pain seared her muscles as it encased the hand at her throat. His eyes narrowed, and he sniffed the air, the only reaction.

"What are you doing?"

His eyes narrowed. "You have Moon magic?"

"No. My painite is a Fire crystal."

He weighed his words to determine her truthfulness, but she didn't really care if he believed her. She gritted her teeth. "Let me go."

"Answer me. Did the Snow Princess send you?"

"I don't know who that is."

His gaze, reflecting the red glimmer of her jewel, bore into hers. "You're after the Sun Stone, aren't you? No lies."

He shook her violently, trying to force a confession. She fought to maintain her composure, fearful of unleashing her magic. It appeared he knew something about her and her plans, and he sought to protect Edmar and his kingdom.

She took calm, measured breaths. "Yes."

Will he tell Edmar?

His grip loosened, then tightened again. "I can help you with the Sun Stone, but you must do something for me first."

Shock eclipsed her surprise. Rivus, the king's confidant, proposed betrayal? Perhaps her assumptions were wrong, but given her failure at stealing the stone, she'd accept the help.

"What must I do?"

"Marry the king."

"No," she whispered, her voice trembling. "I can't. It's wrong."

"It's the only way."

"Why?" She didn't want to marry Edmar, only to steal from him. All she wanted was a home, a heart that beat in unison with hers, yet here she was, considering a union that could shatter the very heart she longed to protect.

"I know she'd permit me to say this where he couldn't, but what I'm about to say cannot be repeated without risking lives. Do you understand?"

"I have no idea what you're talking about."

"Listen, Princess." He pulled her closer as his snout receded, his human face reappearing. His eyes darkened, his voice an urgent whisper. "Edmar bears a heavy curse. One that now binds you too. Refusal to marry him puts his life at stake. I can't... I won't let him die. You must marry him."

Her heart raced, Rivus's threats echoing in her mind. *To save Edmar, to save myself, I must play his game, embrace the role of the deceitful bride.*

The irony wasn't lost on her. Seeking belonging and an impossible love, she found herself further entangled in deceit and danger. She swallowed hard against the hand on her throat.

What choice did she have? She wouldn't risk Edmar's life, even if it meant she'd hurt him with the theft of the Sun Stone.

He leaned in, his cheek brushing hers. "After the wedding, I'll help you steal the Sun Stone and get you far away. Deal?"

Her mind reeled, confusion warring with a flicker of hope. Could she safely exploit his offer? He was betraying his best friend, after all.

She turned her head slightly. "I don't trust you."

"Refuse, Princess, and I'll have no choice but to tell Edmar everything. He'll return you to your father."

"He wouldn't!" The words burst from her. Rivus's assertion clashed violently with her image of Edmar, a man bound by honor and duty.

Rivus must be lying. Yet Edmar hadn't suspected her capable of theft, either. And no lie echoed in Rivus's words, but he seemed to be adept at deceit.

"If you doubt me, why has he already summoned your father?"

"What?" She could swear her heart stopped completely in her chest.

Her father was coming here?

If he knew she was here, having left home without his permission, he'd force her back. So far, she'd been able to avoid that fate because he couldn't track her. The Sea Witch's spell dampened her connection to her gem, and so that would have dampened the connection her father felt to her through the tether. For all he knew, she was dead.

"If Edmar believes you want to marry him, he'll fight for you. You'll stay in Agondray, mermaid, and have your chance to steal the Sun Stone."

Drawing in a shaky breath, she weighed her options. Agreeing to his plan offered a chance to fulfill her deal with the Sea Witch. It meant betraying Edmar, but he'd be safe.

Refusal meant returning home, only to end up in the Sea Witch's Garden of Souls.

A shard of ice pierced her heart as she nodded.

Rivus released her. Fur covered his hands, claws extending from his fingertips. She rubbed her bruised neck, her fingers finding the puncture wounds. Blood clung to her fingertips. Her mind raced, trying to comprehend the surreal encounter, each thought more frantic than the last.

With curiosity, he lifted the hand that had gripped her neck, revealing the red, blistered skin on his palm—the result of her magic. "We're both born of the same Mother Goddess, so we'll heal quickly."

Merfolk healed fast. But what was Rivus?

She would have known, had she been observant. The clues were all there.

The beastly face, the blue in his hair, the wolves that attacked her last night and the one that protected her until Edmar arrived. And Rivus meant "stream" in the old language.

"You're a werewolf of the Water Clan."

"I am."

That didn't explain how he knew her plans. Only the Sea Witch knew, having sent her on this quest. Then she remembered her dream, where she'd revealed her quest to the Water Fae. She narrowed her eyes. "You know Malala?"

"I don't."

"Is she the Snow Princess?"

He thumbed his eyes before meeting her gaze. "Forget I mentioned the Snow Princess. Speaking her name can attract her attention, and you don't want that. Trust me."

Trust? She snorted. *Not likely.*

He muttered his last words before gripping her arm and steering her toward the arch over the chapel exit. "Time to convince daddy you're ready to be married."

CHAPTER 34

EMMY

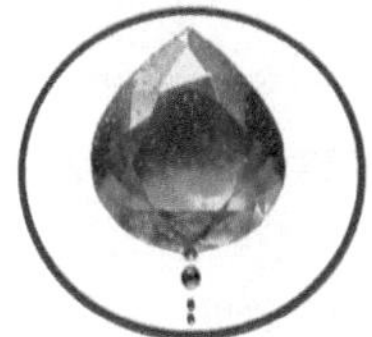

Beside Rivus, Emmy glided into the packed Throne Room, each tiptoe step a stab of pain echoing the dread coiling in her stomach. Towering columns and the vaulted ceiling pressed down, the open space suffocating, whispering her doom. Intricate carvings and paintings blurred into a chaotic swirl of colors and shapes as nausea washed over her.

"Princess Emira." Edmar's voice, sharp as a blade, sliced through the hushed murmurs, sending a shiver down her spine. "You honor us with your presence."

Her gaze darted to the throne. Radiating cold command, he seemed a stranger, a king she barely recognized. Their eyes met, her breath hitching. Then she saw her father.

Standing among his warriors, King Sargon emanated his own chilling power, tightening the air, making it hard for her to breathe. His surprise at seeing her alive vanished, replaced by calculating coldness as his dark eyes flicked from her dim gemstone to her face, a predator assessing prey. His imposing warriors flanked him, their muscular chests bare above their waist cloths.

Anger contorted Sargon's features, his knuckles white against his trident. She recoiled under the frigid glare.

Nowhere left to run. She'd fled the ocean to escape her fate, her killing magic, yet the approaching storm seemed unavoidable.

"Daughter," Sargon's voice thundered, "you've shamed our kingdom, running off like a common fish seeking a different ocean."

She lowered her gaze, his rebuke among the gathered crowd stinging. Her cheeks burned, but the feelings soon swirled into a different kind of heat. He'd meant to sell her, use her as a weapon.

Steeling herself, she raised her eyes to his. "I've been nothing more than a common fish to use for your gain."

Her father's face darkened. "And a common fish you'll always—"

Rising like a vengeful god from his throne, Edmar interrupted, commanding the room's attention. "King Sargon."

Edmar's attention fell to her, and a strange mix of warmth and possessiveness flickered in his eyes. "We've enjoyed your daughter's visit. She lends a certain radiance to our halls."

Heat flooded her cheeks again. Certainly those words could not be true, given she hadn't spoken to him since he stopped her escape. The formality of his tone belied any emotions, so she couldn't hear truth or lie in the words.

Edmar continued. "I invited you here to discuss your daughter."

Sargon's brows furrowed, suspicion hardening his features. "I admit, I thought this was a trick. But now that I see she is alive and unharmed, I will give you a few moments of my time. But speak quickly. I must decide my wayward daughter's punishment."

She nearly snorted. *He doesn't care I'm unharmed, only that I'm still his to command.* Except he couldn't command her right now. With the Sea Witch's suppression spell, the second tether between her father and her gem was absent. Her father would need to take physical possession of her gem to make her obey. He had the power to do that, unless Edmar planned to challenge the King of the Seas.

She turned her gaze to her Dragon King.

Then he leaned forward, ocean-colored eyes glinting. "Your daughter, the Princess Emira, has captured my heart. You dismissed the terms I brought up at our last meeting, but now your daughter is no longer under your control." His gaze, like a blue fire, flicked to hers, holding her captive in a web of unspoken promises and devastating consequences. "So my proposal is to her. I wish to make her my queen, if she will accept."

A proclamation, not a negotiation?

Her heart hammered, the words sinking into the pit of her stomach. Astonished murmurs swept through the court, the air thick with disbelief and anticipation. She swayed, legs weak, gripping her dress for support.

Sargon's scowl deepened, carving harsh lines into his face, his eyes narrowing to slits of icy fury. The room held its breath. He slammed his trident on the floor, a resounding boom reverberating through her. The prongs erupted in a blinding yellow flash of lightning, the air crackling with raw power.

"The princess left without my blessing." His voice silenced the murmurs. "Now that you've alerted me to her whereabouts, I've come to correct this insult and bring her back to the sea."

As if conjured by his wrath, menacing figures materialized. Men and women, hair streaked with various shades of blue and silver, moved with predatory grace, their features shifting, elongating, hands morphing into claws.

Werewolves.

The court erupted, scattering in a panicked flurry of silks and jewels. Courtiers scrambled for the exits, their composure shattered.

Her shaking hands clenched into fists, nails digging into her palms.

The werewolves' silent intensity, focused on her father and his mermen, reminded her of her predicament—return with her father and become part of the Sea Witch's garden or marry Edmar only to betray him.

Beside her, Rivus unsheathed his sword, the polished metal gleaming. His jaw was set, his eyes hard, a warrior ready for battle.

My protector. My jailer.

Even as she resented his manipulation, fear for him pierced her anger. *He'll die if he thinks he can take on my father.*

No one was more powerful than the King of the Seas with his trident.

Sargon eyed the silent werewolves, his gesture dismissive, powerful. His mermen guards stood rigid, their gems aglow. "You would deny a father his right to his *missing* daughter?"

Challenge blazed in Edmar's eyes as a ring of light blue luminance. "She belongs with me."

Her breath caught, dread and guilt warring within her. She loved his loyalty, but if he only knew why she was here and what he was fighting for—that she was here to steal from him.

But then, he was forcing her to marry him. *But he told me he loves me...*

"I will not allow you to use her like a charm," Sargon growled, advancing.

Her heart thundered in her ears. Two powerful kings vied for her fate. A battle of wills, each side supported by magic.

A lifetime of cowering under her father's disgust and hate, she'd vowed never to be controlled again. *No more. I will not be a pawn in their game.*

Meeting Edmar's gaze, she lifted her chin. He offered escape from her father forever. *This is my chance to break free.* Guilt shadowed the thought. She'd break his heart, use him, then disappear.

She approached the dais, Edmar watching her with curiosity until she stopped before him, curtseying deeply. She forced sincerity into her voice. "I accept King Edmar's proposal." She met Edmar's gaze, the blue fire in his eyes reflecting her resolve. "I will marry you."

The crack of Sargon's knuckles filled the tense silence. "You would willingly cast aside your heritage, your people, for this Land-Bound man?"

Rising to her full height, she fully faced her father, years of fearing her power and yearning for his love fueling her defiance. He couldn't control her now with the suppression spell binding her abilities and the tether between him and her. "You meant to marry me to the Seat of the Dwarf, knowing I'd likely kill him with my magic."

She risked a glance at Edmar, catching the flicker of surprise that crossed his face. *He didn't know.* Satisfaction warmed the icy knot in her stomach. He'd known her magic killed her mother, but not the depths of her father's disregard for her life. Now he knew what would happen if he made her return to her father.

Emmy's throat tightened, words lodging there like jagged stones. Acknowledging her father's indifference, voicing her unwanted existence, reopened a deep wound. She swallowed past the lump in her throat. "They would have executed me if I'd killed the dwarves' leader. You'd have been free of your useless daughter, but I reject that future."

She drew her shoulders back. "I will not be your pawn."

She wouldn't be Edmar's either if she could help it. He threatened her return to her father if she didn't marry him. Even knowing now that he would die without their wedding, she couldn't help chafing at these new chains dictating her future.

"Princess Emira has made her choice." Edmar's voice was firm, a challenge to Sargon's authority.

Ignoring him, Sargon grabbed her upper arm, his fingers digging into her flesh. "Where is your magic?"

The werewolves surged forward, snarling. Rivus pressed his sword tip against Sargon's chest. The mermen circled the King of the Seas and his daughter, their gems blazing. A jagged, white-hot lightning bolt arced from a merman's hand, slamming into the floor, halting a charging werewolf with a deafening crack. Icy wind, smelling of snow and ice, rushed through the throne room, swirling between the tense figures. The temperature plummeted, and her breath clouded in the frigid air.

This was madness. They were on the brink of a war that could destroy them all.

"Stop!" Emmy's command rang with a newfound authority.

The werewolves froze, eyes gleaming with restrained fury. Rivus hesitated, his sword still pressed against Sargon's chest, his uncertain gaze seeking hers. The mermen, their magic simmering, watched warily. Only the howling wind continued its icy dance.

She took a deep breath. She had to take control, navigate through this treacherous path. "Rivus," she said, her voice firm despite the tremor in her chest, "remove your sword from my father's chest."

"Your Highness...?" His voice tinged with disbelief.

"My father may act like a monster, but he's not an idiot," she said, meeting Rivus's gaze with a steely resolve that surprised even herself. "He wouldn't hurt the king or disgrace this kingdom. Agondray would hunt him and our people. The merfolk wouldn't know a day of peace, not in these oceans."

The words felt like a gamble, a desperate bluff, but she had to believe them. She had to believe in Edmar's strength, in the loyalty of his brothers, in the power of Agondray to protect its own.

Sargon's sharp gaze pierced her, challenging her defiance. A tremor of fear, an echo of a lifetime under his control, ran through her.

Cursing, Rivus withdrew his sword. The weapon, as if touched by phantom fire, crumbled in his grasp, the metal melting starting at its tip, dripping onto the floor in a shimmering liquid pool.

Rivus yelped, flinging the disintegrating sword away. It clattered against the stone, the sound unnaturally loud in the sudden silence, before dissolving fully into molten silver.

A cruel smile twisted Sargon's lips, a predator savoring its dominance. The casual dismissal of Rivus's threat turned her stomach.

"Answer me, daughter," Sargon said, his voice reverberating in her bones. "Where is your magic?"

Defiance sparked her words. "Let go of me."

What is it with men holding onto me? Always trying to control me, to dictate my fate.

She extracted her arm from his slackened grasp, meeting his gaze with surprising defiance. "I got rid of it."

This wasn't a lie; it was a declaration of a future she was carving for herself. One day, she'd be free from her magic's curse, from the fear and pain it inflicted.

Sargon's eyes narrowed, probing for deceit. But she held his stare, her body filled with newfound strength. A fierce determination to escape his control overshadowed her present fear.

He leaned closer, his voice a menacing whisper. "You resemble your mother most, but her heart was pure. Yours is twisted. At least I don't have to bother transferring your tether to your mate, because from now on, you don't belong to the merfolk. We are not your people, and you are not my daughter."

She jerked as if struck, his words slicing deep. She couldn't feel it, but he'd just severed his connection to her gem, and while she should rejoice, his rejection tore through her, leaving her breathless. Her well of sadness overflowed.

Had I ever truly believed I could go back?

In her deepest desires, she'd yearned for a reconciliation, for her family's love and acceptance she had craved since childhood. But now, facing the bleak truth of his words, cold emptiness settled within her.

That part of my life is over. I have no family. I have no home.

Chapter 35

EMMY

Emmy sat at the wharf's edge, feet dangling in the warm waters of the Lunarclaw River. After her father's departure, Edmar attempted conversation, but she'd ignored him.

Instead, she'd glared at Rivus on her way out, barely keeping her voice steady. Desolation threatened to buckle her knees. What she wouldn't give to slip into a dreamless slumber and forget her life. But she couldn't give in to that, and the urge to lash out was strong.

She had sneered at the werewolf as she'd leaned close to him. "Happy now? Keep your promise, or I will allow my magic to kill you."

Fear, and perhaps a flicker of respect, shone in his eyes.

She'd left then, avoiding Edmar.

Under the waning moon, her voice carried the Ocean's Lament, mingling with the river's whispers. Each note pleaded for release from despair, but without magic, the song's promise was unattainable.

If she severed her connection to her magic, to her gem, she'd no longer be a mermaid, anyway. Deep down, she knew this.

Her fingers toyed with the jewel at her neck. To save Edmar, she was forced to marry him. To save herself, she was forced to betray him.

She'd never know what they could have been, because she wouldn't go on the honeymoon sail. Too much time had been wasted already.

Abruptly, another voice joined hers in the mournful song.

"Sorrow wrapped in waves of our hearts,
A symphony echoing through the sea,
The Ocean's Lament renews our soul,
Release pain and let spirits roam free."

Emmy's voice faded as she closed her eyes, the melody weaving through her, her heart syncing with its beat. It pulled at her, imbued with merfolk power. Easing her, draining her well of sadness, but agonizingly slow.

She recognized the sweet voice granting her reprieve and her heart swelled.

The song trailed off with the gentle lapping of the water. As the soothing sounds faded, she opened her eyes to find her sister, Anjali. Her purple and green tail glowed beneath the surface, casting faint light on her sea foam green skin, which shimmered with silver swirls. Her turquoise eyes were luminous.

"Thank you," Emmy said. She'd almost forgotten what it felt like to have the Ocean's Lament's power soothe pain and sadness.

Anjali drew closer, framed by bubbles in the serene river. "Come home, Emmy."

Shaking her head, she lifted her legs from the water, wrapping her arms around her knees. "You shouldn't be here. Father would be furious."

"I don't care what Father says. You'll always be my sister."

"Emmy." Edmar's voice shattered the serenity like a stone thrown into still water.

Startled, Anjali vanished beneath the surface, her tail's glow fading, leaving only a ripple to disturb the river's calm.

Emmy remained still, suppressing her anger at the interruption. She should have known he'd come; the man was unstoppable.

He sat beside her, folding his long legs beneath him. A quick glance revealed the loose, dark clothing he wore for his nighttime excursions into the city.

"Why did you choose to marry me?" he asked.

His words sent a tremor through her, their implications swirling in her heart. She hesitated, searching for a response, but he raised a hand.

"If your words are lies, don't bother." His face hardened.

Lies?

She'd tried very hard to keep her words as true as possible but hadn't always succeeded. She'd had no choice. *Which lie had he found out?* "What are you talking about, Edmar?"

"Your *Sun* Crystal?"

Oh.

He'd discovered her gem's true nature.

He saw the recognition on her face. "Such a silly lie. And what about your lost magic?"

"I don't know how I used my magic in the forest, but it's been the only time. I still can't access it, and I think it's connected to being part human."

He narrowed his eyes, giving nothing away. "What are you truly after?"

She dropped her head to her knees, defeat lacing her voice. "You do not know what my life has been like."

"Then tell me."

She shook her head, closing her eyes. She yearned to tell him everything, but couldn't.

"Are you marrying me only to avoid going home?" Longing resonated in his voice, as if hoping she'd lie, reveal that she wanted him. "Are you only interested in what my crown can do for you?"

Considering her response, a memory flashed—her younger self, watching through the window as the world moved on without her. She fought back the sadness, wanting to be as truthful as possible.

Her voice faltered as she traced the grain of the wooden dock. "My magic was too powerful, and it frightened everyone—yet I've never felt powerful. To contain it, I was isolated, rarely leaving my Little Palace except for ceremonies. My magic imprisoned me, as much as my father's ambitions did.

"I left to escape captivity. After meeting you, I found that without magic, I no longer felt powerful on my own. I needed something to make me feel powerful, even if it was a lie about my gem. A lie that gave me power because only I knew the truth."

He gazed at the dark river, then up at the sky. "I'd never want you to feel weak. If staying here does that, I'll release you. Marry me first, then if you want to travel to the stars alone, you have my blessing."

Goosebumps prickled her arms. Here was this good man, promising her everything she'd never had. But because he was good, she couldn't stay and endanger him.

She would continue the Sea Witch's quest, using the Sun Stone to find the Metal Stone. Finding the Summer Child was too dangerous, too ridiculous. The child was a threat to Winter creatures.

Would Edmar ever forgive her?

She couldn't think about that. She couldn't control his thoughts, because she couldn't change her actions.

He shifted beside her, his silhouette blending with the darkness, his clothes rustling uneasily.

Her fingers twisted her sleeve, betraying her anxiety. "I've already agreed to marry you. I won't break my word."

He caught the hand tormenting her sleeve, lifting it gently to his mouth. Warmth surged through her as his lips brushed her fingertips, chasing away the icy dread in her stomach. She shivered.

She felt his smile against her skin and shifted uncomfortably. His awareness of his effect on her ignited an uncomfortable heat, but he released her hand before she could embarrass herself further.

"Tomorrow night we marry. A lavish affair followed by a feast. We'll have little time for ourselves. Then we leave for our honeymoon, sailing leisurely down the Cyaneus coast, introducing you as the new queen.

"Then we'll visit Meridonali, where you'll meet my youngest brother, King Zane. We can't stay long. Then we return home within two weeks. Unless you wish to leave before then—before I introduce you to the kingdom?"

Despite her doubts about Rivus's plan, she couldn't board that ship. But Edmar wouldn't leave if he discovered her intentions. He needed to be gone, distracted, long enough for her to achieve her goal, the sole reason she'd come to this kingdom.

"It sounds wonderful." Her voice was a whisper, almost lost to the night. She had to lie yet again. She yearned for the day her life wasn't complicated by lies. "I'll accompany you on the honeymoon."

It could have been wonderful.

He sighed. "I promise to do everything I can so you won't regret marrying me."

Meeting his gaze, she said, "I believe you."

That made him smile. He rose, then paused, seeing she wasn't moving. "I'm going back into the city tonight. Do you want to accompany me?"

She wished she could, but she feared her heart was already too lost to him. She shook her head.

Disappointment flashed briefly in his eyes. "I look forward to tomorrow night, then."

She nodded, and he left.

Anjali surfaced again. "You will marry him?"

She bit her lip, studying her sister's familiar face, which looked so much like hers. "I need your help."

Chapter 36

EMMY

The Grand Hall was transformed into a spectacle of opulence for Emmy's wedding. The air, heavy with the fragrance of countless flowers, sparkled under golden candlelight.

Lords and ladies, adorned in their finest attire, filled the hall. Richly embroidered fabrics, vibrant colors, and gleaming jewels created overwhelming elegance. The atmosphere buzzed with excitement as guests turned, their eyes fixed on her as she entered.

She glided down the blue carpet, flanked by Rivus and another lord. Each step stabbed sharp knives through her tender feet, but she accepted the pain. A sharper pang pierced through her heart. This was the last evening she would ever see her Dragon King, for whom she had to forsake to save him from the curse of her magic.

Each step brought her closer to Edmar, to the life she'd once dreamed of. *You don't deserve him, you lying piece of detritus.*

Her impending betrayal weighed heavily upon her. But she'd steal the Sun Stone, escape the curse of her magic, and finally be free.

Each sharp-edged step offered no absolution, but she bore it willingly.

At the carpet's end, Edmar's posture stiffened slightly when their gazes met—a silent acknowledgment of the weight this moment held for them. She devoured the sight of him through her lace veil.

Standing by the altar, he commanded reverence in flowing dark blue velvet robes edged with ermine, the fabric shot through with silver thread and draped over a silk tunic intricately embroidered with silver knotwork. A jeweled belt low on his hips held a long dagger with a scabbard of polished silver, its sapphire and onyx accents gleaming with the light.

His platinum crown, set with sapphires, topazes, tourmalines, and zircons, complemented his dark blue velvet cap, trimmed with more ermine. Gems on its high arches and the golden sunburst caught the light, sparkling beneath the chandeliers. The beauty of the crown, and the man wearing it, stole her breath more than her constricting dress.

If she could cry, tears would well in her eyes. This had been a mere fantasy, a daydream that continued as she approached him, his eyes fixed solely on her. Each step softened his expression, joy and concern crinkling the corners of his eyes. He offered a barely perceptible nod, a silent reassurance that they were in this together.

If he only knew...

But she discarded that ugly truth, even as her wedding gown felt heavier.

Though she detested the dress, it was undeniably beautiful—swathes of emerald and sapphire silk cascading down her curves, hand-embroidered with silver filigree in swirling ocean motifs. The symbol of Edmar's reign, the compass rose, adorned her bodice. The sleeves cascaded in layers, resembling foamy waves, a subtle nod to her aquatic heritage. And behind her, the gown flowed as a river of white and gold.

He received her at the aisle's end, his hand extended, teal scales glittering on his skin. She took it, and they faced Father Jayasurya, resplendent in his orange and gold vestments. Heavy golden chains weighted with various gold medallions rested on his chest, symbols of his office and authority.

"Dear friends, we gather today to unite this man and woman in joyful matri mony..."

His voice resonated like a steady hymn. The blessings, the promises of love and duty, echoed hollowly, mocking the truth twisting in her gut.

They knelt, reciting their vows, a litany of promises that felt like ashes on her tongue. Two ladies helped her rise, preventing a stumble in the layers of her dress.

Prompted by Father Jayasurya, they turned to face each other. She met Edmar's gaze, wondering at the turmoil swirling in his eyes. His fingers trembled as he took her hands, but their warmth was a comfort.

He bent his head, his voice a tender whisper meant only for her. "You look beautiful."

Her heart pounded, the response hovering on her lips—words heavier than the waiting crown. Each possible reply held a promise their future couldn't fulfill. It wasn't reality, so she held them back, trying to deny them.

But they had always been true.

Her chest ached with the need to respond.

She gazed into his ocean-colored eyes, yearning for him to feel the truth, hoping he might one day forgive her. Even if he didn't, she wanted to be truthful before she left him forever. This was the last evening that she would breathe the same air with him, or gaze upon the starry sky and the deep sea.

"No matter what happens, Edmar, you need to know..." She poured all her feelings into her gaze. "I love you."

Surprise warmed his features, his eyes searching hers, seeking the truth. His fingers tightened around hers, not just in reflex, but as if holding onto something precious and fragile. For a fleeting second, his composure slipped, revealing his raw affection for her.

The Grand Hall, the guests, the flickering candlelight—all faded into a distant murmur. Her confession hung between them, delicate and potent. Edmar's lips parted, a reply forming, but the ceremony reclaimed them too soon.

They exchanged rings. Then the Royal Steward solemnly presented the silver crown, adorned with stars and turquoise jewels, worn by every Queen of Cyaneus.

Edmar took the crown and reverently placed it atop her veiled head. He raised his voice for all to hear. "I crown thee, Queen Emira of Cyaneus."

Father Jayasurya motioned for them to face the guests. He raised the Golden Scepter, the obsidian Sun Stone quiet. "By the power of the Sun God, I proclaim Princess Emira, daughter of King Sargon, the King of the Seas, the King of the Merfolk, as the next Queen of Cyaneus and the consort of King Edmar, ordained by Solis, our Holy Father."

The Sun Stone brightened, bathing everyone in golden light before fading.

He laid the Golden Scepter across her upturned palms, his hands resting on the staff as he said, "Queen Emira will be a kind and virtuous queen who shall lead this kingdom to great prosperity."

Her breath stalled, knowing it was a lie.

Yet, the Sun Stone flared, filling the hall with blinding golden light, and cheers erupted.

She closed her eyes, dazed.

How could it be true?

Perhaps the Sun Stone revealed potential, not certainty. After all, it was not meant to be used to tell the future, only the truth at that moment.

That was the only explanation.

CHAPTER 37
EDMAR

"Where is Queen Emira?" Edmar stepped aboard the *Silver Lily*, searching for his new bride. Named for the silver-petaled flowers that bloomed under a full moon, the royal ship boasted a sleek design. The last glimmer of dusk lit the ship's polished wood and gleaming metal accents in fiery orange. The crew moved with practiced precision on deck.

Mister Morcant, his seasoned first mate, approached with a knowing smile. "Your bride awaits in your cabin, Your Majesty. She's unwell, but insisted on waiting for you to finish the sailing ceremony."

He frowned, unease creeping in. Now married, he could no longer sense Emmy's presence. The constricting band either gone because of the wedding, as it happened with every forced marriage, or because the curse was broken.

At least his scales and hardened skin had receded.

But is my curse broken?

None of his brothers had broken their own curse yet, so he had no reference. He'd waited a thousand years for a woman who loved him and met all the requirements—a maiden with a true heart who could survive the Dragon's Kiss.

Emmy was a maiden he'd kissed many times. If she truly loved him, that should be it. He should be able to shift at will, but that seemed out of reach. He'd know for sure come morning if he was forced to change.

She loves me... The thought, still wondrous and disbelieving, warmed him despite the worry knotting his gut. He longed to be by her side, to hear her repeat those words, but duty called.

"The wheel is ready for you, Your Majesty." The first mate gestured to the helm. "We're ready to sail."

He took the helm, expertly guiding the *Silver Lily* from the harbor. The familiar ritual, usually a source of pride, felt like a tedious delay, his thoughts consumed by his wife waiting for him in his bed. As they left Cyaneus's bustling port, the city sounds faded, replaced by creaking timbers and wind rushing through sails.

Once the ship was on its southerly course, Mister Morcant relieved him. The crew, eager to celebrate, gathered around their king with casks of his best wine. "Aye, Captain, you'll need all your strength tonight!" one sailor roared, his words met with a chorus of laughter and cheers.

He raised his tankard, forcing a smile as his crew toasted his happiness. But the wine, usually a source of warmth and camaraderie, did little to ease the ache in his chest. Each passing moment stretched into an eternity, separating him from the woman who'd captured his heart.

"To King Edmar and his queen!" Helmut, the boatswain, bellowed, raising his tankard high.

Edmar joined the toast, the cheers echoing in the night. He allowed himself a moment of hope, envisioning a future with the curse broken, a future where he and Emmy explored the world, free from fate's shackles.

He drank liberally, the wine warming his insides as the ship sailed under brightening stars. Hours passed, laughter echoing, mingling with the gentle lull of waves.

Amidst the revelry and alcohol, his thoughts constantly returned to Emmy waiting for him in their cabin. His heart quickened, anticipating their reunion. A moment of genuine connection. He envisioned her smile, the softness in her eyes when she looked at him, the gentle touch of her hand—the way she'd been during their wedding when she'd confessed her love.

Then his imagination turned to what she'd look like when he would pleasure her. Naked and willing, a flush darkening her sea-foam skin, her breasts aching for his touch, her rounded hips begging for him to hold tight. The place between her thighs inviting him to finally find a home.

His longing encompassed both the physical and a deep yearning for intimacy, for connection denied by his curse. His thoughts warmed him more than the wine, his body reacting to the thought of her in his arms. Tonight, they'd finally be together. His entire being thrummed with the anticipation of making love to her, and he hoped she felt better now she'd rested.

Unable to resist any longer, he set aside his tankard and strode toward his cabin, heart pounding with anticipation.

"Uh-oh, the queen better be ready. Captain's on a mission!"

"A mission to pleasure his bride."

More hoots and hollers followed, bringing a smile to his flushed face. The sailor was right. He was on a mission to ensure Emmy never wanted to leave him. More importantly, to spend the night in the arms of a woman he'd loved for twenty-five years.

Nothing slowed him as he ducked into the dark cabin, though dizziness made him stumble. He shook his head, closing the door. Faint starlight filtered through gauzy curtains covering the windows behind the bed.

With his entrance, Emmy shifted, bundled atop the mattress.

Familiar with the cabin even in darkness, he crossed the space quickly. He hesitated momentarily. What if she still wasn't well?

But the thought vanished as the figure sat up, long hair a dark halo against the starlight, face shadowed. He reached for her, wrenching her to him, wanting her to feel his desire. She'd forget his previous rejection.

He silenced her surprised cry with a kiss, one hand cupping her head, the other at her back, his lips pressing to hers. She was naked, and he wondered if she was ready for him. He deepened the kiss, his tongue slipping between her lips.

Her body stiffened, not melting into his as it usually did. His heart faltered, confusion seeping into his desire. The alcohol intensified his need. He kissed her, seeking reassurance in the familiarity of her response, but when his hand went to her breast, she recoiled.

Somewhere in his alcohol-soaked brain, he realized this woman did not feel the same.

She pushed him away.

His panic cut through the alcohol haze. Dread filled him—something was wrong.

Suddenly, a dazzling burst of moonlight erupted between them, blinding. An intense surge of emotional energy overwhelmed him, and he staggered back.

This isn't Emmy.

He blinked rapidly, the light throbbing in his eyes, even though the cabin fell dark as the white gem on her throat dimmed. "Who are you?"

She didn't respond.

Dazed, he shook his head, stumbling from the energy wash. His heel caught, and he fell, catching himself on his hands against the wooden floorboards.

The figure remained silent.

His blood ran cold. Whoever she was, she was here instead of Emmy.

Which meant Emmy had left him.

Heaviness settled on his chest. His hands shook so hard that he struggled to regain his feet.

I can't lose her.

They needed to turn back, return to port. He had to find her.

The woman rose from the bed, scattering his already fragmented thoughts.

Her outline sharpened against starlight.

She was too petite, too small.

Who in the eight hells is she?

He opened his mouth to question her, but then she struck him, and everything went black.

Chapter 38

EMMY

Sitting on a rocky cave floor, Emmy glared at Rivus, wringing rainwater from her hair. The curls tangled, catching on the coarse, soaked cloth of her tunic and pants. She hated the fabric against her legs, its confinement reminiscent of the chains that had once weighed down her tail. The memory clawed—rocks hooked to her scales to prevent drifting. A prison in the ocean depths, and now, another on land.

Rivus ignored her, snapping shut a small mirror he'd muttered over before rummaging through wooden boxes and clay jars at the back of the cave. Oil lamps flickered, casting dancing shadows as he stuffed objects into his oiled leather satchel. She had one too, containing spare clothes and unappetizing food.

"Try to sleep, Princess. In a few hours, we start again, and we'll reach the Sun Temple."

"I'm not a princess anymore." The words twisted painfully, reminding her of her father's disownment, the kingdom beneath the waves that would never welcome her back.

Her gaze drifted to the cave entrance, a narrow hole leading to this more spacious room. Outside, the waning moon and twinkling stars offered little light on their second night.

Does Edmar gaze upon these same stars? The thought pierced her heart.

"Would you rather be called Runaway Queen?" Rivus snorted. "You hardly merit the title, especially with no crown or wedding ring."

She frowned, frustration bubbling. Rivus—so infuriating, so full of contradictions. He'd forced her to marry Edmar to save him, and now Rivus was angry she'd left Edmar, returning both his crown and ring.

Rivus was keeping his promise to help her with the Sun Stone, an act that would wound the entire kingdom. Running away from Edmar was painful enough. Stealing the stone would be worse, and Rivus was just as culpable, so he should be mad at himself.

Both Edmar and the kingdom would recover. But her heart ached for Edmar—for his smile, his touch, the impossible future. The thought sliced through her soul like a blade.

Sacrificing love came with no relief. No tears, no Ocean's Lament to ease the burden. Her throat tightened, emotions choking her. She surged to her feet, startling Rivus. Knives slashed into her feet, but she was quick. Before he could react, she grabbed the dagger from his hip.

Rivus froze, eyes widening.

Gripping a thick chunk of her sapphire hair, she yanked it taut. The strands, once freely flowing like ocean currents, felt out of place. Everything bound her, constricted her life, even when she thought she was free. Her long hair held the remnants of her old life.

The men's clothes reflected her life more accurately. The tunic scratched, the pants trapped her legs. A new confining life, but one she could seek to change. She'd mark the beginning of her changes.

Her fingers trembled as she positioned the dagger, the cold handle biting into her palm. With a swift stroke, she sliced through the locks. The severed strands fell, her breath hitching in a half-sob, just another piece of her past abandoned.

Rivus raised his eyebrows, open-mouthed.

She grabbed more hair, slashing through it. Hair cascaded from her open hand, tumbling to the floor, curls flipping and flying in silent rebellion. Each falling strand severed a fragment of her old self, a reminder of the chains that had bound her, of sacrifices she made now to protect those she loved. "If I could trade for Edmar's pain, I would. It stings to know I've caused him the ache of my betrayal." *And gods, I miss him.*

She sliced through another handful, a low croon escaping her throat, mourning the loss of everything they could have had.

When she reached for the hair at the back of her head, Rivus jumped forward, hand out. "Here, let me do it so you don't look like a wild woman afterward."

She handed him the dagger, closing her eyes as he cut. "Why are you angry? You threatened me if I didn't marry him."

"You told him you loved him."

"You're upset I shared my feelings?"

"I'm upset you lied."

She turned to look at him. "I didn't lie."

"Then you lied about your virginity. Why else can't he shift at will?" He straightened her head.

She didn't understand. "What are you talking about?"

"The curse," he said, irritation lacing his voice.

"You've told me everything I know about the curse, which appears to not be enough if I don't understand what you mean."

"A thousand years ago, a vengeful fae cursed the Dragon Princes. The Snow Princess's words doomed them:

"'Our love by chance was tainted with lies and deceit, so I will put a stop to the union between our peoples. Ice and snow will cover your land. The weak shall die. Our people will remain as witnesses. To heal the land, you shall suffer the chains of forced marriage. Again and again, you must marry through the ages, but the choice is never yours. Each bride must come to you by chance, or the beast will take over and ice will return to the land. And if the bride by chance refuses to marry you by the end of a lunar cycle, you shall suffer the fate of your people. Only a maiden who loves you with a true heart can save you if she can survive the Dragon's Kiss.'"

She considered the curse's words, seeking the reason for his anger. "I survived the Dragon's Kiss. You believe I'm not a maiden, or I lied about loving Edmar. Otherwise, his curse would be broken?"

"Exactly."

She considered the curse again. "What if the requirements must be met sequentially?"

He paused. "You mean, first she must be a maiden who loves him, *then* survive the kiss?"

She nodded. "We didn't kiss after I told him."

Rivus hummed noncommittally, falling silent as he resumed cutting.

She closed her eyes, envisioning Edmar at their wedding. Handsome, regal. Her chest ached. Maybe one day, she'd find her way back to him. To survive, she needed a distraction and latched onto her anger at Rivus. "Why couldn't we just steal the Sun Stone from the caravan?"

The memory of that first night, the moonlit pursuit, the agonizing decision to slow down, to hide from the dragon during the next day, still stung. Two nights since her wedding. It felt like an eternity since she'd seen Edmar.

Does he now seek me out of love or obligation? Doubt plagued her.

"Too risky." He circled her, assessing her hair, trimming stray strands. "Too many guards. Someone could get hurt. My plan is cleaner."

"Cleaner?" Emmy scoffed. "The Sun Temple will be swarming with guards and worshippers. How can you guarantee no one gets hurt?"

Rivus's jaw clenched, his features flickering between man and beast. "Trust me, Princess. I know what I'm doing."

She leveled her gaze, fingering her shorn hair where the curls lay just past her chin, considering the man who couldn't decide what form to take. "Really, if you want to be the wolf, then go be the wolf."

She shooed him toward the cave entrance.

Sheathing his dagger, he backed away. "How did Edmar not find you annoying?"

His words stung, but she wouldn't show it. Adopting the stillness perfected over two hundred years, she watched her sapphire curls settle on the cave floor. "Probably for the same reason he didn't realize he had a snake for a friend instead of a wolf."

He laughed mirthlessly. "Look who's talking."

"You're betraying your king, too," she said bitterly. He could have just told Edmar her plans and not help her steal the Sun Stone. "Either Edmar is blind, or you're a master of deception."

Rivus's anger deflated, replaced by a weary sadness. "It's not about personal gain. You wouldn't understand. You have no family loyalty. My decisions are to protect others."

"I do the same."

His brow lowered. "I don't follow."

"My magic is a curse." She fingered the painite gem. "It killed my mother. I need the God's Stone to break free from it, to protect those I love."

Rivus stared, his expression shifting from disbelief to understanding. The memory of his burned hand flickered in his eyes. "Will the Sun Stone be enough?"

She turned away to dig into her leather pack.

"It's a start," she said, withdrawing Edmar's dingy white shirt. His ocean scent clung to the folds. "My magic is mostly dormant, but only temporarily."

Rivus studied her, then drew a deep breath and slowly released it. "Sleep, Princess. In a few hours, we steal the Sun Stone."

Despite his betrayal of his king and friend, she had no choice but to trust him. That night, curled with Edmar's shirt, she dreamed again of the Summer Child. Their eastward journey strengthened the child's pull.

Once more, she asked Emmy to come to her. *You are powerful enough to bring me to life.*

"But I'm trying to get rid of my magic."

With my help, you won't need to. I'll siphon your magic. Isn't that better?

"Will I still be a mermaid?" She couldn't imagine herself as anything else. But without her power, could she still claim her heritage? Merfolk were nothing without their magic.

Yes.

Floating in her mermaid form, she felt fire acid building in her muscles. It was weaker than before, but it was a reminder.

Come to me, give me your magic.

"Will you kill Winter creatures?"

The child didn't answer, and the dream faded, replaced by the flowering courtyard and Malala. The stark difference between the two dreams jolted her. Both locations held power, both were prisons. But while she understood the child's desires, the Water Fae's call remained a mystery.

"You left him?" Malala laughed, sitting beside her on the emerald grass.

Her well of sadness deepened, but she masked her anguish. There was still something about this fae she didn't trust. "I have."

"Left him on the honeymoon night. So sad. But I hope you're pleased the magic picked you again."

Between the fae's tone, the twinkle in her eye, and her wide smile, Emmy hesitated. It seemed as if Malala was saying something important without fully revealing it. Unease filled her. Did the fae somehow influence the ceremony and pick her as the next queen? That seemed preposterous. The fae was stuck in this dream world.

And why did this woman seem to get enjoyment from hurting her Dragon King? "Why are you interested in Edmar?"

Malala waved a lavender hand. "Not him specifically. The Dragon Kings, they all imprisoned me here."

She rubbed her head, recalling the Water Fae saying this before. These dreams always faded upon waking, the details hazy.

"What will you do after stealing the Sun Stone?"

She certainly wouldn't tell her the truth. "I think I'll travel. I've never been allowed to travel anywhere."

Malala rested her chin on her hands. "I miss home."

"Where is home?"

"Nilamora."

"The Sapphire City?"

The Water Fae's head listed to the side, her slate-blue gaze scrutinizing. "Few outside the Water Fae know of Nilamora."

"Except merfolk."

"Have you been there?"

"I've never been allowed anywhere."

"It was a beautiful city. I hear it's been destroyed."

Emmy nodded, her lessons returning. Royalty received extensive education in geography and politics. "The Sun Fae burned it down near the end of the Little Ice Age."

"I have seen none of my people in a very long time."

"I've never met a living Water Fae."

Malala snorted. "And I'm most certainly not alive."

Her tone suggested offense.

"Are you alive?"

"I'm as alive as you. Just trapped. Perhaps it's time to escape, though I do enjoy tormenting the Dragon Kings."

She'd just given Malala another way to torment Edmar. He would hate her forever.

The dream dissolved before she could see its end, Rivus shaking her awake. The sky was only slightly brighter.

"It's time, Princess."

Inhaling deeply, she crawled out of the cave's narrow opening. Today was the day she would finally have the Sun Stone.

CHAPTER 39

EDMAR

Three nights earlier...

A nightmare claimed Edmar, a ghostly echo of a past he'd tried to forget. He stood beside the bed where his wife had labored for many hours. Moonlight streamed through the window, casting a chilly glow on the infant, seemingly asleep in his arms.

My son.

But as his fingers brushed the silken fabric swaddled around the tiny, cold body, he felt heartache all over again, the bone-deep, gut-wrenching, heart-twisting sense of loss for something so innocent.

He moaned a half sob, the sound jarring him awake. An incessant banging, a dull ache echoing in his skull, made him dizzy. The world swam into focus, the wooden floorboards of his cabin tilting beneath him. He blinked, disoriented, the hard surface unfamiliar.

"Your Majesty. We're an hour out from port." The voice, muffled by the cabin door, barely registered.

Attempting to sit up, dizziness swamped him, and he lay back down. His hand went to his head, encountering a tender, throbbing knot.

Emmy.

The name, a whisper, a prayer. The previous night returned. Emptiness settled in his stomach. She was gone. The warmth of her body, the scent of her hair, the soft rhythm of her breath. All absent. He was alone.

Despite their vows, her declaration of love, she'd fled. *Did she lie about her love?*

The approaching sunrise mocked his inability to control his shifting, a reminder of the unbroken curse.

Am I only concerned about her because of my curse?

His reliance on love to break the curse felt like a fool's errand. But what was coerced love, born of obligation? Was he a monster for seeking salvation at such a cost?

No, he loved her, regardless.

He pushed himself up, ignoring the throbbing pain. His gaze fell on the woman sitting on the bed, shoulders hunched, face pale in the faint light. His heart lurched, a painful spasm of recognition.

She wasn't Emmy.

The green skin and sapphire hair were the same, but she was smaller. She stared at him with wide turquoise eyes, clutching the coverlet to her mouth. She looked scared, but he needed answers. Staggering to his feet, he steadied himself against the wall.

The woman watched warily, lowering the coverlet slightly to whisper, "Stay back."

"You're Emmy's sister, Anjali?" he asked, already knowing the answer.

She gave a small, apprehensive nod.

"Where is my wife? Where has Emmy gone?"

Anjali flinched but remained silent.

"Why did she send you?"

"I had no choice. She asked me to keep you from the truth." Anjali's tone held defiance and regret. Her loyalty to Emmy was clear, but she didn't seem to like the plan. "She needed you distracted, long enough to escape."

As he struggled to process Anjali's words, he retreated to the icy numbness of his Frostlands. His veins pulsed with each thunderous heartbeat. Why had Emmy deceived him?

Was it to mock me?

She could have simply refused to sail with him, an option he gave her, but instead, she'd used her sister as a tool for her deception.

Why, why, why?

None of it made sense.

Why all the lies?

The ship listed, and he threw out a hand to steady himself. Anjali slid forward, then scrambled back as he stepped toward her.

"Don't—Don't touch me!" Anjali recoiled, her voice sharp with fear.

He paused, frustration simmering. "Forgive my behavior last night. I mistook you for *my wife*. Can you at least tell me where she went?"

Suddenly, Anjali leaped from the bed, grabbing the quilt and swinging it at him. It billowed out, momentarily blinding him.

He caught a flash of green skin as she darted naked through the doorway. By the time he freed himself, she was gone. He sprinted after her, the quilt falling from his grasp.

Desperation surged. He chased not just Anjali, but the hope of finding answers. On deck, the mermaid's panicked gaze darted among the sailors, their stares curious. Edmar reached for her, a sliver of hope driving him, but she vaulted over the railing, disappearing into the ocean with a final flash of her purple and green tail.

He stood frozen at the wooden railing, struck by the irony. In seeking freedom, fueled by the hope Emmy had given him, he'd only tightened his chains, his heart sinking with her sister.

Mister Morcant joined him at the railing. "Your Majesty, did your wife just jump overboard?"

"Guess one night was all she needed," said a sailor behind him.

"Or maybe it was too long?" another added, sparking more laughter.

Edmar pressed his fingers to his closed eyes, breathing deep. He could hear the rumors now of the queen swimming away from him. He turned to face his men.

"That was not the queen, but an imposter." He addressed his first mate. "Get us to port, give them a few hours, then set sail back to Cyaneus."

"What will you do?"

"I'm going to find my *real* wife." The declaration was as much for himself as for his crew. *Why did she flee?*

He sought answers, questioning the very nature of his centuries-old curse, its resolution pressing upon him anew as he sifted through her belongings in their cabin. Fingers brushing against the soft dresses she'd hated wearing, he pondered the futility of his hopes. As he searched for a clue, a message, anything to explain her departure, he realized he'd hinged everything on her heart, a heart that hadn't truly been open to him.

Is it fair, or right, to burden another with my salvation?

He should just let her go. *But I don't know how.* She'd taken a part of him when she'd left him, and he no longer felt like a whole man.

They reached port as dawn colored the horizon, a signal for him to withdraw. As he distanced himself from the bustling activity, the first rays of the sun kissed his skin, triggering his transformation. He imagined each scale as armor against his vulnerabilities. But as he soared back toward his palace, Emmy's absence gutted him.

For hours, he scoured the land from the sky, suppressing his emotions, surrendering them to the Frostlands. Panic still threaded through the yawning emptiness and settled heavily in his chest. He ground his teeth, refusing to succumb to despair.

I will find her, and she will explain.

The promise fueled his determination.

But the solitude of flight offered no comfort, only a bird's-eye view of his life slipping away. Hours of fruitless searching. The setting sun signaled his need to return. Reluctantly, he landed, his human form heavier than ever. His curse remained, and he had no clues as to Emmy's whereabouts.

Tension vibrated through him as he returned to the palace, his shoulders stiff, fists clenching and unclenching.

How dare she leave without a word? He'd promised to release her. Another lie, her agreeing to the honeymoon. Had she ever been truthful? *Does she even love me, or is that another lie?*

But he remembered the sincerity in her voice, her touch, when she'd confessed her love. *So why did she leave?*

As darkness fell, he returned to the Emerald Palace, finding himself kneeling at the altar. The Golden Scepter and Sun Stone were gone, returning to the Sun Temple. A prayer formed in his mind, but a voice interrupted him.

"Dragon King."

He turned to see Brac, Isa's devoted companion, approaching hesitantly.

"I caught wind of the queen. Saw something you oughta know." He stopped beside the altar. "I overheard—well, not exactly, but the night afore your weddin', the queen and your Marshal crossed paths here. They was talkin' about the Sun Stone."

CHAPTER 40

EDMAR

Edmar stood, frowning. An icy prickle crept up his spine. His heart thudded against his chest, a loud echo in his ears.

"What are you saying?" he asked Brac.

"I can't say for sure what words were tossed about, but your Marshal was breathin' threats at the lass. When they talked about the Sun Stone, I reckoned you were in on it, but I see now that he acted without your say-so. They're plannin' to pilfer it." The bioluminescent green strands in his black hair brightened as they frothed around his shoulders.

A hollow ache settled in his chest. Emira's declaration of love, once a beacon of hope, hadn't broken the curse. Was this the reason? *Can it be true?*

His fingers shook, and he clenched his fists to stop them.

Rivus had planned to leave before the ball, staying at his request. His continued presence through the wedding seemed like support. He closed his eyes, sifting through recent conversations, seeking any sign of their conspiracy, praying for the revelation to be false.

His best friend had never given him cause for suspicion. Rivus had even revealed Emmy's lie about the gem. Perhaps that reinforced his subterfuge. What if Emmy's lie had been a distraction, diverting his attention from her interest in the Sun Stone with all her questions?

He clung to the memory of her confession that she loved him.

"Sorry for the trouble this might stir." Brac's dark hair and luminescent green strands waved rhythmically down his back.

"Thank you for telling me."

Brac nodded. "I'll be takin' my leave, then."

"Back to Isa's side?" A lump formed in his throat. Both had lost the women they loved, but Isa hadn't betrayed Brac. He didn't want to believe either Rivus or Emmy would deceive him, and he still couldn't quite believe it.

"Some old mates just sailed in, and I'm sure they'll be keen to lay eyes on Isa as well." Brac left.

Candle flames danced, shadows whispering betrayal, freezing him in place. He stumbled back, catching himself against a buttress, his knees threatening to buckle. The air, thick with incense and aged wood, suffocated him. Dazed, he pushed away from the buttress and left the chapel.

No. I don't believe it. He hurried through the halls, a frantic energy propelling him forward. He needed proof. Proof that Brac was mistaken, that Rivus hadn't betrayed him, that Emmy hadn't lied.

The one-way mirror. He could see for himself, confirm their whereabouts, dispel the chilling doubt clawing at his insides. He burst into his chambers, his breath ragged, his hands shaking as he opened the drawer where he always stowed the mirror. His fingers swept over the empty space, dread settling in his stomach. *Where is it?*

Maybe he hadn't put it up in the right place the last time he used it. With a desperate urgency, he ransacked his chambers, his heart hammering a frantic tattoo against his ribs. He tore through his belongings, tossing aside clothes, scrolls, and trinkets.

"It has to be here," he muttered, panic rising in his chest. *Think, Edmar.* He had to find it, had to see for himself. He checked the desk, the shelves, under the bed, each void a blow, chipping away at the denial he clung to.

No matter how much he destroyed his chambers, the small one-way mirror was gone. A terrifying thought pierced his panic. *Rivus. He wouldn't... Would he?*

Rivus was intelligent, cunning, always thinking several steps ahead. He knew the power of the one-way mirror, knew how easily Edmar could track them. *If he was planning to disappear, to betray me... He would have taken it.*

Deep down, he had to finally recognize the truth of his best friend's and wife's treachery. The realization was a punch to the gut, stealing his breath. He slumped against the wall, the room tilting precariously, the scattered belongings proof of his unraveling control.

His thoughts churned, confusion and disbelief slowing his reactions. He'd so utterly failed, as a king, as a husband, as a person. He'd been blind to the machinations happening right here, so close to his heart. That heart now hurt, aching in his chest, and he dragged in a ragged breath. Heartbreak shattered his carefully constructed Frostlands, leaving a throbbing, burning agony. Each heartbeat stung, bruising his insides. He pressed a hand to his breast, his vision blurring.

How could she betray me?

Despair warred with dawning anger. Not just her deception, but Rivus's too. How long had they manipulated him? Sharp cracks split the ice of his Frostlands, gouging his armor, releasing centuries of suppressed rage. It threatened to erupt.

In a daze, he wandered into the halls, walking without truly seeing, each step a battle to calm the landscape of his emotional wasteland. He paused before a tapestry, tracing the intricate weavings depicting ancestral legends—heroes facing betrayal with stoic resolve. The vibrant colors and patterns mocked the chaos within him.

Was I just a means to an end? Something to be so easily discarded once I'd fulfilled my purpose.

The two people he'd loved most had left, indifferent to his pain. A guttural growl escaped his lips, anger twisting in his gut. He reached out, fingers digging into the thick fabric, fury demanding release. With a surge of raw power, he ripped the tapestry. Threads snapped, proud images distorted. Perverse satisfaction filled him as the fabric yielded. He embraced the destruction.

Had the Snow Princess felt this same searing betrayal, this love and rage, when she cursed his family?

He flung the ruined tapestry to the floor, its heavy thud echoing. Everything within him felt as torn as that fabric, and he gasped. A fierce rhythm pulsed in his temples. He clenched his jaw, a metallic taste flooding his mouth.

Staring down at his hands, he imagined confronting Emira, demanding answers as he wrapped his fingers around her throat. He'd ruin her, too.

Grigor found him there, the torn tapestry at his feet. He raised a brow and spoke in his usual calm tone. "You have visitors."

The visitors Brac mentioned.

Visitors meant nothing when he wanted to kill his best friend and punish his treacherous wife. But then a husky feminine voice echoed, pulling him from his rage. Its familiarity tugged at memories buried under years of governance and grief.

He heard it again, louder, anguished: "Isamore?"

He was only steps from the Grand Hall—the place where he married Emira. What should have been the happiest day of his life when she'd told him she loved him. The bitter taste of betrayal lingered as he strode toward the voices. Each swallow was acrid, a reminder of the sharp truth of Emira's deceit. Of his best friend's deceit. He needed the distraction of the four figures before his cousin's statue.

Anything to quell the thoughts of what I will do to Emira and Rivus.

He stopped a few feet away, memories surfacing. He recognized one of the two women, though they looked similar. Of the first, her presence was a surprise—a Water Fae, with dark lavender skin and gray-blue eyes. Her hair, a mix of dark tones, green and blue, waved and curled like wind-tossed ocean waves.

The other woman resembled her, but with light gray skin and cerulean eyes. Her hair, similar colors with silver highlights, hung still. Both wore fitted leather vests over bright shirts and dark breeches tucked into knee-high boots. Scuffed leather bracers and belts packed with pouches and daggers hinted at their pirate life.

The first woman tore her gaze from the statue and looked at him, hand over her mouth, tears in her gray-blue eyes. "What happened to her, Edmar?"

"Hello, Adria." This was the Water Fae pirate who'd been close friends with Isa, visiting often in Drakkon before the curse. "She arrived like this, but I'm sure her condition is courtesy of your great-granddaughter."

The woman beside Adria shifted, and the pirate touched her arm. "This is Avi, my daughter, Lutine's grandmother."

Lutine.

A name he hadn't heard in a long time. They usually called her the Snow Princess. Well, Zane called her the Winter Witch after she cursed them. But those weren't her names when they'd first met her, the woman intended for their eldest brother.

Of the other two people standing with Adria and Avi, he knew Brac. The second man was mysterious, cloaked and shadowed, his back looking malformed—maybe wings beneath the cloak? Flashes of a refined nose and his hands revealed milk-white skin with a subtle blue undertone. Some Moon Fae possessed such pale skin, but they were a lost civilization, extinct now because of the Summer Fae Wars.

But something hazy clung to his skin. A sense of death. The man hovered close to Avi, his posture possessive.

Adria narrowed her eyes at the man. "And that is Cielan."

Edmar inclined his head toward the newcomers. "Welcome to the Emerald Palace. While I'm pleased to see you, Adria, two Water Fae will attract attention."

Moon and Water Fae were both Winter Fae, targeted by the Summer Fae for centuries. While the Moon Fae were driven to extinction, the diminishing population of Water Fae survived by going into hiding. Leaving their hidden city was dangerous for any Water Fae, risking a Summer Fae attack.

Adria waved away his concern. "When I heard the first rumor of Isa in centuries, I had to investigate. I knew she wasn't on the continent when Lutine cast her curse, and I've searched everywhere."

The curse. It had linked him to Emira twice, and each time he lost her. "Now you've found Isamore. Your search is at an end. Is there anything you need for your travels back to your ship? You're welcome to stay longer, but unfortunately, I must take my leave."

Adria tilted her head, a cocky smile lifting her scarred left eyebrow. Scars marked her arms and fingers. He'd once considered her the most formidable fae he knew.

Over a thousand years ago, when he'd been just a boy dreaming of adventures beyond the palace walls, she'd been a frequent, exhilarating visitor. He remembered her tales of open seas and starlit skies, sparking his wanderlust.

One crisp evening, watching the stars from the royal gardens, he'd pleaded with her. "Take me with you! I want to see the stars from every corner of the world."

Her husky laughter, warm and inviting, filled the night. Ruffling his hair, she made him a promise. "When you're older, if the sea still calls, come find me."

That moment sealed his admiration. He'd never lost his love of the sea, though he'd chosen his own path on his own ship. Now, his admiration mingled with bitterness.

Adria looked back up at the statue. "Isa had her reasons for coming back, even knowing she'd meet her end. Did she say why?"

Brac answered her with Isa's last words. "'Release the souls from the stones so the dragons can protect me from the Summer Child.'"

The Water Fae frowned, repeating the words as if memorizing them. "Back before the curse, we were studying the Summer Child and its ties to Agondray. We found nothing, then she left my ship. She must have found out something in her solo travels."

Edmar raised his brow. He hadn't realized Isa had been investigating the same thing he had centuries earlier. Now it was too late. Anger tightened his chest.

Between his impending marriage and Isa's arrival, he'd had little time to process her words. His fists clenched, sweat prickling his palms. "Do you know what it means?"

Adria shook her head. "No idea."

A dead end.

He clenched his jaw, considering the deceit surrounding his marriage. "I wish we could unravel these mysteries together, Adria, but I must confront the shadows in my own house."

"It's been a few centuries, but you seem out of sorts."

Anger and betrayal fueled him, yet he yearned for simpler times, when Adria's stories had been his only concerns. "My new wife and best friend ran away together, probably to steal the Sun Stone."

Adria stared, open-mouthed.

He remembered the fae stealing the Sun Stone, before he was born. Isa had told him the story and her role in helping the Water Fae—Adria, cursed with a debilitating skin disease, had bargained with the Sea Witch. The Sun Stone in exchange for her cure.

Adria had her curse removed, but the Sea Witch never got the stone. Edmar's kingdom would be a different place today if Adria had fulfilled her bargain.

But what else has been changed in our world from all the many other successful bargains made with the Sea Witch?

Before he could delve deeper into his thoughts, Avi spoke for the first time, her voice quiet but firm.

"It's all connected." She swayed, but the pale man steadied her with hands on her shoulders.

Adria glanced at her daughter before looking back at him. "We'll join your search."

Dawn was only a few hours away. Soon, he'd be a dragon again.

Before dawn, he left instructions for his council, similar to those for his honeymoon. Then he sank into a chair by the fireplace in the Council Chamber, watching the stars fade.

The familiar surroundings, his favorite star-gazing pastime, offered little comfort. The revelations of the last twenty-four hours replayed in his mind, each one a fresh wound. Emira's betrayal, intertwined with Rivus's, formed a knot of pain he couldn't loosen.

He closed his eyes, conjuring her face—her eyes sparkling when she spoke of the same stars he loved, her voice tender when she'd said she loved him. Each memory, once sweet, now stung with deceit.

Had it all been an act?

Or was there some truth buried beneath the lies? He couldn't afford hope, though the question plagued him.

Fire was the antithesis of his Winter magic, yet it burned within him now, a desire for retribution cracking his Frostlands further.

The approaching dawn, and his inevitable transformation, brought no solace. He felt adrift in a sea of emotions, as vast and turbulent as the oceans Emira had escaped. When dawn broke, he gave Adria and her daughter a smile, hoping it wasn't too feral. "Keep up, if you can."

CHAPTER 41

EMMY

Given the heavy security surrounding the Sun Temple, Emmy appreciated Rivus's presence. During their last hours of travel, he'd thoroughly prepared her for the theft, even making her recite the plan repeatedly.

The northern air, bordering Nordrun, was colder, with winters lasting over half the year. She welcomed the cold, but after Rivus checked his mirror again with some muttering, he gave her a concealing cloak and hood.

Keeping her head down, hidden, made her reliant on him. "Did you name your mirror Edmar?"

"Quiet." With an arm around her shoulders, he led her through the gate and up the wide, blue steps to the golden temple. The hard stone emphasized the pain in her feet, a hurtful reminder that she was about to steal a precious artifact from the man she loved.

At the entrance, a guard asked their purpose.

"My mute niece seeks guidance and healing from our Father."

Rivus's smooth deception granted them entry.

"You lie so easily," she whispered, eyeing him skeptically as they entered the temple's shadow. "No wonder Edmar trusted you."

Rivus squeezed her shoulder, his nails digging in, weakening her knees. The pain seemed to stir her dormant power. A creeping realization accompanied her delayed quest, her powers were returning, stronger each day. A third of her allotted time had passed. The risk of losing control loomed. She closed her eyes, using her mother's breathing technique to find calm in the rhythm of their steps.

Rivus halted. "Temple Hall," he said in a whisper.

Her gaze traveled from the gold-dusted carpet to the iron altar, where the familiar Golden Scepter cradled the Sun Stone. Its dark sheen reflected the flickering red candlelight. A shiver of awe and fear ran through her, the air thrumming with the stone's whispers.

Rivus leaned closer. "This is your mark. I'll need half an hour. Wait for the signal."

As he slipped away, fire acid sparked in her blood, and she gritted her teeth. *Just a minor torment.* She stayed motionless until a small, pale hand reached for the Sun Stone. Her heart skipped a beat. "The Sun Stone is not meant for human hands."

The arm withdrew. "How did you...?"

She chuckled, realizing she hadn't been noticed. She turned slowly. The newcomer was young, but her youth was the least interesting thing about her, overshadowed by her light blue skin and translucent, silver-flecked hair. She was the most spectacular *human* Emmy had ever seen. "But you're not human, are you?"

"I am."

Emmy smiled faintly, minute shocks tingling her face from her returning magic and the turmoil of her feelings. This woman truly believed she was human, the conviction plain in her voice. But she seemed more than that. Almost shrugging it off—a motion Emmy had come to love—her smile faded. "If you are human, do not touch the stone. It will burn you up in an instant."

The young woman's hands twitched in hesitation, then she looked back at the Golden Scepter. Emmy studied her profile, puzzled. This combination of blue skin and the unusual hair did not match any known race from her studies.

The woman looked up. "Are you human?"

"No."

"You are so beautiful. Are you fae?"

Emmy flushed. *Beautiful?* She was no Gilly. "I am not fae, and I'm not of your world, but I want to be."

It is true? Did she wish to be part of this world? Edmar was here, her husband now. While her merfolk heritage was all she knew, she hated being a mermaid bound to her father, forced to obey.

"That is not at all confusing," the woman said.

The *human* waited, but Emmy remained silent, needing to refocus. She hoped the woman would leave before Rivus's signal. Her silence didn't deter the small woman, though.

"I'm Airi, a human who wishes to be a part of a different world."

Candlelight flickered off Airi's silver strands, captivating her. "Perhaps you will be, Airi. My name is Emira, but you can call me Emmy."

She straightened, compelled to present herself well. But Airi's gaze fell to her neck, and she winced inwardly. She'd revealed too much.

Touching her own neck, Airi asked, "Are you a slave to someone here?"

A slave? Forced to obey, her destiny controlled. Imprisoned most of her life. Perhaps she was. Airi's question illuminated the lives of all mermaids.

None truly had a choice. They were tethered to the mermen in their lives, lacking autonomy. No choice in mates, or even in remaining unmated. Eventually, they were all forced to mate. All mermaids were slaves to their gems and the whims of their merman.

She inhaled slowly, little tremors of pain scuttling under her skin. "I've been a slave since my birth, but I'm here to gain my freedom."

She bowed her head, turning back to the scepter with measured movements, hoping Airi would leave.

"Can I do anything to help you?"

Go away. "No."

"I could try to sneak you out of this place. I can help hide you from your master."

Despite Airi's kindness, she remained resolute. "This is where I'm meant to be."

Airi hesitated, as if contemplating whether to intervene, then sighed and stepped away.

Praise the eight gods.

Emmy bowed her head once more, mimicking prayer, meditating as the crowd's murmur washed over her. Tension eased, her pain ebbing. For a while, she stood unnoticed, people coming and going, some praying, but none engaging her.

Then it began.

Roaring booms erupted outside.

Startled patrons voiced their concerns, many heading toward the Temple Hall's entrance. Gray smoke poured into the room, prompting faster exits and persuading the remaining few to reconsider staying. Smaller pops continued after the booms, more smoke spread, and screams rose above the chaos. Everyone scrambled for the exit.

Gray smoke curled around her. Harmless, Rivus had assured her, but she held her breath as it enveloped her, the carpet vanishing beneath its ghostly swirl.

Hands shaking, she reached for the Sun Stone. The scepter's thin golden arms cradled the stone fast, barely bending. Pain whispered in her muscles, but she ignored it. She maneuvered the scepter over a candle flame, hoping the heat would soften the metal. Balancing, the staff strained her, her muscles screaming, as the smoke intensified her anxiety.

Could she harness her magic, even now?

She'd never been clear-headed enough when the pain became overwhelming, but she'd practiced controlling her magic's source with her mother's meditating techniques. She focused, coaxing magic to her fingertips, willing it with faster breaths. Fire acid spurted from her hands, then subsided. *Enough.*

Two golden arms melted into molten threads, and the black Sun Stone loosened. Triumph surged through her. Freedom, finally within reach.

This is the moment that changes everything.

She secured the stone in the waistband of her pants, nestled against her skin. Her triumph was short-lived, though, as deep longing and nausea replaced it.

Edmar's disappointed face, the memory of his touch, sent a jolt of pain through her. The intense emotion triggered a surge of heat, her hands tingling, the familiar hum of magic building again.

Panic seized her.

Never before had she realized how her emotions connected to her power. Her guilt and yearning for Edmar fueled the return of her powers. Inhaling deeply, she plunged into the smoke, following a faint light leading to a hallway. Pain shot through her muscles, but she didn't stop. Orange-robed monks directed people toward the exit. She joined the crowd, focusing on her breathing, walking on her tiptoes, shrinking into her cloak as a dragon roared overhead.

The courtyard buzzed with confusion. She joined a group heading east, counting her steps, managing her fire acid until it subsided. A hand clamped onto her arm, pulling her into the dense evergreens.

"Got it?" Rivus asked.

"I do." A yellow light emanated from her clothes.

Rivus shielded his eyes. "Careful what you say when you have the Sun Stone. Only lies keep it quiet."

"Easy enough. I'll just follow your example." The stone's dim silence supported her lie.

Rivus frowned, rummaging through his satchel. He handed her a metal container. "The Sun Stone came to Agondray in an iron box. Figured iron shields its properties."

She secured the stone inside, holding up the container. "Rivus's company is agonizing, worse than a hundred jellyfish stings."

A faint yellow glimmer appeared. Not enough to attract attention. She tucked the box into her leather bag. Despite her triumph, her heart felt heavy. Freedom's cost, the distance from Edmar, felt like a gaping, raw wound. Rivus's presence reminded her of all she'd lost, yet the thought of him leaving hurt. A sharp, unexpected ache unrelated to her magic. He was the last link to Edmar.

She missed her Dragon King already, and likely always would. Clearing her throat, she said, "I married your king as you asked. You helped me get the Sun Stone in return. Now, you can leave. Our partnership is completed."

"Gods above and below, I wish I could."

She stepped back. He was staying? She already regretted her earlier thoughts of missing him. "You need to leave."

Rivus grabbed her upper arm. "You have no choice, Princess."

"Why?"

"Not anything I can tell you."

Desperately, she tried to summon her magic, but found only pain. "Let me go."

"Ground rules first." His eyes shadowed when the dragon flew overhead, and they hid in an evergreen's low boughs. "You can choose the destination, but I accompany you. And you listen to me when safety is at stake."

Perhaps his company was preferable in a world unfamiliar to her, as much as she detested the idea. She met his gaze with defiance, her lips twisting into a bitter smile. "I suppose it's better you stay with me than return to Edmar and pretend to be his friend again."

CHAPTER 42

EDMAR

The first day's aerial search yielded nothing. As he flew above the land, his mind drifted to those he'd lost... his parents, cousins, aunts, uncles, wife after cursed wife, then the one that tore him apart, the one in his dreams and nightmares. His son.

His empty crib haunted him.

Am I cursed to lose everyone I love?

Now his most recent wife—the one he'd thought of and dreamed of for twenty-five years. Seeing her in his mind became a bitter pill, a cold knot tightening in his chest. Refusing to succumb to despair, he shoved it into his Frostlands. He would find her. He had to. Not just for his kingdom, for the Sun Stone, but for something more... a need to understand why she had left, why she had betrayed the trust he thought they had built.

He reached the Sun Temple within hours, but Adria and Avi needed another day, searching from the ground. At night, he joined the fae women, unconcerned about hiding his transformation, a rare comfort. Both had known the Ice Dragons in better times, when secrecy wasn't a cloak they wore daily.

They camped in the forest, avoiding towns. His face would be recognized, the lack of guards questioned. The appearance of the Water Fae would also cause a stir and not a favorable one once it was known that they were pirates.

And then there was Cielan. Absent all day, he rejoined them an hour after sunset, arriving in a rush of wind. Immediately he crouched beside Avi, his voice too low to be heard, pushing back his hood.

Firelight turned his pale skin translucent blue, like a stormy sky. His long, straight hair, dark gray with blue hints, was feather-light in the breeze, like smoke caught in a draft, wispy around pointed ears.

This was unlike any fae Edmar had ever seen. "What are you?"

Cielan's gaze lifted from Avi, and the intensity in his clear eyes sent a chill of dragon's breath down his spine. He'd never seen eyes so devoid of color.

A slight smile lifted Cielan's sculpted lips. "Vamphyr, or so my maker was called."

He had more questions, but the vamphyr's attention never strayed from Avi after that.

Before the night ended, Cielan departed as quickly as he'd arrived. Then they resumed their journey. Before his sunrise transformation, Adria told him more about Cielan.

Once an Air Fae, he'd had the misfortune of encountering a powerful female entity who drained him of his living blood. He'd died, then been reborn, no longer fae, stronger, faster, with only the sun as his enemy.

"And your daughter?" he asked.

"He helps her. Without him, things would be worse for her with her magic." Despite Cielan's positive influence on Avi, Adria frowned.

Again, he had more questions, but his transformation began. Near midday, he winged over the Sun Temple. All was quiet. The Water Fae wouldn't arrive until later. He continued his vigil, scrutinizing each visitor, but found no sign of Emira or Rivus.

The monks bowed, hands clasped, but their eyes betrayed their discomfort. His presence disturbed the visitors, so he flew off, following the road, then veering into the forest.

He roared his frustrations at finding nothing.

Just past midday, he met his older brother, Kalden, who'd just taken flight from inside the Sun Temple's compound. Where Edmar was more vividly colored with greens and blues, Kalden was nearly all black save for the cobalt glow of his underbelly.

What brings you here? he asked Kalden.

My bride wanted to see the temple. What about you?

Pride prevented him from confiding in Kalden. *Investigating rumors of a possible theft of the Sun Stone.*

If it were missing, we'd know. The monks wouldn't be so calm.

Yes, of course you're right. Which meant that his treacherous wife and friend had not appeared yet, or maybe they were even in the temple now preparing to steal it. He would be here to catch them if that was the case.

They talked for another fifteen minutes, Kalden thanking him for the food and supplies that had just arrived that day.

The cool air dropped several degrees in temperature. Prolonged proximity would create ice storms, thanks to the Snow Princess's curse. In relief, he exhaled cold air when his brother's diminutive bride appeared on the blue-painted steps of the Sun Temple.

Edmar delayed, wind whistling across his scales, the sight of Kalden's predicament tightening his chest. Then he wheeled away.

Good luck, Kalden said.

And to you!

He feared for his brother. Although Emira had married him before leaving, Kalden's bride resisted marriage. If Airian didn't marry him by the next full moon, he could die. Surely Kalden would send her away from Agondray to save himself. The continent would suffer a year of winter, but the curse would relent its hold on the bride by chance and Kalden would live.

Unease settled within him as he soared. Kalden's reluctant bride sparked self-awareness. He pondered his countless brides, fleeting presences, bound by curse, not choice. Relationships driven by duty, not genuine connection. Had he ever truly opened his heart? Or merely played the role, awaiting salvation, the *right* bride?

The question brought little comfort as he faced Emira's departure from his life.

He found Adria and Avi a few hours from the temple, their pace surprisingly swift. Perhaps it would be quick enough.

Halfway back, explosive crackles echoed across the valley, followed by bursts of brilliant light—vivid blues and sulfurous yellows that painted the horizon. His heart sank. Dwarven black powder, unmistakable, the fireworks peddled to his parents long ago.

Emira was stealing the stone right now.

He winged hard for the Sun Temple, each wingbeat drumming his frustration. Helpless anger surged as he roared.

He arrived amid the chaos. Visitors and monks scrambled down the steps, smoke billowing from within. Crowds fled. Frantically, he searched for any sign of Emmy or Rivus, unable to land safely. Hope dwindled, replaced by gnawing despair.

His deafening roar echoed his pounding heart, a rhythm of betrayal. They were escaping. The thought of losing Emira forever clawed at his mind, fueling a fury that grew with each heartbeat.

If she vanished, the trail would go cold.

His thundering heart threatened to burst from his chest, the thought of Emira and Rivus together, laughing and celebrating their theft, making him dizzy.

Did they have a secret love affair?

Had he been so blind?

He'd been so focused on controlling his lust, every time she'd tempted him, sought his kiss.

He grappled with the echoes of betrayal, finding parallels between his own heartbreak and the legendary tale of King Artorius, Queen Guinevere, and Sir Lysander. Their story of love, loyalty, and betrayal intertwined in a tragic dance of destiny.

Radiant Sun God, I beseech you, as the eternal watcher, safeguard your God stone. Safeguard my wife. I don't know what I'll do if I find her.

Desperate, he swept low over the forest, treetops scraping his underbelly. As the sun set, he landed in a clearing near the Sun Temple. Shifted back into his human form, he sprinted to the gates where his men were securing the temple for the night. Shaken, they knelt, heads bowed.

"Your Majesty," several said.

"Rise."

Father Jayasurya spun around, his face contorted in horror—a sight never before seen on the usually composed monk. "News travels fast."

"I was forewarned. Tell me the Sun Stone is safe."

The air reeked of burnt metal and rotten eggs.

The old man bowed his head. "I'm afraid it's gone."

His mind raced, a whirlwind of anger and betrayal. Emira had planned this all along. *And Rivus, my trusted friend, helped her.* He'd been a pawn to them, as much as he was a pawn to the Snow Princess. A sick churning gripped his stomach.

"The explosions came from this." Adria rounded from behind the temple and pushed back the hood of her cloak. Blue and green strands of her dark hair curled around her face, at once foamy and fluid.

Charred paper casings, eerily familiar, lay in her outstretched hand, confirming his fears. Black powder. Not seen in a thousand years. Kalden's bride had revealed its presence in his kingdom. Edmar had hoped it hadn't reached his.

He started to ask about Emira, but Adria answered preemptively. "The moment we arrived, we checked everyone. If your wife had been here to steal the Sun Stone, she and the stone were long gone."

The explosions. The black powder. His heart pounded with sickening thoughts. It couldn't be a coincidence. Emira, Rivus, the dwarves, the Sea Witch—were they all connected? *How?*

The stolen Sun Stone, the black powder, were greater threats than Emira and Rivus's betrayal. For centuries, he'd retreated to his Frostlands, playing his role. But he was tired of sacrificing his emotions, a puppet for the Snow Princess.

Punishing his wife and friend for their crimes offered a chance to feel something real—deep hurt from their deception, fury gnawing his insides. The previous night's thoughts haunted him, leaving him shaken and lost.

He felt utterly alone, rage spiraling into despair.

Chapter 43

EMMY

"The Metal Stone is south of where I face." The Sun Stone lay inert in Emmy's grasp. Even its whispers remained silent.

She sat against a cave wall facing north. Earlier, Rivus had guided them deeper into a secluded part of his cave network, ensuring the stone's glow wouldn't reveal their hideout.

Leaning against the opposite cave wall, Rivus raised an eyebrow, snapping his mirror shut and whistling softly. "Edmar never knew what he was getting himself into with you, did he? A deceitful siren from the sea, gathering all the Gods' Stones."

Edmar's name conjured his ocean-colored eyes, the soft curve of his smile. Her chest tightened, her breath catching.

"You are hateful," she said, her voice echoing in the cave. She closed her eyes as the stone flared, bright and overwhelming.

The light faded, revealing Rivus's scowling face.

"Don't worry, Your Highness," he said, his voice laced with bitterness. "I'm aware of what I am. Are you aware of what you are?"

She pressed her lips together, hands tightening on the Sun Stone. "The Metal Stone is east."

Again, no response.

West, back toward Edmar, was out of the question. Her chest tightened with each thought of him. She swallowed the lump in her throat.

"The Metal Stone is north." The Sun Stone lit up. *Finally, progress.*

It had taken several attempts to find the right phrasing.

"The Metal Stone is still in Agondray." Another flash. Good, she didn't have to go far. But how far? "The Metal Stone is within a day's walk." Silence. "Within two days' walk, then?"

The stone flared, filling her with hope. She jumped up, ignoring the stabbing in her feet. She steadied herself against the cave wall, excitement tempered by the daunting journey ahead and hiding from Edmar.

"What are you doing?" Rivus raised his eyebrows.

"I have to get the Metal Stone."

He shook his head, shaggy hair brushing his cloak. "Not until nightfall. Or have you forgotten Edmar, flying through the skies as a dragon, searching for us?"

She sat back down, her voice a trembling whisper. "Why did you help me steal the Sun Stone? Was it only to force my marriage to Edmar?"

"The curse, remember?"

"The Snow Princess's curse? You thought I worked for her. Tell me about her."

"She's pure evil. Stay far away from her."

"How will I know who she is?"

He shook his head. "Don't say her name. Don't even think about her. Her curse killed all the Ice Dragons in Agondray except the brothers and caused the Little Ice Age. She'll come after you if she thinks you can break Edmar's curse."

From the night they danced at the tavern, she remembered Edmar blaming himself and his brothers for the Little Ice Age. And she recalled the curse's words: *Ice and snow will cover your land. The weak shall die. Our people will remain as witnesses. To heal the land, you shall suffer the chains of forced marriage.*

She could see why Edmar might blame himself with his sense of duty. "They didn't heed the curse at first. That's what caused the Little Ice Age?"

Rivus nodded.

The man made no sense to her. "You care for Edmar. So, why betray him?"

Tension simmered beneath his calm exterior as he approached her. He crouched, eyes intense, a red flush on his cheeks. "Understand this. Everything I do is to protect those I love. I wish to all eight gods I'd never had to hurt Edmar."

His thick brows lowered, his brown eyes, usually warm, now glinted with anger. She pulled back, but hit the wall.

He pointed at her. "If you hadn't arrived in the kingdom when you did, I never would've hurt him directly, and he certainly wouldn't know my loyalties were divided."

"Then I'm glad I exposed you. Edmar deserves a better friend than you."

Rivus slammed his fist into the wall next to her head, the sound reverberating. She flinched. Silence fell in the cave. She inhaled, the reality of their situation—and her own actions—settling heavily on her shoulders.

Dark red stained his entire face, but raw pain echoed in his voice as he shifted away. "I've proven myself for centuries. You, on the other hand, are the worst thing that's ever happened to him."

She held his gaze, her heart breaking. "Edmar didn't deserve any of what we've done. I wish... I..."

That she could take it all back? Then what, let herself become a weapon or a lost soul? *Let this be over. Get the stone, return to the Sea Witch.*

His voice softened unexpectedly, and he handed her his closed mirror. "Touch the surface and say Edmar's name. He cannot see you."

The mysterious mirror Rivus constantly muttered over. She did as he said and gasped when Edmar's likeness as the dragon filled the mirror. He flew through the clear azure sky, surely looking for them. She swallowed a lump in her throat, glancing up and giving a shy smile to Rivus for his kindness.

"Thank you," she whispered.

He nodded as he settled against the opposite wall again, crossing his arms. "Sleep, Princess. We travel tonight."

The cold cave wall pressed against her back as she got comfortable. She rested her head on Edmar's shirt and watched as the beautiful teal and blue dragon soared through the sky. She wished she could have any other life. But that was not her reality.

So she thought of the next stone, of escaping Agondray, of finally being free of Edmar's haunting memory. Each thought twisted a knot in her stomach even as his ocean scent wafted from his shirt. Would she ever not think of him again? She longed for that day.

For over twenty-five years, she'd envisioned a life with him. Fantasies, once something to pass the time while she lay trapped in the Little Palace, alone. But now, as she drifted to sleep, her dreams burst with colors of a potential reality. She dreamed of him—proud, strong, his smile reaching his ocean-colored eyes. She fell into his offered embrace, warm. A rare love she had known only in fleeting moments since her mother's death.

The dream faded, replaced by the cave's chill. Reality returned, reminding her of the painful truth—she was here for a purpose, not for love.

Her next dream brought memories of her wedding, her sister boarding the ship, then the bitter memory of leaving Edmar behind. She never saw him again after the night of their wedding.

Laughter echoed. It wasn't hers. Malala's taunting chortle. *Left him on the honeymoon. So sad.*

The Water Fae's intrusion stopped the dance of a million colors and solidified into something more familiar. The scene shifted in her dream. She stood on a high balcony overlooking the familiar garden, where she often met Malala. The height, and the sight below, surprised her. She gripped the balustrade.

Sunlight glinted off Malala's silver-accented white dress, her blue and green hair rippling, strands rolling over and over each other, reminiscent of sea waves racing toward sandy shores. Clasping the white stone at her neck, she whispered, her words too soft to be heard, meant for the white dire wolf bowing before her.

What about this is wrong? Something about the scene before her caused alarm. The wolf?

At first, she mistook the wolf for Rivus. But this one was smaller, its tail a striking lapis lazuli blue. She sought a closer look, but Malala appeared, gripping her wrist, her hold bruising. The fae's hair whipped around her face. A storm-tossed ocean.

Malala's demanding voice cut through the tension. "Why are you going after the Gods' Stones?"

A quick glance told her the wolf was gone. Returning her gaze to Malala, she adopted the stillness that had once defined her existence. This fae, despite claiming to be imprisoned, always seemed to possess more knowledge than she should.

Until now.

Only three people knew of her actions. The Sea Witch and Gilly. Unlikely, they communicated with this Water Fae. But Rivus had learned of her quest, and now Malala had met with a white wolf...

She wrenched her wrist free, her lip curling with accusation. "The werewolf is your spy."

The fae's hair mellowed, blue and green strands rocking with slower and slower movements. Her eyes widened slightly. "You're not what I expected."

"What do you want?"

Malala stepped closer, towering over her. She fingered her shorn hair. "Bold choice to chop off your beautiful hair."

Her tone yielded a mix of curiosity and appraisal.

Emmy pulled away.

The fae sighed. "You've never trusted me, but I'd like to help, as long as you don't interfere with Agondray."

She squared her shoulders. "I'll be finished soon, then I hope to never see Agondray again."

"Good." She tilted her head, studying her. "What are you hoping to accomplish?"

Sharing her motivations wouldn't hurt. "I want to be rid of my magic."

The fae nodded. "Seeking the Metal Stone makes sense, but without the words to awaken its power, you'll fail. You'd be better off seeking your Father God."

Emmy frowned. That wasn't her reason for seeking the Metal Stone, but the idea was intriguing, first suggested by the Summer Child. "Metallon? But he hasn't been seen in thousands of years."

The fae smirked. "I thought you were smarter than that."

"Has he been seen?" she asked, barely containing her surprise.

If he wasn't asleep, the implications were monumental—surely the merfolk would have noticed their god's return. He must still be slumbering. How would one find a sleeping god?

Before the question finished in her mind, she knew the answer.

The Sun Stone. It could find a sleeping god. The possibility excited her. Hope swelled, leaving her breathless. "But would he help me?"

Malala shrugged and placed lavender hands on her hips, her expression unreadable. "Better to ask a god than a stone."

Finding Metallon would be more productive than finding the Metal Stone. It wasn't her original plan, but the possibility excited and overwhelmed her. She took a moment to let this settle, pondering the unexpected alternative to working for the Sea Witch, if she could find the god before her time was up and she became part of the Garden of Souls.

She could ask Metallon for help instead. That vile creature probably meant to challenge her biological father for the rule of the oceans once she had the stones. Perhaps Emmy shouldn't care. Her father had tried to sacrifice her, but a war would cost many merfolk lives.

"I want to help, Emmy."

She thought about Malala's meeting with the dire wolf. "Then be truthful."

The fae chewed on her bottom lip before continuing. "Have you ever loved someone who betrayed you completely?"

Her heart skipped a beat. Was the question about Edmar? She tried to answer honestly. "My father blames me for my mother's death. I've always tried to please him, hoping for his love. But he tried to sell me in marriage, knowing my magic would kill my husband, leading to my execution."

Horror filled the fae's eyes. "I'm so sorry," she said, gripping Emmy's hands.

Her throat tightened. Once more, she wished for the release of the Ocean's Lament or even tears. "Have you?"

Malala smiled sadly. Her blue eyes misted, darkening to a rich brown. The transformation mesmerized her. Distracted, she allowed Malala to thread an arm with hers and pull her away from the balcony.

The fae took a deep breath. "Let me tell you a story."

Chapter 44
EDMAR

Edmar downed another swallow of warm, bitter beer, his gaze lost in the slowly spinning stars above. Blades of grass poked his head. A campfire crackled at his feet.

"You'd think the Sun Temple had better tasting stuff than this junk." Adria's husky voice floated into his hearing with a slow reverberation. "I could steal better."

His chuckle sounded hollow, tinged with darker thoughts. "You have stolen better from me."

Her laughter reminded him of their first encounter after he'd started sailing on his own, her ship easily outmaneuvering his. He could've frozen her ship solid, but she'd melted the ice as soon as it seized her ship, then manipulated the water, flushing it over his deck and sending his crew sprawling. After that, her crew had swarmed aboard, drank his mead and wine, then left. A valuable first lesson in the dangers of sailing the seas.

A log split with a loud pop in the fire, its heat pushing back against the night's chill. His thoughts inevitably returned to his burdens.

Adria seemed to notice the shift in his mood. "What are you going to do?"

Squinting against the firelight, he closed one eye, reducing the number of Adrias sitting on the other side. Her quiet daughter had wandered off with Cielan into the forest to meditate away from the "man-made light."

Dragon-made light, he'd snorted.

Same difference, she'd said before leaving them.

Adria had shrugged, explaining her daughter had always been a strange child, one not made for a life of piracy. The vamphyr would keep her safe.

Edmar hunched into his drink, something dark and unyielding settling over him. He'd lived by a strict code—a set of ethics that ensured he made just decisions. He allowed hope to live in the useless muscle in his chest, believing goodness would lead to his salvation.

But Emira and Rivus's betrayals shattered that illusion. The bitter taste of the beer mixed with the bitterness swelling inside him. *Why?*

The question haunted him.

He replayed conversations with Emira in his mind, searching for clues, for any hint of deception. Had it all been an act, a calculated performance to gain his trust and steal the Sun Stone? Or had he missed something, some desperation driving her?

Memories surfaced. Emira laughing under the tavern lights when they danced; her eyes alight with joy when they spoke about the stars.

Rivus. The name brought another blow.

He recalled their first meeting, a battlefield encounter that blossomed into an unlikely friendship. Charming and loyal, quick to become his confidante, then his Marshal. For centuries, Rivus had been loyal, a steadfast support. Their kinship a solace through cursed decades. Together, they'd shared duty and camaraderie.

Now that loyalty lay shattered. Rivus had helped Emira. It had to be her plan; Rivus had never shown any interest in the stone before.

Each memory, once sweet, now twisted with betrayal. Goodness didn't guarantee reciprocation. He'd been a fool. *I believed finding love would save me, but I was merely a stepping stone in their schemes.*

He wouldn't be used again. When he caught them, both would face punishment. And he *would* find them.

Somehow.

He gulped his beer, refusing to acknowledge his lack of options. He did not know how to find them now they'd stolen the Sun Stone.

"Do you know why your wife would steal the Sun Stone?" Adria asked.

He rubbed palms against his eyes. "I don't know."

"You haven't said much about her besides her name. Who is Emira? Tell me about her."

"Princess Emira, a mermaid actually. The daughter of King Sargon, King of the Seas."

Adria choked, spitting beer into the fire. Through a hoarse voice, she asked, "Najla's daughter?"

"You know her?"

Dark blue and green hair whipped around her face, parts lightening in the firelight.

"I knew her mother," she said softly, a yearning sadness in her voice. "Long ago. Najla and Isa were my closest friends before Najla married the Sea King."

A pang of empathy resonated in his chest.

"It's hard," he said, remembering faces long gone. Friends and lovers lost to time and tragedy. The loss of his son. Now the loss and betrayal of his best friend and his wife. "Hard to keep opening your heart."

Adria nodded, and firelight glimmered over a faint sheen of tears in her darkened eyes.

"It's all connected," she said softly.

"What was that?"

"Avi's premonition," she said, wiping her cheeks. "Does your wife have a skin ailment?"

Taking another long drink, he stared up at the spinning stars. "None that I know of. Why?"

She grimaced with a deep swallow of her beer, her unfocused gaze on the fire. "Never mind."

What was going on in that pirate brain? Adria was always steps ahead of everyone. "Did you know her magic was destructive? She accidentally killed her mother."

Adria gasped, her fists clenching. "No, it can't be."

"She got rid of it, though. Her magic. She's not a mermaid anymore."

"This is too awful if true, but I think I know what happened." She wiped hands over her face, settling cross-legged. "I think I know what Emira is doing."

He propped himself up on an elbow, the world spinning. "Tell me."

"The Sea Witch took away my curse, my skin disease."

"I remember the story. Isa told me that was when you stole the Sun Stone from my parents."

"There's more to the story." Adria gulped beer from her leather wineskin as if looking for fortification. "The Sea Witch extracted my curse. A living, tangible thing. But she wouldn't release Najla or my husband, unless I found the other Gods' Stones for her. The Sun God intervened. He helped me free them in exchange for abandoning my quest. The Sea Witch, enraged, placed my curse into Najla. But nothing happened, so we thought it was over."

Despite his fuzzy brain, he understood the direction of her assumptions. He recalled Emira's stories—her isolation, her fear, her father's plans. "You think your curse manifested in Emira?"

Adria leaned forward, the fire shining in her eyes. "What if she made a deal with the Sea Witch? The Gods' Stones for removing her magic?"

A little light of hope burned in the center of his chest.

Perhaps her betrayal wasn't malicious, but born of desperation. It painted a picture of a woman driven to extreme measures. The thought softened his anger, replaced by a flicker of empathy.

But why didn't she tell me? She could have. Instead, she'd deceived him, stolen from him, used him. He shook his head, banishing any empathy.

She was a manipulator.

No, she was more than that. She was an enemy, collecting the stones for the Sea Witch.

"She's mad!" His breath quickened with rising anger. "Giving the Sun Stone to the Sea Witch!"

Everything about Adria paused, even her constantly curling hair. "Sometimes we make choices that break our hearts to heal our wounds. I know it's hard to understand, but when you're desperate, even the darkest path can seem like the only way."

"It's selfish, no matter the justification."

Adria shook her head. "Let's just find her. There's more at stake than the Sun Stone if she is working with the Sea Witch."

"How could it be worse?"

"My husband always suspected the Sea Witch wanted to use the Gods' Stones to find, or exploit, the Summer Child."

The Summer Child.

The Summer Child kept resurfacing—the werewolves' report, Isamore's me ssage...

He took another drink, wiped his mouth, and laid back down. "Wonderful. My wife's not just a thief, but conspiring to end the world."

"At least we know where to look." She continued with his raised brow. "She's either returning to the Sea Witch or going after the Metal Stone."

He jerked, the world tilting. Kalden had just told them Lord Galton had the Metal Stone. "The Metal Stone is in Nordrun."

Adria slowly nodded. "It hasn't moved far in twelve hundred years. I was going to retrieve it when the Sun God stopped me."

Will the Sun God intercept Emira? It would be nice if he did and told her to return the Sun Stone. She was heading east or north to Kalden's lands. *Should I warn my brother?*

No, let Kalden handle his own affairs. Edmar could handle his wife.

"Avi and I can head east. Better you go to your brother's lands than pirates."

Suspicion and relief warred within him. He couldn't afford blind trust anymore, but her offer could prove useful. He couldn't be in two places at once, and he'd planned to head north. "I appreciate the help, but it's not fair to involve you."

Adria waved away his concern. "Najla was my dearest friend. Helping Emira is the least I can do, especially if she has my curse."

He narrowed his eyes, assessing her. Emira had stolen a precious artifact, punishable by death. Thinking of her lifeless body made his hand clench around the wineskin. He knew what the path of vengeance might turn him into, the dragon within whispering seductive justifications for cruelty.

And Adria would likely interfere. Maybe he needed her to. Either way, he wouldn't tell the pirate his plans. He searched her face. "Then I accept. I'll head north, you go east. If you find her, detain her at my palace and send word to the Sun Temple."

A subtle stillness settled over Adria, a stillness he only noticed because he was looking for it.

"What will you do when you find your queen?" she asked, her voice low.

The question sank like a stone in his stomach. Lying was unnatural, yet circumstances molded him into a creature of shadows and half-truths. He would lie, like the Iron Dragons, hoarding their secrets. Convincing Adria wouldn't be easy. "If she returns the Sun Stone, I will help her with her magic."

If only she'd told me about her struggles. Now it was too late. He wasn't sure Adria believed him, though she wanted to.

"Do you love her?" she asked.

The question struck him like a blade, twisting in his gut. *I hate what she's done to me. Hate the pain.*

A deep, resonant crack reverberated through the frozen expanse of his Frostlands, like the distant rumble of thunder rolling beneath the surface.

I hate her.

Anger surged, a shield against the deeper ache. He *had* loved her, perhaps still did deep within his heart. His external calm belied the storm within as he struggled to reconcile his love with the betrayal that poisoned it.

Adria sensed his answer, her jaw clenching.

Then stocky dwarves stepped into the firelight, encircling them, weapons drawn.

Chapter 45

EMMY

Beneath a covered walkway, the Water Fae Malala stood silently and gazed into a familiar garden. Twilight deepened the sky to indigo. This Malala seemed younger, her features softer, a gentle smile on her lips.

A tall man approached, reminiscent of Edmar, lean through his hips, broader in the shoulders, and easily wider than her Dragon King. His skin matched the twilight. He stopped behind the younger Malala, barely an inch separating their bodies.

Could he be a Dragon King—one of Edmar's brothers?

His large hands settled on her hips as he whispered in her ear. "All alone, Princess?"

"Merely waiting," she said, leaning back into his embrace, her hand stroking his midnight hair. "For my lover."

He pulled her hips back against him, his lips trailing from her bare shoulder to her throat. Malala moaned, her eyes fluttering shut.

He smiled. "Looks like he missed his chance."

"Missed his chance?"

His hands skimmed up her body, cupping and kneading her breasts.

Heat flushed Emmy's face, sparking warmth in her core. She glanced at the older Malala, who watched, lips parted, pupils dilated.

"Tonight, you're mine," the man said with a possessive undertone.

She arched her body, undulating her hips against him. "But I'm to be married. I vowed to remain pure for my husband."

"Should we stop?"

She stilled, and he lifted his head.

He whispered, "Never have I yearned for anyone like this."

"We only have to wait ten more days."

Emmy, confused, had expected a story, not this vivid reenactment. To her Malala, she asked, "Who is he?"

"My fiancé," Malala said, her gaze fixed on the scene.

He slipped a hand into her dress, rolling her nipple between his fingers. A soft, involuntary sound escaped her lips, her shoulders relaxing. Kissing the spot below her ear, he murmured, "Why wait? We're meant to be together."

"Neither of us has to accept our parents' wishes to marry."

"Do you plan to say no?"

Various emotions crossed her face, none showing refusal. She shook her head. "What about you?"

"I couldn't walk away from you, even if the Sun God himself forbade it."

Malala turned, pulling his face down to hers, her fingers tangled in his hair. He crushed her smaller body in his arms and nearly bent her back with the force of his kiss.

She broke free, breathless. "Make love to me, Rin."

"As you command, Snow Princess." He swept her into his arms, carrying her inside.

Emmy reeled. Malala was the Snow Princess, responsible for the Ice Dragon massacre, the Little Ice Age, the deaths of thousands.

She should have known.

The garden blurred, the memory fading. The courtyard remained, but now bathed in noon sunlight, four handsome, similar-looking men stood within. No mistaking who these men were. The four Dragon Kings: Rin, Kalden, Edmar, and Zane.

She hadn't been alive when all four had been the Dragon Princes before their parents' deaths, but now she knew their faces. She drank in the sight of Edmar, regal yet relaxed, leaning against a short stone wall surrounding a bed of vibrant flowers. He listened to the most imposing of the brothers, Kalden, his deep, smoky voice familiar from her encounter with the Seat of the Dwarf.

Their conversation was muffled, reaching her in fragments as the younger Malala circled the courtyard, unseen.

"You would really allow...?" Kalden gestured toward Rin.

Kalden, like Edmar, had lighter blue skin, but shared Rin's black hair. He was massive, broad-shouldered, his courtly attire straining against his muscled frame. Other than being slightly shorter than Rin, Kalden was the largest of his brothers.

Rin crossed his arms. "... tales. What harm... hobby?"

Zane's laugh was menacing. "... cause chaos ... if they prove true?"

Rin looked between his brothers, his gaze coming to rest on Edmar, before saying something indistinguishable.

"...the Snow Princess before you... a foolish quest..." Edmar's voice tugged at her heart.

Whatever he said prompted Rin to turn away from his brothers, taking a few steps toward the walkway, then pivoting back to his brothers. Malala froze.

His lowered voice paired with his back to Malala obscured the first part of his declaration, but the end came through clearly, each harsh word clipped and said with a sense of finality. "... I will not marry her."

Younger Malala screamed, a raw, shattering cry. Light exploded from her, blue streams crushed beneath white shards of magic. Instinctively, Emmy shielded her eyes. When she looked again, only the older Malala remained, grief etched on her face.

She drew a shaky breath, wondering if Edmar had felt this same betrayal. "That's when you created the curse?"

The Water Fae blinked, shaking off the memory. Slowly, her shoulders straightened, her spine stiffened. Her grief vanished, replaced by an imperial command. The air thickened, charged with power. It was the Snow Princess, standing before her, the very person Rivus had warned her to stay away from.

She stepped back, the fae's blue eyes piercing her. Emmy searched for her magic, but found nothing. *This woman could kill me.* If this was truly Moon Walking and not just a dream, death was possible.

A white aura crackled over Malala's skin. Gripping the stone at her neck, she said, "My fiancé was a predator."

"You seemed to welcome his attentions."

"What did I know?" she snapped, anger flaring. "His touch, his kisses. I never asked for them. That—" She threw out an arm, pointing to the spot where she'd stood when Rin had come up behind her. "That's when I finally gave in, after days of him manipulating me, using me."

Wary of the spiky white light bouncing off Malala's skin, she scooted back, crossing her arms. "He didn't force you."

"Oh. My. Gods!" Malala laughed oddly, rolling her eyes. Then her head whipped down, anger marring her brow. "I was young, foolishly in love. But he took my innocence, then discarded me."

And you cursed thousands to die for your hurt feelings...

She bit back the words as white magic flared, freezing tendrils reaching her, snapping against her arms. Fire acid surged through her and exploded outward. For a terrifying moment, she thought she'd kill Malala, forced to watch her melt beneath fire acid. She screamed, her magic surging. Nausea overwhelmed her, the world a blur. She gasped, smelling salt and brine, then she was submerged, her tail glinting in the water.

She moved from the Snow Princess's realm into another. The Summer Child absorbed her magic, its aura shifting from deep purple to blazing white. Fire acid spewed, boiling the water, the cavern shuddering. The Summer Child, its form flickering white, thrashed within its prison. Its heartbeat was a frantic drumbeat echoing through the cavern. Then the magic subsided. Scalding bubbles surrounded the egg as it regained its color.

Is the child still alive? Is this still Moon Walking, or just another dream? Power was real in a realm shaped by Moon Walking. Just as real as death. Reveling in her mermaid form, Emmy swam toward the egg, but the pale, dark-haired, black-winged woman blocked her with her sword.

Then the child spoke with her aged, soothing voice. *You're close. Come to me.*

She cowered. The encounter with Malala left her tense, fearing the woman meant to kill her. But the Summer Child, the woman guarding it, represented something far worse.

The child spoke again, but this time her tone was menacing. *You would deny me?*

The words echoed in her mind, reverberating off the cavern walls. She yelled, covering her ears, but the vibrations slammed against her, stealing her breath. Darkness swallowed her. She fought for consciousness, preparing for death. "I don't know what you are, but I cannot help you."

The soothing voice returned, a contrast to the words spoken next. *You don't have a choice.* Then the Summer Child sang, a true siren's song.

Chapter 46

EDMAR

A dwarf, broadsword in hand, smiled down at Edmar, where he lay drunk. "When the wolves said you were alone, I thought they lied."

The dwarf, like the others surrounding him, wore metal armor and valor tokens braided into his hair. But this one was different—their leader, second only to the Seat of the Dwarf.

Edmar smiled, spreading his hands, not bothering to stand. "Don't you know I'm never unprotected, Thrandmir?"

Thrandmir, laird of the eastern clans, half-human, had risen ruthlessly through the ranks despite many challenges.

The dwarves' appearance, their dealings with the werewolves, troubled him. *Why are the werewolves and dwarves even talking to each other?*

Neither group owed him loyalty, but they certainly weren't allies.

Thrandmir's smile broadened, landing on Adria. "Who's the pretty lass?"

"This pretty lass can kill you ten ways before you blink."

Thrandmir chuckled. Despite her humor, Adria's gaze darted among the dwarves.

Edmar knew she was worried about Avi. He clenched his jaw, willing himself to sober up. "What are you doing here, Thrandmir?"

The dwarf rubbed his clean-shaven face. Unlike other dwarves, Thrandmir remained beardless. A sign of defiance, but no one dared comment.

His defiance reminded Edmar of Emira. She, too, had defied her people. He admired her boldness in fleeing a destiny she didn't want.

"Isn't it obvious?" He lifted the broadsword a few inches. "I never pass up a chance for fun."

The other dwarves tensed, ready for action.

Unfortunately for Edmar, no weapon lay close at hand, and calling his magic to him would light him up like those fireworks, inciting the dwarves to attack right away before he talked them out of bloodshed. He centered himself, drawing on the night's chill. "What are you doing in my kingdom?"

Peace had reigned for over eight hundred years, since Central Agondray was ceded to the dwarves.

Thrandmir cocked a smile. "What's life without a little rule-breaking?"

The dwarf's words held a rogue's charm, sparking a wistful grin. Now he reminded Edmar of Zane. Perhaps they could have been comrades, sharing more than just fleeting battles and wary truces.

He narrowed his eyes. Two centuries ago, they'd had a far friendlier meeting. Thrandmir, newly appointed leader after his father's death, had been adamant about following the rules.

Something had changed.

His grip tightened on the wineskin, cold seeping through. How often had he been blind to shifting loyalties? "What's really going on?"

Thrandmir's eyes half closed.

"Forces are awakening, Dragon King." He motioned with his broadsword. "Rise and face me."

"Are you sure this is something you want to do?" The unspoken threat suggested this would not be a battle the dwarf could win against him, or that if something happened, his brothers were likely to seek revenge.

On a good day, he could defeat them all. But today wasn't a good day. Numbing himself with alcohol didn't do him any favors. He visualized his magic, dark blue energy tingling in his hands.

Thrandmir grinned. "I enjoy a challenge."

A dwarf shifted forward.

That was enough. Time to act. With a swift motion, he summoned a blast of freezing wind, sending the dwarves sprawling. Two dwarves disappeared into the trees. The others stumbled but regained their balance. Thrandmir stood firm.

"Good shot," Adria said.

"Lucky shot," he said. "I'm still seeing double."

The dwarves charged. Adria leaped to her feet, daggers in hand.

He tried to stand, but the world tilted, and he fell to one knee. Thrandmir chuckled.

Too close.

He surged to his feet, flinging a barrage of ice shards. Then fell back to his knees, dizzy.

The dwarf reacted quickly, his sword a blur, deflecting the ice. One shard pierced his arm, and he grunted, dropping his sword, red blood soaking his sleeve.

Thrandmir yanked the shard free, blood gushing. He stared at Edmar, his sword arm useless.

The clang of metal and Adria's grunts confirmed she was holding her own. He kept his eyes on Thrandmir. "I never took you for one of the rebels the Seat of the Dwarf said he couldn't control."

Thrandmir half-bowed, an awkward gesture for a dwarf. "I respect you, Dragon King, but some desire the end of the Ice Dragons' rule."

"Are you one of them?"

"You know me." The dwarf smiled. "I support my king."

Meaning that what Thrandmir did right now had the support of the Seat of the Dwarf. The Seat was working against them, as they'd suspected. *How many smiles hid daggers?* "Do you agree with your king?"

He shrugged. "It's not my place to judge. Although you know I favor humans."

The fact the Ice Dragons protected the humans and Thrandmir's mother was human had created a bond between them centuries ago. So Thrandmir didn't really agree with his king's decisions. Edmar was glad to know this information. "Perhaps there should be a new Seat."

Thrandmir stilled. Either he'd never considered that or Edmar had spoken too close to his thoughts. The clan leader had told him he had intended to create changes, at least for his clan.

"If you two are done admiring each other, I'd like to end this fight," Adria called from above.

Edmar realized he had heard no fighting for a while. He tilted his head, keeping Thrandmir in sight while trying to locate Adria. She perched high in a tree, a dagger in one hand, another clenched between her teeth, one boot kicking a dwarf in the face. Resourcefulness was second nature to her.

He returned his attention to Thrandmir. "Are you selling Dwarven snow in my kingdom?"

Thrandmir smirked. "What are you doing so far from your palace? Newly married, and yet...where's your bride?"

He closed his eyes with the world still tilting, but slower now. So, everyone knew about Emira. He focused on his magic, although Thrandmir was wounded and unlikely to attack again. "Leave, Thrandmir. And don't come back."

"Give me the Water Fae."

"Not a chance," Adria said.

That made Edmar smile. "Catch her, and she's yours."

"Never gonna happen." Adria laughed.

She sheathed her daggers, then leaped, catching a branch of the next tree. She pulled herself up, ran across the limb, then disappeared into the forest.

"Now there's a woman I'd love to have." Thrandmir smiled. "Think about what I said."

The dwarf rapped a ring against his metal armor, the sound echoing with magic. Edmar sensed the power, but it was not his element, so he couldn't decipher its intentions. The other dwarves abandoned their pursuit, turning to Thrandmir.

The clan leader raised his arm at a ninety-degree angle, fist closed, then dropped it sharply. His men retreated.

"Remember this day, Dragon King." Thrandmir eyed his drink. "I could have taken you prisoner today. The Seat of the Dwarf would value such a bargaining chip."

"Why didn't you?"

"Not all of us agree with these changes. Remember this courtesy."

He nodded, acknowledging the implied debt. "I'm always here for our allies."

Thrandmir left then. Once all the dwarves were gone, he stumbled to the trees and vomited.

"Well, that's fragrant," Adria said as she returned.

"Not safe to stay here anyway," he said, meeting her gaze.

It wasn't safe for anyone, not if the dwarves were breaking the treaty. He'd have to send word back to his council so a warning could be issued to all his citizens.

Adria sighed. "And I was looking forward to sleeping on the ground."

A rustle silenced her chuckle. She spun, crouching, daggers drawn. He groaned, reaching for his magic. Avi and Cielan appeared, their approach deliberately loud.

"Avi!" Adria's relief was palpable.

Avi, her eyes clouded with a strange, filmy whiteness, knelt before Edmar, ignoring her mother. Cielan watched, his face tense.

Avi's slender fingers clasped his, surprisingly strong. "The Metal Stone is a diversion. The real tragedy comes when the god awakens. He'll know what's been lost. All the sleeping gods above and below will weep. But redemption..."

Her voice faltered, eyes closing. "Redemption lies in healing the moon, their stones, smoke and frost, uniting the children of destiny."

Avi swayed forward. Adria and Cielan rushed to her, but Edmar caught her, steady hands on her shoulders, his mind racing. *A diversion? A god awakens?*

But something else caught his attention—something terrifying.

Blood trickled from Avi's eyes, nose, and mouth. Panic spiked through the air. She convulsed violently, her body trembling. Cielan pulled her away. Adria cried out, a sound of pure anguish, as she hovered helplessly.

Cielan cradled Avi's head, his lips parting, revealing sharp fangs.

Edmar froze, disbelieving what he was seeing as Cielan's fangs pierced Avi's neck, sinking deep into the soft flesh. *Is this really happening?*

Avi's convulsions stopped instantly, her body relaxing into the vamphyr's arms.

His stomach churned. *What is this?* He wanted to intervene, but he flicked a glance to Adria to gauge her reaction. She only looked hopeful.

A moan drew his gaze back to Avi and the vamphyr, and he became paralyzed, his mind unable to grasp what he witnessed. This wasn't just survival; it was something darker. He watched, horrified, as not only had Avi's trembling subsided, but her movements had also become sensual. She gasped, a breathless whimper escaping her.

He jerked at the unsettling noise.

Then her body arched, pressing closer to Cielan, her soft mewling sounding too much like pleasure. Cielan curled her tighter to him, his mouth fastened to her neck, drinking from her. There was something so disturbingly intimate in the way her body responded to each pull of her blood, as if the pain had given way to deep, consuming euphoria.

Strange heat thickened the air, charged with unspoken tension. The scene both horrifying and uncomfortably intimate. He tore his gaze away, his pulse pounding in his ears.

He didn't understand how this macabre exchange could be helping. But Avi's response... she seemed lost in ecstasy.

Then Avi sighed, relaxing, tension draining away. Slowly, Cielan withdrew, his fangs slipping free from her neck with a quiet sound that sent a shiver down

Edmar's spine. The vamphyr licked the two puncture marks before loosening his grip enough for Adria to wipe the blood from Avi's face.

Nestled in Cielan's arms, Avi seemed serene, peacefully asleep. He rose to find a tree to sit against, keeping her close to his chest.

The heat faded, leaving Edmar to grapple with what he'd witnessed with Avi's words. His heart still raced. *The Metal Stone is a diversion... the god awakens...*

New chills touched his spine. For many millennia, the gods, save the Sun God, had slumbered. What did their awakening portend? He wished he had time to decipher the warning. As Adria relaxed, Edmar raised his eyebrows questioningly.

"Seers are common in my husband's Moon Fae lineage," she said. "Avi's visions are increasing. It's what brought us here, after hearing Isa left Atheria."

He remembered Adria's husband, half-Moon Fae, half-human. "Will she explain her words when she wakes?"

"She should, but she won't remember what she's even said."

"You won't question her, dragon," Cielan said sharply, his face placid.

His fangs were hidden, but Edmar wondered... Did the vamphyr use them to attack others? He didn't trust Cielan, but knew the vamphyr outmatched him. The twinkle in Cielan's eyes acknowledged his power.

Adria hugged herself, shivering.

"I fear these visions are killing her, but I don't know what to do." Her voice broke, tears glittering on her bottom eyelashes. "Her human side can't handle the magic."

"That's why I'm here," Cielan said. "I'll keep her alive, with her consent."

Avi's mixed heritage highlighted the dangers of interspecies mingling. It reminded him of what he'd lost.

"Dragons mate for life, but we only develop that bond within our species." He swallowed past the lump in his throat. The Snow Princess's curse forced unnatural bonds. In a low voice, he told them about the son he'd lost, a babe who barely took a breath before his heart failed. "We weren't meant to mate with humans."

"I'm so sorry, Edmar. I didn't know."

"You were hiding as you needed to be during the Summer Fae Wars."

Adria drank from a discarded wineskin, her gaze fixed westward.

"There are other bonds," she said. "My husband and I, we're Soul Halves."

The Moon Fae's notion. A single soul, split before birth, destined to reunite, life after life. Adria's gaze sought her other half, looking back the way they had come.

He no longer believed in fate. Emira had entered his life twice by chance—or misfortune—and each time had brought only chaos.

Now it was time for retribution.

He eyed the wineskin, then dismissed the urge. It would be hard to wrap his hands around Emira's throat if he couldn't see straight.

Chapter 47

EMMY

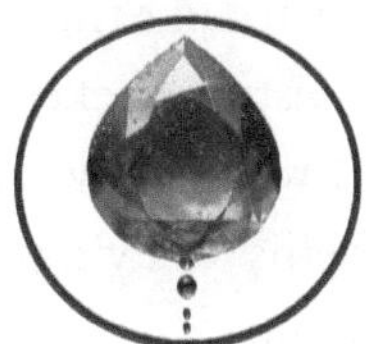

The siren's song vibrated through Emmy, relaxing her tail, lulling her into a languor.

> "Adventure calls, the heart's desire,
> Come, let us set the world on fire.
> In shadows deep, where dreams entwine,
> Together, we'll weave a tale divine."

She yearned to reach the Summer Child, lifting her arms with a smile, ready to serve.

Her eyes flew open.

The Summer Child's dulcet voice continued, an echo in her mind, then distant in the cave tunnel. Rivus snored softly, leaning against the cave wall.

The song's tempo increased.

> "Embrace the call of the endless sea,
> Where woes dissolve and spirits flee.
> With me, dear Emmy, find release,
> In my embrace, find sweet peace."

A stronger haze fell over her mind. She stood, instinctively following the song. Pain stabbed her feet as she tiptoed, then danced lightly through the tunnels. Fire acid simmered in her muscles.

As she ventured deeper, the air thickened with scents of damp earth, ancient minerals, and a faint, underlying heat that seemed to emanate from the very stone itself. She shivered, though the fire acid in her veins often kept her warm. It was as if the earth itself held a secret fire, waiting to be unleashed.

The passageways wound and twisted like the coils of a sea serpent. Phosphorescent moss cast eerie glows from moisture-slickened walls, brighter than the silver swirls on her skin. The gurgling of water grew louder, intertwined with the siren song. Ocean tides moved in her veins, drawing her ever closer to briny streams. The air tasted tangy, infused with salt.

Hours passed, each sense heightening. She walked and walked. Pain faded as the song rooted itself in her soul, replacing all other needs with an all-consuming yearning.

Time ceased to exist. Exhaustion was meaningless. Her muscles quivered, but she continued. Perhaps this would have been the rest of her life.

She'd never know because a woman collided with her in the dark tunnels and knocked her out of her trance. She staggered, suppressing a cry. Fire acid surged in her blood. Clarity returned, bringing agonizing pain. She retreated into meditation, whimpering. Everything hurt. Her feet, her calves, her backside. *How long did I walk?*

Her stomach growled, her mouth parched. *So weak.*

First, she had to control her pain, suppress her power. As fire acid simmered, the other woman's muttering made meditating difficult. She opened her eyes.

Under the moss's bioluminescent glow, they stared at each other.

The woman resembled a Fire Fae. Tall, ebony-skinned. Strikingly beautiful. But her hair, long black curls framing braided sections adorned with gold beads, didn't resemble a living flame, and it remained still.

Her hands were bound together with silver bracelets.

An instinctive shiver coursed through Emmy. Danger emanated from this woman. Despite her beauty, she possessed a lethal aura, like a hidden ocean current concealing strength before surging forth.

The woman's golden eyes glinted with disciplined intensity, reminding her of her own years of training to remain immovable. She knew this fae could kill her easily, even bound.

That realization chilled her despite the fire acid in her muscles.

The fae held up her hands, glancing at her gem. Urgency laced her words. "Can you remove my bonds?"

She hesitated, her heart pounding. Using her magic was risky. What if she lost control? Memories of past accidents, her father's fear in unguarded moments, flashed through her mind.

She empathized, nodding. *Without Gilly and Anjali's support, I would still be trapped, or dead.*

Freeing the fae would also ease her own pain.

The fae approached, hands raised, her steps measured and deliberate, radiating a quiet confidence. Emmy touched the cold metal. *Moonsilver.* She'd never seen any before. It suppressed any magical creature's powers.

What magic does she possess? Her unmoving hair suggested she wasn't fully fae, but some mixed and hybrid fae still had magic, although diminished compared to full fae.

She grasped the bands, her hands shaking, power surging beneath her fingertips. "My magic is unpredictable. This will hurt."

"Free me, and I won't care."

She was under no illusion this fae could kill her without hesitation. *Is it wise to help?*

Abruptly, a gentle softness unmasked the fae's guarded features. "I understand risking much for little hope. I've taken that risk many times in my life."

She held up her bound hands, her gaze pleading.

May the gods above and below take me quickly if I fail...

Inhaling deeply, she channeled the fire acid through her blood and past the barrier of her skin, her heart pounding with power and fear. Stinging pain seized her muscles, but she gritted her teeth. "What's your name?"

"Nira." The Fire Fae's mouth snapped shut on anything else she would have said, and her lips thinned. Her only response as molten fire ate through the metal, singeing her skin. Burned flesh filled the air. Nira shook free the seared metal, blood trailing down her wrists.

Emmy flinched at the sight, her stomach churning. *Will the fae be angry?*

She met Nira's golden gaze, searching for anger or resentment.

Nira's eyes narrowed, but her expression remained soft. "Thank you."

The words offered little comfort. "No moving hair, an odd name for a Fire Fae, and red blood. Are you a mixed or hybrid fae?"

Nira laughed, the sound incongruous in the shadowed, damp tunnel. Emmy jumped, startled.

"I'm a Fa Fa Fa," the fae said, her voice tinged with bitterness.

She searched her memories for her lessons on fae lineage. "I don't know that species."

Nira's lips twitched into a wry smile, her eyes glinting with a mix of mischief and sadness. "Not a species. I'm a Failed Fire Fae. Born without magic."

Her voice was light, mocking, a bitter joke she repeated at her own expense. Nira's humor pierced the tension, and Emmy smiled. Then her smile faded. "But how is that possible? Fae are magical."

"Not all are blessed. And not all curses are visible." Those golden eyes studied her. "But curses can be broken, can't they?" Her gaze slid to the glowing moss. A flicker of something fierce, almost predatory, glinted in her eyes. "And sometimes, from the ashes of one curse, a different power can rise."

Nira spun, steadying herself, holding out her stiff hands, fingers closed together.

A dark blur shot toward Nira, striking with the deadly precision of a shark. An unseen force hurled her upward, slamming her against the ceiling. She hung for a moment, then collapsed to the ground, limp. Blood streamed down Nira's face, stark red against her dark skin.

Clawed fingers dug into Emmy's arms from behind. A whisper brushed across her ears. "She calls you, and you cannot escape her."

Then pain pierced Emmy's neck; teeth sank into her skin. She reached up instinctively. Her fingers brushed cold, unyielding flesh. Panic seized her as the world slowed—the bite, the breached skin, the intimate violation of her body. Fear surged, mingled with a bizarre warmth spreading from the wound.

Her mouth had parted for a silent scream, but now a calming euphoria muddled her senses, her body melting against the cold wall holding her. The pain faded to a dull throb, replaced by a confusing comfort, her limbs heavy, thoughts hazy.

Warmth swept through her, an unexpected sensation, invasive yet soothing. Visions of Edmar filled her mind—his hands gentle on her skin, his lips pressing softly against hers. She moaned, surrendering to the sensations, but the desire vanished. Her mind, a swirling vortex, struggled to comprehend. Fear warred with submission, as if her body had betrayed her.

Suddenly, she fell to her hands and knees, free of the cold wall, the rocky floor digging into her palms, her breathing labored.

The world spun. Hearing the sound of retching brought her back. The Summer Child's protector, on her hands and knees, expelled a dark liquid, her black wings trembling.

The woman's head snapped up, her eyes black voids, pinning Emmy in place. "You are cursed," she said, her fangs stained black.

"My magic is a curse."

The woman moved with blurring speed, wiping her hand across her mouth.

Emmy remembered the sting of teeth on her throat. She touched her neck, wincing as her fingers came away wet with her blood.

"Did you bite me?" she whispered, her voice filled with disbelief.

"Your magic isn't cursed. *You* are. And you're far from a worthy vessel for my charge."

The words struck Emmy like a blow, sending a shiver of dread down her spine. The darkness in the strange woman's eyes left her breathless, her own fears about her curse echoing in the sudden silence that followed. "Who are you?"

Sniffing the air, the woman ignored her, spun, then knelt beside Nira, licking the blood from her cheek. A disturbingly intimate act. The woman growled, a feral sound, then sank her teeth into Nira's neck. The fae stirred, whimpering, but didn't wake.

As if drawing from an ancient, forbidden well, the winged woman drank deeply from the fae's neck, her throat convulsing as she swallowed blood. Nira arched beneath her in a haunting dance of pain and need. She moaned the way Emmy knew she'd moaned when Edmar kissed her.

Desperate to help Nira, she charged at the other woman, only to be flung back by a black wing crashing her into the wall. She gasped, doubling over and struggling for air as the woman collected Nira into her arms.

Black eyes locked on her. "Don't come looking for the Summer Child."

Then she vanished.

CHAPTER 48

EDMAR

After hours of fruitless searching along the northern border, the line between his kingdom and Kalden's northern realm, without a trace of Emira or Rivus, Edmar returned to the golden Sun Temple. He landed in a secluded forest clearing nearby as sunlight faded, the familiar tug of transformation seizing him.

With a gut-wrenching lurch, his body contorted and twisted, scales and claws giving way to flesh and bone in a flash of golden light. The transformation was never pleasant, but tonight, it mirrored the turmoil raging within him. His fists clenched with each shift, his jaw tight. Now fully sober, rage and anguish churned within him.

Memories, once buried and sunk in the depths of his Frostlands, now surged like a frozen tide of ice, eroding his resolve. They came unbidden—his parents' death, his previous wives' faces, his son's tiny form going cold in his arms. He doubled over, a guttural sob tearing from his throat as the losses resurfaced with cruel clarity. Memories whispered, intertwined with the rustling leaves, demanding to be felt. Tears stung his eyes, blurring his vision.

His steps faltered with each jagged breath, the rough bark of trees scraping against his palms as he leaned on them for support. The contact sparked not pain, but raw, simmering anger. *Emira. Rivus.* Names echoing with each heartbeat. Bitterness filled his mouth.

One moment, he shook with fury, visions of vengeance vivid against the treachery. The next, his shoulders slumped and despair numbed him, sapping his strength. He wavered between these two extremes, caught in their merciless tug-of-war.

Beneath the rage and despair, a flicker of doubt remained, a longing for the love he'd lost. He craved closure, answers to questions tormenting him.

Why did Emira leave me after declaring her love? Why did Rivus betray me after centuries of friendship?

What did it say about him that the two people he trusted more than anyone had both deceived him so easily?

Answers he may never receive. But he wouldn't give up.

Emerging from the forest's cloak, he found no comfort in the oppressive vastness of the night sky. The stars he loved so much now reflected his grief. Vengeance beckoned at the edges of his sorrow, a sinister solace with the promise of retribution.

Resolve hardened within him as he approached the temple. An orange-robed monk led him to one of the four golden spires, where Father Jayasurya awaited him.

Standing in the Chamber of Reflection's entrance, the abbot bowed over his clasped hands. "Welcome back, Your Majesty."

He followed the abbot into the opulent chamber, its intricate tapestries and golden-framed artwork a jarring juxtaposition to his turmoil. The Sun God's blessings mocked him. Broken promises, denied dreams. Peace and comfort eluded him. Shadows from flickering candles distorted the windows' stained-glass images. Heavy incense choked the air, stifling peace and clarity.

Father Jayasurya closed a book on the table, its golden inlays shimmering like the gold dust on the dark carpets.

Earlier, Adria and Avi headed east. Avi, her cerulean eyes curious, tilted her head. "The time will be short until we see each other again."

He hadn't known any Moon Seers in his life, so he hadn't known how to interpret her words. He hoped they meant he'd find Emira and Rivus soon.

"Any news from the border settlements?" he now asked the abbot, hoping his orders to track Emira and Rivus would have yielded something.

"Nothing, Your Majesty."

"Then my search continues."

The theft of the Sun Stone was a dual blow, the loss of a sacred artifact and a threat to the kingdom's harmony. Its absence clouded the future with uncertainty.

Concern etched Father Jayasurya's features, and he adjusted his golden mantle. "The council manages the kingdom in your absence, but how long before you return?"

"I won't return until the Sun Stone is recovered and justice is done." He clenched his jaw and traced the golden inlays on the table with one finger. "I appoint you, Father Jayasurya, as head of the council. I'll prepare the necessary documents for you to take back to the Emerald Palace."

The abbot bowed, his palms pressed together.

"Warn the people about the dwarves breaching their treaty. Settlements closer to the Malustra Woods need to be prepared. I also need you to investigate any trade in the Dwarven snow or black powder. The same used to distract everyone during the Sun Stone theft." The empty tubes that held the fireworks also lay on the table. "You'll have to dig deep into underground trading. Find out everything you can—who's selling, who's buying, where it's going. Unearth the truth."

"I will do as you ask." Father Jayasurya slipped his hands into his saffron robe's wide sleeves. "May I ask what you plan to do when you locate the queen?"

Vengeance flashed before him. He'd felt something genuine with Emira, but her actions... "She'll receive the same punishment as anyone else who would steal the Sun Stone."

"You would execute your queen? Is it only justice motivating you?"

Could he truly condemn her to such a fate? Fleeting images of her smile, the warmth in her eyes flashed through his mind. He shook his head. It was all a lie. "Nothing matters more than justice."

The abbot raised his brows. "Not even your heart?"

"It doesn't matter," he said, looking away. "She's a traitor."

The abbot sighed. "Guard your soul, Your Majesty. Vengeance can hollow a man as thoroughly as love can fill him. We need a whole king, not a broken avenger."

A human monk entered the room, bowing. "Forgive the interruption, Father, but dwarves are attacking Sarineton."

Freaking dwarves! Sarineton was less than an hour away.

Father Jayasurya hid his hands in the wide sleeves of his orange robes. "You did well, Brother. How many?"

"At least a dozen. We can spare eight men from the temple to aid Sarineton."

"Make that nine," Edmar said, capturing both men's attention. "I will lead them."

Father Jayasurya scrutinized him.

"I will deal with this threat, then continue my search."

The abbot bowed over clasped hands. "Is there anything I can do to help you? Some words of wisdom about a quest for vengeance?"

He might have responded with any number of things, but vengeance was his steady companion now—after satisfying his need to protect his people and taste blood at the same time. "Do you have any silver?"

Father Jayasurya shrugged, hands sweeping out. "We are in the Sun Temple, surrounded by gold, the radiance of our Father. Do you think we have silver here?"

Chapter 49

EMMY

Silence followed the departure of the Summer Child's protector and Nira. Emmy inhaled deeply, centering herself. She'd used her magic to free Nira, leaving her with none to defend herself against the strange woman. Not that she could have threatened her anyway, not against someone who moved faster than the wind and drank the blood of her victims.

She'd never encountered such a creature in all her lessons.

Breathing evenly, she assessed her aching body. Bruises and scrapes, nothing serious. But her magic was dormant. Satisfied, she stood, surveying the tunnel. *Which way out?*

Retracing her steps, she winced at the pain in her feet. But she quickly became hopelessly lost with each new turn and curve. She barely recalled the descent under the Summer Child's spell. *A siren song?*

Just like the Blue Angel tavern owner had described. The information did little to clarify the mystery. Understanding her didn't matter anymore. The protector had released Emmy.

Now to escape.

Panic seized her. She was lost, and her bag, with the Sun Stone, was left behind with Rivus. She forced herself to calm down, her fire acid smoldering under her skin. *Escape first, worry later.*

Tentatively, she tested her sense of the ocean, moving away from it at every fork. The soles of her feet felt sliced into ribbons. Her muscles screamed. Good thing she healed quickly, a benefit of the merfolk she wasn't sure she still had until the bite marks on her neck closed up.

Exhaustion settled deep in her bones with every step, her legs and eyelids heavy. She yawned repeatedly. *How long have I walked?*

And what did Rivus think of her disappearance?

The thought led to Edmar. She'd avoided thinking about him, which had been easy to do while they chased the Sun Stone, but now...

But now, alone and lost in the dark tunnels, she thought of him. Did he miss her? She'd left without a word, sending her sister in her place. Did he know she'd taken the Sun Stone?

Only Rivus knew her plans. He might not connect her to the theft, but he'd be angry. Either way, he would have been upset at her deception.

He must hate her now.

No matter. Her destructive magic was the priority. She shivered, forcing herself onward. Once more, her fate had nearly been wrested from her control. The Summer Child could have never been an alternative to the Sea Witch's quest, but she had tried to force Emmy to go to her.

The Sea Witch wasn't much better, but what choice did she have?

You'd be better off seeking your Father God. The echo of Malala's words.

That could be a better option. If she ever found her way out and back to the Sun Stone.

She trudged for hours through tunnels blanketed in phosphorus moss, the ocean's pull fading. Perhaps she was nearing the surface, but nothing looked familiar.

Scratches echoed from the walls, growing louder. Then she entered a new tunnel, devoid of the phosphorescent moss. Only the faint glow of her skin's silver swirls accompanied her stumbles through the darkness. She held back her trepidation and fear by keeping one hand on the wall, the knife points in her soles a reminder she was alive, that she still had time.

From the darkness ahead, an ominous scraping intensified and echoed, approaching rapidly. She froze, heart pounding.

Her instinct was to summon her magic, but between the suppression of the Sea Witch's spell and exhaustion, she was powerless, vulnerable, her magic dormant.

What in all eight hells ever made me believe I could take on the Sea Witch's quest? What did she know of this world?

Claws clacked rhythmically, growing louder. A guttural growl, then a spine-chilling hiss. She trembled. Cold, sharp terror spurred her to action. She turned and fled, trying to summon her magic, but it was useless. Her boots slipped on loose stones. Her frantic, aching footsteps pounded a desperate tempo in the dark.

Despite her punishing pace, the ominous scraping intensified—louder, closer—a relentless echo in the dark tunnel as the creature gained ground.

She gasped for breath, her boots thudding against uneven ground, echoing her racing heartbeat. Each step a battle against the dread of the suffocating darkness. Her world narrowed to the relentless pursuit of the unseen horror. Primal fear, unlike anything she had ever known, consumed her mind.

A rock caught her foot, sending her sprawling. Pain exploded through her as she hit the ground. Groaning, she rolled onto her back, just as a hulking, shadowy form towered above her.

She screamed.

Fire acid surged, a desperate attempt to defend herself. But a fleeting spark quickly extinguished itself. Her heart pounded against her ribs. She threw up her hands, but fetid breath, smelling of decay, washed over her. Rough fur brushed her cheek. Spindly legs encircled her, trapping her against the cold ground.

Terror froze her, the creature's gaping maw a dark abyss. She faced death, and only one thought filled her mind.

Edmar. His smile, his warmth, his passion.

What might have been? He'll never know I died here, alone and thinking of him.

The spindly legs tapped the rocky ground. Sharp teeth sank into her arm. She screamed, praying to all the gods.

A thunderous roar, snarling fury.

A massive shadow slammed into the creature, the tunnel echoing with screeches and snapping jaws. A savage symphony of survival.

Hulking forms clashed in the darkness.

She scooted away, clutching her arm. Hope flickered.

The battle raged, with ferocious snarls, tearing flesh. She crawled away, wincing at the pain shooting through her arm.

The uproar ceased, replaced by unnerving silence. She froze, her breath catching. *Is it over?*

Lingering dread of what lay in the darkness and what would come next made her chest heave.

Soft padding sounds grew louder and more distinct with each heartbeat. She squeezed her eyes shut, praying to the gods again for another reprieve.

A cold nose nudged her cheek, and she shrieked.

In the stretched silence, she dared to look. An enormous wolf loomed above her. She whimpered in relief.

If that was Rivus, she could kiss him.

CHAPTER 50

EDMAR

Frigid air, a comforting chill against his simmering rage, clung to Edmar like a shroud. Three moons had risen since Emira and Rivus had shattered his world, fleeing with the Sun Stone and leaving a gaping wound in his soul. The icy wind mirrored the storm within, a storm craving release.

Sarineton, a human village, was a cluster of huddled shadows against the darkness, fear lingering in the air like woodsmoke. The dwarves were bold, attacking so close to the Sun Temple. Grim satisfaction filled him. They would pay for their audacity, and their blood would serve as a meager offering to his anger.

He turned to the eight soldiers who accompanied him, apprehension etched on their faces. Lambs to the slaughter, pawns to support their enraged king.

"Stay close," he commanded, his voice a low growl the wind seemed to snatch away. "And try to keep up."

His magic crackled around him, a dark blue aura punctuated with pinpricks of gold, like a starry night descended upon the battlefield. The Blue Angel did not come this night. Layers of duty and honor usually bound him, now forgotten. A thousand years of festering rage, of suppressed emotions sure to drive anyone insane, erupted, and the Blue Devil emerged, the weapon needed to harness his rage.

He surged forward into the night, boots crunching on the path, each footfall a drumbeat to impending violence. Dwarven voices, the clang of weapons, echoed through the trees.

Ice crystals formed in his hands, each sting heralding the surge of power within. He closed his eyes, picturing Emira's musical laugh, Rivus's easy smile. He imagined the way they looked at each other.

Had there been any shared glances he missed? Secretive longing, looks he hadn't even noticed, which excluded him, mocked him. The ice sharpened, becoming jagged shards, each one a vessel of his fury.

He burst into the clearing, dwarves battling villagers. Men and women. Young and old.

An explosion rocked the village, a house erupting in flames. An orange glow lit the scene of chaos. The metallic smell of black powder filled the air. Terrified villagers tugged on his protective instincts. He focused past them to the nearest dwarf, who swung a two-bladed axe.

In a whirlwind of frost and fury, he launched his ice daggers. The shards pierced the dwarf's armor, burying deep in his back. He fell, his axe landing inches from a young man. No satisfaction filled him from his first kill, only a growing hunger for more. He sprang forward with another ice shard in his fist.

The Sun Temple's soldiers followed, bellowing their allegiance, joining the fray.

A bulky dwarf emerged from the dark house closest to Edmar, dragging a child behind him.

"Mommy!" Terror in her cry.

Without thought, Edmar slammed the shard of ice through the dwarf's neck, puncturing all the way through with a gush of blood splattering Edmar's face.

The child screamed, fleeing back into the house.

The dwarves finally noticed him as the biggest threat. Several encircled him, their eyes burning with battle lust.

He relished their attention, spinning in a dance of frost and destruction, his ice shards erupting from his hands, deadly daggers. Each one found its mark—a throat, an eye, a heart. He didn't just disable, he destroyed. A macabre waltz of death, with winter as his partner.

Their gazes itched along his neck, villagers, soldiers, dwarves.

The Blue Devil inspired awe and terror.

I'm not the honorable king they knew, the protector of the realm.

A shot of guilt twisted deep within him, but it was pushed into his Frostlands so he could embrace his anger and become a force of nature. He was a winter storm given human form, leaving a trail of frozen corpses in its wake. He didn't slow down, not even after a circle of dwarves lay bloody and broken on the ground. Blood painted the grass and pooled in the soil, his boots sloshing through thick mud.

A scream pierced the air.

One of the temple soldiers, barely more than a boy, lay crumpled, a gaping wound in his side. He pleaded for help, for the mercy of his king.

That king is dying. But he hesitated. A war raged within him; the man he once was battling the monster he was becoming.

The monster won. He saw an opportunity to attack the dwarves driving his way, easy prey on the ground, not a life in need of saving.

"Your deaths will be swift!" he roared, his voice echoing through the chaos.

He summoned a blizzard of ice shards, each one shimmering with deadly promise. A lure to the remaining dwarves who had yet to join those charging him. Dwarven war cries filled the air.

He met them head-on, a storm of ice and death. Moving like a wraith, he froze their sweat, encasing them in ice. His eyes burned with a cold fire, mirroring winter.

The young soldier's cries were lost in the cacophony, his pain a mere footnote amid destruction. Edmar fought with a ferocious madness, each kill fueling his rage.

The dwarves thought to flee, but he hunted each one down and slaughtered them in their flight. Then the last dwarf fell, and silence descended upon the village, broken only by crackling flames and whimpers. In the carnage's center, he stood, chest heaving, face splattered with blood. A grim smile twisted at his success.

When he looked down at the young soldier from the temple, who now lay still, his eyes vacant, victory tasted bitter. A hollowness grew beneath Edmar's smile until it slipped from his face.

The remaining soldiers from the Sun Temple regarded him with wariness. He had become the winter he wielded, cold, unforgiving, and utterly ruthless. So he turned away from their condemnation and gazed at the starry sky, the constellation of the doomed lovers shimmering above. The same stars Emira would see, wherever she was, whatever she was doing with Rivus.

A bitter memory of their shared wonder under these stars flashed through his mind. Resentment surged through him. He was no longer the man who had loved his best friend and wife. He was the king who would destroy them.

Raking his hand through his sweat-soaked hair, he pushed it back from his forehead. When he lowered his hand, he stared at a bead of sweat tracing a clean line through the blood and grime on his palm. It rolled down to his wrist.

A single path through the crimson horror darkening against his blue skin. A single virtuous path offering a way to emerge from the fury that had bathed him in blood.

He swiped at the sweat, smearing it all together.

CHAPTER 51

EMMY

Emmy gasped, lying helpless as the near-black tunnel pressed in around her. Damp earth and decay filled her nostrils, her senses sharp and elevated with lingering fear. Cold seeped into her bones, an unwelcome chill that churned her nausea. She was so tired of being afraid, but she had to push—had to escape before something else found her.

Rivus, in wolf form, stood beside her as she rose, the monster's bite throbbing in her arm. She staggered, leaning against the damp wall, struggling to calm her pounding heart. The large, shadowy wolf rubbed against her leg, offering comfort. His heavy breath mingled with the distant drip of water from the tunnel ceiling. Haunting melodies in the oppressive silence.

She was grateful, but why had he come back for her? He could have taken the Sun Stone and left her to die.

A distant noise stalled her breath. Sweat lined her palms, thinking of what might still lurk in the shadows. The wolf backed away, dry twigs snapping followed by a squelching sound. She shuddered as Rivus shifted back.

"Here," he said, thrusting her leather pack against her chest.

She sighed with relief after she found both Edmar's shirt and the iron box with the Sun Stone. She drank greedily of her waterskin, then shouldered her pack as an ungodly moan echoed in the tunnels.

"Quickly now!" The low rumble of Rivus's voice resonated with urgency. He grabbed her wrist and pulled her along. "The Malustra Woods are just above us. We can't linger, or more of those creatures will find us."

He guided them through the dark, winding tunnels. The walls closed around her, much like her own fate, a labyrinth she continued to lose control over.

The Malustra Woods. She had traveled far beneath the land. Dangerous territory, where wild magic twisted animals into monstrous creatures. Only the dragon statues encircling the forest kept the animals bound within. Hours passed, punctuated by the occasional glow of luminescent moss. Adrenaline faded, leaving a dull throbbing of weariness and stuttered thoughts. Her feet ached with every step, a bed of knives beneath her soles, her steps sluggish. At least the monster's bite in her arm healed at a rapid rate.

"Hurry."

Exhaustion clouded her mind. She attempted to match Rivus's pace, but an invisible anchor dragged her down, almost rooting her to the spot like the heavy chains and rocks hooked into her scales back at the little palace. When next they stopped to drink water, the world spun and her eyelids fluttered closed.

"Emmy." His voice, a hand on her shoulder, woke her.

She had slumped against the dark tunnel wall but now straightened, heart pounding as she remembered where she was. "I'm so tired."

With a hand clamped onto Rivus's wrist for support, she stood, wincing at the sharp pain in her feet. She didn't need to see Rivus's face to feel his disapproval.

"Have you slept? It's taken me nearly two days to find you."

Confusion swirled through her foggy brain. Had she been under the song's influence that long? "I haven't slept."

Rivus huffed, a sound of exasperation rather than sympathy. "We are not safe yet. Keep moving."

He gripped her elbow and pulled her along.

A spark of her fire acid snapped in her muscles. *Now it appears!* Not earlier when she needed it against... whatever that was in the tunnel. At least it warded against some of her exhaustion. "What was that?"

"Spider mole."

She shuddered. A nightmare of fur, fangs, and too many legs. How many more lurked in the dark? Shivering again, she allowed him to drag her along, almost grateful for the additional aid. Luminescent moss provided intermittent light, casting dancing shadows.

Two days in these tunnels. The thought was dizzying. Only thirteen days remained before the Sea Witch's spell would no longer hold her volatile magic at bay. Was it enough time? Enough to find the Metal Stone, to wake Metallon? Doubt gnawed at her.

How does one even wake a god?

Rivus's steady pressure kept her moving, but her thoughts drifted to Malala. "I saw you with the Snow Princess."

"Not me."

No, he's right. Sometimes her memories with the Water Fae were hazy, and she seemed to forget a lot of what was said. But she remembered the wolf's differences now, the curled lapis lazuli tail. "Who then?"

He tightened his grip, shaking her arm, but didn't answer.

"More secrets, Rivus?" She would have crossed her arms if they weren't treading dark tunnels so fast. "You know all of mine."

"Do I?"

No. "What do you mean?"

"Care to explain why you disappeared?" Rivus asked, his casualness masking an accusation. His concern was not for her safety but rather, for whatever reason, he refused to leave her on her own.

She barely recalled waking up and following the Summer Child's song. "I think I was under a siren spell."

Her confession said aloud left a residue of dread and confusion. How could she have been so easily manipulated, so utterly controlled? The notion seemed absurd, yet the melody had woven through her consciousness, undeniable and compelling. The thought left her feeling vulnerable and shaken.

Rivus scoffed, releasing her. "A siren underground?"

His disbelief stung. "Do you think me so easily deceived? I didn't have a choice."

"Who could have that power?"

"The Summer Child."

Rivus missed a step but quickly regained his rhythm, albeit slower. "The Summer Child?" His tone became guarded. "You've seen her?"

Perhaps she shouldn't have revealed information about the Summer Child, but she thought he knew already because the Snow Princess knew about her dreams with the powerful child. "Only once. She's been in my dreams since then."

"She used a siren song? Down here? Is that where you saw her?" Now his step lagged, almost stopping.

"No. She's much further away. And she has a powerful protector."

Even without seeing him clearly, she knew he wrestled with something. Did he want to find the Summer Child instead? She still didn't understand his motives, but she didn't want to lose his support right now. "Rivus, we need to escape."

A large sigh. "Of course."

Silence chased their footsteps for many turns and twists before he spoke again. "You cannot go to the Summer Child."

He doesn't know I'd already decided against going to the Summer Child. The Snow Princess didn't know either. A realization that offered insight. The Snow Princess knew a lot about her, but it seemed she only knew what happened in Emmy's dreams and whatever Rivus and any of her other spies told her.

I guess I have more secrets. What secrets did Rivus keep? Could he answer her questions? "I thought sirens only affected men. Why was I entranced?"

"You're thinking of mermaids, the offspring of Metallon and Aqua."

"The Summer Child is not a mermaid?" No mermaid laid such a large egg, but there were similarities.

His fingers flexed tighter on her elbow, then loosened. "The Summer Child is something different. The myths claim her mother was the first mermaid, a love child between Chaos and Aqua. And the Summer Gods were her fathers."

Two fathers? How? But the merfolk had their own story about the first mermaid. "Our legends say the first mermaid died in a war between the Sun and Fire Gods. There's no mention of a child."

He grunted, the sound echoing. His silence, his ambiguity, unnerved her.

Her feet and arm burned. Fire acid thrummed in her veins, a slow, burning throb. How much longer before she lost control? The Sea Witch promised she had until the end of the lunar cycle, but each flare came stronger than the last. The intermittent pain in her muscles kept her awake and provided the only positive note of her growing magic.

Her gem flickered, dark red light pulsing, then vanishing. Rivus must have seen it. He said nothing. Neither did she.

Then, he stopped abruptly. His posture stiffened, eyes scanning the blackness ahead.

"We're close to an exit." His voice lowered. "But we're still in Malustra Woods. And we're not alone."

CHAPTER 52

EMMY

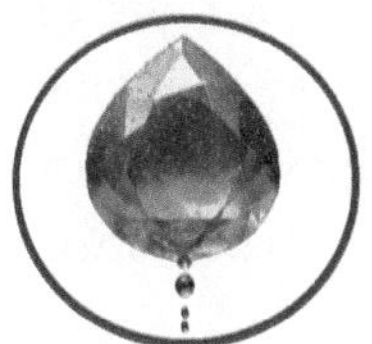

The tunnel brightened gradually, revealing a small cave cluttered with barrels and boxes. Her gem's glow flickered, casting Rivus's silhouette—broad shoulders, muscular back, and... round, brown buttocks—as he dressed.

"Eyes closed, Princess!" Rivus didn't look at her as he snapped the words.

She smirked. Even the werewolf wasn't immune to human modesty. But then, tiny shocks prickled beneath her skin. Magic pulsed like fire in her veins, heating her muscles. It ebbed and flowed, restless as the tide.

Lying on the cool earth, she closed her eyes, breathing deeply. She centered herself and visualized wild flames calming into a gentle glow, waning with each heartbeat and each slow breath. Her magic subsided.

He eyed her curiously where she lay on the ground. "Do you have the mirror?"

The mirror? She frowned.

"The mirror, Princess. The one I gave you to see Edmar?"

Her breath froze. Hadn't she fallen asleep with it in her hand? "It wasn't where I slept?"

"No."

"I must have had it with me when the siren song entranced me, but I don't remember having it when I came out of the trance." She offered an apologetic look. "I must have lost it somewhere in the tunnels."

Rivus's hands balled before he shook them out, running one through his shaggy hair. A tremor of unease entered his voice. "We're on our own."

Her stomach rumbled, reminding her she hadn't eaten in days.

He wiped a hand over his face. "Touch nothing, all right."

"But there are supplies."

"This is another pack's territory. They will smell us next time they come here. If anything's been touched or is missing, they will come after us."

She sat up with a huff and drank from her waterskin.

"What were you doing lying there on the ground, anyway?" he asked.

She grimaced. Warning him was the right thing to do. She never wanted to kill another living being, no matter how annoying or untrustworthy. The image of her mother melting in front of her would haunt her for the rest of her life. "You felt my magic before. It's returning. Not as strong, but it intensifies when I move." *Or with strong negative emotions...*

He threw his hands up into the air. "Great! Not only do I have to babysit a manipulative, deceitful princess, who loses precious artifacts, and then see us through these dangerous woods, but now I have to watch my back, too."

She narrowed her eyes, all her gratitude and remorse gone. "I didn't ask for your help."

"Believe me," he said, crossing his arms and looking down on her, "I wouldn't be here if I had a choice."

"Why are you still here?"

Rivus inhaled deeply. "I'm ensuring your departure from Agondray, permanently."

Each word, every intonation, each inflection hit her and soured in her ears. His words, though true, held a hidden meaning. "Is this about Edmar? You don't want me to break his curse."

Rivus gripped her arm, sharp claws pricking her skin through the coarse linen shirt as he pulled her to her feet.

"Let me go." She yanked at his grip, but his iron hold didn't budge. Her pulse roared in her ears, the same helplessness, the same fear. Her mother's fate flashed behind her eyes.

"I'm tired of your games."

"You play the Snow Princess's games." Silence met her challenge, so she asked, "Who was the wolf with Malala?"

"The reason for everything I do." He dragged her from the cave. "Now stop testing me. These games need to stop."

Sunlight struggled to penetrate the dense canopy as Rivus dragged her through the snowy forest. Shadowed patches of snow piled up against trees. The cold air was welcome, but her isolation, her dependence on someone who despised her, chilled her. She never wanted to depend on anyone again, a burden to those responsible for her.

"What games?" she asked, forcing her voice steady.

"Whatever game you played with Edmar's heart. Whatever game you failed when you attempted to steal the Sun Stone. Whatever game you started with the Summer Child."

"None of that—"

"I'm done!"

"Rivus, listen—"

He spun her, grip bruising, lifting her onto her toes. His face flushed red, canine teeth sharpening as he snarled. "I don't care, Princess. You're leaving on the first ship leaving Agondray, so I can finally be rid of you."

His sudden release left her staggering. Rivus strode away, his broad back a silent rebuke. Loneliness washed over her. "You could have left me in the tunnels to die," she said, nearly in a whisper.

He paused, his head turning toward her but not looking at her. "Edmar cares for you."

But that makes no sense! He saved her because of Edmar, but he was making her leave Agondray because of Edmar.

And he was walking away again.

She ran to catch him, hissing at the pain in her feet. "You saved me because of Edmar, but why does that matter?"

"We don't have time for this," he said over his shoulder. "The magic here is alive, malevolent, and it will seek us out."

She rubbed her arms, then hurried after him, her chest tight, her feet aching.

They hastened through twisted, gnarled trees, the air thick with the scent of something dark, something foul. Roots and vines hidden beneath patches of snow and forest debris threatened to trip them. Whispers and rustles spoke of unseen eyes watching their every move.

She'd never seen snow. It would have been captivating if not for the menace in every shadow. Tiredness quivered in her muscles, eyelids drooping, but she didn't dare stop or complain.

Instead, she followed Rivus, knowing that was her only option right now, even if he forced her to leave Agondray. She could return to the Sea Witch with the Sun Stone, but would that be enough to save her from the creature's wrath?

Probably not. She needed the Metal God, Metallon, wherever he was. And maybe getting on that ship might buy her the time she needed before her powers fully returned.

A guttural roar shattered the silence, rattling the earth beneath her feet.

She had always known a life of safety for herself, if not for others. Her magic had always protected her.

Now, defenseless, she was terrified. First the Sea Witch, then the winged woman, the Snow Princess, the spider mole... *And something else hunts us.*

Her heart pounded with terror.

"Run!" Rivus shouted, grabbing her hand.

The roar sounded again, closer. Fury and hunger. It echoed everywhere, bouncing off the trees and closing in on them with terrifying speed.

They dodged gnarled roots clawing out of the snow and low-hanging branches reaching for them like the fingers of the woods themselves. The underbrush exploded. A grotesque amalgamation of predator and prey. A crocodile's hulking frame, dark, scaled hide glistening, paired with a stag's majestic antlers, a twisted crown reaching skyward.

Piercing green eyes, filled with malevolence, fixed on her as the weakest prey. The long, sinuous creature lunged, its jaws snapping open, revealing razor-sharp teeth.

She yelped as it closed in. A chilling hiss escaped its throat, hot on her neck, pushing her beyond her limits. A ten-foot dragon statue loomed ahead, marking the Forbidden Boundary, an invisible line of promised safety.

"Go!" Rivus shoved her forward. "I'll hold it off!"

He faced the creature and transformed, his frame twisting and expanding, bones snapping. Silver-white fur sprouted, his hands and feet morphing into claws, his new clothes shredded.

Mesmerized, she faltered as he lunged, snarling. Rivus and beast collided, a whirlwind of silver and dark scales. She ran again toward the hulking dragon statue, heart hammering, knowing she might never see him again.

Chapter 53

EMMY

Emmy crossed the invisible, magical boundary, stumbling to a halt, her heart pounding. "I made it, Rivus!"

Rivus fought desperately, then with a final leap, broke away, racing toward her, the crocodile stag snapping at his heels. The monster roared in frustration. Just as the creature lunged, Rivus crossed the boundary, an invisible barrier that held firm. The magic of the stone dragon statue. The creature skidded to a halt, pacing along the line it couldn't breach, its green eyes blazing with fury. It growled, a low rumble of thwarted rage.

Her knees buckled, and she sank to the ground. Never would she take her safety for granted again. Rivus, in his huge dire wolf form, stood unharmed beside her, but for how long?

She missed Edmar keenly at this moment. All of this would have been so much easier with him at her side. Easier for her, though it would have meant risking his safety. And of course, she wouldn't be stealing the Sun Stone.

A howl rose in the distance.

Rivus lowered his massive body next to her. His great brown eyes willing her to understand his message.

She did. His transformation had destroyed his clothes, his pack. Both were back in the Malustra Woods. He'd remain a wolf, for now, providing transportation. Hands shaking, she climbed onto his back, holding tight, legs clamped around his body, hands fisted in his fur. He loped through the forest, a haven compared to the Malustra Woods.

Fresh, crisp air cooled the heat of her veins. Her eyes drifted closed, but she fought sleep, knowing she'd fall. Time slipped as the sun descended.

A dragon roared overhead, its shadow passing over them. *Edmar.* She knew his roar by now, and her heart pounded. Rivus slowed, keeping to the forest's gloomy areas, until the dragon passed. An hour later, they reached the forest's edge, facing flat land with grass tall enough to brush their thighs. Dusk approached, long shadows edging the horizon.

After urging her down, Rivus shifted back, naked. He rummaged through her pack, pulling on her spare pants, which stopped halfway down his calves. He also donned Edmar's shirt, a near-perfect fit, but she begrudged having to share this part of Edmar with him.

"For the love of the gods," she said, "take off that shirt first before you shift."

He lifted the shirt collar to his nose to take a whiff, and his eyebrows rose. She crossed her arms, daring him to say something, but he shrugged.

"We're not safe yet," he said, sniffing the air. Wintry winds curled around them, patches of snow fading into lumpy shadows. "Nordrun. We're north of the temple. We'll head east, but there's open ground to cover."

He pointed to the shadows of buildings on the horizon. "Next stop."

Her stomach growled, and she yawned, her jaw cracking. "No more caves?"

He shook his head. "This isn't our territory."

"I thought all wolves in Agondray belonged to the Water Clan?"

"Several clans, one banner under the Water Lunarclaws. As allies, we value our independence but also our secrecy." He marched into the tall grass. "If we hurry, we'll reach the village by sundown. Hopefully, we'll avoid Edmar in his dragon form."

She struggled to keep up, pain throbbing in her feet. She focused on her breathing in measured heartbeats, centering herself.

When the sun slipped beneath the horizon, Rivus slowed. The sky opened to a sprawling canvas of twilight, painted in strokes of deep orange and dusky pink. Rivus scanned the heavens. "Edmar usually finds a space for his transformation around now. I think we're safe."

In the distance, village lights flickered and pierced the darkening sky. A beacon of hope with the fading day. Stars winked in the darkening sky. The promise of rest and food momentarily lifted her spirits.

At the border of the village, Rivus guided them through the dimly lit streets of packed earth.

"Welcome to Paxsylva," he said. "Sanctuary of the Woods. Just beyond this village lies a forest sacred to my people. We'll find more supplies there, but we can't stay, so we'll get a room for the night at the inn."

"And food?"

"Of course, Princess."

The soft murmur of evening activity surrounded them. The gentle clatter of dishes and the distant laughter of families settling down for the night. Even exhausted, she marveled at the simple single-story houses, thatched roofs, flickering lanterns.

Approaching the only multi-story building, he slowed. He cast a concerned glance back at her, his eyes reflecting the firelight. "We can't sleep long. Traveling at night gives us our best chance at evading Edmar."

Her heart sank. The inn's warm glow promised the rest she so desperately needed. She swallowed her disappointment. She understood the risks, though.

With her nod, he pushed open the heavy wooden door. The scent of roasted meat and fresh bread wafted out. Once more, her stomach gurgled as warmth enveloped her. Lanterns and a roaring fireplace illuminated the low-ceilinged room, casting a soft, golden glow over the rough-hewn wooden tables and benches.

Wood smoke mingled with conversation, raucous laughter, and clinking dishes. The people of Paxsylva gathered here in a camaraderie she'd never known.

Who were her people? The merfolk feared her. Her father disowned her. She'd betrayed the Land Bound, stolen from Edmar and had hurt him, if he truly loved her.

She had no one, no people.

She swallowed hard as Rivus directed her to a table, then spoke to the innkeeper.

He was the only one by her side. The only one who cared to keep her alive. And he despised her as much as she disliked him.

She belonged nowhere.

What was the value of her life?

Curious glances landed on them, quieting some of the noise. Clearly intrigued by her, the patrons seemed unsure what to make of her, a being both familiar and wholly alien.

By existing, I cause more harm than good. How could she be different?

When her magic was gone. But would there be anyone left who'd accept her?

Waves of nervous energy rolled off Rivus as he joined her. His gaze swept the room several times. Most patrons ignored them, but some still glanced their way.

"Edmar never saw us, so he has no way of knowing we're here," she said to reassure him.

With watchful eyes on the villagers, he said, "People are paying too much attention to us, and I heard part of a conversation about a blue-haired woman. I should have known that Edmar would be too smart not to have missives sent out. I think he knows we stole the Sun Stone."

A serving maid brought mugs of beer.

Emmy took a long, greedy gulp, the foam tickling her nose. She blinked sleepily, and for the hundredth time, she yawned. "How long before he finds us?"

Rivus spared her a glance, his brown-eyed gaze shining in the lantern light. "Three men have left through the front door since we've arrived. The innkeeper spoke to a boy after I sat down with you, and the lad took off at a run through the back. Any of them could send a message as we sit here, and I wouldn't bet my mother that he isn't receiving word soon."

A new chill wrapped around her spine again. She missed Edmar, but she couldn't face him, not until her magic was gone. "We have to go."

Now he turned his full attention on her. "I doubt Edmar is close. If I know him as I think I do, he would be back at the Sun Temple, where he would have set up his reception for any messages about us. Even if he leaves now, it's at least a two-hour journey."

The serving maid returned with bowls of stew—vegetables and unidentifiable meat. Although hungry, Emmy felt nauseous and stifled a yawn behind her hand.

Rivus surveyed the room, picking up his spoon. "Eat, Princess. And hurry."

She'd swallowed maybe five spoonfuls of soup when the inn door burst open. A breathless young man, straw-haired and wide-eyed, rushed in.

An explosion rocked the inn.

Conversation died. All eyes turned to the young man.

"Dwarves! We're under attack!"

CHAPTER 54

EMMY

The tavern erupted in chaos, chairs scraping back, falling over, men shouting, scrambling for weapons.

Rivus grabbed Emmy's arm, pulling her toward the back door. "This way."

They darted past the kitchen staff, frozen in confusion. Then they burst into the cool night air, stumbling past a small garden. A narrow path led them between the houses, the crescent moon barely illuminating their way.

They hurried along, the clamor of battle growing. Clashing metal, terrified screams, and guttural roars filled the night. Her heart pounded, echoing the chaos. Sharp pain in her feet battled her rising nausea.

Another explosion rocked the ground.

She pulled her arm free. "We can't run. We have to help."

"And what do you think we can do?" he retorted. "I can fight or protect you."

She understood. Without him, she was defenseless, and she knew nothing about fighting. He didn't wait for an answer before leading her between houses again. Exhaustion made her limbs heavy. Fire acid simmered in her blood. Her gem pulsed, a dark red glow. Pain stole her breath.

Rivus halted, pressing her against a wall in a shadowed alley, his hand stifling her gasp. "Don't move," he whispered in her ear, as two dwarves rounded the corner.

Silhouetted against the moonlight, the dwarves froze, then charged, guttural growls rumbling in their throats. One hefted an ax at Rivus. The other reached for her.

She braced herself.

Energy surged, pain blazing through her. The glow beneath her skin intensified, focusing her will. With a defiant exhale, her magic erupted.

The dwarf melted.

A lump of blackened flesh, twisted metal, charred bone. Her power was weaker now with the Sea Witch's suppression spell.

Nothing had been left of her mother.

The stench of burned flesh and metal sent her reeling. She scrambled away, vomiting. She wiped her mouth, trembling. Her magic was gone again. But she'd killed.

Another dwarf charged toward Rivus. Her breath caught. He was massive, his armor straining against his thick frame, his beard like dark iron, his eyes glinting like a predator.

Rivus half transformed, muscles bulging, face sharpening, shirt and pants stretching but holding tight to his partially shifted body. She needed his ferocity, yet it terrified her.

The dwarf roared, the ax swinging a wide arc. Rivus ducked the blow, slashing the dwarf's arm. Blood gushed. The dwarf stumbled back, but Rivus pressed his attack, his speed ferocious, his claws a blur.

The sounds of their struggle reverberated between the houses—metal clanging, grunts, snarls. She couldn't tear her gaze away from the brutal dance of death playing out before her.

Rivus struck the dwarf's knee, sending him crashing down. He followed with a savage swipe of his claws, aiming for the dwarf's throat. The dwarf raised his arm, but too late. Rivus tore through flesh and bone, past the arm and into his thick neck.

The dwarf's eyes widened, a choked gurgle escaping his ruined throat. He twitched, then he lay still.

Silence descended, broken only by Rivus's ragged breaths. He stood over the body, his body slowly returning to his full human form, Edmar's shirt too loose, her pants torn along the seams most of the way up his legs. Blood dripped from his arms.

His eyes held a darkness she'd never seen.

"Rivus?"

He shook his head, his voice hoarse when he spoke. "Come on. We need to get out of here."

With a firm grip, he took her hand, and they ran, leaving the bodies behind. They slipped between darkened homes, avoiding well-traveled paths, the only sound their soft footsteps on the damp earth.

"Why are they attacking?" she gasped, her voice barely audible above the sound of the dwarves' invasion. Her fire acid simmered again with her heightened fear. "The dwarves have a treaty with the Dragon Kings."

They turned down a deserted street, lit only by a few lamps. The sounds of battle faded.

Rivus shot her a brief look. "Treaties break, Princess, and chaos paves the way for new orders."

If she wasn't so weary and on edge, she'd be curious enough to ask what that meant, but Rivus only cared about getting them away.

As he should.

She couldn't fault him for that, so she silenced her questions for now. They reached the village edge, where the path met a dirt road leading into the forest. The sounds of the attack faded.

She stumbled, her breath ragged. "I need to rest."

Rivus shook his head. "Not yet. We're not safe."

Sleep beckoned, promising oblivion from pain and fear. Her knees weakened, fire acid searing through her. She swayed, gasping for breath, the world tilting precariously.

"You must keep going!" he said. "We're almost there."

"I can't—"

He ignored her, dragging her through the tall grass, rough stalks slapping her skin. Pain stabbed her feet, fire burned in her veins. Her hands and arm glowed.

They reached the trees, her gem illuminating their path. The forest enclosed them in a new, darker world.

"This way," he said, calmer now. "There's a sacred spring ahead. We can stop there."

"Thank the goddess," she whispered. Fiery pain clenched her throat. Darkness edged her vision.

She stumbled through a thicket, branches clawing at her. Then a pool of crystal-clear water shimmered in front of her.

"The Spring of Whispers." Rivus's voice was hushed, reverent. "A sacred place for my people and hidden from most."

Her power, a tidal wave of fire surging forward, threatened to consume this place, this sanctuary. Like it did to her mother as fire acid ate through her. But she couldn't stop. The fire within, a torrent she couldn't control.

Without hesitation, she plunged into the water as her power surged outward. Dark red light filled her vision. Searing pain wracked every part of her body. A thousand reed lashes. Water hissed and bubbled. Spots dotted her vision.

Then the heat faded, replaced by icy exhaustion.

Darkness. Her body a dead weight sinking into warm depths.

Vaguely, she was aware of hands on her arm, pulling her from marshy land.

"What have you done?" Fear laced Rivus's voice.

A shadow loomed over her as she began slipping into oblivion, the last vestiges of her strength failing as a different but deep voice came from above her. "Who are you?"

Chapter 55

EDMAR

Under night's cloak, Edmar arrived at the border village between Cyaneus and Nordrun. His heart synced with his borrowed horse's labored breaths.

When news had arrived about the sighting of Emira and Rivus, he'd acquired a horse. But the image of his wife and best friend together at the inn, limbs entwined, kissing, ignited a fierce rage within him. He imagined catching them in the act, the dark fantasy fueling his resolve.

He and his horse were slick with sweat when yet another messenger caught him on the road, relaying the dwarves' attack.

Now he imagined both dead beneath a dwarf's ax blade, and his heart skipped a beat. Loss twisted inside him, a vulnerability he couldn't afford to acknowledge.

He had urged his horse faster. Two nights, two dwarven attacks. Unease filled him. Things were changing. The fragile peace of the last thousand years had been broken, and he couldn't help his thoughts. War was coming. Not the petty but near-consistent wars with the Fire Fae in southern Agondray.

No, this was something happening right here, in the heart of their land.

The village lay unsettlingly silent, the evidence of the attack stark. Splintered doors and gaping windows like empty eyes, blackened husks. Debris littered the streets. Broken barrels, shattered pottery, and weapons abandoned in haste lay scattered around.

Bloodstains marred the ground, the stench of blood and smoke lingering, an echo of the violence he'd left behind in Sarineton just the night before.

A child's doll lay abandoned in the mud. Cracked porcelain face, sightless eyes staring blankly at the starless sky. His Frostlands remained intact, cracks frozen once more, but a profound sense of loss struck him.

More humans attacked by the dwarves. These weren't his subjects, but his heart ached at the failure of protecting them. He shivered. The silence was oppressive, broken only by his horse's whinny and a distant dog's howl.

At the inn, he dismounted and hurried inside, his fury renewed. The villagers huddled around the tables nearest the fireplace, fear and exhaustion etched on their faces, their wounds bandaged. Whispers of the attack filled the air.

The innkeeper, his face haunted, wiped his hands on a cloth behind the bar's counter.

Edmar approached him. "You sent word of two travelers? A woman with the emerald sea in her eyes and a man with silver and blue in his hair?"

The innkeeper hesitated, choosing his words carefully. "They were here. They left when the dwarves attacked."

Relief spun the room, and he closed his eyes, grateful not to witness Emira's lush body wrapped around his friend. The icy calm of his Frostlands throbbed with a volatile mix of his relief and now frustration. They were always one step ahead, leading him deeper into this web of treachery.

First Thrandmir, boasting of his knowledge that Emira had left him, then this village, ravaged by dwarves shortly after they had been there, and he recalled the other settlement close to here that had suffered a similar fate. His pursuit of them intertwined with the dwarves' movements, their paths converging in a deadly dance. *Coincidence?* He no longer believed in coincidences.

New urgency filled him. "Do you know where they went?"

"We were under attack, so it wasn't my concern." The innkeeper shook his head. "But my boy's taking names of the survivors. He'll know if they're still here. He should be back soon."

"I'll wait." Jaw tightening, he gave the innkeeper a couple of coins. "For your trouble."

He glanced around the room to find a spot to wait when the small, polished two-way mirror in his pocket shook, reminding him of his meeting with his brothers. He turned back to the innkeeper with another coin. "Do you have a private room?"

The man nodded after taking the coin and raised his arm with the towel as he exited from behind the counter. "Follow me."

In the secluded room, he touched the mirror's cool surface, a small comfort as he prepared to connect with his brothers.

"Brothers, I need reinforcements," Kalden said as soon as Edmar appeared. "Lord Galton is defying the slavery ban. He's on the verge of rebellion."

Edmar had worried about the power vacuum his oldest brother would face after decades of hiding and sulking in his lair.

Zane answered before Edmar. "I'm tied up now, but I'll send help as soon as I can."

Expectant eyes turned to Edmar, unaware of the anger and vengeance threatening to expose his Frostlands. It consumed all his thoughts now. "I'm a bit far from home myself, but I'll see what I can do."

Although black scales covered most of Kalden's face, weariness shadowed his dark blue eyes.

Edmar narrowed his eyes. He'd always been the even-tempered one, quick to notice his brothers' varying moods. He recognized Kalden's stage, the time before he spiraled back into his depression. "What else is wrong?"

"The Snow Princess has Airian trapped in her dreams, and I don't know if she'll wake this time."

"Then you have no choice but to send her off the continent." He spoke more bluntly than he'd intended, usually the positive one. His own burdens were heavy enough.

"I can't do that to her," Kalden said.

Sending her away while under the Snow Princess's enthrall risked her spirit being lost. But keeping her risked his brother's life. He thought of when Kalden told him he'd tried to kill himself to avoid another marriage, but the Snow Princess wouldn't allow him to die. Anger tinged his voice. "By not sending the girl away, I hope this is not just an attempt to end your life."

"He loves her." That surprising information from Zane made Edmar's eyes widen.

Kalden, emerging from a twenty-year depression, had fallen in love? He'd always become too attached to his wives, but Edmar hadn't expected it to happen so quickly again. Then he realized how similar their situations were.

Kalden loved Airian, but she refused to marry him, escaping into dreams. Edmar had loved Emira too, but she'd escaped as well. Even though his bride married him, Emira had stolen more than just his heart.

"Something's wrong, Edmar. I thought we just celebrated your nuptials?" Kalden leaned closer to the mirror, as if to discern Edmar's feelings.

"My bride has run away," he said, masking his anger.

"You married her, though, right?" Zane asked.

Zane, the serial womanizer, would think that was all that mattered. The curse only required they marry their brides. No other fidelity was required. Zane married, then left his brides to their own lives. They were provided for, but he lived away from them.

Essentially, in the eyes of his brothers, he was safe. But they didn't know the truth. "I married her. Then she stole the Sun Stone and disappeared."

Zane whistled. "I'd say good riddance, but the Sun Stone? That was the only God's Stone still known in existence until Kalden's Earth Fae claimed to know the whereabouts of the Metal Stone."

This time Edmar barely contained his rage. His voice hardened. "Exactly why I must find her."

Kalden studied him closely. Edmar waited for Zane to crack a joke about him being old, but even Zane seemed unusually serious.

"Where are you guys?" Kalden asked.

"I'm in a rundown tavern at the border between our kingdoms. Someone had a tip about where my *wife* might be." His fists clenched, thinking about Emira with Rivus.

Zane's shift to a cocky smile seemed a world away from Edmar's concealed strife. "You'll never believe me if I tell you where I am. There's a whole other world that exists in the earth beneath Agondray, and currently, I don't know how to get out on my own."

"Like underground? What are you doing there?" Kalden asked.

"It's a long story, but those Fire Fae I followed... they had other interests besides the black powder. The Fire Fae kingdom had wanted Agondray all these millennia not to destroy us, but for the resource located underground. When I know more for sure, I'll let you know."

Underground? He frowned, uneasy. The werewolves had their tunnels, but Zane's description sounded different, more vast, more... ancient. And Rivus's last report mentioned the dwarves delving deeper, seeking something, or perhaps someone.

Could it be the Summer Child? And is the Sea Witch, with her thirst for the Gods' Stones, somehow involved?

Regardless, he feared for his younger brother. Zane didn't know the first thing about living without luxury. Even though he didn't stay in his palace, he spent all his free time in any of his numerous estates, with fancy homes filled with servants and willing women. "You're sure you'll get out?"

"What have I said about underestimating these good looks?" Zane quipped, unbothered. "Don't worry about me. It's all going like a breeze right now."

Kalden rubbed his chest. "Looks like Zane gets to have all the fun again."

That old joke made Edmar smile.

Before the curse, before a time when their very presence together didn't cause massive ice storms, Zane had been the mischievous one to drag them into trouble. It was always fun, if not painful later when their parents inevitably reprimanded them. Now, Zane still treated life like a game, one filled with pleasure and amusement.

He envied Zane's ease.

"The only way to live," Zane said, rubbing his stubble. "I feel bad I can't come to your aid, Kalden."

Kalden shook his head. "Avenge me, brothers, if I lose."

"That won't happen!" Zane said.

Despite Zane's bluster, silence fell.

Edmar pushed a hand through his tangled hair. Kalden's predicament, Zane's safety... once, he would've helped without hesitation. *What's happened to me?* He focused on Kalden. "I'll communicate with my council, directing them to send an army in your support. But, as you know, they tend to deliberate for weeks before deciding on any action. I don't know how your council ever decides anything without you, Zane."

"They have full control, so there are no political games to play against me."

He pushed the thought aside. His own worries were consuming. The urgency to find Emira and Rivus returned, and he was grateful Kalden initiated the end of their conversation. He left the room, ready to depart if the boy hadn't returned.

But his luck turned when the boy appeared and relayed his message.

"They went into Paxsylva Forest," he said. "I tried to follow, but a thick fog... magic, I think. I couldn't go any further."

Chapter 56

EMMY

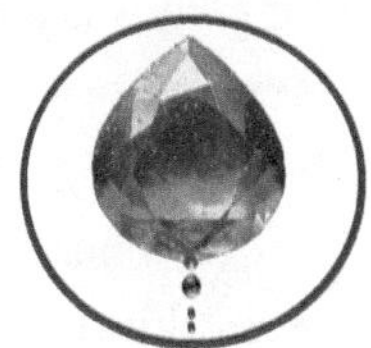

Emmy squinted through a persistent headache as she woke to a room bathed in dim, unnatural light. Smooth, metallic walls emitted soft blue and green light. The room smelled sterile, but a faint, musky scent raised goosebumps on her arms.

Where am I?

She sat up, holding her head, moaning. The musky scent came from the rough blankets of her pallet and beneath that, a metal floor etched with angular markings. Machinery hummed rhythmically, punctuated by distant echoes beyond the walls.

No door appeared on the walls. She was in a box with no escape.

Her surroundings distracted her from the aches in her body. At least her magic was dormant.

Then she remembered.

The dwarves, the attack, Rivus, the spring, her magic exploding...

Panic seized her chest, making her breath hitch.

That had been the second time.

The first time...*Oh, gods.*

She dry heaved.

Her fire acid had taken another life. *I killed again.*

That nightmare had played over and over until the Snow Princess pulled her into a dreamscape, but she had run and run, trying to escape.

The need to escape spurred her to throw off the blankets, then she paused.

What was she wearing?

Something felt wrong.

A clothed band barely contained her generous breasts, and the fabric around her hips reminded her of what the mermen gave her to wear when they visited the Seat of the Dwarf except this was made of cloth. She was alright with the scarcity of her clothes, but something was still wrong.

Her fingers flew to her throat. Her gem was gone.

No, no, no. In all her life, she'd never removed the jewelry. All merfolk knew their life tied directly to the magic within the gems.

Whoever controlled her gem, controlled her.

She could only hope she'd be treated kindly. When her father had disowned her, he severed one of the two tethers with her gem—the one that helped him find her and could have overridden whoever had power over her physical gem. The only tether that existed now was between her and her gem. She could hope that the person with her gem didn't understand the power. She could hope she'd live long enough to see the curse of her magic completely gone. For a day she was no longer tethered to her gem.

But hope felt fragile now. Her dread settled hard in her gut with the realization that her fate had never been hers to command.

The wall hissed as a panel slid open, revealing an imposing woman, similarly dressed. Her long, silver and blue hair was choppy, uneven. The woman's rough edges contrasted with the refinement of the room, as if she didn't belong here any more than Emmy did.

"You're awake, finally." The woman's voice was deep but as sharp as a winter wind. She crouched before Emmy, the wall hissing shut.

"H-how long was I sleeping?" Her words were rough, her voice unused to speaking.

Dark eyes perused her. In the dim light, she barely discerned the woman's faded scars. She had many crisscrossing her face. Even without them, the woman wouldn't have been considered more than handsome, but with them, she was downright imposing. "Two days, Mermaid."

She jerked, her stomach turning.

"Yes, I know what you are." A humorless smile twisted her lips as she opened her palm, revealing her painite, free of its golden band. The room's unnatural light refracted through its dark red color, casting a sinister glow across her face.

She reached for her painite, a desperate plea. "Give it back to me. Please."

The woman laughed. A cold, humorless sound. "You're in no position to demand anything."

"What do you want?" *Does she also have the Sun Stone?*

The woman closed her hand around the gem again. "That I haven't quite figured out yet, but I will make you pay."

Her heart sank. Once again, she was a prisoner, a slave to the holder of her gem. No matter what she tried to do, fate constantly taunted her with freedom, only to take it away. Not allowed to make her own choices, her life forfeit to those stronger than her.

Strains of the Ocean's Lament reverberated in her mind.

Her voice came out small when she spoke. "What am I to pay for?"

The woman jumped to her feet, making Emmy tilt her head back to look up at the woman. "You will address me as Alpha."

She swallowed at the menace in the other's voice, her throat dry. *Another werewolf.* Then she nodded. "Where am I, Alpha?"

"Novacor, the Ironfangs' home lair." She crossed her arms, biceps bulging. "Rivus has not been forthcoming about your identity. So the real question is, what are you doing with the traitor of our kind?"

"Traitor?" When the alpha's brow raise, she amended her question. "Traitor, Alpha?"

"Rivus has interfered too often with his Dwarven snow. Whole villages gone. Blamed on us, when it has all been the work of one wolf."

Dwarven snow? Isn't this what the humans asked the Seat of the Dwarf about when my father had tried to sell me in marriage? She didn't understand. What did Rivus have to do with it? And was he really responsible for so many deaths?

"Not only have you tied yourself to the traitor, you destroyed our sacred spring, turning it into a depleted, marshy pond."

She frowned, recalling the spring. She'd jumped into the water, hoping her magic wouldn't kill Rivus with that cushion between them. Had she damaged the spring? "I didn't mean to—"

"Silence!" The alpha's gaze turned icy, her words a sharp blade. "You will learn your place."

She flashed the painite, pinching it between her fingers and her thumb. "You will obey me, mine to command. Now tell me, who are you?"

Each word sliced through her, ripping away any hope left flickering within her. The tether to her gem compelled her. Defeat made her feel hollow inside. Then a coil of fury sparked in her breast.

She hated how mermaids were so easily controlled by their gems, a tangible object often abused. But she hadn't come so far to be broken by this werewolf.

Squaring her shoulders, she lifted her chin. "I was Princess Emira, daughter of King Sargon, King of the Seas. Now, I'm Queen Emira, wife of King Edmar of Cyaneus, the Dragon King, Alpha."

"A royal? Interesting. I'll take even more pleasure in making you work for me to atone for the damage you've done."

"Your commands will be followed, my will yours, but my magic is dangerous and does not obey any restraints. Not even my own, Alpha."

"We'll see, *Your Majesty*." She said the title with a sneer. "Sleep. Your atonement begins tomorrow."

Chapter 57

EMMY

"Get up, Mermaid," a sharp voice, as cold and unforgiving as the metal walls, shattered Emmy's sleep.

She jerked up, pushing back the rough blankets. Her body ached, each muscle protesting days of relentless travel and exertion, and pain stabbed through her feet. But the pain paled compared to the dread gripping her heart.

The alpha woman stood in the doorway, her imposing figure silhouetted against the faint hallway glow.

Emmy averted her gaze, unable to meet the werewolf's intense scrutiny, feeling the pull of her gem, a silent threat in her fist. "Alpha, please believe me about my magic. If I lose control, I might kill all of you, even if I don't want to."

The alpha toyed with her gem, her eyes distant, pondering. "I control your magic now."

If she commands me not to use my magic, what would happen? Terror gripped her. Her magic could not be contained or suppressed. It would kill the woman and everyone else around her.

She shook her head, desperate to make her understand. "Please—"

"You will stay within twenty feet of me at all times and don't even think about using your magic without my permission. Understand, Mermaid?"

"But my magic—"

"Say you understand me."

She bit her lip to hold back the words, but she couldn't deny this command. "I understand, Alpha."

"Good." The alpha's tension eased, her voice devoid of warmth. "Today, you begin your atonement. This building needs cleaning."

She obeyed, her movements mechanical as she moved through dust-laden hallways and rooms, always within twenty feet of the alpha woman. She scrubbed floors, wiped down surfaces, and emptied overflowing waste bins, her mind a numb void. Her muscles ached as she moved through the corridors with a broom in hand. Every sweep, every rhythmic motion, offered a brief escape from the fear and uncertainty.

Her muscles screamed, but the ache was preferable to the sting of her magic. However, fire acid simmered beneath her skin, its intensity growing with each passing hour. She meditated, seeking control, but the effort was a losing battle. Time was running out.

During the first meal among the pack, she learned she was to serve the alpha, whom the others called Morvella. The alpha's icy gaze observed her while she handed out orders, her commands absolute.

Every meal was the same, but they offered Emmy a chance to observe the pack. All the werewolves gathered in the central hall, a once grand space, now stripped bare. Tension simmered, alliances and rivalries bubbling beneath the surface. She remained silent, observing as she served.

A younger shifter, compared to the rest of the pack, was animated with his news. "All white with silver."

"Are you sure? No one has seen a griffin in over a thousand years."

"I saw it with my own eyes while out on patrol further east."

A burly man dismissed the news with a wave of his hand. "Probably just an eagle owl like those found in these woods. They can get big."

"Or the eastern Ice Dragon. Ain't he all white?"

The younger shifter's face deepened to a reddish-brown color. "I know what I saw. I can't help it if you're too ignorant to understand me."

The burly man slammed his fist on the table, his chair scraping back, glaring at him. "You think you can challenge me, pup?" he growled.

The younger shifter, his hands trembling, held his ground. "I'm not afraid of you," he said, his defiance wavering.

Unspoken threats hung in the air, a battle of wills quelled only by Morvella's sharp glance, her eyes glowing. Whatever she communicated mentally to her pack members deflated the anger.

Perhaps Emmy could exploit their conflicts, create a distraction, so she could grab her gem. It was risky, but desperation made her cunning. *Divide and conquer.*

Except Morvella never let the gem out of her sight.

Emmy hated it. Hated being a slave to her gem, feeling so insignificant in her own life, a mere curiosity to the watchful wolves.

She gleaned very little information from the alpha. Once, she asked about Rivus. While she'd never be fond of him, he'd saved her so many times.

The alpha gave a curt response. "Alive. Still in Novacor." No more information was offered.

After meals, she resumed cleaning, wiping dusty surfaces, scrubbing moss from once-grand windows. Outside, the remnants of the ancient city sprawled. Ivy and tree roots snaked their way through the ruins, reclaiming the land, while the looming silhouette of a great wall rose in the distance. Guards—both human and wolf—patrolled its length, a reminder of her captivity.

That night, she slept in Morvella's chamber. Spacious, austere, more like a vault than a bedroom, keeping echoes of its forgotten purpose. Smooth, metallic walls, etched with faded markings, hummed with residual energy. The only adornment was a low platform draped in dark furs, which seemed out of place, the only softness in a space that felt as barren as a tomb.

Morvella ordered her to stay in the room and promised no harm would come to her, pointing to a pallet on the floor near the massive bed of furs. Emmy curled up on her pallet with two smelly blankets. Throughout the night, Morvella's restless movements heightened her sense of dread, and she barely slept.

She wouldn't escape this nightmare until her magic returned and killed them all. Then she'd be caught in a new nightmare of death and destruction.

The next morning, Morvella asked if she could read the common tongue. With her nod, the werewolf had said, "Good. You will help me look for information and you will tell no one what we are doing."

Emmy's gem tugged at her inner being with the command, and she knew she wouldn't be able to say a word to anyone, not that she'd communicated with any of the other werewolves.

An actual wooden door in this metal building groaned as it opened from Morvella's push, revealing shelves of ancient books and cryptic artifacts. Strange devices of metal and glass, books bound in leather and unknown symbols.

Curiosity piqued, she examined a book, its pages soft as silk but durable. Words etched in a strange language hinted at forgotten knowledge and powerful magic.

The alpha closed the book. "This will not help me. Search through the books and inscribed artifacts on that table over there."

Emmy pulled her hands away. Then she spied the open iron box with the Sun Stone. Hope sped up her heartbeat, but she was aware of Morvella studying her. Perhaps the werewolf didn't know what she had and waited for Emmy's reaction.

She schooled her features to a blank look, and hope faded.

She couldn't do anything about the Sun Stone, not even able to slip it out of the box, because where would she hide it with so little clothing? For once clothing would be useful.

Not that it mattered. Without her gem, she was powerless. She turned toward the table Morvella had gestured to. "What am I looking for?"

"Anything about the Winter Child."

The Winter Child and not the Summer Child? Who is the Winter Child?

Morvella caught her surprise and her quickness in hiding it. "You know of the Winter Child?"

Emmy stiffened, her heart pounding. She'd tried to bury the memories of her encounter with the Summer Child, the terrifying power it possessed, the chilling warning from its protector. "Not the Winter Child."

"Then the Summer Child?" Whatever she saw on Emmy's face sharpened her tone. "Tell me what you know."

Resistance was futile. She relayed what she knew—the siren song, the underwater cavern, the Summer Child's potential awakening. Morvella listened intently, her expression unreadable.

"Our findings confirm your tale. The dwarves we captured... they serve as the Summer Child's guardians, tasked by their Father God, Metallon. They prepare for her return."

Emmy frowned. *Why would Metallon task the dwarves with protecting the Summer Child?* The dwarves were Winter creatures, guarding a child with opposing powers, one who could kill them. It made no sense. Parts of this story were missing. "Is the Winter Child related to the Summer Child?"

"That's what we're searching for. There's an ancient reference," Morvella said, her voice low, "The Winter Child is a being of equal power, destined to oppose the Summer Child's reign... but I've found nothing more. No one knows if he exists."

The werewolf waved her toward the table. "Find me something."

For the next few hours, she leafed through books and artifacts, all the while searching for something to aid her. *A weapon, a tool, a secret that could help me escape.*

Then a breathless messenger interrupted their search. "The Whitewinds agreed to negotiate, Alpha. They demand Rivus's return but are willing to bargain. They'll arrive tomorrow at sundown."

Morvella dismissed the messenger, turning back to Emmy, a wicked gleam in her eyes. "Tomorrow your friend dies."

The words hit her like a punch to the chest. *He's not my friend.* But she didn't want to watch him die, either. Coldness settled around her heart. In eight days, the Sea Witch's suppression spell would wear off. *They will all die.*

"A fine opportunity to showcase my prize," Morvella said, her voice mocking. "The mermaid slave. What do you think, *Your Majesty*? Looking forward to your friend's execution?"

"He was never my friend," she muttered, fighting the urge to lash out. Her fire acid stirred, but it was too weak to protect her. Instead, she bowed her head. "I welcome the chance for fresh air."

Morvella's laugh was sharp. "I'm sure you do."

That night, Morvella wasn't alone. Galerius, a male werewolf, joined her in bed.

Emmy curled up on her pallet, her body aching. The night was shattered by the sounds of their intimacy, a raw, animalistic symphony that made her shiver. She closed her eyes tightly, her thoughts drifting to Edmar, to the love she had betrayed, to the life that was never hers but lost all the same.

The noises finally subsided, but her reprieve was short-lived. Galerius rolled over, his gaze falling on her, light flashing in his eyes, relieving the darkness.

"Several of us would love a turn with the mermaid," he said, his voice low.

Emmy's heart raced, fear gripping her. She wrapped her arms around herself, trying to disappear into the shadows.

Morvella snorted. "Not tonight."

"Maybe we can share her, you and I."

"She's not a plaything for the likes of you. Or anyone." Morvella's voice rapped sharp and commanding. "There are rules. I won't have them broken for your amusement."

Resentment flickered in his eyes, but he backed down, slinking out of the room.

"Get some sleep," she said curtly, settling back into the bed without looking at Emmy. "Tomorrow demands much from us all."

She clutched her blanket tighter, relief and fear keeping her awake long into the night. She longed for Edmar, for his warmth, his forgiveness, but such dreams were fleeting.

Chapter 58

EDMAR

Edmar left the inn the night of the Dwarven attack, spending the hours until dawn tracking Emira and Rivus. Their trail vanished into thick fog.

He followed muddy tracks, the scent of sulfur and burned wood thick in the air, evidence of Emira's magic. The fog, a swirling, ethereal curtain, muted sound and swallowed light. Instinct whispered caution, but he silenced it. He had no patience for second-guessing, not anymore.

The fog thickened, a ghostly force pressing against him. His magic flickered defensively, but he welcomed the cold; it was an echo of his rage, his power, the thing that made men and beasts fear him. He walked for hours, the fog twisting the familiar landscape into a disorienting maze. The tracks disappeared. Silence fell, heavy and unnatural.

Then the fog receded. Wisps of gray smoke lifted, revealing an empty clearing bathed in the soft glow of the rising sun. The trees at the edge rustled gently, as if mocking him. Like his mercy, his patience had worn thin.

They were gone.

A growl rumbled in his throat, low and deadly. He did not curse. He did not pray. Those were weaknesses of men who still believed in salvation.

Instead, he scoured the land for two days, his dragon form a dark specter in the sky. His roars thundered across the mountains and valleys. Let them hear him. Let them fear what was coming.

When the silence stretched too long, when even the wind refused to carry an answer, something inside him cracked. Hairline fractures spiderwebbed through his Frostlands' surface, subtle and insidious. He had spent centuries entombing his grief, his rage, his guilt beneath that unyielding cold. But tonight, the ice did not hold.

Something crept through the cracks, something darker and far sharper. Frost sharpened to a blade's edge, honed by betrayal. A slow, creeping freeze that settled in his bones. The Blue Angel had been a name, a fiction, something that had belonged to a man with restraint. That man was gone, his fragile mask splintered. The Blue Devil remained.

Each night, as dusk settled, he returned to his capital. He met with his council, issued orders, attended to the kingdom's affairs. The duty that once defined him felt like a shackle, yet he upheld it with unwavering resolve.

He did not allow himself to feel disappointment. He did not allow himself to feel anything at all. This was what the Frostlands were for. To consume, to smother, to make sure that nothing touched him too deeply. But something had shifted. The ice was thinning, weakened by betrayal.

He forced them beneath the ice, locking them away with the practiced ease of a man who had spent centuries ensuring his heart would never rule him. But the cracks remained. He could feel them, spreading unseen beneath the surface. And he did not know how much longer the ice would hold.

By the third day, he crossed into Nordrun and spotted a glint of silver. Descending, he found them, dozens of dire wolves gathered in a clearing.

They sensed him. Heads lifted, ears perked, howls rising in both greeting and warning.

As the sun dipped into the horizon, painting the sky in shades of fire and ash, Edmar landed in a nearby meadow, his mind sharpening past fatigue. The sun slipped out of sight, and his forced transition ripped through him. He veiled himself in an aura of icy power, a promise of violence should they cross him.

He entered the clearing. The werewolves parted warily as he approached their leader, Rynthor, Rivus's beta. The massive werewolf shifted, bones snapping, flesh and sinew squelching.

The grotesque sound was a lullaby compared to the screams Edmar wanted to coax from those who had wronged him. Not for pleasure. Not for cruelty. Just to silence them. To end what they had started. To ensure no one mistook his mercy for weakness ever again.

When the transformation finished, Rynthor stood naked before him, tall, muscular, a large diagonal scar slashing his chest. His presence, stern face, and penetrating eyes exuded authority and power.

"Edmar, son of Eldric," the beta said, his voice a deep rumble, carrying a challenging tone, cutting through the twilight stillness. "Your presence is unexpected. You tread dangerous ground coming here alone."

The old name—the one tied to his father's rule, his family's honor—triggered something in him. Once, it had been a name that meant justice. But where had that justice got his father? Honor had a price.

"I'm looking for Rivus. Where is he?"

The leader's lips curled into a snarl, teeth flashing. "Rivus is *our* alpha. His loyalty should be to us, not to you. Yet, he abandoned his duty, always at your beck and call. And now you've driven him to the shadows."

He growled in response, but he kept his voice measured. He would not be part of that old argument. "His choices are his own."

"Yet here you are," Rynthor said. "Hunting him."

His patience frayed. "He betrayed me. Stole from me. If I were a lesser man, I'd have already made an example of someone in his place."

The werewolves shifted uneasily, their hackles raised. They understood what kind of justice he could deliver.

He clenched his fists. "I will see Rivus pay for his treason."

The werewolves exchanged guarded glances, their suspicion and mistrust evident in their glowing eyes as they spoke through their mental links.

Rynthor's gaze bore into Edmar, searching for any hint of deceit. "You made him a traitor when you had him sell Dwarven snow. That black powder has wreaked havoc. Collapsing our tunnels, burning peaceful villages, and killing countless innocents. You won't leave here until you tell us what dark schemes you've entangled him in."

Edmar reeled. Black powder... he and his brothers suspected the dwarves, but he'd never suspected Rivus, his trusted friend. His mind sharpened, cutting through the shock with something colder. He had known Rivus kept secrets when it came to his pack, but this? The betrayal was worse than he'd imagined.

He did not let his anger show. That was weakness.

Instead, he tilted his head, considering Rynthor with a deliberately unreadable expression. "I'd never condone the sale and distribution of Dwarven snow or black powder in my kingdom, and neither would my brothers. If Rivus has been dealing in black powder, he did so without my consent."

The werewolf studied him, eyes narrowing. "And if he has? If he is guilty?"

Edmar smiled then, a slow, cold thing. "Then I will deal with him."

Rynthor crossed his arms. "Will you?"

"I will kill him myself."

A ripple of unease spread through the werewolves. He let it fester. Let them see the lengths to which he was willing to go.

Finally, Rynthor spoke. "Rivus is a captive of the Ironfangs. We're negotiating his release. Tomorrow, we run to their stronghold." A flicker of challenge crossed his face. "All of us."

The words carried an unspoken warning. Edmar did not belong to their pack, their code. If he ran with them, he would be judged by their rules.

He did not care.

He had already made up his mind.

The Blue Devil was coming.

He nodded once. "Then I will fly with you."

Chapter 59

EMMY

Morvella's boot heel dug into Emmy's back, pressing painfully into her bare skin. She knelt before the alpha, her body a footstool, hands and knees braced against the rough ground.

The remnants of the ancient city, bathed in the strategic placement of torches interspersed with metal poles, some dark but others casting a strange bluish-white glow, whispered of a forgotten past. Humans, creating light and power without magic. *Why when there was plenty of magic?*

Except hers, which brought only pain and death instead.

Fire acid circulated in her blood. One week left. *Will the alpha's command stop the return of my magic?*

Sweat dripped from her nose as she held back whimpers against the pain.

"Stop fidgeting." Morvella's voice dripped with condescension as she shifted her weight. The painite illuminated the alpha's hand.

Forced into stillness, she screamed silently. Light glowed in the tips of her fingers, making them translucent.

She meditated, seeking control.

Metal clinked, the only sound among the gathered werewolves, but it drew her back. The soft, eerie glow of twilight bathed members of the pack. Some human, some wolf, gathered around their alpha. They waited in an open area between the ruins, grass covering the ground with patches of old stones crumbling with each step.

Rivus lay nearby, bruised and battered, one eye swollen shut, the other looking at her, but with a vacant expression. A silver collar, etched with runes, encircled his neck. He was gaunt, as if starved for several weeks even though it had only been a few days since the werewolves had captured them. Edmar's shirt hung looser on him.

Her muscles quivered from the strain of holding her position, but she seethed inside from the humiliation of her subjugation, her powerlessness. Shame, hot and bitter. Her skin tingled again with suppressed fire acid, and once more she fought the urges of her magic.

When her fingertips glowed again, Rivus's good eye focused on her. A haunting plea, a silent apology, then defeat. He looked like a man who had been drained of everything—hope, strength, the will to fight.

He looked like he wanted to die.

Her heart twisted. He'd used and manipulated her, betrayed Edmar. But seeing him like this... it wasn't a fate she would wish on anyone.

"You're awfully quiet tonight, Mermaid." Morvella's voice, sharp, shattered the silence.

Well, I can't talk because of your command... When will you figure that out?

Morvella was a queen, Emmy her footstool. Her body throbbed with a deep ache. Each pulse of her gem a reminder of Morvella's command, her power over Emmy's will. Her throat ached with the words she yearned to scream. She'd been a prisoner for too long, too many decades, bleeding into two hundred years.

Morvella patted her head. "There's a certain satisfaction in controlling such a dangerous creature like you. You're nothing here. Less than nothing."

She clenched her jaw. *Is this a dominance display?* Morvella hadn't treated her this roughly before.

A growl shattered the silence.

Massive doors creaked open. Two men walked through the archway, their shadows long from the scant lighting near the entrance.

Her heart leaped. *Edmar.* She recognized his gait, strong and sure, a message of a subtle power commanding respect.

Dire wolves followed, the Whitewinds' gazes fixed on Morvella. They moved with an effortless grace, their muscles rippling beneath their thick fur. Rustling leaves, padding paws, then they stopped a dozen feet away.

When the doors creaked shut, several of the Whitewinds whimpered.

"A precaution," Morvella said loudly. "Otherwise, the creatures of the Malustra Woods would attack."

Emmy's surprise at learning she was back in the Malustra Woods faded when Edmar stepped into the full glow of the torches and metal lights. Her heart thundered against her chest. A flood of emotions spun her thoughts.

His turbulent ocean-colored eyes fixed on her until Morvella spoke again. Whatever emotion tossed in his eyes hardened.

"I don't recall inviting you, Dragon King."

Edmar tore his gaze away to narrow his eyes on the Ironfangs' alpha. "You have something that belongs to me."

"Lose things often?" Morvella laughed, some of her pack joining in. Then her laughter died. "This mermaid desecrated our sacred spring. She's mine."

Edmar stepped forward, anger twisting his features, but the second man restrained him with a hand on his arm. This other man was tall, muscular, with streaks of silver in his hair. He carried himself with nearly the same confidence as her father, a man comfortable with his power.

When Edmar conceded, the man turned his attention to Morvella, touching his chest, forehead, and mouth. With a deep and resonant voice, he said, "Alpha Morvella, we thank you for your hospitality. Our gratitude knows no depths."

"Rynthor, we welcome our sister pack under the peace of our Mother Goddess." Morvella shifted her feet, heels digging into Emmy's back.

Her breath quickened. More pain, more fire acid. Edmar tensed, his hands fisting at his sides.

Morvella continued. "I know you've come for your alpha. We're open to bargains, as long as he's executed before you leave."

The Whitewinds stirred, tension thickening in the air.

"We'll decide his fate," Rynthor said. "But we are open to bargaining his immediate punishment."

"We have one offer. Take it or leave."

In both voices, Emmy heard their iron wills clash. She tensed. *Will this turn violent?*

Edmar relaxed his hands, but his whole body seemed constrained to inaction. "He's not yours. His loyalty was never to the Ironfangs."

Morvella's lip curled in disdain. "You have no say here, Dragon King."

"I have as much say when the same wolf has broken bonds to me and my kingdom, words of loyalty discarded in the name of self-interest."

Morvella jumped to her feet. Emmy sighed with relief, even if she still couldn't move.

"We are not leaving without him, Morvella," Rynthor said.

His tone softened slightly when he said her name. *Is there something between them?*

"You dare to make demands in my territory?" she asked, her voice a whip crack.

Rynthor didn't flinch. "Not a demand." He met her gaze with more unsaid words in his eyes. "A request."

Morvella frowned, her lips curling into a snarl. "He betrayed the entire clan. His actions brought Dwarven snow into our lands, endangering our kind. He answers to us now."

Rynthor shook his head. "His betrayal affects us all. He must face justice before the Water Clan."

"He will face justice," Morvella snapped. "Our justice, if you will not bargain with us to execute him yourself. This is our territory, our law. You have no authority here."

Tension crackled, the threat of violence heavy in the air.

Rynthor crossed his arms. "We're willing to negotiate. We seek a just punishment for Rivus, but one that ensures the safety of all Water Clan werewolves."

"Negotiate?" Morvella laughed, a harsh, mocking sound. "You demand my prisoner, then speak of negotiation? What could you possibly offer that I would desire?"

Edmar stepped forward, a blue aura laced with golden sparks shimmering around him. A chill wind swept through the ruins. Emmy's breath caught in her throat, her heart pounding a frantic rhythm against her ribs. He was so beautiful; it hurt to watch him, but she couldn't tear her gaze away.

For a fleeting second, their eyes met. There was no warmth in his glance, no sympathy. *Only icy indifference.*

"We offer peace," he said to Morvella. "We offer a pledge to end the flow of Dwarven snow and black powder into Nordrun, to protect your borders from Dwarven encroachment."

Rynthor nodded. "We offer a chance for our packs to stand united against the true enemy."

Morvella's gaze narrowed. She seemed to consider the offer, weighing its worth. Almost absently, she pet Emmy's hair. "Your pledge requires the return of Rivus?"

"And the return of my stolen property." Edmar clenched his jaw while he tracked the female alpha's hand on Emmy.

Morvella smiled cruelly. "Stolen, you say? I didn't steal her. She remains mine until her atonement is done. Then she must die."

Die? Her heart raced with the pronouncement of her eventual fate.

Edmar's fists closed again, the wind howling. A distant roar startled the werewolves, but it didn't deter him as he stepped closer. "Release my wife, Morvella."

Morvella's grip tightened in her hair, pulling her up. Pain lanced through her body. Fire acid hungrily filled her muscles.

Edmar halted. "Morvella." His voice held a warning.

Morvella's laughter echoed through the wind. She pulled Emmy close, sniffing the side of her face. "You're in no position to make demands, Dragon King. Not only is this my territory, not only did she destroy something sacred to my people, but have you smelled her magic?"

Smell my magic? Her gem glowed in Morvella's fist with the whisper of her fire acid.

"Your mermaid's magic is a threat. One specifically for our kinds' existence. We were made to rid the earth of such anomalies."

Her cursed magic. It would finally be the death of her.

"You will not touch her," Edmar said through gritted teeth.

Another laugh. "Too late for that, Dragon King!"

Icy wind howled. The ground rumbled.

"Release them." Edmar's crisp voice was unyielding. "They are mine. They answer to me."

"Rivus is a traitor," Morvella said. "He'll face justice here. And the mermaid belongs to me."

Tension crackled in the air, a brewing storm on the brink of breaking. Werewolves on both sides growled low, their eyes gleaming with danger, fingers twitching in anticipation. Several Ironfangs shifted into their wolf forms, muscles coiled, but held their ground.

"Last chance, Morvella." His warning tone echoed as a quiet, razor-edged threat.

"No, Dragon King, it's *your* last chance, or you'll watch your mermaid suffer, too."

"Let her go!"

Morvella released her. She stumbled, her body screaming to obey the last command to not move. Then Morvella punched her, fist smashing into her cheek, sending her flying back.

A black void threatened to claim her. Searing pain flooded her body, and she shrieked as her magic surged.

White-hot magic.

The entire world rocked.

Screams, howling wind, rumbling ground. Fire consumed her, her body convulsing. A wild burning. A torment filling her world.

Her magic, a wild beast finally unleashed, roared.

Chapter 60

EDMAR

Emira's scream, raw and agonizing, split the air. A sound of pure destruction.

Then came the dark red fire.

A torrent of molten energy erupted from her, incinerating everything in its wake. The nearest werewolf had no time to react before molten flames engulfed him, his death cry lost in the inferno.

Blinding light slashed through the battlefield. Edmar shielded his eyes, his body instinctively encased in ice. But the heat still pressed against him, searing away the cold. His magic roiled, a storm of fury churning beneath his skin.

"Emira!" His roar vanished into the inferno, swallowed by her magic, a wild, untamed thing that devoured everything it touched.

The world exploded into chaos. The air reeked of scorched fur and burned flesh. Whitewinds and Ironfangs leaped at each other and clashed in a frenzied storm of claws and steel. The beginning of the battle was the signal.

Edmar gathered more of his magic, and an icy battering ram splintered the compound's wooden doors. Several Whitewinds, left behind to draw the Malustra Woods's monsters, bounded inside, their howls sharp commands echoing through the battlefield.

A tiger elk barreled into the fray, impaling an Ironfang on its massive antlers before tossing the body aside like refuse. Behind it, a turtle scorpion followed, its jagged claws snapping as it lunged at the nearest enemy.

This had been a trap from the beginning. The Whitewinds already within the compound had positioned themselves strategically, forcing the Ironfangs between them and the summoned creatures. The battle belonged to those who controlled the chaos.

Leaving Edmar to his treasonous wife.

He strode forward, unmoved by the carnage. His Frostlands would not allow weakness. Hesitation, mercy, love. Things he had buried long ago.

Then his gaze landed on her.

Emira lay motionless, her skin pale beneath streaks of ash, her breath barely visible in the chilled air. A dead werewolf's charred husk sizzled beside her. Proof of her magic. Another lie she'd told him.

Yet, when her chest rose with her breath, something cracked within him—not relief, not grief. A violent, suffocating pressure, like ice splintering beneath the weight of an avalanche. He did not name it.

She was still alive.

And she was still his.

The thought came unbidden, a truth carved into the marrow of his bones. It did not matter that she had betrayed him. It did not matter that she had run. Emira belonged to him in a way no treachery could sever. *Her magic. Her body. Her soul.* If she still breathed, it was because he allowed it.

And looking at her now—battered, helpless, stripped of the power she had used against him—it was not enough.

It would never be enough.

Something dark stirred beneath his ribs, a cold hunger he did not try to suppress. Let her wake. Let her see who she had made him. Let her know there was no escape.

A slow exhale. The ice within him hardened once more. There was no time for this. The Blue Devil did not dwell. He acted.

And the moment Morvella's boot struck Emira, the decision was made.

Rage. A slow, creeping freeze seeped through his veins, spreading like ice cracking across a lake. It was not an eruption. It was calculated destruction.

Morvella had barely turned before he was upon her. Ice formed mid-air, jagged and deadly, launching toward her like spears. He crashed into her, slamming her against a crumbling stone wall. A dagger pressed into her throat, his grip unyielding.

She gasped, struggling to shift, but he had frozen her mid-transition. The half-formed wolf beneath her skin fought against the ice, but he was stronger. She would break before he did.

"She's a weapon!" Morvella hissed, her voice ragged as her eyes darted to Emira. "A monster! You saw what she did."

"She's mine." His voice was ice and thunder. "Release your claim to her."

Morvella's lips curled in defiance. "I control her, Dragon King. Her will is mine."

Edmar's gaze narrowed. *What does she mean?*

Then he saw it.

The gem.

It had glowed in Morvella's grasp just before Emira's magic erupted. The same gem she had always worn.

Edmar pressed the dagger deeper into the werewolf's throat, enough to draw blood.

"Give it to me." The words carried the weight of a death sentence.

Morvella's pulse quickened in her throat. Her eyes darted, searching for aid, but no one would save her. None dared to interfere with an Ice Dragon.

With a shaking hand, she surrendered the gem.

His fist closed around it. He could feel Emira's presence through it. *Why had Morvella taken it away from Emira?*

But Morvella had taken something else.

"The Sun Stone." His voice was calm, too calm. "I know you have it."

Morvella hesitated, then exhaled in defeat. From the folds of her skirt, she withdrew the dark stone. "I knew the mermaid coveted it, even though she tried to play it off. I just never knew why."

Edmar plucked it from her fingers.

Morvella's eyes burned with quiet rage. "This isn't over, Dragon King."

He laughed softly. "Empty threats. The next time you take what's mine, I will not hesitate to end you."

But he didn't step back yet. Instead, he allowed his cold to seep from his skin into hers. Morvella had dared to take what was his, keep it from him, then lay a boot against it.

That would not go unanswered.

A slow smile curled at his lips, one that held no warmth, no mercy. "Did you think I would let you walk away unscathed, wolf?"

Her breath hitched, but she did not beg. That was fine. She would need whatever fight she had left when he was done with her.

Before she could react, he struck.

Ice flared at his fingertips, wrapping like liquid frost around her throat and shoulders, sinking deep into her skin. Her mouth opened in a silent scream as the cold turned to jagged ice, sinking beneath flesh, claiming her bones.

"Do not think you can keep what belongs to a Dragon King." His voice was soft, but the power beneath it howled like a winter storm.

He squeezed, feeling the delicate snap of cartilage in her shoulder joint, the sickening pop of tendons giving way. Her dominant arm—her weapon—now useless.

A wound that would never fully heal.

A weakness she would never overcome.

She gasped, eyes wide with pain, her breath ragged. A wolf who could not fight was not an Alpha. She knew it. They all knew it.

He leaned in, his breath a frozen whisper against her ear.

"Next time, I won't stop at your arm."

Then, with a final flick of magic, he sent her crashing onto the now frozen ground, the ice in her shoulder locking her arm at an unnatural angle.

He stepped over her as if she were nothing.

Then he was at Emira's side, gathering her limp form into his arms. A tremor ran through his Frostlands. *Possession.*

His wife lay in his arms, but she was no longer the girl he had once known. She was something else. Something dangerous.

And she was his to deal with.

Her eyes flickered open for the briefest moment. "Edmar?"

The sound of his name from her lips did nothing to ease the storm inside him.

She had betrayed him.

And he would decide what she was worth.

Before she could slip back into unconsciousness, he whispered, "You're not leaving me again."

With her weight against his chest, he turned, catching Rynthor's eye. The battlefield had descended into true carnage. The Malustra creatures rampaged inside the city ruins, the Ironfangs now trapped between the snapping claws of the turtle scorpion and the blood-hungry fangs of the Whitewinds.

Edmar did not hesitate.

Ice spears erupted from his hands, jagged and lethal. They aimed for throats. For skulls. For hearts. He was past mercy. The Ironfangs who had once stood in his way now lay bleeding, some encased in ice, their bodies sculpted in their final moments of terror.

A wolverine moth descended upon the battlefield, its wings kicking up a storm of dust and blood. Some Ironfangs tried to flee, but others snarled orders that made them stand their ground. It would not save them with their defenses destroyed.

Edmar turned back to Rynthor. He nodded once.

The Whitewinds retreated with Rynthor's command. Two werewolves dragged Rivus between them.

Edmar carried Emira into the shadowed embrace of the Malustra Woods, the mayhem of the battlefield fading behind them.

The hunt was over.

But the journey had just begun, ending only when she begged for forgiveness before he executed her.

He ran with the wolves for several hours, the thunder of paws and breath filling the space between his thoughts. The rhythm of the hunt, the drive of pursuit, adrenaline pumping through his veins. It was all that existed.

They reached the Forbidden Boundary further south, bordering his lands.

The pack halted atop a low ridge, their gazes fixed on the dragon statue marking the invisible exit. They did not cross. Instead, they threw Rivus down against an ancient oak, its gnarled branches twisting like skeletal fingers reaching for the condemned.

Rynthor shifted, rising before him, naked, but unbothered. "We don't leave in case we decide his fate is to be left to the creatures of the Malustra Woods."

Edmar said nothing, his gaze falling to the broken thing at the base of the tree.

Rivus was barely conscious, his one eye unfocused, the silver collar gleaming against his throat. The very sight of it was a mockery of everything Edmar had once believed.

This was Rivus? The same man who had fought at his side, bled for his kingdom, laughed in the face of death? This hollow, crumpled waste of flesh. His once trusted friend, reduced to this, a symbol of treachery and pain.

How?

Whatever he had expected to feel—triumph, satisfaction, clarity—none of it came. Only a cold, empty weight pressed against his chest, like the ice of his Frostlands closing in.

There was no victory in this.

There never had been.

Several dire wolves growled low, their hackles raised. The shadows moved.

They were not alone.

If the Whitewinds deemed Rivus unworthy of death by a king's hand, the Malustra Woods would finish him instead. Perhaps that would be best. Perhaps it would be a lesson in suffering more fitting than anything Edmar could deliver.

But he still had questions.

He readied himself, his magic licking at his skin, the remnants of winter curling around him like a living thing. The trees seemed to shift, whispering, stretching shadows where there should be none. The air crackled, and from the gloom, a bear-deer lumbered forward, nostrils flaring. It sniffed Rivus, intrigued, hesitant.

Edmar did not hesitate.

A spear of ice erupted from his palm. It did not just scatter the creature. It tore through the ground where it had stood, freezing everything in an instant. The bear-deer bellowed and fled. The clearing fell silent.

He turned back to Rivus.

"You won't get much out of him until the silver collar comes off," Rynthor said, voice calm. A test. Would Edmar free his friend before executing him?

Would it matter?

Edmar had already known the answer before they arrived. The collar was an insult. A mockery—but one he'd intended on using himself if the Sun Temple had any silver. Silver drained werewolves' energy, taking away their will to do anything—to eat and drink, to live.

He didn't do Rivus the honor of looking at his face. Instead, he knelt, laying Emira's body against another tree, her unconscious form forgotten for the moment.

His hand hovered over the collar. "You deserve this."

Rivus did not respond.

For a long moment, Edmar did not move.

He could free Rivus, but who would free him?

The unwelcome thought reared sharp in his mind, but he buried it deep in his Frostlands. He was not the one in chains. He was the one who decided when they came off.

Then his gaze fell on Rivus's shirt.

Not *Rivus's*.

The one he had given to Emira.

Rage slammed through him, cold and pure. His fingers curled into fists, his control fraying at the edges.

Without thought, he ripped the fabric away, tearing it from Rivus's body like it burned him. He cast it aside, breathing hard, before unclasping the collar.

Rivus gasped, the silver no longer draining his will. His one good eye sharpened, his mouth opening, his body returning to itself.

His voice rasped in a raw throat. "Forgive me."

Something dark uncoiled within Edmar. "Not possible."

He turned, shoving the collar into his pack, his shoulders squared. His justice would come later.

Rynthor nodded approvingly, dropping into a crouch before Rivus. "You are a disgrace to the clans. I claim the title of Alpha. Submit to me."

His claws extended, raking down Rivus's chest.

Rivus grunted, his eye rolling back. Blood welled from four deep gouges. He shook his head, then focused on Rynthor. "I concede."

Rivus's easy surrender bothered Edmar. Something about it did not sit right.

It was too easy. Too final.

At odds with the betrayer they all knew him to be now. What did it mean to truly submit out of respect rather than necessity?

Perhaps Rivus's loyalty had always been forced.

The thoughts curled around him like chains, but he shoved them aside.

He met Rynthor's questioning gaze as the werewolf stood. "As the King of Cyaneus, I recognize Rivus's lost status as the Alpha of the Whitewinds, the Cyaneus Water Clan, and I swear I will support you with mutual respect and trust. Your continued alliance with my kingdom is invaluable to me, and I will not forget that or what we've started today."

Rynthor placed a hand over his heart, then touched a finger to his forehead and mouth. "From the lips of the Water Goddess herself, I swear the same."

The new alpha flicked a glance to his old leader. "He will be punished for all crimes?"

Edmar did not hesitate. This was inevitable. A judgment long decided. Not by feeling, not by vengeance—but by duty.

He nodded once. "He will."

The weight of it settled, but did not stir. His Frostlands remained untouched, the storm locked away, buried beneath unyielding ice. There was nothing to rise. No fury. No grief. Just cold, unshaken resolve.

At least, that was the lie he told himself.

Because if this were truly about duty, if it were only about the kingdom, there would be no need for this stillness. No need for the layers of ice, for the practiced suffocation of something far uglier.

Beneath the surface, beneath even his Frostlands, something festered.

Something wounded.

But the Blue Devil had no use for wounds. He only knew how to make them.

Rynthor exhaled, stepping back. "From this day forward, Rivus of the Winter Clan belongs to no pack, and no wolf will follow his leadership or give aid."

Rivus did not answer, looking away.

"They'll come for you," Rynthor said to Edmar. "The Ironfangs."

"I know."

Rynthor nodded, then shifted, leading his pack away, their howls melting into the early light.

Dawn approached. A familiar tingle in Edmar's skin warned of his coming forced transformation.

Edmar knelt beside Rivus.

The dagger was at his Marshal's throat before he even realized he had moved.

A storm howled in his Frostlands, his hand shaking from the force of it.

"You have committed treason by aiding the queen in the theft of the Sun Stone. Your treason continues with your deliberate involvement in the sale of Dwarven snow and black powder in multiple kingdoms."

He could name other things.

He could name his own hurt.

Like my best friend running away with my wife.

He leaned into the dagger, but stopped, seeing the resignation in Rivus's eye. "Why?"

It was more than a question. He needed to understand. Rivus's betrayal shook the foundations of his Frostlands.

"It's not that simple," Rivus murmured.

His heart pounded, each beat a drum of war against the betrayal fracturing his Frostlands. He wanted to scream, to unleash the fury trying to escape through the cracks in the ice. But Rivus's gaze held him, a connection forged through years of camaraderie and friendship.

"The reason..." Rivus struggled to breathe. "It's worth more than my life."

Edmar searched the eyes of his old friend, yearning for an answer, for meaning. But only surrender met his questions. His grip tightened. "Gods damn you. I will kill you, and you'd let your death mean so little?"

Rivus's silence created a void echoing with the ghosts of their shared past. It was in that silence he realized the futility of his quest for understanding. No answer would salve the wounds, no justification would mend what had been broken.

Either he completed his duty and executed Rivus, or he let him go.

"For your treason," he said, placing the tip of the dagger on one side of Rivus's throat, "I sentence you to death."

Then, the voice that should have meant nothing.

"Edmar."

The Frostlands held. He did not look at her. Did not waver.

But the ice cracked anyway.

Rivus lifted his chin, baring his throat further. Edmar only had to pull the blade across. One swipe, and Rivus's life would be forfeited.

"I submit. My life is yours, my king."

That should have satisfied him.

It didn't.

He missed his friend.

But he had made his decision.

The dagger pressed into Rivus's skin—

Then, Emira's voice shattered the moment.

"It's my fault, Edmar. Kill me."

Chapter 61

EMMY

An icy blast slammed into Emmy, brutal and unrelenting. It lifted her off her feet, sent her crashing into a tree. Breath fled her lungs. Snow and shards of ice enveloped her like a frozen coffin, trapping her, suffocating her. She gasped, but the cold stole that too.

When it stopped, Edmar pressed his body into hers, his dagger at her throat. Her breath hitched. Her eyes widened.

Pain throbbed in her muscles, intensified by Edmar's punishing force and the rough bark digging into her skin. Fire acid simmered in her muscles. Bubbles of pain popping beneath her skin.

She closed her eyes, meditating, savoring the conflicting sensations. The pressure of his body against hers, his familiar ocean scent. She whimpered as a dull throb beat low in her belly. Her heart beat a tattoo in her chest.

Vainly pushing away her body's reaction to Edmar, she opened her eyes and searched his, waiting for his proclamation to doom her. Despair climbed up her throat, threatening to choke her, to steal the air from her breath. The forest lightened by degrees, giving her a clearer view of his features.

"Edmar," she whispered. She'd missed him.

Icy granite hardened his face, his gaze unwavering. He seemed a stranger. Still, her stomach fluttered, any other words stuck in her throat. All the things she wanted to say to him. Her fingers curled against his chest.

In his silence, her unease and fear grew, increasing her magic's strength.

Images flashed in her mind—the werewolf, fear twisting his face, halfway shifted into his wolf form, melting. Sharp features, a wide mouth, brown skin, sliding off his skull like candle wax, blood bubbling into black steam. Her stomach roiled.

Fire acid skittered in her veins. She couldn't hurt Edmar, not like that. "Let me go."

His lip curled, his only response. He seemed to battle inner demons, light blue rings glowing in his ocean-colored irises.

"I don't want to hurt you," she said.

The dagger buried into the tree beside her head, the force of it vibrating through the bark, so close she swore she felt the kiss of steel against her skin. She flinched. A mistake. The moment her body recoiled, his fingers closed around her throat. Tight. Merciless. A silent promise that he could take everything from her—breath, power, life—without hesitation.

His lip curled, voice razor-sharp. "Nothing you do can hurt me anymore, Your Majesty."

His words, though cruel, made her heart skip a beat. She hadn't heard his voice since their wedding night, nearly two weeks ago. No matter what passed between them, even if he killed her, she'd always love her Dragon King.

She swallowed the lump in her throat, and his grip tightened. "Before you kill me, please know that I never wanted to lie to you."

"Lie?" Angry violet-red streaks stained Edmar's blue skin. "You did far more than that."

Tighter. She clawed at his wrist.

"Edmar," Rivus rasped, his good eye pleading.

He didn't seem to hear Rivus, his hand tightening further, crushing her throat, something about to give.

She sank nails into his skin. No air to respond, eyelids fluttering, vision blurring. Fire acid roared.

His grip loosened. She gasped and sagged against the tree. One long, shuddering breath, willing her magic to calm. But it remained, a burning heat beneath her skin.

The glow in his eyes dimmed, then flared as he raked his gaze over her, then to Rivus, where the werewolf still leaned against the oak tree.

His icy breath chilled her cheek, a dangerous caress. "Tell me, how long did you and Rivus plan to betray me?"

"No, it wasn't like that—"

"How long have you been giving yourself to him?" His voice slithered over her skin, cold and possessive. "Did he enjoy what belongs to me? Did he lay beside you, wearing my shirt, stripping you of everything that's mine?"

Rivus groaned, a rumble of protest, but Edmar ignored him. Fury consumed the gaze fixed on her. She swallowed, overwhelmed by the deluge of emotions each tearing her apart.

Love, regret, desire, fear. How could so much live in her breast without driving her crazy?

"Never," she whispered. She trembled. Pain seared her, her breath coming in gasps, the intensity growing.

Please help me, Solis. Her first prayer to the Sun God. Anything to save Edmar when her magic erupted again.

His knee forced her legs apart, pressing against the most sensitive part of her. Heat bloomed, traitorous and unwanted. Her breath hitched in a sound dangerously close to a whimper.

"You might have let him touch what is mine, but…" A slow, dangerous smirk curled his lips. He leaned in, his breath icy against her cheek. "Even now, you crave me."

He was right about wanting him still. She wondered how she could possibly still feel this need for him.

Then astonishment filled her as her pain receded.

This simple feeling of pleasure reduced the roar of her fire acid.

Thank the gods.

Then she couldn't help herself, chasing more of that pleasurable feeling. She tilted her hips, seeking… increasing friction against her center. He cupped her breast, his thumb brushing her nipple through the cloth band, and she moaned.

His lips whispered over the corner of her jaw. "So, you never sought his touch like you sought mine?" He lightly pinched her tightening nipple. "Did you want me, or was that all an act?"

She bit her lip and shook her head. "I've always wanted you."

Nothing changed in his expression, and she desperately longed to know his thoughts. She had always craved his touch, ever since the day she'd saved him.

Another tug on her nipple. Her body arched over his leg. Little shocks of pleasure.

He groaned, his expression softening. Then he blinked twice, shaking his head. "Tell me what I want to know," he said, brushing his lips over her cheek, his voice regaining its familiar warmth.

Beneath the gentleness, his anger simmered, making her wary. "What do you want to know?"

"Admit what you've done. You stole the Sun Stone."

A lump stuck in her throat. She wouldn't lie. Not anymore. Not just because she should have been truthful from the beginning or that her guilt and regret demanded it of her now.

It was because she missed him.

She'd known it before, but seeing him again... her lungs had forgotten how to breathe. Her body ached for him, a deep, resonant hum vibrating through her. It was the absence, the gaping hole she hadn't realized was there, that suddenly roared with his presence.

She'd run from him, from his kingdom, from his love, only to realize she'd been running from the pain of his absence, from the pain of losing his love. She had to face him, even if he never loved her again. Right now, honesty was more important than her life. She owed him that.

"I stole the Sun Stone."

"Hmmm," he murmured, his fingers now alternating between tugging and pinching her nipple.

She arched into his hand, whimpering. He kissed the spot below her ear, his lips hot, his breath cold. Everything about the way he touched her sparked a buildup of pleasurable feelings between her legs. She raced toward something, everything tightening in her body. Soft mewling sounds escaped her, but she didn't care, a haze draping over her mind.

"And seducing me..." he murmured. "Was that part of the plan, too?"

She couldn't think clearly. Heat coiled in her belly. Pleasure warred with the demanding man before her. The sensation collided with the fire acid simmering in her muscles, taming parts of it, cooling the fire while fanning the heat in her core.

"Emira." He lightly nipped the corner of her jaw. "Answer me."

She groaned as the hand on her breast stilled. "Yes? I mean...no. Seducing you wasn't part of the plan."

His eyes narrowed, then his hand was at her throat, squeezing, cutting off her air. "More lies."

She bucked against his hold, the hand on her throat. Pleasure fled and fire acid roared back into her blood in thick waves.

He clenched his jaw. "You used me. You planned to steal from me and run away with your lover."

What the eight hells! How could he think that about her?

But Rivus had been wearing his shirt, a terrible coincidence, and he didn't know her, not really. He only knew what she'd shown him in the few nights they were together. She had nothing to prove her true intentions. Scorching pain throbbed in her muscles.

She shook her head, pleading with her eyes. A discordant harmony filled her mind. Lines of the Ocean's Lament, twisted. She'd cry if she could make tears. If she was going to die, she'd tell him the truth one last time—whether he believed her. Blackness crowded her vision, pierced by flashes of light, reminding her of the stars.

The words slipped out as a strangled whisper. "I love you."

Her words were the final sin.

His fingers spasmed, then tightened, as if punishing her for speaking. For existing. For daring to love him when she had ruined him. He did not let go. Not this time.

Familiar heat raged in her body. A thousand needles burrowed into her flesh, tearing her apart from the inside. Stars flickered behind her vision. Her limbs jerked, desperate, but there was no air. No mercy.

And still, he did not let go.

She had never seen death so close. Never felt its lips press against hers, whispering for her to surrender.

And then, as darkness swallowed her whole, light flooded behind her eyelids.

Chapter 62

EMMY

A cold hand tapped Emmy's cheek, rousing her. Snow-laden branches loomed, casting shadows in the faint light. The predawn air hung heavy with mist and silence. Only minutes had passed.

I'm still alive.

But pain throbbed through her. Breathing hurt. Air rasped through her bruised throat. Her muscles ached, her body trembling, protesting days of relentless travel and work. The forest floor was cold, the chill seeping into her bones, weaving fatigue and soreness together.

"Princess," Rivus said, his voice drawing her gaze. He stood hunched, clutching his ribs.

But Edmar, lying motionless, caught her attention, and she pushed past Rivus, crawling to her Dragon King. Her body protested vehemently at the new movement. A deep, burning pain coursed through her, fueling her need to help Edmar, praying she hadn't killed him.

Her throat tightened, words forming silently on her lips. *Please be alive.*

His stillness etched a profound divergence from her frantic heartbeat. His charred chest beneath his tattered tunic seized her breath.

"Edmar?"

The Ocean's Lament stirred within her, a melody of despair. She longed to cry, but tears wouldn't come, her grief pouring out in a song that, for once, seemed to touch her very essence.

"Princess." Rivus crouched beside her, his gaze scanning the forest. Her song died. "We have to go. Now."

The ground trembled. *Something is coming.*

"I can't leave him."

Rivus touched her shoulder, his brown eyes filled with an emotion she couldn't decipher. She didn't understand him at all.

"He might never forgive you."

Her heart lurched. It was true, but she didn't care. She'd hurt him, burned him. Charred skin peeled away from the center of his chest, revealing a deeper wound. Blue blood welled at jagged edges. She shuddered. "I can't leave him. It's my fault."

Her magic's lethal touch stained her soul. Grief, a heavy cloak, settled around her. Her mother, the dwarf, the werewolf...

How many more?

Please, not Edmar.

He bore her scars. Strains of the Ocean's Lament rumbled in her chest, a lament for all harmed by her destructive magic. *I deserve to die.*

Edmar groaned, his beautiful ocean-colored eyes meeting hers with a look she missed, brimming with a love she ached for.

His trembling hand cradled her cheek. "Emmy."

She may deserve to die, but she didn't want to.

She smiled for the first time in days, a fleeting moment of warmth.

His gaze held hers, a tumultuous sea of emotions, sending a whirlwind of hope and fear through her. For a heartbeat, the world seemed to pause, their breaths mingling in the frosty air.

But it was short-lived.

With startling strength, he gripped her, rolling, pinning her beneath him. She gasped, the air driven from her lungs as her back hit the frozen ground. Disoriented, her heart pounded against her ribs.

The chill of the forest floor seeped through her again, icy dread flooding her veins. His face, inches from hers, an enigmatic mask, his intentions unreadable. The warmth in his eyes vanished, replaced by icy resolve.

Metal scraped against leather, followed by the cold kiss of steel against her throat. "Now you die."

Chapter 63

EDMAR

"Don't!" Rivus's voice shattered the moment.

Edmar didn't flinch. His grip on the dagger remained steady, the blade pressing into Emira's throat. "She tried to kill me. I won't give her another chance."

She looked up at him, eyes like deep emerald pools. The same ones he had once dreamed of, the same ones that had reflected love during their wedding. The same ones that had lied.

He pressed the dagger harder, feeling the pulse beneath the blade. Fast. Erratic. A rabbit caught in a snare.

Good. She should be afraid.

Yet, his hand did not move. Not forward. Not across her throat. Not to finish what she had started when she unleashed her magic upon him.

Why?

He had told himself that her life was already forfeit. That she had made her choice when she ran. When she stole from him. When she stood beside Rivus, his best friend—the man he had once called brother. This was justice. This was what had to be done.

So why wasn't it finished? What kind of man would he become if he did?

For a moment, he saw his son's face, so small, so innocent, blurred with Emira's. Fate was a cruel mistress, mocking him. To offer him something so beautiful and innocent, only to take it away before he truly had a chance to revel in that love, for a son, for a wife.

Yet he held Emira's life in his hands now.

"Think, Edmar." Rivus hissed as he rose, still clutching his ribs. "You were choking her. What would you have done?"

He'd fight back with everything he had. "Except she lied. She said she'd gotten rid of her magic."

"Talk to her. Find out why."

His patience was already fraying. Rivus should not be speaking. *Rivus should be dead.* The thought flickered through him, quiet and absolute. It would be easy. *So easy.*

He ignored the werewolf and looked back down at the woman beneath him. His grip on the dagger did not falter, but something unsteady coiled in his chest. Doubt. A sliver of it, buried beneath years of certainty.

If he killed her now, he'd never know why she betrayed him. If she would tell him the truth. Gaze locked onto hers, he spoke only to Rivus. "I'll deal with you in a moment."

Her lips trembled. "I'm trying to get rid of my magic. I never meant to hurt you."

A weak excuse. One she had the audacity to believe he would accept. Still, her sincerity unearthed something he had buried deep. He remembered the night in the city. Her confession about her mother. Her pain. Her truth.

But is it the magic, or is it her? Either way, she was a liar. She had fooled him once. She would not do so again. Rage surged free of his Frostlands, a crack in the ice, a leak in the dam.

"Did you really think you could kill me?" His voice was quiet, lethal.

"Never," she whispered, shaking her head. "Not intentionally."

A lie. A tired, desperate lie.

He shook his head, his fury thickening. He couldn't trust her words or the treacherous yearning clawing through his chest. "More lies."

"I tried to warn you!"

"Warn me?" His control slipped, a tide of wrath surging free of his Frostlands. He slammed the butt of his dagger into the ground beside her head. She flinched. "You seduced me, stole from me, ran away with my best friend."

"Edmar, please." Her voice rasped, rougher than before.

"And now you lie again, trying to distract me. You tried to kill me." He leaned down, his breath frigid against her cheek. "Why shouldn't I end this now?"

"I don't want to kill you."

"Do you even know when you're lying?"

"I don't know what to do to make you believe me, but I would never hurt you on purpose," she said, her eyes wide. "I love you."

The words struck like a blade. A desperate yearning to believe her welled up inside him. To find a reason, a justification for all the pain. More than anything, he longed to believe she loved him. But how could he?

He ached for her, even as the memory of her attack flared in his mind. Everything about her captivated him. The scent of coconut and flowers, the softness of her beneath him. The way she had always felt like his.

He'd wanted her, and she wanted him, too, given her response to his touch. But had she also responded to Rivus that way? The thought gutted him, stealing his breath. She said she loved him… but she'd tried to kill him. Words meant nothing to her. All lies.

How can I trust her words when her actions scream otherwise?

The ground rumbled. Time was running out. He needed to finish this.

"Actions speak louder than words, and your actions have consequences," he said, his voice hollow. Still, he could not move the blade. Could not bring it across her pretty throat.

Her gaze held his, searching. "What do you want?"

He didn't know anymore. The ground trembled beneath them.

"I would have done anything for you," he said, his voice barely above a whisper.

"I know."

"I can't trust you."

The admission felt final. But so did the truth that followed. The truth he could not face. He couldn't kill her.

She had taken advantage of his love, his open heart, and he had let her. He couldn't be that naïve again. He could no longer afford to be the Blue Angel she had known.

"We need to go," Rivus said, his voice hoarse.

Emira looked at Rivus, then back at him. "Kiss me."

"What?"

"Kiss me. For the curse. You'll see I'm telling the truth."

His heart beat loud in his ears. The curse.

"A maiden with a true heart who can survive the *Dragon's Kiss*," she said, emphasizing the last words. "Kiss me. See for yourself."

He frowned.

Could the curse be broken?

If she is telling the truth.

Kiss her and see. And if it isn't?

Then I'll bury what's left of my heart beneath the ice.

Not even his brothers would be able to drag his true feelings from the depths of his Frostlands. It would be the end of everything she'd ever meant to him.

Beneath his anger and despair, a desire to possess Emira's kiss haunted him. Her words gave permission to his yearning.

He sheathed his dagger, then tilted her chin up with his thumb and forefinger.

She sucked in her bottom lip, and he couldn't resist, finally giving in to the urge to kiss her, an urge he'd had since he'd pushed her against that tree. Her mouth opened to his, and they shared their cold breaths. She returned his kiss with the same need he felt.

Magic erupted within him. The curse that had once bound him to the sun's cycle, changing him between man and beast with every sunset and sunrise. A cascade of golden light burst outward.

The spell lifted from his body, as if he'd been wearing a tight sheath all his life. He stood, looking at his hands. The light receded from his skin.

He willed his claws to extend from his fingertips. They slid out easily, then back in. For the first time in his life, he was free.

The curse is broken.

Could it really be true after a thousand years?

But he felt nothing in this moment. Robbed of the joy and triumph he should have felt.

Because she was looking at him, emerald eyes searching his, and the past crashed into him with full force.

He had felt this before. That same moment of false elation. That same fleeting hope, right before she had torn him apart.

From the moment when her father had negotiated her marriage to the Seat of the Dwarf. Since then, his feelings for her had only deepened and intensified, becoming so complex that he couldn't separate his hurt from the love he'd once felt for her.

She loves me.

She hadn't lied about that.

But she's lied about so many things.

Despair coiled in his gut. His love twisted into something ugly.

He hated her.

He hated her for confusing him, for hurting him.

He hated himself for allowing it.

He looked between her and Rivus. They weren't lovers, but they'd betrayed him.

He had loved both of them, but they'd tried to destroy him. They deserved nothing from him.

"You will stand trial for treason." His voice was cold, final.

"Aren't you even going to ask why?" Rivus said.

"It's irrelevant," Edmar said, his fists clenching. He'd wanted to know why before, but it wouldn't stop their punishment.

"That's madness!" Rivus threw up his hands.

Emira shifted to her knees on the ground, kneeling before him. "This isn't you. You are good and kind. Fair and giving to a fault."

No. *This is who they made me.*

The absence of the curse left a hollow space where its grip had once ruled his life. A thousand years of torment—gone in a single breath. But it didn't matter. He couldn't let it matter. Not now. Not when she had manipulated him, stole from him, ran away with his best friend.

He took all the love he'd ever felt for her, all the love he'd given to Rivus as his brother in all but name, and he shoved it beneath the ice of his Frostlands.

Never again.

They were nothing to him now.

Personal vengeance replaced by cold emptiness. They were traitors, deserving of the fate they brought on themselves. He couldn't be the hero they thought him to be. They'd made him their judge.

"You both knew what you were doing when you stole one of the most precious artifacts in the world," he said, his voice hollow, the earth shaking beneath his feet. His entire worldview had tilted. "I'll be the villain you've made me be, the Blue Devil."

"Edmar!" Rivus fell back. "Behind you!"

A hippo fox burst through the foliage, its massive form upending trees and underbrush in a thunderous charge. Its leathery hide shrugged off collisions with sturdier trunks. The sleek, angular features of a fox refined the broad muzzle and gaping jaws. Intelligent eyes, alight with intent, fixed on Emira's kneeling figure.

He stepped between the charging beast and Emira, cold fury filling him.

She's mine!

Earth heaved beneath Edmar, and his form morphed, grace giving way to the might of draconian rage. Scales like armor encased him, his form towering, snout bristling with teeth. The trees were too close for his wings, but he didn't need them.

The creature lunged. He met its charge, sending it crashing through trees. It careened against a rocky outcrop, roaring with a mix of bellow and bark.

He crouched protectively over Emira.

The hippo fox pawed the ground, then a dire wolf slammed into it. The forest echoed with the sounds of their struggle, the wolf's jaws closing around the hippo fox's neck.

Edmar summoned his magic, sculpting moisture from the air into a storm of ice. The hippo fox broke free of the wolf, and he unleashed his storm. Frozen shards slammed into the creature, piercing the thick hide. With anguished cries, it retreated into the shadowed forest.

He scanned the trees. More trouble was coming.

A howl rose in the distance as the sun crested the horizon.

For a fleeting moment, he dreaded the dawn, the agony of his forced transition, then he remembered. *The curse is broken.*

He exhaled, releasing his magic, looking at Emira, who had just found his shirt and now clung to it. His claws flexed.

Her emerald eyes searched his for what he would do next.

Did she think this was over? That protecting her meant mercy?

She would understand soon enough.

She belonged to him now—not as his wife, not as the woman he had once loved, but as the traitor who had stolen from him. As the prisoner who would answer for her crimes.

Whatever that looked like because he couldn't deny one crucial fact.

She loved him.

So why did she betray me?

Another howl, closer.

He scooped Emira into his scaled arms and ran, heading for the western border, Rivus following in wolf form.

Rivus was right.

He needed to know why.

CHAPTER 64

EMMY

The remnants of the Malustra Woods thinned as they crossed the Forbidden Boundary, giving way to rolling meadows bathed in the glow of a mid-morning sun. Edmar lowered Emmy, then shifted back to his human shape.

Even the stabbing pain in her feet couldn't tear her gaze away from him. Golden sunlight kissed his scale-free blue skin, turning it light green, highlighting the translucent depths of his blue-green eyes. It reminded her of the way the sun pierced the top layers of the sea, sparkling in the swirls of nearly clear water.

Her heart thumped loud in her ears. Even in his fury, she understood him.

Anger masked his kindness, but she saw the passionate pursuit of justice in his eyes. It was a defining part of him, this sense of duty, this unwavering commitment to what he believed was right. He would always be her Dragon King, the one who spoke of stars with such excitement that it lit up the darkest nights. His dedication to his kingdom, though sometimes irrational, was proof of his selflessness and sense of duty.

The man who could be so fierce, so driven, could also be gentle, kind, and selfless. It was that duality that had captivated her heart, and even now, facing his icy demeanor, she couldn't help but love him. Leaving him again would destroy her, but she was a danger to him, to everyone. Besides, she'd broken his curse. There wasn't anything else he could want from her. Except the Sun Stone.

Rivus shifted back, his gaze on Edmar.

She plucked the hem of her short skirt, and balled Edmar's dingy shirt in her hands, considering. She hated clothes and felt vastly out of place with the two men comfortable in their skin. Her clothes were hot. The warmth of the sun felt strange after days in the forest. She almost wished for the frost and snow again.

She shivered and discarded the idea of removing her clothes.

"The Sun Stone," Rivus said. "Give it to me."

"You look better." Edmar tossed the pack out of Rivus's reach.

Rivus's bruises were fading, both eyes open, though dark circles remained. "I'm well enough."

Edmar crossed the distance between them in two strides and slammed his fist into Rivus's jaw, sending him sprawling. The sound echoed in the stillness.

She gasped, but her gaze darted to the satchel. *Can I escape?* She had to get the stones. *But then what?*

At least she could take her gem before Edmar understood its significance. She'd never surrender her control again. She'd fight for it. Edging closer to the bag, she looked back at Edmar, his muscles coiled, a blue aura crackling around him. He pressed his knee into Rivus's chest. Rivus groaned, cradling his jaw.

"How long, Rivus?" Edmar said, putting more weight on his knee. "How long have you been betraying the kingdom? Betraying me?"

Rivus strained against Edmar's weight. "Give me the Sun Stone."

She edged closer to the satchel, sharp pain in her soles. But at least her magic lay dormant. She didn't want to leave him, but what choice did she have? All she'd ever wanted was to be loved, but Edmar... She didn't think he held any fondness for her. Not now.

When he'd looked at her before the creature attack, there had been nothing in his eyes.

Just icy disdain.

It made sense to run. She inched closer.

"Tell me," Edmar said. "Why? Why sell Dwarven snow? Why steal from your king? Why run away with my wife? Why—" His voice cracked.

"The stone." Rivus's voice rasped. "Then you'll know I'm telling the truth."

Dwarven snow. Black powder. Rivus, his trusted friend, entangled in this web of treachery. Why had Rivus done all of those things? What possible gain could outweigh the risk, the potential for chaos and destruction?

"Tell me," he said, with a growl, "or I swear—"

She reached for the satchel, but Edmar glanced over his shoulder. She snatched it with a yelp and ran. Her magic woke, circulating in her blood with searing static.

And given that she'd only had legs for a couple of weeks, her legs screamed in protest, her feet aching from knife points.

He tackled her, and they went down. She screamed, struggling, clawing at the ground. Fire acid slipped into her muscles.

"Stop, Emira."

"Get off!"

He rolled her over and pinned her wrists, wrenching the satchel and his shirt away.

"No, please! You don't understand! Let me go." She bucked against him, but it was no use.

Then she felt it, the hardening of his body against hers. He may have erased his love for her, but his body responded to her, his pupils dilating, his gaze tracing her face, lingering on her mouth. She thought he'd kiss her again.

Her magic dissipated. *Pleasurable feelings calm my magic...*

His jaw clenched, icy contempt hardening his eyes. "I won't fall for your tricks again. Your love comes with teeth," he said. "And I'm never letting you go, Emira."

Why? "Your curse is broken. You don't need me anymore."

His eyes closed halfway. "Yes, your love broke the curse." He dropped his head close to hers, his breath freezing against her ear. "How does it feel to love a man who hates you?"

Sharp ice pierced her heart, colder than any ocean depth. *Hate?*

The playful banter, the shared laughter under the starlight, the warmth of his touch. All gone, replaced by chilling emptiness. She'd known she'd hurt him, but she hadn't realized the depth of the wound, the irreversible damage she'd inflicted.

The Ocean's Lament echoed in her soul.

He hated her. But his body... his body still desired her. Maybe this was the key to her freedom. Later, she'd mourn the loss of his love.

Slowly, she ground her hips against him. His eyes fluttered closed, and he growled low in his throat. Heat coiled inside her.

"You may hate me," she whispered, "but your body says otherwise."

He buried his face in her neck, his grip tightening. For a long moment, he didn't move. Was he reconsidering his true feelings? Perhaps his love was not lost.

"Edmar," she said. "Please. Believe me. I never meant to hurt you. It's my magic, it's cursed, and if you don't let me..."

He pushed himself up, grabbing the satchel and shirt, face etched with coldness. Any effect she'd had a moment ago vanished.

"Don't move," he said, pressing her down with his foot.

Heat crept up her neck as he turned away.

Momentarily he looked at the shirt, then with a sound of disgust, he stuffed it into the satchel and retrieved the iron box. He tossed the black Sun Stone to Rivus, who caught it one-handed. A new bruise had formed on his jaw.

Surprise filled Emmy that Edmar would just hand over the stone, but maybe he believed Rivus too weak to run away with it.

Edmar kept the bag in hand, his other clenched as if he wanted to hit Rivus again. "Now. Tell the truth."

CHAPTER 65

EDMAR

Rivus knelt before him, and Edmar tensed.

His Frostlands held. Barely.

Betrayal sat heavy in his chest, but he did not allow it to surface. He would not shatter. Not now. Not yet. If he let go, if he surrendered to the rage, what would be left?

Exhaustion, perhaps, or something worse, a hollowness that might never heal. The Blue Devil never relenting as he visited destruction on everyone.

He rubbed his healed chest, the phantom pain of Emira's attack reminding him of how much it hurt to love anyone. He needed answers but dreaded them. Their treachery overshadowed the joy of his broken curse. Emira loved him. The broken curse was proof enough of that.

And yet, it didn't feel like proof. It felt like another cruel joke. Another game played by the gods at his expense. If she loved him, then why had she run? Why had she stolen from him?

Rivus dropped his head, chin to his chest, and cradled the black Sun Stone. "For centuries, two goals have guided my life. To sow discord within your kingdom, and to ensure you never broke the curse."

The Sun Stone flared, a brilliant yellow light stabbing his eyes. Rivus's confession ripped through him, leaving him reeling. The light faded, but the searing heat of betrayal remained, branding his soul. He forced his voice to remain steady, but a thread of his hurt wavered in his voice. "Why?"

"It doesn't matter now," Rivus hesitated. "But she'll kill me—"

"Speak or I will kill you."

"If it was only my death, I wouldn't care." Amid the stone's yellow glow, Rivus looked up, his face gaunt, sickly in the light, his eyes vast caverns of guilt and fear. "She has my sister."

Understanding crashed down upon Edmar.

She.

The word pulsed with golden light.

There was only one *she* who would continue to lash out at him, who would care about the curse remaining intact.

It all made sense now, Rivus's insistence on Edmar bedding Emira before the wedding, the constant threat of the Dwarven snow... all orchestrated by *her*. He was a pawn in a game he didn't even know he was playing. A game that had spanned centuries.

She couldn't just leave them alone. A thousand years, and she still punished them. Cold rage surged. He wanted to rip the Snow Princess from her icy prison, shred her with his claws, bury her beneath a blizzard she could never escape.

Did her machinations include the Summer Child?

"Edmar!" Emira's voice, sharp with fear, pierced the red haze of his rage.

He blinked, the blizzard vanishing. Hailstones melted on the grass at his feet. She clutched his arm, her face paler, her short sapphire curls plastered to her head.

Shame washed over him. He'd never lost control like that, never felt such an all-consuming rage. Her understanding both soothed and terrified him. She should have no effect on him, but before he could bury the emotions again, the earth rumbled.

It began as a tremor, then intensified, a violent quake shaking them to their core.

He stumbled, fear twisting in his gut. This wasn't him. *This was something else, far more powerful.*

The earth buckled, the grassy plain undulating like the sea, the green rippling outward from the epicenter somewhere deep in the Malustra Woods. Trees swayed, branches snapping. He pulled Emira close, holding her tight.

The earthquake roared, the ground splitting beneath them. He fell, pulling Emira down with him. The world spun, a dizzying chaos of sound and sensation.

Had his rage triggered this cataclysm? Panic clawed at him.

The tremors finally subsided after several minutes, leaving behind a scarred landscape. Dust filled the air, the smell of freshly turned earth sharp in his nostrils. Beside him, Emira leaned into him, her green face pale with shock.

Rivus pushed himself up, his chest heaving. He sat back on his haunches, the Sun Stone in his hands. "I never wanted this." The stone glowed, verifying the truth of his words. "I'm sorry."

"Sorry?" Edmar's voice broke, a brittle edge to his words. "For what, Rivus? For your lies? Your deceit?"

"Yes," Rivus said, pain filling his eyes. "I did what I had to, to protect my sister. But that doesn't change... I love you, Edmar. Like a brother."

Rivus's words, a painful echo of the bond they once shared, and the stone's glow confirmed his sincerity. His brother in all but blood. And he knew what it was to protect those you loved. But the anger remained. "You turned your back on your king. You manipulated me, used my trust to keep me enslaved by that curse."

Rivus shook his head, the silver and blue strands in his brown hair shimmering in the dusty light. Another tremor shook the earth. "I know. But I would do it again. For my sister."

The stone's glow intensified.

Rivus sighed, then tossed the stone back to him.

Edmar caught it, his jaw clenched, the conflict tearing at him. He would do anything to protect his brothers, so he understood Rivus's fierce loyalty, but understanding didn't erase the betrayal, ease the pain. "You will face justice for your crimes."

"Perhaps," Rivus said, shielding his eyes. "One day. But today I must go. The curse is broken. My sister is in danger."

"You won't escape justice." The Sun Stone pulsed in his hand.

"Stop me, if that's what you truly wish," Rivus said, his voice hollow. "Every moment I stay, I risk her life. Every moment I stay, I risk your life, because I would sell every piece of information I have, double-cross a thousand kings, to keep her safe."

Fury threatened to consume him. The air crackled with his magical aura.

"Edmar, stop." Rivus's voice was sharp above the wind. "You'll destroy us all."

He fought for control, forcing the rage down, his icy wind dissipating. "If you leave, you can never return. If you do, you will be tried and hanged as a traitor."

Regret filled Rivus's eyes. "I know. And I accept that."

A complex blend of grief, sadness, and bewilderment filled him. He couldn't believe it had come to this.

With a final, sorrowful look, Rivus stood. "One day, I hope you can forgive me."

Edmar did not answer. There was nothing left to say.

Rivus shifted. The dire wolf, a flash of white and silver, disappeared into the Malustra Woods. His mournful howl echoed in the stillness, but Edmar did not watch him go. The man he once called brother was already gone.

Rivus's centuries of betrayal became a scar that would never heal.

His best friend had left him. Alone with his fury, his grief, and the woman who had deceived him.

He looked at her. Wide emerald eyes glimmered with her own complex emotions. Ones he couldn't decipher. Ones he wasn't sure he wanted to. Her expression remained carefully blank, her eerie stillness unreadable.

How little I understand her.

She loved him, yet she'd shattered his trust. He needed to know why. But knowing wouldn't change what she had done. It wouldn't undo the betrayal, wouldn't make her love mean something again.

Whatever her reasons, regardless of how much he hated her, he could never hurt her.

What now?

He pushed all those emotions into his Frostlands, his icy shield firmly in place. The world should have felt stable now. But it wasn't. Everything was shifting beneath him, just like everything else.

Blinding golden light exploded all around them.

He shielded his eyes, but the light was relentless, consuming the world. Like staring into the heart of the sun, a radiance so intense it seared his very being.

A figure emerged from the light, tall and imposing. So much power. Edmar recognized him, and his breath caught.

The earth trembled as the Sun God descended, forcing Edmar to his knees. His heart pounded a frantic rhythm against his ribs. He set the Sun Stone before him and bowed his head in reverence.

"Children of my brothers and sisters." The Sun God's voice boomed, reverberating through Edmar's soul. "Listen."

CHAPTER 66

EMMY

The Sun God?

Impossible—he hadn't been seen in centuries—yet, here he was. Emmy knelt beside Edmar, shielding her eyes. The ground trembled. Once more, it struck her that Edmar worshiped a deity not his own.

Then the Sun God spoke. His voice was like thunder, deep and resonant, vibrating through her bones. "You have nothing to fear."

She cautiously looked up, squinting against the radiant light. The figure shimmered like the sun, a being of pure white light. Power crackled in the air, making her skin tingle, her head swim.

"I do not fear you, my lord," Edmar said, his head still bowed. "But why do you seek this servant?"

The Sun God glanced at Edmar, warmth flickering in his brilliance. *Unsettling.*

The light figure flickered in and out of existence, his stance slightly shifting each time it solidified. "You have the honor of your kind, Ice Dragon. Let honor be your guide."

"As you command, my lord."

The Sun God chuckled. "Do not think to deceive me, Edmar. My light reveals the truth, and I see the anger simmering within you. You must set it aside."

"My lord—"

"Silence," the Sun God commanded, and the word seemed to echo through her very being, cutting through her thoughts, her doubts, her very will.

"Betrayal is as old as the gods, and betrayal between brothers is a play performed over and over through the ages. But anger is a dangerous path. It leads to vengeance, and vengeance is why the other gods sleep.

"I imprisoned them," Solis said, his voice heavy with regret. "Vengeance was my downfall. And now, I need them. The Summer Child is free."

The Summer Child?

The words sent a tremor through the ground. She gripped the earth, her heart pounding. Somehow the powerful child had been brought to life without her, but that meant a terrible power had been unleashed, one that could kill all Winter creatures—the merfolk, Ice Dragons, Water Fae, and so many lesser-known species.

"The child exists?" Edmar asked, disbelief in his tone.

"She exists," Solis confirmed. "Her very presence warps the fabric of this world. Already, creatures of darkness stir, drawn to her power. Ancient beings of Winter and Summer awakening. And this is only the beginning."

The Sun God laid a hand over his heart. "In nine months, my daughter will be born."

Her breath stalled. *His daughter?* She thought of all the stories she heard about the Summer Child being fathered by both the Sun God and the Fire God. "Then it's true. She's so powerful because the Summer gods are her fathers. But who is her mother?"

In time, Little Mermaid. The voice spoke directly in her mind, just like the Sea Witch had, ancient and powerful, silencing her. Solis continued, as if her questions hadn't interrupted him. "I've seen visions." His form flickered in agitation. "She will burn this world to cinders. The oceans will boil, the very mountains will crumble, leaving only a molten husk."

From the god's words, the image flashed in her mind: a world consumed by fire, nothing left but melting rock and rivers of silver. Dizzying visions overwhelmed her.

Beside her, Edmar stiffened, hands clenching. Even with his head bowed, his radiating tension matched her terror.

But she remembered what Morvella had said. "What about the Winter Child?"

The Sun God's form flickered. "I have found nothing to confirm his existence. It has taken me many millennia to even confirm my daughter still lived."

Edmar stirred, shaking out his fists. "What can I do?"

"The Seven Sleepers must awaken."

Hope sparked within her. The Seven Sleepers. This was her chance. Waking the Metal God, freeing herself from her curse. It all felt like a distant dream suddenly within reach.

But at what cost? She'd learned that everything came at a cost, and it seemed that waking a god would be a high one indeed.

"Will they help?" Edmar asked, his voice tight. "Will they stand against the Summer Child?"

She hadn't considered that. It just seemed natural to her that the gods would protect their creations from such a destructive being.

"They will." The Sun God's light dimmed slightly. "But waking them... will be difficult."

Exactly her thought. However, one question had always remained when she thought about finding her Father God. She asked it now. "How do I wake Metallon?"

"You seek Metallon first? Journey to his resting place. Spill the blood of one of his creations over my stone, and he will awaken. This same procedure must be done for each of my siblings."

Solis's form dimmed, sadness radiating from him. The world paused; her breath caught in her throat. She felt the weight of his sorrow and the gravity of what he asked of them.

Blood of Metallon's creations, like the merfolk. Surely it won't be a simple cut across her hand. No, the gods always took so much more. *My life for his awakening.*

Was this truly her fate?

Solis's words rattled through her mind. The Summer Child is free. The world could burn, the oceans could boil, and everything she'd ever known could turn to cinders. And yet... all she could think about was her own end.

It was selfish, wasn't it? With an apocalypse on the horizon, why did her thoughts cling to herself? But maybe because, for the first time in her life, she had a choice. A real one. And it was terrifying.

If the Sun God was right, this mission gave her more than just a task. It gave her time. Time to understand. Time to fight. Maybe even time to make Edmar see the truth before the end. But to what end? Would that time only serve to drag her to her final purpose?

This is what my life was always supposed to be. A means to an end for someone else's desires. First, my father would have used my death for his gain. Then Sea Witch, then Edmar with his desire to break the curse, and now the Sun God.

In almost every instance, she was to give up her desires to lead a life filled with safety, with love. Her death would make everyone happy.

Even Edmar.

Despair drowned her thoughts.

"You will do this, Little Mermaid," the Sun God said. "Once, I gave your mother a quest, but she failed. Now you can atone for her failure."

My mother? Her heart hammered against her ribs, every breath a struggle. Did Solis know she had killed her mother? The memory of her mother's death hit her, the cold sea around them, her fire acid boiling the water away. Her mother's calm, soothing voice absolving her. *"It's not your fault."*

Najla's fate was sealed long before her demise. Solis's voice echoed in her mind, and a sense of finality filtered in his tone.

Demise? Such an impersonal word for the tragic death of her mother. Did the gods feel this way about all of them, that their death meant nothing more than a footnote in history, along with their failures?

Had her mother's last words to her been an offer of forgiveness or a clue to why Emmy wasn't at fault? "What did you ask my mother to do?"

The light around the Sun God intensified, pulsing. "Careful of your thoughts, Little Mermaid! I gave your mother more power than I've ever given any other. She could have used her power to complete her quest, but she fell in love with the very person she was to kill."

"You asked her to kill someone?" She couldn't help her anger. Her sweet mother, an assassin?

Solis's radiance grew, heat overwhelming her. It was so hot, it stole the breath from her throat, leaving her parched, near choking on the dryness of her throat. Then it faded, revealing a tall, handsome man with golden-orange skin and a halo of golden hair.

"I've made many mistakes since the birth of our children." Despondency echoed in his voice. "I never discount any. But your mother knew the risks in accepting my power and her quest. Her success would have protected the one I love the most and saved us from this future."

Who do you love the most? Is it the Summer Child's mother?

But Solis didn't answer, saying instead, *I hope you don't let me down, too.*

She fisted her hands with resentment.

Edmar, silent during the last few moments and unaware of her internal conversation with Solis, asked, "Where is Metallon's resting place?"

Such a sensible question. It would save time instead of drawing out the answer from the Sun Stone.

A new golden-white aura surrounded the Sun God, and his human form partially dissolved into the light. "Aelunis."

Her breath hitched. *The shrouded land?* Aelunis remained hidden from the world by the Ever Mist for nine years before opening for a single year. It was open this year, but...

"Impossible," Edmar said, shaking his head. "Those waters are cursed. No one returns from Aelunis."

Merfolk avoided the waters close around the island, too. Their senses completely scrambled, lateral lines unable to reliably predict water flow or detect movement. Panic clutched her heart. "Even if we reach Aelunis... how will he return? How will we—"

Emmy couldn't finish the question that consumed her soul. She wanted to ask if the Sun God's request meant her death.

His light softened, resembling the gentle caress of the morning sun, but his silence was torment.

I don't want to die.

A hint of fondness caressed his voice. "Worry not, child. You have allies. You'll find all your answers on Aelunis."

But am I to die?

The question burned in her throat, unspoken.

Edmar rose, his expression grim but resolute. "It will be done."

Her heart pounded. *Did he understand?* Did he realize what this meant for her? Perhaps he didn't understand how punishing the gods could be. Or perhaps he wanted to honor the request of his precious Sun God and see her sacrificed to wake a god.

Fear choked her. Either she would die trying to wake her Father God, or she would become part of the Sea Witch's Garden of Souls. No escape, no peace. The Ocean's Lament rumbled within her, but she lifted her chin. "Why not awaken the Sleepers yourself?"

Solis solidified, his golden eyes holding hers. He was beautiful, powerful, alluring. Face stern but not unkind. Easy grace in his movements as he approached her, and she rose, refusing to kneel any longer.

He took her shoulders, heat radiating from his hands and body, his touch surprisingly gentle. "I grieve for what she has become, the one I love. Once, she was not the monster you know today. She was graceful and kind. But now vengeance drives her—that and a mother's love."

The god's overwhelming heat smothered her. So many questions, all making her dizzy. Who was this *she* he spoke of? "I don't understand."

"I can't wake them," Solis said, stepping back. "They would seek retribution for what I have done."

A blessed wind cooled her skin where the Sun God had touched her, but she laid hands over her churning stomach. *If he couldn't wake them, what hope do I have of surviving this?*

"And for this reason, I must leave soon. I will not be back for a long time, if ever," Solis said, his form blurring. "The world's fate rests with you. Wake the Sleepers. Save my daughter from the monster she'll become, and I'll ensure her mother doesn't interfere when our daughter is born."

The edges of the Sun God's form melted into light.

She glanced at Edmar, his jaw clenched.

He would feel the burden of responsibility more than her with his sense of duty and honor. This etched lines into his usually smooth features, but he peered into the light. "I swear to complete this duty, my lord."

She still had so many questions. *Who is the Summer Child's mother?*

The answer to her question sounded in her mind. *The Sea Witch.*

A dizzying torrent of what-ifs and hows swirled in her thoughts.

Why didn't the Sea Witch give birth to her own daughter? How could the Sea Witch, a creature of water, be the mother of the Sun and Fire Gods' child—opposing magics? What retribution did the Sea Witch seek?

And how did any of this involve her?

Some questions are better left unanswered, Solis said.

His golden light faded like a setting sun, Solis gone, leaving her alone with Edmar in the silent clearing. She rubbed her palms over her thighs, desperately seeking something solid. Solis's quest echoed—her curse, the Summer Child, the Sea Witch, Aelunis. The price of waking the Metal God.

It's too much.

Solis was gone, perhaps forever.

He wasn't her god, but he'd been the only one watching, the only one protecting the world. Now they were alone.

Until they woke the gods. Woke Metallon, the very thing that would likely kill her.

How did she dare take another step toward that terrible future?

What choice did she have?

None that she could see.

She shivered, wrapping her arms around herself. *A sacrifice to a god who didn't know her name.*

Even Edmar wished he'd never known her name. Loneliness threatened to suffocate her. She'd always been lonely, but never like this. Never had she felt so utterly abandoned.

CHAPTER 67

EDMAR

Heavy, cold silence fell, replacing the Sun God's radiance. Solis's pronouncements reverberated in the quiet clearing.

The Summer Child. Aelunis. The Seven Sleepers.

A dizzying array of urgency and dread swirled in Edmar's thoughts. The fate of the world rested on a quest as daunting as it was unexpected. A millennium spent seeking freedom from the curse, only to be burdened with a greater responsibility.

Nine months.

Nine months to awaken gods who had slumbered for eons, to unite them against a world-ending threat. The task felt impossible. And dangerous.

The real tragedy comes when the god awakens. He'll know what's been lost. All the sleeping gods above and below will weep.

Avi's words came back to him.

But what did it all mean?

He scrubbed a hand over his face. From his pursuit of Emira and Rivus, exhaustion settled deep in his bones, an ache in his empty heart.

His gaze drifted to Emira, her stillness unsettling against the backdrop of the fractured earth. A jagged fissure near her, a gaping wound in the ground, echoed the split between them. Tremors resonated from the earthquake. He realized they were the signs of the Summer Child's arrival.

The Summer Child Isa mentioned in her message. The Summer Child Adria warned would be exploited or aided by the Sea Witch with all the Gods' Stones. And now, the Summer Child who threatened the world.

And Emira was at the center of it all.

Was she collecting the stones for the Sea Witch, and would this new quest change her mind?

What am I to do about her? The question surfaced through the numbness of his Frostlands. She'd betrayed him, lied to him, stolen from him, tried to kill him. He should hate her, as he told her. *Yet...*

He looked at her, really looked at her, the curve of her jaw, the fragility in her eyes. He felt only emptiness. Because of her, he broke free from the curse, but he felt more trapped than ever. Retreating to his mental Frostlands soothed the pain, a semblance of freedom.

He picked up the Sun Stone, his fingers brushing against its cool, smooth surface, a symbol of his kingdom, its familiar weight grounding him. Duty called. Stashing it in his satchel, resolve solidified within him. A new sense of purpose rooted in his core, allowing him to move beyond his numbness.

He would not falter in the Sun God's quest.

"What now?" Emira asked, her voice tight despite her carefully composed features. Her gaze fixed on the satchel.

"Aelunis." The name heavy on his tongue.

"And me?" she asked, meeting his gaze. "Do you still plan to kill me?"

His inner dragon growled at the thought of losing her. Before Solis arrived, he'd been ready to punish Rivus and Emira. But he'd let Rivus leave. He understood the lengths one would go to for family. That left him with Emira and a holy quest. He couldn't let her go, but could he forgive her after what she'd done? He couldn't trust her, so what now?

"What will you do with *me*?" she asked again, her voice barely a whisper.

An emphasis on her words caught his ear, but he couldn't discern her intent until her gaze flicked to the satchel again. Understanding dawned. Morvella's words echoed in his mind: *"Her will is mine."*

He reached into the bag, his fingers closing around the small, deep red stone that had always graced her neck. Her gem.

"Tell me, Emira," his voice low, dangerous, "what does this mean?"

She inhaled sharply, her gaze darting to the gem in his hand, then back to his face, color draining from her face. Her voice strained. "Our gems are our magic.

Tied to our life force. One tether binds us to our parents. For males, it breaks at adulthood. For females—"

"I know this already, Emira." He ran his thumb over the gem. She trembled, and something twisted inside him. He should have felt satisfaction. But the feeling was muddled, tainted by something else—something dangerously close to regret.

He continued, his voice soft. "If there's one tether, that means there's another one. Tell me about the second tether."

Her jaw clenched, defiance and fear warring in her eyes. "You control me," she said, the words a strangled whisper. "Anything you command... I must obey."

He couldn't deny a certain satisfaction, knowing that she wouldn't be able to leave him again if he commanded her to stay. The thought both tempted and repelled him. How far did this control extend? "Morvella commanded you to kneel before her, to use you. If I ordered the same, you would have to obey?"

"Yes," she said through gritted teeth. "Is that what you want?"

The heat of her anger crossed the space between them even as he held up her dark-red gem. *So much power in this tiny stone.*

No wonder merfolk avoided the Land Bound. To have their very will bound to a physical object. It made them vulnerable, easily controlled. *Had her life always been like this? Controlled, manipulated?*

Now he held that control. The power to command her, to strip her of free will, to keep her bound to his side forever.

The thought should have satisfied him. But it didn't.

Because if he did that, if he wielded that power over her, what separated him from the ones who had manipulated and used her all her life? How did that not make him as terrible as the Snow Princess?

But he didn't want to let her go.

A flash of her fragility etched in the lines of her brow. Then it was gone. Despite her betrayal, he wrestled with the idea of making her stay with him and what kind of monster that would make of him.

At least he could say with absolute certainty that he wouldn't kill her. But could he ever atone for almost doing it?

He had pressed a blade to her throat. Had choked the breath from her body. Had watched as she gasped, as she clawed at his grip, as the life drained from her eyes.

And still, even now, she stood before him. Not with hatred. Not with vengeance. But with something else entirely.

Understanding.

What did all of that say about his true feelings?

Do I still love her?

A shock stabbed through his heart, catching his breath. Immediately he pushed the pain into his Frostlands, burying it beneath the icy landscape. The question of his love disappeared as the Blue Devil took over, leaving numbness where she was concerned. He couldn't let her hurt him again. She'd nearly destroyed him.

She was his queen, but wholly untrustworthy. He didn't dare trust her with the Sun Stone, not fully aware of her magical capabilities. That left their future as bleak as his Frostlands. Not a future with love-filled passion, as he'd always hoped for.

Her presence tortures me. Yet the thought of her gone is worse.

His Frostlands should have swallowed his pain by now. But it wasn't working. The ice cracked, and emotions leaked through the fractures, raw and relentless. Maybe retreating forever into his Frostlands was his only option. Maybe it was the only way to survive her.

But no, she was too dangerous. Too unpredictable. He had to keep her close, had to ensure she couldn't use her magic against him again.

"Emira."

She crossed her arms, wary.

"You will stay with me," he commanded, his voice firm. "And you will not use your magic."

"That won't work," she said, her voice flat.

He frowned at the stubborn set to her jaw. "Why not?"

"My magic is dangerous, uncontrollable." Her tone was not a taunt. She sounded afraid of her powers.

Why? Phantom pain flared on his chest. He rubbed the spot, fingers tracing the raw, healing skin. *Had she not meant to hurt me?* "Explain."

"I told you. It's cursed. I can't control it."

If that was true, she was a danger to everyone. How could he take her back to the palace, to the city and his people, if she could hurt them?

How could he keep her by his side if she could kill him at any moment? But her explanation didn't answer everything. "Your magic seems under control now. It wasn't a problem before we married."

"My control is temporary. The Sea Witch suppressed it, but the spell is fading. Soon, I won't be able to control it at all."

Her revelation crashed through him, supporting all his assumptions, but he wished it had been otherwise. "You are working with the Sea Witch."

Her gaze turned guarded.

"Is she having you collect all the Gods' Stones?"

As much as she tried to master her expression, her brows twitched up.

"Don't," he warned, his voice tight. "Don't lie to me."

"I swear I never wanted to."

He remembered her smile at their wedding, the warmth in her eyes. She loved him, but it was all a mockery of the life they could have had. So many instances of her lies, questions about the Sun Stone, diverting his attention from her true purpose.

"But you did," he said, his voice cold. "By omission, and by deliberate deceit, you've lied."

"You wouldn't have understood," she said, her emerald eyes shimmering with anger.

"You never gave me a chance—"

"You would have stopped me! With your sense of duty, you wouldn't have let me take the Sun Stone—"

"Of course not—"

"You would have imprisoned me, just like my father!"

"I am nothing like your father."

Her eyebrows slashed down. "You're just like him. You think you're always right, that everyone must obey your righteous path. You can see no way other than your own."

His balled fists twitched. She mocked everything he took pride in. He inhaled slowly, seeking the icy calm of his Frostlands. He'd always striven for justice and peace. His kingdom flourished under his rule, unlike his brothers. Once, he'd thought she liked that part of him.

What a wonder she loved him at all.

He wouldn't waste any more time arguing. He'd stop her from completing the Sea Witch's quest. "When you told me about your mother, you said you knew what to do to avoid using your magic. How?"

Guarded skepticism fell over her face again, and she pursed her lips, not speaking.

"Your father knew. That's why he isolated you. How did he control your magic?"

"You told me once that you wouldn't make me reveal my secrets."

A tic jumped in his jaw. "That was before you betrayed me."

Her eyes narrowed. "Where is the Edmar who embodied patience and kindness?"

"Dead. Stabbed in the back by his wife and best friend." His fist clenched around her gem. "Answer me. How did you keep everyone safe from your magic?"

She flinched at his command. "I didn't move."

Memories of her flashed in his mind. The way she'd watched him from Siren's Cove twenty-five years ago, frozen in place. The way she'd stood like a statue, her head bowed, when they'd met with the Seat of the Dwarf. The way she often completely immobilized herself, her face a blank mask, her emotions locked away.

"Not moving keeps it dormant."

She blinked slowly. "Yes."

She was hiding something, but this was enough. He had to ensure she remained harmless. Had to contain the danger she posed.

Will she hate me for this?

Does it matter?

Holding her gem should have made him feel secure, victorious. Instead, it felt like a shackle around his own throat.

But only until he could find a better way for her curse to be broken than through the Sea Witch. Once they finished their quest for the Sun God, he wouldn't stop until he found a way to break her curse.

"Emira." She'd just have to hate him until he could help her. "I command you to live as you did before—"

"No!" she cried, her hands rising, her eyes pleading. "Please, don't! I can't—"

"Silence," he said coldly, retreating into his Frostlands. Her pleas had too much power. He couldn't allow her to sway him. "I command you to stop speaking and to stop moving. You will do nothing that will make you lose control of your magic."

She froze, defiance blazing in her eyes. Whatever words she had for him remained behind closed lips.

Doubt gnawed at him. Cracks spread through his Frostlands.

Why? He was regaining control over everything, so why did his Frostlands suffer?

For a thousand years, he'd done his duty and protected his people. He'd sacrificed his autonomy in choosing his queens, silently mourning them as they died too young. Over and over, he'd married against his will, yielding to the curse's compulsion so that his people could prosper, live, and be happy... even when he wasn't allowed to find the same happiness.

His duty was always to his kingdom, and it would continue. Even if it meant silencing her.

New frigidity solidified in his Frostlands, hardening against the doubt that threatened to take root.

She was a threat. That much, he could not forget. She had stolen from him, deceived him, nearly killed him. And for what?

The Sea Witch's plan? A power she refused to control? A cause greater than the kingdom she had sworn to serve as its queen?

She didn't care about his sacrifices. She didn't care about his kingdom. She didn't care who got hurt, so long as she had what she wanted.

That, he could never forgive.

He turned away from the fire in her eyes, shifting. Pain lanced through him as bones cracked and reformed, scales replacing skin. He unfurled his wings, their shadows falling across the shattered earth.

He gathered her into his scaled arms, drawing in a large breath to warm his torso. Her cheek fell against the thinner skin of his chest, her touch sending a jolt through him, a confusing mix of anger and longing.

He couldn't reconcile the two. The deceit and the devotion, the pain and the pleasure. The hate and the something else, clawing at the edges of his mind, demanding to be acknowledged.

With a roar of frustration, he launched into the sky, leaving behind the shattered earth and devastating revelations.

CHAPTER 68

EDMAR

Behind Edmar, the earthquake's devastation stretched as far as the eye could see. Trees, ancient and tall, lay uprooted, scattered like matchsticks. Deep fissures scarred the earth. Ahead, the landscape remained untouched, his kingdom of gentle hills giving way to flattened fields, villages, and pastures.

As they soared through the air, his mind churned with a dizzying mix of emotions: relief at the curse's end, fury at Emira's betrayal, fear for the world's future, and a deep, haunting sorrow he couldn't shake. He struggled to bury the emotions in his Frostlands.

Controlling Emira worked against every fiber of his being. No one should control another like that, but she was a danger. Her attack proved that.

What if her magic is truly uncontrollable? She'd never be able to move again. *Maybe that is why she went to the Sea Witch.*

But it didn't excuse her betrayal. There was still so much he didn't know or understand.

Maybe returning her to her father would be best. She'd be imprisoned again, but at least she'd be safe. At least his people would be safe. At least he wouldn't have to fight this war within himself every time he looked at her.

But the thought of never seeing her again hurt his heart almost as much as the thought that he might still love her. His soul lay empty without her.

What should I do?

He tightened his grip, fear battling a possessive urge to keep her close. He didn't understand. Not her magic, not her motives, not her betrayal. Anger, his constant companion these days, faded, replaced by a hollow ache. Emptiness threatened to consume him as her ocean homeland glimmered on the horizon. They reached the capital quickly. The stone and silver city sprawled beneath him, the Lunarclaw River a shimmering vein of light.

Relief washed over him. The capital was untouched by the devastation he'd witnessed inland. *My people are safe... for now.*

He didn't go to the palace. Not yet. He needed to understand her motivations. He flew south, descending to the secluded beach nestled at the base of the cliffs beneath his palace. If he truly had to keep her immobile, he needed answers to decide what to do next.

Shifting back was agony, each bone cracking, each muscle screaming. His new skin was tight, burn marks still visible on his chest. He set her down, her scent a torment, stirring a longing he couldn't suppress.

He turned away, needing space. Waves crashed against the shore.

He had questions. He needed answers. But he dreaded them.

Yet ignoring them wouldn't help. He turned back to her. "You may speak. But don't attempt to escape. Tell me why you stole the Sun Stone."

Her emerald eyes met his.

"You want to know why I betrayed you?" she whispered, her voice laced with a bitterness he didn't understand. "My magic is a prison I've endured for two hundred years. The Sea Witch offered me freedom, unlike you."

Her words were a slap, a cut deeper than any blade. A fleeting image—his son's tiny face, his cheek turning cold in his last moments—flashed through his mind, a bitter reminder of the curse that bound him, that had taken so much from him.

He'd been a fool to trust her, to believe in their shared future. The Blue Devil roared out his Frostlands, the ice cracking, thawing, releasing a torrent of fury. His voice hardened. "And you think freedom justifies your choices? Your deceit?"

"What choices? I had no choices." She shook her head, defiance flickering in her eyes. "I had to be free."

"Free?" he said, stepping closer, his shadow falling over her. "At what cost? Did you consider the consequences?"

"I was dangerous," she said, her voice breaking. "My magic wouldn't hurt anyone if I were free of it."

"The cost of your freedom is too great, and you were only a danger if you moved."

Her sea-foam green skin darkened. "That's not a life! That's a prison I endured far too long. What was I supposed to do? Kill myself?"

No. He'd never want that. But what would he have done?

He didn't believe for one moment that he would have ever made a choice that deliberately put others in danger, but living in a silent, unmoving hell would have driven him insane.

"I understand your desperation, Emira." He truly did. "I know what it's like to be chained to a curse. I spent a thousand years with mine, forced into empty unions, my heart a barren wasteland." He paused. "But I don't understand why you helped the Sea Witch. You know what she's capable of."

"As I said, I had no choices, but you don't seem to understand this."

"No? I lived the same life. I followed the rules. I sacrificed love, freedom, everything, for my people. And you? You ran. You stole. You lied. And now you tell me I don't understand?"

"You think sacrificing your heart is the same as having your body stolen from you? You think choosing to follow the rules is the same as never having a choice at all?" Her emerald eyes became chips of stone. "I lived with literal chains holding me down every day."

He scrubbed hands over his face. "I feel I'll never exit this endless loop of betrayal, pain, and incomprehension with you."

His gaze lingered on the lines of tension etched around her eyes, still seeing the mermaid who had first captured his attention and heart. His breath stuttered.

He brushed a strand of hair from her cheek, the touch electric. She inhaled sharply, her chest rising, then falling. Had she felt the same connection between them? He was certain that at least their physical attraction was still there. She wanted him as much as he wanted her. But fear and anger held him back from taking her in his arms.

Panic surged. *What about Rivus?* Had she turned to the werewolf, loving his best friend even if their relationship remained chaste?

"Tell me everything, Emira." His heart pounded. "Why did Rivus help you in your quest? Tell me...why did you leave?"

Why did you leave me?

For a moment, their eyes met, and hope flickered. Perhaps beneath the layers of betrayal and deceit, love survived—survived in a form he understood and recognized, because this wasn't something that made any sense to him. But then she looked away to the sea.

Sharp and unforgiving frustration twisted in his gut. Her silence was a fortress, and he was locked outside, pounding at the gates. He wanted to shake her, force her to look at him, to acknowledge what she had done to him. To his kingdom. To them.

He yelled into the void of his Frostlands but found no relief.

"Why?" he asked, his voice rough. "Don't I deserve an answer?"

Her body remained rigid, her face a carefully blank mask, but her emerald eyes… they flickered with fear. It was a subtle shift, but it was there.

Was she afraid of him?

"You can tell me." He softened his tone. "I won't hurt you."

"I'm not afraid of you."

"Then what?" he asked, his voice low. "What frightens you?"

She swallowed, her gaze darting to the sea. Still evading him. He resented the fact that he might have to force the truth from her.

"Don't lie," he said, his voice sharp.

She stiffened further. "I have no reason to lie."

"Yet you're hiding something."

"You wouldn't understand."

"Try me."

"You know my father wanted to use me to kill the Seat of the Dwarf," she said, her eyes blazing. "That's why I fled. If I'd stayed, I would have killed again. Then I would have died."

"That would have been more honorable than working with the Sea Witch."

"Just as I thought. You don't understand." She narrowed her eyes. "The Sea Witch would have removed my magic. I'd be free, never worrying about killing anyone again. I could have been your wife in more than name."

With each word, his anger grew, widening cracks in his glaciers, deep chasms threatening to separate into individual icebergs. "What will the Sea Witch do with the Gods' Stones?"

"I don't know," she said, her gaze falling to the water.

A sharp crack sounded in his mind as a chunk of ice broke free in his Frostlands. "You wanted to not worry about killing anyone by putting that power directly into the hands of one who lacks the same scruples, who would use that power to kill, and you'd still be responsible. How could you be so reckless?"

Her voice was small. "I never meant to hurt anyone."

"You've said that." He stomped away from her, running a hand through his hair, then pivoted back. "You used me, used my kingdom. You've joined forces with the Sea Witch. Did you even think about her plans?"

Her shoulders trembled, her eyes sorrowful, but she didn't answer.

So he gave her the answer. "She wants to use the stones to control the Summer Child."

Her chin snapped up. "She wouldn't do that."

Her certainty gave him pause. "How would you know?"

"The Summer Child is her daughter. The Sun God told me in my mind."

The Sun God had also spoken into his mind, but Solis hadn't passed on that information. The Sun God and the Sea Witch had a daughter. No wonder the Summer Child was dangerous to the world with such conflicting magics, like the Ember Wraith.

And Emira would have given her the stones. "You're a danger, Emira. To everyone."

She looked away. "What choice did I have?"

"I would have never helped the Sea Witch."

"Must be nice to be so honor bound. To have the luxury of choosing your duty. I never got that. That's why I could never tell you."

Her words were a slap, a painful reminder of his fears.

"How could you have been falling in love with me when you didn't even trust me with yourself?" The words ripped from him, raw and ragged. He wanted to deny her love, but he knew it was true. She'd broken his curse.

"I never said that." Her voice was flat, emotionless.

Fury replaced hurt. He didn't understand her. Love and betrayal, desire and flight... How could she reconcile such contradictions?

How could this sane, rational, beautiful creature, this woman who'd stolen his heart with her stories and a shared love for the stars, be the same as the woman who only thought of herself, caring nothing about the threat she represented?

How could she love him, yet steal from him and run away with his best friend?

He couldn't shake the image of her with Rivus, the thought of their shared betrayal. Scheming. Planning. Deciding his fate without him. Keeping him blind while they took everything from him. Whispering behind his back, making choices he hadn't even known existed. Had she ever truly been his, or had he only been a fool in a game he never understood?

Her scent drifted to him on the breeze, a torment, a temptation. He wanted her, despite everything. That was the cruelest part. His own need defied reason.

His mind yelled at him to stop—that touching her was like a drug he couldn't deny—but he didn't listen. Stepping up behind her, his hands closed on her hips. His thumbs brushed the bare skin above the short skirt, tracing the lush curve of her waist.

She closed her eyes, shivering, her skin erupting in goosebumps.

A tremor of desire, not fear.

One of his hands traveled up her body to tangle in her short hair, gently tilting her head. He kissed her neck, her pulse fluttering beneath his lips.

For a moment, she leaned back into him, then stiffened, her breath catching.

He stilled, but didn't want to release her yet as questions bombarded him.

Why had she chosen him? Why did she betray him? Why had she gone to *Rivus*?

"Tell me, Emira," he said against her skin, his voice rough with barely controlled need. "Did you lie to him the way you lied to me? Did you try to seduce him, too?"

Her body went rigid. "What?" she asked, her voice sharp with confusion.

He released her, stepping back. "Did you climb on top of Rivus like you did with me?" he asked, his voice harsh. "Did you let him believe he was the only one you wanted, too?"

Do I really want to know the answer?

If she said yes, would it change anything? Would it make hating her easier? Would it make wanting her stop if he learned he'd never been special to her at all?

Her expression shifted from shock to anger, her emerald eyes flashing with fury. "Why would you ask me that?"

"Because I don't know what was real," he admitted, his voice raw. "You swore yourself to me, made me believe I was yours. And yet you ran to Rivus. So tell me, Emira, did you use him the same way?"

Hurt flickered across her face, but she lifted her chin. "I already told you I didn't give myself to him, which you know the truth about, or I couldn't have broken your curse."

He ignored the ache in his chest, the voice that told him she was right, that she had already proven her love. But self-doubt whispered he continued to be the fool for even caring. "That doesn't mean you didn't let him kiss you, touch you."

"No one touched me," she said, her voice trembling with anger. "Only you. And that... that seems to be a mistake now."

Her words cut him open, exposing something raw and ugly inside him. He could either bleed or freeze it over. He chose the latter, latching onto anger instead of pain. It was easier that way.

Anger that once more she thought him a fool when only a moment ago her body had responded to him. "Lying again?"

"I did what I had to. I kept you safe." Emira trembled, her arms wrapping around her waist. "Don't you understand? I love you. I don't know why, but I do."

His Frostlands fractured, and for one agonizing moment, he almost believed her. Almost let himself fall into the impossible hope of it.

But then he remembered.

The stolen Sun Stone. The lies. The choices she made without him.

"You say you love me, but I don't know how to believe you." His heart raced as he circled around to face her. "How can love be so deceitful? How can you love me when our values don't match?"

"But they do," she said, yearning in her voice.

He shook his head. "You were reckless. You didn't care about the consequences of your actions, gathering the stones for the Sea Witch."

"I had no choice!" A glow lit beneath her skin. "Should I have continued to live in silence? To watch everyone around me flinch when they had to touch me? Should I have allowed my father to sell me in marriage knowing I was going to kill? To be a monster—"

"Emira—"

"You're right, Edmar. I am an idiot for the choices I've made, and we have nothing in common. So look down on me from your high throne of self-righteousness, and do what you must."

"Emmy, stop!"

She closed her eyes, deep red light flaring, her hands turning translucent.

He held his breath, wondering if he should shift and take flight. He slipped the satchel from his shoulder, unsure what would happen if he took her gem with him. Regardless of what she'd done to him, he didn't want to hurt her.

Dark red light spilled from the satchel, then dimmed. Her breathing slowed; her skin returned to her normal sea foam-green color.

She opened her eyes.

"You can control your magic." He searched her face, seeking an answer to yet another lie, but finding only weary resignation.

"Only if I catch it in time," she said, her voice strained. "The Sea Witch's spell... it's waning. I'll have very little influence over my power when I'm at full strength again at the next full moon."

The danger she posed, not just to him, but to everyone around her...

Free from one curse, only to be shackled by another. He'd help her find a way to overcome her curse, but right now, he was exhausted, drained, utterly conflicted.

One part of him was a fierce need, an urgent possessiveness to both keep her safe and to never let her leave again. That part warred with the anger and hurt of her betrayal, with the rage of knowing what she had meant to do with the Gods' Stones. She was willing to allow the world to burn around her if it meant she had her freedom.

He couldn't trust her. Not ever.

Another iceberg collapsed in his Frostlands. "Emira, until we break this curse on your magic..."

He looked at her, the woman who had shattered him, the woman he couldn't let go. His emotions churned, breaking free, spiraling out of his control. He didn't know what else to do.

He retreated into his Frostlands, sealing the cracks before they could destroy him.

"You will be as you were before. Silent. Still. Safe."

Chapter 69

EDMAR

With both of them dressed in decent clothes retrieved from his cave along the beach, Edmar returned to the palace, carrying Emira while he climbed the long flight of marble steps. Grigor, his steward, met him in the Grand Hall, surprise evident on his thin face. One look at Edmar, and he fell silent, following him through the halls.

Grigor's surprise was understandable. He'd never appeared during daylight hours. Even without knowing about his curse, everyone knew he disappeared during the hours between sunrise and sunset, never to be seen nor found.

"Prepare my trunks for a two-week voyage," he said to Grigor, "and the queen's."

He could count on his steward's meticulousness and organization to see his orders followed. Grigor was one who had never failed him, a large part of the Emerald Palace's success.

With his dragon form always accessible now, he could fly to Aelunis, but not with Emira. The extra load would hinder his navigation through the storms surrounding the island, making it treacherous, even without the Evermist.

And he wouldn't leave without her.

Despite the hurt she caused, despite the rage still simmering beneath his skin—no matter how much he should hate her—he couldn't let her go. Not yet. Maybe not ever. That truth sat like a stone in his chest, heavy, immovable.

She was a vital part of him, a living extension of his soul.

Soul Half. Adria's words echoed in his mind.

Maybe not, but he still wouldn't leave her behind in the Emerald Palace.

Wherever his adventure took him, wherever he had to sail, she'd be with him, and he began to think of his northern trip to Aelunis and what that would look like. He'd already considered how he'd navigate the icebergs and massive ice sheets as well as the storms. The waters were treacherous the further north they traveled, and they'd have to go slowly to avoid a collision and sinking.

Yet Emira's magic returned in a week. Hopefully, they'd learn more after waking Metallon. Understanding a little more about her cursed magic, he now knew why she'd questioned Solis about the Metal God. Did she think that would provide answers, or an alternate solution to helping the Sea Witch?

Even though she'd said she wouldn't lie to him anymore, she was not forthcoming with information without him pulling it from her.

Grigor followed him into the solar, a private sitting room with large windows, bowing. "Your trunks remain packed from your honeymoon, Your Majesty."

Honeymoon. The word tasted like ash. "Have them put on my ship, the *Silver Lily.*"

"Of course, Your Majesty. I will see it done."

Edmar placed Emira in a cozy seat overlooking the garden. Anger etched lines around her eyes, but she refused to meet his gaze.

His own fury and rage agitated in the widening cracks of his Frostlands, their heat melting the ice. Her betrayal, her recklessness, created a maelstrom of conflict that allowed his weak emotions to surface from the fractures.

He would let her believe this was a punishment for her crimes, but it wasn't.

Though he'd never want to control another being, her dangerous magic left him little choice. Risking his people's safety was not an option. It was this or leave her outside his city, somewhere far from him, but he didn't want to leave her, not even for a moment.

With a sigh, not really wanting to leave her side, he turned to Grigor. "Where is Father Jayasurya?"

"The Council Hall, Your Majesty."

He climbed the stairs to meet with his regent. Emira's painite, tucked away in one fist, tugged toward her, stronger the further he traveled away from her. With her gem, he'd always know how to find her. *Handy.*

The abbot stood by the fireplace in the Council Hall, his brow furrowed with concern as Edmar explained about the Dwarven snow and Rivus's role in the sale and distribution in the kingdom.

"That explains a lot," Father Jayasurya said. "Several smaller villages in the far south of our kingdom have been wiped out by the black powder, completely burned down to the ground. Most bordered the Malustra Woods."

"Why didn't we have reports from those villages before now?"

"Few survived, Your Majesty. Since these villages were far apart, there was little travel and communication between them, and the attacks were recent. Our scouts are just now returning."

He went to the floor-length windows, looking out at the same view Emira would have one floor below him, and he brushed his fingertips over her gem. Questions persisted, but the Sun God's quest was urgent.

Centuries of relative peace in Cyaneus, now shattered. The Snow Princess had used Rivus to create disruption with the black powder and to push him toward Emira, who intended to steal the Sun Stone.

Does Emira know the Snow Princess?

A question for later.

"Did the earthquake reach the city?" he asked, already knowing the answer.

A faint rustle of cloth. The abbot shook his head. "Some rumors of tremors further east, but nothing here."

"Good."

"The queen is still alive," the abbot said. "I'm glad you've overcome your vengeance."

"Age should bring wisdom," he said, glancing at the man. "But injustice clouds judgment."

Father Jayasurya didn't know about the curse, but Edmar had always believed he handled it better than his brothers. Kalden becoming more and more reclusive, Zane giving up ruling his kingdom to be a womanizer, and Rin completely ignoring the curse, stuck forever as a dragon.

He'd met the curse's dictates and ruled his kingdom with the most pragmatism. But really, he'd just buried all of his anger and resentment in his Frostlands until Emira resurrected everything by breaching his icy domain.

Those aged brown eyes seemed to peer deep into his very being. "So, all is well between you?"

He shrugged, unsure how to answer.

"I saw you arrive with a queen who had fire in her eyes."

"I don't wish to burden you when everything is close to being resolved."

"Is it?" The skepticism in his tone lay heavy in the air.

He shifted uncomfortably. He couldn't tell him everything. Not about his curse or her cursed magic.

The abbot waved a hand. "It is not my business what happened. We all have secrets, and we've all made mistakes. I know you cared about the queen. Has she done something so terrible to damage your love for her?"

It was the very question he wrestled with. A question he refused to answer. Because if the answer was yes—if he still loved her—what did that make him? A fool? Or something worse?

Father Jayasurya sighed. "If all is close to a resolution, and you have everything you've wanted, then you cannot let mistakes define your future relationship. Life will offer few rewards if you hold onto your anger. It will take hard work to overcome these trials, but won't it be worth it?"

A glimmer of what the future could hold for him and Emira crossed his mind. He didn't want to always feel anger toward her, an anger so hot that he'd learn to hate her more than he'd ever love her.

"I have faith in you." The abbot smiled. "You retrieved the Sun Stone?"

"I did."

Father Jayasurya made a noise of contentment.

"But I need to keep it for a while." He fully faced the abbot, who wore a look of concern. "The Sun God gave me a holy quest," he said. "It requires the stone."

The abbot's eyes widened, and he placed a hand on Edmar's shoulder, his touch both gentle and firm. "A divine mission is a great honor, Your Majesty."

A great honor?

The abbot continued. "This will test you. Prepare yourself, body and soul. I'll offer whatever guidance and support I can."

A god had sought him and had given him a holy quest. Long dormant, excitement coursed through his veins. "I entrust you with the secret but share with no one else. Powerful forces might try to stop me."

"By the light of the Sun God, I swear to aid you and keep your secret," he said, his voice resonant with conviction. His expression softened with a mix of pride and concern. "I remember the day you first came to me, seeking guidance. You have always been a remarkable leader, but do not forget to take care of your own soul. You don't have to bear this burden alone."

Not alone. He'd felt alone for so long. Emira had been the first light in his loneliness.

"What is this quest?" the abbot asked.

Once, Edmar trusted the abbot nearly as much as Rivus. His ability to detect loyal friends now felt flawed. He didn't know who to trust. But there was no one better to rule in his absence. "I'm to awaken the gods."

The abbot stared at him. "I'm sorry, Your Majesty," he said. "I must have misheard."

Excitement leaked into his voice. "The Sun God tasked me with awakening his brothers and sisters."

"Deus meus." The abbot raised praying hands to his face, touching the top of his fingers to his forehead, his face paling.

The abbot's reaction surprised him.

"You're worried?" Unease settled in his chest when he remembered Avi's premonition about awakening the gods.

The abbot nodded. "Yes, Your Majesty, I am fearful. For you. You have your wife back and the weight of a divine task. This can be overwhelming for any man. Promise me you will seek counsel, not just from the gods, but from those who care about you."

"I will endeavor to fulfill my duty to this kingdom and not lose myself in the holy quest."

"Good. Because I'm worried about this quest."

"Why?"

"The Chaos Lore," the abbot whispered, turning toward the fire, his hands trembling. "One of the last Moon Fae prophecies spoke of the gods' awakenings. It's the beginning of the end. The Chaos Lore."

The Chaos Lore. Now there was something he hadn't heard about in a long time. Although it was part of the Serpent's Embrace constellation story he'd told Emira.

An ancient legend, foretelling the end of magic, a doomsday for magical creatures. For all dragons. For him. It was a future in which humans wouldn't be as defenseless, and they would no longer need dragons to protect them. He'd heard the stories before, dismissed them as superstition. But the abbot's fear was real, and that unsettled him more than he wanted to admit.

The Chaos Lore was also the last thing he and his brothers had argued about when the Snow Princess had unleashed her curse. Those thoughts dampened his mood. He hoped it wasn't true. He hoped Avi's premonition and this prophecy were wrong. But the Sun God had commanded him, and he would see that he completed his holy orders.

"I'll pray for your success, Your Majesty." Father Jayasurya's voice was firm and unwavering. He stepped closer, his eyes meeting Edmar's with a steady gaze. "And I'll rally the faithful. You've always been our beacon. Now, we'll be yours."

A knock sounded at the door.

"Enter," Edmar said.

Grigor bowed his way in.

Edmar glanced at the abbot, a warning for silence, then smiled at Grigor. "Yes?"

"Pardon, Your Majesty, but I thought you should know the pirate captain has returned."

The steward wrinkled his nose at the words *pirate captain*, which almost made Edmar laugh. He tried to keep the humor from his voice. "Captain Adria is back in port?"

With a sniff, the man crossed his hands over each other in front of him, his chin raised. "She never left, Your Majesty. But she's returned to the palace now, speaking with the queen."

Chapter 70

EDMAR

"Met her at the Coral Gardens, I did, on her twentieth birthday. Wasn't supposed to be there, but I snuck off my mother's ship. After that, Najla and I were as close as a pair of pirates." Adria's voice echoed down the hall, quickening Edmar's pace.

He recalled Adria telling him she'd been best friends with Emira's mother. And that it was all connected. *But how?* He really didn't want to think too hard about that right now. *A long bath and maybe even sleep, though sunset was still hours away... But first, the pirate.*

His eyelids felt heavy, as if weighted with sand. Each step a monumental effort, legs protesting every movement. The events of the past few days had left him feeling raw. He'd always prided himself on his control, but his Frostlands had begun to crack. Great icebergs floated away from the mental land, releasing too many emotions.

Adria clasped Emira's hand as he entered. "You look so much like your mother. If you had her sapphire eyes, I'd swear you were her."

Bathed in the afternoon sun's golden rays, Emira blinked in response to Adria's words. The vision of her stole his breath.

Her emerald gaze was a placid sea, yet he sensed the fiery current of magic rippling beneath that surface. Untamed, volatile, a haunting echo of her attack earlier. Her concealed fury, masked by her forced obedience, mocked him, stirring the storm within his own chest.

He yearned for the ease they'd once shared, the way she had once looked at him without walls between them. But the memories couldn't erase the damage of her lies, her theft.

Adria dropped Emira's hand, rising, a scowl darkening her blue-gray eyes. Today the pirate was dressed in a ruffled, bright blue shirt paired with soft, brown trousers, and her signature pair of daggers sheathed on the belt around her hips. "Very little rattles me, Edmar."

Moisture filled the air, pulled from somewhere that would have awed him if not for the very real, very angry Water Fae pirate before him. Her hair frothed around her face.

"She's none of your concern, Adria," he said, his voice colder than he intended. The Frostlands beckoned, offering refuge.

"Like hells she isn't!" Moisture thickened, droplets gathering on the intricate carvings of the ceiling. "Her mother was my closest friend. I won't see her daughter treated like this."

"Friendship means little to me. Friends are more likely to stab you in the back than enemies."

Rivus's betrayal was a wound that wouldn't heal.

"Give me her gem." She extended her hand. "No matter her deeds, she deserves to walk free. I know this life. Lived it myself when I was cursed."

He chuckled darkly. "*My wife* will not escape me again. Besides, this is for everyone's safety. You are unaware of the danger she poses."

"Danger? Look at the poor lass! Can't move, can't speak. She's no danger to anyone."

"Adria," he said with a growl. "When she moves, her magic becomes unstable."

The Water Fae hesitated only a moment. "Give her a fair chance to learn her own limits. This ain't right, what you're doing."

Is she right? Emira had said she could control it right now. And Rivus had said the only reason she'd attacked him was because of his own actions.

Water swirled around Adria's hand, ready to attack.

"Adriavata, stop!"

The water splashed down. A fae's true name had the power to control them, the Fae Willing, so Adria's true name should have given him complete control. But as a royal, Adria retained a spark of resistance. Still, he'd suppressed her magic for now.

Her face flushed a deep purple with anger, and she seethed through her teeth. "Your command won't last forever. And when it breaks, you'll have me to reckon with."

"I'll lock you up if you interfere," he threatened. He'd idolized her once, but she had no right to interfere.

She laughed, her dark blue and green hair swirling like violent waves. "Go on, try it, kid. Even if you break through my magic, you'll have my husband and crew to face."

They stared each other down, a silent battle of wills.

Incarcerating Adria crossed his mind, but the consequences were too steep. He couldn't bear losing another friend, especially when the ice beneath his feet was already cracking. And then there was her husband to consider—a former Moon Fae Prince whose sense of duty and justice aligned with his own. The hybrid fae's love for Adria knew no limits.

His grip on Emira's gem tightened. Giving it back meant giving up control. Letting her move meant taking a risk he wasn't ready for. But Adria wouldn't let this go, and the weight of it—of everything—was crushing him. His fingers curled tighter around the gem before he forced himself to give in.

Adria's expression softened, recognizing his acquiescence. She exasperated him.

"You are free to move, Emira," Edmar said, his voice flat, devoid of the tenderness he once reserved for her. "But if your magic returns, you'll be immobile again. Understood?"

Her lips parted on a sigh and everything within him was drawn to her, an urge to bridge the distance separating them and breathe the air that left her mouth. He ruthlessly suppressed the impulse, reminding himself of the chasm her betrayal had created.

"Thank you, Adria," Emira said, her voice soft. "I'd love to hear more about my mother."

Adria smiled. "Anytime!"

Emira smiled back, and another crack spider-webbed across his Frostlands. The sight of their easy connection, the warmth in Emira's voice, twisted something inside him. He yearned for that same warmth, that unguarded smile, but it felt lost forever, lost in the wreckage of her actions.

Emira rose, her movements slow and graceful. He kept a wary eye on her and her gem, searching for any sign of her magic returning—the light beneath her skin or the red glow in the jewel. For now, the signs didn't appear.

"Can I ask a favor?" Emira asked Adria. "This is not just for me, but it's very important."

"I'll do what I can to help you, no matter what," Adria said.

"Can you take me to Aelunis?"

He stiffened. "You will sail with *me*, Emira."

She turned to him, her emerald eyes cool and distant. "I do not wish to be near you unless necessary."

Her words, though spoken softly, cut through him like a blade. He had told himself he didn't care. That her betrayal had burned away any tenderness he had left for her. But the ice in his Frostlands cracked further, a sharp fracture splitting deep. She meant them, evident in every line of her body, upset with him for making her immobile. But she had no right to her anger when she was in the wrong, when her actions put the world in danger.

When her actions had led to the emergence of the Blue Devil, a side of him he hated in his more lucid times.

But the Blue Devil's control faltered, increasingly fragile, tightening his voice. "I will not allow you to leave my side."

"I want to be anywhere but at your side." Her chin lifted in defiance. A blush rose in her cheeks and at the tip of her nose. The darkening color gave lie to her words.

The memory of the night she came to his room flashed through his mind. An image of her beneath him, her body arching, her breath a plea in his night-shrouded bedroom. She'd wanted him, craved his touch... but now her gaze was guarded.

She didn't want to want him.

He didn't want to want her, either. He didn't want her lying ways near him—he didn't want to be near her influence, her seductive scent, her intense gaze. The pain of her deceit still throbbed deep inside his Frostlands, creating new fissures.

Yet he couldn't just let her go.

Heated looks volleyed between them, each serve coming with narrowing eyes. Waiting for the other to break.

"Sailing to Aelunis, are we?" Adria's voice broke the stalemate.

Edmar internally shook himself and gazed at the pirate. "I have a quest that takes me there."

"*We* have a quest," Emira said.

Adria's mouth opened in surprise. "Why Aelunis?"

Emira replied before he could. "We are to wake the Metal God."

"Emira!" He didn't want to broadcast their quest or the reasons behind it, but the mermaid and pirate ignored him.

"Awaken Metallon? How?"

"With the Sun Stone," Emira said.

Edmar recognized how Adria's quick mind processed this information. He pressed his knuckles against his temple, his control slipping further. His Frostlands succumbed, thawing.

"Our quest is dangerous," Emira said. "You should know that before you agree to take me to Aelunis."

"Ah, there's nothing I love more than a bit of danger." Adria's eyes glittered.

"Don't get involved, Adria." He didn't want to put anyone's life at risk, even though he knew he was asking it of his crew.

A sharp pain slashed through his chest as he realized he was putting his crew in danger.

His *human* crew.

Dragons were created to protect humans, making it impossible to harm humans unless dragons felt directly threatened. He couldn't sail with his human crew. His biology wouldn't allow him, knowing the dangers. No one ever returned from Aelunis.

He had to find a new crew, but where would he find enough non-humans in time to sail by tomorrow?

"I owe it to Najla." Adria's mirth faded. She gripped Emira's hand. "I will take you to Aelunis aboard *my* ship."

Edmar rubbed his chest, the pain easing with Adria's alternative. "I don't want to risk your crew and family."

Emira winced. "We might encounter the Sea Witch if she learns what I'm doing."

That brought a quick smile to Adria's face. "We're pirates! The sea's where the real adventure lies, and no pirate worth their salt would leave a friend stranded. Besides, I've faced the Sea Witch before and bested her." She turned her smile to him. "Do you remember what I always used to say?"

"Smart pirates have plans within plans," he said, reciting her motto.

"Exactly." Her eyes sparkled. "And I have a secret. I know the words that'll unlock the Sun Stone's true power."

"Tell me," he said.

"I can't. Solis forbade it."

"You're not taking both my wife and the Sun Stone." His possessive instincts flared.

Adria crossed her arms. "Why're you being so thick-headed?"

He caught Emira's faint smile and felt another fissure split his carefully controlled facade. He recognized the inevitability of the situation.

"Fine," he said, conceding. Resentment stuck in his throat. "But I'm coming too, and you will not interfere between my wife and me again."

Adria's expression became fierce, like when she led her crew to plunder. This was the pirate he never wanted to face. "If you harm her or strip her of her rights, I'll toss you overboard myself."

He didn't think she could carry out her threat, but he saw the wisdom in accepting Adria's offer, however grudgingly. "I don't intend to harm her."

Emira clasped the pirate's hands. "Thank you, Adria. This means more to me than you know."

He ordered their trunks transferred to her ship. He couldn't help but steal a glance at Emira, expecting smugness, but her expression was open, listening to Adria weave another sea adventure story. The stories Adria had once shared with him.

The last vestiges of his control shattered. His Frostlands shook, chunks of ice thawing and crumbling. He strode away, needing to escape the sight of their easy camaraderie, the warmth they shared so effortlessly. But every step felt unstable, every thought a struggle to maintain control when rawness left him aching.

He loved her. He hated her. He needed her. He couldn't trust her.

He had given her freedom, but he still felt trapped. Trapped between the past and the future. Between duty and desire. Between the man he was and the monster she had made him into.

Tomorrow, they sailed to Aelunis. Tomorrow, they would face the unknown together.

But right now, he needed something else—someone else—to help him navigate the jagged, icy wasteland of his Frostlands.

CHAPTER 71

EDMAR

Edmar retreated to his chambers, his Frostlands fracturing, the icy calm teetering on the edge of chaos. The strict dichotomy between his Blue Angel and Blue Devil personas wavered.

How can she love me, yet work against me so relentlessly?

The question clawed at him, a shard digging into his wounded heart. A lingering tightness pulled at his scarred skin as he rubbed his chest. Before the tall mirror he paused, its dark, smooth surface offering no answers. He needed his brothers—their shared history, the understanding that spanned a millennium—to ground him.

He activated the mirror, focusing on Zane, always the lighthearted one, the most likely source of comfort. The surface rippled, then cleared, revealing his brother's reflection. He was holding a small, handheld mirror, angled to capture his image from below.

"Zane," he said, relief flooding him at the sight of his brother, confirmation that he was alive and well.

But Zane didn't respond. His face, usually mischievous, was drawn and pale. His eyes, normally sparkling with a playful light, were shadowed, almost... haunted.

"Zane, what's wrong?" Edmar asked, his concern rising. "Can you hear me?"

Zane nodded slowly, his gaze fixed on something beyond the mirror's reflection. He opened his mouth as if to speak, then closed it again, a muscle twitching in his jaw.

A chill went through him, a deeper, unsettling cold. He'd never seen Zane like this. "Are you hurt?"

Zane shook his head, his silence heavy. He was still underground, and Edmar could swear he'd been crying. Zane never cried.

"What happened?"

His brother finally met his gaze with a pained expression. "I must go," he whispered, his voice hoarse. "I'm sorry, Edmar. I can't—"

The connection snapped, leaving Edmar staring at his reflection. Zane's obvious pain hung in the room like a phantom. A chill coated the air because his younger brother had never looked like that before.

With a quick prayer to the gods for Zane, he focused on Kalden, hoping for reassurance. The mirror rippled, revealing his older brother, an aura of familiar melancholy in his brooding gaze.

"Kalden," he said, his voice weary.

His older brother nodded, a flicker of concern in his dark eyes. "Edmar. Glad to see you back home. Is everything alright?"

"The Sun Stone is safe," he said, needing to offer his own reassurance. "My wife has returned."

"Thank the gods." Kalden sighed, his shoulders slumping slightly.

He hesitated. He longed to share his curse was broken. Yet his wife had devastated him—from her betrayal and her admission to conspiracy with the Sea Witch.

While his brother would be happy for him, he could not divorce the good parts from the terrible. How could he deliver such news and encumber his brother further? Kalden's tendency to retreat into despair was a constant source of worry. His brother faced his own struggles with his bride by chance. Airian lay trapped and fading in a distant dreamscape with the Snow Princess. "How are you holding up?"

Kalden sighed, his despair palpable even through the mirror. "Winter grows harsher, and Airian grows weaker."

The old Edmar knew the exact right thing to say, and he would have believed what he said. Now he struggled to bring the words forward. But he had to. He'd always been the light for his brothers, the voice of reason. "She's still with you, Kalden. There's hope. We'll find a way."

The words sounded empty in his ears.

But they are the right words.

Kalden's eyes flickered with a brief light. "Thank you. It helps to have your support. How did you become wiser than either of your older brothers?"

It's all a lie. A rumble echoed in his Frostlands. He wanted to tell Kalden everything, to unburden his soul, but he couldn't do that to him. "Stay strong. We will overcome this curse one day."

Kalden's image faded, leaving him alone once more.

He stood before the now-empty mirror, his reflection a stranger. His Frostlands churned, ice fracturing into unstable, floating shards. A battlefield of crumbling glaciers, emotions threatening to surface through the cracks. Zane's silent pain, Kalden's veiled grief, Rivus's sabotage, Emira's betrayal—it was all too much.

He needed control. He needed to bury it deeper because if he let it all go, let himself feel, there would be nothing left of him.

He stepped out onto the balcony, and a blanket of sticky, hot air instantly plastered his shirt to his back. Shadows trickled past the eastern horizon as the sky shifted from afternoon to early evening. The looming darkness beckoned him.

Except for the twenty-year period where Kalden spiraled into his depression, Edmar couldn't recall any other time since the curse had settled upon him that any of his brothers didn't confide in each other. They were each other's anchors, a bulwark against the demands of the curse. Except Rin...

For the first time in centuries, he considered Rin. His oldest brother, the one who had refused the curse's dictates and embraced his dragon form permanently. Rin, who lived in a desolate, frozen wasteland, devoid of all life.

Rin understands.

The solitude of his brother's frozen kingdom beckoned, whispering the solace of true emotional isolation, a promised refuge, a place where hearts turned to stone, incapable of feeling loss or love. He envied that ease as he launched himself into the cooling air. His body rippled with power as he shifted into his dragon form. He soared eastward, toward the mountains that separated Central Agondray from Rin's icy domain.

Even with his exhaustion, the journey was swift, the wind screaming past his scales. The landscape blurred beneath him, the Malustra Woods a dense shadow on the ground. As he approached the border, the air grew colder.

He landed on a mountain peak on the far east side of the Malustra Woods, the highest point for miles around. Eastward, a vista of breathtaking desolation.

A vast expanse of ice and snow, a frozen, white ocean stretching to the horizon. Ruins of an old palace courtyard emerged halfway out of the ice like broken teeth, the only sight offering a break in the deserted ice land. A haunting sight—his childhood home, a life long gone with so many lost—his parents, family, friends.

Pain, long buried, stirred within him. The bleak landscape, howling wind, and shifting ice bore witness to his buried rage and grief.

He drew in a deep breath, the cold air welcomed into his lungs. He spread his wings wide and let out a low, rumbling roar, his dragon's call to Rin echoing across the frozen expanse. The guttural sound barely registered above the wind's howl.

Rin. He reached out, testing their mental connection.

Nothing.

He scanned the landscape. Where would a dragon even take shelter in this forsaken place?

He roared again, frustration building. His thunderous demand shook the mountains, sheets of snow and ice sliding down jagged peaks. *Rin! I know you're here. Answer me!*

Icy power slammed into him, a mental backlash.

Must you be so loud, little brother? Rin's voice reverberated in his mind, a deep, grating sound laced with irritation.

He blinked, momentarily disoriented. He couldn't see Rin, but he sensed him, a cold intelligence woven into the landscape.

I can't see you. His confusion battled with rising anxiety. The storm intensified, the wind howling with fury.

What do you want, Edmar?

Where are you?

A dragon's growl accompanied Rin's words in his mind. *A thousand years as a dragon have taught me to delve deeper into our abilities. We do not need a direct line of sight to communicate, but our proximity still stirs the Snow Princess's curse. You should not have come here.*

Rin's mental tone edged with dismissive impatience.

He looked east across the glacial ice sheet. Storm clouds churned with more force, the wind whipping snow into a blinding frenzy. The combined presence of Rin and himself created this gale. The brewing tempest would only strengthen the longer they stayed near each other.

I didn't come to make things worse, he said.

Why did you come?

This land... He struggled to find the right words. He looked out at the endless expanse of ice, a landscape as barren and unforgiving as his own Frostlands. He envied Rin's icy tranquility, a simple world devoid of emotional complexity. If only his Frostlands were so complete.

My wife... He couldn't think of her betrayals without anger rising. *This is where she sent my heart.*

Don't come to me with your sorrows. Rin's retort lacked empathy. A harsh dismissal. *Go back home.*

His brother had become like his land, hard, unyielding. He was the Frostlands, a being of ice and shadow, detached from the world, from emotion, from hope.

Where before Edmar might have accepted that coldness, embraced his older brother's unyielding cynicism, resentment now sparked an icy rage. A world without passion—it wasn't what he desired. It felt empty, pointless, his heart twisting under its heavy burden of longing for a love he now saw as unreachable.

The storm thickened and swirled around him. *Your land is empty.*

A rumble of discontent echoed from Rin's mind. *You've come here to tell me this?*

Resentment snapped in his next words. *Have you found peace here? Have you conquered your feelings for the Snow Princess or simply fled from her and her reach?*

Rin growled, the sound echoing between the mountain peaks. *And what would you have me do, Edmar? Embrace the curse? Break it and set my fiancé free?*

He hesitated, the thought chilling him. If they broke their curses, would that set the Snow Princess free? After she unleashed her curse on them and wiped out the rest of the Ice Dragons, he and his brothers encased her in ice. She hadn't been free in a thousand years. They didn't need another threat loose in Agondray. *No. I don't want her free any more than you do. But there has to be another way.*

You think there's hope for us? Look around you, Edmar. This is what hope looks like... the hope that comes from giving your love fully to someone who doesn't deserve it.

He understood the sentiment, but he was unwilling to surrender to his Frostlands entirely. *Why must I hold these contradictory, destructive desires—my love for her entangled with disdain and hate, vengeance warping with acceptance?*

I was once in love. Rin's anguish infused those words. *Once, a path of happiness and trust lay ahead for both of us. But the love I felt... It didn't save me, and it didn't protect those closest to me.*

He remembered Rin's cries, a thousand years ago, when the curse was cast, when Lutine cursed the Ice Dragons, a cold snap of winter wind howling across the frozen land. Suddenly, he understood why Rin sought this existence. Oblivion and true detachment from all things—love, trust, joy—was truly the only path out of despair. *I envy your peace.*

There's no peace here, brother, Rin said. *Only oblivion.*

Was this his future? The end of one curse only to be trapped in another? A life where he felt nothing, where even rage faded into silence? His brother had become the Frostlands itself. Unfeeling, unchanging. Would he, too, forget the warmth of a lover's touch? The sound of laughter? Would he, too, wake one day and find nothing left of himself but ice and wind?

His grip tightened, digits clenching until claws sliced through the rock he perched on. The earth quaked, a deep growl. *My wife betrayed me. But the very act set me free. She lied, stole, threatened everything.* His Frostlands cracked, fragmented under the pressure of his warring emotions. *And still, I long for her.*

Just like Rin once longed for the Snow Princess.

Rin had learned. He had severed himself from all of it. And he had survived.

Edmar would do the same. That was the only way to survive this.

Let go of warmth. Let go of hope. Let go of her.

His Frostlands thickened around him, encasing his heart in ice. Yes. This was the only way to survive.

His brother's voice came across just as cold. *Your journey isn't mine to tread. There is no reprieve, only endless silence in a tomb of our making.*

She's broken my curse.

Sounds like a reason to celebrate. Rin's voice sharpened, piercing his usual apathy. *So why are you here bothering me?*

He hesitated, the words catching in his throat. How could he explain the tangled mess of his emotions, the love and betrayal, the kiss that had both freed and shattered him?

I don't know, he said.

Go away then, little brother. I have no time nor patience for the drama of your love life. Rin's mental reply carried no trace of caring, a whisper of ice and shadow.

Let go of her, his Frostlands whispered. Embrace the Blue Devil fully. Yes, that's what he would do, but not forever. Not like Rin's wasteland.

He launched himself into the sky. *One day, brother...* A silent vow formed in his heart. *One day, I'll come back for you so we can both leave our Frostlands.*

A snort of derision followed him as he left Rin in his desolate kingdom.

Chapter 72

EMMY

The large arched windows framed the night, faint silvery moonlight filtering into the room where Edmar had left Emmy hours ago. Adria's husky voice wove through the stillness, a soothing comfort with Emmy's fatigue. Despite her weariness, she found herself drawn to the stories, especially those about her mother. Adria's lack of judgment over the Sun Stone theft brought a warmth Emmy hadn't realized she needed. There was also something vaguely familiar about the Water Fae that comforted her.

She forced her thoughts onto what lay ahead. Edmar's curse was broken, but he wouldn't let her go. She couldn't trick herself into believing he cared.

No, he wants to punish me.

Tomorrow they'd set sail for Aelunis, an island shrouded in mystery and danger. There, she'd either meet her end trying to awaken the Metal God or finally break free from the curse that had haunted her for so long.

She traced the emptiness on her throat where her painite would lie. Where had Edmar gone? Perhaps she should ask for a bedchamber. She was exhausted.

Then his presence filled the room, cold and commanding. He looked weary, shadows under his eyes, his expression unreadable.

She'd sensed him before he entered—not with that invisible tether of her gem between them, but with the ice in his eyes that always seemed to settle over her as a caress... an emotion she hated while relishing it. Reminiscent of those first stolen glances from the sky, when he flew past her at Siren's Cove, embodying a grace she envied.

And with every inhale, his presence solidified in the room. A king returned to his domain.

She hated him even more.

Except her hatred would fade when she was free. As much as she detested him right now, she was tied to him by more than marriage vows. He was a part of her, a missing piece that completed her when she was with him. With every separation, that became more clear. Her soul burned within her, tugging her toward him. When sleep separated them, she dreamed about him, his kisses, his touch...

She attempted to quell the warmth rushing to her center. *Foolish woman.*

He was angry with her because of what she had done. Her betrayal, once necessary, now tasted bitter. Her heart ached.

"Come here, Emira." His voice was flat, a harsh discord.

It wasn't a request. Not a true one when his grip on her gem had so far echoed with his demand, leaving her trembling to submit.

Adria's lips thinned, but she remained silent.

Obey. Or fight. Or flee.

Delusional. She possessed only the illusion of autonomy. How she despised her gem and its leash to slavery. Even if losing her magic meant forfeiting her identity as a mermaid, she longed for the day when she would no longer be bound to another's whims.

Even Edmar's. And that was the hardest part, knowing she didn't truly want to leave him. Yet here she was, his prisoner not by choice, but by decree. All her decisions were his now, until her will meant something again.

Just as it had been with her father.

Her time as her own master had been so fleeting.

Her blood roared with rising fury. Maybe he recognized her pinched lips, her darkening skin, because she shivered with his touch on her gem, a slow sweep. A shadow of a warning of what he could make her do.

The compulsion was subtle but undeniable. She stood, knife points pricking her feet, and walked toward him. She didn't look at him at first, and when she finally did, he wasn't looking at her either. His gaze distant, cold. His frigidity radiated into a quiet stretch when she stopped in front of him. She held her breath, controlling her anger.

He finally broke the unnerving silence. "Time to retire."

Why did her stomach leap at those words? Nothing kind or remorseful in his declaration. It should have chilled her.

On the beach earlier today, it had felt like he wanted her, desired her still. She'd been determined to stop her reactions to his touch. But maybe he hadn't wanted her at all. Had he been playing with her?

His coldness made her doubt everything.

He left the room, expecting her to follow. When they entered the hallway and neared his chamber door first, her heart pounded. He could have brought them the other way if he'd intended to escort her to her previous chambers.

Every part of her yearned to get lost in his arms, to feel his lips on hers again, to lose her breath to his kisses, but that warred with the idea of him as her master. He couldn't control her feelings, but he could control her actions, forcing her to submit to him.

Would he do that?

Not the honor-bound Edmar. At least, not the one she'd known before, but this man in front of her was someone different. *The Blue Devil? What will he do?*

Her heart raced, and before they reached his door, she blurted out, "I don't want to sleep with you."

Edmar halted, his stiff shoulders a rebuke. "Do you really think I'd subject myself to your touch again? I do not want you in my bed either."

Shame scorched through her, hot and swift, pushing past the dull ache that he no longer desired her. Her fears that he'd force her into submission now seemed foolish.

Her throat tightened. The air in the hallway felt thick, suffocating.

Wordlessly, he led her past his chambers, a space whispering of their past intimacies and toward those that held a different kind of truth now. Once inside her old chambers, he motioned her ahead, but he waited at the threshold.

His expression was hard. "You will not leave this room. You will not use your magic. You will not enlist in anyone's help to subvert my commands. Do you understand?"

"I'm a prisoner."

"What else?" His voice was flat. "You cannot be trusted, and you lost all citizen rights because of your treachery."

She nodded.

Resentment burned in his ocean-colored eyes. The rest of him cold, controlled, but was there pain behind it? "The journey ahead will be rough, and the holy quest cannot be compromised by your wayward magic. Try to stay out of my way."

His tone was clipped, final. His gaze held hers, unwavering, but in that chilly space, an unwelcome knowledge settled—maybe he would never forgive her. He didn't want her now. *Will he ever, one day, perhaps, when I'm no longer a threat?*

He tightened his grip on the doorknob. His composure wavered, then his voice softened to a whisper that still held the edge of a sword. "Remember, Emira, actions have consequences."

With that, he left, locking the door behind him. The silence of her confinement pressed down on her, his presence lingering with a taste of bitterness. She stood at the window, gazing at the cold, distant stars. The Ocean's Lament rumbled within her.

Her resolve hardened. She would break free from this curse of her gem and her magic. She would reclaim her autonomy. And she would confront the emotions that Edmar stirred within her, emotions as turbulent as the sea she came from.

That night, she dreamed of Malala. She hadn't seen the Snow Princess since the Water Fae attacked, when Emmy had fought back. This time, they weren't in the garden where they usually met, but on a balcony overlooking it. Peering over the balustrade, she caught sight of a sleeping woman—the same one she'd seen in the Sun Temple. Airi, with her translucent, silver hair, the one who believed she was human.

"You have broken the curse for Cyaneus's Dragon King," Malala said, drawing her attention.

"And you're the Snow Princess. Is Malala even your given name?"

Malala narrowed her eyes, then shrugged. "I have been given many names and have embraced a few myself. My true name is known only to my mother, who no longer graces our world, and to my fiancé."

"What do you want, Malala?"

"Someday soon, we will meet. I want us to be on the same side."

What? Does the Water Fae see into the future? "And why would I ever be on your side after all you've done?"

Malala looked back over the balustrade, her eyes softening as she gazed upon the sleeping Airi. "I dread the day I must face my consequences, but it looms closer." A pale lavender hand flattened on her stomach when she met Emmy's gaze again. "We will need all the magic and allies we can find to stand against the Summer Child."

Malala was right, exactly the reason she was on a quest to wake the gods, but she wouldn't reveal any of that to the woman. "And why would anyone trust you?"

"No one has to trust me to save our world from the Summer Child. If they'd listened, I would have killed her before she gained power. But now, there's no stopping her unless we band together."

"You knew about her?" Emmy asked, surprised. "For how long?"

"Reading about ancient lore has captivated me since I was a child, consuming every book I could find. I came to believe that she existed, but it was a matter of finding her." Malala's eyes turned distant. "Then I saw her in visions, saw what she was capable of. I was certain she was in this land when I came here to meet my fiancé. But no one believed me. And you know what happened after that."

Longing and sadness etched lines on her face, but they soon smoothed away. "I know you've been feared and used your whole life for what your magic can do. Little more than a puppet. I found myself in similar circumstances, and I've made terrible choices."

"You've killed thousands with your choices."

"And you would have caused just as many deaths if you hadn't been stopped," she said, countering her. "We both made mistakes. I understand why you've done what you have, and I'm not judging you. Let's do better. We need each other. We need a powerful alliance for what's coming."

Silence fell between them as she looked away. Big, puffy white clouds filled the spaces beyond the garden below with the sleeping woman. It was all serene, but her heart thudded too hard.

Malala echoed Edmar's words. Her choices would have killed many. She'd been as selfish as the Snow Princess. The only difference being that she had sought a different choice. Before Solis appeared, she'd already decided to find Metallon and not collect the stones for the Sea Witch.

But she hadn't told that to Edmar. He believed her to be the person who would have made the Sea Witch powerful enough to cause destruction. That had been her, but not her intention. Now, she needed to be honest, to tell Edmar everything, no matter that she was angry at him for controlling her through her gem or that she was afraid of making him hate her more.

Below, Airi shifted in her sleep, cradling a book.

She raised her eyebrows at Malala. "Why is Airi here?"

Malala glanced down at the sleeping girl, a soft smile on her face. "She's my friend."

"What's her role in all of this?"

The Snow Princess shook her head, lips pursing, fingers caressing a white stone on a silver chain.

More evasiveness. Emmy didn't like how that made her feel, yet she'd done the same thing to Edmar. *I should have told him the truth from the beginning.* "I've learned secrets are as bad as lies."

"Not all information is useful."

"According to you."

"There are too many things happening right now, too many threads. I see them all coming together, but if we're not careful, it could be the end of the world."

She covered Malala's lavender hand with her own. "You don't have to keep this burden alone. Share with me or others. Let us truly work together."

For a moment, she thought Malala would confide in her, but the Water Fae straightened her shoulders, pulling away from her hand.

She dropped her arm back to her side, disappointed. "You've learned nothing from your years in isolation." Part of her felt bad for the Snow Princess, but the woman was ignorant. "Find me when you're ready to be honest. Until then, stay out of my dreams."

In the ruins of Drakkon, a large block of ice, containing the most powerful magical being the land had ever known to curse it, groaned with a low, resonant creak. A series of high-pitched pops echoed faintly as smaller pieces splintered off, filling the air with a sense of something delicate, like glass under stress. The Snow Princess sighed, "One more."

Chapter 73

EMMY

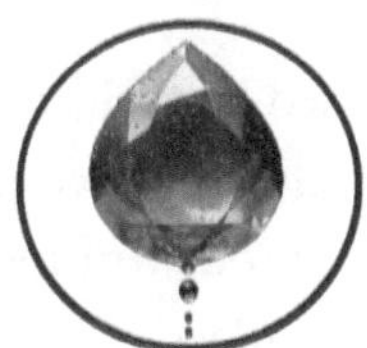

In the Grand Hall, the stone dragon's gaze pierced Emmy, a silent judgment. She traced a finger along its outstretched wing, the rough texture different from Edmar's smooth, cool scales.

Who are you? Her gaze rested on the statue's cupped hands, frozen in a gesture of supplication. *What secrets do you hold?*

A shiver coursed through her, a mix of the predawn chill and the unsettling awareness of Edmar's presence behind her. His magic, a pale blue aura flecked with gold, illuminated the space between them, an irritating reminder of the invisible tether that bound her to him. She refused to look at him, her emotions still raw after her encounter with Malala. She'd been ready to tell Edmar everything, all that beat in her heart and lived in the dark recesses of her mind.

"Emira." His voice, low and impatient. "Move on."

Another command.

He'd bombarded her with commands all morning. *Get out of bed. Hold still for Lida.*

He hadn't even left while she dressed. She'd have preferred to remain nude, but the Land Bound... His icy gaze as she dressed had been infuriating.

Every word chafed, every glance sparked a yearning she couldn't indulge. She remembered his rejection last night. But it wasn't just anger, was it? He didn't trust her. Maybe he never would.

That realization settled over her like a stone. She had done that. She had taken something from him, something fragile and unseen, and he wasn't willing to offer it again. Maybe she deserved this coldness. But did he really think she'd try to manipulate him again?

She wouldn't—but how could he know that? Still, anger at his words simmered beneath her calm exterior.

"But you said..." She meant the words to sound hard, but they were more of a plea.

"We're wasting time." He caressed her painite, sending a shiver through her.

Upon reaching the open doors, she hummed the Ocean's Lament. New magic stirred within her. This song, the mournful melody a source of solace for her people, had always threatened to unleash her destructive power. But now, its magic wove through her, soothing the ache in her chest.

Each note was a whispered promise to her sister, a beacon across the miles that separated them.

Edmar shadowed her, silent now but watchful, her gem glowing intermittently.

Beneath fading stars, shadows and scents permeating the garden, she strode toward the path to the Lunarclaw River. Morning humidity slicked her skin. Each step led her closer to her fate, a sacrifice that might await her on Aelunis. But as she walked to the edge of the dock, a flicker of hope ignited within her.

Maybe, just maybe, she was wrong and the Metal God wouldn't require her sacrifice. In a perfect world, she'd live and he'd free her of her magic.

At the river, she waited, her heart heavy with what was to come. Less than twenty minutes later, her breath hitched as Anjali emerged from the river, her sapphire hair shimmering.

"Emmy!" Relief and concern laced Anjali's whispered cry. Her turquoise eyes, wide and glowing in the strengthening light, darted from Emmy's face to her short hair, then to her bare neck. "You're all right? I've heard nothing for many days... I thought..."

Relief washed over her as she knelt on the dock. Embracing her sister, a comfort she'd craved for so long, a wave of joy momentarily eclipsed the dread of her impending voyage. For now, she was here, with her sister, beneath the watchful gaze of the man who held her fate, her heart, in his hands.

In the back of her mind, she recalled Anjali acting in her stead for her honeymoon cruise, and she hoped it didn't upset Edmar too much to see her sister again. A shiver coursed through her from his caress of her gem, probably a note that he did indeed remember her sister and what they had done.

"I'm safe."

"But your painite..." Anjali's gaze dropped to her bare neck. "Where is it?"

Behind her, Edmar shifted, tension radiating from him.

"Edmar has it," she said, her voice tight.

Anjali's eyebrows shot up. "He controls your gem?"

"I can't talk about it right now." Emmy pushed down the urge to explain the reasons behind Edmar's control. It was a truth too complex, too fraught with betrayal and fear.

"I hate our gems!" Anjali's vehemence surprised her.

Her sister had never said anything about their gems before. "What's wrong?"

A furrow creased her sister's brow. "Father is making me marry Tarinor."

Pure anguish flashed in her sister's eyes, and Emmy shared her silence. Their father was marrying off his last daughter, to a king who ruled over a smaller kingdom on the other side of the planet. Tarinor had visited her father's court often. Although Emmy had been kept at the Little Palace, having met none of her brothers-in-law before their untimely deaths, Anjali kept her updated and had been enamored of the young king.

Anjali clasped hands to her mouth, the Ocean's Lament rumbling in her breast. "I love him, Emmy. But father will send him to war, just like the others. I can't let him die."

Heat coiled in Emmy's chest, a slow, seething burn. Then a rush of fire acid filled her veins. She'd always thought of her own sorry existence under the rule of her father, but it wasn't just her. All mermaids and mermatrons suffered. They were all subjugated to their mermen. Her father made it worse, making his daughters all into weapons.

"Emira," Edmar said sharply, drawing her back. "Control your magic!"

Immediately, she meditated, calming her magic. "I'm sorry, Anjali." The Ocean's Lament echoed in her mind to follow her sister's. "I wish I could help."

Is there something I can do? She was on her way to see Metallon, the god responsible for their tethered gems. The one responsible for them being slaves to the mermen, even if that had not been the god's intention. Could he help? She pushed the question from her mind for now.

Anjali gripped her hands. "You have your life to worry about. Forget I said anything."

How can I? But time was running out. "Anjali, I may not come back from what I'm doing next."

Edmar's subtle movement caught her eye, his disapproval clear, yet he remained silent, allowing her to speak. Before Anjali could respond to her words, a familiar figure emerged from the depths.

Gilly, her amethyst eyes shimmering, a mix of relief and urgency in her expression. She spoke with a lowered voice. "Do you have the Gods' Stones?"

Her joy at seeing her friend curdled into bitterness. Why was she more concerned about the stones than about her?

Gilly responded to her thoughts. *I worry about the Sea Witch's wrath. The moon cycle is nearly complete.*

I know, she said in her mind before pushing the resentment aside to say aloud, "The Sun God has given me a different task. We're sailing soon... to a dangerous place. I will probably not return."

Edmar cleared his throat, his caress steady on her gem. She'd snap at him if she wasn't giving her sister and best friend all of her attention.

"But the Sea Witch—" Gilly tried again to warn her.

"The Sea Witch can rot in the deepest trench for all I care." Her anger boiled again. "You don't even ask how I am, what I've been through. All you care about are the stones!"

"Emmy, that's not true." Gilly's words of protest rang hollow.

Her suspicions flared. This wasn't like Gilly. Her friend had always been kind, compassionate, yet now...

"What's happening?" Anjali asked nervously. "Where are you going?"

She hesitated, then sighed, knowing Edmar wouldn't be happy. "Aelunis."

"Emira, please," Edmar said, frustration and weariness in his voice. "Why must you tell everyone our plans?"

Emmy met his gaze, her defiance hardening when his jaw clenched. "Why do you get to decide what I should do, Edmar?"

"When you make the right decisions, then I won't make them for you."

Her sister's breath hitched, breaking the tense atmosphere. "Aelunis? But E mmy... no merfolk has ever returned from there."

Fear shadowed Anjali's face.

She gripped her sister's hand, the familiar feel of her satiny skin a comfort. "Thank you, Anjali," she said, her voice lower. "Thank you for everything, for always accepting me. I love you."

Her sister's eyes widened, understanding dawning.

Edmar's voice cut through their exchange. "Emira." He placed a hand on her shoulder, his gaze softening when she looked up at him. "We need to leave."

Anjali's gaze flicked to Edmar, distrust hardening her features. The hummed strains of the Ocean's Lament vibrated louder in her sister's chest, her sorrow at their forced separation.

Gilly, too, watched Edmar warily, suspicion dimming her eyes. No song filled the beautiful mermaid, a difference from her sister's reaction. With a light-blue hand, her best friend pressed a necklace into Emmy's hand. "This has healing properties,"

She examined the small seashell strung on a gold chain. *We're mermaids. We heal fast already.*

"It's also blessed by Pheronis." A minor god known for guiding people. "He will protect the traveler who wears this."

Grateful for her friend's gift, she slipped the necklace over her head. Regret for her earlier suspicion filled her, a wish to take it back lodged in her throat. Gilly's last memory of her shouldn't be clouded by her doubt. *Thank you for your thoughtfulness. How did you come by something so wondrous?*

You should know me by now, a woman with mysterious ways. Gilly smiled.

Emmy returned her smile. "Thank you."

"Enough, Emira. Say your goodbyes."

Edmar's cold command made her back straighten, but she refused to look at him. He hadn't required that. Instead, she hugged her sister and her friend.

"Please come back to me." Anjali squeezed her hand, then disappeared beneath the surface, along with Gilly.

Emmy's throat tightened. *Is that the last time I'll see them?* The last time she'd have any chance to connect with them? She stood, trembling, sadness gripping her heart. The Ocean's Lament echoed faintly, offering no relief. Fire pulsed in her veins, a rolling furnace in her stomach, tumbling, all sharp edges, punching her insides.

She whirled on Edmar, her fists clenched. "Why can't you hold your misery long enough to allow me a proper goodbye?"

A spark ignited between their gazes, a flash of the connection they had once shared.

His jaw tightened, the blue glow around his irises intensifying, as if he recognized the same flare, the same pull. His Frostlands trembled, his grip on the icy wasteland weaker than before. But just as quickly, he shuttered his gaze, a wall of ice slamming down, sealing off the warmth before it could spread. "Why tell everyone our plans? We'll have enough obstacles without your blatant admissions."

Her fury nearly made her miss the flicker of regret in his eyes.

A maelstrom of emotions buffeted her—sadness, defiance, anger—but overall, a desperate yearning for him to understand. But the words wouldn't come, caught in the tightening knot of her throat.

"Come," he said, his voice commanding, with a hint of hesitancy.

He lifted his hand, an indecisive gesture stopping short of touching her. For a moment, she thought he might make that connection, offer some semblance of comfort, but then his hand clenched into a fist at his side.

"We have a ship to catch." His gaze fixed on the palace doors, as if he couldn't bear to look at her.

CHAPTER 74

EMMY

The port bustled with a chaotic energy assaulting Emmy's senses. It took her mind off the pain stabbing her toes through her soft leather boots. Morning sunlight, sharp and fresh, glinted off the water, a million dancing diamonds mocking the dull ache in her chest.

Gull cries mingled with the shouts of dockworkers, the creak of rigging, and the rumble of cargo being unloaded. The scents of fresh fish and ship tar thickened in the air. But the smell of the ocean made her heart ache with a deep, almost desperate longing.

The Longing.

She struggled to suppress the urge to leap off the dock into the water. With the waning of the Sea Witch's suppression spell, the Longing intensified. *Just a few more days and I'll be free of this yearning, this... Longing.*

Two days to Aelunis, Adria had said. Emmy would either be a step closer to her death or have freedom from her magic.

"Who was the mermaid with your sister?" Suspicion tinged Edmar's voice.

He walked beside her in a loose emerald shirt and snug pants tucked into knee-high boots, his gaze fixed on the harbor. With each long, heavy stride, his jaw clenched tighter, a muscle ticking in his cheek. Several times, his scrutiny pricked the hairs on her neck, but she never caught his eye.

The leather satchel, with the Sun Stone and her painite, was slung over his shoulder, while she clutched her own smaller satchel, her fingers brushing against his shirt tucked inside. Pain throbbed in her feet, sharp as knives scraping bone with each step.

"Gilly. My best friend."

"I don't trust her." His tone was icy.

"I think the feeling's mutual."

His eyes narrowed. "She brought you to the surface the day you came back into my life, but she didn't leave the water. You would have drowned if I hadn't dived in to save you."

"Maybe you missed something." Simmering resentment tightened her voice. She couldn't help but feel like he was accusing Gilly, finding fault where none existed. She touched Gilly's gift, the seashell necklace.

"Perhaps," he muttered, his gaze distant, his jaw tight.

She couldn't shake the feeling he didn't believe her, that he still suspected Gilly of some unspoken treachery. Perhaps he saw treachery everywhere now. She hurried ahead, keeping Adria in sight.

The Water Fae pirate, a whirlwind of motion with her own bag bumping on her shoulder, navigated the crowded docks with ease. Her attire spoke of a different kind of freedom. Loose trousers tucked into low boots, and a billowing emerald shirt with a crimson sash. Emmy still preferred dresses to the more restrictive trousers.

Adria stopped at a ship—the *Tempest Queen*. The ship was massive, its towering masts thick like a giant squid, its woven ropes intricate as a spiderweb. Above the ropes and fabric sails, platforms jutted out like the arms of a starfish. Women scurried about these and on all the decks. They dressed in an array of bright colors, flamboyant feathers, metal chains, some with vivid sashes while others wore belts, some with hats or scarves, their shouts echoing across to each other.

A tattered black flag, a kraken skull with writhing bone-white tentacles, snapped on the tallest mast. The kraken's eye sockets stared into the depths of her soul. She shivered. She'd never seen anything like it.

Adria smiled, then bounded across the gangplank, a sturdy wooden board connecting the dock to the ship. She hesitated at the edge of the dock. The ocean called to her, almost overwhelming. Edmar's hand clamped onto her elbow, his grip hard, startling her. Her gaze flew to his.

"Don't even think about it," he said, his eyes like chips of ice.

Adria squealed, and Emmy pulled free, crossing the gangplank just as the pirate launched herself at a tall man on deck, who wore nondescript, simple clothes compared to the others.

"Husband!" Adria's joyous cry pierced the harbor's din.

The man, his steel-gray skin and silver hair gleaming, caught her, his laughter a deep rumble. He held her close, their kiss speaking of years of love and adventure.

"You just saw me yesterday, wife." He chuckled, his cerulean eyes twinkling.

"But it feels like ages since I've been in your arms, Lian." Adria wrapped her legs around him.

Their passion tugged at Emmy, captivating her, sparking a yearning for a similar connection, so profound, so unshakeable. A pang of longing twisted in her chest.

"Emira." Edmar's hand tightened on her elbow again, pulling her forward, then helping her onto the deck.

The ship spoke of age and loving care with its intricate carvings. A hive of activity animated the wooden deck. Mostly Water Fae women in all shades of blue and purple skin tones, their faces weathered by sun and salt, their eyes sharp. Veiled and robed men hovered in the shadows, avoiding eye contact with anyone.

Adria finally climbed down from her husband's embrace and turned to her. "I want you to meet my daughter, Avi."

A young woman with pale gray skin and striking cerulean eyes stepped forward. Her dark hair, streaked with blue, green, and silver, hung still, a mark of her mixed heritage, like her father. Avi took Emmy's hand, and a strange warmth flowed between them.

"The path ahead..." Avi began, her voice a low murmur, her gaze intense, "it holds such darkness—"

The world abruptly silenced, and every movement stilled. A haunting melody drifted across the harbor, capturing all attention. Unintelligible words echoed in the wind, yet the song pulsed with magic—reminiscent of the Ocean's Lament but different, more compelling, more menacing, like the Summer Child's siren song. Emmy's mind tumbled into a darkening abyss. Her sense of self spiraling, lost in a growing void. A jerk on her neck swept the darkness away.

Avi swayed against her, her hand tangled in Emmy's necklace, her eyes wide, her face pale, blood trickling from her nose. Then she collapsed. The melody softened, more subdued.

"Avi!" Adria's cry shattered the eerie stillness.

The song faded. In one moment, every head on deck and at port had been turned toward the ocean, mesmerized. In the next, people blinked their eyes as if waking from a dream, resuming their tasks like nothing had happened.

"Lian," Adria yelled, panicked, crouching beside her daughter.

Lian swept up Avi, creases etched around his eyes. The door leading to the cabins flew open, revealing a tall, dark figure barely discernible in the shadows. The figure held out pale arms to take Avi from her father.

Before Adria rose, she swept Emmy's seashell necklace up from the deck and offered it to her. "I believe this is yours?"

She touched her bare throat but shook her head. "Keep it for Avi. It aids in healing."

Adria nodded, clutching the necklace in her fist. "We'll get you settled soon." Then she barked a command to a sturdy, formidable-looking Water Fae woman, her voice sharp and commanding. "Jesi, set sail! Get us out of port. Chart a course north."

The ship groaned as the pirates scrambled, following Jesi's orders.

"That melody was like a siren song," she mumbled, glancing at Edmar. *Can we just talk now, without it turning into another fight? Are we there yet—will we ever be? Or are we still trapped in the wreckage of everything unsaid?*

"What song?" He scanned the harbor, not even looking at her. His voice was flat, as if the idea wasn't even worth considering. "There was nothing."

She shook her head, frowning. No one seemed to remember—no one was asking questions about it. They moved around her like nothing had happened, laughing, calling out orders, carrying on as if the world hadn't just trembled beneath their feet. A chill turned her insides to salt water.

The shoreline receded as the ship pulled away. She was leaving Agondray, and something about that felt final. She left a land that had once offered her hope, and she now headed toward a precarious future. Avi's cryptic message, the quest, the Summer Child, the Sea Witch, Metallon... A long list of threats, each possibly seeking her death. Despair threatened to drown her.

Despite her fear, she was excited. She'd never been on a ship before. But as the ship groaned and waves slapped the wooden sides, she thought of one more forbidding thing that seemed to seek her out, warning her.

The haunting siren song.

Just what was that mysterious melody? *And why does it seem like no one remembers it?*

Chapter 75

EMMY

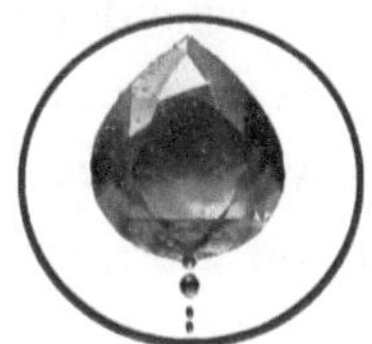

Emmy stood at the ship's railing, a cool spray of saltwater misting her face. The sun was now well above the horizon, casting over the bustling deck in a warm, deceptive light. But the endless ocean echoed her unease. The rhythmic sway of the ship was a disconcerting lullaby. A reminder of her powerlessness.

Of all mermaids' powerlessness, really, when she recalled Anjali's message about her impending marriage. *She'll lose the man she loves because our father decides our fates.*

The creak of timbers, the shouts of the Water Fae crew, the salty tang of the sea—they mingled in a strange harmony to draw her out of her misery. But in unsettling moments, the Longing pulsed with increasing urgency. Her fingers tightened over the wooden railing. Disquiet echoed in the churning waves.

She closed her eyes, fighting the urge to jump overboard.

Breathe.

"Your first sea voyage?" Adria's warm, husky voice interrupted her. Wind swelled and rippled within her emerald shirt.

"Yes." She shifted slightly to face the pirate captain. Muscles protested the stillness she forced upon herself, fire acid threatening within. Every breath a constant, conscious effort. *Six days left.*

Behind Adria, the Water Fae's usual social order, a dominant female culture, shifted. The line between genders blurred as the men shucked their robes and veils, now dressed in styles similar to those worn by the women. Out here, on the open sea, men and women worked side by side, their voices carrying equal weight.

So different from merfolk society. A merman's word was law and a merwoman's place was firmly beneath the waves.

"The sea has a way of calling to us, doesn't it?" Adria leaned against the railing, her gaze distant.

"It's different from being beneath the water. The open ocean feels boundless. Life doesn't end with the surface but expands into the heavens." The ocean's immensity should have dwarfed her, yet she found strange freedom in the relentless ballet of turquoise and sapphire waves. *Or is that the Longing?*

Adria's lips curved into a genuine smile, her eyes sparkling. "I've sailed the world a hundred times over, and the sea's still got her charm."

A hundred times over... She envied the fae's freedom. Her casual mention of a life lived on her own terms. A life of adventure with a loving family. That prompted her thoughts about the song and Avi's reaction. "How is your daughter?"

A shadow, fleeting but undeniable, crossed Adria's face. "She's sleeping. Happens from time to time."

Her keen ears picked up the nuance in her tone. "But something's not right this time."

Adria sighed, settling onto a nearby barrel with a fluidity that spoke of someone born of the sea. "Aye, you're right. It's happened before, those visions... but never this long. Usually, I can rouse her quick, or her lover can, but this time..."

A heavy silence filled with the creaking of the ship and the distant cries of seabirds. She glanced toward the quarterdeck, a shiver running down her spine with Edmar's casual stroke of her painite.

Not so casual, perhaps. He was thinking of her.

Was she vexed by his constant reminder of control or thrilled by his attention? The line blurred, confusing her further.

Edmar moved across the rocking deck, his forced indifference unconvincing to her. Occasionally, his easy confidence and grace returned only to change, his shoulders stiffening, his eyes wary. She couldn't tell if this new tension stemmed from the ship's uneven surface or her presence. Currently, he spoke with Jesi, their conversation too distant to decipher, his hand gesturing toward the chart the helmsman studied.

Since leaving Agondray, he'd made a point of interacting with the crew, both men and women, his inherent leadership resonating with the very rhythm of the ship. Observing him in these interactions, she felt a curious warmth bloom within her chest. Unwelcome yet persistent. At those times, she forgot her painite in his pocket.

His authority, so cold and distant to her, carried a hint of his passion for the sea—a side of him she hadn't glimpsed before. She loved his passion for things, the way it animated him.

"Tell me, what do you remember of your mother?" Adria's voice pulled her attention from Edmar. "Was she happy?"

The fae's childlike face, marred by a jagged scar above her left eyebrow, sent a flicker of unease through her. Not for the first time, her features tugged at Emmy's memory, vaguely familiar yet strangely out of reach.

"She always seemed sad to me until her best friend visited." She pictured her mother's gentle smile, the way her eyes lit up with Carina. "But father didn't like Carina and often drove her away. I don't have many other memories. She died when I was ten."

Adria took one of her hands in both of hers and took a deep breath. Her eyelids drooped at the corners, inner eyebrows slanting. "I heard of her death. I'm so sorry, Emmy."

The memory of her mother's death choked her.

"I loved your mother, and as you know, she was once my best friend," Adria said with her soft, husky voice.

That bit of information had made her curious before. Why hadn't she known Adria if her mother had been her best friend? She understood what would have drawn her mother to this pirate. The seasoned resilience, the aura of adventure, and beneath it all, a raw vulnerability.

The pirate captain both fascinated and intimidated her, but it was her unguarded softness that resonated with her, a painful echo of her mother's heart. "What happened to your friendship?"

Adria rubbed scarred hands over her face. "The sea's always been in my blood." A deep yearning resonated in her husky tone, drawing Emmy in. "I was cursed once, too. Every move felt like agony, but the ocean. It called to me. When I dove beneath the waves, my affliction vanished. Najla wanted me to stay with her. I could've stayed, found peace in the deep."

She frowned. *Pain with movement, like mine, but not the same.* "But you didn't stay, and you're cured. How?"

Adria winced. "I swiped the Sun Stone for the Sea Witch."

Alarms sounded in her head, and now Adria's familiarity made sense. Her likeness similar to another, her story one partially told by both Edmar and Malala.

"You're the pirate who stole the Sun Stone. You're the Snow Princess's great grandmother."

Her head spun. *There was something else, something she was missing.*

Adria nodded, her face earnest. "Listen to me, Emmy. I know you struck a deal with the Sea Witch, but her promises are pure temptation. She ensnares you with what you think you need, but every step is part of her game, and it's rigged from the start. Believe me, no one wins her games. If the Sun God hadn't intervened, I wouldn't have escaped her clutches. Don't let her win."

"But you're cured."

"The Sea Witch took the curse out of me when I brought her the Sun Stone, but she'd already taken your mother and Lian captive. Held 'em prisoner until I brought her the rest of the Gods' Stones. Thank the gods that never happened. Solis ensured the Sea Witch released my loved ones without me needing to fulfill the bargain."

She considered Adria's words, something still tugging at her.

Adria had lived a life of pain, like me. The Sea Witch had removed the curse—no, her exact words were, took the curse out of me, *as if it was a tangible thing. And her mother had been the Sea Witch's captive.*

The intricate network of scars etched on Adria's dark lavender skin each told a story, choices made... "Is it possible your curse was given to my mother?"

Guilt washed over Adria's face. "I'd heard tell the Sea Witch cast my curse into Najla, but when nothing happened—had I ever truly suspected..." She trailed off, her eyes brimming with regret. Dread drained the pirate's skin of nearly all color.

Emmy touched her bare throat. This fae woman, who spoke so freely of love for the sea and longing for a life unburdened, was the source of all her pain. She turned back to the sea, unable to meet her gaze. Grief and resentment warred within her, stealing her breath.

Adria laid a hesitant hand on her arm. "Forgive me, please. I hadn't any idea my curse... If I'd known, I'd never have taken the Sea Witch's help."

A bitter knot twisted in her stomach, souring all reason. She stared at Adria again. This woman, who spoke of love and freedom, was the origin of everything awful in her life. If she hadn't befriended her mother, if she hadn't been so selfish... "You loved Najla?"

A whisper of sadness in her husky voice. "Yes."

The air thickened, grief blooming into something more defined. Anger, sharp and hot, simmered beneath her skin. She wanted to hurt Adria, to make her feel all her pain.

She chose her words to exact that agony on the pirate. "Your curse killed my mother."

"I know."

The admission unleashed a torrent of rage. Pain snapped and shocked her muscles. She clenched her jaw. "She died painfully. Fire acid builds in my blood, in my muscles, the more I move."

Her body trembled with the effort of controlling her magic. Agony wracked her, her breath short, but she continued. "One day, I lost control. I didn't understand what I would lose that day. My mother melted in front of me..."

A sheen of tears mirrored in Adria's eyes. "Oh, Najla."

"But that shouldn't have happened, should it, Adria? Not if you'd only kept your curse?"

"Emmy—"

"No!" Her vision blurred with red, fire acid roaring through her veins, engulfing her, the pain a balm for her loss. "You were reckless with your own curse, with your friends, selfish in the decisions you made!"

Haven't you been just as reckless, choosing to work for the Sea Witch?

The voice, a whisper in the back of her mind, sounded so much like Edmar she almost thought he was in her head. She shoved the thought away, knowing she'd already chosen a different course. Her anger was a living thing now, coiling tight within her.

Adria held up her hands, frowning, eyes widening with alarm. "Easy now, Emmy. Calm yourself."

"This is your fault!" She shrieked, her control snapping. "Don't lecture me about choices!"

"Emmy, stop!" Edmar's command cut through her rage.

She whirled around, her gaze clashing with his. His face was a mask of icy fury. Ocean-colored eyes smoldered with an intensity that stole her breath.

"Not another word." His voice rang with absolute finality, a decree she could not defy. The blue ring glowed in his eyes, fighting against the dark red light of her pulsing painite, his will pressing against hers.

"You're endangering everyone." He tightened his grip on the painite. For one fleeting second, something shifted in his expression, something almost uncertain, almost reluctant. Then his face hardened like chiseled ice. "Don't move. Don't speak. Until I release you."

There was no warmth in his words, no hesitation, just a cold, brutal decree. Not anger, not passion—just emptiness. Her fury surged, directed at him this time. But she couldn't say anything.

His eyes glinted with a recognition of her rage toward him.

"This isn't about control, Emira," he said, but she could hear the distance in his voice, feel it in the way his gaze didn't quite meet hers. "It's about keeping everyone safe. Including you."

Realizing just how close her power was to erupting, terror washed away some of her anger. But she wouldn't be here, about to engulf the ship in flames if Adria hadn't loved her mother, hadn't sought a way to rid herself of her curse. Emmy wouldn't be here right now, completely controlled by the man she loved.

With one last searing glare, she met his gaze—unflinching, burning with everything she couldn't say. She wanted him to feel it. To feel her hatred. Her grief. To feel anything.

But he didn't even flinch.

He simply looked at her the way he had before. As if he had already decided she didn't matter anymore.

A sharp pain lanced through her chest, worse than any fire acid burning her veins.

So she closed her eyes. And let herself disappear.

Chapter 76
EDMAR

The confrontation with Emira confirmed what he already knew—she was a danger. To him. To this ship. To everything. The moment her magic had surged, it had confirmed all his worst fears.

He buried the rest, the guile, the turmoil, the exhaustion. He would not let it touch him.

His Frostlands sealed shut, winds howling over barren ice, swallowing everything. This was where he thrived, where the Blue Devil reigned. Here, there was no guilt. No longing.

Just control.

And control meant she would not move.

Once again, he had commanded her silence, her stillness. Necessary. For her safety. For the crew's safety. For everyone.

That was all this was. Necessity.

Not control. Not cruelty.

He wouldn't make the same mistake again.

Still, the thought crawled under his skin like a parasite, whispering unwanted truths. His Frostlands groaned. He had imprisoned her, just like her father. Just like she feared.

The realization should have meant nothing. It didn't matter what she thought. It didn't matter what she felt. His fingers twitched, the sharp sting of his nails biting into his palm.

She was dangerous. Unstable. She had proved it repeatedly.

And yet—even now, as she stood motionless, her sapphire hair whipping in the wind, she still burned like an ember refusing to die.

She was chaos. He was order.

For centuries, he'd sought solace in duty, in logic, in the cold detachment of his frozen wasteland. Emira, with her fiery spirit and her turbulent magic, threatened to melt the ice, to unleash the storms he'd kept imprisoned for so long.

But he could not afford to let her consume him again.

Her magic pulsed erratically, white light flickering beneath her skin, threatening to spiral out of control again. He could not allow that. He would not.

What had she been thinking?

His hands were steady as he lifted her, the weight of her in his arms light compared to the burdens she had already placed upon him. He should have felt nothing...

No tenderness. No hesitation. Just action.

But the feel of her soft curves against his chest did something to him. A rush of heat, an unwelcome yearning. The memory of her touch, the cool frost of her breath against his skin, remained like a phantom, and his breath caught in his throat. It shouldn't have been possible. He should have been immune to her now, to the way his heart traitorously leaped in his chest at her nearness.

For all she'd done, somehow, she anchored him in ways he couldn't explain. She would be his undoing, but she was also a part of him. But even that was too much to acknowledge. His sanity threatened a break from reality.

He crushed the feelings beneath the ice of his Frostlands.

She would not be his undoing.

She was his responsibility.

That was all.

And that was everything.

The ship creaked as he descended the narrow staircase below deck, shadows closing in around them. The scent of brine and old wood filled the dim hallway, the walls pressing tighter, the flickering lanterns casting strange patterns over the rough planks.

Inside her cabin, the air thickened, heavy with the scent of coconut and flowers—her scent. He inhaled sharply, then exhaled through his nose. *Irrelevant.*

Yet, he laid her gently on the bed, not wanting to let her go.

Even with blazing light vibrating beneath her skin, she looked small, breakable. Vulnerable in a way that unsettled him. She was never supposed to be vulnerable.

She was supposed to be strong enough to resist betrayal. Strong enough to fight beside him, not against him.

Sapphire curls fanned across the pillow, her emerald gaze fixed on the ceiling, refusing to look at him. The ship's creaking and crew's distant murmur the only sounds.

Good. Let her stay silent. Let her stew in the consequences of her own recklessness.

His fingers hovered at his side, clenched, then relaxed. He shouldn't touch her. Not now. Not ever.

And yet—

His hand moved anyway.

His fingers brushed her wrist, the delicate curve of her pulse. Warm. Soft. Alive.

The ice in his Frostlands hissed at the contact. A warning. A crack forming beneath his feet. He told himself it was just to steady her, to ensure her magic had settled. Nothing more.

But he didn't let go. Didn't want to.

His fingers traced the delicate blue veins, more visible beneath her translucent sea foam-green complexion.

Her pulse jumped. Emerald eyes snapped to his, wary.

But he continued to stroke her soft wrist. Back and forth. Steady as the rocking ship. Her warmth transferred through his calloused fingers. A tether to something he refused to name.

He longed to lean down, to taste the salt on her skin, to feel the pulse of her magic against his lips. His breath hitched, his control slipping, unraveling in ways he hadn't expected. He clenched his jaw, fighting the urge.

Her magic dimmed, the glow in her veins darkening.

This should have felt like victory. Like proof that control worked, that she was no longer a threat. But the way his hand lingered, the way his own pulse pounded beneath his skin—this was not control.

This was weakness.

The illusion of his Frostlands shook.

As the Blue Devil, he had reclaimed the cold, untouchable sanctuary of his mind. But touching her now destroyed his control.

He had tricked himself into believing his Frostlands had been restored. But he had only buried the damage beneath ice too thin to hold.

A fool's mirage.

That realization crushed him. He was not untouchable. He had never been.

His Frostlands groaned under the weight of something unwanted.

He had failed to rebuild what he lost. He was still broken.

And now she knew it too.

But she didn't have to.

He still needed the cold comfort of his Frostlands, the icy detachment that had shielded him for centuries. He needed to force himself back into the ice. To make this fracture mean nothing.

But his lingering touch on her wrist hadn't changed.

He should have stopped by now.

He didn't.

"Emira," he began, his voice rough, the sound unfamiliar in the cabin. "I..." He faltered, unsure how to begin. Unsure if he should begin at all.

If he spoke—if he let this moment mean something—it would undo everything. The ice, the detachment, the control.

But this quiet wouldn't fix it either.

"I hate this." His voice scraped against the silence. "I hate that I can't trust you. You've made me question everything I thought I knew about love, about loyalty, about myself."

He hated that touching her didn't feel like victory. It felt like surrender.

Her lips parted, her breath shallow. A faint blush warmed her cheeks, the silver swirls on her skin shimmering. Even in her stillness, she captivated him, enthralling him. He took a shaky breath, reminding himself of the danger she posed. Her magic, a volatile force, could erupt at any moment.

He needed to let her go.

Instead, his fingers continued stroking her wrist. The warmth of her skin tethered him to something beyond the ice.

"I'm torn between my duty to my kingdom and these feelings I can't seem to shake. I thought I could hate you, but seeing you struggle like this... it's not that simple."

His Frostlands ached, his grasp on them weakened—but not broken.

Not yet.

"For centuries, I've lived by a strict code, believing that honor and duty would guide me to a better future. I thought, no—I believed—" His voice wavered, something catching in his throat. He exhaled sharply, his grip flexing against her skin. "I believed it would be enough."

A truth he had never dared to say aloud. That it was easier to sacrifice than to hope.

Hope meant wanting. It meant risk. It meant failure.

He had spent a thousand years convincing himself that sacrifice made a man righteous. That the things he gave up—love, freedom, choice—were necessary for the greater good.

And then she came along, and for a moment, he thought he could have both.

He scoffed bitterly, shaking his head at his own foolishness. *What a lie.*

His fingers curled around her wrist, and she closed her eyes. Her muscles relaxed, her breath growing steadier. The luminance beneath her skin faded completely, the threat diminishing.

She was safe.

But his Frostlands weren't whole. They never had been.

She had always been the one thing that could expose it.

And here she was, undoing him all over again.

His fingers twitched against her skin, a moment of hesitation, a moment of dangerous indecision. He had spent so long convincing himself that feeling nothing was the answer. That detachment was survival. That pain was only weakness when acknowledged.

But here, now, with her warmth bleeding into him, with her breath steady under his touch, something lurched inside him. A pull. A fracture. A whisper of something he couldn't drown in ice.

What if… just for a moment… he let himself feel it?

Would it be worse than this constant battle to bury what had already surfaced?

The thought made his grip tighten. *A risk.* He wasn't sure if he was willing to take it.

And yet, his next words betrayed him.

He sighed. "You may speak, Emira, but do not move otherwise."

He observed her closely, his heart a frantic drum against his ribs. The painite in his pocket pulsed with a dying glow. He still held control—the control she desperately craved.

He wanted nothing more than to give it back to her.

Using the Sun Stone to test her control, her credibility, was a thought that had crossed his mind before, but her ability to blend truth with deception stopped him. They'd have to find their own way, or none at all.

Her eyes fluttered open, their emerald depths reflecting a mix of defiance and something like relief and hope.

"Thank you," she said, her voice hoarse.

He forced himself to nod, not trusting his voice. The thank you felt undeserved. Yet, a part of him—one he despised—wanted to believe it meant something.

Hope, he knew, was a dangerous thing.

"You can release all of me now." Her voice was steady, but he sensed the urgency beneath her words, the desperate need for autonomy.

His heart ached at her request, but he couldn't bring himself to trust her completely—to trust that she would know when to stop herself. "I'm sure you feel in control of your magic now, but—"

Her expression darkened. "You said you hate this. But I think you secretly love having so much control over me."

He stilled.

Her words cut.

Did he?

No. He didn't want this. He never wanted this. And yet...

"You think that's who I am?" His chest ached, a sharp pressure that felt too much like regret. "Right now, I'm more concerned about all the lives in jeopardy on this ship than any genuine need to control you."

A slight narrowing of her eyes saw into him. "But you force me to stay with you. You have the Sun Stone back. You could have allowed me to leave, like Rivus."

The thought of her leaving him stole his breath. He wanted to continue hating her, to dismiss her as a manipulative liar, but he didn't know how to let her go.

Even without his response, she read him, and her eyes flashed. "Why are you still holding onto me?"

Why? He didn't know. Couldn't allow the answer to rise out of his Frostlands.

Her next words were a whisper, but they struck like a blade. "Your curse is broken. You hate me. The only reason you keep me is to punish me for your twisted version of justice."

His pulse thundered in his ears.

"I don't hate you," he said, his voice a whisper with the realization of that truth.

Her expression softened for a fraction of a second. A moment he could have reached for. A moment he could have stepped into.

"Then release me."

He hesitated.

Then—

"No."

Her skin shaded with anger, and she shut her eyes, her expression closing off as if he wasn't even there.

His breath caught.

Fool.

For one brief, ridiculous moment, he had let himself believe they could move forward.

But nothing had changed.

The moment slipped through his fingers like melting snow, and his Frostlands lurched back into place, chasms groaning as fractures began to seal again.

Still, he hesitated. "You won't speak to me?"

The words slipped out before he could stop them. He hadn't meant to ask. Hadn't meant to care. But her silence stretched, suffocating. It wasn't just defiance—it was distance. An abyss he had no way of crossing.

"Choices have consequences, Emira."

Still silence.

His fingers twitched at his sides, the urge to touch her returning with a vengeance. To make her look at him. To fix this—

No.

It was already broken. They were already broken.

His throat tightened, but he smothered it down.

Fine. Let her be silent. Let her keep her distance.

He would do the same.

The Blue Devil stirred, rising to take dominion of his Frostlands. Hope was the cruelest lie of all. A mistake he would not make again.

"If silence is what you want, then I'll leave you to it," he said, his voice colder, more distant. A judge passing a sentence.

His fingers curled into fists.

If she wanted him to be the monster, so be it. He had been reforged in ice before—he would do it again. The Blue Devil left nothing behind.

He turned on his heel and slammed the door with finality, severing whatever moment of warmth had almost existed between them.

CHAPTER 77

EMMY

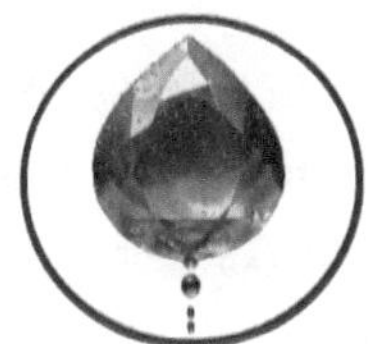

The incessant creak of the ship's timbers grated on Emmy's nerves, a mocking rhythm to her caged heartbeat. The salty air, usually welcome, felt oppressive. Confined, she could only listen and think as the sun climbed toward midday.

A restless fire burned in her gut, fueled by what she'd learned about Adria and the source of Emmy's curse. Thinking of it again incited a fury like she'd never known, compounded by Edmar's control, by his harsh words, by the injustice of it all. Trapped in her cabin, bound by his command again.

Every muscle ached for release. The urge to feel the solid deck beneath her feet, to lash out at something, anything, to vent the frustration that coiled tight within her, pulsed as an urgent need through her veins.

How dare he lecture her about choices, about consequences, as if her life hadn't been shaped by the very curse Adria had rid herself of, making a bargain with the same Sea Witch? *Does he not understand the desperation that drove Adria to such extremes had also driven me?*

Her father had imprisoned her, but never like this—he hadn't taken away her ability to move. At least with him she knew her place, knew the rules of her confinement.

A nagging whisper echoed in her mind. *Father hadn't limited your movement because the consequences had been enough to keep you still. But now you face those same consequences without restraining yourself, and you've killed again when you didn't want to.*

Everything was so confusing—anger, tenderness, control, and a yearning that made her heart ache. Edmar's caress had been both soothing and tormenting. He'd carried her with gentleness. A treacherous heat lingered on her wrist, a phantom sensation where he'd stroked her. She hated the way his touch affected her, hated the weakness it revealed. And all of this contrasted harshly with his command to stop moving.

How long will he leave me like this?! Will he come back and touch me again?

Like before, when his caress ignited desire within her, her magic calmed faster than she would have managed alone. A sobering thought, one muddling her anger with a craving for more of his caresses.

A craving that softened her when she thought of his curse, the struggles he'd had, his fears for the kingdom. He'd seen the world turn to ice, had faced betrayal and loss starting a thousand years ago—much longer than she'd dealt with her own curse. She'd glimpsed the shadows in his eyes, the burden of his centuries-old duty.

But does he see my fears, too? My curse, the terror of my power?

The waves against the hull drew her gaze to the porthole. The yearning to be free, to dive into the ocean and escape this prison, surged within her. A siren song of freedom promised by the Longing's appeal.

Escape. Oblivion.

An endless expanse of water, cold depths bewitching her, calling her home.

But the sea offers no refuge. Only imprisonment by either her father or the Sea Witch. She must fight the call.

She hummed unconsciously, the Ocean's Lament weaving through her. Like the last time she'd sung the melody, its magic soothed the ache in her heart until she remembered her sister. *Anjali might hear.* She stopped humming, the melody fading into the rhythm of the waves against the hull.

Then anger, a dark tide, rose within her, seeking a different release. This fury summoned by Edmar's commands, fed by Adria's revelations. She started a different song, a ballad of vengeance other mermaids sang. A tale of a mermaid luring a deceitful man to his watery grave.

"Oh, lover false, with honeyed tongue,
You wove your lies, a web so strong.

Now taste the depths, the cold embrace,
Where truth is drowned, and shadows chase."

The song matched her dark mood, and the sunlight dimmed, bowing to her gloomy lyrics. The sky beyond turned a brooding gray.

A subtle shift in the air, a sudden chill prickling her skin, drew her from the song's embrace. She held her breath, her gaze darting as far as she could see without being able to turn her head toward the door.

Did Edmar return?

She could smell him, his ocean scent blended with his body's musk, but it was hard to tell if it remained from when he carried her here, from this new appearance, or maybe from his shirt close to her head, which she'd unpacked earlier after she'd been given her cabin.

Silence stretched, heavy and expectant. Her heart pounded, a frantic drum against her ribs. Then, a rush of movement, a whisper of displaced air, and darkness fell as a curtain closed over the porthole, plunging the cabin into near darkness.

A tall, imposing figure silhouetted against the faint light, his back to her, dressed in all black. Long, dark gray hair with hints of blue flowed between a pair of midnight wings. The wings draped close together like curtains, twitching subtly, casting an oily blue sheen as if a dark liquid drenched them. So different from Edmar's leathery dragon wings.

He turned. His gaze, clear and piercing, locked onto hers, expression as impassive as a statue's. "Don't sing again, mermaid."

A dark aura clung to his pale, milky-blue skin. Shadows whispered around him, carrying a sense of decay. His features, disturbingly handsome, held a grim expression. He reminded her of the Summer Child's protector, a harbinger of death. But while her eyes were completely black, his seemed almost normal, except for their unnaturally light color, nearly void of any pigment. She wondered if, up close, she might see into his soul.

"Who... who are you?" Her voice came out in a shaky whisper.

Is he as powerful as the Summer Child's protector?

His gaze fixed on her, unblinking. "Your Siren's Call is making the men jump overboard. Normally I'd watch in amusement. Let the idiots jump, but I can't afford it this time."

He spoke in a monotone, devoid of any inflection, his attention already elsewhere, drifting around the room. He sighed, the sound almost imperceptible.

She couldn't mask her disgust at his callousness. "How can you value their lives so little?"

"I couldn't care less about the pirates' fate, but it took considerable effort to restrain Avi's father." His flat voice sharpened by the end of his last words, barely discernible, but she caught it. "Avi wouldn't want to see him come to harm."

Avi's name softened his voice. *Interesting.*

His careless words still bothered her. Not that jumping overboard would kill most of the pirates. The majority were Water Fae, with bodies adaptable to living in the water. Regardless... "Everyone's life matters."

Yet even she hadn't considered everyone or anyone else when she went to the Sea Witch. *Edmar is right in that respect.*

But would she make the deal with the Sea Witch again if it was her only choice? Or could she die to ensure others were safe?

"Only Avi's life matters to me." One shoulder lifted in a careless shrug, a fluid movement devoid of energy, as if even that simple action required too much effort. "The rest, no. It's hard to care when you've seen the things I have."

Pain flickered across his face, quickly masked. His lips made a thin, bloodless line. His words resonated with a haunting familiarity. Edmar, too, had spoken of loss in the same way. The same that echoed in her soul.

Who did he lose?

"Did you say Siren's Call?" she asked, remembering his words.

One fine gray eyebrow arched on his pale face. "Please don't tell me we have an idiot on board who can make men do anything she wants."

Me? But she didn't have that power... or did she? She'd never sang before the suppression spell, so she hadn't known the magic merfolk imbued into their songs or the spell of a siren.

The legends must be true for mere mermaids. As her merfolk nature returned, with all the pain and destruction of her magic, so too did the power of the Siren's Call. But curiously, unless she was wrong, this dark creature appeared to be male. "Why didn't my song affect you?"

"The Siren's Call only works on living males."

"You're not alive?" *How is that possible?*

"Undead," he said, his correction sounding as enthusiastic as the dead, but bloodless lips curved into a stiff smile.

Her mind raced with questions. "What does that mean—being undead? What race are you? Are you connected to the Summer Child's protector? Do you have a name?"

"I'm not interested in wasting time with pointless chatter." He turned to leave, his wings rustling like clothes as they swayed back and forth.

"Wait!" Her voice gained more strength. "You must answer my questions, or I will start singing again."

He paused, his shoulders stiffening. "You're a troublesome creature," he muttered, a hint of frustration tinged with begrudging admiration.

"And you're a controlling one."

"I don't care to be manipulated, mermaid." He turned back, his movements graceful, and their gazes clashed. Finally, he conceded with a sigh. "Cielan."

Cielan meant the sky on a clear day or an airy day. A name heavy with meaning, with one of the eight magical elements included. Fae liked those types of names.

Her own name was much simpler. Emira meant princess. "Emmy."

"I didn't ask." His impatience wasn't concealed. "To be undead means I walk between life and death, not one or the other. I was an Air Fae once, but now I'm some perversion of my previous life. The Summer Child's protector is unknown to me. Anything else?"

He'd clearly answered many questions before. She plunged into her next set.

"How did you become undead? What does that even mean? Do you have magic?"

He raised a hand to stop her, then opened his thin mouth to answer.

A jarring impact rocked the ship, throwing her against the wall. A groaning tremor echoed through the ship. Wood splintered, glass shattered, and panicked shouts all combined right before the ship tilted violently again.

CHAPTER 78

EMMY

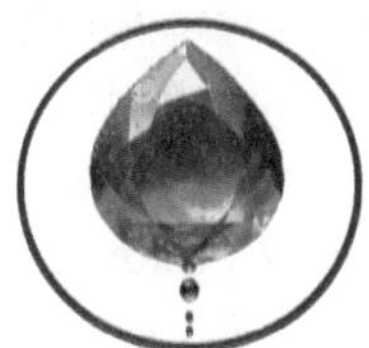

The world whipped back and forth. Timbers groaned. Salt and fear filled the air. With the next brutal pitch, Emmy tumbled from the bed with a cry, her body a helpless weight.

Cold arms caught her, a rush of wind against her skin. She gasped from the sudden shift in gravity. Cielan held her, his face grim, lips pressed hard together. He tilted his head toward the door, as if listening to a distant conversation.

"You hear something?" she asked.

He didn't look at her. "Enhanced senses."

A deafening roar, then a massive impact. The ship shuddered, timbers splintering. The vessel lurched. Cielan winced, tightening his grip.

Her heart lurched. "What's happening?"

"Moon-Tide Leviathan. We're under attack."

Terror gripped her. The legendary Moon-Tide Leviathan—a colossal sea serpent, harbinger of storms and shipwrecks. Said to dwell in the darkest depths of the ocean, though no one had seen it for several thousand years. An ancient Winter being, a creature of darkness drawn to the Summer Child's power just as the Sun God warned.

His expression remained impassive, but concern flickered in his eyes, a tremor in his voice betraying his unease. "Several crew members lost already."

She wondered who had been lost, and her thoughts flew to Edmar. She whispered his name, her voice lost in the creature's roar.

Cielan started to lower her back onto the bed. "You're safer here."

A surge of defiance battled her fear. "Is it male?"

His blank look revealed nothing but a subtle show of distaste. "Do I look like I have time to figure that out?"

"Take me to the deck," she said, her voice stronger. "Now."

He arched a brow, then tightened his hold, moving with blinding speed. The rush of air stole her breath.

Chaos reigned. The deck tilted precariously. The Moon-Tide Leviathan, a monstrous serpent, coiled around the ship, its silver scales glinting. A sail-like fin burst up from the waves, followed by its dragon head, crowned with metal spikes.

Red glowing eyes fixed on the crew. Pirates attacked with swords and cutlasses, some hanging from the rigging. One screamed as the creature's jaws closed around her.

Emmy's heart pounded as she searched for Edmar. She spotted Avi, the slim fae clinging to a mast, her gaze fixed on the sea serpent, her expression blank.

"Dolcivita, get below!" Cielan shouted.

Avi looked at him, her expression unchanged.

What is she doing?

Then she saw Edmar, his blue-emblazoned form battling the creature with ice magic. A blizzard of frozen shards erupted from his hands, his expression fierce.

He hadn't noticed her yet, his focus entirely on the battle.

"Hurry, mermaid." Cielan gasped, dropping to one knee, sweat beading on his forehead.

His wings trembled with the effort to stay upright. Despite his struggle, he kept a firm hold on her. Not wasting another moment, she started singing, hoping it would work.

> "Oh, ancient one, of depths untold,
> Your anger stirs, a tale unfolds.
> But peace awaits, a tranquil tide,
> Where shadows sleep, and storms subside."

Designed to soothe and compel, her song resonated across the deck, penetrating the battle's mayhem, reaching the Moon-Tide Leviathan. She poured her will into the melody, a desperate plea for calm.

"Turn from this path, find solace deep,
Where dreams of silver softly sleep."

She infused a subtle command, a warning to the male crew to stay on the ship, directing her Siren's Call solely to the creature.

"Let land's embrace not be your goal,
But ocean's depths, a calming soul."

The Moon-Tide Leviathan paused, its glowing eyes softening, shifting from red to blue. It loosened its grip on the ship, its massive body uncoiling, the metallic spikes retracting. Slowly, it turned, silver scales flashing in the churning waves.

She kept singing, not sure how long the creature needed to get him far enough away. Then her voice faltered, and she stopped.

Silence fell. The crew stood frozen, eyes wide, jaws slack.

An older pirate near the helm brought a fist to her chest, the silver rings on her fingers glinting in the sunlight. Two sharp taps of her thumb against her breastbone echoed across the deck, a silent plea to Nerithra, the goddess of sea monsters.

A younger pirate, gripping the arm of his companion, knuckles white against sun-weathered blue skin, mimicked the ancient signal. Fist clenched, thumb tapping twice against his chest. Others followed, making Nerithra's sign, whispering prayers, and seeking her protection from the retreating creature.

Only the ship's groans and the Leviathan's receding roar accompanied the whispers. Then the pirate crew turned their gazes to her. Gratitude and suspicion filled their stares equally.

She ignored them to look at Edmar, their eyes finally meeting across the ravaged deck.

Relief washed over his features, but a shadow of apprehension remained in their depths. The blue glow around his irises pulsed.

Her heart pounded, a frantic rhythm against her ribs, and exhaustion washed over her. But a strange exhilaration replaced some of her weariness. The creature, monstrous as it was, had heeded her song. It had obeyed her. She'd wielded a power she hadn't known she possessed.

Cielan released a groan of pain, his grip slackening, his body trembling.

Adria barked orders, her voice booming, breaking the silence, and the crew jumped to obey. A flood of raucous conversation spilled forth, mostly the awe in seeing the legendary creature. There was also talk about her, a mermaid with a siren's voice.

Edmar approached, his gaze never leaving hers, his fingers brushing her painite. She shivered, her heart pounding. If her heart didn't slow down, it would leap right out of her chest.

She held her breath.

She'd displayed her power, an ability to control and command with her song.

Would he be wary of her again, his control tightening further even though she'd saved them? Perhaps now he would command her to stop speaking all the time.

Chapter 79

EDMAR

Cielan slumped against a mast, his body trembling. His other knee buckled, grip weakening. Edmar saw it before it happened, saw the vamphyr's strength failing.

And Emira—still immobile—was slipping from his arms.

Edmar moved before he could think, boots skidding on the blood-slicked deck. His heart slammed against his ribs as he caught her, pulling her tight against him. *Mine.* The thought came unbidden, raw, visceral.

His Frostlands groaned, shaking apart.

He ignored it.

Cielan collapsed, his head hitting the deck.

Edmar tore his gaze away from Emira. "Get him below deck. Quickly!"

The vamphyr succumbed to the sun's unforgiving rays. Skin, already pale as death, turned ashen, a sickly gray tinge spreading beneath sweat. Spidery black lines crawled beneath his skin.

A metallic tang of blood and the acrid scent of magic thickened the air. He held Emira close as the crew moved around him, the nearest ones scrambling to lift Cielan and carry the unconscious vamphyr away, wearing looks of revulsion. No one seemed to like the man.

And yet, it wasn't the vamphyr that held Edmar's attention.

It was her.

He shifted her in his arms, steadying her. She blinked up at him, her emerald eyes hazy, wary. Her breath came quick and shallow, her body still, but she was whole. Unharmed.

Then everything he'd felt when he first saw her on deck with the sea serpent came rushing back. Anger, fear, and frustration.

Anger at her recklessness, in leaving the cabin, fear for her safety, frustration at her defiance. No matter what he did to ensure he protected both her and the pirates, he couldn't seem to keep everyone from harm.

He couldn't seem to keep his emotions buried around her, because despite all of this, relief crashed into him, fierce and unrelenting. She was safe. And beyond that, she'd saved them all with her magic.

Magic that could kill every one of us.

The turmoil of emotions churned free of his Frostlands, slamming into him one after another after centuries of holding them back. He struggled to clear his mind, to draw a steady breath. His nostrils flared in panic, then he caught her scent.

His thoughts hyperfocused on an awareness of her.

Fingers curled over the curve of her waist, the softness of her hip. Her short curls tantalizing him as they brushed over his skin. He fought to rise above the flood of emotions, so he latched onto the thing that had captured his attention yet seemed unimportant in the face of her betrayals.

"Why did you cut your hair?" he asked, his voice husky.

Surprise flashed in her eyes. She had not been expecting his question, and some of the wariness faded. "I cut ties to the woman who had no control over her destiny."

"And have you gained that control?"

"Not yet. But I refused to be her again."

Fire burned in her eyes, a promise, not defiance. The fire frustrated him but also roused him. Heat, that had nothing to do with the battle or the sun beating down on the deck, flushed through him. The way her body fit against him, the way her breath hitched. This was dangerous.

Her gaze softened for a fraction of a second, and he forgot to breathe. She wasn't supposed to look at him like that. Like he was still the man she wanted.

He swallowed, something thick settling in his chest. Just for a moment, she wasn't his betrayer, his prisoner, or the dangerous wielder of magic that haunted him. She was simply Emira, and it was enough to leave him unsteady.

I want her. The thought, raw and unwelcome, pulsed through him.

His fingers tightened for reasons he didn't want to name, and he forced his desire into his rumbling Frostlands, taking a breath.

Too many things remained unresolved.

Remembering that, a treacherous current of anger won against his craving for her. He had commanded her not to move.

"You..." he began, his voice strained. What was the right word? She hadn't disobeyed his commands, not technically. But she'd used magic when she knew she lacked control.

And he had seen nothing like it. She had controlled the Leviathan with nothing more than her voice.

But there was a deeper hurt. Recalling the night they had danced at the Blue Angel tavern, he realized once more the depths of her deceptions. She hadn't been truthful with him even then.

"You lied to me." The accusation ripped from him, a shard of ice against the burgeoning heat in his blood. "The Siren's Call."

Her eyes widened slightly, as if realizing what he meant. "I didn't know."

No quaver in her voice. No flicker of deceit.

But how could he believe that?

He searched her, desperate for a lie, for something to make his distrust feel justified. But there was no evasion, no shift in her expression. Only quiet certainty.

A strong wind swept over the deck, whipping her short sapphire curls, surrounding him in her scent, drowning him, threatening his ability to reason. He shifted her in his arms again, her weight a delicious torment against his chest.

But he remembered how easily lies fell from her pretty mouth.

She was the woman who had stolen from him, lied to him.

And yet somehow still anchored him in ways he couldn't explain. She wasn't just his completion. She was his undoing.

He couldn't look away.

His lungs tightened, as if grappling with the impossible balance of pain and longing.

She watched him closely, her expression unreadable. But beneath the exhaustion in her gaze, something flickered.

Something that made him want to believe her.

His throat tightened. No. That was dangerous. That was how she had destroyed him before.

Finally, he broke their eye contact, his gaze sweeping the wreckage of the deck, the place where the Leviathan had nearly destroyed them.

"You could have killed all the men." The tales of sirens, their songs weaving madness and destruction, echoed in his mind. "You could have killed me."

She shook her head. "I wouldn't."

He turned back to her, eyes narrowing. "How can I believe that?"

She didn't flinch, didn't look away. "Because it's the truth. I only hoped to protect the ship. To protect you."

And gods help him, he wanted to believe her.

His brows lifted at the caress in her last words, echoing in his mind, creating yet another fissure in his icy landscape. She had protected him. *Her.* The woman who had betrayed him, stolen from him... had used her power to save him and everyone else. Did she really possess such selflessness?

Or is it a trick?

Trust was not something easily regained. Not when it had already cost him everything.

But her song had saved them, controlled the leviathan.

Frustration warred with his growing sense of awe. Using only her mind and words, she'd found a way to convince the vamphyr, who couldn't be in the sun, to bring her on deck so she could fight the Moon-Tide Leviathan. All while immobile. Her ingenuity unnerved and captured him.

And he wanted her. He wanted her with a fierceness that shook him to his core, her nearness a torment, her soft body a silent invitation. He drew in a shaky breath, her scent filling his lungs.

I have to get away from her. His gaze dropped to her lips, full and inviting. He forced himself to look away, focusing on the horizon, the endless expanse of the sea. "I'm releasing you."

A small gasp escaped her lips as he slowly lowered her to the deck. But he didn't let go immediately. Her body slid against his, her heat branding him, her breath a whisper against his throat. A sharp pang of desire shot through him.

He gritted his teeth. *Damn her.*

He forced his hands to loosen, to let her go before he kissed her—kissing her now would make him the biggest fool. But stepping back felt like tearing something from his soul.

She wobbled slightly but caught herself, her eyes wide with disbelief.

"I'm releasing you from all my commands," he repeated.

Relief and uncertainty flickered over her face, but so did something else. Something that had nothing to do with freedom.

And he recognized it instantly.

Desire.

She wanted him still.

And that shattered something deep inside of him.

He clenched his fists. *Not here. Not now.*

Trying to reconcile all of her actions with the simmering pain and rage within him, with the unwelcome heat of desire, proved impossible, unbearable. His Frostlands staggered against something he had no defense for. He had believed he could patch the fractures, reclaim the cold, but with each breath, each stolen glance at her, the ice weakened.

He needed to rebuild the walls before they shattered entirely.

Backing away, he put distance between them, but his heart pounded relentlessly.

Space. He needed space to think.

"So help me, Emira." His fists clenched. He could do nothing to hurt her, but if she became a danger, he'd get her away from everyone, even if it meant his death. "If you put anyone at risk..."

He shook his head. "All our fates are in your hands."

A warning. A truth.

She didn't look away. "I know."

Relief and uncertainty flitted in her eyes.

He couldn't deny a similar relief, releasing her. And he understood her uncertainty. He kept her gem, the small red painite, in his fist. A reminder of the control he still held. But she was also still dangerous, and trust was a different matter.

Perhaps it was better if she was still wary of him. Maybe this incessant need to take her into his arms and finally make love to his wife would eventually go away, because that would only lead him into worse danger.

To break the tension between them, he scanned the deck. The crew watched them, their expressions curious but also wary. He caught Avi in the doorway leading down to the cabins, her cerulean eyes unreadable, her presence unsettling.

Why isn't she with Cielan? Aren't they...?

A sense of unease filtered over him, but he shoved the thought away. There were more immediate concerns. He had a quest to complete and a woman with a dangerous power to watch. He needed to be vigilant to protect himself and everyone from the woman who loved him.

The woman he couldn't trust nor resist.

He turned abruptly, forcing himself to walk away.

He wanted to be far away from her, and he wanted nothing more than to pull her into his arms, to lose himself in her.

The conflict raged.

The Blue Devil had cracked in his mental fortress. He needed to hold on to his Frostlands. If he let them crumble now, there would be no rebuilding them. And he needed them. He needed the cold. He needed the Blue Devil. And for the first time, he wasn't sure if he could fortify his icy wastelands again.

Chapter 80

EMMY

The ship rocked gently as the evening meal came to a close in the galley. The savory scents of fish, spiced vegetables, and something earthy wafted in the air. Lanterns swayed, casting flickering shadows across the faces of the crew. Emmy sat amidst the rowdy pirates at a rough-hewn table, yet alone in her silence.

"—and then the blasted sea serpent reared up, teeth as big as harpoons before it released its grip on the ship, body as thick as a rowboat slithering back into the depths, leaving us bobbing like a cork in a whirlpool!"

Laughter erupted, mingling with the ship's creaking and the splash of waves against the hull. She glanced at the dark water visible through the porthole. Most of the day she'd spent in contemplation, watching the horizon and the crew.

Edmar had released her, but his distrust remained evident in his actions, his avoidance of her.

She didn't know how to feel about that. Not when his gaze landed on her several times throughout the day, revealing equal parts heat and anguish.

It deflated all of her anger.

"Aye," Adria chimed in, a mischievous glint in her eyes, "and you were all white as ghosts, clinging to the rigging for dear life."

"Speak for yourself, wife." Lian chuckled, his arm around Adria, where they sat across from her. "I was just admiring the view."

Avi sat quietly beside them, her cerulean eyes keen on every interaction. She seemed more lucent than in those first few minutes of meeting Emmy when they first boarded the ship. Gilly's golden necklace rested with the seashell nestled between her breasts.

What had she tried to tell me at port?

Unease churned the meal in her stomach. Adria's revelations, Edmar, waking the Metal God—each thought tangled together, leaving her restless. Now that she'd set aside her anger, the sick feeling only grew, filling the space it left behind.

She longed for something simpler, a chance to rebuild with the woman who had been her mother's best friend. To speak with Edmar without tension, without the unspoken words hanging between them like a barrier. But since freeing her from her bonds earlier, he'd kept his distance.

Edmar sat at the other end of the table, his focus on the conversation near him. His occasional touch to her gem relayed a silent signal, a reminder. The distance between them was more than just physical.

As much as he'd watched her, she'd also observed him from afar, drawn to his every movement, the way his fingers traced the charts, the beautiful smile that touched his lips when he spoke with others.

She loved this man, a deep-sea current that could not be turned. But with each passing hour and each league sailed, her impending sacrifice pressed down on her. They had little time left. Little time for a reconciliation.

The camaraderie of the pirate crew, their laughter and boisterous tales, faded as the meal wound down and many dispersed. The room's atmosphere shifted to one of relaxed ease. Adria and Lian whispered, sharing a smile. Lian brushed a lock of hair from Adria's face, which latched onto his finger as a curled wave of solid water.

The evident love in their tender gestures made her heart ache. She longed to repair the distance between herself and Edmar.

A faint chill, a shift in the air, drew her attention to Cielan. He stood in the shadows, shaking out his wings, then folding them again. Throughout the meal he hadn't moved, gaze fixed on Avi. With his deliberate movement, he finally received a reaction from the focus of his scrutiny. Avi stiffened, turning away from her parents, toying with a silver ring.

Emmy wondered why he hadn't eaten, then remembered the Summer Child's protector. *He probably fed differently.* She shuddered at the ghost of fangs sinking into her neck.

Edmar stood.

His continued silence fortified her newfound resolve. She couldn't let this be their ending. She wanted to mend what had been broken, what she had broken when she'd stolen the Sun Stone and left him. If it was possible.

"Thank you for the meal and the hospitality." Edmar's normally sensual voice was devoid of emotion. He left, disappearing into the dimly lit corridor.

She hesitated, the clatter of dishes echoing her own emptiness. Then, taking a deep, fortifying breath, she followed him, pain stabbing her feet. Guided by the invisible thread of her gem, she found him lying on the forecastle deck, gazing at the stars. His love for the night sky was clear in his serene face, the small smile on his lips.

The space beside him was invitingly empty. She hesitated, her confidence waning, replaced by anger and resentment rising within her again. They'd never get anywhere if she didn't overcome those feelings.

Remember, you love him. With a sigh, she lowered herself onto the deck, lying beside him, the wood cool against her skin. Immediate relief in her feet. *Thank the gods.*

He glanced at her, then away, his smile fading.

More silence. She'd started that silence when she'd refused to talk to him earlier. Now the quiet was only broken by the creaking ship and whispering wind. The stars tugged at her heart, a familiar ache of cherished memories—the stars Anjali painted in her chambers, the constellation stories she'd exchanged with Edmar.

"They are beautiful, aren't they?" she said, her voice barely a whisper over the gentle lapping of waves against the hull.

Starlight illuminated his profile, a quick smile at the corner of his eye, then gone. "Yes."

She had to press on and not be deterred by his abruptness. She hoped that deep within, he still loved her, too. Even though he'd avoided her the entire day, the constant caress of her stone was a sure sign his thoughts had never been far from her. "Do you remember the night we talked about the stars?"

Did he remember their shared passion, the moment they'd realized a common love between them?

He remained silent for a moment more, his jaw clenched, before finally relenting with a sigh. "I do."

Her glimmer of hope ignited into fierce determination. Perhaps he wasn't entirely lost to her, perhaps a part of him still longed for their connection. She prayed she wasn't deceiving herself. She lowered her voice. "The doomed lovers. Lost souls separated by the coils of the serpent."

No words, nothing in reply. Her hope deflated. Would they ever be more than this?

"I miss that." Her hands trembled, her openness becoming isolating. "I miss us."

Edmar finally looked at her, his eyes reflecting the starlight, his expression guarded. "That 'us' was built on lies, Emira."

Shame washed over her, but she pressed on, her voice a plea for understanding. "I know, and I'm sorry. But I had no choice."

"You keep saying that, but there's always a choice." He looked away.

Closing her eyes, she replayed his words, listening to each syllable, feeling the emotions hidden in their layers. The same arguments couldn't continue, not if they hoped for even a sliver of friendship.

Sitting up, hand over her heart, she gazed down at his profile, the long nose, the full lips. Heat spread through her core, a warmth intensified by her fire acid, the flickering painite in his pocket a telltale sign. "I thought I was right, but I understand you would have made different choices. I can't change the past. So how can we move forward?"

He continued his perusal of the sky.

She swallowed the grief climbing up her throat. "I'm truly sorry, Edmar. For everything. No matter my intentions, I hurt you, and I regret it. I'll never forgive myself for that."

His silence stretched, taut and uncomfortable. Then his agonized gaze met hers. "Why the Sea Witch? Why not trust *me* to find another way?"

His question was a barb, twisting in her heart. The Ocean's Lament, a harmony of sorrow, echoed in her soul, a reminder of the darkness she carried. "My magi c..."

"Tell me about it." He scrutinized her with half-closed eyes. "Tell me about your life, about what it meant to live with this curse."

She hesitated, memories flooding back—the isolation of the Little Palace, her father's fear-laced gaze, the chilling truth of her mother's sacrifice, her sisters' hatred. It was a past she'd tried to escape, yet it clung to her like a shadow. In a halting voice, she spoke of the restrictions, the constant vigilance, the desperate need to suppress her magic to keep those she loved safe, to reduce her pain.

"Pain? You've never mentioned this before."

"I've lived with it all my life. As magic increases in my blood, it floods my muscles with pain."

"Every time?"

She nodded.

The information roused anger, followed by sympathy in his eyes. Then they cleared of all emotion with his next inquiry. "And the Sea Witch? What are her plans?"

"You're asking me the same questions," she said, her voice tinged with frustration. "But I'll answer them a thousand times if that's what you need, Edmar. I'll tell you the truth, again and again, until you finally believe me. I didn't lie before, and I swear, I don't know why she wants the Gods' Stones."

"Then I need to know you'll give this up. That you'll give up going after the stones. I need to know that you're not in league with the Sea Witch."

"I already made that choice. Before the Sun God appeared. Before the werewolves."

He frowned, clear confusion giving way to relief. "What choice?"

"To stop." She closed her eyes, her voice barely audible. "To stop seeking the stones, to stop… betraying you."

"But you stole the Sun Stone."

"My choice came afterward. I would have used it to find Metallon." Her eyebrows drew together in a plea. "To free me from my magic. Permanently."

"I still don't understand why you didn't just tell me." The hurt in his voice was undeniable. "We could have worked together to find a solution."

"I believed you wouldn't have understood. That you wouldn't have allowed any of the choices I had."

"I understand desperation, Emira. I know what it means to be trapped because I lived it."

"It's not the same," she said, shaking her head. "You live by a code. Duty. Honor. Sacrifice. I trusted you would have found another way, a 'noble' way, but I couldn't risk that if it meant more imprisonment or the Sea Witch finding her revenge. I needed to be free. I had to be free."

A wet sheen appeared briefly in his eyes, then it was gone. "And you didn't think I could help you. Even after everything. After we got to know each other?"

She shook her head. "You hadn't seen my magic yet. I was afraid."

"Of what?"

She bit her lip. "Everyone fears my magic. I never dreamed anyone would accept me. Then I fell in love with you, even though I didn't want to. I fought it." She closed her eyes. "I didn't want to be a danger to you."

With his silence, she opened her eyes. *What is he thinking?*

His brow furrowed, skepticism clear in his gaze. Whatever he thought about her words, he didn't share as he lay his head back. When he spoke again, all the hurt had disappeared. "And Rivus? What was his role in this?"

"He never explained his reasons, and I didn't tell him what I was doing. He threatened to expose me, so I let him help me steal the Sun Stone. Considering what we learned from him, I don't doubt the Snow Princess involved him."

His eyes narrowed. "What do you know of the Snow Princess?"

With a deep breath, she nodded. This wasn't something he knew about her, and she would tell him anything and everything he wanted to know. She recounted every moment she spent with Malala, all of their conversations, and even her encounters with the Summer Child and her dark protector.

Slowly, Edmar rose to a seated position, his full attention on her. She mirrored his movement, their knees touching after they crossed their legs. By the end of her explanation, the tension seemed to drain from his shoulders, his posture relaxing. The furrow in his brow eased, and for a fleeting moment, a flicker of warmth lit his ocean-colored eyes, the ice melting to reveal a glimpse of the man she loved beneath the mask of detachment and anger, the Blue Devil she was sure had taken over him. This was a vulnerability she hadn't seen in him since before she'd taken the Sun Stone.

When she finished, fresh pain crossed his features, but an openness shimmered in the depths of his eyes. His voice was low, stripped of its usual command. "What do you want from me, Emira?"

She hesitated, her heart pounding, the words she longed to speak catching in her throat. The painite glowed through his pocket again, and searing pain raced through her limbs. She quickly calmed her heart, taking a deep breath before revealing her dreams. "If I were free to choose my own path, I would choose to spend my life with you."

"My curse is broken," he said, a quiet tremor in his voice. "You could be free of your marriage to me. It's a promise I made to you before, so no platitudes. I can set you free if that's what you really want."

"I choose you," she said again, her hand reaching for his, a desperate plea for understanding. "I love you, Edmar. I pray to all the gods that we have a chance..."

She couldn't finish the thought, certain that her death came at the end of this voyage.

His fingers laced with hers, a smile starting on his lips. A flicker of the love she craved rekindled in his eyes. "I also pray for—"

A hauntingly familiar melody drifted through the air, silencing him. Her heart skipped a beat. *Another siren song?*

Edmar turned toward the sound.

Avi stood at the far end of the deck, singing the enchanting tune. He stood, taking a step toward the fae.

Emmy leaped to her feet, fingers digging into his arm. "What were you going to say?"

He looked down at her with a blank expression, his voice cold and distant. "I'll never forgive you, Emira. Stop bothering me."

His words cut through her with the sharp precision of a blade, but she had no choice but to follow his command, her gem ensuring her compliance. She watched helplessly as he approached Avi, who leaned into him with a hand on his chest, the song nothing more than a memory on the wind.

Hurt, alarm, and an unsettling sense of something terribly wrong seized her. A chilling premonition seized her heart.

This isn't Edmar.

Something else, something darker, had taken hold of him. As Avi's lips moved, whispering words she couldn't hear, her hands shook, and she wanted to throw up.

CHAPTER 81

EDMAR

An inexplicable urge drew Edmar toward Avi. He found her at the railing, her slender form silhouetted against the vast expanse of the star-dusted sky. The ship creaked, waves lapping against the hull, a soothing rhythm against his turbulent emotions.

"The stars are breathtaking. I've always loved them." Her voice was soft and melodic. Leaning toward him, she turned a beautiful smile up at him, laying her gray hand on his chest.

He looked down at the hand, startled but feeling warm. His gaze was then drawn to her loose, lacy crimson shirt, the wide collar hanging open as she angled her body lower, revealing the smooth skin of her small breasts and a hint of her dark nipples.

Remembering his honor, he tore his gaze away to take in her lovely face, surprised he never noticed how attractive she was for a hybrid fae. "Breathtaking."

Her beauty was a song, a subtle melody. He didn't actually lose his breath. Only one woman did that... but he couldn't remember her. He frowned.

A delicate flush covered Avi's usual pallor, highlighting the silver strands woven through her dark hair. Her cerulean eyes, normally distant and veiled, shimmered with an intensity that both captivated and unnerved him.

"Have you ever watched them with someone you..." she paused, her gaze dropping to his lips, her cheeks tinged with a rosy hue, "care about?"

He felt a tug in his chest, a distant echo of some other woman's laughter, the warmth of her hand in his. *Emmy.* The name, a whisper in his mind, was quickly swallowed by the mesmerizing pull of Avi's presence, a melody on the wind.

"I have," he murmured, his voice softening.

His gaze drifted toward Emira, who stood on the opposite side of the deck, her eyes fixed on them. She held a hand over her heart, everything about her broadcasting alarm and sadness. He backed away from Avi. His memories filtered back in.

He saw Cielan then, looming in the shadows, his eyes glowing, his body tense.

Edmar swallowed. He knew little about vamphyrs, only what he'd learned since his earlier journey with Adria. Besides being stronger and faster than others, he had super senses and fed on magical blood. While the sun was his only enemy, it wouldn't kill him. It seemed nothing could kill a vamphyr.

This one, Cielan, had an obsession with Avi, who didn't appear to return his affections. Edmar didn't want to be the one to come between the vamphyr and his obsession.

But the hybrid fae's small fingers danced on his wrist, drawing his attention away from Emira and Cielan, making him forget that anyone else even existed beyond this enchanting fae. The scent of saltwater and silver lilies, intoxicating and alluring, enveloped him. He inhaled deeply, the fragrance triggering an urge to possess, to claim.

"Perhaps," she said, whispering, "we could watch them together sometime?"

Her words, a subtle invitation, ignited a fire within him. She was a beautiful woman, free of complications, free of lies and deceit. A haunting melody promised him she was what he'd been missing.

A need to touch her, to feel her naked skin against his, to lose himself in the depths of those cerulean eyes, surged through him. Part of him didn't understand what he was doing, but the delicate dance of seduction soothed the wounds of a betrayal he couldn't remember.

He leaned in, his voice husky. "Perhaps we could."

Her lips curved into a smile, and a warmth, as potent as the sun's embrace, radiated from her. His gaze locked with hers, an elusive, compelling melody echoing in his mind.

The world around him faded. The ship, the crew, the vast expanse of the sea, even the stars, all dissolved into a hazy backdrop as Avi's presence filled his senses. Peace settled over him, a calmness he hadn't known in years.

"You're troubled," Avi said softly, concern in her voice. "Tell me, what weighs so heavily on your heart?"

Her empathy, her genuine interest, struck a chord within him. For a moment, a flicker of doubt, a distant memory of pain-filled emerald eyes, surfaced. Avi offered an escape to the complexities of his feelings for this unknown woman. That shadow woman was cold cynicism and suspicion. Avi, by contrast, was free of such darkness, only offering warmth and desire. Thoughts of the other woman extinguished under the stimulating allure of Avi's presence. He yearned to confide in her, to share the burden he carried.

"The Sun God," he began, his voice barely a whisper, "he appeared to me."

Avi gave a sympathetic nod. "What did he say?"

"He gave me a holy quest."

She stepped closer, her shoulder brushing against his arm, her voice a soft murmur in his ear. "Tell me, Edmar, why are you going to Aelunis? What is your holy quest?"

His mind, clouded by her nearness, struggled to find the truth. "We need to wake the Metal God."

She tilted her head, her smile lovely. "How do you plan to wake him?"

"Blood," he replied, his voice distant. "The Sun God said we need to spill the blood of one of the god's creations on the Sun Stone."

She raised an eyebrow, her lips curving into a sly smile. "So that's why the mermaid is on this trip?"

"Yes," he said, then frowned. How had he forgotten the mermaid had been there, too? *Who is she?* That didn't matter. Something told him he needed to protect her. "No. Solis gave her the quest, too, but her blood will wake Metallon."

I shouldn't be telling her this. His mind screamed at him to stop, to recognize the danger of revealing so much. But every time he tried to focus on the warning, something about Avi and her lyrical voice drew him back, her smile reassuring him he was doing the right thing.

"Interesting. So, the Little Mermaid is offering herself to wake a god?" Her question was more of a statement, followed by a soft laugh.

"Offering herself?" *What does that mean?*

"Sacrificing. What else could wake a sleeping god than a full sacrifice? Gods are so unforgiving."

"No." He shook his head at the thought of the mermaid dying. "I can't let her..."

Avi placed a pale gray hand on his chest again, and his thoughts scrambled. His heart beat faster. A sweet melody filled his mind, erasing his fear, dismissing his reason for alarm, making him forget there was a mermaid.

The fae's distracting aroma of saltwater and silver lilies spun his mind, reminding him of his mother, and he wrapped his arms around her. At first, her thin frame felt wrong against his body. Usually, he preferred women with full curves, but the melody continued, and he held her tighter.

"What else did Solis say to you?"

"We need to wake all the gods." He nuzzled the side of her neck, wanting to taste her.

She pushed him back gently. "Tell me all of it, Edmar."

He recounted the Sun God's words—the Summer Child's impending birth, the need to awaken all the gods to save the world from her, his first mission for the Metal God, the journey to the shrouded land of Aelunis, and now the possibility of sacrificing the gods' children to awaken each of them.

Avi listened intently to his story, her gaze never leaving his face, fascination and dread swirling in her eyes. Each time her attention dropped to his lips, a burning fire strengthened within him, urging him to claim a kiss, to run his hands over her body.

His hands swept down her back, resting at the top of her buttocks. His fingers dug into her slim hips, wanting to pull her hard against him. Once more, he was reminded she differed from his preference. From someone else.

"Aelunis," she said, her voice barely audible. "A perilous journey indeed. And the Sun Stone. It holds the key." Her gaze, intense and searching, met his. Her tone became light and playful, but with an edge of insistence beneath the surface. "May I see it, Edmar?"

Doubt crept through the haze in his mind. He hesitated, the veil's grip on his thoughts loosening. He'd retrieved the Sun Stone from someone, fought for it, even broken his curse while trying to possess it again.

Avi laughed at his hesitation. "I only want to see it, not take it from you."

Something wasn't right. His instincts flared, and he released her, taking a step back. "No."

Avi laughed again, the sound like tinkling bells.

"Of course, of course," she said, brushing off his denial with a wave of her hand. She leaned into him, her fingers lingering on his arm, her breath a warm caress against his cheek. "But if you ever change your mind, you can trust me."

Her closeness, the subtle allure of her voice, eroded his hesitation. He needed to trust someone. He'd been betrayed by those closest to him, left with wounds continually festering in his heart. But Avi, with her gentle fingers and understanding gaze, offered a solace he hadn't known in centuries. His doubts began to fade.

"Edmar," she said softly, her fingers tracing patterns on his arm. Her voice dropped to a conspiratorial whisper. "You need to be careful with the mermaid."

The mermaid? Her caress ignited the fire within him again, but his heart stuttered at her words. "What do you mean?"

"She's dangerous, Edmar. Be careful. The future... it's not always clear, but I sense... I sense she will be your undoing. You cannot trust her."

He stiffened, the mermaid's face flashing before his eyes. His hand instinctively reached for her gem, a possessive urge quickly reeled back by the warmth of Avi's stroking, a hypnotic melody weaving through his thoughts.

"She will betray you again. She will bring you ruin."

The disparity between Avi's gentle touch and the venom in her words made him uneasy. Yet, he couldn't dismiss the feeling she was right. The mermaid had already betrayed him, gutting him, ripping out his heart. He couldn't trust her.

Avi's words validated the mistrust he harbored for the mermaid. They reinforced everything he'd tried to suppress.

He glanced toward where she had last stood, but the mermaid wasn't there. Who was she? He frowned, touching the gem in his pocket, realizing it belonged to the mermaid. Every move she made communicated through the painite.

But he hadn't felt her leave. *Strange.* How had he missed it? With a bit of concentration through his muddled thoughts, he discerned her location, below deck, in her cabin.

"Let her go, Edmar," Avi whispered, her voice a lyrical refrain, weaving through his senses. "She's not worth the pain, the risk. Trust me. I can give you everything she promised, and more."

He turned to her, his heart pounding. Her cerulean eyes shimmered with her promises of something deeper, something more profound than he'd ever known. He leaned in, his lips parting, his breath catching in his throat.

"May I kiss you, Avi?" he whispered, the question a plea for something real, something lasting, in a world where love seemed to fade like distant stars swallowed by the dawn.

Avi's musical laugh sent shivers down his spine. Her fingers traced his jaw, and desire for her surged through him.

"Patience, my king." Her eyes sparkled with mischief. "Perhaps once you let me hold the Sun Stone, then you'll have all the kisses you want from me."

A hint of something darker, something more than the innocent maiden, flashed with her mischief. But as he gazed into the blue depths of her eyes, a wave of desire, powerful and consuming, washed over him, drowning out the whispers of doubt and the lingering ache of betrayal.

"Go find your sleep," Avi said, her voice soothing. "We'll talk tomorrow."

He nodded, his mind clouded, his heart heavy.

"Just remember my divination. Don't be fooled by the mermaid. You're the one in control."

Then she raised up on her tiptoes and kissed his cheek. When he would have taken her in his arms again, she pushed him toward the stern, toward the door leading down into the cabins.

As he walked away, the lingering scent of saltwater and silver lilies filled his senses, the memory of Avi's touch burning in his mind. But beneath the intoxicating aroma, a faint, familiar fragrance tugged at his heart—a delicate blend of coconut and flowers, a phantom scent that whispered a name he'd forgotten.

Emmy.

The memories of her rushed back, and confusion filled his thoughts. Then her gem pulsed with urgency in his pocket and faded. He couldn't sense her anymore.

CHAPTER 82

EMMY

Emmy stood on the deck, her eyes transfixed by Edmar and Avi under the star-laden sky. The ship's gentle sway did little to soothe the storm brewing within her. Little shocks pricked over her body, a warning of her returning magic.

Edmar leaned closer to Avi, his laughter a warm caress in the night air. The coldness he reserved for her—the distrust that shadowed his every word to her—now softened as he spoke to Avi. She couldn't deny the open affection, the tenderness in his voice, the easy way he interacted with the hybrid fae. Every touch, every glance, was a dagger to her heart.

Faint strains of a siren song, a haunting melody steeped in magic, wove through the air.

Is Avi using magic to control Edmar? Or is there genuine interest?

The thought twisted her insides. Fire acid simmered in her veins and arteries, making her gasp.

She couldn't watch anymore. She turned, heading for the stairs to the cabins, each step stabbing pain into her feet. Cielan stood in the shadows, his clear eyes fixed on Avi with an intensity that made her skin crawl.

Why isn't he stopping her?

She halted next to him, taking deep breaths to calm her magic. "Either intervene or stop watching her like a stalker."

"Go away," he said, not looking at her.

The need to understand what was happening between Avi and Edmar tormented her. It just didn't seem natural. *I have to do something.* "Do you hear the siren song?"

His eyes narrowed without looking at her as he ignored her question. "Manipulative mermaid."

She hardened her voice, not giving up. "Do you hear it?"

He sighed and finally gave his attention to her. "I don't think I like you very much."

"What does that matter right now?" She gestured to Avi and Edmar. "Does Avi have the powers of a siren?"

A barely noticeable shake of his head, then his eyes flicked back to the pair. "She has no magic beyond divination."

Edmar couldn't be attracted to Avi—that would kill Emmy. To know he wanted another while she stood before him. *But no, I know what I heard.* "There's something at work here, the magic of a siren."

"Do you think your Siren's Call could pull him away?" His suggestion was clipped, a subtle challenge.

For a fleeting moment, frustration filled her at Cielan's lack of answers, but then she couldn't deny the temptation he offered. She could use her song, bend Edmar to her will, reclaim him from Avi's grasp.

But the thought left her stomach sour. She had spent a lifetime fighting against control, against the shackles of her magic, against the dictates of her father.

"No," she said, resolute. "I won't do that to him. To anyone, if I can help it."

And she'd always wondered if he really wanted her, not Avi.

Cielan's eyebrows rose. "Your restraint is admirable. When I was alive, I craved that power, to control, to dominate..." He trailed off, his gaze distant, a shadow of regret flitting across his face. "It's a curse, mermaid, to yearn for what destroys."

She leaned closer to him to catch the tones under his words, a strange mix of longing and bitterness. So much emotion for such a stoic creature. *Is this the loss I heard in his voice before?*

Nostrils flaring, Cielan pushed her back with two fingers against her chest. "Avi's been different since we set sail."

"Has she ever returned your affections?" she asked, her voice gentle, hoping the question wouldn't upset him. She still wasn't sure what he had become now that he was an undead Air Fae, but like the Summer Child's protector, he could move faster than the eye could follow. That made him dangerous.

In the shadows, his nearly clear eyes illuminated from deep within. "In her own way, she has. But she's dying. She fights her love for me, thinking it unfair to promise herself to me or anyone."

"So flirting with Edmar, that's not like her?"

He closed his eyes, hiding his feelings, before continuing. "As much as she fights me, she has never turned down my help. But since leaving Agondray, she won't even let me touch her."

His voice cracked, displaying a rarity in his emotional depth.

"Why does she need your help?"

"Her magic is corrupted. It's killing her. I drain her, just enough to take away her magic, to save her for one more day."

Drain? She touched her throat, remembering the Summer Child's protector biting her neck, sucking her blood. *But he takes away her magic!* "How does that take away her magic?"

This time, a scowl crossed his face as he used two fingers to push her back once more. She hadn't even noticed leaning close again.

"What don't you understand about my dislike for you?"

She rubbed the spot on her chest where he'd poked her twice now. "But I'm not trying to manipulate you."

Disgust twisted his mouth. "It's your blood. It calls to me."

"So you don't like me because I manipulate you, or because my blood calls to you?"

"Both."

"I promise to endeavor never to manipulate you again. But I'm not sure what I can do about my blood."

"Nothing can be done. I know this scent, and I know I would enjoy tasting it."

"I wouldn't suggest it," she said, recalling how the protector threw up her blood. "A curse runs in my blood."

He smiled, but he looked like he was in pain. "Exactly the type of blood that calls to me."

He didn't move, but somehow the space in the shadows seemed much smaller. She swallowed hard. "I think we need to figure out what is going on. Figure out whatever magic Avi is using."

"And how do you propose we do that?" His gaze was sharp, skeptical. "The dragon has you bound, your magic leashed. Do you want to tell me why he limits your abilities, your movements?"

"He's not controlling my magic, though I wish he could. My magic is dangerous, and I'm losing the ability to control it."

Cielan's eyes traveled down to her neck, his pupils widening.

She took a reactive step back, wincing at the stabbing in her soles. But she forced herself to square her shoulders and ask her next questions, because maybe he could help her. "Blood sustains you? Not food?"

"In a way. Magic sustains us. The magic of our ancestors is in our blood."

Almost everyone was magical in some way save the humans, so there were plenty of people for Cielan to have fed from. But he looked hungry. "Have you fed recently?"

Slowly, his eyes rose to meet hers, and he almost looked offended. "You should ask your real question."

"Would... would you...?" She hesitated, her heart pounding, swallowing hard. The unsettling encounter with the Summer Child's protector, her teeth sinking into her neck, the invasive warmth, the loss of control. Even though she wondered if Cielan could help her, he scared her. What if he was like the protector?

He took a step toward her, forcing her against a wall. "Would I feed from you without consent?"

She nodded, swallowing again, her throat suddenly parched.

He smiled, showing his fangs. "No and no, mermaid. I haven't fed in a while, but I'm very good at controlling myself." He bent his head to sniff her, his eyes closing. "The corruption in your blood is strong. I've resisted so far, but perhaps you should go to your cabin now."

What if Avi continued to refuse him? How long could he restrain himself?

"You're thinking too hard, mermaid, when you should be walking away." A slight tremor shook his shoulders.

"You would like to drink my blood."

"Already established," he said through gritted teeth.

"You need to feed, and I want my magic gone."

He tilted his head, studying her. "You're offering yourself to me?"

Desperation outweighed her fear. If Cielan could help her master her magic, she would risk anything. She nodded.

"Not good enough, mermaid. I need to hear you say exactly what you want me to do."

Now she trembled, but she clenched her fists. "I want you to take my blood. Help me with my magic."

The last word barely escaped her lips when her world tilted and everything blurred with dizziness. A moment later, she stood in her cabin with Cielan. His tall frame nearly touched the low ceiling, his dark wings brushing the walls as they fluttered wide, as if in anticipation.

She pressed a hand to her churning stomach. "Why are we in my cabin?"

The scent of seawater and old wood wafted in the cramped space, and now his storm-like aroma added to the smells.

He took her gently into his arms. "You will be very tired afterward. Having a bed nearby is handy."

The mention of the bed brought her eyes to it, falling to Edmar's shirt next to her pillow. But then her thoughts spun back to Cielan when he took a hold of her chin. His touch was surprisingly soft, but his body was hard, unyielding, cold as ice.

"What are you?"

"Vamphyr." He tilted her head to the side, his fingers brushing her throat, a strange mix of tenderness and menace in his touch. "A race contaminated by the Sun God's dark magic."

"The Sun God cursed you?"

"Solis did this to my maker. No more questions," he murmured, his breath a winter breeze against her skin. "This won't hurt."

He licked her neck, the sensation unexpected—a hard coldness far from sensual but sending shivers down her body.

"What are you—?"

"My saliva has many unique qualities. For now, it acts as a numbing agent." His explanation was a soothing whisper. "You won't feel the bite. Mostly."

She trembled again, but squeezed her eyes shut and braced herself, resolute.

His fangs pierced her skin.

The initial pain was minimal, quickly replaced by a familiar wave of intense warmth, a delicious heat pulsing through veins as blood rushed to her throat. Euphoria flooded her, her body relaxing, her limbs heavy.

Edmar held her, kissing her, fingers playing over her nipple like he did before, stimulating her senses. She was racing toward something, chasing a feeling, and she wanted it. She moaned and begged, her hands digging into his hair, pulling him closer.

Her body arched against his, seeking something... *release*.

The door slammed against the wall, the sound a thunderclap in the small cabin. Her eyes flew open, a haze of desire still enthralling her.

Edmar stood there, his face shocked. *But he's holding me, kissing me...*

Then she remembered.

Cielan.

The vamphyr's hard mouth on her throat, fangs piercing her skin. And she clung to him like a lover.

Murderous rage shook Edmar. "Get away from her!"

CHAPTER 83

EDMAR

A glacial storm raged within Edmar.

Cielan's mouth pressed to Emira's throat, his arms around her, like she belonged to him.

Mine. The thought slammed into Edmar, raw and visceral, a guttural snarl echoing in his mind.

Ice lanced through his veins, turning his rage into something more dangerous. His fury had always been cold, honed to a blade's edge. His Frostlands froze solid, his emotions sealed beneath the unyielding tundra of his will.

"Get. Away. From. Her." His voice was lethal in its quiet restraint.

Cielan didn't flinch. The vamphyr's eyes gleamed with a sinister satisfaction as he continued feeding. His smirk sent a challenge, a silent duel of wills. Then Emira moaned softly—

Crack.

The fissure in Edmar's Frostlands sent a warning shudder through his control. The world around him vanished. All of it blurred to irrelevance as his focus narrowed to the scene before him.

Cielan. Feeding on her. Holding her.

His restraint shattered.

Cold surged through him, and his magic lashed out. Spears of ice erupted from his fingertips, a blizzard of blue light and gold sparks, aimed straight for the vamphyr.

Cielan chuckled, the ice shards shattering harmlessly against him, leaving a dusting of frost. He released Emira, her blood staining his lips. And she sighed, her eyes fluttering closed as she leaned into the vamphyr.

"Such futile gestures, dragon," he said, dark amusement lacing his voice.

Edmar's breath came sharp through his nose.

Cielan tossed Emira onto the bed like discarded silk. He turned to face Edmar fully, his movements languid, deliberate. The vamphyr's expression was not one of concern, not fear, but of something far worse.

Amusement.

Edmar readied another attack, but then Cielan moved.

A blur of darkness, a rush of wind. Iron fingers clamped around Edmar's throat.

With impossible strength, the vamphyr slammed him against the wall, pinning him a foot off the ground. Edmar's vision blurred for a moment as his breath caught.

It had been centuries since someone had bested him in speed.

Cielan, it seemed, had decided to remind him he was not invincible.

"Such theatrics." The vamphyr's cool voice came from lips still stained with her blood. "You are terribly possessive, more so than the average dragon."

Edmar's growl was low, primal. "If you ever touch her again, I *will* find a way to kill you."

A pause.

Then, unexpectedly, Cielan laughed before his expression sobered again. "Touch Avi again, and I'll return the favor."

"Avi?" Confusion momentarily eclipsed his anger, but something teased him at the corner of his memory. "Let me go, you bloodsucking fiend."

"Pathetic." Cold dark eyes seemed to bore into Edmar's soul. "Do you hear yourself, dragon?"

His grip on Edmar's throat loosened, just enough to let him breathe easier, but not escape.

"The way you talk about her, the way you act?" A storm tossed in Cielan's clear gaze. "Examine your own desires for control, dragon. I once thought it was my right to command the woman I loved. It cost me everything. Her love, my home, my friends, my *life*."

For a single, sharp moment, Edmar felt something unfamiliar.

Doubt.

Crack.

Another fracture in his Frostlands, but he refused to acknowledge it. He clung to his ice, clung to his fury.

Cielan's expression remained intense, unreadable. "Think carefully about your next move."

The vamphyr exhaled, as if suddenly tired of the entire exchange. Then he let go.

Edmar dropped to the floor, his body trembling, his magic fading even though he wanted to attack the vamphyr.

For the first time, he wasn't entirely sure why he held back.

Cielan studied him, then turned his gaze to Emira. A lingering look. Not possession. Not attraction.

Something softer. Something Edmar couldn't understand.

Then Cielan nodded curtly and vanished in a gust of cold air.

Edmar barely had a moment to process before Emira sat up, clutching her head, her movements slow, exhausted. His gaze snapped to her.

Is she hurt? His heart pounded with an overwhelming need to go to her.

Then a fresh wave of anger and something else he refused to name flooded him.

She stood on wobbly legs, her sapphire hair a dark halo around her paler face. The sight of her sent a confusing mix of anger and protectiveness through his chest. But she only appeared vulnerable because she allowed the vamphyr to drink from her.

She will betray you again. She will bring you ruin. He'd just heard this, but he couldn't remember where or from whom. However, the voice echoed in his head.

"You," he said, his voice harsh with anger.

Her green eyes widened slightly. A flicker of fear.

He took a step closer. "You treacherous—"

But his words faltered.

Something caught his eye. Something small. Insignificant, yet shattering.

A familiar worn shirt, balled on the bed, his shirt—the one he had given her long ago.

His world tilted. Contradictions slammed into him all at once.

She kept his shirt, some sign of devotion. She bore another man's mark.

He couldn't make sense of it.

She had betrayed him, but she clung to him in ways she didn't even realize.

His fury wavered. Just for a second when a coral color flushed across her cheeks, her mouth tightening. A tremor ran through her body, and he felt a flicker of unwelcome tenderness before shoving it ruthlessly into his Frostlands. She didn't deserve it.

"You think you can betray me, again and again," he said, his voice as cold as the ice beneath his skin, each word laced with vehemence sharp enough to cut, "and then run to him?"

Emira flinched, but she squared her shoulders. He could see the effort it took to hold herself together, the way her breath caught, how she backed up against her bed.

His fist clenched around her gem. He took a step closer, but then it happened again.

Air vanished from his lungs.

His Frostlands trembled beneath him, his control slipping, and it was because of her. Always her. Even now, even after this, being near her did something to him he couldn't explain, something infuriating, something dangerous.

But he had to find the breath to say whatever he needed to get her to stay away from the vamphyr.

Her gaze hardened, fire igniting in her emerald eyes. "And you think you can bust into my cabin, after what you did with Avi?" Her voice cracked, a shaky, breathless sound, betraying her exhaustion. "You're delusional, Edmar."

He stared at her, confusion rippling through the ice of his mind. "What are you talking about? Avi? I—"

A foggy memory surfaced, a haze of moonlight and silver lilies, the intoxicating warmth of her touch, soft hands brushing over his skin. But the details were blurred, lost in a fog.

Emira trembled, but her voice was iron. "She's controlling you with a siren song."

He scoffed. "That's absurd. She's not a mermaid. She doesn't have that power."

Her hands clenched into fists, her breathing uneven. "Why don't you believe me?" Despair edged her voice.

"Why should I? Your history speaks for itself, Emira."

"And you think I sought Cielan's company for no other reason than some affair?" She threw her hands up in the air, but wavered on her feet. She collapsed back onto the bed, and his muscles tensed, an instinctive move toward her, before he stopped himself.

Her eyes burned, and her voice broke.

"It's obvious you'll never see me clearly, and I can't keep doing this. It hurts too much."

Crack.

He stiffened.

She shook her head, pressing a trembling hand to her chest. "If we survive this quest, it would be better if we part ways."

Everything in him went still.

Tightness clenched his heart, a physical ache, a cold fist squeezing his lungs, stealing his breath.

No.

He staggered back, catching himself against the wall, his vision blurring. Cracks already present in his Frostlands splintered like shattered glass, groaning as they widened, deeper, deeper—he couldn't stop it.

I can't lose her.

Not again.

But then he saw the pain in her eyes, the despair shadowing her features. And it gutted him.

She meant it.

Cielan's words echoed in his mind: *I once thought it was my right to command the woman I loved. It cost me everything.*

For a long moment he couldn't draw a breath.

The Blue Devil snarled within him, raging against this, demanding he take control, make her stay, make her see reason.

But something else, something quieter, something infinitely more dangerous, rose instead.

What if... he had already lost?

The more he fought to hold on to her, the more he pushed her away.

His breath shuddered out. She was slipping further from him, and he felt helpless to stop it.

And that was what terrified him most.

His voice was lower when he finally spoke. Unsteady.

"Why was Cielan here?" He swallowed the sharpness from his tone, forcing himself to meet her gaze. "Tell me. I promise, I'll listen."

A flicker of hesitation. Wary, uncertain. But then... something in her relaxed, like she hadn't expected him to say that.

Her voice was soft, halting, as she explained how Cielan fed on corrupted magic, how it silenced the power coursing through her veins. "It works, Edmar. I don't feel my power or my fire acid. No pain."

Edmar barely noticed himself moving, but suddenly he was closer. Studying her face. The way she was watching him, waiting.

Waiting for him to accuse her again.

Waiting for him to turn away.

And he couldn't.

The truth was in her eyes. In the lines of her face—the exhaustion, the vulnerability, the years of isolation she had endured.

"I'm sorry, Emmy." He also knew it to be the truth because he couldn't feel her through her gem, her magic depleted, her gem inactive. "I shouldn't have jumped to conclusions."

His heart ached in ways he wasn't ready to name.

His fingers found her pulse, ghosting over the twin marks on her throat, his thumb tracing the smooth skin. His touch was light, barely there, yet she shivered.

His hand slid higher, along the column of her throat, cupping her jaw.

Her pulse fluttered.

New torment wracked him, an aching need to pull her into his arms. Her pulse quickened, a frantic rhythm. The same mesmerizing desire flared in her emerald eyes, laced with wariness.

He understood.

Desperation clawed at him, a hunger to touch more, to consume her, not as an extension of himself but as something vital, a living, breathing part of him.

It was too much.

The distance between them, this unbearable, aching space. He couldn't stand it.

But restraint won over impulse.

His thumb ghosted across her lower lip, soft and full, and she sighed. Everything about Emira was a heady rush, unraveling him, drowning out the betrayal, the anger, the fear.

Leaning in, he surrendered, their breaths mingling.

Just before their lips touched, she whispered against his mouth, "You're insane if you think you can kiss me after Avi was in your arms."

He jerked back as if burned.

What?

His hand dropped, his body locking up, the memory ripping through the haze.

Avi.

Her hands on him. The scent of saltwater and silver lilies. The way her voice had wrapped around him, soft as silk, and yet...

How could he have been so easily swayed? *Is my mind that weak, my heart that fickle?*

It wasn't real.

None of it was real.

And yet, he had let it happen.

His throat went dry. His Frostlands shuddered, unsteady.

He could feel it, the weight of her accusation, the way she was looking at him.

And worse—the way she was waiting for him to say something.

The Blue Devil sneered. *Defend yourself.*

But Edmar knew the truth, and for the first time, he didn't know how to face it.

His voice came raw, unsteady. "I don't remember..."

The words sounded like a weak excuse, and he hated it.

He knew, with a certainty that shook him to his core, his feelings for Emira were real.

Even if those feelings, no matter how deep, clashed with the gnawing doubt that had rooted itself in his heart. The thought of losing her, of watching her walk away and out of his life, sent a sharp pang through his chest. He couldn't bear the idea of their connection severed permanently, never seeing her again. It would kill him.

All those emotions made his voice raw. "Avi means nothing. I don't know what that was, but my feelings for you are real."

Her gaze searched his, her thoughts digging into his words, weighing their worth, and it nearly destroyed him. "If this is true, then I just need to know one thing."

"Ask me."

"Do you trust me?"

He wanted to erase the hurt, the doubt, to say yes. To embrace the hope she was offering.

Can I trust her?

When he thought about saying yes, visualizing his mouth moving through the word, the memory of her betrayal, the fear of her power, loomed like an enormous shadow, threatening to never let him go.

"I don't know," he said, a tortured whisper.

The instant pain in her eyes gutted him.

His Frostlands groaned, struggling to hold beneath the weight of something it wasn't built to contain—doubt.

The Blue Devil snarled, recoiling, demanding retreat. Control. Ice. Anything but this.

But his ice wasn't working anymore.

He left her, the uncertainty crushing his soul.

CHAPTER 84

EMMY

Emmy lay sprawled on her narrow bunk, her body heavy and drained, as if all the strength had been sapped from her limbs. Her confrontation with Edmar played on a loop behind her heavy eyelids, his accusations echoing in the silence.

Treacherous. The word branded her soul.

As if she were the only one who had broken vows, who had shattered trust. He'd imprisoned her with her own magic, silenced her with his command, yet he judged her?

She shifted, dizziness halting her. She wanted to rise, to pace, to shake off the pain, but her body refused to obey. Anger simmered beneath her skin, heat flushing her, accompanied by a faint tingling where Cielan had bitten her.

Cielan.

His name surfaced in the fog of her exhaustion.

The memory of him drinking her blood, the belief that she'd wrapped herself in Edmar while he brought her pleasure, the strange absence of pain afterward, and the unsettling calmness that had followed. An eerie silence had settled where her magic usually roared. That calmness wrapped around her now, a rare reprieve that felt too close to weakness.

Her body ached, fatigue pulling her toward sleep. She curled Edmar's shirt against her cheek, falling asleep to his scent. When she woke later, the night had deepened. The ship creaked. Waves whispered against the hull. She lay still, listening, her body heavy and drained, yet strangely restless.

The cabin walls seemed to press in on her as everything rushed back to her awareness. *He'll never trust me.*

She clutched Edmar's shirt as she sang broken lines of the Ocean's Lament. But without her magic, the song failed to soothe her. Her fire acid felt distant—muted. Doubt crept in, insidious and cold, wrapping around her heart. *Will he ever love me again?*

Can anyone love me?

Her heart squeezed at the thought of her mother, who had loved her unconditionally and had paid the price. And after the ceremony to honor her mother's passing, her father had looked at her with sorrow, only to retreat behind an impenetrable wall. Since then, his gaze had never softened, never held any warmth for her again.

Maybe that is my fate, to be loved only to lose it. Perhaps it is safer for Edmar to see me as treacherous, a danger, just as my father had, than to risk the pain of loving me.

Her curse a barrier that would forever separate her from those she cared about. For a few fleeting moments, she allowed herself to drift to sleep, surrendering to exhaustion. But just as quickly, her eyes fluttered open again, her thoughts circling back to Edmar, the way he had once looked at her with love, the nights they'd shared beneath the stars.

A hollow ache filled her chest, vast and unrelenting. It spread through her, curling into the spaces where love had once lived, where trust had once felt unshakable. Loss pressed down, sharp and suffocating, leaving behind an emptiness that no whispered song could soothe.

The uncertainty of their future, Edmar's distrust, kept her tethered to wakefulness, but her small cabin suffocated her. She had to get out, to breathe, to escape the stifling confines of her thoughts and his smell. With a groan, she sat up. The room tilted, alarming her until it righted itself. Ignoring the lingering dizziness, she threw off the blanket and stumbled toward the door.

A fresh wave of stabbing in her feet reminded her of a pain she'd never outrun. She gritted her teeth and walked on her tiptoes. The sounds of slumbering pirates echoed in the dimly lit hallways. She turned a corner, then stopped.

At the end of the hallway, Cielan pressed Avi against the wall, his wings half-unfurled, midnight with a blue oily sheen, his gaze possessive.

"Stop avoiding me, Avi," he said, his voice low.

Everything about the scene should have alarmed Emmy, but Avi didn't appear distressed.

The fae tilted her head with an amusing smile. "You know why I do."

Cielan's low growl barely restrained his anger. "I do not appreciate you playing with the dragon."

"Do you finally want to play with me, demon?" Avi asked, a predatory glint in her cerulean eyes.

He gripped her hair, yanking her head back, his lips hovering over hers. "You know I do. But I won't kiss you until you admit you love me, Dolcivita."

Avi's smile didn't falter. "You'll be sent to the eight hells first."

Cielan stared down at her, his face unreadable, but a storm brewed in his pale eyes. Then, with a frustrated growl, he released her, shoving her back against the wall.

Avi laughed, a sharp sound that echoed down the hallway. "Stop being a baby. Just fuck me so I can focus on more important matters."

"I don't even know you anymore," he said, pain flickering in his eyes. His agony surprised Emmy. "You're not my Avi."

Is that how Edmar sees me now? As someone changed from who he knew, doubting his own love for me.

Cielan stalked away, his soft wings brushing against Emmy as he passed her. She shivered. The intensity of their exchange, the raw emotions on both sides, left her feeling uneasy. Cielan's claim Avi had changed deepened her fears about the dangerous game the fae played with Edmar. Emmy prayed it was over.

She shook off the tension, heading for the deck, drawn by the Longing. A crisp chill, unnatural for the heart of summer, settled over the night, whispering of their approach to Aelunis.

Stars pierced the inky darkness like a million pinpricks of light. The ocean lay tranquil, its surface smooth as glass, reflecting the flawless night above. Beauty, yes, but laced with a stillness that stole her breath, the ominous hush before a storm's fury. She gripped the railing, tension crackling in the air. The world, it seemed, held its breath.

The Longing, a low thrum in her blood, whispered promises of home, quieter than before, but still there, a persistent ache. *Home isn't a place.* It was Edmar.

Just as Anjali and Gilly had been her home for two hundred years. She missed both of them. What were their lives becoming without her? Would Anjali marry soon? Who did Gilly visit now that Emmy no longer burdened her days?

They were better off without her, without the *burden* she had always been. *When had I ever been useful to anyone?*

She stared out at the sea, her thoughts turning dark. *If my life is the price for waking the Metal God, then let it mean something.*

When she'd said goodbye to Anjali, she wondered if there was anything she could do to help her sister. She knew what that was now. *Let me leave a legacy of good, a gift to my people. I will beg Metallon if I have to.* Even if her people never knew it was her, at least she would have done something good. *Finally.*

A soft footfall made her turn.

"Hello, Emmy," Adria said, her husky voice tentative.

"Adria," she said, surprised by her own lack of anger. But she turned back to the mirror-like sea.

"Glad to see you aren't still riled up."

Emmy shook her head. "I had no right. I was a hypocrite to be mad when I made the same choices."

Adria sighed, moving to stand beside her. "Why aren't you catching any shut-eye?"

"I can't." She'd never been one to confide in anyone—she couldn't without being able to talk, and Gilly always knew her thoughts—but right now, an overwhelming urge pushed the confession through her lips. "Edmar hates me. And he has every right to. I betrayed him, his trust."

The Ocean's Lament vibrated in her breast, and she swallowed a tearless sob with the ache in her chest.

Adria placed a comforting hand on her arm. "We've both made choices driven by pain and fear. Choices we've come to regret."

"Does it justify it?"

"Nay, but we can't change the past. All we can do is stay true to who we are and set our sights on the future."

"But he doesn't trust me. What future can we have?"

Adria chuckled softly. "I'm sorry. I see your pain, and I don't mean to laugh. But I've known Edmar and his brothers since they were wee lads. Those Dragon Kings are as stubborn as barnacles on a ship's hull. Edmar's the most level-headed of 'em, so I've no doubt he'll come around in time."

But there might not be time. Her heart clenched thinking about what would happen on Aelunis. And Avi... What if the fae was continuing to weave her spell on Edmar? How could Emmy compete unless she used the same magic on him?

She'd never do that. There had to be another way.

"Have you noticed any changes in Avi?"

"She's always been a bit different." Adria frowned. "But aye, something's changed. I've never known her when her visions weren't tearing her apart. But now her visions be gone, which is a blessing, don't get me wrong." Worry creased her face, then vanished, replaced by a shadow of concern. "Her human half ain't strong enough to bear that magic. But this quiet, it's got me worried, too. Wondering what's coming next."

Emmy nearly swallowed her next question, but she had to know. "Has she expressed an interest in Edmar?"

Adria's childlike face scrunched. "Nay, but she ain't been much for talking to me on this sail. Be something amiss?"

She chose her words carefully, not wanting to create a rift. "I'm not sure." The whole situation made her uncomfortable, unable to forget the song or that Cielan hadn't fed on Avi since they'd set sail, and she looked for a way to change the conversation. "Maybe what Cielan is doing has helped more long term, giving her more energy?"

Adria's frown deepened. "Much as I've no love for the vamphyr, I can't deny he's helped her."

"I've never met a vamphyr before."

"Dangerous creatures. Keep your wits about you with 'em."

"Where do they come from?"

"Mind your curiosity." Her voice dropped to a whisper. "Vamphyrs were born from a powerful woman the Sun God raised from the dead over a thousand years ago."

"Why would the Sun God resurrect someone?" For what purpose instead of allowing her to reincarnate or move on to rest her soul for eternity?

"No one knows for certain," Adria said, her voice laced with a hint of fear. "But legends tell that the Sun God gave her great magic and strength, creating a creature meant to be unbreakable. But bringing the dead back, it wasn't natural. A perversion of life, they say. So the god's magic twisted, making her weak under the sun, a curse she passed down to her children."

"Cielan is one of her children?"

Adria nodded. "Vamphyr, she called herself, and she birthed others just like her. Cielan had the ill luck of crossing paths with her before she disappeared. Her offspring, they call themselves the Vamphyrians."

She shuddered. How much of Cielan's humanity remained? Was he a monster, or a victim? "I thought I knew all the races of the world."

"Don't mistake 'em for a true race. They can't breed naturally. Only turn others into their kind, like she did with Cielan. Be wary around him, Emmy."

She nodded, her mind drifting to Cielan. She was already cautious of him. *But I might need his help again.*

Adria patted her shoulder, then sauntered away.

She gripped the railing, staring at the distant stars scattered across the endless black night sky. Edmar's continued distrust stung, especially after he'd flirted with Avi, even knowing he was likely under a spell. She touched her throat, where her painite usually rested.

A sudden brush along her spine drew her attention across the deck, her connection to her gem slowly returning, but the signal was weak. Edmar stood there, watching her, his silhouette a stark outline against starlight. When their eyes met, he turned away.

Had he come here to watch me, investigating why I left my cabin? Would he never really trust her?

Her heart ached. At this point, she didn't believe they'd ever find their way back to the connection they'd once had.

Chapter 85

EDMAR

Morning sunlight bathed the ship, the air alive with the scent of salt and the creak of timbers. Edmar stepped onto the main deck, the ship swaying gently, the crew moving with practiced efficiency. Their voices hummed low against the steady rhythm of the waves.

He squinted against a bright sun, but beneath its warmth, a cold unease coiled in his chest.

His Frostlands groaned, unsteady. The Blue Devil lay silent, no longer at the helm

The ship swayed gently beneath him, but his balance had never felt more precarious.

He ascended the stairs onto the quarterdeck, his hands gripping the rail as his gaze drifted over the ship.

Emira.

The air around him seemed to thicken, as if her presence alone could steal the breath from his lungs.

On coiled rope, she sat near the mainmast, her sapphire hair gleaming in the morning. A simple sky-blue dress pooled around her as she worked, her focus intent. She was weaving rope, repairing a frayed net, her fingers deftly looping and knotting the strands with surprising precision. The sight of her—not moving in defiance, not wielding uncontrollable magic, but *calm, deliberate, steady*—sent an unexpected ache through his chest.

The midday light softened her features, accentuating the quiet strength in her expression. A strength that had always been there, beneath the chaos.

His fingers tightened around the railing. It was the first time he'd seen her like this, in daylight, without the haze of anger clouding his vision. Instead, he found a haunting beauty in the sight.

The snap of sails caught the wind, drawing him back to the present. A steady breeze propelled them closer to Aelunis.

He forced his attention away from her.

His conversation with Kalden before last night's dinner stuck with him. His older brother had admitted that Airian—his bride by chance—still slept. Kalden hadn't sent her away yet, though the full moon loomed less than a week away. And now, his forces struggled against increasing dwarven raids along the southeastern border.

Kalden's on the verge of despair again, and Zane's missing. At least, he couldn't get through to Zane. Kalden promised to use his one-way mirror to find him, even if they couldn't talk to him. Edmar would have used his own, except Rivus had taken his only one-way mirror, which would have allowed him to spy on anyone.

Rivus. Will this bitter twist in my gut ever stop at the thought of my former friend?

Maybe it was better that he didn't have the one-way mirror anymore. He might have been tempted to spy on Emira. And that way led to more distrust.

He exhaled sharply, turning his attention to the crew.

Lian, silver hair gleaming, stood with him on the quarterdeck, conferring with the helmsman, Jesi, his sharp eyes scanning the horizon. A watchful presence commanding the vessel with quiet authority—just the type of first mate Edmar liked.

He stepped closer to the hybrid fae. "You're making good speed this morning, making up for the delay from the Moon-Tide Leviathan."

"Aye." Lian nodded, a steady eye on the ocean.

Today he stood barefoot with a simple, sleeveless vest left open against his weathered gray skin, his dark patched shorts rolled up at the knees. The image of a man who had spent a lifetime at sea. "The ocean is calm for now."

"For now," Edmar echoed.

He turned his gaze to the horizon, to the endless stretch of blue that separated them from Aelunis. *Soon.* "What hour do you think we'll reach the island?"

Lian cast him a sidelong glance.

"Shortly after midnight, if the charts are accurate." His expression darkened. "But the storm is another matter."

Edmar studied the sky, searching for any signs of trouble, but all he saw was clear blue. "What do we know?"

"Not much," Lian said, his lips thinning. He exchanged a glance with Jesi before lowering his voice. "The storms surrounding Aelunis are unpredictable. They can swallow ships whole, disorient even the most seasoned navigators. They're unlike anything I've seen. Fierce winds, jagged lightning, rogue waves. We'll need to be prepared for anything."

He hesitated, then met Edmar's gaze with something unreadable. "Come. I'll show you what we know."

Edmar followed, but his gaze drifted back down to Emira as he descended the stairs. She had stilled.

She no longer worked, her hands clenched around the rope in her lap. She stared at the net she had been mending, eyes unfocused, a grimace flickering across her face.

Her pain—and her magic—were returning.

He could feel it.

Last night, he had lost the connection to her gem when Cielan had drained enough of her blood to weaken her magic. Now, it stirred again. He'd hoped the vamphyr's solution would last longer, offer her more relief. That was the whole reason for the vamphyr being in her cabin last night.

Edmar's fingers closed into a fist.

Recalling the image of Cielan, his teeth in Emira while her fingers entangled in his hair, their bodies pressed close together, made his gut twist, his heart pounding faster. A searing flare of jealousy, irrational and unwelcome, flashed through him. He couldn't kill the vamphyr, but he'd ensured Cielan stayed away from Emira.

At least she was out here in the sun, so he didn't have to be concerned about it right now.

She shifted, uncomfortable, and as if drawn by the invisible thread between them, her gaze lifted, locking onto his.

Something passed between them, something unspoken, something fragile.

A shadow of sadness clouded her features. They had yet to speak to each other this morning. He didn't know what to say.

His fingers closed around her gem, a cool comfort against his palm. He brushed his thumb across its smooth surface. A familiar pulse responded, a subtle vibration thrumming through him. A reminder that, no matter what had changed between them, he still held this piece of her.

Emira flinched.

Her shoulders squared, her expression tightening. Resentment flickered in her eyes, but it didn't reach the raw betrayal he had seen in her before.

It looked... defeated.

A knot formed in his gut. He didn't know what to do with that.

She turned back to her work, refusing to look at him again.

He followed Lian toward the lower deck, but that cold unease snaked tighter around his ribs. He hadn't kept his distance because he wanted to, but because he didn't know how to trust himself around her anymore.

Because, despite everything, he still wanted her.

And that terrified him.

Lian led him into the chart room off the main deck. Dimly lit and smelling of parchment and ink, the space felt smaller than before. Stifling. He resisted the urge to roll his shoulders, to push away the invisible weight pressing down on him.

Lian unfurled a chart on the table, its aged surface crisscrossed with lines and markings. He traced the jagged outline of Aelunis with a calloused finger.

"The storms usually hug the coastline." He tapped a cluster of symbols swirling around the island. "But it shifts, expands, contracts, without warning." He pointed to an area west of the island. "They say the storms weaken on the west side, but it's still a treacherous barrier."

"That's where we'll sail through?"

"We'll try that way first. But..." Lian's sharp gaze flicked up. "Right now, it's your face that worries me, Edmar." His voice gentled. "Something tells me the storm is brewing in your mind, not on the horizon."

Edmar exhaled through his nose, but the familiar cold didn't settle.

He had always been the strong one. The steady one. The brother who kept his emotions locked beneath the ice of his Frostlands, sealed beneath unyielding tundra. But Emira had cracked the ice, had sent the ground beneath him shifting.

"You could say that," he admitted, his voice low. "Seems I've found myself at odds with more than just the elements." His jaw tightened. His grip on the Blue Devil wavered. "My wife has proven herself to be deceitful. But I can't stop thinking about her."

Lian's expression was thoughtful. Then, with the patience of a man who had been in these waters before, he said, "That's how it starts."

Edmar shot him a sharp look.

Lian's lips quirked. "Before Adria and I found our way together, I had many a restless night, believing I was navigating a course to ruin. Perhaps you're sailing in familiar waters?"

The door swung open.

Adria strode in, her presence always impossible to ignore. Lavender skin glowing in the light, dark brown shirt fitted beneath a corset with laced cuffs. She was every bit the pirate queen, the woman who had once stolen from a prince and made him love her for it.

She kissed Lian, her touch lingering.

Edmar looked away. Not out of discomfort, but because envy was a slow poison in his veins.

"Just checking on my first mate," she said, her voice husky. "Making sure he ain't lost himself in his charts again."

Lian's focus turned fully on her, the warmth in his gaze almost smoldering. "Have you had enough rest,? You were up for most of the night watch."

"Sleep? On a day like this? The sea's calling, my love." She laughed and winked at Edmar.

Lian chuckled.

"You know Adria stole the Sun Stone from me," Lian said, his voice quiet, a distant echo of his wife's carefree laughter. "But did you know she convinced me to help her deliver it to the Sea Witch?"

"There wasn't a choice, really," Adria added. "He foiled my first attempt at stealing the stone."

Their laughter filled the cabin.

Edmar's fingers curled against the edge of the table. The words hit harder than they should have.

He had known the story, but hearing it now, seeing them like this—*as if betrayal could be undone, as if love could bloom in the ashes of broken trust*—made something inside him twist.

Could Emira have convinced him to help her?

No. He couldn't imagine it.

"I was so righteous then," Lian admitted, shaking his head. "I believed that I, the Moon Fae Prince, could keep a pirate from stealing it. Such arrogance as I was soon to find out."

"The second time," Adria added smugly, "I was forced to kidnap him along with the stone because he'd locked it away with his blood."

Lian wrapped an arm around his wife's waist, drawing her closer. His eyes were only for her.

Edmar stared at the map, unseeing.

He should have left. He should have walked away from this conversation, ignored the sinking feeling in his gut.

But he stayed.

And then Lian's voice softened. "When she succeeded the second time, I was furious. I wanted to punish her, to make her pay for what she'd done." A pause. A slow, exhale. "But the more time we spent together, the more I understood her desperation. The curse she carried was a torment."

Edmar's throat felt tight.

Lian looked up at him, cerulean eyes filled with a knowing sadness. "Empathy, Edmar. That's the key. Understand her pain, her reasons. Sometimes we make choices out of fear, out of desperation. Those choices don't define us."

His Frostlands rumbled.

Empathy.

The word did not belong in the world of the Blue Devil.

He had spent centuries believing actions defined a person, that choices were made, consequences followed.

How could he simply excuse what she had done?

He swallowed, his voice strained. "And trust?"

Lian's gaze didn't waver. "Trust is a journey, not a destination."

The hybrid fae gazed at Adria, his eyes filled with all the love he had for her.

Adria leaned into him, smiling. "It can be broken, yes, but it can also be rebuilt."

Their words settled inside him, deep and uncertain. Hope, a fragile sprout in his Frostlands, broke free. For the first time, he let himself consider it.

Lian and Adria had found their way through the wreckage of their past. Could he and Emira do the same?

His stomach twisted. Otherwise...

I have to let her go.

Or worse.

She would leave him.

His breath shuddered out, uneven. His Frostlands trembled. The idea of her leaving tore something apart inside him.

I need her.

The realization struck with the force of a tidal wave. He couldn't live without her. It wasn't just wanting her.

He couldn't imagine waking up to a day she was not a part of, without seeing her, hearing her musical voice, being near her. There would be no reason to live into the next day if she left him.

It was a truth as deep as the ocean.

But trust—how? "It's hard to forget everything that's happened."

Harder still to forgive.

Lian gave him a knowing look. "Do you love her?"

Yes. The truth had always been there. But he feared to admit it aloud.

"I know you do," Lian said, answering for him. "Love is a powerful force. It can heal the deepest wounds, bridge the widest trenches. Don't give up."

"It takes more than a storm to keep a strong bond down." Adria nodded, her attention on Edmar for only a moment before leaning into her husband's arms, reaching a hand to cup Lian's jaw. "If you ever flounder, look at us."

"I'd rather he not look at the moment, though." Lian's voice slowly receded, with a subtle shift in the air as his focus turned fully to Adria. "I missed you in our bed last night. Perhaps we can..."

Edmar turned away, his thoughts a violent storm.

Then—a shiver of unseen energy buzzed in his ears. Strange warmth spread through him, pooling at the base of his spine. A slow, insistent pull. Like the tide, dragging him toward the open sea. A soft melody, almost imperceptible, skimmed the edge of his awareness. He frowned, tilting his head slightly.

"Do you hear that?" His voice came out rougher than intended, uneven.

Lian didn't respond. Didn't even glance up from where he was now lifting Adria onto the sturdy table.

Edmar exhaled sharply, rubbing his forehead, trying to shake the heaviness creeping into his mind. The edges of his thoughts blurred, shifting in and out of focus.

Something felt familiar. A melody he had heard before. Hadn't he?

The thought slipped away before he could grasp it.

A trick of exhaustion, of stress.

But the pull deepened, curling around him, sinking into his bones, spreading through him like warmth from a long-forgotten sun.

Before he even realized what he was doing, he was moving. Leaving the room.

The shift from the dim chart room to the bright deck was jarring. Salt-laden air filled his lungs, kissed his lips. His boots struck the wooden planks with steady, measured steps.

He stopped.

A woman sat near the mainmast, her blue hair curling over the top of her shoulders. Something about her stilled him.

Her hands moved with careful precision over the rope in her lap, weaving, twisting, untangling.

His breath caught. Something about her was familiar.

But why?

A flicker of emerald. A question in her eyes.

Recognition stirred at the edges of his mind—but before it could take hold, the symphony surged.

A chorus of voices, layered and endless. A lullaby that soothed, that whispered—*don't think, don't fight, just listen.*

His muscles loosened. Everything that had felt wrong no longer mattered. He released the breath that had stalled in his lungs as the woman with blue hair faded from his focus. A shadow, nothing more.

Because Avi was waiting for him.

At the ship's railing, she stood, her silhouette outlined against the horizon. The pale yellow of her shirt glowed under the midday sun, a soft contrast to the deep cerulean of her eyes.

His chest tightened. *Gods, she's beautiful.*

He needed to be near her.

Why am I drawn to Avi like this?

It's not right.

She doesn't fulfill me like—

Like... *like what?*

The thought drifted, dissolving into the warmth pooling in his limbs. Music wrapped him in layers of warmth and ease, a spell of peace.

He stepped past the blue-haired woman without acknowledging her, wondering why she stared at him, why her fingers faltered against the rope in her hands.

Any doubts he had drowned in his overwhelming desire for Avi.

His voice dropped to a husky whisper as he leaned close to her ear. "I've missed you, Avi."

Her lips curled, eyes gleaming with an unnatural brilliance. "Will you show me the Sun Stone today?"

"I cannot." The words left his mouth, but he frowned, the fog shifting—no, thickening.

She sighed, her breath warm against his cheek.

The melody rose again, softer now, stroking the edges of his mind. And the moment of resistance vanished.

Her breast brushed against his arm, and a sharp pang of desire shot through him, instant, consuming. Her perfect mouth pouted, and it took everything within him to restrain himself, to be respectful. He barely registered his own voice as he spoke.

"Can I kiss you?"

Avi slid two fingers under the low collar of his shirt, her touch a brand. "Why don't we go back to your cabin? I've been dying to be alone with you."

The ease with which Avi's touch ignited his desire startled him.

This was simpler.

No tangled history. No pain. No betrayal.

It felt good—too good.

Deep down, he wondered if this comfort was real or just an escape from the pain that always accompanied—

Who?

The question never fully formed.

The slow movement of Avi's fingers against his chest erased all thoughts of anything else.

He grabbed her hand. "Come. I'll give you what you want."

When he passed the blue-haired woman, he barely noticed the way her shoulders tensed, the way her fingers tightened around the rope.

Something flickered in her eyes.

Despair?

He couldn't discern why.

His fleeting pang of guilt was smothered before it could surface.

It didn't matter.

Avi was all that mattered now.

Her song filled his head, her warmth wrapped around him, and the rest of the world ceased to exist.

Chapter 86

EMMY

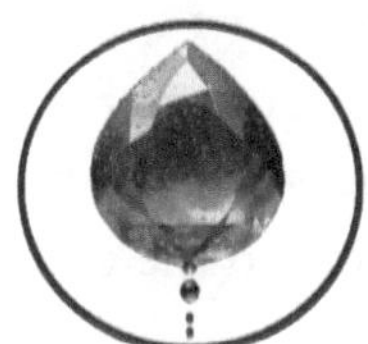

Emmy's heart sank as she watched Edmar and Avi walk away, their hands intertwined, his gaze fixed on the hybrid fae with an intensity that twisted a knife in her gut. He hadn't even glanced back at her, his dismissal of her silent plea a crushing blow.

Anger and jealousy warred within her, a storm of emotions threatening to consume her. Fire acid flared in her veins, turning her knuckles white as she gripped the rough coil of rope. She wanted to rush after them, to tear them apart, to demand an explanation. But what good would it do?

Edmar was clearly under Avi's spell, his judgment clouded, his heart ensnared.

It was her own fault. Her secrets and theft had left him vulnerable, his heart easy prey for another. As her magic dimmed, a deeper instinct clawed through the hollow ache, chasing away her self-doubt. *None of this is true.*

Something darker was at play, a sinister force she couldn't fully grasp. Avi's interest in Edmar, her haunting song—it was all too calculated, too deliberate.

This isn't him. And that thought spurred her to her feet. She couldn't let this *thing* control him.

He's mine.

Each step a slice to her heels, she hurried across the deck toward the cabins. "Cielan, I need you!" Her call held a desperate plea. "It's Avi. Edmar's cabin."

The vamphyr, with his heightened hearing and unwavering devotion to Avi, was the only one who might have the power to intervene. Without waiting for a response, she bolted toward Edmar's cabin, her heart hammering in her chest. A gust of cold air signaled Cielan's arrival at her side just as she reached the door. His piercing eyes burned with intensity, his expression an enigmatic mask.

"Stop them," she whispered, her voice strained.

He tilted his head, listening, then without hesitation, slammed the door open, splintering wood.

Edmar straddled Avi on his bed, hands fumbling with the ties of Avi's yellow shirt, while he kissed the bare skin of her chest. She arched into him.

A whirlwind of dark fury, Cielan gripped Edmar's throat and hurled him across the room. Edmar crashed into the wall and crumpled to the floor.

Will he kill Edmar? She prayed to the gods above and below the vamphyr restrained himself.

Unfazed by Cielan's anger, as he stood over her, Avi sat up in the rumpled bed, her shirt hanging open, exposing far too much. She returned Cielan's glare with a humorless smile, her cerulean eyes blazing, her voice taunting. "Stop ruining my fun, demon. You had your chance to fuck me."

Cielan ignored her, turning instead to a dazed and confused Edmar. "You live another day, dragon, only because the fault does not lie with you."

He grabbed Avi's wrist, yanking her from the bed.

"Are you going to pleasure me finally?" Avi said with a laugh that sounded brittle, almost desperate.

Cielan's jaw tightened as he dragged her from the cabin.

Alone with her Dragon King now, Emmy crouched beside him, her heart pounding. "Edmar."

A flicker of the man she loved—trapped beneath Avi's spell—struggled to break free. But he tensed at her touch.

"Get out." His rough voice made her blood run cold.

The resentment in his eyes, the way he recoiled from her touch, told her he didn't want her there. The sting of his rejection cut deeper than any blade, but she took a deep, steadying breath. This wasn't the time. He needed space to clear his head, to fight the magic that held him captive.

"Edmar, I—" She stopped, unable to find the words, her throat tightening with the effort to keep her emotions in check.

She understood, she did. Despite that, she turned and fled.

She sought peace in the rhythmic practice of her breathing exercises. But even in the solitude of her cabin, the fire acid in her veins burned hotter with every passing hour.

By midafternoon, the air turned frigid. Through the porthole, she gaped at massive icebergs, their jagged peaks glistening under a sun offering no warmth. It was a sight both beautiful and terrifying.

She ventured onto the deck, drawn by the cold, crisp air and the need to stretch her aching muscles. The ship had slowed down, carefully navigating the treacherous waters the farther north they traveled.

Adria stood on the prow, the forwardmost area of the ship. Like her husband, she went barefoot, with only a leather vest and cropped trousers. Her hand motions directed swirls of lavender magic. Icebergs parted before them, groaning.

Around her, the crew spoke of Aelunis and the coming storm. The storm was the last barrier before they reached the island, the point of no return. Whoever braved the storm to reach the Shrouded Land was never seen again. Currently, it was still just a dark smudge on the horizon, hours away. They'd reach the point of no return at midnight.

Edmar watched the storm from the railing, wind tousling his brown locks. She longed to approach him, to seek even the smallest connection, but his icy gaze sent her a clear message: stay away.

His familiar caress of her gem was gone, replaced by an aching emptiness. Despair threatened to consume her. She wanted to believe his coldness, his distance, resulted from the siren song, but a chilling doubt whispered in her mind. *What if he truly desires Avi?*

Then he walked toward Avi, drawn by the faint lure of the siren song and her welcoming smile. A suffocating coldness pressed down on Emmy's chest like the weight of a glacier descending, heavy and immovable.

Though free from the weight of rocks and chains, she felt just as alone as she had in her prison in the Little Palace. The only difference now was that she could finally fight for something larger than herself, even if it meant sacrificing everything to wake a sleeping god—one who would protect the world from the Summer Child.

She turned away from the sight of her husband with the hybrid fae.

Hours later, as the setting sun dipped below the waves, staining the sky in hues of a twilight tide pool, a fleeting wall of lavender and sea-foam green, a desperate urge to talk to Edmar spurred her forward. She had to try one last time to reach him, to find some semblance of peace, even if it was only friendship.

Her heart yearned for harmony before she faced her destiny.

But as she approached him, Avi materialized before her, her words a venomous caress. "He's mine now, desiring only me, and you've lost. Give up before it's just too pathetic to even look at you."

Avi's smile held a dark cruelty, mirroring the darkening sky, her bright eyes gleaming with malicious triumph.

"Why?" The question was more than just why the fae had used her magic to enthrall Edmar. It was a question that delved into why she'd chosen Edmar. Emmy had thought about this all day.

Who is Avi really? An agent for the Snow Princess? The Summer Child?

"Poor, lost mermaid," Avi cooed, her voice thick with false sympathy. "Did you really think you could keep him? The Dragon King was never meant for someone as weak as you. He belongs with me, and there's nothing you can do about it."

Turning the words over in her ears, she broke down each tone, each inflection. What she heard confirmed her thoughts with sickening certainty: this was more than just a rivalry for Edmar's affections. Nausea welled, stealing her breath and blurring her vision. With an effort of will, she forced her eyes to focus, refusing to give Avi the satisfaction of seeing her weakness.

But fire acid roared in her veins, defying her control. A whimper escaped her lips.

Control yourself, Emmy!

Clenching her fists, she focused on the distant silhouette of Mariskust to the far west, the closest Agondray city, just five miles from the island of Aelunis. She drew strength from the city's enduring presence, the largest city in the northern kingdom.

She glared at the fae, her voice trembling with rage. "Edmar isn't a prize to be won."

"And yet, I've won." Avi's cruel smile widened with smug confidence. "You'll never again know how his cold kisses scorch your skin, how his skillful fingers play with your nipples, how deliciously wonderful it feels to be filled with him."

Avi's words ignited a fire that even the icy wind couldn't cool. Her magic flared, fire acid boiling in her veins, her muscles swelling with her power. Light sparked at her fingertips. A familiar tug, a tingling sensation, cut through the haze of her rage.

Edmar. Across the deck, he stared at the glowing painite in his hand, his thumb rubbing across its surface.

Spasms wracked her muscles, stealing her breath. She stumbled toward the cabins, desperate to escape and meditate, but Avi blocked her path. Purple lightning split the sky behind her, giving the fae an otherworldly appearance. Her hair whipped around her face.

Emmy recalled similar purple lightning, once, long ago, the day Edmar, as the dragon, had been struck out of the sky. The day she'd saved him.

Not knowing what that meant, she instead dropped her voice low with a warning to Avi. "You don't know what you're doing."

"You're the one who doesn't know." Avi laughed, a chilling sound. Low thunder rumbled. "Let me tell you a story. Two powerful gods once loved the same mermaid. When she chose wrong, the other, consumed by rage, raped her, tore her apart, and bathed her in a baptism of fire."

"What kind of story is that?" Fear turned her insides to salt water.

"The lesson, mermaid: if you don't back down, Edmar will suffer the same fate. Choose wisely."

Avi's words, laced with a veiled threat, sent her fire acid flaring. Pain buckled her knees, spinning her world. She desperately struggled to maintain control.

A gust of icy wind, harbinger of the approaching storm, swept the deck, stirring the once-calm sea. The faintest taste of magic lingered in the air.

From the island? Or something else?

She trembled, barely containing her magic. "You're either insane or pathetic. He's only with you because of your spell."

Avi's smile was predatory. "He desires me. Craves me. You can't penetrate his devotion."

Wind whipped around them, echoing the rising fury of both the storm and Emmy's magic. Waves crashed against the hull as a distant rumble of thunder echoed the storm of emotions building within her.

"He doesn't really desire you." Emmy clung to the railing as waves crashed over the bow, soaking her. "You're controlling him!"

"Controlling?" Avi laughed, a sharp, cruel sound. "No one controls a Dragon King."

"You're wrong!" Despair threatened to drown her. "I know him. This isn't him."

"This is who he is meant to be." Avi's voice hardened. "And now you'll be who you were meant to be."

The air crackled with a surge of energy. Waves slammed into the boat, forcing creaking groans.

A deafening boom, a blinding flash of purple lightning. Then the sea swelled, a monstrous wave crashing over the bow and sending the ship lurching violently, throwing Emmy off balance.

She screamed, sliding helplessly across the slick deck.

Chapter 87

EMMY

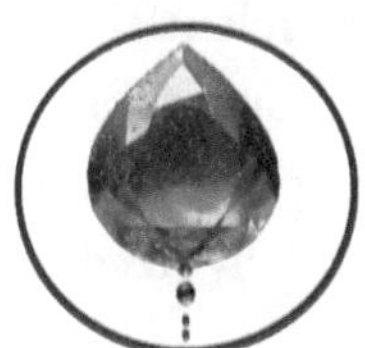

The world exploded in a deafening fury. Emmy was flung across the deck like flotsam in a violent current, the storm howling and tearing at the ship. Ship timbers groaned, the air thick with salt and seaweed as the ocean roared its rage. Icy rain lashed her skin, soaking her to the bone as she gasped, struggling to stay upright on the slick deck.

Panic clawed at her throat, but she forced herself to focus, desperately seeking a solid handhold. When the ship lurched, slamming her into a rolling barrel, her fire acid roared to life. Searing pain ripped through her, raging hotter and hotter. She cried out as she scrambled for the foremast, clinging to it, burning fire ripping through her blood.

She dug deep, drawing on every ounce of strength to control her magic. Slowly, the agony eased enough to breathe.

A flash of purple lightning illuminated pale faces emerging from below deck, determination etched with terror. Sparks of magic—blue, green, silver—lit the churning darkness as the crew fought back against the storm.

She searched frantically for Edmar.

There! A flash of blue amidst the darkness.

He battled the storm near the helm, his magic a whirlwind. Their eyes met, a fleeting connection. Concern, urgency flared in his gaze as he glanced at the glowing red gem in his pocket. He struggled to reach her, but stopped when the storm buffeted him, forcing him to fight with every ounce of strength to stay on his feet. A blue aura, laced with gold, whipped around him, redirecting the wind, reinforcing the hull, freezing leaks—all the while keeping her in his sight.

The rest of the crew fought just as fiercely. Adria, with savage grace, manipulated waves and icebergs away from the hull, while Lian, face grim, conjured shimmering shields of Moon magic, protecting small groups from the storm's fury within invisible barriers. Many of the crew also used magic in defense. The air crackled alive with the hum of power, sparks of light defying the storm's fury.

But still the storm pressed on, relentless. The ship groaned under the onslaught. Deep dread settled in her bones. *This storm seeks to destroy us.*

She had to get to Edmar. Leaving the mast, she fought her way across the deck, the combined magic of the crew briefly steadying the ship, until she reached the stairs down to the main deck.

The sea surged, lifting her into the air before slamming her against the deck again. Pain exploded in her shoulder and hip, stealing her breath, her thoughts—her control. She screamed. Stinging rain and water lashed her body. Searing heat flooded her veins, the glow beneath her skin pulsing brighter, hotter.

She fought for command of her magic, her pain, but the storm, the fear, her fiery power—it was all too much.

Fire acid threatened to consume her from the inside.

Agony overwhelmed her body, her mind. Light erupted from her fingertips.

Hands grabbed her, pulling her toward the mast. Thick rope tight around her middle, securing her.

"No," she shouted. "Stop!" But the wind ripped away her words.

She thrashed against the ropes, but she weakened, the person already gone. Her magic surged, a tide of fire searing, fusing her muscles into convulsions of unbearable torment. Flames burned her alive from the inside.

She screeched and wailed at the torture, even as she centered her thoughts, not releasing her magic while she was tied up. *I can't let it out. I can't hurt anyone else.*

But her strength was failing.

Never had she held her magic for so long and never had it been so strong. It coursed through her like lava. Despair battled her will as another scream tore from her.

She cried. Not the salt tears of the Land Bound, but her own blue blood.

Through the haze of her thick, dark tears, she locked onto her pulsing painite, a beacon in Edmar's pocket. As if sensing her struggle, he looked at her, his eyes reflecting her agony.

His magic flickered, died, and he charged toward her, only to be thrown back by the wind and waves, swept away. She shouted when he disappeared beneath the water, then sagged with relief when he reappeared. Further away from her but still on the ship.

Fierce, desperate love warred with her own certainty. She couldn't allow her magic to hurt him again.

She twisted, writhed, numb fingers fumbling with the knot, but her magic only surged stronger. The inferno beneath her skin pulsed with each agonizing throb of her heart. Veins burning like molten rivers beneath translucent flesh burned brighter, threatening to engulf her. Raindrops sizzled against her heated skin.

She didn't have much time, her control waning.

Finally, the rope fell away. She stumbled forward, vision blurring, body burning, parched despite the torrent of water. Whimpering, she stumbled toward the railing, each step a torment.

Across the ravaged deck, desperation filled Edmar's eyes, a silent plea. But he couldn't reach her in time. Nothing could help her now. She slipped, fell, then scrambled back up, gaze fixed on the churning sea.

Memories, sharp and fragmented, flashed through her mind—her mother's resigned face, engulfed in flames. Her father's cold, accusing eyes. The suffocating solitude of the Little Palace. Anjali's warm smile. And the nights spent with Edmar, sharing stories under the stars, his laughter echoing in her heart.

Wind buffeted her against the railing, and she latched on with another whimper, her vision blackening at the edges as her body failed.

Edmar frantically shouted, calling her name. But she couldn't stop. Couldn't turn back. Not when her entire being threatened annihilation.

Gripping the railing, she screamed through hauling herself up, agony nearly collapsing her arms, steam rising from her burning skin as the storm raged around her.

If only we had more time, Edmar.

And then, with the last of her strength, she jumped.

Icy water closed over her, a suffocating shroud. For a fleeting moment, blessed numbness. Then, her magic returned with a rush, leaking from her transparent skin. Her silver swirls blazed white-hot, illuminating the ocean depths. She was a living sun, her magic a raging inferno.

Her entire being ignited, fire acid erupting in a violent explosion. Water boiled, icy blue, turning into a seething cauldron of steam as her magic clashed with the ocean's depths. She was the epicenter, a conduit for unimaginable power.

Her body convulsed, the last vestiges of fire acid sputtering out. Around her, the boiling water settled into an eerie stillness. Her magic receded, exhausted, a dying flame. A deep, bone-chilling cold replaced the inferno.

Her torment was at an end.

Her body, now impossibly heavy, sank into the abyss. The last sparks of magic flickered beneath her skin, fading until only the cold, dark void remained.

Her lungs burned, the need for air becoming unbearable. She accepted it. She only wished she'd been able to tell Edmar she loved him one more time.

Now she lacked the strength to continue the fight, the storm's fury fading to a distant whisper.

Her end.

Her sacrifice.

And then there was only darkness.

Chapter 88

EDMAR

Time stopped.

Shock.

Emmy jumped overboard.

Gone.

Edmar stared at the empty space where she'd just stood, mind blank, body frozen. Rain, a deluge, pelted the *Tempest Queen* sideways. Yet all he could see was her empty spot, an impossible vacancy where she'd been only a heartbeat ago.

And in that heartbeat, the walls of his mind—his Frostlands—cracked, splintered. The void he'd maintained for centuries shuddered, as if his soul itself was breaking.

Denial ripped through him, a silent scream against the impossible. But he'd *seen* her reckless jump.

His entire being locked, the air catching in his lungs as though he'd never drawn a breath before.

And then the shock imploded. His magic roared in response, as if the cracks in his heart bled into the surrounding storm.

But amidst the chaos, a single image seared itself into his mind, her hand, reaching. Not flailing, not panicked. Just... reaching. For what? For help? For him?

Or had she already known there was no saving herself?

His breath caught, the agony sharper than any blade.

No. No, she does not get to surrender.

His breath hitched as a tsunami of emotions broke free: anguish, love, guilt, all crashing into him in waves of despair threatening to drown him.

I can't lose her. Not like this.

His distrust, his accusations, *Avi*—he'd driven her to this.

A piercing ache shot through him, and his magic surged outward, merging with the storm, a torrent barely leashed.

Then something shifted. A deep, resonant crack echoed through his being, the sound of a thousand years of icy control shattering, his Frostlands completely collapsing, leaving him exposed to the full force of his grief.

A guttural sob tore from his throat, the sound lost in the storm's fury. Memories, long buried, surged forth—frozen shards of his memories breaking free, floating past him in an endless, searing tide. His parents' terrified faces, the cries of a son he'd only known for an instant, the faces of his countless brides, their eyes vacant, their bodies cold.

All of it was there, whole and inescapable. He staggered, his knees buckling, the weight of a millennium of loss crushing him.

Emmy. Her name, a desperate prayer, a silent wail against the storm raging within.

For an instant, he glimpsed her again, a shadow beneath the waves, slipping away.

A voice howled inside him, primal, unforgiving.

She left you.

The Blue Devil bared his fangs, his fury sharpening like a blade. This wasn't how it ended. Not like this. She had no right. He was the one who decided who stayed, who left.

And yet, here she was, slipping through his fingers, making the choice he never saw coming.

For one frozen breath, he teetered on the edge, caught between rage and something infinitely more terrifying.

Loss.

The realization gutted him.

And then, blinding light flashed beneath the ocean's surface, and a feral scream tore from his throat, a sound that was at once rage and agony, desperate and wild.

The Blue Devil roared. *Take control. Bind the pain. Don't let it touch you.*

Edmar reached for him. A thousand years of instinct, of shutting out the world, of turning himself to ice. His fingers closed around empty air.

Nothing.

Panic clawed at his chest. Where was his armor? His walls? His ice?

The answer was suffocating. His Frostlands were gone, melted into a raw, agonizing emptiness, silent fields of obliterated ice. Once it promised safety in his detachment, escaping pain. Now no more.

Rage, fear, and loss surged unchecked, sparking out of him, bleeding into the storm's fury. Magic he'd once kept firmly contained now sparked wildly, feeding the storm's fury, a reckless force without his Frostlands to bind it.

Wind howled in response. The ship groaned, the crew's shouts all swallowed by the tempest raging within him and around them.

"Edmar!" Adria's shout.

A hand on his arm. He blinked at her, unseeing.

Emira. My Emmy. My love.

Somewhere in the dark, churning depths below, she was alone.

He couldn't see her, couldn't feel her. His mind spiraled into the ruin of his own memories, into darkness.

"Edmar, please!"

A beat, a breath—Emira.

He forced a shuddering breath, reeling in his magic.

But Emira...

I have to save her.

His unnamed son, a silent whisper on his lips. He wouldn't fail again. Not this time. The anguish and despair of a thousand years, now unleashed, unburdened by the icy walls of his Frostlands, fueled his actions, a fierce, desperate determination to find her.

For a moment, the siren song surfaced. He always forgot it until he heard it again. But this time, he shoved it aside.

He could not bear this life without Emira.

He thrust the painite at Adria and vaulted off the ship, shifting mid-air. Bones cracked, muscles spasmed, clothes shredded as scales and wings erupted. A roar ripped from his throat as he plunged into the icy water.

Can I save her?

The question seared him, a brand against his soul.

What if he was too late? The thought clawed at him. The loved ones he'd failed to protect, his parents, his son, barely a breath from his lips before...

Vestiges of his Frostlands trembled, a brief flicker of cold, as if the ice in him didn't want to let go. He shut down his instinct to protect himself again. Instead of burying it all again, he acknowledged it and moved on with a single-minded goal.

Only one thought, one driving purpose: *Find her.*

I have to save her.

Leathery wings folded tight against his body as he streamlined himself. His powerful tail propelled him through the water, a spear cleaving through the inky blackness. Ocean currents fought him, but he plunged deeper.

A faint flicker of light, a tiny beacon in the suffocating blackness.

Hold on, Emmy.

He pushed harder, praying to all eight gods, praying to Solis. The darkness pressed in, but with each sweep of his tail, he shot through the water faster, fueled by desperation.

Another flicker. This time, he saw her, a pale shadow sinking into the abyss. Fear stabbed at him, but he banished it. *Get her to safety. Get her help.*

With a powerful downward arc, he swept past her, catching her limp body, pulling her tight. He surged upward, tail whipping through the water as he shot toward the surface.

The ocean roared as he broke free, wings snapping open. His momentum shot him into the sky, rain and seawater trailing from his leathery wings like silvered streaks in the storm.

With a deep, rumbling growl, he struggled to hold steady, wings battling the wind. Below, the *Tempest Queen* was a toy in the grip of a raging beast. Pirates scrambled across the slick deck, fighting to keep the vessel afloat.

He scanned the heaving deck, aiming for a spot between the rigging and the swaying masts. With one powerful sweep of his wings, he closed the distance, rain pelting his scales, his claws tightening around Emira.

He hovered, searching for who could help her. He found Cielan waiting, his sinister clear gaze on him.

Hells no!

"Make way for the Dragon King!" a pirate shouted, her voice trembling.

He hesitated, claws curling protectively around Emira. Every instinct screamed at him to protect her, even from Cielan. Scales bristled, a growl building in his chest.

But he couldn't tell if she was even breathing.

I have no choice, and there's no one stronger who could protect her.

With a roar, he forced himself to surrender her to Cielan's waiting arms. Every instinct rebelled, claws tightening around her fragile body. He knew he had to let go. He knew. But gods, it felt like tearing himself apart.

Cielan's cold fingers brushed against his scales as he took her, a calculated movement, too smooth, too practiced. A reminder that she was no longer his to hold.

Edmar bared his fangs, a guttural snarl curling deep in his chest. *If you fail her, I will end you.* The words weren't spoken, but Cielan's sharp gaze met his, unreadable, a silent acknowledgment of the threat.

Then, she was gone from his grasp, and the absence of her weight left him hollow.

His body tensed, magic sparking. He despised Cielan, but he was Emira's best chance of survival. *Trust*. A bitter pill. The Frostlands, once his refuge, offered no solace now, only the echoing emptiness of his grief.

What are his motives?

Fragmented memories—Avi's cool touch, her lips—assaulted him. He shook his head, disgusted. Cielan could use this, seek revenge. He didn't understand it, didn't want to, but the fear was there.

With a frustrated roar, he launched himself back into the storm.

The *Tempest Queen* lurched in the waters, battered and off course. Guilt twisted in his chest. He'd left them, left everyone, for her. But now he could guide them, at least, by using an aerial view to set them back on course. Even if it killed him.

He flew, dodging lightning, battling winds that tore at his wings. Magic flickered, strength waned, but still he pushed onward.

Save them. Save her.

The mantra drove him, pushing him beyond his limits as he guided the ship toward Aelunis.

When he allowed himself to think, she was there. Emira. Her pale face, her stillness. *Is she alive?*

It whispered of numbness, that familiar chill of distance.

The ghost of his Frostlands beckoned him with icy fingers, a whisper of numbness in the face of another unbearable loss. But he couldn't afford the promise of cold detachment now. No more Blue Devil. Not when she needed him warm, whole. He banished the wasteland forever, his mental Frostlands, and clung to duty, to hope. *She has to be alive.*

Slowly, the storm weakened. The wind lessened, rain became a drizzle, and a sliver of a star-studded night appeared on the horizon.

His wings beat sluggishly, exhaustion pressing down on him. But beneath the storm's dying breath, another whisper called to him. One he hadn't realized had been spiraling through his mind.

A silent, desperate cry, reaching beyond reason.

Over and over, a prayer to the gods, to the sea, to the storm itself.

Emira.

It was carved into every frantic beat of his wings, into every pulse of his magic, into every breath he still forced into his aching lungs.

The wind howled in response, indifferent. She wasn't there to hear it. But the ache in his chest remained, raw and unrelenting.

Wings leaden, he turned back toward the ship, a shadow against the fading storm.

He descended, heart pounding with a single question.

Is she alive?

Please, gods, let her live.

CHAPTER 89

EDMAR

Rain fell in a steady drizzle as Edmar descended toward the ship, dragon form shifting back to human just before he reached the deck. The storm loomed nearby, a brooding presence refusing to leave.

Barely registering the appreciative whistles of the crew with his nakedness, his gaze swept the deck, frantic, searching. Avi approached, cerulean eyes glinting, a seductive smile on her lips. He brushed past her, his entire being focused on finding Emira.

"She's alive." Adria's husky voice cut through the noise. "Cielan took her to her cabin."

Relief warred with a surge of tension. *Cielan. Alone with Emira.* He spared Adria a curt nod and raced below, worry and suspicion twisting in his gut. He burst into Emira's cabin. Cielan sat at the desk, quill scratching parchment, unfazed. Emira lay asleep in her bed, covers pulled up to her chin. He rushed to her side, touching her face, concern overriding his mistrust of Cielan. Her skin was icy cold. She shivered. *She's alive!*

"Glad to be off babysitting duty." Cielan rose with languid grace. He folded the parchment with meticulous care. "She's all yours, Dragon King."

Don't expect that I'm not aware of what you actually want. After his recent experiences with betrayal, trust was a dangerous thing to offer anyone, and especially a creature like Cielan. Noticing her bare shoulder peeking from beneath the blanket, he lifted the edge, heart skipping a beat. She was naked. The soft curve of her hip, the smoothness of her skin—it stirred something deep inside him. Desire and a fierce protectiveness warred within him.

He rounded on Cielan, fists clenched. "Did you undress her?"

The vamphyr raised an eyebrow, his expression a mask of unconcerned amusement. "Did you want me to leave her in wet clothes?"

"You could have asked someone else more appropriate."

"Was I to ask the crew while they fought for their lives?" Cielan scoffed. "And Avi, let's be honest, she wouldn't have been much help."

Rage warred with grudging acceptance, the vamphyr's logic sound. Cielan was right. But the thought of him touching her was unbearable. "Why weren't you helping on deck? There was no sun."

One shoulder shrugged, a slow, deliberate movement. "I save my energy for important things. I'm sure the crew appreciated my absence, considering their disposition toward me."

"What if the ship went down?"

"I'm impervious to death."

"But Avi isn't." Cielan's one weakness.

"Exactly. I would need my strength to save her—to keep her alive."

"That's selfish when you could save everyone."

"Selfish?" A flicker of something cold crossed his features. "Not in my estimation. Why save those who would see me dead?"

He shook his head, knowing this conversation could go around in circles with the vamphyr's unapologetic nature.

As Cielan tucked the folded paper into his sleeve, his gaze flicked over Edmar's nakedness. One thin eyebrow arched again. "Considering your similar states of undress, perhaps you can finally consummate your marriage. Now that you're her savior."

The vamphyr's provocative smile and his casual disregard for propriety irritated Edmar. "Get. Out."

"Not even a thank you, dragon?"

"Don't think I don't know why you helped her." He was sure Cielan was waiting for the opportunity to feed from Emira again. Yet, his honor demanded it. "Thank you," he ground out.

Cielan nodded once, then leisurely glided to the door. At the threshold, he looked back. "Such a temptation," he murmured, glancing at Emira. "Her charms are… considerable."

Then he vanished. Quick, like a shadow under a noon sun. As Edmar moved to close the door, Avi was suddenly there, blocking the doorway. Cerulean eyes gleamed. A seashell necklace rested in the valley between her breasts, drawing attention to her open shirt, indecently inviting. Edmar blocked her entrance when she attempted to cross the threshold.

Her gaze raked down his body, lingering. A slow smile spread across her lips. "Perhaps we can pick up where we left off?"

Her hand trailed over his stomach, and he flinched, nauseous. Saltwater and silver lilies. Her cloying scent hit him, triggering a dizzying urge he couldn't understand. He grabbed her wrist and shoved her back with a growl. "Not interested."

Avi pressed closer, her body a tempting heat. A familiar melody drifted over him, seductive, intoxicating. He remembered.

"You were interested last night." Cerulean eyes promised untold pleasures. "I can make you interested again."

Anger warred with a seductive pull he couldn't quite shake. The forgotten melody wound around his thoughts, hauntingly familiar, yet—this time, something clicked. He shook his head. *She's bewitching me.*

He shoved her back into the hallway. "Stay away from me."

Fury contorted Avi's features, her cheeks flushed a deep wine-red color. "You'll regret this."

"I don't think so."

She turned on her heel and stomped away, passing Cielan, who leaned against the wall.

Something dark gleamed in the vamphyr's eyes. "Very good, dragon."

And then he was gone, leaving a breath of cold air behind. Edmar remained frozen in place, his pulse hammering in his ears. *The spell is gone.* Not just the magic—her hold on him. Avi had manipulated him, twisted his thoughts, but it wasn't just her magic that had made him weak. He had let her in. Because it had been easier.

Easier to let himself be pulled into her warmth than to face the wreckage of his trust in Emira. Easier to believe he didn't love her anymore. Easier to justify his doubts instead of risking hope. And it had almost cost him everything.

He squeezed his eyes shut. He'd been so blinded by betrayal, so desperate to protect himself, that he had left himself open to something worse. Never again. The thought settled deep, unshakable. He would never fall under Avi's spell again—not because her magic had broken, but because the moment Emira leapt into the sea, he had broken.

He turned the lock behind him. Then he faced the only woman who had ever truly mattered.

Sapphire curls framed her face, dark lashes fanned against her cheeks. Each breath was a victory.

She's alive.

The thought, the reality, nearly shattered him. Without his Frostlands, he shook, a tremble reaching his core.

Shoulders twitching, he wiped a hand over moist eyes. He'd wasted time on anger, on pain, on his own wounded pride. And he'd nearly lost her. A cost too high to pay. He didn't understand it, this fierce, unyielding love, but it pulsed through him, strong and true.

He slid into the bed beside her, his breath catching in his throat at the simple act of being this close to her again. Gathering her close, he inhaled, her scent of coconut and flowers filling his lungs, a dizzying elixir. She shivered, then relaxed against his warmth. Her soft curves against his body created a familiar ache through him, a longing that would never die for this woman.

The rhythm of her breathing, the patter of rain against the hull, lulled him into a restless slumber. He woke to her movement, to the feel of her pulling away. Rain still fell, the cabin lit by the soft glow of a lantern.

Wide-eyed, she sat up and scooted away from him, putting distance between them until her back hit the wall.

His heart pounded against his ribs, blood surging in his veins at the sight of her. Full breasts, dusky green nipples, sapphire hair a dark halo around her face—she was breathtaking. Each breath labored, the air thick. Desire flared hot and urgent, but he forced himself still, fingers clawing into the sheets.

Control, a constant battle with her, left his body tense. An undeniable urge to possess her, to make her truly his, warred within him. He wanted her, fiercely, desperately, but shadows lingered in her eyes, in the space between them.

"Why?" Her voice was soft, hesitant. "Why are you here? What happened?"

"I..." He dragged in a ragged breath. "I'm so relieved you're safe."

She closed her eyes, drawing her own shaky breath. "I lost control of my magic."

"Yes."

"But I jumped into the ocean."

He sat up. They nearly touched, the space between them suddenly too full of what he'd almost lost. "What you did was a very foolish, very dangerous—"

"Please don't tell me I've made the wrong decision again."

"—very smart, very brave, courageous thing to do." He longed to touch her, to stroke her face, to show her just how precious she was to him. But she was too skittish right now. He stayed his hands. "You were willing to sacrifice yourself to save us, Emira. You amaze me."

Color bloomed on her cheeks, a beautiful blush against her green skin. He ached to pull her close, to erase the shadows in her eyes, but her expression remained guarded.

"Why are you *really* here?" she asked. Her question seemed to ask something else from the accusing tone. "Why not..." Her lips twitched. "Why not Avi's bed?"

That's what she wanted to know, if he really wanted Avi. Fragmented memories of the last day with Avi—it all felt hazy, disjointed. Regret filled him, even if he couldn't remember making any specific decision to pursue Avi. "You were right. She was using magic on me. But it's gone now. The spell, the hold she had. It's gone."

Wariness lurked in the depths of her emerald eyes.

His fingers itched to grasp her hand, but once more, he controlled his natural instinct. She may never want him to touch her again, and he'd live with that, no matter how much it killed him. Instead, he laid a hand on his chest. "There's no one else in my heart, Emira. There never was."

Her gaze slid down to where his palm rested on his chest. Her lips parted, but she didn't say anything.

"Emira, please." He needed to be closer to her, to touch her, to chase away the shadows he saw in her eyes. "Let me hold you."

Hesitantly, she nodded, and he slipped his arms around her, tucking her head under his chin. He held her there, eyes closing, thanking the gods. This was all that mattered, the feel of her in his arms, the scent of her hair, the warmth of her skin against his. After several tense heartbeats, she finally melted against him, burying her face in his chest. And then she stiffened.

"Edmar." Her voice was breathless, strained. She pulled back slightly, her gaze dropping to where the blanket did little to conceal his arousal. Her gaze lifted to his, filled with uncertainty.

He winced. He hadn't meant for this to happen. "Do you want me to leave?"

She shook her head, another slow, hesitant movement while she bit her lip. But the shadows still haunted her face, a reflection of the pain he'd caused.

How many shadows had he cast upon her? His anger, his accusations, the memory of the night he'd choked her when he caught her? Or were there deeper ones, something from her past, from the years of suffering she'd endured?

Or maybe it was Avi. Blurry flashes of Avi arching her body under his kisses filled his mind.

He had hurt Emira, and those wounds ran deep.

"About Avi." He stopped, searching for the right words. "I wasn't myself. What I did, what I—" He closed his eyes, unable to voice the guilt and shame that clawed at him, but he tore the words from his soul, whispering to her, "I'm so sorry."

"I know," she whispered back, her hand finding his. "I believe you because I know you. The honor and duty that binds you. I forgive you, Edmar."

Her forgiveness, so easily given, stung. If their roles had been reversed, he knew he would have been consumed by rage and jealousy. Yet here she was, offering him understanding and compassion, even when he felt he didn't deserve it. "You have more honor than I would have in this moment."

"My forgiveness comes with understanding, but," a tremor ran through her, "it still hurts."

"I understand." He squeezed his eyes shut, feeling her loss again. His heart ached that he was responsible for her pain. "I'll go."

"No," she said quickly. "Please... stay."

He gathered her close and cradled her against him, burying his face in her hair, drawing strength from her courage, her quiet, inner strength, and her compassion. As he lay down with her, she snuggled against his chest, her breathing soon evening out.

Desire warred with guilt, tenderness with the lingering fear of what he'd almost lost. He closed his eyes, the rhythm of her breathing his only solace. Aelunis awaited. But even here, in the quiet of her cabin, Emira in his arms, a sliver of unease remained when he thought about how she sacrificed herself to save everyone.

A whisper of Avi's words came back to him with clarity, a chilling premonition. *What else could wake a sleeping god than a full sacrifice?*

Chapter 90

EMMY

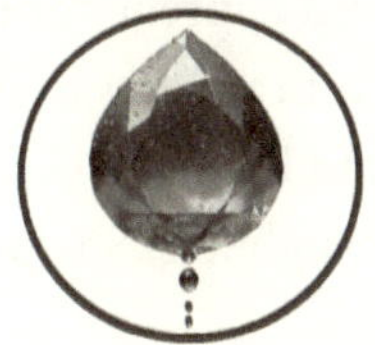

Sunlight streamed through the porthole, painting Emmy's cabin in a golden glow. The storm had passed, leaving only the gentle rocking of the ship and the murmur of the sea. Serenity mingled with a lingering sense of unease.

Awareness returned in layers. Warmth. The comforting weight of a body pressed against hers, an arm over her waist. A steady rise and fall of a chest beneath her cheek. And then the scent, the sea, mingled with something uniquely Edmar.

Edmar.

He'd stayed. Just as she'd known he would. The memory of his gaze—the longing, the vulnerability, when he said no one else had his heart—sent a wave of heat through her. Nestling closer, she savored his warmth, the solid presence of his body along the length of hers. The intimacy was a heady rush, desire pulling deep in her core, heat pooling between her thighs. Twenty-five years she'd dreamed of this. Now it was real. And yet...

Fear, a cold fist, clenched around her heart.

Avi's naked chest. The way Edmar had kissed her, with a passion Emmy had once thought he reserved for her alone. Revulsion and pain twisted through her.

She'd forgiven him. She *knew* he'd been bewitched. But the images, the memories, still stung. Avi's words, a venomous whisper, echoed in her mind: *He's mine now, desiring only me, and you've lost.*

Insecurities gnawed at her. *Even free from the siren's spell, does he truly want me? He still doesn't trust me.*

A lifetime imprisoned, by her magic, by her father, by the curse that had kept her from true intimacy. But now, she was free. Free to experience Edmar's love, to fulfill the desires that burned within her.

The heat between her legs throbbed, a pulsing need. She shifted, her hip brushing against his hardness. Her breath caught. *Did I wake him?*

A low chuckle rumbled in his chest.

"Good morning," he murmured, his voice husky with sleep.

Her throat tightened. Desire and apprehension warred within her.

"Morning," she said, hating the breathless tremor in her voice.

He shifted, as if to pull away, but her hand darted out, a hesitant weight on his arm. Urgent yearning surged through her. She pressed his hand to her stomach, her skin tingling beneath his touch.

"Don't," she whispered. "Don't go yet."

He stilled, his ocean-colored eyes searching hers. What emotions churned there? But her mounting desire erased her question. She guided his hand lower to the ache that throbbed between her legs.

His hand hovered, his touch a promise, waiting for the right words. "Are you sure?"

Fierce joy curved her lips. "Make me feel breathless."

His brows twitched up as the tension between them grew, each second an eternity. Then, his touch—a featherlight brush against her throbbing clit—sent a jolt of pleasure racing up her spine. She gasped, eyes closing as a different fire ignited within her. Her body arched instinctively, seeking relief.

His hand, his breath against her skin, sent tremors cascading down her back. He understood her unspoken plea, teasing her with a slow, deliberate rhythm before increasing the pressure and speed, stoking the fire in her veins. She gasped, her body craving more.

The sensations were unlike anything she'd ever known. Her magic had always been a barrier, a threat that kept her hand still and others at a distance. Now she knew what exquisite pleasure she'd been missing.

She met his gaze—dark, possessive, a look that sent a spark tingling over her skin.

He kissed her shoulder. "You always leave me breathless."

A rush of heat flooded her with his admission. Then he nudged her onto her back, a finger gliding into her heat, and she gasped at the novel sensation, a moan escaping her lips. He moved his finger in and out, slowly. Then another finger joined the first.

Her hips lifted against his hand, wanting more. With a touch both tender and demanding, he understood her every reaction, his eyes intense on her. He teased her, fingers alternating speed, while his thumb swept over her clit.

Her whole being strained toward him, her moans growing louder, breath hitching as waves of sensation rushed over her, each one building. Desire surged within her, a powerful current she longed to surrender to. As pleasure coiled tighter, sharper, she bucked against his hand.

Then he stole her moan and breath when he kissed her, his tongue tangling with hers. His hand moved faster, hitting a spot that sent her spiraling toward oblivion. But even as she crested her pleasure, she stayed right there on the edge, chasing something illusory. Her body quivered, her breath coming in short, sharp gasps. She whimpered, desperate for release.

"Please." She didn't know what she begged for.

He moved down her body, taking a nipple into his mouth. An unexpected rush of sensations shot through her core, pleasure shifting, building higher. He sucked the tight bud harder and harder, flicking it with his tongue.

Such torment swelled inside her, so much closer, but she still chased the elusive euphoria she'd yet to find. Her head fell back, her eyes closing, whimpering.

His fingers curled inside her, moving faster. Then, he bit down on her nipple, and she bowed off the bed with her cry, the darkness exploding into a million stars. Ecstasy crashed over her, shattering, consuming. A devastating release, breaking boundaries. A freedom she'd never dared to imagine.

Aftershocks of pleasure rippled through her, and she floated in the feeling for long moments. Then she opened her eyes, meeting his stormy gaze.

"You're so beautiful," he said, and the awe in his voice reflected in the ocean of his eyes.

For a heartbeat, the world shrank to just the two of them. Nothing else existed outside of this bed, this cabin, this ship. Then the intensity faded. He slipped his fingers free, leaving her breathless, aching.

He started to withdraw from the bed again, but she caught his hand. "I don't want to stop. I want more."

Immediately, he came back to her, framing her face with his hands. "I've wanted this for so long." His voice was rough with unsated desire. Something more than wonder filled his eyes—sadness, regret, relief. A depth of emotions that stole her breath. His thumb traced her cheekbone. "And I almost—" His voice broke. "I almost lost the chance."

He swallowed audibly, his eyes briefly closing. Then his voice, deep and sorrowful, filled with all the tones she'd heard when he'd spoken of his son. "When I thought I'd lost you… I never knew I could need someone like this."

"I'm here." Her fingers tightened around his on her face. "I'm here, Edmar."

He brought their linked hands to his mouth, pressing a warm kiss to hers.

She gasped at the tingle of pleasure, thinking about that mouth on her breast.

"Edmar." The ache returned with a vengeance to her core. She still felt so empty. "I want you."

Desire flared in his eyes, obvious in the hardness pressed against her.

"I want to give you everything you want," he murmured. "I'll give you as much pleasure as you'll allow me."

Heat coiled in her belly, a delicious ache. She hesitated for only a moment, emboldened by the intimacy that thrummed between them. "What about your release? You didn't receive any pleasure from what you did."

"Seeing your pleasure is enough for me."

His sincerity, the raw need in his eyes, touched her deeply. But it wasn't enough. She needed a deeper connection. She wanted to feel breathless. "Kiss me."

He obliged, his lips claiming her, a searing, possessive kiss that first stole her breath, then fanned heat deep within her core. His hands sank into her hair, his tongue an invasion she welcomed, each touch stoking the fire within her. She hooked a leg over his, pressing closer, her core throbbing against his hardness.

And then he paused. His forehead rested against hers, his breath cold against her skin.

"Don't stop." She pressed herself closer.

His gaze searched hers. Then he pushed her onto her back, his kiss a claim, his body against hers, the hard length of him a hot torment on her belly. She wrapped her legs around him, arching into him.

His hands tangled in her hair, angling her head for a deeper kiss. He trailed kisses down her neck, his touch igniting a firestorm within her. She moaned his name, her body writhing, craving a new release.

But then he stopped again.

Tension radiated from him, a battle raging beneath his skin. His hands loosened, and he looked up at her, a clear struggle in his gaze. "We should wait."

"Why?" Alarm chased away the lingering pleasure, her legs loosening their hold. "Did I do something wrong?"

"No, never." The struggle vanished, replaced by a tenderness that warmed her. "There is something I must do first."

Hope, fragile but persistent, bloomed in her chest.

"More important than this?" she whispered, her palm grazing over his whisker-rough cheek.

He nodded.

"Besides, I want to savor this," he murmured, his gaze intense. "To take my time with you."

"I think we've waited long enough."

He chuckled, then his lips brushed against her neck. "I want you to be so sedated with pleasure that you'll be ready to welcome me within you."

"I'm ready now," she breathed, her body aching to close the distance between them.

He smiled against her skin. "I know."

His hand drifted down her body, cupping her breast as he kissed a path down her neck to her breast. Her breath hitched with anticipation.

"I'll make you come," he whispered against her skin, "again and again. Before I take you the first time."

His thumb flicked over her nipple, sending pleasure through her. Then he sucked the nipple hard into his mouth. A cry tore from her throat, her body bowing off the bed. He softened the sucking, teasing her nipple with his tongue before finally releasing it with a soft kiss. "I want to learn all your secrets."

"Everything feels good," she breathed, her body thrumming with need.

He chuckled, a low, rumbling sound. "Oh, we'll find the things that feel *better*."

He flicked his tongue across her nipple. A whimper, half moan, half groan, escaped her lips.

His smile widened. "So sensitive," he said, a cold breath brushing her skin. He latched onto her nipple again, teasing it with his teeth before releasing it with a sigh. "So much fun to be had."

He sucked her, nipping lightly, sending waves of pleasure over her. She tangled her fingers in his hair, wanting to pull him closer, to push him away, lost in the sweet torment.

Urgent shouts erupted from above, shattering the sensual haze.

Edmar lifted his head, listening. "Aelunis," he said, his voice a rough mix of excitement and lingering desire.

Fear became a cold shadow lurking beneath her breast. *Aelunis.* Her destiny. Either her cure or her doom.

Then she focused on Edmar. She'd always thought about what Aelunis might hold for her, but she'd never considered what it might mean for him.

If she died, what would that do to him?

Terror clawed at her. *He needs a purpose, something to fight for.*

"Promise me you'll do whatever it takes," she whispered, grasping one of his hands. "Wake every god. Don't stop, no matter what."

He frowned, his gaze searching hers. "What?"

"Promise me," she insisted, her voice urgent.

He hesitated, then nodded, the frown easing from his face. "I promise."

Then he rolled off the bed.

"Come," he said, eagerness dancing in his eyes, a hand held out to her. "Let's go see the infamous island no one returns from."

CHAPTER 91

EMMY

Salty air, heavy with humidity, clung to Emmy's skin like a heated blanket, a desolate departure from the cold ice fields they'd left behind on the other side of the storm. Ahead, Aelunis rose from the sea, shrouded in mist, its shoreline obscured by an ethereal embrace of fog.

Aelunis. The island of no return.

The air crackled with anticipation, tension palpable in the crew's hushed whispers and wary glances. Even the ship seemed to hold its breath, timbers creaking softly as waves lapped against its hull.

Mountains cloaked in dense jungle appeared and disappeared as the mist shifted, their jagged peaks dark silhouettes against the hazy sky. And always, behind them, the storm. A swirling curtain of dark clouds encircling the island, a menacing presence for those trying to leave.

But between the island and the storm stretched a band of tranquil water, an invitation she couldn't resist, drawing her to the railing. The walk from her cabin had been agony, each step searing pain. Despite expelling her magic the day before, fire acid simmered beneath her skin, a constant threat.

A life without pain... Is it even possible? Her power grew as the suppression spell faded. *Four days left.*

They were so close to finding Metallon. But how could she navigate this treacherous island without her magic erupting, without risking the lives of the crew? *Without risking Edmar?*

He'd left her cabin before she'd even dressed, their shared intimacy a fleeting memory against the backdrop of this dangerous quest. She hadn't seen him since, and a cold knot of uncertainty tightened in her chest. Where did they stand now? Had their moment of closeness, their shared vulnerability, meant anything? Or had the shadows of her betrayal already returned?

How will he react when I tell him what I must do before we depart? His mistrust of her could make things complicated.

As if summoned by her thoughts, he appeared on the deck below. Her stomach fluttered, heat pooling low in her belly. Her Dragon King looked so handsome, the loose pirate garb doing little to hide his strength. His gaze swept the deck, finding hers, and a smile lit his eyes. She returned it, her heart quickening as he took a step toward her. But then Adria's voice broke their connection.

"Where to, Edmar?" Her husky voice boomed across the ship, her gaze sharp and assessing.

His reluctance transparent, Edmar joined Adria on the quarterdeck. Emmy longed for his touch, for the closeness they'd shared, too impatient to wait. As he pulled out the Sun Stone, his gaze met hers, and for a fleeting moment, she thought she saw the same longing reflected in his eyes.

The small, black gem fit perfectly in his palm. "We need to sail north around the island to find Metallon's resting place."

Everyone, including her, held their breath, but the stone didn't change. Avi emerged from below at that moment, her gaze fixed on Edmar. For the briefest moment, Adria's eyes flicked to her daughter, her lips pressing into a thin line. She said nothing, but the moment passed like a shadow moving over the deck.

"We need to sail south around the island to find Metallon's resting place." Again, no response from the stone. Puzzling. How many other choices did they have to find the Metal God?

He lifted his hand higher. "We need to sail straight at the island to find Metallon's resting place."

The Sun Stone flared, bathing the deck in brilliant golden light so intense she had to shield her eyes. Then silence fell as the light subsided, broken only by the sharp exhales of the crew.

Adria propped a hand on her hip. "Straight?" Her voice was sharp, incredulous.

He nodded, his jaw set. "Straight through the fog."

Shaking her head, Adria bounded down to the main deck. "If we wreck, Edmar, you'll be the first I toss overboard—dead or alive!"

Adria took her position at the prow, a lavender aura swirling around her.

"Damnable fog," she muttered. "Jesi, keep her steady as she goes. I'll see to the obstacles."

The pirate captain's movements mesmerized Emmy. This was the first time she could watch magic happening in front of her without the threat of attacking dire wolves, raging beasts and creatures, lumbering icebergs emerging from quiet mists, or an uncontrollable storm. Adria swept her arms in several arcs, her magic spreading, descending into the ocean. The ship surged forward, into the heart of the unknown.

Strong arms encircled her from behind, a hot mouth pressing against her neck. She leaned back against Edmar, a sigh escaping her lips. He chuckled, his breath brushing an icy chill over her skin, making her shiver, and kissed her again. Desire pooled in her core, moaning before she could stop it.

"I have a burning need for you," she whispered the confession.

"And I for you," he murmured back, his voice thick.

He kissed her once more, a lingering kiss that left her breathless as usual, then straightened, his hands gripping the railing on either side of her, effectively caging her between his body and the ship's railing. She looked up at him, his gaze bright with excitement as he surveyed the island rising above the swirling mist.

"You look like a young mermaid who's just found her first shiny pearl." She teased him with a smile.

He laughed, the sound warm and familiar.

"Once, long ago, I dreamed of adventure, Emmy." Wistful longing tinged his words. "A third prince, with no crown, no destiny, just the freedom to explore, to experience the world."

She liked that he called her Emmy more often now rather than Emira.

"And who will you tell your tales to if we don't escape this island?" Dark humor accompanied her question.

What if I don't survive waking Metallon?

"My wife, of course." His eyes twinkled. "You'll always be there to listen to my tales of adventure."

She smiled despite her fears, until her gaze landed on Avi, not far from them. She lowered her voice. "Are you really free of her?"

Edmar stiffened, a flash of anger in his eyes when he looked at the hybrid fae. It melted when his gaze returned to her.

"She only had power over me because I let her. Because I—" He swallowed. "Because I was too afraid of opening myself again to you." His thumb brushed over her knuckles. "That fear is gone now."

Relief filled her, but the fae still felt dangerous. "Then why does it feel like no one sees what she's doing?"

He shook his head. "What would it change? I tried to speak to Adria and Lian this morning, but they want to believe she's better. That Cielan has been helping her keep her visions away."

"They don't see what we do."

"No," he said. "I feel Cielan knows something is not right, but his devotion to her comes first for him."

Yes, she could understand that about the vamphyr.

"Besides, I—" He exhaled. "I don't care what happens to her. I care about us."

His words settled the fluttering in her heart, then their attention was drawn to the barrier ahead of the ship.

The world dissolved into a wall of white and gray as they entered the swirling fog. The air thickened, pressing down on them, the silence broken only by Adria's sharp commands and the creak of the ship as she navigated the treacherous waters. Jagged rocks, hidden beneath the surface, appeared like the teeth of some great beast, looming out of the fog before disappearing just as quickly.

She gripped the railing, knuckles white, fire acid simmering beneath her skin. Stinging heat made her gasp, but then it faded with her deep breaths.

"We'll find our way," he murmured, his hand closing over hers.

How will he react to my plan? Her insides turned into cold salt water with the thought he might return to hating her. She had to tell him. But the words wouldn't come, her mouth dry. For now, she'd savor his warmth, his touch, the unexpected tenderness that chased away the shadows of doubt. *Sun God, let me survive this. Let me have a life with him.*

But was she worthy of that life, if she couldn't be honest with him right now?

She turned, facing him, her back against the railing, her hands on his chest. His heart leaped beneath her hand. Ocean eyes swallowed her, holding her captive.

Everything about him in this moment—his warmth, his touch, his gaze—offered a reassurance she hadn't dared to hope for. He was the Edmar she'd fallen in love with, the man who'd shared her love for the stars, who'd made her laugh, who'd looked at her with tenderness and trust. The man she'd almost lost, might lose again if he didn't understand.

She curled her fingers in his shirt, her heart pounding with a mix of hope and fear. She didn't want to lose this version of him again. Her voice caught in her throat before she could finally get words out. "Edmar, there's something I need to tell you."

"Me too." Hope and yearning entered the light of his eyes. "But let me go first?"

She nodded, heart pounding. He reached into his pocket, placing something in her palm, his fingers closing over hers.

My painite! Warmth flooded her as the connection reasserted itself, a familiar hum beneath her skin.

"It's yours. It should never have been taken from you."

Hope surged, bright and unexpected. *He trusts me.* "Edmar, there's something—"

Promises filled his gaze, and for a moment, she was lost in the tenderness she'd craved for so long. But he shook his head, silencing her.

"I was wrong." His voice, rough with emotion, faltered. "Terribly wrong. When I thought I'd lost you..." Shaking his head, he trailed off. "Judging your choices was never my right. I may think I know what I would have done in your situation, but the truth is, I don't. I don't know if I would have been any stronger, any braver."

He paused, brushing his thumb lightly against her knuckles. "I was a fool. A stubborn, arrogant fool too rigid in my ideals. I'm sorry I wasn't there for you, that I wasn't someone you could trust. I failed you. And I don't know how to make it up to you. I don't know how—"

"Edmar, stop." She pressed her hand against his chest, feeling the steady beat of his heart beneath her palm. "That stubborn, arrogant fool is the man I fell in love with." Emotion welled within her, a knot of pain and love she couldn't swallow. If only she could cry, let the tears wash it all away. "I should have trusted you."

Regret whispered thickly in her words as she continued. "But I was afraid. I've been alone most of my life, with few people to trust and even fewer to love." She took a shaky breath. "I'm sorry, Edmar. For everything. For hurting you. I never wanted to hurt you."

"And I never want to control you again," he said, his gaze intense. "I shouldn't have used your gem against you. I'm so sorry, Emmy. From now on, I want to be the man you *can* trust. The one you can talk to, the one you can lean on."

A nervous laugh escaped her.

"I hope so, too." She hesitated, her gaze dropping to her hand on his chest. "Which is why... You might wish you still had my gem when you hear what I'm about to say."

He frowned, his brow furrowing deeply.

"Thank you for trusting me again," she said softly, lifting her gaze to his. "But I need to ask Cielan for help. Before we go ashore."

His face hardened, his sky-blue skin darkening to a stormy violet. "No. Absolutely not."

"I don't have a choice, Edmar." Her voice was firm, despite the tremor in her chest. "My magic is coming back. I can't risk hurting anyone."

"There has to be another way." Desperation edged his voice. "I'll carry you. I'll protect you."

"You can't carry me *everywhere*." Frustration laced her words. "And this is *my* choice. My magic. My body."

The anguish in his eyes twisted her heart. He didn't want this. She knew that. But... "We don't know how long it'll take to find Metallon," she said, her gaze pleading with him to understand.

"It won't be long," a sharp voice cut in. Avi stood a few feet away, her cerulean eyes narrowed. "I'm pretty sure that's where he is."

Emmy returned to the railing, drawn by a sudden shift in the air. They were emerging from the fog, and there, looming before them, was the island. Rugged, imposing. The air grew thick, the scent of salt and something else, something ancient, metallic.

The taste of metal, sharp and tangy, hit her tongue.

Metallon. He was here. She felt him, deep inside her, a resonance that vibrated through her very being.

Edmar's arm slid around her waist, drawing her close as the ship glided toward the jagged cliffs that rose from the sea. Nestled within the rugged mountain face, an ancient temple, its dark stone stark against the vibrant green of the jungle. Metal glinted under the bright sun.

A shiver of awe and dread ran through her. The temple, carved from the mountain itself, ominous above them, its entrance guarded by two towering statues whose metallic gaze seemed to pierce the very air.

Metallon.

An endless staircase wound its way up to the temple's entrance, hinting at the arduous journey ahead, a journey that filled her with both fear and a strange, compelling fascination.

Edmar's hand tightened around hers, a silent reassurance. They were here. The first task of the Sun God's quest. But first, she needed to see Cielan, and she prayed this didn't shatter the fragile trust they'd just begun to rebuild.

Chapter 92

EMMY

A suffocating wall of jungle pressed in, thick and humid, sweat trickling down Emmy's neck. Shirt and trousers clung to her sticky skin, and she longed for the ocean's cool embrace. She was a creature of Winter, ill-suited to this sweltering heat.

"This be no place for a pirate," Adria grumbled, her husky voice barely audible over the buzz of insects. With a practiced swing of her cutlass, she hacked through a tangle of vines. The Water Fae pirate led the group beside her husband. "Where's the sea breeze when you need it?"

Lian, sweat gleaming on his steel-gray skin, chuckled and swung his massive ax, clearing a path through the ferns. "You love a good challenge, Adria. Or has the jungle finally bested the great pirate captain?"

"Watch yourself, or I'll have you swabbing the deck when we get back." She winked, voice laced with teasing affection.

Avi walked ahead of Emmy, dark hair limp, but her steps were light, confident. Emmy gritted her teeth, each step an effort. She wiped sweat from her forehead, pushing back damp curls, and waved off the persistent gnats. The jungle felt alive in a way that made the hair on the back of her neck rise. Watching, waiting.

Avi glanced back and smirked. "Charming, isn't it? Perhaps this island was cursed just to spite us. Or perhaps your curse followed you here."

Emmy shot her a look. "You could always turn back."

"Don't worry, Little Mermaid." Avi pushed a clump of low-hanging branches aside to pass through. She laughed, a sharp, mocking sound. "I wouldn't dream of leaving you—and Edmar—without my talents."

As she followed Avi, the branches snapped back, whipping against her face. Heat flared in her cheeks, anger simmering beneath the surface. She bit back a retort, swallowing the sting of pain and humiliation.

Avi laughed.

This is one time I actually wish I could use my magic on someone.

Thankfully, it remained dormant. She didn't trust herself not to lash out, not with the jungle's oppressive heat amplifying her anger.

A hand on her shoulder stopped her. *Edmar.* His gaze, dark with anger for most of the day, softened as he cupped her face, his thumb gently brushing her cheek. She hissed, the touch stinging a cut there.

"I'll talk to her." His jaw tightened. "This has to stop."

She shook her head, frowning. "Just stay away from her."

He dropped his hands, taking a step away from her. "She has no power over me."

She gritted her teeth, her voice tight with a jealousy she couldn't quite conceal. "She cannot do worse to me unless she means to work against our mission."

"How are you feeling?" he asked, his voice quiet but concerned. She knew his real concern. Her magic. Cielan's *help*.

"Fine," she said, forcing a smile. "My magic's quiet."

"Are you sure?" He hesitated, his gaze lingering on her face.

This was the longest he'd looked at her since...

"I had no idea that would happen," she whispered. Her cheeks still heated with what happened earlier today with Cielan, and she wished she could forget it.

"I don't want to think about that." The hard glint in his eyes lasted only a moment. "Are you not telling me something else?"

"What?"

His brow furrowed. "You seem in pain."

"It's the spell," she said, her voice dropping to a whisper. "A side effect of the Sea Witch's magic. It's a constant pain. Like knives in my feet."

A scowl darkened his features. "You've been in pain this whole time?"

She shrugged, trying to make light of it. "It's manageable."

"Manageable?" His voice was rough as he cupped her face, his touch both tender and fierce. "Why didn't you tell me?"

"What could you have done?" she asked, her voice laced with a bitterness she couldn't quite suppress.

He shook his head, his jaw clenched.

"Don't," she said, pulling away, hating the pity she saw in his eyes. "I'm not helpless, Edmar."

"I know. But I want to help, so please let me."

Her heart leaped with those words, but she shook her head, her throat tight. "You can't. There's nothing you can do." She paused, unable to think of how he could help without her becoming a burden, yet knowing this wouldn't satisfy him. She'd been a burden to enough people in her life. "But I promise, if it gets worse, I'll tell you."

His concerned words reassured her, though. Perhaps he was moving beyond what happened earlier, but as they resumed their trek, his silence returned, a wall between them. He avoided touching her, looking at her. A knot of tension tightened in her chest.

He hasn't forgiven me for what happened with Cielan before they left the ship.

He moved ahead, putting himself between her and Avi, his curved sword a blur as he cleared a path through the dense foliage. She hadn't realized he was so skilled with a blade.

A handful of pirates brought up the rear of the group. Not a single member of their group took well to the jungle's oppressive temperatures. All of them were Winter beings. Soon, the heat, the cloying scent of exotic flowers, made her head spin. Exhaustion dragged at her, but she concealed it, determined not to be a burden.

She stumbled, a gnarled root catching her foot, twisting her ankle. She cried out. Edmar was instantly at her side, concern etched on his face, masking the anger that still simmered beneath the surface. No words escaped his pursed lips.

"I'm fine," she said, but relief flooded her as he steadied her, his touch a silent apology. He took her pack, slinging it over his shoulder, a brief, encouraging smile touching his lips. Her heart skipped a beat.

"Look at the Dragon King," Adria teased. "Soft as a summer breeze when it comes to his queen."

"Perhaps," Edmar said, a smirk playing on his lips. "But better a soft heart than a soft head."

Lian chuckled. "Don't go getting too soft now. We'll need that ice in your belly before this is through."

After a quick water break, ensuring Emmy could still travel with her ankle, they continued their journey, the silence between Edmar and her growing heavier with each step. Despite his protective gestures, anger simmered.

Why does he have to hate Cielan? Why did Cielan insist on provoking him? Her stomach churned, but she refused to regret her actions when they protected everyone.

The memory of Cielan's help, of Edmar's icy fury, flashed through her mind. She hadn't expected the tension, the silent battle that had unfolded in her cabin earlier. Edmar insisted on being there, which she understood. But she'd been so naïve, so focused on controlling her magic, that she hadn't considered what could happen and the consequences. *Or Avi's presence.*

Cielan's cold hand had cradled her head, tilting it, exposing her neck. She hadn't seen his expression with him standing behind her, but she'd felt the silent challenge in the way his arm snaked around her waist, pulling her back against his chest.

Edmar's fists had clenched, his jaw tight. Her quick frown had stopped him when he took a step toward them.

Cielan's touch had been a slow, deliberate caress, his tongue a sliver of ice against her heated skin.

Edmar's face had tightened, his skin darkening to that stormy violet color again.

Cielan's fangs had grazed her neck, and then... oblivion. A wave of warmth, of pure, liquid desire, had swept through her, leaving her limbs heavy, her mind falling into a seductive euphoria.

She'd been back in her bed with Edmar, his fingers moving in her, his mouth on her nipple, stoking a firestorm within her. She writhed and moaned. So much pleasure, building and building. The intensity of the heat contrasted with a coldness invading her limbs, each sensation amplifying the other. And then the world had exploded in a shower of golden stars, a wrenching groan escaping her lips as wave after wave of ecstasy washed over her.

She'd sagged, awareness returning slowly, painfully.

Then the realization. She wasn't in bed with Edmar. Instead, Cielan's arm, a cold band of steel, held her upright, her head resting against his chest. She blinked, the hazy warmth of pleasure clinging to her, a world she'd rather not leave.

I came. In Cielan's arms. Mortification washed over her, hot and suffocating. *What must Edmar think? And Avi...*

The temperature in the cabin had plummeted, Edmar's icy magic flaring, his aura crackling with navy-blue light. But Avi's gaze remained fixed on Cielan, a strange gleam in her eyes.

Cielan licked her neck. "Delicious," he murmured against her skin. "Even better than last time."

He deposited her, limp and weak, into Edmar's arms, his gaze meeting her Dragon King's with cool indifference. "My saliva will heal her quickly this time," he said, his voice smooth, addressing Edmar, but his gaze locked on Avi. "Prevent scarring." He turned to the hybrid fae, his hand brushing her arm possessively. "She'll be weak for a few hours. Take care of her."

Then they were both gone, a whisper of displaced air.

She shuddered, the memory still raw, still painful. *It had been the right decision. Hadn't it?* The thought of Avi watching, of Edmar's icy gaze, while she found her pleasure in the vamphyr's embrace, sent a wave of revulsion through her.

Edmar had held her until she felt strong enough to leave the ship, but he didn't talk to her, barely made eye contact. The distance between them now left her breathless. She understood his reaction, but it still hurt. *It's not like I wanted* that *from Cielan.*

Hours later, the path grew steeper, the air thicker. And then, through the trees, she saw it closer—the temple, a dark silhouette against the misty sky.

Edmar stopped next to her, looking up at the temple. "Emira..." His voice was quieter now. "That night... when I taught you to dance..." He hesitated, still not looking at her. "Were you in pain?"

She grimaced, more from the heat and discomfort she felt now. "Yes, but I didn't care. Being with you, dancing. It was worth it."

"I should have known, should have noticed your pain. I'm sorry."

"Every step was a dream come true." Her fingers brushed his, and he finally looked at her, warmth in his eyes, followed by a look of someone lost.

For a heartbeat, the tension between them eased. Then they walked again.

The mist thinned, revealing the mountains' shadows and the temple in all its imposing grandeur. The massive statues flanking the entrance, carved from dark, weathered stone and clad in metallic armor, seemed to watch their every move.

Ahead of them, two pirates exchanged uneasy glances.

"This place..." one muttered. "It feels wrong."

"Captain knows what she's about," the other said, but her voice lacked conviction.

Despite the statues' fearsome appearances, Emmy didn't feel afraid. A strange sense of familiarity settled over her, a pull, deep and resonant, as if she were coming home.

"The Metal God," she whispered, her voice barely audible. "He's waiting for me."

Edmar glanced at her. "What was that?"

"Nothing," she said, shaking her head, dismissing the unsettling feeling.

The jungle pressed in, the air thick with anticipation. It felt like more than just the god watched them. Unseen eyes surveying them from the dense undergrowth.

Does Metallon know I'm coming to wake him?

"Careful, Emmy," Avi's voice, smooth as silk, cut through the humid air. The fae gave her a knowing smile over her shoulder. "This island brings out the darkness. Wicked desires. Uncontrollable impulses."

Heat touched Emmy's cheeks despite her glare. Edmar's hand brushed her arm, a silent reassurance.

Near sunset, when long shadows crawled across the jungle floor, they made camp in a small clearing. The oppressive heat gave way to a humid, but welcome, coolness. While the others set up camp, Edmar left to patrol.

Adria moved swiftly to set traps around the perimeter of their camp. Ever since the Sun God had first appeared and tasked them with this holy quest, Emmy had wanted to question the Water Fae pirate.

Adria crouched to press a wax paper pouch of black powder into the ground, looping hemp twine around a sliver of steel next to flint.

"Anyone who trips this will set off the powder," she said, dusting dirt over the setup. "They'll create a very loud explosion."

Emmy cleared her throat, summoning courage. "Did you know about my mother's quest from the Sun God?"

Adria's gaze flicked toward her, blue and green strands glinting as she worked. "I did."

"Why did she fail?" Not that she could see her mother killing anyone.

Adria's fingers paused on the twine, her voice soft. "Because she fell in love with me."

At her silence, Adria continued. "Solis commanded her to kill me to prevent Sygilla from finding her daughter, to protect both her and their daughter from a future he saw. One of fire and pain. He promised Najla freedom from your father in return." She met Emmy's gaze, her voice heavy with regret. "She chose to save me, because she loved me."

Emmy felt a pang for yet another mermaid, her mother, unable to choose her own future. "She was being forced to marry my father, wasn't she?"

With resignation, Adria nodded. "Yes. She was already betrothed to him, but she didn't love him."

Her heart ached for her mother, for the sacrifices made in the name of love. "Why didn't you save her?"

"She saw my love for Lian. She didn't want to force me to stay with her, just as your father was forcing her. With the Goddess of Love's help, she chose to forget me."

Understanding dawned. That was why she'd never known about Adria from her mother's stories. "Why didn't Solis kill you himself?"

Adria shrugged. "I don't know why he didn't. But after I met the Sea Witch, it was too late. By helping me, he bought himself time to prepare for what he saw coming."

Adria finished setting the last of the traps and Emmy, her mind reeling, wandered back into the camp and sat on her pack several feet away from a fire meant to ward off wild animals.

With sunset, Cielan arrived, his presence a sudden chill in the humid air, his movements effortless, graceful. A wry smile touched his lips, unreturned by the others. His gaze found Avi, and a silent exchange passed between them, a knowing smirk playing on the fae's lips. They spoke in hushed tones, and Emmy's stomach churned. *What does Cielan see in that woman?*

Cielan approached her next, his gaze lingering on her neck. He crouched before her, his presence a sudden chill despite the warmth of the fire.

"How is your magic?" he asked, his voice smooth but laced with a disturbing hunger. "Has my assistance proved effective?"

"It helped," she said, unable to meet his unsettling stare. The memory of his feeding, of the pleasure that had ripped through her, sent a shiver down her spine. *I can't risk turning down his help if my magic reappears, but how would Edmar cope?*

"Does that happen every time?" she blurted out, the question escaping before she could stop it.

Amusement flickered in his eyes. "Does *what* happen, mermaid?"

Heat flooded her cheeks as she avoided his knowing gaze. "The... the feelings."

"Are you asking if my feeding will always bring you such exquisite pleasure? Make you scream with your release?"

"I didn't scream," she said, the words barely a whisper.

He chuckled. "There's nothing wrong with your response. But to answer your question, it depends. Short feedings rarely result in an orgasm. However, a deeper feeding, one that drains your magic," a slow shrug, "it's likely you'll receive immense pleasure from what I'm doing."

"You could have warned me." Her cheeks burned.

"Would it have changed your mind?" His gaze pierced hers, and she knew he already knew the answer. A slow smile curved his lips. "Let me know if you need my *services* again."

He started to rise, but she caught his hand, forcing herself to meet his gaze. "Thank you," she said, her voice low.

He tilted his head, his gaze dropping to where her fingers curled around his. She released him, but he didn't move, a strange expression flickering across his face.

"Interesting," he said, meeting her gaze again as he stood. "Once, in another life, I would have asked if you thanked me for the pleasure or for helping you with your magic." He smiled, a touch of amusement in his eyes. "Now I don't care."

He left before her response, but she still muttered it under her breath, knowing his hearing would pick it up. "Not for pleasure!"

Next to Avi, he smiled.

After a meal of dried meat and bananas, the pirates gathered around the fire, sharing stories and laughter, their voices competing over each other. Adria and Lian's voices rose in song, their harmonies blending with the crackling fire. A mix of envy and longing filled her, wishing for the same ease in her relationship with Edmar. *One day.*

Avoiding the rum, Edmar volunteered to take first watch, silently setting up their tent, ensuring she had what she needed. As she said goodnight to everyone in camp, he stopped beside her, a dark, almost feral gleam in his eyes. Heat sparked in her belly. He cupped her face, his thumb tracing across her lips. Her heart raced, wanting to kiss him but unsure if he'd welcome that.

"One day," he said, capturing her exact sentiment from earlier. Her heart beat faster. "I hope we have all the time in the world to share stories, watch the stars, and dream of our future."

He kissed her, his cold meeting hers with the force of a storm. Once more his kiss made her breathless. He lifted his head, his gaze intense, unwavering, before he released her.

She lay down inside the tent, the scent of him clinging to his shirt as she curled it to her cheek. His absence left an ache in her chest. She closed her eyes, seeking solace in the memory of his touch, falling asleep to a dream of his embrace.

A hand clamped over her mouth, stifling her scream. She was dragged from the tent, thrown into the darkness, her heart pounding against her ribs. A cold blade pressed against her throat, the whisper of steel against her skin.

Chapter 93

EMMY

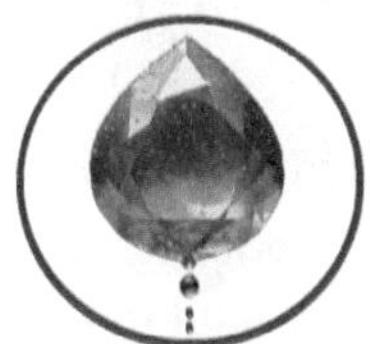

"Don't move." A blade pressed against Emmy's throat, a cold whisper of steel against her skin. "Don't make a sound. Or I will slice your throat."

Her heart raced. She tried to nod, but the blade pressed harder, drawing a bead of warm blood down her neck. Her attacker deftly switched his hands, one gripping her throat, fingers digging into her skin, while the other patted her down.

Darkness. The fire was gone, extinguished. *Edmar.* The thought of him out there, unaware, hurt, sent a wave of panic through her.

A shadow loomed. She screamed.

Her attacker crushed her throat with a shake, and for a heartbeat, she lost consciousness.

"What did I say! Don't make—"

An explosion rocked the ground in a crash of blinding light.

Chaos erupted. A sudden inferno of noise and energy engulfed the camp.

"We're under attack!" Adria's husky voice. "Protect the mermaid!"

Darkness swallowed her, the sounds of ripping fabric and clashing weapons a cacophony in the night.

Her attacker's grip faltered. She twisted to free herself, but his hold tightened, his fingers biting into her throat.

"Where is it?" His free hand swept over her chest, exploring every curve and crevice, a violation that made her legs weak.

Flashes of magical light revealed dark figures, phantoms moving with chilling efficiency, striking and vanishing like serpents weaving through the undergrowth. Everything around her became a blur of shadowy figures clashing in aural lights, the air filling with the scent of blood and the sound of grunts and ragged breaths.

Blazing in a silver energy glow, Lian awakened the campfire with a muttered curse. Silver flames roared, casting dancing shadows over the chaotic camp. Attackers in muted colors, hoods and masks obscuring their features, their eyes gleaming in the firelight as they attacked pirates pulled from sleep.

"Emmy!" Edmar's voice, a roar, cut through the madness. He charged, half-shifted, a blur of scales and firelight, his sword flashing, his claws tearing through the attackers. "Get your hands off her!"

Her heart soared, but her attacker held tight, his grip merciless. Edmar fought his way toward her, his eyes burning with fury, his scales ablaze with magic. He fought valiantly, but they were relentless. More attackers surged forward, swarming like a tide. With shallow breaths, heart racing, her hands and feet numb, her sight narrowed. It slowly retreated to a pinpoint of light, the silver flames.

Suddenly, searing heat ripped through her, a surge of magic reawakening, unstoppable. She screamed, legs buckling beneath her.

Too soon... but her terror unleashed her fire acid.

Her attacker held her, trying to speak, but she was deaf to his words.

No, not now. Please. Desperation fueled the flames, her fire acid raging out of control. She choked, unable to breathe.

Her gem pulsed from inside her tent, a beacon of warning, but her fire acid was unstoppable. It burned through her muscles, searing, agonizing pain wracking her body. She screamed.

Dimly, she was aware of lying on the ground, sobbing with no tears.

Her attacker stood over her, the gem in his hand, a mask obscuring his features, but his eyes, silver with streaks of red, burned into her. She shuddered, exposed, vulnerable, in the hands of a stranger. *Powerless again.*

But her attacker gave her no space to recover, hauling her across the camp, and he deposited her before a tall, lean figure. The leader was clad in shadows, their mask obscuring half their face. Her attacker handed over the gem, a silent exchange of power.

The leader squatted. "Is it true, Sapphira Syrēna?" A feminine voice, commanding but with an underlying tone of awe. "Does this gem control you?"

She hesitated, her defiance a dying ember in the face of her pain and hopelessness. Whoever these people were, they seemed to know exactly what the gem did. Why else attack and purposefully search for the gem?

"Answer me!"

She couldn't resist the compulsion. "Yes."

Why did they target me? Her heart raced too fast.

The woman lurched to her feet, her voice booming. "I have control of your mermaid. Stand down, or she dies!"

The camp froze.

Forcing herself to breathe deeply, calming the storm within, her mind raced with questions. *Who were they? What did they want?*

The pirates, eyes darting between the leader, her, and the masked figures, held their breath. Adria, reluctant, lowered her weapons. The rest followed suit. Fury blazed in Edmar's eyes, but he threw his curved sword to the ground, his hands clenched tightly as he shifted back into his human form.

They were allowed to pack up camp, strap on their gear, and then, one by one, the masked figures bound the pirates' hands. Only she remained free, but then a hand grasped her, pulling her upright. She hissed, sharp pain radiating through her feet.

The leader, silver eyes narrowed, studied the gem. "How do I turn off the light?"

She swallowed hard, hating the feeling of helplessness crawling inside her skin beneath the fire acid. "If I move, the light will intensify. But if I stay still, it will dim and I can control my magic."

The leader made a sharp clicking sound with her tongue. A hulking figure, taller than the leader and twice as wide, stepped forward. Silent gestures passed between them, and he swiftly lifted Emmy into his arms, his grip strong and sure.

Another set of clicking sounds. A second attacker disappeared into the shadows.

She tensed, aware of the hulking figure's strength, the vulnerability of her position.

"Control your magic, mermaid. Put out this light," the leader said.

She hated this. *Powerless. A pawn.* Only this time, she didn't know what they wanted from her. Her magic pulsed beneath the surface, a volatile force threatening to erupt with her fear.

She scanned the faces, searching. Cielan was gone. Avi, too. All the rest still alive, if bloody, and one with a broken arm.

Edmar's eyes met hers, burning with fury.

They were prisoners, surrounded by an enemy they didn't understand. But the attackers had shown restraint, leaving them alive. That thought, a lifeline, kept her going.

She closed her eyes, seeking refuge in the familiar rhythm of her breath, the familiar calm of her meditative state. Control her magic. Control her pain.

When she opened her eyes, the leader nodded, Emmy's gem dim again. More sharp clicking sounds emanated from the leader's lips, and the attackers pushed the group forward, their movements silent and efficient, no light to lead their way as they moved swiftly through the night.

After that, the journey became a blur of sensations—the darkness, the heat, the humidity, the oppressive scent of so many plants—all amplified by her fear and the growing pressure of her magic.

Her limbs grew heavy, thoughts clouded by exhaustion. She tried to track their movements, but the darkness was impenetrable. The attackers navigated the jungle as if they were blind.

But who are they?

The silver eyes suggested fae. Most likely Metal Fae, considering their location. But the man who carried her... his eyes were darker. A hybrid? A human? Not all of them were fae.

When they entered a network of tunnels, her pulse quickened. The tunnels pressed in, a suffocating darkness that sent a wave of panic through her. Dripping water, echoing silence, earthy scents. It was a horrifying echo of the tunnels she'd been trapped in with the Summer Child's Siren Call. Beneath the Malustra Woods, with the spider mole.

She shivered, drawing deep breaths. This time was different. She wasn't alone. But the fear persisted. "Where are we going?" She whispered, hoping the leader wouldn't hear.

Her bearer didn't respond.

"Please," she said. "Talk to me. Anything. Anything to distract me from this fear."

He grunted, a low, guttural sound. She wished she could see his face.

"Will you kill me?" Her voice trembled. "Will you kill us?"

This time, his body tensed, his fingers tightening just slightly. "No."

A rush of relief released the tension in her shoulders, but her fear remained. Her breathing sped up, her heart beating faster. "Tell me a story?"

"Quiet," was all he said.

After that, she didn't try to talk again. Instead, she delved into a meditative state to control her fear, worried about what these people planned, and wondering about Cielan and Avi.

Are they in danger? Never mind that. *Are we in danger?*

Maybe this was why no one ever returned from Aelunis. Death was not always the worst outcome.

Hours later, they emerged from the tunnels into the dawn, the sky washed in shades of dark violet and magenta. Fresh air washed over her, a welcome reprieve from the suffocating tunnels.

But the jungle's heat and humidity returned with a vengeance, stealing the last of her strength. Fire acid smoldered beneath her skin, spreading through her limbs like wildfire. She gritted her teeth, her jaw aching with the effort to hold her magic in check.

She had to hold on, refusing to give in. She'd survived too much to break now.

Then she looked up. *The temple.* Looming closer than before, a dark stone monument to ancient power and gods. They were allowed a brief respite, a chance to relieve themselves, drink water, and adjust their packs before being bound again.

Her bearer allowed her the same respite before picking her up again.

She scanned the crowd, searching for Edmar. His hands were bound, his clothes torn from his partial shift, but even from a distance, his gaze held her captive, a simmering intensity that made her stomach flip.

Will it ever be our time?

Before leaving the area, she took advantage of the time to assess their captors. Loose pants and tunics in dark shades of green and brown, most with silver eyes, light tawny to gray skin. Mostly Metal Fae, as she thought, but still with hoods covering their hair and ears, some could be fae hybrids. At least two humans with dark eyes and brown skin.

With a renewed sense of urgency, the attackers pushed them forward.

They marched through the dense jungle, their silent efficiency unnerving. No one spoke, their focus solely on reaching their destination. No doubt, it was the Metal God's temple, which still called to her, compelling her as much as her gem. Thrilling and terrifying.

By midday, they reached the temple, a towering monument carved into the mountain, its entrance guarded by two statues whose metallic eyes and armored bodies glinted under the high sun.

Two large forces met them at the foot of the stairs, winding up into the temple. The first, clad in muted greens and browns, their faces obscured by hoods and masks. The second, warriors in gleaming armor and full helmets, bearing a dark red star etched into their breastplates: two intersecting tetrahedrons.

Two figures in deep crimson robes stood before the warriors. Embroidered on their robes, the Flower of Life, an ancient symbol of creation.

The geometric pattern seemed to thrum with an unseen energy.

What does it mean?

Was it connected to the Metal God?

The leader of their warriors flashed hand signals. Her bearer lowered her, her feet hitting the ground with a jarring thud. Sharp, stabbing pain shot up her legs, sending a wave of nausea through her.

When the female leader came to her side to push her forward, she stumbled, crashing to the ground. She gasped, her head hanging low as fire acid pulsed through her muscles. She counted her breaths, her mother's voice echoing in her mind.

"Stop!" Edmar roared, his voice a storm of fury.

Over a dozen weapons whispered, leaving their sheaths at Edmar's shout. She raised her head to find him, but too many legs surrounded her.

The legs parted before her, creating a path. One of the crimson-robed figures crouched in front of her. The man lowered his hood, revealing silver-streaked black hair and mismatched eyes: one blue, one brown. An intricate tattoo, elegant but sharp lines like a map of forgotten knowledge, curled on one side of his face.

His gaze was unsettling, piercing. It felt as though he could see beyond her flesh and bone, into the very core of her being. Her heart pounded, and she sucked in breath, vainly trying to rein in her magic.

The jungle fell silent, the air thick with anticipation. A sense of inevitability settled over her. She'd faced gods and monsters, men who thought themselves invincible. But this man felt different. Stronger. Older.

And then he spoke, his voice resonating through the silent jungle. "We've been waiting for you, Sapphira Syrēna."

Chapter 94

EDMAR

The midday sun beat down, its heat doing little to soothe the cold fury festering in Edmar's chest. He stood at the foot of the temple steps, his gaze fixed on Emira, an enraged beast caged beneath his skin.

"We've been waiting for you, Sapphira Syrēna." The words echoed in the oppressive silence.

What in the eight hells did that mean?

At least they were still alive. No casualties. He'd already noted the two enemy forces. One he recognized. Templars, warriors in full armor, dedicated to serving one of the gods.

At least we're in the right place.

The other group, those ninja-like warriors, remained a mystery. He didn't recognize them, nor the robes worn by the two men, adorned with the intricate Flower of Life embroidered on crimson fabric. Their hostility put him on edge.

The taller of the robed men, with dark silver-streaked hair, placed his hands on Emira's shoulders where she sat on the ground, his gaze lingering on her with a possessive intensity that set his blood on fire.

Edmar ripped free of his restraints, his fury blazing, and half shifted into his draconian form. "Get your hands off my wife!" he roared.

He surged forward, his strength a whirlwind of rage, dragging the warriors with him, knocking them aside. Cold, sharp spears ringed his neck, forcing him to stop. He snarled, mist swirling around him.

The man stood, gaze upon him, assessing him. Contempt and something else—a flicker of recognition, perhaps, or dark amusement—blazed in his mismatched eyes. The man dismissed him and turned back to Emira.

"You are married to this... *Ice Dragon*?"

The disdain in the man's voice was unmistakable, and the emphasis on "Ice Dragon" drove Edmar to scrape his claws against his scales, a harsh screech that echoed off the mountains, causing the Templars to flinch.

The ninja-like warriors, though, remained stoic.

The man who touched Emira also did not react. His face was a mask, the tattoo unwavering.

What's his problem with me? Before he could demand answers, Emira's hands glowed faintly, volatile magic crackling beneath her skin.

"Are we your prisoners?" Her voice, strained but steady, sliced through the tension.

"That depends." The man smiled, his mismatched eyes betraying no warmth. "Can you stay a few days at the temple?"

"This was our destination."

He nodded. "Good. Let's go inside the Temple of Khalanthrax where we can learn more about each other."

The Temple of Khalanthrax—the Iron Fortress.

Fitting for the Metal God's resting place.

The female leader of the ambush party approached the shorter robed man, a silent exchange passing between them, their hands moving swiftly. She handed him Emira's gem.

Edmar didn't recognize any of the sign language the ninja-like warriors used.

Then a silent exchange passed between the two robed men before the taller one turned back to Emira, a charming smile playing on his lips. "Let's get our guests settled."

Edmar wasn't fooled. The glint in the man's eyes was anything but welcoming. *He's toying with us.*

The shorter man made a series of hand signals, and the attackers, with a coordinated organization that bordered on supernatural, sprang into action. Before Edmar could react, the same warrior who'd carried Emira now swept her up into his arms. She closed her eyes, her magic subdued, and disappeared into the mass of robed figures.

"Where are you taking her?" he roared.

Spears pressed into his neck again, silencing his protest. They prodded him toward the temple. Climbing the stairs took nearly an hour, and he cursed every step. He could have flown faster than this, but spears could tear through leathery wings just as easily as the skin of his neck.

At the top, he passed between the towering statues of the Metal God, their metallic eyes seeming to follow him, weighing him, judging him. A pulsing energy, ancient and powerful, vibrated through the stone. The hair on his arms stood on end.

A vast hall stretched before him, its high ceiling supported by massive metal columns. Every step echoed on the polished stone floor, inlaid with intricate geometric patterns, triangles within triangles. A large altar, crafted from various metals and centered by a brazier, hinted at sacred rituals. The lack of dried blood on its surface eased some of Edmar's worry.

Monks, their robes shimmering with woven metal threads, moved with silent grace and precise discipline, their eyes fixed on some distant point. Warriors, clad in gleaming armor, stood guard, vigilant.

A guard escorted him down a narrow corridor to a small room, the heavy door slamming shut behind him. Confined, he paced, jerking at each turn, his stomach hardening, his mind a whirlwind. *Emira.* He had to find her. The thought of her in pain was unbearable. He smashed his fist against the unyielding stone wall, leaving a trail of blue blood.

After what felt like an eternity, a monk arrived, silently gesturing for him to follow.

A large communal bathhouse awaited. In the center, a sunken pool steamed gently, the rhythmic splashing of water the only sound. Monks, clad in shimmering robes, moved silently about, their presence calm and unnerving.

Lian sat in the pool, his shoulders slumped, his gaze distant. Edmar joined him, his mind churning. He grabbed a bar of soap from a silver plate.

"Where's Adria?" he asked, his voice low.

"They separated us," Lian said, his voice tight, although he looked in the direction that his Soul Half probably called to him. "And I haven't seen Avi."

"Damn vamphyr," Edmar muttered, his anger flaring. "He took the first chance to abandon us, likely taking Avi with him."

Lian nodded grimly. "At least my daughter is safe."

While Edmar washed, he surreptitiously scanned the room. It seemed to be made of stone and steel, every exit guarded by warriors clad in armor bearing the two intersecting tetrahedrons.

The air thickened, a shift in the atmosphere. The two red-robed figures from earlier entered the room. Edmar didn't move, but he felt the taller man's regard lingering on him, assessing him.

Teal scales layered down his arms and the back of his hands, a natural response to the man's intensity. The other man's skin, pale blue, almost periwinkle, was unusual. His ears weren't pointed. So, a fae hybrid? A silver circlet of gemstones sparkled against his dark, silver-threaded hair. Some type of royalty, quickly confirmed by the man's words.

"Hello, King Edmar of Cyaneus. I am Vayushin." His bitter voice carried a commanding air. "Lord and Regent of Aelunis."

Edmar's jaw tightened. "Where is my wife?"

Vayushin ignored the question and gestured to the second man. "And this is my Royal Secretary and High Templar, Solvrev."

His eyes narrowed. *High Templar?* Two powerful figures, one ruling the people, the other charged with their salvation. They seemed to have a long-standing, comfortable partnership.

Neither appeared older, Vayushin's silver streaks a result of his heritage, which also applied to Solvrev's shock of white hair, severely pulled back into a long ponytail. Both had deep-set, hooded eyes. But there the similarities ended between the two. Vayushin's periwinkle skin a complement to Solvrev's dark gray skin.

However young they appeared, Vayushin's eyes gleamed with an ancient and knowing gaze, holding a depth that Edmar couldn't decipher. "I've spoken with the Sapphira Syrēna, your wife. I know why you've come to Aelunis."

His muscles tensed, a low growl rumbling in his throat. A blue aura shot through with golden sparks flared around him, the air crackling with energy. He took a step forward, his claws extending, his fangs bared in a silent snarl. *The man spoke to my wife without me?* This was no true royal to disregard the social norms expected from all nobility.

"As long as you remain peaceful," Vayushin said, his voice smooth, controlled. "You are free to move about the temple."

His reply was brusque. "Am I allowed to see my wife now?"

Vayushin's gaze drifted over his chest, then lower, lingering before returning to meet his eyes. The heat in the man's gaze was unmistakable, something charged and unsettling, and it only fueled his frustration.

"Once you've finished your bath," Vayushin said, his voice smooth, controlled, "you will be reunited with your queen. We'll dine together this evening."

He narrowed his eyes. There was a hidden message in his words, a warning. As soon as the men departed, he vented to Lian. "The man hates me. But I don't know why?"

Lian frowned, his gaze fixed on the receding figures. "He looks familiar." A hint of uncertainty in his voice. "I feel like I know him, but..."

Unease intensified as Edmar dressed in silence, slipping on a knee-length linen tunic and a sarong-style wrap. Something about all of this didn't sit right, but he didn't know why.

Chapter 95
EDMAR

A monk escorted Edmar to a set of interconnected spacious chambers, walls adorned with intricate metal tapestries depicting scenes from Metallon's life and his time on the planet. A tropical breeze, fragrant and warm, beckoned him forward, leading him to the last chamber. Here, a balcony opened to a view of the jungle below on the backside of the mountain.

Relief flooded him when he saw Emira lying on a wide bed, his old shirt in her hands. He rushed to her side, whispering her name. When her eyes fluttered open, there was a moment of quiet understanding between them.

Her sapphire curls were damp, and she wore a light aqua silk dress tied with a decorative white and silver sash. The clothing was different, but her beauty was breathtaking. With a heart beating too fast, he took her hand, their fingers intertwining. Her skin was cool beneath his touch, her face a mask of serenity.

"Kiss me," she whispered, her voice barely a sigh.

Even though he worried about causing more pain, he couldn't deny her request. His gaze lingered on her lips, soft and slightly parted, the faintest tremble at the corner of her mouth making his pulse stutter. The scent of her, the delicate mix of coconut and flowers, filled his lungs, grounding him and making his head swim all at once.

His hand touched her cheek. The world seemed to slow, their precarious position and the coming quest fading, until the only thing that existed was her. The rise and fall of her chest, the flutter of her lashes as she closed her eyes. His thumb brushed across her cheek, barely a whisper, and she leaned into him, that tiny movement unlocking something in his chest, freeing the tension coiled so tightly there since she was taken in the ambush.

When their lips finally met, it was soft at first, tentative. A gentle press, making him shudder, igniting his skin with a sudden, overwhelming warmth. His other hand skimmed along her shoulder, down her side, feeling the soft curve of her waist beneath his fingertips, a potent reminder of how deeply he desired her.

She breathed a sigh into his mouth. The sound sent his heart thudding wildly, and he imagined a lifetime of these moments, these breathless, stolen kisses, with her.

When she guided his hand to her breast, he hesitated, concern outweighing desire. "Your magic?"

Her large emerald eyes looked up at him, sleepy, but filled with her desires. "Arousal calms my magic. I had hoped we could test the theory that it might also have lingering effects, reduce the possibility of it flaring again."

Every fiber of him thrummed with the need to claim her, to possess her completely. The thought of their union calming her magic sent a surge of desire through him. He kissed her again, a deeper, more demanding kiss this time.

"Emmy," he whispered against her lips, "Tell me if it hurts."

With her nod, he kicked off his sandals and straddled her. Their kiss deepened, and the world seemed to tilt, spinning away, leaving just the two of them wrapped in heat and need. Every inch of his body surged with sensation—the way her lips moved against his, matching the rhythm of his own, her fingers curling into his shirt.

He longed to lose himself in her, but as he untied the sash, his fingers trembled. *Is this too much?* Surely she would tell him to stop if she was in pain.

Slipping his fingers along the dress's edge where it wrapped around her, the delicate silk whispered over her breasts, her hardened nipples easily seen through the fabric.

He closed his mouth over one, sucking it lightly through the silk. A tremor ran through her with a moan. He hesitated, gauging her reaction, searching for signs of pain.

"Is this working?" he asked

She opened her eyes. "Don't stop," she said with a whimper. Her hands tightened in his hair.

Uncertainly, he unwrapped the dress, letting it fall away, revealing a white cotton slip tied at the shoulders. He met her open gaze as he untied the slip. Looking for any signal to stop, any flicker of pain in her eyes.

Slowly, he pulled the slip down over her breasts, but he kept it taut so that it flicked over her nipples. He loved seeing her reactions, the way her eyes rolled back, the sounds she made. She was so easily aroused by her breasts. But he was constantly on edge, waiting for any sign that he needed to stop.

He shook with his need to bury himself in her, which warred with his fear of hurting her.

He cupped her breasts, feeling their fullness, the heat of her arousal. Her body arched instinctively, and he jumped back and left the bed.

She sat up, blinking her large eyes. "What is it?"

She was a goddess, her breasts full and inviting, her lips swollen from his kisses. *How many times do I have to hold myself back from her?*

He paced, a storm raging within him. "I cannot stop worrying about hurting you." He shook his head at being a fool. "I shouldn't have done this."

"Edmar."

He turned, his heart pounding as she moved, worried about her pain.

She knelt on the bed, her dress discarded, the slip hanging low on her hips. "You haven't hurt me," she said, her voice thick with desire. "You've eased the pain." She held up a hand. "Please."

He clenched his fists, knowing he couldn't continue to seduce his wife, but also wanting to give into her plea, because he also wanted her.

"Cabezon!" Frustration darkened her cheeks.

"What?"

"Cabezon," she said, a touch of humor in her voice. "You're just as stubborn as the most stubborn sea creature I know." She tried to get off the bed, but when she put a foot down on the floor, she hissed with pain.

Instinct made him move, but she waved him back. He stopped. This was the test. He would push through his objections and fears, give her all the ecstasy she asked for if it saved her magic from returning.

Squaring her shoulders—a movement thrusting her breasts forward—she walked toward him. His breath caught. His body throbbed, responding to the sight of her, wanting, needing... This goddess came to him, and he was powerless.

At first, relief lit her eyes. Then the last step to him, she crumpled with a cry. He caught her, taking her back to the bed.

With her eyes closed, her skin a paler shade of green, and her fingertips glowing, she used her breathing exercises to calm her fire acid. He leaned over, taking one of her nipples into his mouth, hoping to ease the pain.

When pleasurable moans broke her silence, he lifted his head to look at her. They didn't need to say anything. They both knew he couldn't help her with controlling her magic enough to allow continued movement. He could only soothe and calm any magic that flared within her.

"I need Cielan," she whispered, her voice ragged.

The admission cut through him. He tried to nod, but jealousy, a sharp, bitter taste, filled his mouth. "I don't know where he is," he said, forcing the words out. "But if he's coming, we won't see him until sunset."

"Please." Her musical voice had lost its harmony.

He hated she needed the vamphyr, hated the thought of Cielan touching her, draining her blood. But he couldn't deny her. He squeezed her hand gently. "I'll find him and bring him to you."

He'd do anything for her, even if it meant accepting the vamphyr touching her again.

As he sat by her side, so much pressed down on him. For a moment, he lost himself in her, tasting her, touching her. But he couldn't forget their reason for being here. To wake a god, hoping he could cure her and not demand her life in return.

When stressed, he relied on his Frostlands to feel like he had some command of his life. But it had failed him ever since Emira had thrown herself into the ocean to save everyone.

The temple, Vayushin, Cielan—it was all spiraling out of his control. But one thing remained clear. He would do whatever Emira wanted, no matter the cost.

CHAPTER 96

EDMAR

Fading sunlight slanted through the open balcony, casting long shadows across the room. Edmar paced restlessly, his eyes flicking from the sturdy metal door to Emira's sleeping form on the bed. He had already checked the halls and noted the armored templars stationed outside. Their presence grated on him, silent sentinels watching his every move.

Prisoners in all but name.

Escape routes unraveled in his mind, each plan highlighting weaknesses in the temple's layout, guard positions, and defenses. He would secure weapons; he would find a way out.

Yet, his thoughts always circled back to Emira. He couldn't leave her, and right now, she couldn't even move to wake Metallon or leave the temple. In her current condition, he feared what that meant for their quest.

But then Cielan was an option, if he appeared tonight.

Desire warred with fear and dread, with no place to go, no Frostlands to bury his emotions. But the need to protect her eclipsed all else.

He wished he could speak with his brothers once the sun set, but his two-way mirror was cracked during the attack on their camp, the magic released from the glass. So, it was just him and the pirates—and the vamphyr who would likely help no one but Avi, and maybe Emira, if he found them this night.

A sharp knock at the door shattered the silence.

"Edmar." Lian's voice was tense, urgent.

He opened the door, and Lian slipped inside, his face grim. "I lost the Kraken."

Code for Vayushin.

Frustration tightened his jaw as he shut the door. "What happened?"

"There are tunnels within this place, hidden well. He slipped through one, didn't even leave a ripple."

Silver hair askew, Lian recounted his and Adria's attempts to follow Vayushin and Solvrev. They'd split up when the men parted ways, but Vayushin vanished down a hallway with no visible exit.

"Either he's hiding something," Lian said, his voice low. "Or he knew I was on his tail."

"And Adria?"

Before Lian could answer, Adria burst into the room, her eyes sharp and alert. "The Eel..." she began, then stopped, her gaze falling on Emira. "Is she?"

"Asleep," Edmar said, his voice tight.

With a slight easing of her shoulders, Adria joined them at the table. Their voices dropped to hushed tones.

"The Eel's the one you've got to keep both eyes on," she said without preamble, the Eel being code for Solvrev. "He's got the current flowing his way, just as much pull as the Kraken."

His suspicions about Vayushin deepened as they discussed the templars' tight surveillance and the hidden doors within the temple.

"These templars move like clockwork, and every cog turns when the Eel says so. The Kraken might steer the ship, but the Eel, he's the real rudder. They don't move without his nod."

An interesting dynamic: the templars following Solvrev in faith, Solvrev answering to Vayushin in politics. But there was still the unanswered question of the warriors who had ambushed them. Who were they and who did they answer to?

She leaned closer, her voice barely a whisper. "I found a door, deep in the mountain's heart. Big as a galleon, with templars swarming like sharks. That's where the treasure lies. Where Metallon waits."

"I wasn't able to find out much about the warriors who ambushed us." A headache pulsed behind Edmar's eyes. "I couldn't get close to one without them vanishing, and the templars won't speak about them. This might cause trouble later."

Despite the disciplined warriors surrounding them, he knew they needed an exit plan, and quickly.

"I believe they are a Nintura," Lian said.

Adria looked up at him. "A secret order?"

"Ninexjutsu," Lian said, confirming. "A way of moving taught to all the orders. I may not have finished my training for the Order of the Winter Child, but I recognize the forms."

"The Winter Child?" Emira's weak voice barely pitched loud enough for Edmar to hear.

Relief and longing warred within him as he crossed to her side. She'd been sleeping most of the day. Kneeling, he took her hand. "Do you know something?"

"Not really." She took a long, deep breath. "Morvella, the Ironfang werewolf. She was searching for the Winter Child. She believes he can oppose the Summer Child."

"The Summer Child?" Both Adria and Lian asked at the same time.

Edmar explained the Sun God's prophecy, the Summer Child's coming birth, the reason for the holy quest. At this point, it didn't matter if they knew everything. He turned back to Emira. "How much does the Kraken—Vayushin—know about what we're doing here?"

"He knows about the Sun God's request to wake Metallon. I didn't mention the other gods," she said, her voice soft but steady.

"Does he know we have the Sun Stone?"

"No." Emira closed her eyes with a deep breath. Then opened them again. "I don't think he means us harm, Edmar. He returned my gem."

The tension in his chest remained despite the relief. He couldn't shake the feeling of danger. Before he could question her further, the door swung open, Cielan entering with Avi on his heels.

Adria's gaze snapped to the vamphyr. "What be you doing here? You should've taken her back to the ship!"

Cielan smiled, nonchalant as always, eyes glinting. "She wanted to be here. I couldn't refuse her." The vamphyr's gaze flew to Emira, a shadow falling over his eyes as his fangs descended. "The taint in her blood grows stronger."

While Edmar completely sympathized with the vamphyr's inability to refuse Avi anything, he used every bit of his energy to contain his anger, fists shaking. The depth of his feelings for Emira drove him to speak now. "She asked for you."

Frustration and resignation warred on Adria's face as she linked her arm with Avi's. "Come on, darling. We'll find you a room. Lian?"

Avi pulled away from her mother. "I would like to watch again. It was so enlightening last time."

"Avi, what be getting into you?" A thunderous look crossed Adria's face.

The hybrid fae lifted her chin as if looking down on her mother. "I'm finally living my life my way without you shadowing me all the time."

A flash of hurt quickly left Adria's eyes when her gaze flicked to Emira. "There be no call for being mean to others."

"Cielan doesn't mind."

Edmar cleared his throat. "Adria, I appreciate your intervention, but I really want to get this over with. To give Emira relief."

"I understand." But she gave her daughter a frown while letting Lian pull her away.

Cielan tilted his head, inquisitive eyes now on Edmar. "Knowing what I offer, what she will feel, you would still allow this?"

Through gritted teeth, he said, "Help her."

Cielan crossed the room in a blur, hovering over Emira before he could react. The vamphyr climbed onto the bed, caging her with his body. Her eyes opened as he brushed her hair aside.

"Your blood sings to me," he murmured, gaze fixed on the pulse in her throat. "Do you consent to me drinking from you?"

Emira looked at him, concern heavy in her glassy eyes, but he also saw her pain. Tight-lipped, he gave her a nod.

But then she caught sight of Avi.

"Not with her here." She grimaced, as if speaking hurt.

The vamphyr's gaze never left her throat, almost spellbound by her pulse. However, he spoke loud enough for Avi to hear. "Leave."

Avi crossed her arms with a smirk. "I don't think so."

Cielan lifted Avi off the ground in a rush of wind, his hand a vise around her throat. His usual stoicism was a grotesque mockery as his face twisted. "You deny me your blood, Dolcivita. I am starving, so you will obey me in this."

Avi's face turned a mottled wine-red as she struggled, hands scrabbling at his wrist. Finally, she choked out a nod. He lowered her to the ground, letting her go.

Fear and fury battled on the fae's face. She shot Emira a venomous look, rubbing her throat, but left without another word.

The vamphyr was on Emira again in a heartbeat. "May I feed from you?"

Emira nodded, her voice a faint whisper. "Please."

"I need your words, mermaid."

"I consent to you feeding from me."

Cielan tilted Emira's head, his thumb tracing her pulse before he licked her skin, fangs gleaming. Ice crept into Edmar's veins, magic surging, frosting the walls. The temperature plummeted as he fought for control.

"Don't worry, dragon," Cielan said, amusement in his eyes. "She's in good hands."

Then Cielan sank his fangs into Emira's neck.

His vision blurred, fists clenching. He hated it all. Cielan's touch, Emira's involuntary responses, the soft moans, her hands pulling the vamphyr closer, her body arching into his, then that final groan with her release. He wanted to tear Cielan away from her, to shield her from his dark embrace, but he held himself rigid.

He had to allow it. Emira needed this.

"What can kill you?" Edmar gritted out, his voice tight. One day, he would ensure Emira no longer needed the vamphyr.

Cielan released Emira with a final, lingering lick. His gaze, devoid of color, settled on Edmar. "Nothing yet, dragon. But I'm always open to suggestions."

CHAPTER 97

EDMAR

A templar arrived to escort them to dinner a couple of hours later. Emira, though still pale and just waking from sleep, moved more easily, wincing only occasionally. She blamed the lingering sting of the Sea Witch's spell.

She leaned into Edmar as they walked, her voice low. "When Cielan drinks my blood..."

The mere mention of the vamphyr made his fists clench.

She continued. "I see us. His magic, whatever he does, I don't remember he's there until it's done."

Part of his tension eased, even if he didn't really know what she meant. "What do you see about us?"

A blush warmed her cheeks as she lowered her gaze. "I see you touching me, kissing me." Her fingers tightened on his arm. "But more than seeing, I feel it. All the sensations, as if it's happening again. It feels real."

"Comforting, though I still wouldn't wish him touching you."

He studied the templar escorting them. Controlled, disciplined, his focus was absolute. These warriors were different. Their fanatical devotion, their precision, hinted at something beyond obedience.

She tilted her gaze up to him. "Do you think all vamphyrs do this? Offer this euphoria to ensure their prey returns?"

Clever woman. He hadn't considered that. His own emotions were a maelstrom when Cielan fed, the Frostlands lost to a dark, icy sea. "I love how your mind works," he murmured.

The scent of roasted meat, unfamiliar spices, and something sharp and tangy hung heavy in the Temple's Hearth—the name given for their dining area. Flickering torches cast long shadows over tables laden with food, platters of glistening fish, delicately wrapped rolls, and steaming bowls emitting a fragrant umami-rich aroma. Templars guided them to their seats. He found himself at the far end, away from Vayushin, though Solvrev sat beside him.

He shoved his chair back as Emira was led to the opposite end, beside Vayushin. Instantly, templars moved, hands hovering near sword hilts.

Vayushin arched a bored eyebrow, though his mismatched eyes held a glint of challenge. "A problem, *Ice Dragon*?"

Emira flashed him a warning look.

They needed to placate their host, at least until they woke Metallon. Though Vayushin knew of their quest, his stance remained unclear. He might yet try to stop them or imprison them or sacrifice all of them in some bizarre ritual. Who knew? Best to maintain a facade of civility.

He inclined his head in a small bow of deference.

He expected triumph or mockery from Vayushin, but saw something else, a flicker of confusion. It mirrored the expression Vayushin had worn in the baths. Edmar sat again, and the templars relaxed.

As dinner was served, his attention shifted briefly to the spread on the granite table inlaid with intricate geometric patterns of bronze and gold. Nearby, small dumplings floated in a savory broth, their delicate skins translucent in the golden glow of brass lanterns suspended from chains above. The light refracted off polished metal sconces, casting soft, dancing patterns across lacquered bowls with colorful, unfamiliar dishes. Thin slices of raw fish shimmered like gemstones atop wooden boards arranged beside mounds of what looked like finely shredded radish, strange pickled roots, and bright green paste. He eyed it all with suspicion, hesitating, unsure of how to eat such fare, but the aroma was undeniably enticing.

He tried to focus on the conversation, but his gaze was drawn back to Emira again and again. Fury simmered, fueled by Vayushin's barbed comments about the Ice Dragon's attractiveness blinding everyone to his faults and his apparent failings as a protector.

"Patience, Edmar," Solvrev murmured, leaning close. His sharp brown eyes flashed with something wild, barely contained. "You do not yet have the full picture."

"Then enlighten me."

"Turnabout is fair play," Solvrev said, with a sly smile. "Do you wish to return his challenge?"

He frowned, picking up a pair of smooth wooden sticks, his unfamiliarity with the utensils evident. *Is this a game?*

An intrigued smile touched Solvrev's lips. "Come closer, Your Majesty."

Was the Eel truly about to share secrets? He inclined his head, while noticing others using the wooden sticks with practiced ease to lift morsels of food to their mouths.

"Do not watch your queen," Solvrev said, whispering in his ear. "Watch Vayushin. What does he do?"

"Whispering in my wife's ear."

"Now smile like you've just received the best head from your queen."

"What?" He jerked back.

Solvrev sighed, waiting until he leaned in again. "Let us use your surprise to your advantage. Is Vayushin watching?"

"Yes." He attempted to mimic the others with the wooden sticks with little success, dropping a piece of grilled fish back into its small dish. Frustrated, he stabbed the fish with the sticks. He recalled Emira at his table for their first meal, the unfamiliar utensils, and empathized all over again.

"Good. Now, think of something that brings you peace. A favorite place, a cherished memory."

Setting the wooden sticks aside, he snatched a piece of the fish with his fingers, ignoring the curious glances from the others. While chewing the surprisingly delicious food, he thought of stargazing with Emira, a smile touching his lips.

"Answer my next questions with a bit of huskiness in your tone." He paused in his instructions. "Is your queen in your thoughts?"

"Yes," he said, making his voice husky.

"And you pull her close, kiss her?"

"Yes."

"Now close your eyes," Solvrev whispered. "Imagine her beneath you."

He didn't need further prompting. Emira, pliant and willing, her moans his alone...

"Good."

The image shattered at Solvrev's word. He opened his eyes, jerking back from the Eel's knowing gaze.

"Look at Vayushin."

The regent no longer spoke with Emira. A dark scowl marred his face.

"I don't understand."

"You needn't," Solvrev said, sitting back. "You've accomplished your goal."

What game was that? But the man didn't seem inclined to say anything else.

Across the table, Adria caught his eye. Her gaze swept the room, cataloging exits, noting the templars' numbers and positions. She leaned close to Lian, murmuring something.

Know your surroundings. Create plans for an escape. And then plan for when that plan fails. Plans within plans. Adria's lessons stayed with him.

"Tell me, Lian," Vayushin said, his voice cutting through the chatter. "What is your lineage? Moon Fae? Metal Fae?"

"My mother was Moon Fae," Lian replied, his voice guarded, "my father human."

A knowing look entered Vayushin's mismatched eyes. "You speak of the past. They are gone?"

Lian's eyes darkened. "Yes."

"My condolences." But his tone was flat.

Lian's gaze didn't waver. "I knew someone, long ago, with mismatched eyes like yours."

Vayushin's lips twitched. "A rare distinction."

"If we weren't on Aelunis..." Lian's voice grew sharper. "I would say it is impossible. But I must ask, are you Kyran Silverwing?"

"What would a pirate know of Kyran Silverwing?" Vayushin chuckled, a harsh, grating sound.

"I was not always a pirate." Lian straightened. "I was once a prince, heir to the Moon Fae throne. Kyran Silverwing was my uncle, wed to my aunt, Aysima."

Silence descended.

Finally, Vayushin spoke, his gaze sliding toward Edmar. "Kyran Silverwing, King of the Griffins, has been missing for over a thousand years." His gaze swept the table. "Kyran is my cousin, the last of our line save myself. I await the day he returns to his people."

His people? The griffins! How many remained?

Vayushin's animosity made sense now. Edmar's parents, The Scorching, the griffins' desperate pleas for help.

A shadow of guilt twisted inside him, a sour tang settling on his tongue. He'd learned the truth through years of quiet research—the brutal war, the systematic genocide of the griffins, the Ice Dragons' refusal to intervene.

The griffins and Ice Dragons had been allies, but his parents were bound to protect humankind. The griffins' request would have meant sacrificing innocent lives. Vayushin should know this. But grief could blind even the most rational mind.

After The Scorching, everyone had believed the griffins extinct.

His fingers tightened around his goblet, the metal biting into his skin. He wanted to apologize, to explain his parents' decision, but pride choked the words. Guilt, anger, and a grudging understanding of Vayushin's hatred warred within him.

Vayushin smirked, as if sensing his epiphany. Then, deliberately, he turned back to Emira, his voice deceptively gentle. "You look unwell, despite your assurances."

"Just weary from travel and my magic."

Vayushin's gaze flicked back to him. Tension crackled, reaching a breaking point. A challenge burned in the griffin's mismatched eyes, a mocking smile playing on his lips. "I'm surprised you haven't already lost your queen, Ice Dragon. Your protection seems... ineffective. Like father, like son."

His fists clenched. The griffin was deliberately goading him, but he couldn't rise to the bait. "What are you hiding, Vayushin?"

The griffin narrowed his eyes.

Emira's hand settled on Vayushin's arm. "Why were you waiting for me?"

The griffin's smile softened as he turned to her. "Patience, Sapphira Syrēna. All will be revealed. But first, you must rest. Regain your strength."

He glanced again at Edmar, a warning in his mismatched eyes. "Waking the Metal God may kill you."

CHAPTER 98

EMMY

We need a lot of your blood...

Vayushin's words echoed in her mind as she paced restlessly, a silk skirt and tunic swirling around her. He'd explained very little about the ritual last night at dinner. Really nothing other than that she was needed, that she didn't need to move but needed to be at full strength, then evaded the rest of her questions.

The painite gem, warm against her skin on a chain around her neck—Morvella having taken her golden band—rose and fell with each breath. Each step sent a sharp sting through her feet, a welcome ache compared to the fire acid that could simmer in her veins. She had risked everything to escape her father, to find a cure. Fear, even the fear of death, couldn't stop her now.

Her gaze drifted to Edmar, seated at the writing desk, his brow furrowed in concentration. Even in this moment of quiet contemplation, he exuded a raw energy that drew her in. He glanced up, concern in his ocean-colored eyes. But there was something more, too, in the way his gaze lingered on her as she paced, the way his eyes darkened momentarily. Heat curled in her belly, stealing her breath.

He masked whatever he'd been thinking behind concern—about her magic—but she sensed a deeper longing, a hunger like hers.

Rested, her magic stable, she felt Metallon's power more keenly. A deep, resonant hum vibrated through the temple, through her very being. Last night, she'd dreamed of her Father God, his voice a rumble of raw energy, his eyes like molten silver. He called to her, and she yearned to answer, to understand. But now every attempt to leave the chamber was met by impassive templars blocking her way.

I need answers. I need to see Vayushin.

"Emmy." Edmar's voice, soft yet firm, cut through her thoughts. He crossed the room, resting his hands on her shoulders. Heat spread through her from his touch, leaving her breathless. "You need to calm down. Your magic—"

"I'm terrified," she said, the words escaping in a shaky whisper.

He pulled her close, his arms strong and sure. She breathed in the sea's scent, letting his warmth chase away the fear.

"We will make it through this together. I cannot imagine it any other way," he said against her hair. "I promise to keep you safe."

Fierce determination resonated in his words, stirring an answering heat within her. She focused on the feel of his body pressed against hers, the solid strength beneath her hands.

His fingers brushed a stray curl from her cheek, lingering a heartbeat too long. Then his lips were on hers, soft yet insistent. Desire flared, a powerful current threatening to sweep her away, making her breathless.

Reality crashed back over her, the ritual, the danger. The griffin's vague reassurances offered little comfort.

She pulled away, heart pounding. "Vayushin claims I'm important," she said, frustration lacing her voice. "Yet he can't spare a few moments to answer my questions? I'm done waiting."

She pivoted toward the door.

Edmar muttered something under his breath, and she caught the words, "...t ired of other men coming between us."

She glanced back, catching a flicker of longing, perhaps regret, in his gaze. Her pulse quickened at the thought of kissing Edmar... and of where kisses like this might eventually lead. She turned back to the door. The templars stood like statues, barring her way.

"Let me pass, or I'll find another way," she said firmly. Not that she knew how. Maybe the balcony, but it came out on the opposite side of the mountain.

The templars exchanged a look. One disappeared down the corridor. The other gestured for her to follow. Edmar kept pace beside her.

"I'm glad you don't need Cielan anymore."

"Not that I don't need him." She shook her head. "But his help comes with a price."

A bigger price than her having an orgasm in his arms, as they had found out after dinner last night.

Cielan had revealed, with infuriating nonchalance, that a bond formed between vamphyr and donor. The more he fed, the stronger that bond, the more she would crave him. Her insides had turned into salt water with the fear of that happening, and Edmar... his fury had been almost as unnerving as Cielan's revelation.

"He waited until the last minute to tell us. That arrogant—" Edmar's voice cut off.

"Vayushin says the ritual can be done without me moving," she said. "So, if my magic returns, then as long as I remain still, silent, well, I can still awaken Metallon." She brushed against him, heat rising to her cheeks. "Thank you for your patience. With Cielan. It means a lot, knowing how you feel about him."

"I'd do anything to protect you. Even watch another man put his mouth on you." His promise lay under the roughness of his voice.

His gaze dropped to her neck, and her skin tingled under his scrutiny. She imagined Cielan's icy touch, then pictured Edmar's lips against her skin, his dragon fangs grazing her, a forbidden fantasy that made her breath catch in her throat.

She wished she hadn't been so quick to leave. Last night, after they'd kissed, she'd wanted more, but he had pulled away, urging her to rest. She loved his respect for her health, but hated that it stood between them.

She brushed against him again, a thrill shooting through her. The tension of the upcoming ritual was almost a tangible thing, but so was the unspoken tension between them.

They descended deep into the mountain, finally reaching a massive metal door guarded by half a dozen templars. Vayushin and Solvrev awaited them, expressions expectant.

"What is this ritual to awaken Metallon?" she asked Vayushin.

Vayushin smiled faintly. "Follow me, Sapphira Syrēna."

Beyond the door, another staircase descended. The air grew colder, heavy with the scent of metal. At last, they reached a vast, windowless chamber. Massive columns disappeared into the shadowed heights. Hieroglyphics and paintings, illuminated by an intricate system of gears and mirrors, covered the walls.

Vayushin stopped before a wall covered in hieroglyphics. "The prophecy foretold your coming. The Sapphire Mermaid, the Sapphira Syrēna, bearing a red gem, destined to awaken the Metal God."

He traced a finger along the wall, illuminating the glyphs. They depicted a mermaid, hair like sapphire-blue fire, a red gem blazing on her chest. The enormity of his words sank into her like an anchor, heavy and unavoidable. *Was I always meant to come here?*

"This temple," he said, his gaze lifting to the shadowed ceiling, "was built to commemorate Metallon's creation of the first Metal Fae. It was a place of pilgrimage, a repository of knowledge, a sanctuary. And it is here the Metal God slumbers, lending his essence to this place. And this prophecy foretold your arrival before Metallon was laid to sleep."

"The ritual," Vayushin continued, "requires a blood sacrifice."

"So we've been told." She studied the glyphs, but they offered no answers, no clues as to her fate.

Edmar slipped an arm around her waist. "Is there no guarantee she'll survive?"

Vayushin and Solvrev exchanged swift, silent hand signs. Her heart hammered at their silence until the griffin finally spoke.

"This quest was given to you by the Sun God. The choice is yours. Proceed, or abandon your duty."

A growl rumbled in Edmar's chest. "That's not good enough."

She turned to him, her fingers catching in his silk tunic. "This is my choice. I'd rather face this ritual than live in fear. Success means a chance at a normal life. And even if I die, it's a better fate than the one the Sea Witch plans for me."

"Emmy—"

"Let me do this," she said, her voice firm. "For me. For all of us."

Vayushin's gaze sharpened, his mismatched eyes burning with intensity. "You seem stronger today, Sapphira Syrēna."

"I feel more myself. I'm ready." She forced a smile, though dread still pulsed beneath the surface. She looked at Edmar, longing for more time with him. *I don't want to die. Not before I have a chance to experience so many things.*

"We wait one more day," Vayushin said. "The ritual will commence tomorrow, at dawn."

"Tell me about the ritual," she said. "I need to know what to expect."

He nodded, leading them toward the center of the chamber. Cielan and Avi emerged from the shadows, their expressions unreadable.

How long were they there?

Her question disappeared as she was drawn to a three-dimensional silver star, no larger than her fist, that hovered over a triangular depression in the floor. Three more triangles, points angled towards the center, surrounded it.

As she neared, energy shimmered in the air, a charge of magic she sensed deep within her being.

"The Mer-Ka-Ba," Solvrev said, his voice filled with reverence. A humming resonated from the star, stealing her breath. "A gateway to Metallon's slumbering consciousness, created by the Metal God to channel the world's energy. Harmony, wisdom, understanding." He paused. "Sensing the imbalance caused by the Summer Child, Metallon has communicated through it to us. He knew the Sun God would seek to awaken him. This ritual will allow it."

The Summer Child. It always came back to that egg.

"The power of three is essential." Solvrev continued, his voice dropping to a reverent murmur. "You, Vayushin, and I will stand within the triangles, linking our energies through the Mer-Ka-Ba. We each offer our blood upon the Sun Stone, but yours, Sapphira Syrēna, is the key."

Something in Solvrev's smooth, practiced tone, the way his gaze flickered to Vayushin, raised gooseflesh on her arms. Something in his voice alerted her. Was there more to this ritual than he revealed?

"Why is this power of three essential?" Edmar asked. "The Sun God said we needed only the blood of one of the god's creatures. And as a griffin, Vayushin is not a child of the Metal God." He gestured to Solvrev. "I don't know what you are."

"Most of my kind remain hidden," Solvrev said with a small smile, "now that Aelunis is home to the last of the griffins."

The High Templar shot the griffin a look, then bowed deeply, his form shimmering like a visual melody. "Watashi wa Ongaku Kitsune to iu mono desu." Silver fox ears and multiple tails materialized as the surrounding air hummed with an otherworldly harmony. "I am what is called an Ongaku Kitsune, and Metallon is my Father God."

A kitsune? Benevolent helpers or malicious tricksters. She never thought she'd see one, their extinction had been recorded alongside the Moon Fae and griffins. But which was he—a helper or a trickster?

"A Sound Kitsune?" Edmar asked, translating the kitsune type from Solvrev's explanation.

"You are familiar with my kind?"

"Only from books." Edmar glanced at the Mer-Ka-Ba. "Which still fails to explain why you're both needed."

The two men hesitated, exchanging hand signals.

"Our combined energies ensure the ritual's success, and safeguards your queen," Vayushin said finally. "We have waited a long time for this. Her blood is precious to us, as is her life."

"You will give more than we," Solvrev said to her, one ear twitching as Cielan and Avi drew closer. "But we will keep you alive."

Hope flickered. She would live. But Solvrev's reassurances did little to alleviate the feeling that they weren't telling her everything.

"Will it work?" Edmar asked, his voice tight.

"It has to," Vayushin said.

Avi tsked. "Poor, Little Mermaid. Are you sure you're up to this? Perhaps you should reconsider."

"This ritual reeks of deception," Cielan said, frowning at Avi before turning his gaze to her. The message in his colorless eyes was clear. *It is not as simple as they claim.*

"The ritual is as I have described," Solvrev said stiffly. "What would someone like *you* know of such things?"

Her pulse quickened. Cielan also sensed their deception. *What are they hiding?*

"And the Sun Stone?" Edmar asked.

Good question to see what Vayushin and Solvrev's plan was for the Sun Stone if they didn't have it.

Vayushin's smile was wintry. "I'm not a fool, Ice Dragon. I assume you have it."

"Our quest does not end here," Edmar said, his eyes narrowing. "The Sun Stone remains with me."

"Rest assured," Solvrev interjected, "you will be free to continue your quest with the Sun Stone once the ritual is complete."

They're lying. She met Edmar's gaze, a silent warning passing between them.

Cielan chuckled, a low, unsettling sound. "Charming. The griffin and the tricky kitsune." He gestured to Solvrev. "Not as benevolent as he appears with his smooth words."

"Don't be so dramatic, Cielan." Avi rolled her eyes. "It will be fine."

But Cielan ignored her. His gaze held Emmy's for a long moment, distrust burning in his eyes, before he vanished in a rush of cold air, taking a startled Avi with him.

As Edmar pressed the others for details, she felt a pull toward the Mer-Ka-Ba, toward Metallon. It pulsed with energy, a silent call she felt deep within her soul.

This is my destiny. She'd felt that for many days now, and it was true. She took a deep breath, steeling herself. Whatever happened, she had to do this. For Edmar. For the world. For herself. "I'll be ready tomorrow."

"Excellent." Vayushin smiled. "Then let us retire for now. The Mer-Ka-Ba's pull strengthens the longer we remain. We don't want to be caught in its thrall."

Edmar captured her, a thumb brushing her lips as he murmured, "A moment without me, please. I must speak with Vayushin, alone."

What can't be said in front of me? Edmar had changed. He seemed almost like the gentle man she'd first met, but now he had an edge to him, a simmering intensity that worried her.

Please, Edmar. Her heart ached. *Be careful.*

She nodded, giving him a smile. He kissed her before letting her go, leaving her chasing her breath as Solvrev gestured for her to follow him, his voice surprisingly gentle. "Perhaps you would like to see the temple? We have tranquil meditation rooms. They might interest you, Sapphira Syrēna."

Meditation, centering herself... She needed such peace. "I would like that."

She glanced back at the Mer-Ka-Ba, its silvery light a beacon in the growing darkness, before following Solvrev.

Chapter 99

EDMAR

Edmar watched Emira disappear into the temple corridors with Solvrev, desire an ache wracking his body. The need to claim her battled with the frustration of ensuring she was safe and his suspicions about her role here.

The ritual, the secrets, the sense of something far more dangerous lurking beneath the surface. His gaze snapped to Vayushin. *Does he plan to keep her?* Somehow, she was linked to this temple. But Edmar wouldn't let her go unless she asked it of him—but not to this griffin. *She's mine.*

He slammed Vayushin against a column, his forearm a vise across the griffin's throat. Vayushin's raw strength flexed against him, a dangerous reminder he was outmatched. But he didn't care.

Templars moved, hands on sword hilts, but Vayushin stilled them with a raised hand. The griffin's breath hitched, but he didn't fight back, his mismatched eyes burning with a strange light.

"I am a griffin, Ice Dragon." Quiet menace and a promise Edmar didn't understand laced his words. "Don't overestimate your power."

He knew the truth of those words. Griffins were apex predators when it came to Winter creatures, their strength and magic unparalleled—and the reason the Summer Fae sought to annihilate them. But this wasn't just about power. Vayushin's interest in Emira ran deeper than mere power.

"You want something from her," he said, pressing harder against Vayushin's throat. "And it's not just about this ritual. You *want* her."

Vayushin reversed their positions with effortless strength, pinning him to the column. His breath hitched as Vayushin leaned close, amusement gleaming in his mismatched eyes.

"Do you think you can stop me?" Vayushin asked, his voice a cool whisper.

He couldn't. *Not alone.* "I understand your hatred for me," he said, forcing his voice to remain steady. "I wish things could have been different for our peoples. But that doesn't give you the right to use my wife."

"And what if," Vayushin murmured, his gaze softening slightly, "my interest in your wife has nothing to do with hatred? Or even desire for her?"

"Then what is this about?" He narrowed his eyes, refusing to be misled.

"I admit, I played on your emotions," Vayushin said. "But Emira is important. Her blood holds the key to breaking the storms surrounding Aelunis. Only a Water creature of her power, combined with Metallon's awakening, can restore balance. We need her alive for that."

He searched Vayushin's eyes, seeking deception. But the griffin's sincerity was undeniable. "Why not tell us this before?"

"Would you have believed me?" Vayushin's gaze held a flicker of vulnerability. "You still don't trust me, Ice Dragon. And with good reason."

"We're on the same side," he said. "We need to trust each other. At least insofar as not stealing my wife or the Sun Stone."

Vayushin offered no such assurance. The silence was more unsettling than any threat.

"What do you want?"

Vayushin leaned closer, his breath ghosting over his skin. For a moment, he thought the griffin meant to kiss him, but then Vayushin's lips brushed his ear.

"What if, Edmar," he murmured, "the animosity you sense has less to do with your people's betrayal... and more to do with you having a wife?"

His breath hitched. *Is this what Solvrev meant?* The kitsune had known. His heart belonged to Emira, but there was a truth to Vayushin's words he couldn't deny.

The griffin wanted *him*. The evidence lay hard against his stomach.

Vayushin pulled away, a whisper of a smile touching his lips. "I'd rather entice you to my bed than your wife, Ice Dragon. How's that for irony?" A flicker of...regret? crossed his face. "But I know you're not interested."

Vayushin's words, his confession, hung heavy in the air. Edmar's gaze drifted to the doorway, the memory of Emira's smile, the warmth of her touch markedly different from the griffin's cold desire.

He belonged to Emira. She belonged to him.

With a final lingering glance, Vayushin walked away.

Relief warred with confusion. He was relieved Vayushin wasn't after Emira, but the confession and Edmar's rejection... what did it mean for their already fragile alliance? Whatever it meant, all he knew was that it was past time he gave in to his desires for his wife.

He needed to find Emira. Be with her, lose himself in her, forget the griffin's confession. His body ached for her, every step a reminder of the desire burning through him.

He found her, finally, in a meditation room. She knelt before a small altar, bathed in the soft glow of an oil lamp, her sapphire hair a flame in the dimly lit room.

Relief and desire crashed over him. He crossed the room, pulling her into his arms, kissing her with a fierceness he'd been holding back for far too long. The kiss was feral, possessive—a declaration of his love and his determination to have her.

"What was that for?" she asked, her voice breathless against his lips.

"I need you." He scooped her into his arms, ignoring the curious looks of the templars as he carried her back to their chambers.

"Do not disturb us," he ordered the guards at the door

He laid her on the bed, his voice husky. "Any objections, Emmy? State them now because I don't think I can stop myself."

Emira smiled up at him, her emerald eyes filled with the same desire that consumed him. "I've waited long enough."

Chapter 100

EMMY

Edmar's shadow fell over her, and her pulse quickened—not from nervousness, but from the anticipation that had been building between them for so long. Desire, no longer ignorable, thrummed beneath her skin. His gaze, the memory of his kiss, sent shivers down her spine. She'd seen him angry, gentle, fierce—but this... this was new. His gaze held a storm of emotions she couldn't decipher.

Yet, he hesitated.

"Edmar." His name was a breath on her lips.

He braced a knee on the bed, his hand resting on her thigh. The simple touch sent a jolt of need straight to her core. She had waited for this moment, hoped for it, dreamed about it, but now that it was here, the strength of it overwhelmed her. This wasn't just about satisfying their physical desires. It was about something deeper. A reconnection of their souls, a mending of what had been broken.

He cupped her jaw, his thumb tracing across her lower lips. His pupils dilated, the blue-green color nearly consumed by black. "I've always been a sensible, rational person. But since you've come back into my life, you've made me more reckless, illogical. You've destroyed my Frostlands."

She frowned, wondering where he was going with this.

He tugged gently on her lip, and she parted her mouth for him, her tongue darting out to taste the salt of his skin. *Home.* He sucked in a breath, holding it.

She didn't know what possessed her to do that, but she loved tasting him.

He released his breath slowly, his gaze dropping to the pulse fluttering in her neck, then lower, to where the gem disappeared beneath her tunic. "I feel like I know everything I need to know about you. At the same time, I feel like I'll never know enough to understand you."

Purposefully she arched her body into his, yearning for his touch, yet he still held back even though his eyes flicked lower.

"I'm not sure this is how seduction works, Edmar."

A wild fierceness filled the depths of his eyes, and he shifted, settling beside her on the bed, and cupped the back of her head, drawing her close. Their lips were a whisper apart. "My need for you scares me."

"It doesn't scare me."

She brushed his lips with her tongue. He shuddered, eyes closing. The struggle within him was a tangible thing.

"I don't think you understand," he said, his voice rough with restrained need. His hand drifted over her shoulder, down her side, settling on her hip. "I desire control and commitment. They are in my nature. So if I give into my need for you, I'll never let you go."

His fingers tightened on her hip, a note of his possessiveness, and a moan escaped her lips. She wanted his touch, for him to hold her, fill her with the power of his desire.

"Think hard, Emmy." He licked his bottom lip. "If you don't want this, this marriage that was forced upon you, now is the time for you to say so. To leave."

Think hard. She didn't need to do that, did she? Tomorrow loomed, the threat of the ritual. But there was something else, something she couldn't ignore, lingering in her mind and in her heart. "Do you trust me?"

He'd returned her gem, a symbol of trusting her, but the words had never been spoken. His hand relaxed on her hip, and the pressure loss hurt her heart, like he was letting her go when that was not what she wanted.

She looked away, her chest tight. "How can we do this when you don't trust me?"

Gently, he lifted her chin, his gaze holding hers. "I was deceived because I trusted too easily. But now I'm living in torment because I don't trust enough. And that, I fear, breeds more mistrust. But I am trying, Emmy. I'm really trying. And I believe together we can rebuild that trust."

Sincerity resonated in his voice, in the depths of his eyes. Full trust might not be there yet, but maybe he was right. They could rebuild it, and that offered her hope. Underneath the affection he carried for her, devotion clearly bled through.

Could she live with that?

Maybe she sought permission, whatever the reason, to finally be with her Dragon King, but she didn't care. She wanted him, all of him.

Tentatively, she traced a fingertip along his collarbone, marveling at the feel of his sky-blue skin, the strength beneath. Her hand drifted up, fingers threading through his hair. He inhaled sharply.

Desire hung heavy between them. He squeezed her hip again, then brought her hand to his mouth, pressing a kiss to her knuckles.

"What do you want, Emmy?" His voice was thick with longing. "More time? Or..."

"I need..." she whispered, "to feel you."

Understanding flickered in his eyes. He shifted, bracing himself above her, his cool breath ghosting her sensitive skin. Excitement, a frisson of nerves, thrummed through her. "I need you to kiss me," she said.

Dim lamp light danced over his skin, shadows moving in rhythm with his breathing. Then he kissed her, and the world shifted. His kiss was fierce, demanding, and she met it with an answering hunger.

Cold danced along his tongue as it danced with hers, an ice storm that awakened a hunger she'd never known until him. She met his urgency with her own, arching into him, hands roaming the contours of his muscled back, breathless from his kisses. Salt and sea, a reminder of their intertwined lives, filled her senses.

He lifted his head, gaze intense. "After tonight, no other will touch you. No man will put his mouth on you. I will claim you."

She would agree a thousand times over, but fear still haunted her. "What if Metallon doesn't cure me? I can't go back to the life I had before. I'd rather die."

He shook his head, his eyes stormy. "We will find a way. You are not allowed to die, Emmy. Trust me."

What if the ritual is my death? "Promise me, again," she said, her voice tight, "you will continue the Sun God's holy quest."

He searched her gaze, seeking something she couldn't give. She wrapped her arms around him. "Your honor, your duty. They come first."

His jaw tightened, but he nodded. He kissed her then, a desperate kiss, long and deep. With his breath cool against her heated skin, he trailed kisses down her jaw. He found the pulse point in her neck, the same Cielan always fed from, and his teeth grazed her skin, then lightly nipped her. The sound that escaped her was almost a sob. He was recreating her fantasy, and her body thrummed with a spark of ecstasy.

His sharp intake of breath made her open her eyes. The silver swirls on her skin shimmered like diamonds under a sunlit sea.

"Like stars," he breathed, his fingertip tracing the patterns on her chest.

Goosebumps rose beneath his touch, multiplying with the reverence in his voice.

"Edmar." Her plea sounded almost like a whine.

Meeting her gaze again, he smiled, his eyes dark with desire. One hand slid into her hair, cupping the back of her head. "Tell me what you want," he insisted.

Her breath trembled. "I want you," she whispered. "Make me yours, Edmar."

He groaned, his control fracturing. He kissed her again, his hands moving to the hem of her tunic, pulling it free. Her skin tingled in the cool air.

He kissed a path down her neck, teeth grazing her sensitive skin. She shuddered, her body alive to his every touch. She tilted her head back, exposing more of her neck to his eager mouth while his hands skimmed over her skin.

One hand splayed across her stomach, cool and reassuring. She shivered as his fingers traced lazy circles, the sensation both foreign and intoxicating. He skimmed higher, his hand gliding over her ribs, then lingering, the pressure increasing as he explored the curve beneath her breast.

She arched into the touch, a wave of heat washing over her. Anticipation, a delicious agony, vibrated through her. She needed more.

His breath, a cool breeze against her heated skin, ghosted across her nipples, sending shivers through her. His tongue traced the outline of her areola. The sensation so unexpected, so exquisite, it drew a gasp from her lips. She tangled her fingers in his hair.

He chuckled as his gaze swept over her, lingering on the dusky green of her nipples. "You're so beautiful," he whispered, catching one between his fingers. He rubbed it slowly, then faster, the pressure increasing, the friction sending sparks of pleasurable fire through her veins.

Her body bowed, followed by her breathy whimper. It felt so good, and the ache in her core intensified. His mouth replaced his fingers, his tongue swirling around her nipple before drawing it deep with a gentle suck. She cried out, her body writhing as he teased and tormented, alternating between licking and sucking, his fingers returning to the other aching bud.

He bit down gently, and the sharp sensation sent a shockwave of pleasure through her. She twisted and bucked beneath him. "More, more, more..." she gasped the words, her body aching for the pleasure he'd given her before, the pleasure he promised now.

He chuckled, a low rumble in his chest. "So needy, my love?"

"Only for you."

Her response incited him, and his mouth claimed hers once more with rougher possession. His fingers returned to tease her breasts, continuing his delicious torture, pinching, twisting, pulling at her nipples until she thought she'd shatter. Her vision blurred, her breath coming in ragged gasps as wave after wave of pleasure crashed over her. Her nails dug into his skin.

His mouth found the same sensitive spot on her neck, his tongue licking away the memory of another man's touch.

"Mine," he said, his dragon teeth growing and sharpening.

Then his teeth sank into her skin, and with a final twist of his fingers on her nipple, the world exploded.

Pleasure, sharp and bright, ripped through her, leaving her breathless and trembling in its wake.

Chapter 101

EMMY

The afterglow of pleasure faded, leaving a warmth pulsing through Emmy's veins like a gentle current. Yet it left a strange restlessness in its wake. The longing, the heat in her core. It remained.

Is this normal? Her gaze traced the tangled sheets, the shadows dancing on the chamber walls. An unsated need pulsed through her, leaving her trembling.

She touched her neck, the skin tender, broken. She marveled at the pleasure it brought to feel Edmar's teeth. He shifted, his body pressing against hers, his hardness against her thigh. He kissed her, the kiss urgent, demanding, his hand possessively cupping her breast. Desire, a living thing, pulsed between them.

She melted into the breathless kiss, her hands finding his broad chest, tracing the hard muscles beneath his tunic. The fabric was a barrier, one she yearned to remove.

"I love seeing you come undone." Obvious need made his voice rough.

"But..." *How to express this lingering hunger?*

He sensed her hesitation. "What is it?"

"I just... I feel..." Her cheeks flushed with heat.

He smiled. "You want more?"

She nodded, biting her lip.

"Tell me," he urged, his fingers tracing lazy circles on her hip.

With quiet urgency, she tugged at his clothes, her fingers fumbling with the ties. He helped her, his touch sending a delicious shiver down her spine.

Their breaths mingled as they undressed each other until each faced the other, fully naked. He straddled her, his gaze raked over her lush curves—her full breasts, her wide hips—and desire blew his pupils wide.

She studied him in return, his lean, muscled body, the sky-blue of his skin, the power he radiated. Then she saw it, his erection, hard and pulsing. Heat, laced with a touch of fear, flooded her. *He looks too big for me.*

He eased between her legs, his touch a question, a promise. She thrilled as his hand curved over her thigh, lingering at the juncture of hip and leg.

His finger brushed light but purposefully between her legs, then slid down between her slick folds, and a guttural gasp escaped her.

He groaned. "So wet."

"Is that good?"

"It is," he whispered, his thumb stroking her clit. Pleasure shot through her as he kissed her, his fingers continuing their exploration between her legs. "It means you're almost ready for me."

"But I've been ready," she said with a frown.

"In your mind, yes." He delved deeper and slid a finger inside her tight body, and she gasped. "But you've never had a man invade your body the way I want you, and dragons are well endowed."

Another finger joined the first, and she welcomed it with a gasp. Her body craved his fingers, clenching around them with hunger.

"I don't want to hurt you," he murmured, nipping her lower lip as she arched into his touch. He shifted, sliding down her body until his head was between her legs.

"What are you doing?" she asked with panic, gripping his hair. She thought she'd finally feel him inside her.

A wicked smile touched his lips. "I told you I wanted you to be so sedated with pleasure that you'll be ready to welcome me within you," he said, his voice a husky murmur. "I intend to keep that promise."

He licked her, a long, slow stroke from her entrance to her clit.

"Gods, you taste incredible," he breathed.

The rumble of his words and their meaning elicited a shiver, and goosebumps erupted on her skin. Then his mouth closed over her clit, the sensation both hot and cold. Two fingers delved into her again, circling, then withdrawing, then plunging back in. His other hand cupped her breast, teasing her already sensitive nipple. The faint sting only heightened the pleasure.

She reveled in the wanton sensations, her body relaxing beneath his ministrations, unbelieving of all the ways her Dragon King made her feel.

"Good, Emmy," he said against her skin. "Almost there."

She barely heard him, but warmed at his compliment. He watched her as he sucked on her, his fingers moving in her. She whimpered, her entire body aching and screaming for yet another release.

"Oh gods, Edmar." She babbled without awareness. "I need... I need—Please—" Her voice rose with the dangerous intensity of her pleasure peaking.

He chuckled, a dark sound against her skin. His tongue lapped at her, a third finger joining the others, stretching, filling, faster, faster.

He pinched her nipple, then his teeth scraped over her clit and her next release crashed over her. It carried her in a darkened world with brief flashes of light, her body clenching tight, convulsing with the power of her orgasm. She was barely aware of him shifting until she felt him nudging at her entrance. He gathered her into his arms.

"Last chance, Emmy," he murmured, his voice thick with desire.

Her pulse raced, wanting this moment when he'd finally claim her. She nodded, biting her lip. Her breath caught as he pushed inside her, slowly, carefully. His tenderness was almost unbearable. Her need grew too intense, too overwhelming to endure any more waiting.

She needed him—now.

With a desperate cry, she wrapped her legs around his hips, and she pulled him into her. A sharp pain, a momentary resistance, then he filled her completely.

"Emmy!" He froze, eyes wide.

"Move." She gasped.

He hesitated only a heartbeat, then moved, slowly, deliberately. The swelling of him inside her, the pressure of his body becoming part of her, sent waves of pleasure rippling through her body. It was better than she ever imagined it could be, here in her Dragon King's arms.

His rhythm quickened, tension coiling within her. Pleasure intensified, cool skin against heated flesh, the taste of him, the scent of their mingled arousal.

"Gods, you feel so good," he growled against her throat as his thrust quickened, pushing harder.

She wanted to answer, but he moved faster, harder, pushing her closer to the edge. She gripped him, her breath coming in short gasps. His arms curled around her, fingers digging into her flesh.

Then she was lost, pleasure a supernova exploding behind her eyelids. Her body trembled, an ocean of pleasure crashing over her, so intense, so overwhelming, it felt like she was shattering into a million pieces.

He cried out, his release coming after hers. A shudder ran through him, his body tightening above her before he gave in, pressing against her as if he could melt into her skin. She felt the trembling tension in his muscles, the way his breath stuttered, breaking apart like waves over her shoulder. The power of it—the raw vulnerability in the way he let go—sent warmth pooling low in her belly.

He withdrew, collapsing beside her, his chest still rising and falling with uneven breaths. Without hesitation, he gathered her into his arms, as if needing to hold her just as much as she needed to be held. They lay tangled together, slick with sweat, their breathing ragged. She had never felt so content.

Her vision of the world had changed. It felt like she'd been torn apart and reassembled anew, the old Emmy replaced by this new version, one more aware of life's secrets and pleasures, what it meant to fully love another person.

He kissed her languidly, his touch gentle.

"Did I hurt you?" he asked, his voice husky.

"No. It was incredible." Emmy sighed, a soft smile playing on her lips. Then reality crashed back. "I only wish we had more time."

"More time for...?"

"For this. For us." Fear tightened her throat. "What if I don't survive the ritual?"

He held her tight, his embrace a shield against the encroaching fear. "You will live, Emmy. Vayushin will protect you. And I won't let anything happen to you."

His words, laced with such fierce conviction, touched her heart. But fear remained, an icy knot in her stomach.

"But what if he's lying?" she whispered, her voice trembling. "What if the Metal God... What if..." She couldn't voice the fear gnawing at her soul.

"Metallon won't harm you," he said, lifting her chin so their gazes met. "You're his creation. He'll help you. I have to believe that."

"But what if he can't?" she asked, despair threatening to overwhelm her. "What if it's impossible to separate me from my magic?"

"Whatever happens, I will be with you," he said, his words a vow. "We'll find a way. I'll never leave you to face your challenges alone."

Alone. Something that had defined her existence for so long, and now this man in front of her promised to never allow her to go back to that dark place again.

Love, fierce and overwhelming, surged through her, erasing fear and doubt. She traced the line of his jaw, the smooth coolness of his throat. Her lips brushed his skin. "I love your strength, your stubbornness, your unwavering belief in what's right, even when it hurts."

He groaned, his breath harsh. "I love your spirit. Your fire. Your laughter. The way you look at the stars, and the way you make me forget a thousand years of loneliness."

She searched his eyes, the flood of emotions too numerous to untangle, but the tone of his words... Honesty, vulnerability. It was all there. He hadn't spoken of love since their wedding day.

He caressed her cheek, tucking a stray strand of hair behind her ear.

"I never thought I'd be swept away so completely by anyone," he murmured. "Your strength, your resilience in refusing to be broken by anyone. You faced a life of solitude and pain, yet never lost your courage. You melted the ice around my heart, showed me a world beyond duty, beyond control."

She kissed him, a sensual but chaste meeting of their lips. Something electric arced between them. He pulled back, drawing a deep breath.

"You take my breath away," he said, his voice deep with adoration. "Nothing or no one can change the way I love you. There's nothing you could do to change my need for you. I cannot imagine a world without you beside me."

His words, raw and honest, struck her with unexpected force. She'd doubted, feared her curse would forever keep love at bay. But Edmar saw her, all of her, her strength, her flaws, her magic, and loved her still. She stared into his eyes, trying to absorb the immensity of it.

She wouldn't face tomorrow's ritual alone.

Pulling him closer, she explored the contours of his face with her mouth, kissing him. His skin tasted of salt and sea. Her lips trailed down his neck, and one of his hands teased her nipple again. *Are his nipples as sensitive as mine?* She circled one with her tongue, then drew it into her mouth.

He moaned, a sweet reward. His control slipped, his hand tight on her breast.

"Emmy," his voice was rough, "I need you again."

His arousal pressed against her, a hard reminder. With a hand in her hair, he pulled her away with a playful gleam in his eye. He flipped her over, guiding her onto her hands and knees, positioning himself behind her, hands gripping her hips.

He leaned over her.

"This time," he murmured in her ear, his voice a blend of authority and promise, "I'm in control."

Anticipation, not fear, shivered through her. She'd promised herself she'd never surrender her control again, but with him, it felt right. Safe. Exhilarating. This was more than just physical dominance; it was a trust she'd never given to anyone, a sign of the depth of their hard-won bond.

He thrust into her, the force of it making her gasp. The angle sent radiating pleasure through her, and she moaned as he pulled almost all the way out of her, only to dig his fingers into her flesh and yank her back onto his length with another forceful thrust.

She cried out, a mixture of pain and pleasure.

Then he set a punishing pace, his movements powerful, yet graceful. The intensity of it, the way he claimed her, sent her spiraling toward release.

She matched his rhythm, their bodies moving as one, an icy storm of surrender and possession. And this time, when they peaked, it was a shared explosion, a blinding fusion of their energies, their souls merging. They collapsed onto the bed, spent.

She lay tangled in his arms, her heart overflowing. Whatever happened tomorrow, this moment, this love, would carry her through.

Chapter 102

EMMY

Emmy woke with a gasp, nausea twisting her stomach. An invisible hand squeezed her chest, a sickening pull from her gem.

"Get up!"

Avi stood above her—*no, this isn't Avi.* Cold amethyst fire burned where cerulean blue should be. Emmy's heart hammered against her ribs.

An irresistible force yanked her from the bed, her body a puppet.

"Get dressed," the creature commanded.

Hot knives seared through her soles with each step.

Edmar's eyes snapped open, his confused gaze on her as she pulled on his old shirt, the one that reminded her of one of the best days of her life, the day fate had guided her to the beach where he walked.

Then he noticed Avi. "What are you doing?"

Fear flickered in his eyes as he scrambled out of bed, his hands already manipulating his magic. Ice shards streaked toward Avi.

A chilling laugh echoed in the chamber as a wave of pearlescent magic shattered the ice shards before they struck. The air crackled with power, the temperature plummeting.

"Stop me, Ice Dragon, and your mermaid dies." Avi's voice was a viper's hiss, devoid of warmth, while she held up the painite. Pearlescent magic lashed out, searing his skin.

He roared, pain and fury battling in his voice. Ice magic surged in a desperate defense, frost covering everything, but her magic was stronger, forcing him back. He staggered, disbelief in his eyes.

"Stop!" Emmy cried, throwing herself between them. "Don't hurt him!"

Avi laughed, the sound echoing.

"I'd rather take the dragon, anyway." Her cold and calculating gaze swept over Edmar. "His magic is stronger than that useless hybrid. Much stronger."

A chill ran down Emmy's spine. *Lian.* This was definitely not Avi to be talking about her own father that way.

"The Sun Stone," Avi said, her voice cold. "We have a god to awaken."

She retrieved the stone as Edmar pulled on his pants. "But—"

Avi shoved her out the door, Edmar following.

"We're waking Metallon in the morning," Emmy said, undeterred. "Why are you doing this?"

Silence.

The journey was a blur. Avi pushed them forward whenever they slowed. Darkness clung to the temple, the air heavy with incense and metal.

Avi ignored her questions. Whenever they encountered templars or monks, a haunting melody filled the air, leaving them blank-faced and unseeing.

A shadow detached itself from a wall, disappearing into the darkness.

Friend or foe? Her fear mounted. *Please let it be Cielan.* Would he help, though?

Her mind rebelled as Avi's command forced her on.

Edmar's hand found hers, a silent reassurance. His warmth, a flicker of humanity, seeped into her. *Not alone,* his eyes said. *Together.*

But inside, she crumbled. The coerced obedience, the violation of her will. She thought those days of suffocating powerlessness were over.

They stopped in the ritual chamber, the air thick with metal and incense. The Mer-Ka-Ba pulsed with silvery light, calling to her.

Then her heart sank.

Adria and Lian lay bound and gagged within two of the triangles, their eyes wide with shock. They hadn't known Avi to be capable of what she did now.

"The Sun Stone," Avi commanded, shoving her toward the basin. "Then stand in the triangle. Don't move."

Her heart pounded as she obeyed, the sight of the pirates fueling her desperation.

Cielan emerged from the shadows, his gaze fixed on Avi. "Who are you?" he asked, his voice tight. "And what have you done with Avi?"

I was right. Not Avi. But then, who was she?

"I like you, Cielan." She laughed, the sound devoid of humor.

Snaking lines of pearlescent magic shot out from her and bound him where he stood. "Twisted by fate, just like me. We could have had so much fun." Her tone hardened. "Be a good vamphyr, and I'll release your precious Avi when I'm done."

He nodded, and her magic dissipated. Next, blazing amethyst eyes turned to Lian. With a flick of her wrist, she sent him flying across the stone floor.

"Your place, Dragon King," she said, her gaze promising violence as she gestured to the open triangle. "Obey, or your mermaid pays the price."

Emmy's heart shattered as Edmar stepped into the triangle. Avi, or whoever she was, had gained more power than Edmar could beat. All who would help couldn't or didn't. She saw no way out of this situation. Edmar seemed to have similar thoughts.

Fear, mirroring her own, filled his eyes.

I love you. Did he understand?

"Avi, please." She swallowed hard. "Why can't we wait?"

"To awaken the Metal God?"

"You know we planned this. And we can do it safely."

"How convenient," Avi said, her laughter a menacing sound, her voice deeper. "Our goals align. We should be happy."

"This is a quest from the Sun God." Desperation laced her voice. "Unless there is something else you want?"

"A quest from the Sun God?" Avi scoffed. "How *noble*. He sends you to awaken his brother, but forgets to mention the havoc he wrought? He forgets how he plunged his own kin into eternal slumber, ripped families apart, left me... *alone*."

For a heartbeat, pain flickered across her face, then vanished, replaced by icy fury.

"No, Little Mermaid. This isn't about some righteous quest," she said, her lip curled in a snarl. "This is about revenge."

"I understand abandonment," Emmy said. "I understand your pain."

Avi sneered. "You understand nothing. Thousands of centuries of pain, of betrayal, of desertion. You know nothing of such things."

She circled Edmar, her movements predatory. She drew a knife from her voluminous shirt. Long, curved, the bone handle studded with jewels. It glinted in her hand. "The ritual blade," she said with a smile. "Those fools didn't tell you about this, about a knife that would barely drain them," she glanced at Emmy, "but would take all the blood they could from you."

Emmy closed her eyes against the truth. Of course, they'd suspected Vayushin and Solvrev hadn't been entirely forthcoming, but she had to believe that they had not meant to kill her with the ritual.

Avi traced the knife's tip from Edmar's shoulder to his upper arm. "Ingenious really. A blade infused with magic. Every cut yields enough blood to satisfy the wielder's intent."

She sliced down Edmar's arm, drawing a hiss. Blue blood welled on his skin. The knife glinted as she sliced across his chest, then his abdomen, shallow cuts. She cut him again and again, his hisses turning to gasps as his jaw clenched. Her eyes flared amethyst, her hair darkening to a deep black. Her features shifted, shimmering, before settling back into those of the hybrid fae.

But Emmy recognized her, her blood turning to ice.

"Gilly?" Betrayal laced the whispered word.

It couldn't be Gilly. Not her best friend, the one person besides Anjali who had accepted her, never feared her. Even taken care of her, a source of comfort after she'd killed her mother. They had shared so many confidences over the decades.

Delight flashed in her amethyst eyes as Emmy realized who she really was. "Oh, goody!" Avi—Gilly—clapped her hands, a delighted smile on her face. "You figured it out."

Horror filled her. *Emmy* had shared confidences. Gilly had only listened, empathized. Her horror leaked into her whispered words.

"How long?" She shook her head, unbelieving. "You were my friend, my whole life. You were just waiting for this day? To what? To use me?"

She couldn't believe this was her best friend.

Avi—Gilly—waved her hand. "Time is irrelevant when you're immortal."

Her mind reeled, bitterness twisted her stomach. "But why?"

Gilly smirked, not answering her.

She swallowed hard to face reality, and now there really were only two questions left. "How and where is Avi?"

Even with her fear a tangible thing, her magic remained dormant.

Avi—Gilly—smirked again. "You were so tiresome sometimes, Emmy." Mock amusement danced in her eyes. "For someone who was mute, you did a lot of complaining. Whining about your magic, your freedom."

"Gilly, this isn't you—"

"None of this is really your fault, though," Gilly said, her voice softening, though a cruel gleam remained in her eyes. "And now you're delivering on the promise your life held."

What does that mean?

"Please," she begged. "You don't have to do this."

"But I do." Gilly turned back to Edmar, her fingers caressing his face. "Such beauty. Wasted on an idiot who can't decide whether to trust the one woman who loves him." Her hand flitted down to his bare chest. "Hold still, Dragon King."

The knife tip sliced down his chest, leaving a trail of blue blood crisscrossing other lines. "I never really wanted you, foolish dragon. You were a means to an end. The Sun Stone, and diverting Emmy's attention. Although I wouldn't have minded a bit of fun, too."

She lapped at the blood on his chest. "Dragon blood. Not much different from Water or Moon fae. Did Adria ever tell you how foolish she was?" She glanced at the Water Fae. "Bringing her friends into my domain. Remember Adria? So careless. You thought you could bargain with me. Your little hybrid fae, he could have been mine."

What is she talking about? She knows Adria?

"A pity," Gilly said, a cruel smile on her lips as she looked at Lian. "I would've enjoyed breaking him."

Adria struggled, her eyes wide with terror. "Mmf! Mmmf!"

Lian roared, his muffled cries echoing.

They were trying to tell her something, their gazes pleading. *What?*

Little jagged streaks of purple lightning lanced from Gilly to both Adria and Lian, striking both to silence.

"Quiet!" Gilly said. "My story isn't finished."

Emmy gasped. Her once-best friend shouldn't have this much power. This power of purple lightning, seen when it struck Edmar out of the sky and again when she'd fought with Avi on the ship.

Who is she?

Gilly grabbed Edmar's arm, twisting it outward, exposing his wrist. The blade sliced down his arm, from elbow to wrist, and Emmy screamed. Gilly delighted in the venous gush of pale blue blood. Other cuts dripped onto the triangle, pooling in the basin.

"That's a good dragon. Now stay just like that." Gilly approached Adria with her blue-coated knife.

"Dolcivita, I know you're in there!" Cielan said. "You don't want to hurt your mother."

Gilly laughed. "Avi has no power."

Adria cried out in a muffled denial, tears streaming down her face.

"I don't believe you," Cielan snarled, striding forward. "Fight, Avi!"

She whirled, pearlescent magic slamming into Cielan. He flew against the wall, purple sparks flying. One seared into Edmar's shoulder. He grunted, his head bowing.

"Edmar!" Emmy wanted to reach for him, but couldn't move. He met her gaze, shaking his head, his lips a thin line, his face too pale.

"Give up, Cielan." Gilly's voice was deeper, more menacing than before. "Or I destroy this body, and you will surely never get her back."

Adria and Lian struggled against their bonds.

Cielan hesitated, a storm of emotions raging in his gaze. Then, with a resigned sigh, he stepped back, his eyes following Gilly as she turned toward Adria.

"Shhh, Adria," she murmured. "You thought you could escape me." She knelt beside the bound pirate, her magic forcing Adria onto her back.

Tears shimmered in Adria's eyes.

"Foolish woman. Now I have my revenge." She pulled Adria's wrists above her head, the knife glinting. She sliced with a swift, cruel motion across one wrist. Adria screamed, her blood a vibrant stain against her lavender skin. Lian thrashed, his cries echoing his wife's agony.

Gilly laughed, her voice cold.

"I may have let your friends go, but I kept your curse." Her voice softened, a strange tenderness in her next words. "And I used it to create something *spectacular*. The Daughter of Ruin."

CHAPTER 103

EMMY

Gilly looked up at Emmy, a triumphant gleam in her eyes. Dread coiled in Emmy's gut. Only one being had ever called her that.

"You know this story, child," Gilly said, a knowing glint in her amethyst eyes. "A curse passed down, destined to destroy. *The Daughter of Ruin.* You carry that curse, Emmy. You know that pain, that fear, just like me."

Her heart pounded. Everything Gilly had said about Adria, about the ritual, about Emmy herself... This was no longer just Gilly. This was something far darker, far more dangerous.

The Sea Witch.

Terror, cold and consuming, washed over her. A spark of her fire acid stung in her veins.

Avi—Gilly—the Sea Witch nodded, her smile unwavering. *Yes, Daughter of Ruin.* She read Emmy's thoughts, her voice echoing in her mind. *All the same, for the moment.*

All these years you were my friend, but you had always been the Sea Witch? It just didn't seem possible.

"You can call me Gilly. A nickname from Sygilla, the name my mother gave me. A name lost to history, like the truth of my existence, just like how it forgot I was the first mermaid."

Emmy needed to buy time and keep Gilly talking. Maybe someone in the temple would come down, maybe Vayushin or Solvrev, if given enough time to become curious when they found their guests were missing. "What did you do with Avi?"

She's here. "I control her mind."

Adria's trembling cry broke through her gag.

"You knew I was sailing for Aelunis," she said. "I told both you and Anjali before we left. Why not just join me? Why take Avi?"

Gilly tapped the knife against her gray cheek, leaving a smear of blue blood. "My story's been lost to time, so I'll tell you. But first..."

She leaned over Adria, her voice nearly a whisper. "Your daughter is broken. Not just from her magic, but from your family's stone. The reason her granddaughter is twisted."

Emmy didn't understand what any of that meant, but her thoughts stilled when Gilly looked back at her.

"The Daughter of Ruin unknowingly gave me access, and Avi was so easy to invade, easy to control. Fortuitous for me."

What access? Emmy vainly searched the reason behind everything Gilly did. So many years her friend had manipulated her. But for what reasons? *You tried to kill Edmar twenty-five years ago. Why?*

That fool Snow Princess uses the Dragon Kings, and I didn't want her to send them after my most precious treasure. The Sea Witch continued aloud, speaking to Adria. "You've never known true fear, thwarting destiny at every turn. But today you will feel it. You will know what it is to lose a daughter, a daughter you should have never had."

Like how the Sea Witch lost her daughter, a daughter that defies nature. Her child with the Sun God.

Gilly glanced at her, her black hair replacing Avi's again. *What secrets did he tell you, Daughter of Ruin?*

Emmy shut down her thoughts.

Gilly smiled, revealing sharp teeth.

Her heart pounded as reality settled in, piece by piece. Gilly—her friend, her confidante—was wholly gone, replaced by something ancient and vengeful. Every word from the Sea Witch's lips felt like a knife twisting in her gut.

Gilly was Sygilla, the Sea Witch.

The Sea Witch turned back to Adria, venom dripping from her words. "What did you do to earn the Sun God's favor, allowing him to give you the words to unlock his stone, Water Fae? Did you seduce him?"

Adria closed her eyes, tears tracing paths on her lavender skin.

"You used his power against me," the Sea Witch said, her voice softer now, more menacing. "Do you remember?"

Adria sobbed. Lian thrashed, a roar of anguish escaping him.

"He was mine before you had him." The Sea Witch leaned closer to hiss in her ear. "I hated pretending to be your daughter. But revenge is sweet, even if it's twelve hundred years late."

Then, with a swift, merciless motion, she sliced Adria's other wrist, nearly severing the hand.

Adria screamed. Lian's struggles ceased, his face slack, eyes wide on his wife's face, tears hitting the stone ground. Adria's blood flowed into the basin, mingling with Edmar's.

Emmy begged her magic to rush forward, willing to take the searing pain if only it could save Adria, save all of them, but it had fallen dormant again. The Ocean's Lament resonated in her breast, the tune rising through her body, offering solace.

Just as she realized that she might have the powers of a siren still, the Sea Witch rose, her gaze shifting from the weeping Lian to Emmy.

"Ah, ah, ah." She wagged a finger. "You will not sing or use your magic without my permission.

Magic left Emmy's song, leaving her feeling empty, creating space again for terror to fill her.

A flicker of sympathy crossed the Sea Witch's features.

"Poor mermaid," she murmured. "Caught in the middle. Adria's choices led you to me, and you led me here, to my father's resting place." She shook her head, a humorless smile on her lips. "The irony."

"Your father?"

"Metallon," she said with a dismissive wave of her bloodstained hand. "He adopted me, raised me when Chaos abandoned me in this world."

"Chaos?" Other than the story of the eight gods birthed by the primordial force, no other tales had been written about it, a presence most dismissed as nothing more than raw magic.

"The beginning and the end. Chaos is all our mothers and fathers, everything in between and everything encompassed by all." The amethyst eyes looked far away, perhaps looking back eons ago. "They loved their children, an extension of themselves. But desire clouded that love, particularly for my mother, the Water Goddess. I was born of that longing, the first mermaid."

"If you are the first mermaid, why do our legends name the Water Goddess as our mother?"

"Enough, Daughter of Ruin!" She stepped toward her.

Emmy raised her eyes to Edmar's, and her heart twisted. A lifetime of promises reflected there in his ocean-colored eyes.

We had only just begun coming back to each other...

So much blood. The smell of copper strengthening in the air.

"Why are you doing this?" Her throat spasmed as she asked her next question. "What do you want with the Gods' Stones?"

Ignoring her questions, the woman cupped her cheek, her touch unexpectedly gentle, but slick with blood. "What happened to your mother wasn't your fault, Emmy. But you should thank me. I'm getting revenge for you."

"No!" Defiance filled her voice. Her mother's words, a soft reassurance, echoed in her mind. *It's not your fault.* "Adria isn't responsible for my mother's death. I'm not responsible. *You* are! You have caused every terrible thing in my life. Losing my mother, the trauma of her death, the pain I've lived with every single day of my life."

The fleeting sympathy vanished from the Sea Witch's hardened face.

"Let me tell you about trauma, loss, and a mother's love." Her voice was a low growl. "Remember the story, Daughter of Ruin? Two gods loved one mermaid, but she chose the wrong god? I was that mermaid."

She circled Emmy, raising the knife.

"The Fire God—" Her voice cracked, filled with rage. "Ignis raped me. Burned me. Tore me apart. Shattered my body. Stole my future."

The blade traced a chilling path along Emmy's arm, and she flinched.

"I am *the* Immortal Child, unable to die. My father put me back together, melding metal magic with my flesh. Ignis is the reason I can't walk on land anymore." The Sea Witch hissed through her teeth as if reliving her pain. "But that loss, it doesn't compare to what he truly stole. Ignis took my unborn daughter from me, destroyed her when he ripped my body apart and burned my pieces. Or so I thought for thousands of years."

The Sea Witch stopped behind her, one arm coming around her shoulder, pulling her back against her thin body. The seashell necklace dug into her back.

"Metallon lied," she whispered, her voice raw. "He told me Ignis killed her, the baby in my womb. But he *hid* her, *imprisoned* her. He thought to contain her power. He underestimated me. Never underestimate a mother's love."

Metallon is Sygilla's father, and he hid the Summer Child, his granddaughter. That was the missing piece to the puzzle of why the dwarves were tasked by him to protect her.

Sygilla's voice rose with her next words. "That's why I'm here," she said, coldly. "To protect her. And to confront the one who betrayed me. He will help me. Or he will suffer."

The ritual knife pressed against Emmy's throat.

"Remember your promise, Sygilla," Edmar yelled. The promise the Sea Witch wouldn't kill her if Edmar did as he was told. His navy aura bloomed across his skin.

Without looking at him, the Sea Witch threw her pearlescent magic over him, binding him in place. He bucked against the lines wrapped around him, anchored to the ground.

"Hurt her, and I won't stop hunting you. I'll spend every breath promising my vengeance while I chase you to the ends of the earth." He growled, half shifting into his dragon form within the limitations of the binding magic. "I will kill you!"

The Sea Witch's dark chuckle was the only reply.

"Please," Emmy whimpered, the Ocean's Lament a mournful memory she wished to feel echoing in her chest. "Don't kill me."

As the words left her lips, her mind raced through everything she would be losing with Edmar—their future together, stolen before it could begin. The ache in her heart overshadowed the physical pain, her love for him a lifeline she couldn't bear to lose.

"I've only killed a mother today," the Sea Witch said, her voice flat. "I wouldn't want to deprive you of that experience. But I can't take chances."

Pressure on the blade, then a hesitation, her hand trembling.

"I never wanted this," she said softly, sadness in her voice. "But I have no choice, my Daughter of Ruin."

Emmy closed her eyes, her body shaking, fire acid surging in her veins. It wouldn't be enough.

"You're not alone," Edmar said.

Her eyes opened to meet his across the Mer-Ka-Ba. Ocean-colored eyes filled with love and fear, a light blue aura circling in the irises.

She nodded, fire acid searing her insides.

"I love you, Emmy."

She almost returned his words, but her mind sharpened. "The necklace, Edmar! Destroy it—"

The ritual blade yanked across her throat. Pain exploded, and she gasped, blood filling her mouth, slipping into her lungs.

"Sygilla!" Edmar screamed.

Darkness, a navy field pierced by stars, flooded her vision. She coughed and coughed, but her blood choked her.

Gently, the Sea Witch lowered her, brushing her hair back with a tenderness that felt like mockery. She smiled, surrounded by a shimmery pearlescent aura.

"I understand your pain, child," she whispered. "But sacrifices must be made. Even by those we love."

Then she left Emmy's side. Gilly. Her best friend. The Sea Witch. The woman who had killed her mother.

She lay dazed, vision blurring, choking on the coppery taste of blood, her life spilling into the basin, mingling with the Sun Stone. The gem pulsed with golden light, growing in intensity at the corner of her vision. She couldn't turn her head to see it, to see Metallon awaken, the very reason she had to die.

Chaos erupted. Shouts. Clashes of metal. Magic flared—pearlescent, lavender, and navy exploding above her. Such pretty colors, so much prettier than red. What color would a child between her and Edmar have used?

Maybe purple, her red and his blue. Purple like Gilly.

She wished she could have seen it.

"Hold on, Emmy! Wait for me!" Edmar's voice, laced with despair, pierced through her haze. But she couldn't move to tell him she didn't have a choice. The world was slipping away from her. He was slipping away.

The Sun Stone blazed, a blinding white light. Energy surged through her, warmth chasing away the cold, calming her fire acid.

Metallon.

Her Father was calling her home.

Fighting encroaching darkness, she clung to consciousness. She couldn't let go, not yet. She had to stay awake. Had to talk to him. Had to plead for her freedom, for her people, the mermaids enslaved to their gems. Had to plead for a life she hadn't lived with Edmar, a future they deserved.

Her mother's face, beautiful and serene, flashed before her eyes. Then Edmar—the way he looked that first night at dinner, standing by the window, starlight framing his silhouette, a smile that made her heart ache.

She didn't want to let go, but it was too late.

I love you, Edmar.

Darkness closed in, taking all her dreams and memories away.

Chapter 104
EDMAR

The world stopped and narrowed to a single point. Emira, lying limp on the cold stone, the Sea Witch looming over her. Sapphire hair darkened with blood.

No.

For a heartbeat, he was paralyzed, his eyes locked on Emira's pale face. The pain in his arm became insignificant, a distant throb. His magic coiled, a serpent of ice and fury thrumming beneath his skin. Her blood, her life, spilled out before him.

Rage exploded.

He finally broke through the magic that bound him. Ice shards, jagged edges glinting in the torchlight, hurtled toward the Sea Witch. She was distracted, her back to him. She didn't see them coming.

The impact sent her tumbling. A crash echoed from the shadows.

The chamber trembled, the Mer-Ka-Ba spinning faster, its energy a crushing weight. It hummed louder and louder, a whirring noise added to its cadence.

He barely registered it. Only Emira mattered.

"Emmy!" He rushed to her, his heart a frantic drum in his chest. He gathered her into his arms, his hand over her throat, trying to staunch the flow of blood.

Too much blood. It spilled between his fingers.

"Emira?" His voice broke. "Emmy, please… I'm here. You're not alone."

But she was unresponsive, her skin losing its warmth, blood on her lips.

Panic clawed at his throat. *No, no, no. This can't be happening.* This wasn't how it was supposed to end. He'd only just stopped being an idiot. They were supposed to have more time. He looked around wildly. Cielan, face a mask, tore through the ropes binding Adria. Lian was already at his side.

"Help!" His voice echoed, raw with anguish. "Cielan, please!"

Cielan knelt beside him in a heartbeat. His colorless eyes scanned Emira's wound. He looked up at Edmar and shook his head, then vanished into the shadows.

The chamber shook with rocking vibrations, dust raining down. The Mer-Ka-Ba accelerated, its whirring rising into a shrill whine, accompanied by a deep whump whump whump.

Footsteps from the entrance. Solvrev appeared, his gaze taking in the chaotic scene with calm intensity. He was at Edmar's side in an instant, tearing off his tunic to press it against her neck.

"So much blood," Edmar choked out, barely able to form the words.

"Vayushin is coming," Solvrev said grimly. "He is the strongest healer we have."

The chamber groaned, tremors intensifying. The ground shook.

Then Vayushin appeared, alarm in his mismatched eyes. He rushed to Adria, seeing her first, silver light flowing from his fingertips as he wove a healing spell around her mangled wrists.

"Help her!" Edmar cried, his voice breaking. "Please, Vayushin!"

But Vayushin didn't respond, his focus on Adria, his brow furrowed in concentration. Adria attempted to rise, but the griffin pushed her back down.

"Stay still, love," Lian pleaded, his silver hair tangled.

Adria, her eyes glazed with pain, weak from blood loss, ignored him. She broke through both men and crawled toward the basin, her movements labored, her good hand reaching for the Sun Stone.

"Adria, no." Lian's cry was lost in the roar of the Mer-Ka-Ba.

Cielan emerged from the shadows, carrying a dazed Avi.

Destroy the necklace. Emira's last words. The seashell necklace Gilly gave her before they left, the same she offered to Adria to protect Avi.

Before he could warn Cielan, Avi's gaze landed on the Mer-Ka-Ba. She climbed down from the vamphyr's arms, eyes blazing with amethyst light as the Sea Witch took her over again. Whips of pearlescent magic aimed for Adria.

Lian's silvery-blue magic shielded her, but it was too weak, the Sea Witch crashing through his magic.

More figures entered the chamber—templars and monks, even Nintura warriors—but they hesitated, unsure how to intervene.

One brave templar rushed forward, breaking the Sea Witch's concentration. She turned, lashing out with her magic, pearlescent lines grabbing each limb and yanking him apart. He exploded in a spray of blood, bones, and internal organs.

The others stalled, some beginning to pray.

"Stay back!" Solvrev shouted above the noise. "She's too powerful!"

The Sea Witch turned back toward the Mer-Ka-Ba. The chamber trembled. Raw power thickened the air. The Mer-Ka-Ba spun faster, a blinding vortex of white light. Edmar shielded Emira instinctively.

Then it stopped.

The noise, the shaking temple.

It all stilled.

Edmar raised his head.

A figure of molten silver materialized, great metal wings like an eagle's stretched out behind him. His eyes burned like forge fires.

Metallon.

Edmar stared, awe and terror warring within him. He felt small, insignificant, in the presence of this ancient power, just as he'd felt with Solis.

"Please," he whispered, his voice choked with emotion. "Save her."

Metallon's silver gaze touched on him, then swept over the chamber, eyes cold and assessing. No emotion revealed itself on his placid, shiny face. Then his eyes fell on Avi, and his expression darkened, his anger a controlled inferno.

"Sygilla," Metallon's voice rumbled like thunder. "What have you done?"

"Father." The Sea Witch, her form radiating power from Avi's body, stood defiantly in front of Cielan. Her voice trembled with rage. "Why did you hide her? Why tell me she was dead?"

Metallon's gaze softened, a flicker of sadness in his fiery eyes.

"I did what I thought was best, Sygilla." His voice was laced with a weary grief. "To protect her. To protect the world."

"She's my daughter." The Sea Witch' voice cracked. "You imprisoned her, condemned her to a life of solitude! You betrayed me!"

Sorrow and resolve warred on Metallon's face. "I understand, daughter. But your path is dangerous. Your pursuit of the Gods' Stones, your manipulation of the merfolk. You threaten to destroy us all by helping your daughter."

"I do what I have to," she hissed. "To protect her. And I will continue to do so."

"No, Sygilla." A plea laced his voice. "Abandon this quest. Help me restore balance. We will save her."

"You would kill her."

"I did not before," Metallon said, extending a hand. "Trust me."

"Never!" Sygilla's eyes blazed.

Vayushin moved silently to Edmar's side, his silver magic hovering over Emira. He looked weary, strained.

Edmar couldn't feel her heartbeat. His despair reflected in the Metal God's face.

But then Metallon hid his emotions with resolute restraint. "I will stop your daughter, with or without your help."

The Sea Witch attacked, pearlescent energy slamming into the god. He slid back, unharmed. He didn't retaliate, his gaze fixed on her, an ocean of sadness in his burning eyes. "You break my heart, Sygilla."

Rage twisted her face.

"I will protect her," she hissed, magic flaring again. "Even if I have to destroy you."

"One last time," Metallon said, his voice resolute. "Abandon this quest. Or face the consequences."

A grunt stole Edmar's attention.

Adria, face pale and contorted with pain, plucked the black Sun Stone out of its bloody bath, clutching it in her hand. Whispered words unlocked its power. Black smoke erupted from the stone, wrapping around her, turning her skin dark.

"The necklace!" he shouted to her.

Adria's eyes flickered to him, an unnatural glow pulsing in them, then to her daughter. She lifted the Sun Stone.

"Show me the truth," she said low, her voice a rasp.

The gem blazed, golden light devouring the black smoke. It shot forward, pushing Cielan back, enveloping the Sea Witch. She screamed in rage, but the light held her fast, its power undeniable.

Cielan rushed forward, but the magic repelled him, and his eyes filled with desperation.

The Sea Witch's form flickered.

Adria's eyes illuminated with crimson and gold light, her skin a darkened shimmer.

"Leave my daughter, Sygilla!" Her voice, amplified, ancient, resonated through the chamber.

The Sea Witch fought back, her magic a desperate storm. Lian's magic joined Adria's, pressing against the Sea Witch.

"The chain," Adria's aged voice reverberated, and the magic sliced through the gold chain holding the seashell. It clattered to the ground. A whip of black smoke pounded the seashell against the stone ground, smashing it.

The Sea Witch screeched, and the chamber trembled anew.

For a moment, the Sea Witch was visible—not as Avi or even Gilly, the beautiful mermaid, but as herself, her true form. Black octopus legs writhing, metal gleaming on her skin, her one amethyst eye cold and merciless, the other a metal telescope with a dot of red. Her expression twisted with rage and despair.

The Sun Stone's golden light intensified until Sygilla's form was barely visible within it, a writhing silhouette trapped in a storm of magic. She screamed, and golden light exploded outward, sending shockwaves through the chamber.

Silence reigned until the light faded.

She was gone.

But Avi stood there, her body swaying, her eyes flickering back to cerulean blue, her hair her own again. Then, with a shuddering gasp, she collapsed.

With supernatural speed, Cielan caught her, his face pale.

"Dolcivita." Cielan's voice cracked with anguish as he cradled her, walking away into the darkness.

Edmar's fingers tightened on Emira. Vayushin, sweat beading on his face, frowned.

"Please," he whispered to her, his voice raw and broken. "Don't leave me, Emmy."

Metallon, his liquid metal form radiating power, stepped forward, the fire in his eyes gone, leaving behind a shimmering pool of silver. He stooped for a moment to grasp the fallen ritual blade, the weapon disappearing. Then he straightened. His imposing presence offered waves of alternating cold and heat, yet there was a gentleness in his demeanor.

He looked down at Emira, his fiery gaze softening. He reached out, and his magic, a luminous bronze netting, settled over her, sinking and vanishing into her body. Then his hand landed on Edmar's shoulder.

"She is a true daughter of the sea," Metallon said, grief lacing his voice. "What she gave today will not be forgotten."

"No, you have to save her," Edmar begged, tears on his cheeks.

Metallon's gaze remained a moment longer, but he said nothing and then he was gone, vanishing in a shimmering silver light.

Heavy silence filled the chamber, the echoes of Metallon's power fading away. Edmar cradled Emira, his heart a dragon's stone in his chest.

Her skin was cold. Her eyes closed, lips parted, chest still.

Despair deepened. Not even with all the magic in the world could he save her. He pressed his forehead against hers, tears mingling with her blood.

"Emmy?" he whispered, his voice a broken plea.

Silence.

Chapter 105

EMMY

Emmy woke to an unsettling silence. She lay on a bed of soft moss, the air cool, tinged with metal. Silvery fog swirled around her, patches of mist twinkling above like clouds moving across the sky. A deep calm settled over her, erasing the memory of pain, of the Sea Witch, of blood.

What is this?

Her voice didn't echo in the vast silence. It didn't even seem to reach her own ears. Silence, profound and unsettling, surrounded her, wrapping around her like a shroud. This wasn't death as she'd imagined.

She sat up. Warmth washed her chest, and her hands automatically touched her throat.

Blue blood coated her fingertips. A ragged slice split her neck.

How interesting. No pain.

A towering figure of molten silver with great metal eagle wings materialized. His eyes glowed with a warm, inner fire. Metallon, the Metal God, her divine Father.

"You have my gratitude, Daughter of Water and Metal," Metallon's voice, a deep, resonant hum, vibrated through her. "You have awakened me from a long slumber."

Her throat refused to work. Panic tightened her chest.

Speak to me in your mind, he said.

Where am I?

"The Nexi, a crossroads for my children with Aqua. What you would call the Sea of Shadows." His gaze softened. "You are between worlds, Daughter. You are dying."

Dying? Not dead but dying, waiting to move on to the Celestial Firmament. The surrounding calm did nothing to quell the panic rising within her. She wasn't ready. There was so much left undone. *Edmar...*

"I can stop your soul from crossing over." A blend of power and compassion filled his words. "Keep you tethered to the mortal realm. But the magic, it might have unintended consequences."

Unintended consequences. Her fear intensified. She recalled the stories of the Vamphyrians, the first vamphyr, and the curse that bound her children to a shadow life, an insatiable thirst for blood magic.

I don't want to be a vamphyr.

"This is different, Emira." His gaze held hers, the warmth in his eyes a reassurance against the fear threatening to consume her. "You are not dead, not yet. The magic is not the same. But I offer you a choice, to remain or to move on. And in return for your sacrifice, for awakening me, I will grant you one boon. Any favor within my power."

A boon. The word sparked a conflicting swirl of hope and uncertainty within her, making her hesitate before answering. A review of her life unfolded—destructive powers, pain inflicted, both physical and emotional, a burdensome existence marked by the selfish choice to free herself, granting untold power to an evil being. A different path had always seemed beyond reach, yet Edmar had offered her a glimpse of something more.

She could make a choice for herself, ask for her magic to be stripped, but where would that leave her? Who would that serve other than herself?

She'd been a burden. First to her mother, then to her father and sisters. Most of all, to Anjali, who had cared for her, comforted her by painting stars in her room. Anjali, now likely wed, would soon mourn her husband. Her father would see to that, to gain control of the new kingdom and of his daughter again.

She knew what her one boon would be. *Can I accept one but not the other?*

"Explain," he said, his silver brow furrowing.

If I can only have one boon, then I'll take the one favor, but I would rather you allow my soul to cross over. I don't want to return to the life I had.

Curiosity flickered in his eyes. "What boon do you seek, Daughter?"

Free the mermaids. She steadied herself. This was too important to get wrong. *They are tethered to their gems, enslaved to their fathers, then to their mates. It's a curse, a life of servitude and subjugation. Sever their binding tethers to their gems. Release them from bondage.*

Metallon frowned, his silver expression troubled, his voice edged with frustration. "I created that connection to protect them. You know the history, the abuse, the abandonment. It was meant to ensure their safety."

The tethers became another form of abuse, she countered. *Many mermaids are forced to live forever with their abusers. Some are treated better than others, but the bond didn't change the mermen. It only changed the way they control us.* Silence. She held his gaze, pleading. *It's better to be free, Metallon. Even if it means facing danger.*

He sighed, a deep, weary sound that reverberated through the stillness. "It will not be easy, Emira," he said, his voice heavy. "There will be consequences, repercussions that could devastate merfolk societies."

You are wise, Father. You will find a way, and their futures will be brighter.

He studied her for a long moment, his molten silver form shimmering. "So be it," he said finally. "Your boon is granted."

Thank you, Father. Relief and gratitude filled her.

"You could have chosen something for yourself," Metallon said, his fiery gaze searching hers. "More power, riches, magic. I'm impressed by your dedication to your people. Why this selfless act?"

She shook her head. *Freedom matters more. I wouldn't want to live in a world where mermaids are still enslaved.*

He tilted his head, intrigued. "And you still wish to cross over?"

Though her heart ached, she forced herself to remain composed. She longed to tell him about her magic, about her own desire for freedom, but she'd used her boon. Risking what she had gained for the mermaids was not an option. A delicate approach was needed, one that might gain his compassion.

She chose her words carefully. *It's better if I move on. I'm a threat.*

His gaze narrowed, and for a moment, she feared she'd said too much. Then amusement flickered across his silver face. He'd given her the opening to pique his interest, and she'd taken advantage of it without revealing her true motive. A mystery to intrigue him.

"Why a threat?" he asked.

Internally, she sighed, grateful she had his attention still. Now to reveal her truth. *My magic. It's uncontrollable and destructive. If I had another boon, I would ask you to take it away.*

His interest deepened. He stepped closer, his presence overwhelming as he took her hands in his. His touch was both warm and cool, a strange sensation that made her shiver.

His fully silver-eyed gaze peered deeply into her, reaching down into her soul. *Show me your life, Emira.*

She obeyed.

She closed her eyes, and her life's memories flooded her awareness. The searing pain of her magic, her mother's death, her father's coldness, her people's fear of her power, the crushing loneliness of the Little Palace, Edmar's love, his anger, his forgiveness, the desperate hope they'd found again...

It was all there, a whirlwind of emotions, a life lived on the edge of either abandonment or destruction.

She opened her eyes.

Metallon stepped back, sorrow etched on his face. "Your magic is not cursed, Emira," he said. "*You* are."

The Sea Witch and the Summer Child's protector had said something similar. She'd hoped it was a lie.

"It's a power woven into your very being, a force you cannot escape without the right magic. Magic I don't have."

Her heart sank. *Is there nothing you can do?*

"I could take away your magic, and you'd be free from its dangers. But you would be mortal, and the pain from moving would remain. You'd live your life as a statue yet again."

Hope died, leaving only a cold emptiness. She could go back. But what kind of life awaited her?

Living on the land as a mortal, without her sister. A life without magic. But still with pain. A life where she could never truly touch Edmar, never dance again, never mate with him again.

Never experience the freedom she craved without suffering. She'd be a burden once more. It was no life at all, and she couldn't do that to Edmar.

I don't want to die. The Ocean's Lament played in the shimmering air, not coming from her, but from mist in the sky—the shapes moving over her, twinkling in time with the song.

Other merfolk, crossing over, sorrowful for her. She sent a prayer of thanks to them before giving her final response to her Father.

I'd rather die than live a life of pain, a life without love, a life without Edmar's breathless kisses.

Metallon nodded, his gaze filled with sadness.

"As you wish, Daughter."

The silvery light around him faded.

"May the sea guide your soul to peace."

CHAPTER 106

EDMAR

Edmar cradled Emira, searching for any flicker of life, any sign of the warmth that had always burned within her. Vayushin's silver magic pulsed over her, closing the wound at her throat, but the griffin's expression spoke volumes.

"I'm too late," Vayushin said, his voice hollow.

He wanted to scream, to break the world that had taken her from him, but all that came was a strangled breath. An invisible, suffocating grip choked his throat.

Anguish, unlike anything he'd known, drowned him in a sea of grief. The chaos of the room—Cielan's frantic words, Adria's labored breaths, the murmurs of the templars and monks—blurred into a distant hum, fading into insignificance.

The world had narrowed to this one point, and nothing beyond mattered. Not when all he could see was the radiant smile and the twinkle in emerald eyes lifted toward the night sky. The sound of laughter, unrestrained and full of sheer exuberance, as she learned to dance despite the pain in her feet.

The way she had demanded he make love to her after impaling herself on him. Nails clawing his back. A long, breathless moan as her release seized her—the look of pure ecstasy etched across her face, sending him over the edge.

These were the things that mattered. The spark of life within her, the unrelenting joy of existence. He clung to those memories.

A hand on his heavy shoulder, warm then cold, pulled him from the abyss he desperately wanted to fall into.

Metallon knelt before him, his silver eyes clouded with sorrow. He looked down at Emira with the same grief Edmar felt in his soul. "She is truly a rare gem to mourn."

He's seen her! Jealousy struck his heart, stolen moments the god spent with her, ones Edmar wished he'd had with Emira. "Then she's gone?"

Metallon shook his head slowly. "She wished to move on to the afterlife even after I offered to save her."

"What do you mean? She couldn't have chosen to *die*." His voice cracked, a hoarse whisper. "Why would she choose to leave me?" The question reeked of his desperation, but whatever her reasons, he knew Metallon spoke the truth.

"I could not release her curse." True regret lay in his explanation. "She didn't want to return to a life of pain. To be a burden to those she loved."

I told her we would find a way... that I wouldn't give up. The suffocating grip returned, crushing his chest. He opened his mouth, but he struggled to draw a full breath. His lungs rattled, frantic for air. *How easy is it to choose to simply stop breathing?*

"How can I live in a world without her?" *This. This is what Kalden felt in the depths of his despair.* The answer to his question was simple. He squeezed his eyes shut, willing his heart to stop. "I can't live without her."

Promise me you will continue the Sun God's holy quest. Her silvery and ethereal voice, a light musical tone. The voice of an angel.

He'd made that promise, and his heart remembered, refusing to stop beating. "It's too unfair!" He glanced up at Metallon. "If you can't bring back what was taken from me, then give her my life. Let me trade my life for hers."

"I'm sorry, Edmar. I don't have the power for this." Such deep sorrow reflected in the silver lines of the god's face. "But I offered her one boon. Yet, she asked for nothing for herself."

An invaluable treasure, Metallon said into his mind. He told Edmar about Emira's selfless wish. "And this has been done, causing great upheaval among my children."

What could he care when the one person who mattered most to him lay lifeless in his arms?

Care, Metallon said, *because she did.*

He bowed his head, a pang of guilt stabbing him. He'd been the one to push her to see how her actions affected those beyond herself. And in her death, she had shown great honor. *What more could I have asked for in a mate?*

"Do you know the source of her curse?" Metallon asked.

The question made little sense, lost in his grief. *Why does it matter?*

"It is Moon magic." Metallon's silver eyes searching his. "Without knowing the source, there are few options for breaking her curse."

Moon magic... Deep in his brain, he remembered a conversation with Rivus, just weeks ago. It felt like years now. A renewed sense of betrayal reared in his heart, striking painfully as he remembered how his friend had nearly destroyed him. But his words remained. *When she unleashed her power, we smelled a storm of Fire and Moon magic, intertwined, yet volatile.*

Emira had never mentioned knowing the source of her curse, but could it have come from the Snow Princess, the same as his curse?

"If she was cursed by your Snow Princess, then she might yet help her," Metallon said, knowing his thoughts.

Edmar frowned, confusion swirling through his jumbled thoughts. Words came to his tongue and escaped just as quickly. *Why is Metallon talking about her curse as if it still mattered?*

Adria knelt before them, the Sun Stone pulsing in her hand. Her lavender skin had darkened to an ebony shimmer. Crimson and golden lines radiated in her eyes, like twin suns pulsing in the sky. "The curse was mine given to me by a Moon seer." Adria's voice resonated with ancient power. "She believed my line would bear the Chaos Lore, and she sought to stop that future from happening. The Sea Witch transferred the curse to Emmy's mother."

Lian joined her, and she glanced at him, but those eyes seemed to look far away.

Metallon shifted uneasily, his silver gaze on the dark Sun Stone. "Then we need only find this seer."

Adria shook her head, black smoke coiling from the stone, wrapping around her fingers. "My mother killed her."

"Then we have a problem." Metallon leaned away. "But Adria, daughter of my life partner, Aqua, you must put this God stone away from you before the power corrupts you."

Anger blazed in the twin suns of her eyes. "You wish to take this power!"

"Adria," Lian said, drawing her attention. "Tell me you don't love me."

"Lies," she hissed, her face twisted in disgust.

"Say it." Lian's gaze never flinched from his wife's. "Tell me you don't love me."

She glanced at the stone. The twin suns in her eyes vibrated, curling with black smoke. So much power pulsed from her aura. Then whispered words fell from her lips, and the black smoke withdrew. Her skin returned to its normal hue, her eyes to gray-blue again.

She looked up at Lian, a smile on her lips. "I love you. Always."

The hybrid fae nodded, taking the Sun Stone from her, wincing until he put it away from himself, and away from Adria. His wife grasped his hand, now blistered and reddened, and used magic to heal him. Only Lian's fae half allowed him to survive touching the stone.

"I don't understand." All eyes turned to Edmar as he continued. "Why all this talk about Emmy's curse when she has crossed over?"

"I did not honor her wish." The god laid a hand on Emira's forehead. "She believes she has crossed over, but I tethered her soul to a dream realm."

Edmar's chest tightened. *Can it be true?* But of course it is. The god wouldn't lie. Tension drained from his shoulders as he exhaled, the heavy grip loosening from his throat. He took a deep breath, the first in what felt like an eternity. A faint light sparked within him, tenuous and defying the darkness. "She's alive?"

Metallon laid a hand on his chest, the place where his heart would beat. "I am humbled by her selfless act. My own act, in not fulfilling her wishes, lacks the honor she showed. I will beg her forgiveness for this."

Edmar shook his head vehemently, looking down at Emira. Her chest didn't rise, her skin still cold. "I would give all my honor away to save her."

"You may yet have to." The god sighed. "I will keep her in her suspended state until you break the curse. But your choices are limited."

His muscles tightened in readiness. "I'm going to bring her back. Whatever it takes."

"Three choices, then. You could ask Sygilla to remove the curse." Metallon frowned over this. "I wouldn't want her to have that power again, but it is an option."

"How was Sygilla able to remove the curse from Adria, yet you cannot remove it from Emmy?"

The god blinked at him slowly, and unease filled at the thought that he'd offended Metallon somehow, but then the god answered him.

"Sygilla has collected thousands of merfolk souls all tied to magic. She has the power to rival all but Chaos themselves."

Why would the Sea Witch have ever needed the Gods' Stones?

The Gods' Stones together could control Chaos, Metallon whispered in his mind.

Edmar shook his head, imagining the devastation the Sea Witch could unleash with all the Gods' Stones in her grasp. Returning Emira's curse to Sygilla was equally unthinkable. "The Sea Witch would sooner kill us, and even if she didn't, it's not a possibility I can accept."

"You are likely right. Then you have two choices," Metallon said. "The first is to find a Moon Fae with the affinity to undo curses."

Wonderful. In a world without Moon Fae, his choices looked bleak. "Could a half-blood do it, or any fae with Moon blood?"

Metallon touched a finger to his chin. "It is possible, but highly dangerous. For both the fae and Emira, especially if they don't have the knowledge to undo curses. Extreme caution would be needed. It is better to find a full-blooded Moon Fae."

His heart sank. "I know of none like that left alive."

Metallon smiled. "There are two full Moon Fae yet walking in this world. Perhaps you could seek one out."

Seek one out? He glanced at the Sun Stone. It could help in finding one of the Moon Fae, but that might be dangerous itself. Whoever these Moon Fae were, they would be in hiding and likely ready to attack any who sought them.

The god nodded, reading his thoughts.

"I'll find them. We'll undo the curse." Edmar vowed this as his gaze fixed on Emira. His love for her, the need to protect her, a fierce ache in his chest. "I will search the entire earth for whatever is needed to save her."

"There is yet one other choice," Metallon said. "Seek the Moon Goddess. She can eradicate any curse made with her magic."

Once more hope filled him. He was to wake all the gods, anyway. Seeking the Moon Goddess to help Emira coincided with his duty.

But Metallon shook his head. "Luna is a fickle woman with fickle ways. There is no telling how she'll react to your request. But I do know she is not inclined to help those who are not her children. Other supplicants have met their death by asking for any boon."

Those were his choices, limited but a path forward. Find a full-blooded Moon Fae or ask the Moon Goddess for help. He wouldn't consider the Sea Witch. Even if they survived, he'd never give her the magic to wield against another innocent person, or to use it as a weapon while she helped the Summer Child gain dominance in the world.

Each path felt impossible, a daunting task in a world that had already taken so much from him, but they gave him hope. He wouldn't give up. He couldn't.

First, he'd lean on Lian and Avi to at least try to help Emira. If they could remove the curse, that would solve every problem. "I will not rest until I bring her back."

Metallon's gaze softened, and he lowered his voice with a final warning. "She's in a fragile state. Her soul is tethered to a dream. If she's moved, her soul may not find its way back to her body."

"I understand." He couldn't bear to leave her side, but if Lian and Avi failed to undo the curse...

He'd have to seek one of the two Moon Fae or the Moon Goddess.

And he'd have to leave Emira behind while he searched the world for her cure. The thought twisted a knife in his gut, a pain almost as unbearable as losing her completely.

Metallon leaned down, placing a gentle kiss on Emira's forehead, a gesture so tender that Edmar's throat tightened. "May the sea guide her soul," the god murmured, before starting to fade.

"Father," Solvrev said, catching the god's attention. "A boon, if you would please, Father, for the honor of your people, we need your help."

Metallon's form solidified as he stood, facing Solvrev and Vayushin. "Speak, my son."

"While the Sapphira Syrēna's blood is still fresh," Solvrev crossed his hands over his chest and bowed toward the Mer-Ka-Ba with the basin filled with blue blood. "We would ask your assistance to stop the storms around the island."

Edmar snarled, scales erupting along his arms, his body lengthening. "You would use her as she dies?"

"I mean no disrespect to our Sapphira Syrēna." Solvrev gave him the same bow. "We will pray for her to return, and we will fiercely protect her until that time. All of Aelunis will know of her sacrifice, and she will be celebrated for waking Metallon." Triumph gleamed in his eyes now. "But how will you seek her cure if you cannot leave the island?"

The kitsune was right. His anger deflated, his body returning to its human form, while despair clawed in his chest once more.

Metallon reached for the Mer-Ka-Ba, holding the three-dimensional star in his silver hand. "I will do this. The storms were created to protect me. After that, I must be gone."

As the god chanted, his bronze-colored magic glowing around him, expanding, encompassing the room, Edmar sat there, alone with Emira, his grief mingling with the fragile hope Metallon had given him. "I promise. I will not let you go. I will bring you back to me."

He had plans to create. *Plans within plans,* as Adria had taught him.

Anything to save her.

CHAPTER 107

EDMAR

Days turned into nights and back into days, a blur of restless sleep and anxious pacing. He couldn't stay in that chamber, the ritual chamber, the chamber where Emira lay, a fragile echo of the woman who had stormed into his life, shattered his Frostlands, and warmed his heart.

But he couldn't leave her.

"She needs you strong, Edmar," Adria had said, her voice firm. "Not ill with worry. Get out. Find fresh air."

So he walked in the temple gardens, worry a constant companion. Lian's attempt to break the curse had failed. His Moon Fae magic too diluted.

"Avi wants to try," Lian had said, hope weary in his voice. "She believes her visions, her connection to the affinity for prophecy, might hold the key."

But Cielan insisted they wait. Avi was too weak, spending most of her time sleeping.

She looked so different, her face gaunt, her eyes haunted. "I saw it all," she'd said in a rare moment of wakefulness. "Felt it all. But I had no control over my body. I'm so sorry, Edmar."

"There's nothing to forgive," he'd said, and she'd fallen asleep again.

"She's not strong enough yet," Cielan said, his love for Avi a shield against the darkness that still shadowed them. "A few more days."

A few more days.

An eternity.

He clung to that hope. It was better than embarking on a desperate search for a Moon Fae or risking the wrath of the Moon Goddess. Either way meant leaving Emira, and that possibility frightened him.

"Why are you so devoted to Avi?" he asked the vamphyr. He'd wondered this many times, when she hadn't necessarily reciprocated Cielan's affections.

"She knew me before I became this." The vamphyr's stoic mask fell away when he looked at Avi. "I loved her even then, but I was different. I only knew how to master and rule those I claimed as mine. And for a time, she was mine."

He'd wiped a hand over his face. "She left me. Broken, I wandered, until I met my fate with Vamphyr. Now I live to serve Avi, to atone for all my misdeeds, both to her and the other women I claimed when I was alive."

It explained so much—their history, the unspoken darkness that kept Avi from trusting him. Cielan would forever strive to prove his loyalty to her.

Edmar went back to pacing the temple gardens, the scent of exotic flowers a cloying reminder of a world that no longer held any joy. He extended his dragon claws, then retracted them. When the first stars of the early evening appeared, he longed to fly toward them. It had been a thousand years since he'd flown at night.

Then he rounded a corner and stopped. A man, wrapped in sandy-colored linen, approached Vayushin and Solvrev. He looked like a mummy, only his dark eyes visible beneath the bandages.

Edmar paused, listening.

The man prostrated himself before Vayushin. "I have returned, Grand Anthos."

"Rise, Bian," Vayushin said, warmth in his voice.

The man—Bian—turned to Solvrev, bowing. "It is good to see you, Sentinel."

"And you, Master of Shadows," Solvrev replied with a bow of his own.

Grand Anthos? Sentinel? Master of Shadows? Suspicion coiled in his chest.

Vayushin embraced Bian, genuine affection in the gesture. "Welcome home, old friend. Did you succeed?"

Bian nodded, pulling out a small, iridescent gray labradorite.

"The Metal Stone," Vayushin said, his voice hushed. "Excellent. And you still have the Moon Stone?"

The Metal Stone, the Moon Stone... How many did they have?

Kalden had mentioned the Metal Stone was in his kingdom. But it was here now.

"Our Ninjactus is to destroy them," Bian said, bowing his head.

Ninjactus. Their primary mission. To destroy the stones. *But how?* Lian's lessons about Ninturas and their missions didn't include this information.

Solvrev scowled. "Where is this going—"

"I swear to all eight gods, Bian, don't tell me you've lost it," Vayushin said.

Bian bowed lower. "Forgive this servant's insolence." He didn't rise from his bow, not even when no response was given. Once more, he prostrated himself, face smashed to the stone pavements. "I give my life for this grievous offense."

Anger twisted their faces. *What will the griffin and kitsune do?*

Vayushin blew out a large breath and lifted Bian, his anger fading as he embraced him again, a hand cradling his head. "I could never take your life, my friend."

Bian clung to him, his face buried against Vayushin's robes. *Lovers? Or just very close friends?*

"Of course, neither would I," Solvrev said, rolling his eyes. "But tell us what happened."

Bian stepped away from Vayushin, who looked bereft. "A half stone is indestructible, and finding the other half has been like looking for a bee queen in a haystack."

"Bian..." Solvrev whined. "What happened to the Moon Stone?"

"The queen has it. She will find the princess. They will be reunited."

Does he ever make sense? Vayushin and Solvrev looked as if they found him equally confusing.

"It will be whole again," Bian added.

Solvrev narrowed his eyes. "You've seen this?"

"I have."

Is he a seer? But he couldn't be a full-blooded fae with his dark eyes.

"We still have to figure out how to get the Sun Stone," Solvrev said, his gaze sharp, alert.

Edmar gasped, his heart skipping a beat. *They would take the Sun Stone from me.*

Bian signed something, and Vayushin replied in kind. A tense silence fell over them. *They're planning how to get it.*

"The news came to me of Kyran's death," Bian said, breaking the silence.

Vayushin turned abruptly away, hiding his face in the fall of his dark hair. Then he returned, his face a little less composed. "A reliable source, Bian?" His voice was tight.

The last Griffin King dead. But most thought all the griffins extinct.

"The Consort told me."

"You've seen the queen?" Vayushin's voice rose.

"Many queens. The bee queen less important, in this instance, even if it stung me. But yes."

How do they accomplish anything with this man?

"The Sun Stone, Vayushin," Solvrev insisted. "It's our duty. The Chaos Lore—"

Edmar shivered at the words. *The Chaos Lore.* A prophecy of destruction. Father Jayasurya's warning echoed in his mind—a Moon Fae prophecy intertwining the awakening of the gods with the Chaos Lore. *Is that why they have this Ninjactus?*

But only the Sun Stone could awaken the gods. Their mission had been corrupted.

He had to protect the stone.

"It is our sacred duty to gather the Gods' Stones," Solvrev said. "To protect our world."

"But we need the gods, too," Vayushin said, his gaze hardening. "What if thwarting the Ice Dragon's quest hinders our goal? We need more magic."

Edmar frowned over their words, but also because Bian was gone. *Has he gone to steal the Sun Stone?* The thought of the man rifling through his chambers made him sick.

"The Sun Stone belongs to the Order," Solvrev said coldly. "Not to some dragon."

Edmar turned to leave—a blade pressed against his throat.

"Caught you," Bian whispered. "A dragon in my net." His dark eyes perused his face. "Not as big as the other one, but you have the look of him."

Vayushin and Solvrev walked toward them, their expressions unreadable, as if they had known Edmar had been there. He must have given himself away.

"I won't give you the stone," Edmar growled. "It belongs to my people."

Vayushin silenced the others with a raised hand. "We will not steal from you, Ice Dragon." He signed to Bian, who lowered the blade. "But let us negotiate how we can help each other. We may have a solution to save your mermaid."

"Like I could trust you."

Heat filled Vayushin's eyes, not all anger. "Give me a chance to *earn* your trust and explain why the Sun Stone must be returned to Aelunis. To *us* when you're done with your holy quest."

How in eight hells does he know about our holy quest? Emira had only told him about awakening Metallon.

Vayushin smiled. "Not much escapes the Kraken."

Edmar laughed.

Obviously, they had been caught in their planning. Vayushin was playing with them. *But why? Because he desires me?* At this point, Edmar couldn't trust any other reason.

"Then let us negotiate, Griffin."

Chapter 108

EMMY

Emmy wandered through a garden bathed in ethereal sunlight. Fragrant flowers bloomed in a riot of color, their petals shimmering with a delicate, silvery light. A gentle breeze carried the scent of the sea. Beautiful sights and sounds, pleasant warmth, but no sounds. She continued to live in a muted world.

She recognized the winding paths, the stone fountain, the roses climbing the trellis archway. Edmar's garden, recreated in this strange, otherworldly realm. Memories surfaced—laughter beneath the starlit sky, whispered stories, the warmth of his hand in hers.

The familiar ache of the Longing tugged at her heart, but it wasn't as overwhelming as before. It was a gentle whisper, a reminder of the life she'd left. *If only Edmar were here.*

But even the beauty of this place, the peace that surrounded her, couldn't fill the emptiness within. She was still alone.

"Where are you, Edmar?" she whispered, her voice a lonely echo in the stillness.

A beautiful prison with no one to share it with? No one to talk to?

She'd been walking for an eternity. Time had no meaning here. Just an endless expanse of beauty, of serene silence.

Is this the afterlife?

She thought she'd at least meet her Mother Goddess here, but she'd seen no one.

She longed for Edmar's touch, his laughter, the way he made her feel alive, the way he looked at her with a love that burned brighter than any star.

She sang softly, a haunting melody of longing and sorrow. Her voice, once a weapon, now a solace, echoed through the empty garden.

Malala appeared on the garden path, wearing her usual white dress with silver accents. Purple, green, and blue strands of her hair intertwined and meshed together into rivers of water flowing around her face.

Why her? She would have literally taken anyone else. With a sigh, she halted in her perpetual walk. "Are you dead?"

The Water Fae's pretty face crumpled, and she trembled. "I don't know." She touched a gash on her temple. Blue blood trickled down her face. Tears slipped down her cheeks. "It hurts, Emmy."

She gathered the fae in her arms. "It's a shock when you first cross over."

She hadn't felt pain herself, but the revelation of Malala's end in the world could be enough to be painful.

The fae cried against her shoulder. Emmy felt her pain, her sorrow, and yet she couldn't cry herself. She sang the Ocean's Lament.

Finally, Malala pulled away, her face wet with tears. "I'm lost."

"You're in the Celestial Firmament."

"I can't be dead." Even straightening her shoulders, the fae still trembled. "This isn't right."

"You're confused." She wiped one of the fae's wet cheeks. "It'll pass."

Malala shook her head and said, in a small voice, "I belong in the eight hells."

Her slate-blue gaze dropped to the broken white stone hanging from her silver chain. She grasped it in her hands, her eyes fluttering closed.

When she opened her eyes after several silent moments, a beautiful smile spread across her face. "They're with me still."

"Who?"

"The ancestors of Moon magic." She offered the stone to Emmy.

Skeptically, she took the stone. Whispers filled her ears, warm and welcoming—just like the Sun Stone. She closed her eyes, letting the magic pull her in.

Voices ran through her mind, promising power. And loss.

The power to manipulate the oceans, change the tides, reshape the underwater kingdoms. But at a terrible cost. Many would die.

It offered a way to change her fate.

But I'm dead, she yelled into the void.

She left us, she left us, she left us—the voices clamored.

Who? She reached for the voices, and found a broken edge, an abyss. Danger hummed, the crack buzzing with angry energy.

She pulled back.

Emmy. Edmar's voice.

She turned, but he was gone.

This is wrong. Slowly, she untangled herself from the evil taint of magic. The voices offered her more power, but she didn't need more power. *Such power has corrupted our world. There's too much magic. Everyone fights for more.*

We won't, we won't, we won't, they said in a chorus. *Free us.*

But her thoughts had already moved into a different vein of the stone, leaving the voices behind.

Could the Chaos Lore heal our world? No magic, no wars? She shook her incorporeal head. *No. People would always fight for power.*

Magic didn't have to go away, but they needed better leadership.

The gods. Waking them could bring balance back to the world. *But I'm dead.*

She withdrew from the stone, opening her eyes.

A wild frenzy shone in Malala's eyes. "Did they tell you?"

"Tell me what?"

"They can break your curse. You only have to accept them." She smiled. "Accept them into your soul. Let them intertwine their magic with your core, and they will free you."

She knocked the stone out of the fae's hands. It swung on its chain, and Malala stared at her, mouth open. "We're dead, Snow Princess."

Malala closed her mouth, shaking her head. Then fear filled her face. "I remember. They are coming for me." She gripped Emmy's shoulders. "Help me! *Please.* They'll kill me."

Then Malala vanished.

She spun around. There was no sign of her. She lifted her chin to the sky. "A diversion?" she asked the empty air. "Entertainment because I was bored?"

But there was only the ethereal sunlight and silence.

She continued walking the garden path, alone once more.

Chapter 109
EDMAR

Several days of negotiations added to Edmar's torment of waiting and uncertainty. All talks with Vayushin had been a delicate dance, a careful balance of power and desperation. He'd learned about the Nintura, the Order of the Flower of Life—a secret society dedicated to protecting magic. But most of their secrets remained shrouded in frustrating ambiguity.

If Avi couldn't help Emira today, he would have to accept Vayushin's terms.

He prayed for Avi's success.

Pacing the ritual chamber restlessly, he closed and opened his fists, frustration mounting. Seven days of watching Emira lie motionless on the makeshift bed, her body a fragile shell, her soul lost in a dream world. Seven days spent wandering the temple gardens, the lush fragrance of exotic flowers a mockery.

Now Avi sat beside his wife, her brow furrowed in concentration, a cool, silvery blue light emanating from her fingertips.

Despite his impatience, he clung to the fragile hope that Avi might succeed. He couldn't bear the thought of leaving Emira behind or accepting Vayushin's terms.

Adria and Lian, healed and eager for adventure, were ready to leave. "We'll sail with you to find the Moon Goddess," Adria had said, her eyes gleaming with the thrill of a new quest.

But Emira was all that mattered.

"It's not working," Avi said, her voice laced with exhaustion. Her magic sputtered.

Emira was unchanged.

"Enough," Cielan said, concern etched on his face. He placed a hand on Avi's shoulder. "You're pushing too hard."

"But I'm the reason she's like this!" Avi's eyes brimmed with tears. "It should be me. I should be the one to—"

"It wasn't your fault, Dolcivita," Cielan said, his voice soothing. "It was the Sea Witch. She's gone now. You're safe."

"But Emmy—"

"No." Cielan's gaze hardened, a protective fire in his clear gaze. "You need to rest." Gingerly, the vamphyr lifted Avi into his arms, glancing at Edmar. "I wish things were different."

Then he vanished in a gust of cool wind, stirring the stale air of the ritual chamber.

Edmar had no choice but to accept Vayushin's terms. Bian would find and bring back a Moon Fae in exchange for joining Edmar on his holy quest to awaken all the gods. He didn't trust Bian, the man responsible for stealing the Metal Stone from Kalden's kingdom.

Before daylight fell, Bian left.

Now he was forced to wait yet again.

But this time, the wait was short.

Bian returned the next day, and they gathered in the ritual chamber. As the Moon Fae entered, everyone but Bryn gasped.

"I know her," she said.

"Aunt Aysima?" Lian stepped forward.

The gray Moon Fae was a figure of ethereal beauty. Small and slender, fragile looking, dressed in simple white garments flowing around her like moonlight. Her hair, a cascade of silver and clear strands, shimmered, the curls twisting and weaving as if alive. Two pairs of gossamer wings fluttered gently behind her.

She flitted toward Lian with a bright smile, her blue eyes sparkling. "Nephew. Wonderful to see you!"

Bian followed behind the fae and introduced her. "This is Aysima dal Aybek, one of the last Moon Fae, also known as Aysima Silverwing, the consort to the late Kyran Silverwing, Queen of the Griffins."

"Hello!" Aysima's voice was melodic, easing the tension. "It's so lovely to be here!"

Vayushin stepped toward her, his eyes shimmering, a hand raised, but Aysima glided past him, her gaze on Emira. The Moon Fae's movements were graceful, her eyes unsettlingly cheerful.

"Oh, you poor darling." She cooed her words at Emira, her expression a mix of concern and childlike wonder. "You look so uncomfortable."

Edmar approached, apprehension warring with hope. Something about this fae felt off.

The Moon Fae hovered her small hands over Emira. Jagged scars, newly healed, marred the fae's wrists.

"Did Bian hurt you?" he asked quietly.

Aysima, oblivious to his worry, placed her hands on Emira's forehead. "My scars? Silly stories. Love and chains. Family and farewells. But it all worked out in the end, didn't it?"

Her words made no sense, but he didn't press for an explanation. He was desperate.

"Don't worry, darling." Aysima smiled down at his wife. "I'll take care of you."

Cool, silvery energy flowed from her hands. Emira's body relaxed, and for the first time in days, she breathed. Edmar's heart stalled as Aysima chanted, a low melodic hum. The air shimmered.

Now his heart pounded with ferocity. He didn't understand this magic, this strange Moon Fae with her whimsical words and powerful aura.

But he clung to the hope she offered.

He would give anything to see Emira look at him and smile again.

CHAPTER 110

EMMY

Emmy continued her endless walk under the ethereal sun. Fragrant flowers, dazzling colors.

But always silence.

It was like she was half alive.

Then, a woman appeared. Delicate as a willow, her clear and silver hair flowed around her like moonlight. Gossamer wings, tinged with rainbow hues, fluttered behind her.

A Moon Fae.

She looked familiar.

"Hello," the woman said, her voice light and melodic. "I'm Aysima."

Why this new diversion?

"Come, sit." Aysima gestured toward a stone bench beside the fountain.

She joined her, the sound of the fountain a soothing rhythm she'd never heard before.

"Did you ever dance with a griffin under a sky full of stars?" Aysima asked, her blue eyes sparkling. The fae glanced up at the sky.

"With a dragon," she said. "We loved the stars."

Her throat felt tight thinking of Edmar.

"As much as I love the moon," Aysima sighed, her gaze drifting to the fountain. "Sometimes even the brightest stars can fall from the sky, can't they?"

Her heart ached. Aysima touched her arm, and she noticed the scars on her wrists. "What happened?"

"Pain for family," Aysima murmured, her voice distant, eyes clouded with sadness, "but worth it."

The response made little sense, but she let the gentle quiet grow between them, punctuated by moments of reflection. A strange comfort emanated from Aysima, a warmth that eased the ache of loneliness. The silence was no longer empty. Water gently splashing and trees whispering in the breeze.

A thoughtful frown creased Aysima's brow. "Oh, this is the afterlife?" she asked, her voice giddy. "Seems rather empty, doesn't it?"

"It's not what I expected." A peculiar calm permeated their shared observation.

"Well, it's not *quite* the afterlife," Aysima said, tilting her head.

"I never thought so." She blinked, surprised at her admission. *Why hadn't I realized before?* "Metallon said I could cross over. But my curse..."

"Oh, I forgot to tell you." Aysima's smile widened, a mischievous glint in her eyes as she took Emmy's hands into hers. "You're free."

She frowned. "I'm already free. I'm dead."

Aysima giggled, the sound like wind chimes. "This is the in-between place, silly. A dreamscape. You can still go back! And a handsome Dragon King awaits."

Go back? But I'm dead.

Unless she wasn't.

Aysima nodded, as if following her thoughts.

Looking around at the garden that had held such silence and loneliness, it all finally made sense. *I'm not in the afterlife.*

Had Malala been real?

"Metallon did this?" she asked, hope flickering amid the confusion.

"No, silly!" Aysima laughed. "*I* did."

But I don't know her. Maybe the fae was a Moon Walker, moving between dreams. Which meant she was in a dream. *But of whose making?*

"I would have done it anyway," Aysima continued, "even if that dreadful man hadn't kidnapped me." She tapped her chin. "Although he *is* rather handsome. You wouldn't know it with his disguise."

"You created this dreamscape?"

"Goodness, where is my mind?" Aysima giggled. "It's been lost to the ages. But this world is not my creation. I took your curse away."

Emmy closed her eyes, dizzy. The fae woman barely made sense. *No curse?* "I can go back?" Her breath caught in her throat. "To Edmar? Free of my curse?"

"Dissolved into the ether." Aysima nodded. "All the dragon princes turned into such beautiful men." She squeezed Emmy's hands. "Go!"

Exhilaration, a lightness she'd never known, surged through her. Pure ecstasy and joy filled her chest, emotions she hadn't experienced fully since—*How long?*

Never. She'd never known a time of true happiness without a foreboding shadow, but now it all seemed possible.

The world shifted. The garden faded, replaced by the familiar feel of the Temple of Khalanthrax, a vibrating connection to Metallon, a metallic tang in her nose. Her eyelids fluttered, focusing on a blurry world.

The ritual chamber with its ceiling lost to shadows. Whispered voices. Faces swam into view. Aysima, the Moon Fae. Adria and Lian. Cielan holding Avi. Many others, but she only searched for one—Edmar.

He was there, his face etched with worry, then their gazes met, an instantly electrified moment. *Relief. Joy. Love.* He suddenly looked younger, as if a thousand years had fallen away.

She smiled. It didn't hurt. Her magic thrummed within her, a source of power, not pain.

The curse is gone.

She wondered how Metallon's magic changed her by bringing her back so close to death. *A worry for another time.* She opened her arms, and Edmar pulled her close, an embrace of warmth, of peace, of belonging.

"You're real," she said against his neck, breathing in his sea scent.

"I thought I'd lost you forever," he said, his voice thick. He pulled back to cup her face. "I've been a fool. I should have cherished every moment we had together. Life is not a guarantee, and yours is precious to me. Never again will I waste a second I can spend with you. I promise—"

"I'm here," she said, her finger against his lips silencing him. "We're together."

He smiled, kissing her finger. She gasped, heat flaring where his lips touched her skin.

"Together," he whispered.

Without a word, she lifted her chin and kissed him. It was a reunion of what their souls and bodies had always known. A kiss that banished the chaos and uncertainty of the world.

There was only this moment, this breathless kiss.

Their breathless kiss. A promise of a future filled with love, laughter, and adventure. But the best gift was a future promising the freedom to finally be *together.*

EPILOGUE 1

EDMAR

"I feel stronger than ever," Emira said, her laughter echoing through the garden, light and carefree.

She twirled, sapphire hair shimmering in the fading sunlight, her movements fluid and graceful. She wore a simple silk dress that rippled with her steps, and Edmar was thankful she'd given up the idea of wearing his old shirt—now stained with her blood. Although she agreed to the dress, she kept his shirt, and he could only shake his head, knowing he'd give her whatever she wanted.

"No pain. Not even the knives in my feet!" More of her laughter filled the air, the sound musical.

His heart swelled with love and relief. It was a miracle she was alive, a gift from the gods he'd never take for granted. But he couldn't shake the memory of her lifeless body in his arms, no breath, blood staining his hands. He hovered close, constantly checking for any sign of weakness, any flicker of pain. His love for her, once clouded by fear and doubt, now burned with fierce protectiveness.

"Edmar," she said, her smile softening. "I'm alright. Truly. You don't have to treat me like I'm made of glass."

No, definitely not glass. She'd changed. The scar on her throat was the most obvious. Her skin, too, held a metallic sheen now, shifting her sea foam skin color from a light green to a darker teal depending on the angle of light.

A shimmering gemstone.

There were other changes, subtle, unexplored. Metallon had warned of unintended consequences from bringing her back so close to death.

At least her appetite for normal food remained. *No blood magic!*

He chuckled as she danced. When she twirled past him, he pulled her close, loving her curves melding to his body, a comforting haven.

"Perhaps not glass," he murmured into her hair. "But you are precious to me. More precious than any gem, any treasure."

He kissed her, a slow, lingering kiss that spoke of a thousand unspoken promises. He'd never want to control her again. Her magic, her freedom, her choices—they were all part of the woman he loved. But is he what she really wanted? Without the curse of pain or hurting others, she could choose to do anything else with her life.

"Emira?"

She opened her eyes, large emeralds refracting the setting sun.

"Do you want me?" he asked, the question a plea, a fear he couldn't quite suppress.

He'd lost so much, had loved and lost, and for a moment, the terror of repeating that cycle crippled him, a freezing fist clenching around his heart. A son gone too soon, a friend who had betrayed him. Could he trust this fragile hope, this second chance at love?

She rose on tiptoes in his arms, pressing her body against his, her teeth capturing his bottom lip while she sank her hands into his hair. "I want you, Edmar."

His eyes closed on a groan. Relief, so profound it stole his breath, washed over him, chasing away the shadows. Seizing the moment of his lowered defenses, she kissed him, her coconut and floral scent filling his senses. His body tightened, heat rushing to his center. Blood pounded in his ears.

Then he gently gripped her hair and pulled her head back, breaking the kiss before he took her right here in the garden for all in the temple to see. The devious smile and twinkle in her eye nearly destroyed his control.

"To clarify, besides wanting me in the physical sense, do you want to be with me, to stay married to me?"

She lifted her chin, short sapphire curls falling away from her neck, revealing another faint scar, the place where he'd bitten her. A low growl started at the back of his throat, everything within him wanting to claim her again.

The look on her face confirmed she was aware of this calculated movement.

He released her, afraid of what he'd do if he kept touching her. "Emira..."

"Aysima is a wonder, isn't she?" She skipped down the garden path, looking over the flowers.

"Godsent," he mumbled, and he shuddered, remembering the Sea Witch, the terror. He'd been so close to losing his wife.

"I like her. I'm glad she's coming with us."

He couldn't agree. Both she and Bian were the same type of strange, a little too peculiar to him.

Alive too long, Aysima had said. Was that true for Bian, too?

What fate awaited all immortals?

"The company will be good," she said, her emerald eyes twinkling again as she snapped off a flower from a bush, smelling it.

Is she teasing me? "Are you purposefully not answering my question?"

She looked up at him through her eyelashes, a smile hiding behind the flower. "What question?"

"You're torturing me intentionally."

She dropped her hand, her smile gone. With purpose, she turned back to him. They'd had two idyllic days of rest, and her energy had returned with incredible strength, evident in her driven stride.

Another consequence?

In front of him, she poked him in the chest. "You are confusing."

"What?"

"Actions have consequences," she said, poking him with each word. "How many times and variations of that phrase have you said to me?"

He crossed his arms over his chest. Not that her poking hurt. "The words are vaguely familiar."

"You've believed my actions to be my whole truth, even when I've revealed my honesty in words."

She looked at him expectantly.

He was missing something. "Please, just tell me what I'm not understanding."

"Cabezon!" she said, throwing up her hands and twirling away.

He caught her back to him, yanking her against his body and wrapping his arms around her. She gasped, but she didn't resist him.

"A stubborn fish?" He searched her eyes, hoping to see his answers, but she was being just as stubborn. "Perhaps so, but not on purpose."

Still no give in her eyes, so he lowered his head to brush a kiss to the corner of her jaw.

A quick inhale, her body tightening.

At least she wasn't mad at him anymore. Or not in this moment.

He trailed more kisses down her throat, moving to the very spot she'd teased him with a moment ago.

"You are amazing, Emira." Reverence filled his voice. She shivered, and he smiled. He kissed his bite mark. "So strong, so resilient."

"We've both grown, Edmar." She was breathless.

He kissed her mouth, but when she tried to deepen it, he lifted his head away. "We are amazing together like this."

She licked her lips. "Yes."

"I know you want this part of me, but do you want more, a life with me? If we didn't have this holy quest?"

She sighed. "I've spent the last two days under your near-constant supervision when I've felt fine from the beginning. But this satisfied your need to take care of me, even if it felt like another prison for me." Her fingers curled into his shirt as she leaned into him for emphasis on her next words. "I'm sailing with you in two days for the next part of our life's adventure. A dangerous journey to wake the Moon Goddess, chosen for the very woman who tried to seduce you away from me. So, for someone so determined to believe that actions mean everything, what do you think my actions say to you?"

He closed his eyes as he leaned his forehead against hers. He nodded, holding her close. "You're right. I just... Sometimes..."

"I understand," she said, softly. Her fingertips caressed the side of his face, and he shivered. "Sometimes it's nice to hear the words."

Her fingers moved to cup his face. "We faced challenges and succeeded together. We faced our fears together. We will continue our journey together."

Together. Not alone.

She wanted to be with him, not because of some curse or because she'd been forced to marry him. He turned his head and kissed her palm. "I like the sound of that."

Her fingers tangled in his hair to draw him down for a kiss. He let her.

She was fearless, forging her life into what she wanted, leaving the only world she'd known for two hundred years, escaping one tyranny for another, but never quitting, until she'd reached the end, and given a choice of life, she'd liberated all mermaids and refused to make herself a burden for others.

No matter what plans he came up with for their future, he knew she'd only follow the ones that would allow her to amuse him, and the rest would be the path she blazed.

And he'd follow her.

"But let's set one thing straight," he said. "That wasn't the real Avi who used the spell on me."

"I know."

Again he searched her eyes to understand her, and he thought perhaps he finally did. At least a little. Avi had the unfortunate position of reminding Emira of what she'd witnessed, but Emira also understood the fae woman continued to deteriorate, so waking the Moon Goddess next was the most logical decision.

To save Avi. The daughter of her mother's best friend.

The first stars appeared in the twilight sky, a silver tapestry against the deepening blue. A waning crescent moon hung low on the horizon. She looked up, her eyes reflecting the starlight.

"Edmar?" Her voice was soft, filled with longing. "Can you take me up there? The stars always seemed so far away, so unreachable. But now I feel like anything is possible, as long as I have you."

His heart swelled at her words. She wanted him, not for his crown, not because she'd been cornered into marrying him. She truly wanted him. "I'd fly you to the moon."

She laughed, a musical sound he'd never get used to. "I'd rather touch a star."

This woman—she was his heart. He kissed her, a slow, sensual promise of a thousand stars for all their tomorrows. He lifted her into his arms and groaned.

She frowned. "Too heavy?"

"Never," he said. "But you're not as light as you used to be. Another consequence of Metallon's magic? Perhaps you're part metal now, like the Sea Witch."

She crossed her arms, unconvinced. "Fishy story."

He kissed her, rough and demanding, summoning his magic. Her moan spread a tingling warmth through his body.

"As I told you once before," he murmured against her skin, his lips trailing across her scar. "You're perfect."

EPILOGUE 2

EMMY

The Ocean's Lament, a song of sorrow and longing, echoed across the moonlit beach. Emmy stood at the water's edge, her voice blending with the waves, the cool spray a welcome caress against her skin.

The ocean's familiar pull was a whisper now, not a roar. Another consequence of Metallon's magic. The sea felt it, too, retreating from her more often than not.

Even as she teased Edmar about her weight, she knew her body was different now.

Her curse was gone, her magic under her control, and she was free to choose where she belonged.

She touched the painite gem at her throat, its warmth a reassurance. She didn't need it anymore, her magic melded to her soul, the gem no longer controlling her. Now her merfolk power imbued the song with the melody that vibrated in her bones and wove through her body, her heart syncing with its beat.

It soothed her.

After they flew as close as they dared to reach the stars, Edmar had brought her to the beach. She needed this, one last moment with this sea, before they embarked on their journey for the Moon Goddess and left the waters of her home. He stayed back, giving her space, but his presence was a comfort.

His love, his unwavering support, anchored her as she faced the ocean that had once defined her existence.

"Thank you, Metallon," she whispered, her prayer mingling with the song. "Thank you for saving me. For my wish. For freeing my people."

Summoned by her song, a figure emerged from the waves. Anjali, sapphire hair shimmering, a crown of pearls on her head. She didn't come closer. Emmy didn't move toward the water. They remained in their separate worlds, both changed, yet bound by a shared history.

"You're alive." Joy and relief filled her sister's voice. Though it was subdued, tinged with something darker. "You look different."

"I'm finally free." She smiled, hoping to see Anjali's usual smile. "And you? Our tethers are gone, so you're free, too."

A shadow crossed Anjali's delicate features. A merman, handsome, wearing a crown, joined her in the shallow water.

"The kingdoms are in chaos." Anjali gestured to the merman. "My husband, Tarinor, and I are trying to maintain order, but many struggle to adapt."

"Change is never easy," she said, her throat tight. "But it's a new beginning. A chance for a better future."

Anjali narrowed her eyes. "You had something to do with this?"

"A boon from Metallon."

"It's more than you bargained for," Anjali said, a stricken look on her face. "Many of our sisters and their granddaughters, married to the leaders of the powerful kingdoms and nations, have killed their husbands and taken control. They call themselves the Forgotten Queens." Anjali paused to collect herself. "Then there are the Cleansers. Mermen purging their female relatives to take power back."

Her heart sank. *Metallon, guide your children.* "But you're safe?"

Anjali glanced at Tarinor, a smile trembling on her lips. "For now. But it's only a matter of time."

"I will pray for you."

Anjali gave her a strange look. "Pray? Since when?"

"I have Metallon's favor."

Tarinor touched Anjali's arm, and she nodded. "Are you coming home?"

Slowly, she shook her head. "My place is with my Dragon King while we fulfill the Sun God's quest. We must awaken all the gods before the Summer Child is born."

"The Summer Child?" Anjali glanced at her husband. "We've heard rumors of her after several sea monsters appeared in the kingdoms."

"She's the daughter of the Sea Witch. Also, be wary of the Sea Witch. She was posing as Gilly."

A deep frown marred her sister's brow. "I never trusted Gilly. But if she was the Sea Witch, then she shouldn't trouble us further. She's either retreated from the world or she's dead. All the merfolk were suddenly released from her Garden of Souls."

"How?"

"They only said there was a battle and a great release of magic, but none of the merfolk saw what happened."

Something to ponder for another day. At least they didn't have to worry about the Sea Witch looking for retribution.

"I'll miss you," Anjali said, the Ocean's Lament resounded in her breast and heart. So much passed between their gazes, the bond between them unspoken but strong despite their different worlds now. "Be safe, Emmy."

"And you."

Then Anjali and Tarinor disappeared beneath the waves.

She remained on the shore, her heart heavy. She'd freed the mermaids, but at a cost, and she couldn't do anything about it. The Summer Child loomed. That was the threat they had to face. A threat in Edmar's home. Her home.

She turned from the water, seeking Edmar beyond the dunes. He stood at the edge of the trees, moonlight framing his silhouette. Naked, fresh from his transformation. A breathtaking sight, a creature of raw strength and grace, and the sight of him stirred something deep within her. Desire, unexpected but welcome, fluttered in her belly. They hadn't mated since the night of the ritual.

He'd been too careful of her while she *recovered*.

She smiled, her heart swelling with a love that had weathered storms, a love that had been tested and found true. She shed her clothes as she approached him, glorying in her nudity, her skin free to breathe like it always should. "Why can't we live all our days naked?"

A playful smile ticked up one side of his mouth. His graceful fingers captured a curl blowing across her face and tucked it behind an ear. The simple touch sent a thrill through her, goosebumps raising on her arms.

"Ready to leave in two days?" he asked, his voice a low rumble. "Or do you have another request you would make of me?"

"What could you offer?" Her breath caught with anticipation.

"Make you see more stars than those in the sky," he murmured.

Desire, a glorious fire, burned in her veins. She tilted her head, loving the hunger reflected in his darkening gaze.

"I'm lucky to have you." His thumb traced her jawline.

She remembered his fear from the garden earlier. He thought that with her curse gone, she'd leave him. But she couldn't envision a future without him. She gave the reassurance he sought in words. "I choose you," she said. "Always."

"And I choose you," he echoed. "Always."

Those words bound him by his own code, his sense of duty and honor. She understood this about him. "I am yours, and you are mine."

Something crossed his face with her declaration, a light blue ring swirling in his eyes, his gaze dropping to his bite mark on her neck. But he waited. Waited to see if she really wanted this, if she was ready after having almost died.

She pulled him close, pressing her lips to his. The only signal he needed. He devoured her lips, bearing her down onto the soft grass. *Breathless kisses.*

Moonlight bathed them in a soft glow. He lay over her, trapping her between his body and the earth, his gaze intense, possessive. She gasped as his hardness pressed against her softness, the sensation exquisitely pleasurable.

Their kisses slowed, lingering explorations, each touch a reminder of everything they had fought for, everything they had endured. His hands moved over her with aching tenderness, yet with an urgency beneath it all—a need to reclaim what they'd lost, to reaffirm their bond in the most intimate of ways.

His hands traced her curves, and she arched into him, her fingers trailing over the smooth contours of his back. Then over his strong chest. His heart beat a steady thrum beneath her fingertips.

Their kisses deepened, passion swelling like the pull of the tides. Their deliberate movements fanned their desires, each touch calculated to elicit the greatest response, the most profound pleasure.

Her legs parted, inviting him. He entered her slowly, the friction sparking a current that flowed through her veins, connecting her to him on a level deeper than mere flesh. She dug her nails into his back, her body bowing into his, urging him on.

He set a slow rhythm at first, a gentle rocking that built in intensity with each passing moment. He watched her, his expression rapt, his love for her clear in his eyes.

As he quickened their pace, the air filled with her soft moans, his ragged breaths, the rustle of grass beneath their entangled limbs. She closed her eyes, lost in the sensations. Her world narrowed to the place where they became one, where their souls intertwined. The rest faded away, the stars forgotten as they created their own constellations in the night.

His thrusts grew urgent, his need for release building with each stroke. She matched him, her body responding to his every move, her pleasure cresting like a wave ready to crash upon the shore. With a final powerful surge, they tumbled into the abyss together.

Her body convulsed in a torrent of pleasure, seeing the stars he promised her. Long moments of it radiating from her core.

They lay entwined in the aftermath, his heartbeat a lullaby beneath her ear, the cool breeze brushing over their slick skin. The world, and their coming adventure, forgotten. For now.

They lay there for long moments, simply breathing, simply being.

And as the moon bathed them in her silvery light, they were no longer the destructive, manipulative mermaid and the cursed, vengeful dragon. No longer a queen and a king from different worlds.

They were simply...

Emmy and Edmar.

Do you want to know more of what happens between Sun God and Sygilla before this final epilogue, the reason why the Sea Witch is missing? What happens when the Sun loves the Sea, but the world drowns in their ruin? This is a mythic dark fantasy of gods, betrayal, and the love that doomed creation. Join my newsletter and get that tragic but spicy short story, **Forsaken by Sun & Sea** or go to https://tinyurl.com/Forsaken-by-Sun-and-Sea.

The next book in this series with Zane & Nira, *A Curse of Spikes & Smoke...*

A CURSE OF SPIKES & SMOKE PREVIEW OF ROUGH DRAFT CHAPTERS!

Prologue: Zane

The dim light of the Dragon's Haven tavern swallowed the edges of Zane's vision, leaving only the amber glow of ale sloshing in his tankard and a dull ache in his chest. Another wife lost to the curse that held him and his brothers prisoner.

Another sacrifice.

He'd learned her name when they'd married twenty years ago, but the rest he'd avoided after providing everything she needed to be happy, then leaving her.

This was a deliberate distance he maintained, a shield against the inevitable grief. He swirled the ale, the scent of hops and barley doing little to soothe the bitter taste in his mouth.

The tavern was alive with revelry, a cacophony of shouts, clinking mugs, and bawdy sea shanties echoing through the air. The door creaked open, spilling in a wave of noise and laughter. A port city crowd—sailors, merchants, the occasional flash of fae finery.

Quite a few women in the crowd.

He'd have to pick one soon. If he didn't, the cruel curse would randomly choose a new bride for him this night.

By picking one of these women, he'd avoid that fate.

At least for tonight.

A loophole in a curse that wouldn't let them choose their own wives.

His gaze drifted toward the dance floor, where bodies swayed and twirled to the rhythmic pulse of a lute. And then he heard it. A laugh, clear and bright, cutting through the din.

He shifted at the table, leaning a bit, drawn by the sound, his gaze snagging on a figure bathed in the warm glow of the tavern's hearth. A woman amid the whirl of bodies on the dance floor.

Not just any woman. A presence.

She moved with a fluid grace, her attire a riot of vibrant hues, a vivid clash of blues and greens against her dark skin, rippling with her every step, mesmerizing him. She was tall, lean, a silhouette of a moonless night in the firelight, subdued yet commanding all attention.

A familiar prickle of suspicion rose within him. Only Fire Fae had that dark skin tone, and he hated the Fire Fae.

Yet, her hair, a cascade of black curls, fell to her hips, unmoving, defying the usual flickering fire hair of her kind. Light caught on the thin braids threaded with gold woven all throughout the loose curls, golden beads on each braid clicked with her movements. Her hair wasn't the red he so despised.

But gold? Such a bold choice.

He'd always been drawn to its warm gleam, a symbol of wealth and power, things he once craved above all else. Now, more gold than he could ever spend surrounded him.

Their eyes met across the crowded room. Time seemed to stutter, the music fading into background noise as an electric current arced between them. In that instant, he knew.

The recognition in her golden eyes, framed by a daring streak of gold eyeliner, was a silent acknowledgment of the raw attraction pulsing between them. She knew as well, and they were both aware of this pull that wanted to draw them together.

Yet what intrigued him about her also unsettled him.

Power. She radiated power with quiet confidence. Not magical power as far as he could tell, just something in the way she carried herself. Her demeanor held with an assuredness he hadn't encountered before, and it ignited a spark of interest that warred with his ingrained prejudice.

She tossed her head with a wide smile, and the beads in her hair clinked, an odd harmony against the thudding boots and jests around her. Her presence, her poise, the elegance of her swaying body drew every eye, the room made smaller. Every patron hung on her laugh.

He hung on her next laugh, hungrily watching her, gaze lingering on those shimmery gold strands and beads woven into her braids, the thin gold necklace laying between her breasts. The gold glint in her eyes, a lustrous gold burnished with knowing power.

She didn't belong here. Her fearlessness and assuredness made her stand out among the rough-and-tumble sailors and merchants like a flicker of flame against frost. But it wasn't just her beauty or her attire that stirred something dormant in him. It was her laugh, the sound of it, warm and unrestrained, as if the world held no sway over her. That kind of freedom both fascinated and infuriated him.

He stood before he realized what he was doing, the scraped legs of his chair lost in the noise. He wove through the crowd, ignoring the smirks and nudges from the drunken patrons who recognized their errant king emerging from the tavern's shadows.

Not that it mattered. They could think what they wanted. Right now, his focus fixed on her.

"I choose her." The words under his breath. But they were needed. He had to choose someone before the curse could, and he had to mean it, so he let her magnetic pull drag him into her ring of admirers.

He joined a line dance that snaked across the floor, a strategic maneuver to close the distance. As they danced, their bodies brushed, a fleeting contact that sent a jolt of awareness and desire through him. A scent curled around him, unexpected yet compelling. Rich and warm, like sunlit spice and rain-kissed embers, laced with something dark and elusive beneath her polished exterior.

Her gaze came to him, pinning him.

Golden eyes gleaming like polished gold coins, their brightness sharp and impenetrable. Strength reflected there, as though forged in the crucible of fire itself. Looking into them was like staring at the sun, dazzling, overwhelming, and impossible to hold for too long.

Once more her power stunned him.

Some people feigned confidence. But not her. Hers was rooted, unshakable. He'd always been a sucker for a confident woman.

Her gaze delved into his, and she saw him. In that look, he felt stripped bare. For once, the masks he wore seemed flimsy, and the man beneath them... vulnerable.

He wasn't sure he liked it.

"You're staring," she said, her voice smooth, lilting. Her lips quirked into a smile that was as much a challenge as it was an invitation. She didn't stop dancing, her hips swaying in time to the music as she studied him.

"And you're laughing." A smirk tugged at his own lips. "Seems fair."

Her brows rose, amused, but she said nothing, instead holding out her hand. He took it before his mind could catch up with his body, and she pulled him further into the swirling chaos of the dance floor. The heat of her palm against his was startling, almost electric.

As they moved, he noted the small details—her height, nearly matching his own, the lean strength in her frame, the sharp intelligence in her gaze. She wasn't what he usually desired in a woman. Yet, she was everything he couldn't resist.

"You're not from Nova Porta," he said, their steps weaving together in the rhythm of the dance. "Are you Fire Fae?"

He hadn't felt magic when she spoke, power usually shifting in a fae's words, yet her higher-than-normal body heat suggested close Fire Fae ancestry or some other creature with Summer blood.

"Not exactly." Her voice lowered for his ears alone. "And you, King Zane, don't belong on a dance floor in some dirty tavern."

He faltered, though only slightly, not expecting a stranger to know who he was. "You know who I am."

"Hard not to with that dark blue-gray skin and deep indigo eyes."

He relaxed into a smile. "Then you know you're dancing with a dangerous person."

She laughed, the sound that had first drawn him to her. "If you mean your reputation as a rake and wastrel, the once-king of Meridonali, then yes, so dangerous."

He chuckled, a flash of his usual charm surfacing. "Still king, technically." He wagged a playful finger. "And I prefer the term *Homo Ludens*."

"Man at play?" Her lips curved into a knowing smile, golden eyes gleaming with mischief. Then, her voice dropped to a conspiratorial whisper, and she said, "*Drakkon Ludens* fits better."

Dragon at play.

The old language. The specific dialect of the lost city. She knows. An icy chill danced down his spine. She knew he was a dragon, and she knew where he came from.

His grip on her waist tightened, his mind racing.

How did she know about the city of his birth, Drakkon? That name tied him to a time long buried, a time before the Snow Princess's curse destroyed most of the Ice Dragons, a past he kept hidden for survival.

How much does she know?

This woman was more than a random dancer in a tavern. His mind sharpened through the haze of the ale he'd drunk, through the bewitching smell of the woman in his arms. Centuries of training reminded him to never let his guard down.

"You know the old language." He kept his voice carefully neutral. Very aware that he needed to keep choosing her or the curse would.

"I know many things," she replied with unnerving intensity in the depths of her gaze.

He felt a flicker of unease, his attraction battling with a rising tide of suspicion. He forced a smile, the mask of nonchalance slipping back into place.

They danced, their bodies moving closer with each turn, their breathing syncing. The magnetic force between them quickened his pulse, his blood running hot, hotter than he thought possible for someone like him, a creature of Winter. But there was something more beneath the surface. A danger in her laughter, a sharpness in her eyes whispering of secrets and scars.

Danger called to him as much as this woman so the combination became intoxicating, his unease slipping away even as a part of his mind blared a warning.

As their steps slowed, he leaned closer, his lips near her ear. "Who are you?"

Her reply was a whisper against his neck, warm enough to make his skin prickle. "Someone you shouldn't trust."

Then she laughed at his consternation as she twirled away from him.

His body tightened, his heart beating too fast as she came back to him, nearly looking him in the eye with her height. "I don't like women who are as tall as me."

"And?"

His hands slid to her slim hips, pulling her closer. "I don't like women who lack curves to hold on to."

"A shame." She wound her lean arms around his neck, her full lips curving into a smile that was more of a smirk. "I'm sure you'll manage."

With the next dance step, she pressed her lithe body against his, her fingernails sinking into the back of his neck. He gasped at the sting, heat flushing him with desire.

Who is this woman? "I don't like women who are mysterious."

She tilted her hips into him, a part of him instantly hardening, and he groaned.

Her golden eyes sparkled with amusement. "But you like me."

"Yes." The word caught in his throat. The single-syllable word was charged with an honesty that surprised even him. *Bloody gods help him.* He'd chosen her to ward off the curse but he'd never felt such charged desire. *Not since...*

Not going there.

Her smile widened, and he found himself lost in the simple movement. He would have sworn any vow she asked of him for the feel of her lips on him.

The dance continued, their movements growing more intimate, their bodies mirroring each other with a growing sense of familiarity. He wanted her, a visceral urge that went beyond mere lust. It was a consuming hunger, a desire to possess her completely.

But who was she, and why was she here tonight, in his tavern?

As if picking up on his hesitancy, she leaned into him the next time she was in his arms. "Let's just enjoy ourselves tonight."

Her words created an ache inside him. When had he ever just allowed himself to let his guard down? *Not for over six hundred years.*

The constant mask was exhausting.

Now her words tempted him to let himself relax.

The loophole he exploited by choosing her meant he had to open his heart to the idea of loving whichever woman he chose for the night. An unending string of broken hearts for him, loving and losing women every night.

But not only did he now tumble into love with the woman in his arms, heat flushed through his body, a throbbing need to have her, to be the man he once was.

It had been decades since he'd slept with a woman.

Sliding a hand up from her waist and over her ribs, he brushed his thumb along the soft underswell of her small breast. "I can think of more enjoyable things to do with you at the moment."

Her pupils grew, becoming black bottomless pits in the center of molten gold rings. She wanted him, too. Fingernails dug into his neck. "Show me."

The challenge of her words spurred him. Grabbing her hand, he led them to an empty room in a darkened hallway at the back of the tavern. Anticipation charged the thick air, his heart hammering.

Before the door closed them in near darkness, their hands fumbled with the other's clothes. He kissed her across her jaw and down her neck as he walked her back to the bed.

He yearned to taste her lips, but he carefully avoided her mouth. Even if she wasn't Fire Fae, she could be some type of hybrid, mix, or mostly human. Kissing her would seal her death because his cold breath would steal her heat.

He was an Ice Dragon after all.

When he laid her on the bed, her dress fell open to her hips, revealing her small breasts with only the shine of a gold necklace against her dark skin. He palmed one breast, the mound just fitting into his hand while he traced the line of her jaw with his kisses, lingering on her smooth skin. She moaned and arched her body into his, her legs opening to invite him into her heat, and he pressed against her, his trousers the only barrier between them.

Her hands smoothed over his bare chest, following the lines of his thick muscles, then slid around to his back. He groaned, wanting to bury himself in her right then but also wanting to savor the taste of her and show her what pleasure he could give her. He raised above her to grab her hips and pull her tight against his hard length.

"Gods, I want you." His voice thickened with his need.

"Take me," she whispered.

For the first time, her voice wavered as if unsure, and it was almost enough to push him over the edge, this small amount of uncertainty in the face of her overwhelming confidence. But then, whether from his enhanced dragon sight in darkness or the shine of a half-moon through the small window, or both, something caught his eye right below her left breast. He ran a hand up her body to touch it and felt the raised tattoo.

The playful banter, the shared laughter, the burgeoning desire—all of it curdled into a sickening mockery. The heat of their touches, a moment ago intoxicating, now scorched.

Fire Fae.

The words slammed into him, an invisible punch to his gut, the sting of frost flooding his senses, replacing the sweetness he'd just tasted on her skin. Each breath felt tainted, the air thick with the stench of his own stupidity. He'd been so caught up in the moment, in the heady dance of their flirtation, that he'd failed to see the truth burning beneath the surface.

A Fire Fae. Here. In my arms.

Revulsion twisted in his gut, a visceral recoil from the very essence of her. *How could I have been so blind?*

He lifted away from her, the motion abrupt, almost violent, staring at her as if she'd transformed into something monstrous before his very eyes.

"You *are* Fire Fae," he said, his accusation laced with a loathing he couldn't conceal. Only full Fire Fae marked their bodies with the sigil of their Firekin, their clan.

The thought was a physical violation, a betrayal of everything he held sacred. He stumbled back, the need to escape, to cleanse himself of her touch, overriding every other impulse.

But then he stopped. If he didn't continue choosing her, the damned curse would, and he couldn't be tied to a Fire Fae. His people would revolt, and for the next twenty years, he'd be sick with the thought of being married to a fucking Fire Fae.

She raised to her elbows, her golden eyes shiny in the moonlight, and he couldn't help his gaze dropping to her breasts, his cock still hard for her even if his mind warred against her nature.

Her eyes narrowed, yet her words were silky when she spoke. With fluid grace, she stood. Her steps swallowed the space between them, and she leaned into him, brushing her hardened nipples against his bare chest. "Do you dislike Fire Fae?"

Dislike? A tame word for how he felt for the fae who'd constantly invaded his home, bringing war and destruction to his shores for decades at a time. The fae responsible for the death of too many, for the final death of...

No. He couldn't think of *her* if he had to continue choosing this Fire Fae in front of him.

With a growl, he wrapped his arms around the woman and bit her neck, fighting against his revulsion for her kind while still needing her desperately. "I would banish all Fire Fae to the eight hells if I could."

"Hmmm..."

Whatever she would have said stalled in her mouth when his hand found her breast again, and he pinched her nipple. She gasped, then she dug her nails into his back. He hissed but enjoyed the pain, a reminder that she was the enemy even if had to love her this night.

She maneuvered him until he was on the bed on his back, her straddling him.

His cock jumped as her hips settled over his, straining against his trousers, ready to bury himself in her. When she rose above him like some dark goddess, beautiful and deadly, preparing to suck every last bit of desire from him, he forgot she was Fire Fae, forgot he should hate her as his heart opened, the possibility of love growing there again. He groaned as she arched her back, thrusting her small breasts forward, and rubbed her core over him.

"Such vehemence for my race, yet you still want me."

"Yes." The sound was tortured coming from his lips, knowing the dichotomy in his thoughts and actions and not understanding it beyond the curse. Only that he needed her, loved her, because to do otherwise would allow the curse to rule his life.

She leaned over him, her lips barely an inch from his own, and he held his breath, not wanting his cold to harm her. He was so distracted by the feel of her laying along him, the heat of her breath ghosting over his skin, her face so close, that he was taken by surprise when she said, "Too bad I no longer want you."

And before her words settled into his desire-addled brain, she lifted away from him and in a flash of smoke, she was gone.

He coughed, waving a hand through the acrid veil of smoke, but beneath the bitterness, her scent lingered. Rich, dark and spiced, like sun-scorched petals and something wilder, something untamed. It curled through the room, clinging to his sheets, his skin, his breath. A cruel echo of what had just slipped from his grasp.

She'd left him.

Left him alone in a dimly lit room, half-naked, the ghost of her scent taunting him, mocking the desire that had burned so fiercely for the enemy of his people. His body still thrummed with want, but he willed disgust to drown out the ache of longing.

The Fire Fae had destroyed him. Had taken everything from him.

I cannot desire her!

A sudden lurch of sickness seized him, and he vomited over the side of the bed, each heave wringing out his fury, his shame, his hatred. He wiped his mouth with the back of his hand, a growl rumbling low in his throat.

Good riddance.

He hoped he never saw her, or any of those godsdamn Fire Fae, again.

But even as the thought formed, his body betrayed him, refusing to accept that the beautiful woman he'd danced with all night had left him. His fingers twitched, aching for the feel of her skin. His breath hitched, remembering the press of her lips so near his own. And her scent. Gods, her scent still haunted him, curling in the shadows like a promise unfulfilled.

And he knew, despite everything, that if she came back to him now, he'd gladly take her into his arms again and love her until dawn.

Chapter 1: Nira

Six months later, the memory of the Dragon King still tried to surface whenever she let her guard slip. Nira shoved it down where it belonged and fixed her attention on the table in front of her.

The pavilion pulsed with revelry, a maelstrom of flickering firelight, cascading laughter, and the rich scent of spiced wine. The Summer Solstice festival had begun, a month-long celebration that set the capital city of Pyrrhios ablaze with feasts, performances, and endless gambling. The same festivities would be happening across all of the habitable Fire Fae Isles.

Nira sat at a rough-hewn obsidian table beneath one of the pavilion's sweeping arches, the molten glow from a nearby lava trench casting shadows along her emerald silk dress. Around her, Fire Fae merchants, Sun Fae emissaries, and visiting gamblers drank, shouted wagers, and clashed metal mugs together in raucous cheers.

This was her kind of crowd, loose with drink, reckless with coin, and distracted by the wild, golden glow of the city-wide celebrations.

She let her fingers toy with the edges of her Tekkō Karuta, her iron playing cards. She was here for one man, but to everyone else, she was just another gambler, another reveler playing her luck beneath the festival's burning banners.

Her gaze fixed on the fae man across from her. He was handsome, in a conventional way, with the pointed ears of the Fire Fae, shifting fire hair, and the luminous golden eyes common to her kind.

Her perusal remained sharp despite the air of careless amusement she projected. She leaned back in her chair, and her legs crossed, the movement drawing attention to the slit in her skirt that bared a long, lean thigh. The men around her alternated between throwing glances her way and focusing on the cards, each one torn between winning the hand and imagining what it might cost to win her favor.

Except one.

The fae man across from her.

What does he want?

Every one of them sat at this table with the same surface perception, here to play a card game while the festival roared around them. Each saw himself at the center of his own little universe.

But when she layered her perception over the man across from her, tried on his perspective like a cloak, the picture sharpened. Twice the information, twice the leverage.

His name was Atheron, a Fire Fae merchant recently widowed, his wife and child lost in childbirth a year ago. Nira knew all this, of course. She knew everything about Atheron.

His reputation as a savvy negotiator and innovator in economic policy. His role as de facto head of the regional merchant guild on the island of Scorcharis, where he had pioneered new trade routes and resource exchanges for the island's famous enchanted glass. His proposals had emphasized commerce and mutual prosperity, all to strengthen the Fire Fae people.

Business aside, he often spent his evenings playing cards, a recent habit after several months mourning. He also attended many Kindling showings at the Lystra Houses, although he hadn't taken a lover since the death of his wife.

Highly unusual.

With declining Fire Fae birth rates in the last thirteen hundred years, they were encouraged in all activities leading to reproduction. Even she had been to a few Kindlings, though more for research and knowledge than practical use.

Right now, Atheron's attention was entirely on his cards.

Until it wasn't.

When he thought she wasn't looking, his gaze wandered, lingering on the curve of her smile, the beads in her hair, the delicate gold at her wrist, the necklace resting between her breasts. His warm eyes, unguarded in those moments, made him seem more approachable than most fae men of his station. He even moved like a human, a bit clumsy as he tried to hide his growing interest.

Her lips quirked. The decent ones were always harder. Now she understood his perspective. He was willing to watch all the shows, to sit among the debauchery, but he believed joining in would dishonor his wife's memory.

If the object of his desire fell into his lap, though...

She toyed with one of her iron Tekkō Karuta cards, letting it spin between her fingers. The smooth glide of metal against skin was a reassuring weight. A weapon hidden in plain sight. The men around her had no idea what the cards really were, or how precisely they could cut. Or worse.

Atheron glanced at her again, longer this time, desire flickering in his eyes. She answered a slow, deliberate smile, letting her gaze linger on his lips while she swept black curls over her shoulder to give him a better view of her breasts, where the corset beneath her dress pushed up her meager assets.

She dealt another hand of cards with a different deck, her fingers dancing over her Tekkō Karuta occasionally. Those she kept as a distraction, never something she actually played with. The other men at the table grumbled and cursed, their attention fixed on their hands.

Good. The less they noticed, the better.

Atheron's gaze, however, kept returning to her, drawn to the emerald silk that clung to her accentuated curves and the promise in her eyes.

The game had gone on long enough. One by one, the other players folded, their coin purses lighter and their pride heavier. Soon, only Atheron and a burly Fire Fae remained, along with one more gambler, a drunken, hybrid man, part human, part Fire Fae, who had more luck than skill.

With glassy eyes from firewine, the hybrid's wagers became more erratic, until he laid a small, silver locket among the gold coins. The locket was old, worn, well-loved, the kind of thing no one would part with unless desperate.

"My grandmother's," the hybrid said.

When the burly Fire Fae raked in his winnings with a smug grin on the next hand, the hybrid clutched his cup and stared at the jewelry with wet-eyed regret.

"Unlucky night, friend." The fae sneered, turning the locket between thick fingers before slipping it into a pouch on his belt.

The hybrid exhaled sharply through his nose, forcing a smile, but his face crumpled beneath the effort. He was too far gone to argue, too drunk to fight, and the loss weighed on him more than all the coin he had already thrown away.

Her fingers tightened on her Tekkō Karuta as she picked up one of the iron cards and set it spinning. *Idiots.*

"Have some heart, Aethek." Atheron leaned forward, his face suddenly serious. "This is a time of celebration. Let him keep his grandmother's locket."

Surprise, surprise. Atheron the decent one indeed.

Aethek scoffed and brushed off the hybrid's hopeful look until the man was forced to leave the table.

Still, Atheron's civility didn't matter. Decency didn't change what she'd come to do.

But first...

She hadn't planned to intervene. Normally she would have let the hybrid learn his lesson about gambling while drunk. But she had been watching Aethek all night, and she had seen what the others had not.

He'd cheated.

He'd been palming cards when he thought no one was looking, shifting the game in his favor with clumsy sleight of hand that might've fooled most, but not her. She was doing the same, just much better.

She let out a soft tsk between her teeth, just loud enough for Aethek attention. When he glanced up, she met his eyes with a slow, indulgent smile and lifted her cup in a silent toast, as if admiring his victory.

Let him think he's won.

Maintaining her seductive facade, she reached out and "accidentally" brushed Aethek's thigh with her hand, a light enough touch to feel like an invitation, her fingers sliding up his leg. Her lips curved into a smile that promised trouble.

His grin widened, lecherous and smug.

Her fingers slipped over the pouch at his belt. The movement was brief, quick as a breath. A casual flick of her wrist. He thought she attempted to caress his hardening cock.

A second later, the locket was free.

Tucked beneath her sleeve.

He never even noticed, his voice slurring with drink. "I knew you'd come around."

Her smile didn't waver as she pressed a small iron needle into his leg, her ring the perfect hiding place.

Iron could kill a fae.

But not her.

She withdrew the needle quickly, letting the poison on the iron do its work. It was only meant to make someone violently ill, and the brief touch of iron would not truly harm him. She kept her expression loose and indifferent, swirling her drink lazily, feigning amusement while Aethek turned back to his cards, still grinning at his own brilliance.

Pride made men careless.

The burly Fire Fae suddenly jerked, his bravado faltering as nausea replaced his grin. He paled and excused himself from the table with a stammer. The others laughed, oblivious, as he stumbled toward the door.

Her smile faded as she turned back to her cards. One distraction down, and a rude one at that.

Now it was time to focus on Atheron.

"Lucky night?" she asked, her tone playful.

He chuckled, a soft sound, and shrugged. "I suppose so. Luck has a way of turning, though."

"It does."

If only he knew.

She rose from her seat, circling the table with slow, deliberate steps. His eyes followed her, his hand slowing mid shuffle. When she reached his side, she perched on his knee and draped an arm around his shoulders as if they were old lovers.

"Maybe I'll double your luck for you."

He tensed, then relaxed, a hopeful smile spreading over his face. His breathing quickened, and she smiled to herself. The furtive glance at her breasts told her everything she needed. Men like him rarely believed a woman wore a corset and a smirk for anything except seduction.

She caught his hand and guided it toward the coins on the table. "What are these for?"

His fingers trembled as he picked up a gold piece.

"For you," he said, his voice husky. "If... if you want."

Her laughter was soft, genuine enough, as she pulled the edge of her blouse aside, exposing the laces of her corset and a bit more of her swelling breasts. Her breath ghosted over his ear. "Go ahead. Tuck it in."

His fingers grazed her skin as he slid the coin into her corset. He lingered, his touch hesitant but warm. Then his hand cupped her breast, and his lips grazed her throat.

She hid her flinch that wanted to rise. She was very good at hiding her true self.

"I've never done this before," he murmured, his voice filled with wonder. "But you... there's something about you."

He went on about her wild beauty, about how she reminded him of a desert flower, vibrant and dangerous. His mouth slipped lower, his tongue following the curve of her breast.

Her stomach twisted with a familiar unease that she smothered ruthlessly. She hated this part when the target was someone like Atheron, someone decent, but after five hundred years of training she was the best at her job.

She slipped a needle-thin blade of iron into his spine at the base of his neck.

He jerked, but the paralysis was swift and merciless. His eyes widened with shock and fear as his head sagged toward the table. She left the iron in place, letting it do what it was crafted to do.

"What, why?" His voice was weak, words slurred.

She sighed and stroked his hair as if to soothe him. "I do not know," she admitted, her voice flat. "Orders. That is all I need to know."

Asking why was a dangerous game. Questions became cracks in her wall of detachment, a flicker of empathy that could unravel everything.

His eyes, filled with confusion and pain, searched hers.

"You should ask...," he whispered, his words barely audible as the paralysis took hold. "Ask why a man must die."

His words struck a chord, a discordant note, resonating with her growing unease over the last hundred years. Things had shifted, changed within her Nintura, but her Order had saved her life. She shook off the feeling.

She leaned closer, lips near his ear. "You deserve better. So I'll make it quick."

One of her twin blades found its mark, swift and precise, and his soul left this world. She closed his eyes with gentle fingers, her expression carefully maintained.

As she rose, the weight of the festival settled back around her. Flames flickered across the pavilion's banners. Drunken cheers rose and fell. Fire Dancers spun trails of golden embers into the night. Nira straightened her dress and slipped her cards into a hidden pouch. Normally she carried the Tekkō Karuta in her bracers, but that was not tonight's uniform.

Men at the makeshift bar jeered as she passed, their calls following her through the pavilion. She ignored them.

Near the entrance, the drunken hybrid gambler from earlier sat slumped against a pillar, staring at the floor in silent grief. Her fingers brushed the locket in her sleeve. As she passed him, she let it fall beside his hand with a flick of her wrist. A silent return he would never question.

Then she was through the archway and into the humid night, her thoughts already turning elsewhere.

Adar.

Her brother's golden eyes flashed in her mind. He'd never understood her need to kill, the way each completed mission soothed the inadequacies of being a Failed Fire Fae, a fae born without magic.

Now his face was a reminder that her loyalties were no longer simple.

He had been missing for five years, and tonight's work was another step toward finding him. With this mission complete, she could request another assignment to Agondray and follow the next lead of his trail.

Brushing down the silken folds of her dress, she disappeared into the shadows, leaving the festivities behind. She did not let herself think of humid ports or indigo eyes or a Dragon King who had almost been a mistake.

Adar was what mattered. The rest was just ghosts.

Also by S.D. Huston

THE CHAOS UNIVERSE
Epic Romantasy

Brides of the Dragon Kings

A Curse of Scales & Feathers
A Curse of Wings & Gems
A Curse of Spikes & Smoke (Coming to Kickstarter in 2026)

Novellas

The Sun Stone & the Hybrid Prince
The Florist's Budding Desire (16 March 2026)

Short Spicy Romantasy Reads

Wildfire & the Sun Prince (24 April 2026)
Starling & the Moon Blade (4 May 2026)
Shadow & the Air Trickster (4 June 2026)
Lotus & the Earth Son (6 July 2026)
Flicker & the Fire Scion (3 August 2026)
Tidegift & the Water Guardian (4 September 2026)

Viper & the Wood Warder (5 October 2026)
Tarnish & the Metal Knight (4 November 2026)

Romantasy Adventures

Silence Beyond the the Seal
Try a new experience of story telling! A six-month romantasy mystery delivered by mail.
Choose your character. Shape their fate.

FREE with Newsletter Signup

"Forsaken by Sun & Sea"
"Bound in Sunlight"

FREE

"Lies of the Sun Stone & the Hybrid Prince"

CLASH OF GODDESSES
Epic Fantasy

Blood of the Lily
Soul of a Rose
Tears of the Marigold
Clash of Goddesses: The Complete Series

ACKNOWLEDGEMENTS

This book was a challenge. There were moments, more than I care to admit, where I lost hope and seriously questioned whether this story deserved to see the light of day. That it has is in large part thanks to two phenomenal individuals who acted as my personal cheerleaders when my spirits flagged. Victoria and Lisa—thank you. Your encouragement was a lifeline, and without your support, this manuscript might well have been abandoned.

To my family—my wonderful husband and our two amazing kiddos—your constant support and belief in me and my work sustains me daily. Thank you for understanding the late nights, the distracted conversations, and for always being my most enthusiastic fans.

A story evolves with feedback, and I owe a significant debt to my critique partner, Morgan Lee, and all my Alpha and Beta readers. Thank you for diving into the early versions and providing the insights needed to shape this narrative. Special thanks to Victoria, Michelle, Lisa, Catharina, and Rachel for your honest insights and encouragement that shaped this book into what it is today.

To my Typo Buster Team, thank you for saving me from myself, one misplaced comma at a time. A special shout-out to Victoria, Miranda, Matthew, and Linda for your eagle eyes and patience.

I owe immense gratitude to my editors, Nissa and Malcolm, whose guidance and expertise elevated this story. Your thoughtful questions and suggestions challenged me to dig deeper and pushed this book to places I couldn't have reached alone.

Finally, my heartfelt thanks to all my Kickstarter backers who believed in this project enough to support it financially. Your early faith in this book made its publication possible. Special appreciation to Caitlin Millsaps, Devon Gambrell, S. W. Eon, Billye Herndon, Vanjia Thomas, Alexandra Corrsin, Vicki Hsu, Sheryl

SB, Morgan Lee, with extra gratitude to Rita Slanina and Vanessa Lee. Your generosity and enthusiasm were truly inspiring.

Books are never created in isolation, and this one is no exception. To everyone mentioned above, and anyone else who offered a word of encouragement along the way, thank you.

ABOUT THE AUTHOR

S.D. Huston is an epic romantasy and fantasy author with a soft spot for broken characters who would burn the world before they let the people they love fall. Her stories follow wounded heroes and heroines as they face impossible choices, brutal, war-torn worlds, and the kind of magic that always demands a price in blood.

She is obsessed with enemies to lovers, slow burn tension,and relationships that survive monsters, politics, and their own flaws. Her worlds lean to the darker side of epic fantasy, full of war, loss, and powerfulforces that do not play fair. Her characters carry often carry emotional scars from past hurts and injustices, which can include family wounds, grief, bullying, or the urge to give up entirely. At the heart of every book is their fight to grow, to heal, and to become someone they can finally love.

If you pick up one of her books, you can expect sweeping worlds, emotional stakes, and love that stubbornly refuses to die. There may or may not be dragons, but there is always a hard-fought love story at the heart of the fire.

Connect with S.D. Huston on her website at https://www.sdhuston.com/.

www.ingramcontent.com/pod-product-compliance
Lightning Source LLC
Chambersburg PA
CBHW020324030826
48979CB00022B/984

* 9 7 8 1 9 6 2 7 6 1 0 4 8 *